ANTHROPOLOGY
OF AN
AMERICAN GIRL

ANTHROPOLOGY

OF AN

AMERICAN GIRL

A Novel

Hilary Thayer Hamann

SPIEGEL & GRAU

NEW YORK

2010

Anthropology of an American Girl is a work of fiction. Names, characters, places, and incidents are the products of the author's imagination or are used fictitiously. Any resemblance to actual events, locales, or persons, living or dead, is entirely coincidental.

Copyright © 2010 by Hilary Thayer Hamann
Copyright © 2003, 2004 by H. T. Hamann

All rights reserved.

Published in the United States by Spiegel & Grau,
an imprint of The Random House Publishing Group,
a division of Random House, Inc., New York.

SPIEGEL & GRAU is a trademark of Random House, Inc.

This is a completely revised edition of a work originally published
in 2003 and subsequently in a second edition in 2004
by Vernacular Press, New York.

Permissions Acknowledgments can be found on page 601.

LIBRARY OF CONGRESS CATALOGING-IN-PUBLICATION DATA
Hamann, H. T. (Hilary Thayer).
Anthropology of an American girl : a novel / Hilary Thayer Hamann.
p.   cm.
ISBN 978-0-385-52714-9
eBook ISBN 978-1-588-36938-3
1. Young women—United States—Fiction.   2. Self-actualization (Psychology)—
Fiction.   3. Self-realization in women—Fiction.   I. Title.
PS3608.A549437A84 2009
813'.6—dc22   2009012847

Printed in the United States of America on acid-free paper

www.spiegelandgrau.com

2 4 6 8 9 7 5 3 1

FIRST SPIEGEL & GRAU EDITION

Book design and title page illustration by Dana Leigh Blanchette

*For Vee,
Emmanuelle,
and Rainier*

And for Maman

We shall not cease from exploration
And the end of all our exploring
Will be to arrive where we started
And know the place for the first time

—T. S. ELIOT

ANTHROPOLOGY

OF AN

AMERICAN GIRL

OPAL

Autumn 1979

High school is closer to the core of the
American experience than anything else I can think of.

—KURT VONNEGUT, JR.

1

Kate turned to check the darkening clouds and the white arc of her throat looked long like the neck of a preening swan. We pedaled past the mansions on Lily Pond Lane and the sky set down, resting its gravid belly against the earth.

"Hurry," I heard her call through the clack of spokes. "Rain's coming."

She rode faster, and I did also, though I liked the rain and I felt grateful for the changes it wrought. Nothing is worse than the mixture of boredom and anticipation, the way the two twist together, breeding malcontentedly. I opened my mouth to the mist, trapping some of the raindrops that were just forming, and I could feel the membranes pop as I passed, which was sad, like breaking a spider's web. Sometimes you can't help but destroy the intricate things in life.

At Georgica Beach we sat on the concrete step of the empty lifeguard building. The bicycles lay collapsed at our ankles, rear wheels lightly spinning. Kate lit a joint and passed it to me. I drew from it slowly. It burned my throat, searing and disinfecting it, making me think of animal skins tanned to make teepees. Indians used to get high, and when they did, they felt high just the same as me.

"Still *do* get high," I corrected myself. Indians aren't extinct.

"What did you say?" Kate asked.

"Nothing," I said. "Just thinking of Indians."

Her left foot and my right foot were touching. They were the same size and we shared shoes. I leaned forward and played with the plastic-coated tip of her sneaker lace, poking it into the rivet holes of my Tretorns as the rain began to descend halfheartedly before us. In my knapsack I found some paper and a piece of broken charcoal, and I began to sketch Kate. The atmosphere conformed to her bones the way a pillow meets a sleeping head. I tried to recall the story of the cloth of St. Veronica—something about Christ leaving his portrait in blood or sweat on a woman's handkerchief. I imagined the impression of Kate's face remaining in the air after she moved away.

"Know what I mean?" she was asking, as she freed a frail charm from her turtleneck, a *C* for Catherine, lavishly scripted.

"Yes, I do," I said, though I wasn't really sure. I sensed I *probably* knew what she meant. Sometimes our thoughts would intertwine, and in my mind I could see them, little threads of topaz paving a tiny Persian byway.

My hand sawed across the paper I was sketching on, moving mechanically, because that's the way to move hands when you're high and sitting in an autumn rain. Autumn rains are different from summer ones. When I was seven, there were lots of summer rains. Or maybe seven is just the age when you become conscious of rain. That's when I learned that when it rains in one place, it doesn't rain all over the world. My dad and I were driving through a shower, and we reached a line where the water ended. Sun rays windmilled down, and our faces and arms turned gilded pink, the color of flamingos—or was it flamencos?

"Flamingos," Kate corrected. *"Flamenco* is a type of dance."

I remember spinning around in the front seat of the car to see water continuing to fall behind us on the highway. That was the same year I learned that everyone gets eyeglasses eventually and that there's no beginning to traffic. That last thing bothered me a lot. Whenever I got into a car, I used to think, *Today might be the day we reach the front.*

The rain let up. I stood and gave Kate my hand. "Let's go to the water."

She stood too, wiping the sand off the back of her pants, half-turning to check herself, stretching one leg out at a five o'clock angle, the way girls do. We walked our bikes to the crest of the asphalt lot and leaned them against the split rail fence.

The sea was bloated from the tide. It was dark and thick on top: you could tell that underneath there was churning. A hurricane was forming off the coast of Cuba, and Cuba isn't far from where we lived on the South Shore of Long Island, not in terms of weather. Surfers in black rubber sat slope-backed on boards near the jetty, waiting for waves, steady as insects feeding off a deeply breathing beast, lifting and dropping with each wheeze of their massive host. I stripped down to my underwear and T-shirt and left my clothes in a pile. Kate did the same.

The sand closest to the shore was inscribed with drop marks from the rain, and there were springy bits of seaweed the color of iodine gyrating in the chalky foam. I pushed through until I couldn't see my calves anymore. The water was purplish and rough, and it knocked against me, setting me off balance. It felt good to succumb—sometimes you get tired, always having to be strong in yourself.

Dad said that in Normandy during World War II soldiers had to climb from ships into the sea and then onto shore. They had waded through the ocean with packs on their backs and guns in their arms. He hadn't fought in Normandy; he just knew about it because he knows lots of things and he's always reading. He said the men had to get on the beach and kill or be killed. I wondered what those soldiers had eaten for breakfast—scrambled eggs, maybe—all the boys lining two sides of a galley's gangling table, hanging their heads and taking dismal forkfuls while thinking about what was awaiting them on the shore. Maybe they were thinking of getting one last thing from their lockers, where they kept pictures of their families or of their girls, or maybe just Betty Grable pinups.

It's one thing to *say* you're willing to die for your country, but it's another thing to have to do so when the moment actually presents itself. I could not have imagined Jack or Denny or anyone from my class dying to defend America, though everyone said that war was coming again, and also the draft, just like with Vietnam. *The Russians are crazy*, people said. *This time it's going to be nuclear. This time we're all going to go in one atomic blush.*

Kate came alongside me. "God, this water is black."

My mother refuses to go into the ocean. She respects it, she says, which is basically the same as saying she's afraid. I go in *because* it scares me, because certain fears are natural and it's good to distract yourself from unnatural, more terrifying kinds. For example, the ocean can kill you just like a bomb can kill you, but at least the ocean is not awful like bombs or surreal like overgrown greenhouses, or alarming like the barking sounds that flushing toilets make.

In elementary school we used to have emergency civil defense drills. The lights would go out, and we would rise in synchronized silence, obeying hushed orders and furtive hand signals, rustling like herds of terrified mice—if in fact it can be said that mice manifest in herds rather than as random runners. No one ever told us which particular emergency we were drilling to avoid. Probably Russians then too. The thought of Russians attacking eastern Long Island seemed unlikely, though it is true that East Hampton has beaches like the ones in Normandy. Beaches are a threshold.

I asked Kate if she remembered yellow alerts.

She said she did. "And red ones."

"Didn't we have to kneel under our desks for one kind, like this?" I put my head to my chest and locked my fingers around my neck.

"And with the other type," Kate said, "we had to do the same thing, only in the hall."

"Right," I said with a shiver. "That is so fucked up."

She cupped her mouth and imitated an implausibly tranquil public address warning. It was like a European airport voice, like the one we heard at Charles de Gaulle airport when we went to France with the French Club—sterile and cybernetic, glassy and opaque, like rocks at the bottom of a fishbowl. Kate was good with voices.

"This is a yellow alert. This is a yellow alert. Remain calm and follow the instructions of your teacher."

"Which is which?" I asked. "Like, what do the colors mean?"

"Bombs, probably," she said. "Different styles."

"But a bomb is a bomb. We wouldn't have been any safer in the hallway than in the classrooms. Why not just stay at our desks?"

There was a rush of water. Kate lost her footing.

I continued to speculate. "They must have moved us out because the classrooms had something the halls didn't have—*windows*. And the only reason they would have wanted us away from windows was if something was outside, like, coming in."

Kate said, "*Christ*, Evie!"

"A land attack. Gunfire. Grenades. *Red* alert. Death by blood. Yellow meant gas. Death by bombs. *Nukes.*" Jack was always talking about the *massive radiation release* that was coming.

The rain had passed; all that remained up above was a series of garnet streaks. The sea slapped ominously, confessing its strategic impartiality. The sea is an international sea, and the sky a universal sky. Often we forget that. Often we think that what is verging upon us is ours alone. We forget that there are other sides entirely.

Kate and I waded quickly back to shore. As soon as we could, we broke free of the backward pull of the waves and started running. We dressed, yanking our Levi's up over our wet legs, one side, then the other. Sand got in, sticking awfully.

"Shit," she said as we scaled the dune to the lot. "I'm never getting high with you again."

At Mill Hill Lane Kate cut left across Main Street, and I followed. The lane was steep and tree-lined. As we rounded the bend making a right onto Meadow Way, Kate's foot lifted from the pedal, and her leg swung straight back over the seat, parallel to the ground, making me think of fancy skaters. She hopped off in front of a brown ranch house—her house—lying low, like a softly sleeping thing beneath a custodial cover of tree branches. A small sign marked the rim of the lawn—FOR SALE. LAMB AGENCY. Kate bent to collect fallen leaves and twigs from around the crooked slate walkway, which seemed like a lonely project. Once when we were little, maybe about nine, Kate swore she had the distances between the slate pieces of the walkway memorized. At the time I called her a liar, not because she was one but because that's the sort of thing to say when you're nine. But Kate had skipped to the first tile, closed her eyes, and continued along the twisting, broken path, never missing a step, never touching grass.

"Hey, Kate," I called. She turned to me, her face tilting into the half-light. "Remember walking on the slate with our eyes closed?"

"Of course," she said.

"Can you still do it?"

"Sure." She set down the sticks she'd collected and she did it like it was nothing. When she was done, she said, "You try."

I couldn't exactly say no, since it had been my idea in the first place. My bike made a thumping sound when I dropped it. I went to the beginning and closed my eyes, trying to imagine the path I'd taken hundreds of times before. My neck felt vulnerable with my eyes closed, as though some famished thing might come and bite it.

"No grass," I heard her say. I raised my right leg, and while considering where to step, my foot fell, landing inches ahead, slightly to one side. "Whoa," she said. "You just made it."

I only had to decide where my foot was going to go before I lifted it. I only had to imagine the next step. I stepped again, and life moved to greet me. I felt particulate, like pieces matching pieces. I heard the benign crinkle of the trees as the wind swept into the branches, and the music of birds popping to life like individual instruments singled out from an orchestra. I'd gone over ten pieces of slate; four more remained. I half-swung my right leg to the right, then lowered it. My heel left a pulpy impression.

"Grass!" Kate shouted. "I win!"

I opened my eyes to a flare of light. All that endured of the dark was a nostalgic radiance, like when you shut off a television and the shadow of the picture lingers like a minuscule ghost on the screen.

Kate and I sat on the front step of her parents' house, watching the orphan moon elude the embrace of the trees. She was silent. I wondered if she too was waiting for the yellow porch light to click on, for the screen door to creak open from inside, for her mother to say, *On rentre, mes cheries.* Come back in, my loves.

The last time the door opened on us, Maman didn't smile. That was May. Maman's birthday is in May, *was* in May—I'm not sure how it goes with birthdays, whether they die when you do. Her arm unbended with difficulty to prop the door; when it snapped back on her, I caught it.

"*Bon soir,* Eveline," she murmured.

When Kate's mother said my name, she did not say *Ev-a-line*, the way most people did, but *E-vleen*, the first part coming from her mouth, the last part escaping from the cage of her throat. We embraced. Her shoulders floated waifishly within the vigorous circle of my arms. I wondered, *When did she get so small?* Kate and I followed her from room to room, and the floorboards grunted. In the dining room, her fingers skimmed the keys of her husband's piano. He'd died one year before; immediately after burying him, Maman had become terminally ill. Sometimes you hear of people who are so much in love that they die together.

"I did have this piano tuned yesterday, Catherine," Maman said in hobbled English, "in case you do ever wish to play again." *Ca-trine.*

I adjusted the armchair Kate and I had moved to the kitchen weeks before, when the side effects of the chemotherapy had started to become severe. We lowered Maman down by the armpits, the way you bring a toddler to a stand, only in reverse. I tucked the chair under the table, inching her closer until she sighed, *"Ah bien."*

Kate prepared dinner, and the room came to life with daunting pops and sizzles. It's shocking sometimes, the grief-stricken noises of food. I drew a chair alongside Maman's. I hoped it was a somewhat happy birthday with us there, and all her treasures from France—linen and glass and those plates with painted peasants. I wondered what treasures I would keep when I got older. No one in East Hampton really made anything, at least not in the specialty manufacturing sense. I'd probably have to settle for an old map of the bay or a jar of sand. Kate and I once bought these clamshell dolls in Sag Harbor, an undersea barbershop quartet, but they were not exactly keepsakes. They had clipped feathers for eyebrows and mussel-shell shoes and crab-claw hands. They were funny for about a week, then they got really depressing.

On a slender strip of wall near the window to Maman's left was a tiny oil painting, my first. She kept it in an elaborately carved frame without glass, with just a hole on top for a nail. The painting looked nice that way. I liked to prop things I drew or painted against the posts in the barn behind my mother's house, or else thumbtack them to the shelves around her desk. My dad would always stick things I gave him into the sun visor of his car or into some book he happened to be reading. "Pretty good," he'd say, "but off-center." According to him, everything I did was *pretty good but off-center.* Unless it was a photograph, in which case, he'd say, "Pretty good, but you cropped the head. *And* it's off-center."

The painting I'd given to Kate's mother was an oil of a white rose, overblown and beginning to withdraw. Maman had the same quality of a flower receding. There was something eloquent about her admission of resign, something august about the inalterability of her position. I squinted to make her young again. If she could no longer be called beautiful, she possessed something better—a knowledge of beauty, its inflated value, its inevitable loss.

Maman spoke that day of the sea. In her velvety drone, she recalled sailing by ship to America. "The sea is generous," she said. "She is there when you need her. Like a mother." Her dying voice was a black sonata; it defied time. Though it was May, I could think only of the coming autumn, of a world without her in it. *"Ecoutez,"* she said. *"La mer, et la mère. Eh?"*

I heard Kate say something. I looked across the kitchen, but she was not there, the kitchen was not there, not the food, not Maman. Everything had disappeared. The sweet castle of my hallucination had gone down, vanished. We were still sitting on the porch, Kate's knee knocking against mine. Our eyes resisted communion; they scanned the new jet sky, contemplating the black, wondering whether heavens, whether angels.

2

"Big John's coming over tonight," my mother said. She was next to me, wiping the kitchen counter, her thin arms making sweeping circles on the blade- and burn-scarred Formica. "He's Powell's friend from the Merchant Marines. Did I mention that he's an expert birder?"

I was eating my usual dinner of spinach out of a can, and, as usual, green juice dripped onto my shirt. My mother rubbed the spots with her sponge. "Hold still," she said, somewhat exasperated. Softly she added, "Be sure to ask John about his duck decoys."

Later that night, Big John's voice cut past the opened windows and into the yard. I was outside, moving my things from the barn, where I'd stayed for the summer, back to the front house for the school year, and every time he let loose with another bird whistle I could almost see the breeze from his breath in the leaves. He kept going on about *ducks* this and *ducks* that—*coots, broadbills, ringnecks, widgeons.*

I ventured into the kitchen at eleven o'clock. Mom perked up when she saw me. "Hi!"

Big John waved. He was a beefy, black-bearded man. Everything he did was loud. He talked loud, he breathed loud, he even sat loud. His chair creaked and moaned as gross spurts of wind shot out of his nose before getting recalled through his teeth. People who amplify like that are scary, especially when they do so at the beach or on a public phone or in your kitchen late at night.

"Big John's telling me about—" My mother faltered elegantly. She turned back to him. "What is it that you're telling me about?"

"ATVs," he said with a giant sniff.

"All-terrain vehicles," she said experimentally. "Fascinating." She patted the seat next to hers. "Come. Join us."

I went to the sink for a glass of water. "No, thanks. School starts tomorrow." My back was turned; I could hear a match burst to life.

"Oh," she said, drawing in on her cigarette. "Right. And when is Jack back from Oregon?"

"What's he doing up in Oregon?" Big John interrupted.

"Eveline's boyfriend does Outward Bound," Mom said. "River rafting. Mountain climbing."

"I'm not sure when he'll be back," I said. "I haven't heard from him."

She tilted her head and squinted, smoking, lost in thought.

Big John cleared his throat, and my mother and I startled. "My brother runs a Harley dealership in Hauppauge," he shouted to no one in particular. "He's got ATVs, dirt bikes, mopeds, bicycles, skateboards—the whole gamut, basically."

"Let's just say John's brother is *into wheels*," Mom joked lightly.

"Basically."

"Well," I said. "Kate told me she gets up at six. I'm going to turn off the stereo."

"Six?" Mom said. "We're a ten-minute walk from the school!"

"I guess she has to do stuff."

"What kind of stuff?"

"I don't know—hair, ironing."

"Ironing? I don't know if we even have an iron."

"I think she brought her own," I said.

My mother seemed blue. Maybe she was upset about Kate's not having a home anymore except for our ironless one. Maybe she was worried about where Jack had disappeared to and what trouble he might be in. Most likely she was dreading the prospect of hearing Big John's voice without the muffling accompaniment of the stereo or without me as a distraction. I took the electric fan from the top of the refrigerator.

"Hot?" John inquired.

"No, not at all," I said. "It'll just cut down on noise."

"Okay, then, night," he offered, waving again. His hand knocked the edge of the glass table. There was a nasty *crack*.

Mom lurched across, examining the table. "Is it broken?"

"Nah." He looked at the glow-blue school ring throttling his pinky finger. "It's fine."

"I meant the table," she said.

He inspected it. "Oh, *that*. Just a small scratch."

As I set the fan on my desk and plugged it in, the 11:07 passed, filling the bedroom with light. The Long Island Rail Road ran fifty feet from the side of my mother's house. The windows rattled and the furnishings skidded and the pictures cocked sideways when trains passed, but it was a quaint intrusion, a topic of conversation, more amusing than threatening. The LIRR travels between the farmland of the East End of Long Island through the sprawling cemeteries and housing projects of Queens, into the center of Manhattan. In the middle of the ride there are identical houses with identical yards. Each lawn indicates nature. Each box indicates home.

"It's not dying that scares me," Jack would say whenever we went to my father's apartment in the city. "It's Levittown." He planned to live in the mountains with guns. "The Rockies probably. You coming?"

"Yes," I would lie. I could never live on the toothy tip of anything, but it wasn't good to make Jack sad. When Jack felt sad, he hung his head and you couldn't lift it if you tried. I preferred the apocalyptic terrain of cities—the melting asphalt, the artificial illumination. Unlike Jack, I looked forward to the future. At least when things are as bad as they can get, they can't get worse. The future would be untouchable, hypervisual, and intuitive, a place where logic and progress have been played out to such absurd extremes that survival no longer requires the application of either.

"Notice how all it takes is the Force to blow up the entire Death Star?" I would tell Jack. "The future won't be jet packs and space stations; it'll be aboriginal. The language of the physical will atrophy. Our minds will coil inward, and our eyes will grow large to see beyond the seeable. No one dies in the future. We'll all preserve ourselves to be reconstituted."

"That's the whole fucking problem," Jack would say. "I don't *want* to live forever. I'm having trouble with the idea of Tuesday."

I held my face close to the air from the fan and said "Ahhh," with my voice going choppy. In the mirror on the desktop, I could see my hair blowing up. It wasn't a lot of hair, but it felt like a lot in the wind. I was squinting, so my eyes looked like cat eyes.

"They're the color of absinthe," my father likes to say, which is an odd compliment, since the definition of absinthe is *a green drink of bitter wormwood oil*—whatever that is.

My eyes are pointed at the ends like cartoon flames or the acuminate tips of certain leaves. Beneath the green are smoldering circles. They mark the place my skin is thinnest, and so my soul the closest. Mom's boyfriend, Powell, says that the soul is contained in the body. He says if instruments are made from your bones when you die, the music tells your story. Powell got his bachelor's in anthropology from Stanford and his master's in engineering from Columbia, then he joined the navy before moving on to oil rigs. He goes away for months at a time to places like Alaska or the Gulf, where he reads meters and plays harmonica. Powell can play "This Land Is Your Land" on harmonica better than anyone.

One disorienting fact about staring into a mirror is that the person you see is the opposite of what you truly look like. I tried to explain it once to Kate. She was playing with her hair, looking in a mirror, changing the part from left to right.

She said, "It looks better on the left."

"Actually," I said, "though your hair is parted on the left of your true head, it's parted on the *right* of your mirror head. What you mean is, *It looks better on the right.*"

"That's *not* what I mean." She probed her scalp. "It's on the left of my head *here*," she said, holding the spot, "and it doesn't switch places *there*." Kate tapped the mirror.

"You have to *inhabit* the image," I explained. "If you inhabit the image, the part is on the right. But, if we were in the world, looking at the girl in the mirror—"

"We *are* in the world," she interrupted flatly, and by her voice, I knew she was done. Kate could be reluctant to explore topics that require a detachment from vanity.

"Anyway," I sighed. "What you see is the opposite of what everyone else sees."

Kate brushed steadily. "No, Evie. What *you* see is the opposite of what everyone else sees."

Later, Kate tried her makeup on me—cover stick and frosted eye shadow and face powder and Bonne Bell lip gloss. She was applying all these layers, saying the job of cosmetics is not to conceal but *to enhance*. She turned me to face the mirror. "Ta da!"

I looked rubbery, sort of embalmed. My cheekbones were gone and my lips glittered like one of those plastic bracelets with sparkly stuff inside. My eyes burned and my skin felt itchy. I smelled like cherry gum. I made my way to the sink, groping walls. As I rinsed, I watched myself—anyway, the *opposite* of myself—reappear in the mirror. Kate's reflection buoyed and skulked next to my own. She seemed to think I was being difficult. I felt bad about her thinking that. Something felt different between us—I felt something coming, not obvious like a wave but sneaky like a drip, a subtle sort of rising.

It's true that I can be difficult, though that is no fault of my parents. They are extremely good-natured people. They remained friends even after they got divorced. My father always says he married the prettiest Irish girl in New York, and my mother says she married the one funny German. It's true my father is funny, and true as well that my mother is pretty like her sister, Lowie, even if Lowie walks with a cane. Lowie had a fever when she was little. Maybe not a fever. Maybe *fever* is just what everyone says.

As for me, I arrived dark and detached, and though everyone waited, I became nothing like anyone else in my family. Even my birth was hard for my mother. I was breech. She tore, she vomited, she got more stitches than there are states. When the nurse handed me over, my mom was terrified. "I'm supposed to take care of *that?*" she says whenever she tells the story. "She looked like an owl."

My aunt Lowie is a midwife, so I've seen three childbirth films. When babies come out, they wear a bewildered grimace as though they have arrived by train and are peeping about the platform for the friend who promised to pick them up. It's not nice to think of myself as having been left at the station. I know my mother loves me; she frequently says she does. But it's one thing for a child to be the recipient of an affection that is conscious of its lack, and it's another to know fervent devotion, to be a blessing in the flush and the sweat of loving arms.

You cannot recover from a bad birth. The stigma lingers for a lifetime the way bad luck really does last seven years after a mirror breaks. The special gravity of a mother's first disappointed glance impresses itself on the infant's waxy blue skin. On my forehead is just such a mark, slightly off-center, to the left—that is to say, to *my* left. You can't actually see it, but you can sense that it's there. There is a prohibitive aspect to my looks, just as some rivers run too wild for a person to cross.

In the beginning of that summer, before Maman died, Dad and his girlfriend, Marilyn, took me to see an Italian movie, *L'Avventura,* which is about disillusionment and other sixties stuff. Afterward my dad asked what I thought of the film. I told him that I liked Monica Vitti, the film's star. Monica Vitti has this mesmerizing way of leaning against walls and staring out to view nothing, as though the horizon is millimeters away, as though the great distance we all dream into is bearing pestilently upon her skin.

"I think she's my favorite actress," I said.

Marilyn tapped Dad's arm. "See?"

Dad nodded. "I'm impressed, Marilyn."

"During the film I told your dad that you remind me of her," Marilyn said.

Did I really seem so sad? Monica Vitti seemed sad to me. She gave the impression of having lived a better past, of having returned to the present to discover how pointless things have become. She is untouchable, unsaveable: she too has *the mark*.

"You guys want to catch a cab?" Dad asked.

It was drizzling on Second Avenue. The sidewalk was not completely wet, but there was already that dusty smell of rain on cement.

"Mind if we walk?" I said.

Later that night, while my father was reading in the living room, Marilyn and I went into their bedroom. The only light came from the street, so I could scarcely make out the furniture—the walnut armoire with its pewter-finish grill of bamboo shoots, or the matching bureau loaded with bargain books from the Strand and old jewels in tortoiseshell boxes and a terra-cotta bowl of photographs, mostly of me. Or the low bed that was neatly dressed in one of those grandmotherly white spreads with nubby protuberances.

We knelt at the open window, reaching to feel the rain. Cars swished dreamily up Elizabeth Street. Tangerine strands of hair broke free from Marilyn's braid and fluttered in the breeze like kite tails. Her skin was powdered. It's always nice to kiss her cheek; it brings to mind the gentler things.

"Do you think I'm pretty?" I asked.

She turned to face me. "I do."

"But not like Kate." Everyone always said how pretty Kate was.

"No, not like Kate," Marilyn said, adjusting her elbows on the slanted, overpainted sill. "You're more beautiful than Kate."

I felt bad, like I'd forced a compliment from her; I hadn't meant to. "My parents don't think that."

She turned back to look out. "I think they're afraid of the way you look."

I didn't feel frightening, the way my parents found me to be, or difficult, the way others seemed to see me. I felt nothing, really, other than a sense that inside I was very small. Maybe all that anyone perceived was their inability to inspire my trust.

Though Jack was not there, I needed him to be there, so I imagined him. I often did this, and often we would speak. I asked him if getting older means you can't trust anyone. In the mirror, I focused until my burning eyes became his burning eyes, with the hue changing from bottle green to bright Wedgwood blue.

"You never *can* trust anyone," he seemed to answer. "But when you get old, you finally figure it out."

Possibly he was right. You're old when you learn that needs are to be eclipsed by civility. You're old when you join the sticky, stenchy morass of concealed neediness that is society. You're old when you give up trying to change people because then they might want to change you too. When you're young, needs are explicit, possibilities endless, formalities undiscovered, and proofs of allegiance direct. If only there were a way to keep the world new, where every day remains a wonder.

"Jack," I said. "Remember how easy it used to be? Remember when friends used to cut themselves and share blood?"

3

The sun was a mean wall behind us, shoving up against our backs, and the tar that coated the railroad ties was sticky. A resin smell filled the air. I could feel it creeping the way molasses drips, only upward, burning the inside of my nose. Kate didn't like the tar to touch her shoes, so she stepped with perfect strides on the gravel between the ties. I took the rail.

When we reached Newtown Lane I hesitated, teetering on the strip of steel. "I'm just gonna run across the street and grab a cup of coffee."

Her face screwed up into the sunlight. "We're going to be late."

"I'll go fast." I jogged into the street, dodging minor morning traffic.

Three bells on a crooked wire tinked and jangled against the store's glass door. Bucket's Deli was full of laborers in T-shirts, shorts, and Timberlands waiting patiently for egg sandwiches—*patiently* because the city people had gone back and there wasn't much work for them to do. I made my way to the counter and ordered. Joe, the counter-guy, filled one of those jumbo Styrofoam cups with ice cubes and cold coffee from a plastic coffee storage container that was grossly discolored. The radio near the meat slicer played a song by Genesis that reminded me of summertime.

> *I will follow you, will you follow me?*
> *All the days and nights that we know will be.*

"All set for school today, Evie?" Joe asked. "Senior year at last."

I shrugged. "I guess."

"C'mon now," he said, throwing back his head slightly to one side with a smile. When he smiled, I noticed a gap between his teeth. I'd never noticed a gap there before.

I turned away. Outside looked hot, hotter even than when I'd come in. It's hard to start school when the weather is still like summer. Sometimes a time ends or a person dies and you have to move on, though reminders are everywhere. I paid for the coffee real slow, knocking the coins around with one finger.

Joe started ringing up the guy behind me. "Forget about it, Ev."

"It's okay. I've got it." I funneled the change into one of his hands.

I stepped back out into the sluggish heat. It was tipping against the glass door of the deli like a chair you use for a lock. As I crossed the street and climbed the grass embankment onto the sidewalk, I pushed the damp paper off the straw. Kate extended her hand and took the paper from me, putting it into her pocketbook, and we started walking. I wondered if straws were named after real straw, the kind animals eat. Maybe some farmer started chewing a piece and accidentally sucked through it.

I pulled at my shirt, blowing down. "It's got to be ninety degrees out." I said.

Kate did not reply; she just kept stepping eagerly. I thought I should feel eager too, but eagerness is impossible to simulate without seeming phony. I drew in the last mouthful of coffee. The straw probed the empty avenues between the cubes, hunting profitlessly for more liquid.

We turned onto the high school driveway. The building appeared exceptionally horizontal, lower and longer than usual, like a block of grass rising up off a flatland. The parking lot was full, though the main entrance was vacant because no one ever hangs out on school steps and sings, the way they do in movies. As soon as people arrive, they go inside, stop at their lockers, then just walk around the building until classes begin.

Jodie Palumbo and Dee Dee Barnes were smoking in an alcove at the side entrance, near the language and math wing. Jodie was hideously tanned. Her freckles looked three-dimensional, like popped boxes.

Kate paused and offered a bright hello. I edged past.

Dee Dee stretched her lips. "How ya doin'?"

Jodie flapped the tops of her fingers but said nothing since she had just inhaled. It must not have gone down right because she lurched forward and began to cough. It was the rolling, mucousy kind of cough that sounds totally contagious.

Through the double doors behind the girls the school corridor was packed with bodies. I took a breath and went in because nothing is worse than being on the verge of doing something, teetering like a jackass. It'd been a long time since I'd been around so many eyes. In schools eyes are everywhere, there are twice as many eyes as bodies, and in our school there were about a thousand bodies. High schools offer nothing compelling for all those eyes to regard, nothing other than the vista of teenaged bodies, which is sort of the entire fucking problem.

Madame Murat filled the doorway to her classroom, blocking the light from the windows at her back, forming a shadow lagoon in the hallway. She was not fat, just inexplicably large. In profile she seemed to be carrying a basket of laundry.

"*Bonjour,* Mademoiselle Auerbach, Mademoiselle Cassirer."

"*Bonjour,* Madame Murat," we recited in unison. Jack called her *Madman* Murat, which Mom said sounded like the name of a Turkish assassin.

"*Je comprends que je ne vous verrai pas en classe cette année, Ca-trine. C'est vrai?*" Madame said to Kate.

"*Oui, c'est vrai,*" Kate responded, and Madame nodded from top to bottom and over to the left, ushering us along. "Great," Kate whispered. "Now she hates me."

"Maybe," I said. It was hard to know for sure. It could have been that Madame felt sorry for Kate's loss, and understood that that was what had motivated Kate to drop the class. Though it was also possible that Madame felt offended. French people are funny that way.

Kate went onto her toes. "Denny's there with Alicia Ross and Sara Eden. Want to run up?"

"No, thanks," I said. Having to talk to people was one thing, but soliciting conversation was something else. If I acted squirmy or didn't make eye contact, they would want to know what was wrong, and I would have to say, *Nothing,* since nothing really *was* wrong. Nothing is an easy thing to feel but a difficult thing to express.

By the time the bell was about to ring, we had made it three times around the loop of classrooms. You could tell when the bell was about to ring because suddenly everything accelerated. Personal time drew to a close, and people responded to the pressure by acting bigger. I prepared myself for the change. My shoulders drew inward. My face dipped down as though to dodge a blow. From the top of the science hall, we heard a group of girls shrieking at the other end.

"*Oh, my God!*"

"*That is the cutest T-shirt!*"

"*You look, like, soooo unbelievably skinny!*"

Coco Hale spotted us, and she started waving like crazy, calling Kate over as though it was a complete surprise to see her. "Kate! Kate Cassirer!" Something flashed between Kate and me, nothing you could name, not really.

"Do you mind if I go say hi?" Kate asked politely.

"Not at all," I replied, politely also.

She leaned forward and peered at me. "You're not just saying that, are you?"

I filled my cheeks and expelled the air slowly, who knows why. It's just a thing people do. "No, I'm not just saying that."

One time Jack made me explain why I disliked Coco.

I said, "She's, like, witchy, or something."

He was picking at his guitar. "Be specific." We were sitting on the farm table in the barn out back, and his head was cast down over the strings.

"Okay," I said. "Her teeth." She had two rows of miniature teeth, undifferentiated, same-size squares that appeared glossy even in the dark. They were like those miniature corn cobs. "They're witchy."

Jack considered that. "Good one," he agreed. "Next."

"Her eyes." Her eyes shuddered in their sockets when she was being insincere, as if resisting affiliation with her body. "Do you know those earthquake monitors, the rolling graphs with attached pens that measure tremors?"

He looked up with part of his face. "Seismographs."

"She has eyes like that, only they measure her lies."

"Seismographic eyes," he said contemplatively. "That's great." He pulled a felt-tip from his pocket and wrote the phrase on the sole of his blue suede Puma. Suddenly the mirror near the door fell off the wall and into the center of the room, shattering. "Holy shit!" Jack lifted one of the curved triangular shards. "She *is* a witch."

As Kate was about to break away to Coco, the bell rang. *Bwoop!* I made a hard right down the English hall and was drawn instantly into the belly of the crowd. I could hear Kate's voice trailing me—"Evie! Eveline!" I didn't turn, even though the way she called me was better than the way Coco had called her. My name from Kate's lips sounded shy, pining and bare. I felt sad about that, but also I felt a mixture of relief and release just to be alone. My body lightened, and when people said hello to me, I answered, "Hello."

Kate and Coco had gone into the music room probably; probably they were cleaning their flutes, sitting with mingling meringue hair, and all four hands polishing buttons and spitty levers. Perhaps they were discussing me, with Coco saying through rows of tiny teeth how I seemed envious, her eyes shaking.

It was not hard to envy Coco. Her family lived on David's Lane, one of the nicest streets in the village, in a house with a corrugated roof like in picture books of Spain. She wore Lacoste shirts and cloth-covered headbands from Mark, Fore & Strike, the golf-lady clothing store on Main Street, and she rode a kiwi-colored Motobecane bicycle to the beach after private tennis lessons. She had a collection of those Pappagallo purses with the wood handles and the button-on fabric covers. According to Kate, Coco paid forty-five dollars for a style and a blow-dry at that special salon in town next to O'Malley's pub. Mrs. Hale drove a new Mercedes with basketballs and bags of groceries in back, and unlike my mother, she never had beer breath or wore hip-huggers with peace sign patches or hung around with merchant marines and lab technicians. Mrs. Hale did not belong to Mensa.

Once, when my mom and I saw Mrs. Hale collecting tickets at the Ladies Village Improvement Society Fair, she was wearing a straw bonnet with big paper peonies; she'd made it herself.

"Who has time for such nonsense?" my mother asked. "Does that woman ever *read*?"

Despite the energy crisis, Mr. Hale would take his family on long summer trips on *My Romeo II*, their ultra-sleek cabin cruiser, to Block Island or Nantucket or Martha's Vineyard, where Coco and her boating friends would meet prep school boys. Every September, the photos would make the rounds—Coco and Breanne Engel or Pip Harriman, honey-brown and curly blond—hugging boys in Duke University sweatshirts, beige docksiders, and puka shell necklaces. Coco never had to go on trips to Gettysburg, West Point, Old Sturbridge Village, or those World War I air shows up in Rhinebeck like I always had to with Dad and Marilyn. All the family photographs are of me in blinding sunlight, dressed in plaid shorts and ribbed white knee socks and lace-up Earth shoes leaning on some cannon or posing before acres of headstones in Civil War cemeteries. And my mother had never once taken a vacation; she did not even own a camera.

Sometimes I couldn't help but feel meager compared to Coco, and then to confuse meagerness with envy and envy with hate. Everyone always says you shouldn't feel hate or even say the word.

"Bullshit!" Jack once barked. "Who told you that?"

"People." I couldn't think of anyone at the time.

"Words are constructs, like houses. Say whatever the fuck you want. Besides," he added lovingly, "you are incapable of true hatred."

Jack was right. Some feelings just occur, and giving them nicer names does not make them go away. If what I termed *hate* could be more accurately described as *an aversion to the witchy way that Coco acted,* it would have changed nothing inside of me.

Envy is awful. Unlike jealousy, which comes from the threat of losing what you cherish, envy is a dark desire for things over which you have no right or claim. Once I realized that she couldn't possibly take what I loved, and I didn't really want a life of privilege, especially when having such a life seemed to require flaunting it to those who had nothing, I was overtaken by an enormous boredom with Coco. A soaking rain type of boredom, liberating and complete, touching down everywhere in equal amounts. From that moment I was done. I realized it was a lot like doing math. She was *quantifiable.* I was not.

I entered the first class of my senior year early, which meant I was one step closer to getting out, for the day and for life. Sometimes it's best to focus on practical matters, just to *get through.* After Maman died that summer, life became very mechanical. I would eat dinner right after lunch and get ready for bed before night. I marked time. I would consider the task at hand until it was completed, then I would consider the next, never giving my mind a minute to scramble in the circuits of its cage. There's something to be said for automatic living. It makes looking forward to things seem unreasonable. When you stop looking forward to things, you get used to low expectations and you realize, *What's the big deal about success anyway?* If we're all to attain everything we've been conditioned to desire—wealth, fame, education, prestige, security—then those things will become so prevalent that they'll be meaningless. And it's a populated planet. Such uniform comfort would not come without a cost. Someone somewhere would have to pay for all that success.

According to Jack, the only way to maintain dignity is to give up wishes before they don't come true. Maybe that's too extreme. Maybe the best you can do is to refrain from wishing for wishes that are not your own, such as for ranch houses and nice cars, for capri pants and lamb chop dinners and husbands with good haircuts. Sometimes you have no choice; you inherit your parents' wishes. Some parents work hard to guarantee their children's progress. They don't want any slipping back. That's why every now and then you meet some poor kid whose life is controlled as if by committee.

My particular future was not so vigilantly guarded. I was to start from scratch. The best thing about my family's indifference was that I had the freedom to fail miserably.

I stepped behind the teacher's desk to reach the blackboard, and I pulled down the map of the Soviet Union. Kate always said that when she made a lot of money she was going to buy a wall map for me, the kind with lots of sheets. I took a seat in the corner of the room, alone by the window, wondering what Kate was going to do to earn all that money.

Annie McCabe, Breanne Engel, and Darlene Nappa slipped through the door kind of all at once and assembled in an L-shaped cluster in chairs near the teacher's desk. Annie began to whisper, and their three heads probed forward rigidly like construction cranes. I looked at the clock—two minutes to eight. And they were all so *done*. Annie was wearing stockings and a long straight silk skirt. Base makeup covered her from forehead to chest. A stringy ring of mocha stained the collar of her blouse.

Wow, I thought, and on such a hot day! Girls are truly game as soldiers, with the brave things they do to their bodies and the harsh conditions they are able to tolerate.

Darlene looked jaundiced, like a past-due celery stalk, concave and green with bushy stuff on top, and Breanne was beige and emaciated with a kind of polymer quality to her complexion—she looked trapped beneath her skin, like food through Tupperware. Her frosted hair was dry and frazzled at the ends and tied in such a way as to be neither up nor down. Her eyes were wide and shaking. Kate said Breanne takes Dexatrim.

———

About a month or so after the funeral, Kate and I saw those girls at Main Beach. It must have been late August because there was litter and guys with cigars. Litter and guys with cigars usually appear in the Hamptons around late August. That's when the group-house renters come. Breanne had gotten so thin her skin appeared to have been shucked off and reglued. She reminded me of this candy my father used to get for us in Chinatown, the kind with a translucent rice wrapper that's like paper, only you eat it, and it melts in your mouth.

"She looks like one of those Chinese candies my dad gets," I said to Kate.

Kate tilted her head furtively into the shady spot between our shoulders, going, *Sshhh!* We were on our stomachs facing the water. It was late afternoon, and the beach was changing, the way beaches do in the late afternoon—young people go and older ones come, and suddenly there are dogs. A yellow Lab was making wide, dripping circles around an abandoned sand castle, and a couple in hats sat near us, facing their chairs to the west.

"She makes herself throw up," Kate whispered.

I didn't understand. I said, "What do you mean?"

"After she eats, she throws up."

"How do you do that?"

"You put your finger in your mouth. And it just comes out—*I guess.*"

"You're kidding me." I hated to throw up. I avoided it at all costs.

"I wouldn't kid about a thing like that," she said.

Breanne really must have despised her parents in order to deprive their baby girl of sustenance. It was impossible to know for sure, but her mom probably clapped at her first steps and dressed her in eyelet rompers when she was an infant and kissed her shampooed curls. I'd been to the Engels' house. How pathetic Breanne must have looked, leaning over the turquoise toilet in their immaculate bathroom, feet and knees sinking into the plush of the matching turquoise carpet, breathing in the gladiola aroma of those gooey obelisk air fresheners, the kind where if you look inside the shaft, you can see the gel sinking into its own neon-green hip.

"It seems kind of extreme," I said. I didn't think Breanne had such a bad life. I thought of poor Dorothy Becker, who'd been abused at home. Dorothy had cragged seams on her wrists from what she'd tried to do.

Kate returned to *Seventeen*. "You're *so* selfish."

I wasn't sure what Kate meant by *selfish*. If she meant concerned excessively with my own advantage, I didn't feel very selfish. Of course, it was possible she didn't think I was selfish at all, but simply called me that because she couldn't think of anything else to say. I scooped up sand, wondering how many grains were in my hands, which is a cliché thing to wonder at the beach, but stupefying nonetheless. Kate kept licking the tip of her finger, then flipping the pages of her magazine—*snap, snap, snap.*

I don't know how or why, but I suddenly suspected that she had made herself throw up before too. I felt myself stand.

"Where're you going?" she asked nervously, leaning up.

I wasn't sure. "To the water," I said.

I walked along the rim of the shore. Though the day had almost passed, occidental light poured across the sky, making a pink and pious vault. I faced the ocean and remembered the way Maman had once described the water to me as a woman, a mother. *La mer, et la mère. Eh? The sea is there when you need her,* she'd said, though she herself could not be.

I turned back to see Kate sitting with those girls. It didn't bother me that they'd waited until I was gone to extend an invitation to her, or that she'd accepted. But I did wonder what it was that she wanted from them and what it was that they wanted from her, and whether either party stood the remotest chance of satisfaction.

Be a friend to Catherine, Maman had also said to me. And although I was superstitious about things such as last wishes, Kate was beginning to require a type of friendship that I wasn't sure I knew how to handle.

The bell rang again—8:00 A.M. and still no teacher.

Stephen Auchard stepped cautiously past the boys who punched and swatted at one another around the doorway. He chose the desk next to mine and nodded uncomfortably. Last time he'd seen me I'd been crying, which in high school is sort of like seeing someone naked.

At Maman's funeral he'd worn pressed khakis and a blue jacket with anchor buttons. His mother had had glasses with gold rectangular frames, and her auburn hair had been drawn into a sublime twist. She'd conferred with her son in ethereal French, leaning close, calling him *Etienne.* Kate's mother had been related to Stephen's father, and that was how the Cassirer family had found East Hampton. Outside Williams Funeral Home, Mrs. Auchard had held my shoulders and kissed both of my cheeks, kisses like accidental butterflies. Her skin had been dewy and fragrant, cold as packed talc. "Claire did love you," she'd said to me. *Deed luff.*

"What's your locker number?" Stephen asked. Our last names were letters apart, *Auchard* and *Auerbach;* our lockers had been side by side every year.

"591," I said. "What's yours?"

"590," he answered.

I nodded, and he nodded again, and we watched Nico Gerardi and Billy Martinson saunter in. I wasn't surprised to see them in an Advanced Placement class, though they were awful students. Jocks were pretty much exempt from the standards that bound the rest of us. Teachers and administrators humor them because it's in everyone's interests to coax them through school and get them out of the building. Since it's unethical to turn them loose on society, they get sent to college to be kept out of the mix until their frontal lobes develop more fully. As enticement they are given sports scholarships that will later amount to nothing, not even good health.

Stephen fingered the corner of his notebook. He was going to be valedictorian. I wondered if he was annoyed by Nico and Billy and others like them, by the way they occupied the classroom, establishing through body language a right of place that their brains could not. The contrast between their physical conceit and their intellectual timidity made me think of men in small clothes. They'd been given the basics—food, shelter, girls, trouble to cause—but deep down, they were on to the game. You could catch this tiny light in their eyes, this proto-consciousness of slipping supremacy.

Nico had changed over vacation. His football jersey hung closer to his waist than to his legs, his butt was more muscular, his crotch had thickened. I could not help but notice the way the denim of his Levi's was rounded and slightly whiter there. I knew I should despise him as Jack did, the way he and his friends flirted with female teachers and played buddy with the male teachers, the way they gave congenial grabs to girls in hallways and relied on family ties to get them out of trouble. When Nico got caught stealing from summer houses, Judge Baby released him to his parents without so much as a meaningful reprimand. The boys called him Judge Baby because of the way he talked. Every day they played Judge Baby, cracking themselves up. *"I cew-tin-wey hope you've gotten the boyish pwanks out of your system, wittle man. You have gweat pwomise."*

Billy had never been in trouble with the police, not that anyone knew of, except he did go through a bay window at his house once when he rode his mother's spare wheelchair down the staircase, and at several parties he'd swallowed goldfish.

Boys will be boys, that's what people say. No one ever mentions how girls have to be something other than themselves altogether. We are expected to stifle the same feelings that boys are encouraged to express. We are to use gossip as a means of policing ourselves. This way those who do succumb to the lure of sex but are not damaged by it are damaged instead by peer malice. We are to remain united in cruelty, ignorance, and aversion. We are to starve the flesh from our bones, penalizing the body for its nature, castigating ourselves for advances from men that we are powerless to prevent. We are to make false promises, then resist the attentions solicited. Basically we are to become expert liars.

Nico and Billy were talking to Annie McCabe. Her voice was inaudible except for the random coo and peep, and the edges of her fine brown hair came forward like crepe curtains to hide her face. I wondered if she had ever masturbated. Probably not. I couldn't imagine her manicured hands reaching to touch such a damp and pulpy place. Did she have the urge but resist? Or could the situation be precisely as it appeared—that she longed for nothing?

Nico's simian eyes scanned for a target and rested on me. He swaggered strategically into my aisle, and Billy Martinson followed. I curled over my notebook to draw.

"Hey, Steve," Nico said in his weedy voice, "looks like you got the hot seat."

"Guess so," Stephen replied.

Nico sat sideways in the chair in front of mine with his knees poking into the aisle. He put his elbow on my desk and leaned close, his breath coming in humid strokes. "Hey, baby."

I said hi and returned to my sketch. My pen moved boldly. It swirled to wobbly heights, making me think of "Irises" or "Starry Night." Billy settled his lanky frame into the seat in front of Stephen, the four of us carving out a strange chunk in the back of the room.

Breanne said something to Darlene, probably about me.

"What's that, Breanne?" Billy leaned diagonally to shake her seat.

Nico said, "No whispering. Speak up or forever hold your peace."

"That's right," Billy growled. "Speak up or forever hold my *piece*."

Everyone laughed except Breanne, who whined, "Stop it, Billy," in a voice that vibrated because her chair was shaking.

"*St-o-o-p i-it B-il-ly,*" Billy imitated, and the late bell rang. Mr. Shepard finally drifted in, coffee mug in hand. He lingered by the door, talking about golf with the AV teacher.

Nico dug deep into his pocket and removed a fistful of stuff—coins, bills, gum, and erasers, those awful ones that fit on top of pencils. He laid the erasers on the desk. Most of the other boys did the same, except for Stephen, who didn't budge, and Marcus Payne, who was facing back from his seat in the front row, observing.

"This is gonna be great," Nico said.

Marcus stood, addressing everyone with a series of panoramic nods. Whenever I saw him, I felt bad for the way he was treated but also inspired by his stamina. I secretly admired the gentlemanly way he always managed to face off with his oppressors.

"Now, listen up, people." His eyelids fluttered and his top teeth gnawed at the air. His head cocked to one side, and his arms came out from his shoulders at a preacherly incline. "Watch out for my head with those things."

"Shut up, Marcus," Bobby Tabor said. Bobby's parents owned the liquor store and every night at dinner the whole family got drunk on good wine. Bobby got invited to all the parties. "Pouilly-Fuissé," he would say to his teen host, rotating a bottle lovingly in his hands to feature the label. "1974."

"Yeah, *Carcus*. If you don't wanna get hit, *move*," Mike Stern warned as he emptied a snack bag full of erasers onto his desktop.

"It doesn't matter where you sit, Payne," Billy said. "We're gonna hit you anyway."

Mr. Shepard closed the door behind him.

I asked Nico what was going on.

"Everyone's supposed to toss erasers at Shep when he makes a bad joke," Nico said.

"You can't do that," I said.

"It's tradition," Nico stated defensively. "I didn't invent it."

I looked around the room. All the boys were seated properly and staring ahead; the only signs of impudence were the piles of erasers on most desks. It was tradition; of course they wouldn't be punished. It was a preliminary test of gender loyalty, a distinct part of the male experience—next came fraternities, bachelor parties, firefighters, the police, politics, war. It wasn't *girl* tradition. Girls had no traditions—anyway, none that teachers and boys would participate in willingly.

"Relax, baby." Nico leaned into my face. "We're just gonna have a little fun."

4

There was a line I always liked to walk, a single discolored plank that went from the east to the west wall of the barn behind my house. I called it a barn because it was shaped like one, but actually it was just a shed, twenty by twelve, with no plumbing, no heat, and no insulation. The light inside was gauzy, like light in a tent. I went there almost every day to paint or to study.

One warm night, in the spring of my junior year, I fell asleep on the floor. When Mom couldn't find me in the house in the morning, she checked the barn and saw me curled up in the corner. That afternoon,

Kate and I found Mom's Plymouth Scamp parked in front of the high school. The car was old but anxious to please. It leaned forward like a pollen-yellow rhombus. We approached cautiously; we'd never seen my mom at school.

"Maybe she got fired," Kate whispered as we exited the building.

"Maybe she has cancer too," I said.

Mom waved. "Hop in, you two! We're going to Sears!"

We headed toward Amagansett on Pantigo Road. At Sears, Mom ordered a piece of foam from a catalog. "A mattress," she said. "Now you can crash in the barn whenever you're working late. It'll be your studio." She tore a plain blue check from her wallet. On top was her name, Irene Ruane, and our post office box number, and East Hampton, New York, 11937. The amount was forty dollars.

"I wrote it on the bottom, Laura," she told Kiki Hauser's mom, who worked behind the counter. Mrs. Hauser had asked for our phone number even though she knew us. My mother refused to allow the insult to dampen her spirits. As we waited for processing, she brushed my cheek with her hand. "Isn't this exciting? You can sleep there all summer if you want."

Afterward we stopped at A&B Snowflake to celebrate with soft-serve ice cream, then we dropped Kate at her house on Mill Hill Lane. Maman was still alive then, though very sick. When we pulled away, we waved to Kate and I felt sad. It's sad to leave a friend, especially at four-fifteen in the afternoon, especially when her mother is dying but yours is not—but, then again, everything is sad at four-fifteen in the afternoon.

In the barn I always walked that same line—pacing along the plank to the overpainted brown door in back that opened onto no place in particular, just a stall with a potting bench. When I reached the wooden ladder to the sleeping loft, I turned, keeping every inch of my body centered and upright. In some parts of the world, steadiness is a requirement. In some places, children carry baskets on their heads. In America, we don't need balance, except maybe in school athletics.

Pip Harriman was perfectly balanced when she climbed the ropes for the presidential physical fitness exam in gym that morning. It wasn't the *ac-*

tual presidential physical fitness test but a simulated version to determine our "health entry points," from which we were expected to improve by the year's end.

Pip's hands went fast, fist over fist, with her legs crossed like wishful fingers, pinching to maintain counterbalance. Even in the gymnasium's fluorescent light, her hair gleamed like a length of satin ribbon.

Coach Slater took advantage of Pip's sterling example by making a speech. "Rope climbing is noncompetitive, okay ladies?" Coach shouted didactically in a stirring bit of showmanship. Her voice echoed from the freshly polyurethaned floors to the soaring metal rafters. "A climb is a personal challenge, okay? It's an opportunity for you to top your own best performance."

It seemed pretty competitive nonetheless, with Pip effortlessly mounting the one available rope while the rest of us sat slumped and cross-legged, averting our eyes and praying like mad for time to run out before Coach got around to calling our names. If they really wanted it to be noncompetitive, they should have divided us into groups, then added up the total number of inches climbed by each team. Then at least we'd all root for one another to go higher—every single inch gained by one would make a difference for all. I wasn't sure what it had to do with fitness anyway, since the entire gym class was spent sitting and waiting. And obviously the ropes weren't important enough to practice on a regular basis, since they only got dropped from the ceiling for tests. It's not exactly a usable life skill, except maybe in the circus or the army.

"Can you imagine?" I whispered to Kate. "Pip under the Big Top?"

Kate shushed me. She didn't want me to draw Coach's attention to us. I would tell her later, at dinner, and we would laugh. My mother liked to laugh about Pip.

Once we were all standing in Kate's parents' driveway—it was probably freshman year.

"What is it with these children's names?" Mom asked. "Claire, have you heard them?"

"Oui," Maman replied in her turbid accent, "Pip." *Peep*.

"What are the others?" Mom asked.

Kate made a list. "Coco and Kiki, Bobum, Winn."

"Skip," I added, "Colt, Duff, Leaf. Fick."

"Fick!" my mother said, laughing so much she needed her asthma inhaler.

Maman didn't think it was funny. "It is very sad, Irene," she scolded, "this American custom of calling a child by the name of a dog."

Pip hopped off the rope, triumphant and breathless, and Coach made a check mark on the fitness report form. Coach called, "*Palmer*, Ellie!"

The worst thing about the ropes was the panic you felt when you stood up, knowing everyone was staring. Though I sympathized with whomever was up there, I would stare too, since you were wise to feign interest. Ellie rose reluctantly, yanked her T-shirt down around her hips, went dutifully to the swinging rope, tilted her head as if wondering how to begin, then looked pathetically to Coach for some kind of break. But coaches never give breaks. They take their jobs seriously—you can tell by the way they wedge their clipboards into their bulging bellies, blow silver whistles up close and indoors, and wear neat-looking Adidas sweat suits, though they never break a sweat.

Coach Slater had to be forced to give Alice Lee a break. Before class started, Alice had handed Coach a doctor's note saying to excuse her from the exam because it was *that time of the month*. Coach was especially irritated when Alice asked if she could stay there in the locker room or go to the nurse's office for privacy because we were going to be sharing the gym with the boys.

"Are you enrolled in this class?" Coach shouted.

"What do you mean?" Alice asked suspiciously.

Coach shook her head like Alice was dumb. "I *mean*, are you enrolled in this class?"

"I *guess*." Alice's head sank meekly, but her eyes lit up with hatred.

"Then you're my responsibility. *You* go where the *class* goes."

Coach turned from Alice and blasted her whistle harshly, then pointed to the gymnasium and commanded the rest of us to "Get out there and do three laps." The boys had already started, so we ran in place in the corner until they reached the far side of the room, then we moved ahead in a big group. Every time the boys passed Alice, who was sitting on the floor under the water fountains, hugging her knees to her chest, they would say mean things. The coaches did nothing to stop them—they seemed to be using Alice as an example. They seemed to say that the gym is a realm unburdened by sloughing wombs and engorged breasts. It was confusing, frankly, the way everyone stared at our bodies even as they tried to erase the ideas of our bodies from our minds. We were supposed to get over ourselves, but no one was supposed to get over us. The female body was our worst handicap and our best advantage—the surest means to success, the surest course to failure.

"It's her own fault," Jodie Palumbo exhaled.

"God, it's *so* gross." Annie McCabe shuddered.

Pip said something, which I couldn't hear, and they laughed. They didn't like Alice, though they didn't know her. They were sorting, or classifying. It's easy—anyone dressed funny is the enemy, especially if they reject your supremacy or do not acknowledge school as entertainment. If the enemy tries to look like you and act like you, only in more affordable clothes, that person is *still* the enemy, only of a more contemptible, less terrifying variety—the sort you can be seen with *if absolutely necessary,* for instance if you are soliciting float-making help for homecoming or votes for yourself in the class election.

I passed the girls, though it brought me to the rear of the boys. Actually, the rear of the boys was a nicer class of people than the front of the girls, which is a carryover fact for life. I mixed in with Roy Field, who rebuilt radios and ate seven bowls of Trix a day; Tommy Gardner, who had impetigo and a heart murmur; and Daryl Sackler, who was six-foot-four but refused to play basketball even though they offered to let him start, because he had a job mowing lawns after school. Daryl Sackler *buries cats and mows their heads off,* that's what everybody said.

"Actually," Jack said of Daryl, "I like him. Most freaks like that would kill for fucking basketball hero status. But he *chooses* to remain a loser. Either he's a total retard or a complete man of honor. Besides, you know how I feel about cats."

I ran hard, really hard. At the end I sprinted to finish and bent to catch my breath. Others finished after me, forming a docile line at the girls' water fountain. Alice shifted miserably, as though protecting herself from us, like we might kick her or spit, but she didn't shift too far, since her predicament was legitimate; in fact, her predicament was *our* predicament. I felt I was with her, though my body stood apart and my voice was silent. In *Jules and Jim,* Jim blows Catherine a kiss when she jumps into the Seine River after Jules insults women, and Jim says, *I admired her. I was swimming with her in my mind.*

I twisted the knob and drank the water, which was icy cold by the time I got to the front of the line; I had this trick of letting everyone cut in front of me. I wiped my mouth on my shoulder and looked back to Alice. I didn't know what she'd endured beyond the school walls, but her look was knowing. If my eyes met her eyes, I wondered what message mine should convey. Not pity, since I am a woman too, and therefore as pitiful as Alice. I considered sitting next to her, but then I would have gotten detention. It's weird how teachers belong to a union and they teach about revolutions and labor strikes, but they discourage solidarity among students.

Kate and I saw her doctor's note halfway unfolded on Coach's desk when we were sent to return the relay cones to the equipment room behind the office. We could only make out parts. *Please excuse Alice Lee from physical activity due to severe menstrual*—the second paragraph fell into a crease. Something, something—*requiring medication.*

In the hallway Kate said, "How awful."

By that she meant Alice. Kate thought Alice was a poor thing. I thought the awful part was the note. It was written by an expert, by someone who believed what he or she was writing; then it was dispatched into the world, only to be casually disregarded by some *other* expert. It's hard to believe in anything anyone says when experts are constantly contradicting each other. Pip was as sure in gym as I was in art, but Alice was also sure about something, and so was Coach, and Alice's doctor. It's too bad that certain things matter so much when *you* are the one they matter to, but in the grand scheme, no one else cares, not really. I wondered who else besides Coach thought rope climbing mattered to girls but periods didn't.

The barn had become dark. Though I could see very little, I could hear many things: the echo of my footsteps in the room I occupied, the sound of night beyond those walls, my mother's laughter, ascending the hill from the house, traveling on the platform of a breeze. I could almost smell the Chablis on her breath and the mint from the package of gum in her coat pocket—the smells were like fairies escaping. I could almost see her reenact the drama of her day for her friends—bodies wedged into couches and chairs, denim legs jutting across tabletops, drowsy hands passing a joint, passing a bottle, wrists exposed, voices going, "So what happened next, Rene?" *Reen,* short for Irene.

Her friends were always there. If ever it looked like they might leave, they wouldn't. Someone might stand and stretch but then just use the toilet, or tuck in a loose shirt and ask if anyone felt like making a run for more beer. If I ever passed through, they would confer with me congenially, dipping close to my eyes with cigarettes, natted hair, and home-sewn clothes stinking of patchouli and musk.

If my upbringing made me sensitive to affectations of tolerance and to the irony of that particular hypocrisy, I could hardly be blamed. All I ever heard as a child was how *everything is cool* and *everyone should be cool,* and yet they were so very quick to judge new shoes or a clean car or to cogitate over the dementia behind matching furniture or monogrammed stationery. I couldn't help but have developed an aversion to the epoxied stench of incense and the smut of overfilled ashtrays and the sticky liquor rings on tables that had to be cleaned on Sunday mornings. Hiding in my room at bedtime as a little girl, I would drink my dinner of chocolate milk and bury myself beneath hundreds of stuffed animals tied together in twos with rescued ribbon and bits of yarn, one neck fastened to another or belly to belly, buddied up in case of fire, in case they would have to be tossed from the window. I would rub my feet together to distract myself from the noise of the party, the singing, the laughter, the music—Joplin, Dylan, Hendrix.

"I love you," she would say. My mother, popping her head in.

I was sitting on the barn floor, drawing rooftops. There were all these great rooftops by my dad's place in Little Italy. My father was good about taking me up to the roof of his building whenever I wanted. He always waited while I drew, either reading or just looking around. It wasn't necessary for him to wait, but between him and his business partner, Tony Abbruscato, they had about a thousand rooftop horror stories.

Kneeling before my paper, I looked deep into the space Jack might have occupied, and imagining him, I smiled. I thought of him smiling also, a fair angel's smile, his features transmitting a regard so strong as to defy the inconvenience of his factual absence. Had he been there actually, he would have persuaded me to join the party in the house. Jack hated to miss a party. Though I missed him, I was thankful to be beyond the influence of his flesh, the lips that could nudge me with an inflexible kiss through the door of my own home.

"Mom's back, you know." Not Jack, but Kate. She was leaning in the doorway, her head poking through. "Feel like coming up front?"

Yes, my mother, I knew. The laughter and the mint. The sweet wine and music. I wasn't sure what I felt like, being alone or being with people. Neither seemed good. I wondered what was expected of me; if I had known what was expected, I might have done it. I tried to think, but at the same time there was something I needed to forget, something of which an answer to her question might have reminded me.

Kate waited for an answer, and when none came, she left. Her feet clocked down the wood steps outside. In a few seconds the screen door in the back of the house squeaked open and slapped shut. Then nothing. Not silence so much as the absence of sounds affiliated with me. There was the loose, careless clank of silverware, and cabinet doors smacking, and the thud of the plumbing every time the kitchen faucet was shut off. There was the distant muffle of voices—Kate rejoining the party, Mom asking if I was coming. Maybe not. Maybe she did not ask about me at all.

5

When I came home from shopping at the A&P on Saturday, he was there, at my mother's desk, swiveling in her chair, slumped and belligerent, the way you sit at ice cream counters, like at the Candy Kitchen in Bridgehampton. It was as if he'd always been there, all summer long, occupying that very chair.

A scratchy copper beard dusted his chin, making a wafery layer like penny-colored frost on a windowpane. His hair touched the base of his neck. It was the color of gleaming wheat. Jack might have looked healthy, except that beneath his crystalline blue eyes were velvety pouches, and his cheeks were raw and drawn very far in, like a pair of inside-out parentheses. It was possible he had not eaten or slept in days. It's strange to realize you have sustained yourself on a memory of a person that has become untrue. The phantom face of my summer was not the face before me. And, yet, it was Jack.

"Your hair grew," he said. His voice was the same, still so beautiful.

I stopped at the base of the stairs and lowered the groceries to the floor. "I hate it."

"So cut it," he said, moving toward me, lifting me, and we spun.

I tested his existence; my hands felt for the body beneath the shell of his clothes. I confirmed the feathery pressure of his hair on my cheeks. The solid wall of his slender chest, the subtle protrusion of his right shoulder blade. He was real, with a smell that was real and a slightly sticky gleam to his skin. I rested my head in the bony basin between his ear and his shoulder.

"Are you crying?" he asked. He tightened his grip. "What's wrong?"

"It's just, you kept coming, like a ghost, like, floating." For a long while I couldn't speak. "Sometimes I would feel that you were with me, and you seemed so real. Now you're here, but I'm not sure. You seem less real than before."

His eyes studied mine, scanning cautiously. He breathed deeply, heavily, as if taking some of me down with the air.

"Have I changed too?" I asked.

"You have." He drew back my hair one side at a time, trailing with his gaze the path of his fingers. Adding gravely, "But it's okay."

Jack kissed me and his lips on mine were dry. He tasted like black licorice, like anise.

"My mother told me everything," he said, "about Kate's mom." He touched my cheek over and over with a chapped finger. "I'm sorry I wasn't here."

My eyes opened wide, admitting light from my mother's desk lamp. If you don't want to cry, you can stop yourself by looking into light. It's better to keep grief inside. Grief inside works like bees or ants, building curious and perfect structures, complicating you. Grief outside means you want something from someone, and chances are good you won't get it.

Later we were sitting on opposite ends of the couch, drinking black coffee. Our legs were interlocking and I was rubbing my feet together beneath Jack's tailbone. I used to rub my feet behind my dad's back when he was reading or when he and Marilyn were watching that old detective show, *Mannix,* or the crazy Dean Martin program, the one with the spiral staircase. My father's apartment was always freezing.

"They're whirring like a little machine!" Jack said of my feet, and right then WPLR played "Maybe I'm Amazed." The song had played the first time we met, and by coincidence we often heard it play, which sort of made it our song, even though everyone said it was queer to like Wings. Jack left my feet exposed when he stood to raise the volume.

"I want to cover this song with the band," he said, plopping back down. He and Dan Lewis and Dan's cousin Marvin, also known as Smokey Cologne, had a band—Atomic Tangerine. In a moderate shriek, Jack sang along with the radio. *"Der ner ne ner ner ner ne ne."*

When the song was over, we heard a sound behind us. We tilted our heads back over the couch arms. Kate was standing in the entry near the front door.

"Katie!" Jack called. He stood and started to step around the couch, probably to give her a hug or say sorry about her mother dying.

"Hey, Jack," Kate said dismissively, avoiding eye contact.

There was a pause, which made it hard for him to know what to do. He darkened and returned to me. For a while we just sat. Kate craned her neck to regard herself in the mirror over the fireplace, then she removed her sweater and dropped it playfully on top of me.

"How did Drama Club go?" I asked.

"Fine," she said, shaking her hair loose. "We did improvisations."

"A school club on a Saturday?" Jack asked with derision. "Is it a *Communist* club?"

Kate approached the mantel and stepped on the hearth to regard herself more closely. "It's *theater*, Jack," she said. "You have to be committed." She turned and smiled falsely. "Oh, well. I'll leave you two lovebirds alone." She stomped up the stairs, the door slammed, and her stereo switched on. *Her* stereo, not the house stereo. All of a sudden there were two. We soon heard the sounds of Joni Mitchell's "Chelsea Morning" blasting through the ceiling.

"Did she flip her lid when her mother died, or what?" Jack looked to the stairs. "*Lovebirds? Theater?* She's turning into fucking Blanche DuBois." He plucked her sweater from my chest, pinching it and draping it across the coffee table. "How long has this been going on?"

I shook my head. I couldn't remember the time before, or the way it used to be. There were the things we used to do, factual things, and those were easy to recall—playing, biking, singing. As for the things we'd conjured and believed, those were harder to recapture. I wondered if ideals existed only because there was so much to be learned in the loss of them.

Jack pulled me close, kissing my head. "I never thought I'd say this, but let's get the fuck out of here and go to my house."

It was almost seven. We had only a half hour to be alone at Jack's house. His parents were finishing dinner at Gordon's in Amagansett, where they'd had a six o'clock reservation. At seven-fifteen his mother would deliver his father to the Jitney, and by seven-thirty, she would be home.

Mr. Fleming would be back in Manhattan two and a half hours after that. They had an apartment on Madison Avenue and Eighty-seventh Street. He worked at Ogilvy & Mather, the advertising agency.

"Nothing creative," Jack would say; he was always quick to set people straight before they tried to connect Jack to his dad. "He's senior account manager for Schweppes. You know, the carbonated sodas. *Schwepperves-cence.*"

"How come your father's going back on a Saturday?" I asked.

"Because *I* came home today," Jack said. "He can't get away fast enough."

At the Fleming house, Jack's sister's dog Mariah barked, so he gave it a kick. Not really a kick, just a kind of dragging push to one side with the top of his foot. Inside, the air was heavy with the scent of cologne. It spooked me to think of Mr. Fleming's barrel-chested shadow appearing suddenly to block a doorway.

"What perfume does he wear?" I wrinkled my nose. "Lagerfeld?"

"Cat Piss," Jack said. He yanked open the refrigerator door. It smacked the counter and glass bottles clanked. "He must think he's gonna get laid on the bus." Jack grabbed a yogurt, tore off the lid, and flung it into the sink like a Frisbee. He tilted his head back and drank from the cup. Halfway through he paused. "Want some?"

"What flavor is it?"

"I don't know," he said. "I haven't hit fruit yet." He swallowed a little more. "Not the kind you like. It tastes purple."

"Blueberry," I said. "Forget it."

Mariah skulked past our ankles as we moved to the hallway. "Keep away from that beast," Jack warned. "It's an operative."

I asked what an operative was. He said like a spy.

He started up the stairs, his filthy sneakers knocking into the shallow depths. There was something wretched about the sight. "I'll wait here," I said. Mr. and Mrs. Fleming didn't like us to go upstairs when they were out.

Jack reached for my hand. "C'mon, Evie. I swear, we'll just be a minute."

On the southwest side of the attic, Jack had constructed a retreat for himself. He liked to say it was the only room in the house uncontaminated by damask and deodorizer. The windows were shuttered, the paint on the walls was charcoal gray, and the floors were bare wood because three months after we'd met, Jack had torn out the rug. It was the day before he was supposed to leave for boarding school—Labor Day Sunday, 1978. He'd intended to destroy the whole room and after that, the whole house, including the carport.

"Especially the carport," he'd declared. I had no doubt that he meant it. Unlike most people who say they hate their parents, Jack really did.

He'd tried in all sincerity to talk to them, to apologize for certain things, to reason with them about his feelings, to ask them to please let him spend his junior and senior years in East Hampton, to not send him away. I'd gone with him for moral support—only not all the way. I waited at the end of the street, on the porch of the Presbyterian Church. I brought a book, figuring it might take a while. But Jack reappeared in ten minutes.

"That was fast," I said. "What happened?"

"What happened," Jack repeated. "*Hmmm,* let's see." He took my book from me and began to slap it against his thigh. "I try to reconcile. I swear to conform. I sit there, totally fucking humiliating myself. I tell them that I don't want to lose you."

"And," I prodded softly.

"My mother's sure we'll *stay friends.* She says, 'You can write.' "

I hated to hear his voice sound desperate and alone when it did not have to be, not when I was right there.

"Then," Jack said, "the fat bastard goes to the barbecue grill, totally ignoring me, and says, 'C'mon, Susan. I don't want those ribs to char.' "

"Char," I said, "Wow. Who uses a word like *char?*"

"Fat bastards," Jack stated. "Ad agency homos. Neocons. That's who."

At dawn the following morning, he took a knife to his room. After cutting the curtains and shredding the carpet, he'd intended to start on the walls, but beneath the rug in the center of the room, he'd discovered a very old Christmas card with stained edges that looked like it could have been from around the early 1900s. Inside, in childish handwriting, it said, *Eveline.*

He jammed the open card into my hands. I was in my underwear and a T-shirt, and we were standing in the driveway by the garage because it was early and that was the back way to my bedroom if you didn't want to wake up other people. He was winded from running and covered in the fine white matter of demolition. He yanked me into the sunlight, handed over the card, set his hands on his thighs, and bent to catch his breath.

I looked from the card to his face. "I don't understand."

"I found it! In my room. I was pulling out the carpet."

I asked was he sure.

"Of course I'm sure!"

"Maybe someone put it there," I said. "Like, planted it."

"That rug's been there for years," he said. "Besides, no one we know is that interesting. What would be the point?"

He dropped to the dew-soaked grass. I dropped too.

"Listen," he instructed. "I'm cutting and tearing out the rug, I'm throwing the pieces down the stairs, and I'm raising all kinds of dust and shit to really piss them off, and just when I'm about to bust the windows or pry off the molding, I see this paper on the floor." Jack gestured with his hands as he spoke, which he almost never did. "I go to the paper, I lift it. It's a Christmas card. There are angels on front. Did you see the angels?" he asked.

"I saw them," I said.

"Look at the fucking angels," he insisted, pushing the card back at me.

"Yes," I swore. "I see."

"And this, did you see this?" Jack opened it again and tapped at my name. It was scrawled in loopy script that dipped to the right, in old-fashioned penmanship—*Eveline*. "I might have killed him," he said. "I might have done it this time, if he came up those stairs." He looked at the ground, numb. "You had to see me. I had a knife in one hand, and in the other hand I had the card."

He left for boarding school in Kent, Connecticut, later that day without a fight. He took the card with him, and in the Flemings' driveway, where we said goodbye, he vowed to me privately, but before God and whomever the fuck else, to take it with him everywhere he went for the rest of his sorry fucking life, as a mystic but tangible reminder that no matter how far apart he and I might grow, at the core we were one, that we were meant to be one, that things would work out as nature intended, and that no one could prevent destiny's unfolding, not even us, because we were connected—*spiritually*. "Understand?" he said, as his sister, Elizabeth, leaned on the horn of the family's New Yorker.

"I understand," I said, because truly I did, and to seal the vow we kissed. He popped the passenger door. Before getting in, he gave a final wave of the middle finger to his parents, who were largely concealed behind the living room drapes. Then he left, and he stayed away at Kent until he dropped out at Thanksgiving. He was gone just three months, though it had felt more like a thousand years.

Jack was emptying his knapsack from summer. It smelled like heath and wax and mold, and it was covered in President Carter campaign buttons from 1976: JERSEY LOVES CARTER-MONDALE, UAW FOR CARTER-MONDALE, END THE NIXON LEGACY—VOTE JIMMY CARTER, and Jack's particular favorite, CARTER É BRAVISSIMO. The smell was probably from camping in the mountains, but with Jack you never knew. He pulled the card from deep inside his bag and laid it on the desktop. I touched it, the inside part with my name, for luck, then I sat on the bed. Jack's bed was built into the room, wedged square and high into the corner. When you sat, your feet did not touch ground. Attached to the long wall above it was a shelf for shells, fossils, field guides, and bottled things such as butterflies, and also bones and books. *A World of Fungi, The Stranger, Demian.* In *Demian,* Jack had found Abraxas.

"Like on the Santana album—*Abraxas*. There's a quote from Hermann Hesse on the cover," he'd said. "How cool is it that Santana reads Hesse?"

Across from the bed, his Technics stereo system was set carefully on milk crates from Schwenk's, the local dairy farm, twelve of them stacked four wide, three tall, and all filled with albums—some rock, some punk, but mostly jazz and blues. Above that were five guitars, including a 1968 Martin D-28 with a Brazilian rosewood bridge, and a Gibson Les Paul Standard with sunburst finish and humbucking pickups. Near his pillow was a stuffed mouse I'd made in seventh-grade home economics, the only thing I'd ever sewn.

"I can't believe you still have this mouse," I said. I was terrible at sewing. "Do you really like it, or do you just feel sorry for me?"

"I really like it. Though I also happen to feel sorry for you." He kissed my eyelids and lowered himself on top of me.

"Jack," I whispered uncomfortably, pushing him. "Let's get out of here."

We stopped to see the trees on Main Street. The giant elms in East Hampton were dying from Dutch elm disease and many had been marked for removal.

"I went straight to your house," Jack explained. "I didn't get a chance to check the trees."

Jack lay in the grass across from the Hunnting Inn, his head hanging off the curb into the gutter. I watched the car tires whizzing past his extended neck, wondering if he would be decapitated. His untucked Jethro Tull T-shirt crept up his chest, and his jeans slid to reveal the waistband of a pair of boxer shorts. The design on them was of red go-go dancers. The shorts were mine, anyway my father's, from the fifties. Jack's apricot belly was marked by a V of muscle low in the center and a narrow ladder of hair that mounted the middle. I crawled through the grass and got next to him, facing up also. "This one's awesome," he said. "The branch over Main Street is like an arm bent at the elbow. Pretty soon it will be gone."

The streets of the village were full of fog. Along the way to the pizza place, I kept putting up my hands as if to part curtains. Jack was saying how in Wyoming juniper trees have round blue cones like grapes and how Rick Ruddle said that inhaling labdanum tranquilizes the mind. Rick Ruddle was Jack's hike leader and a sound engineer from Portland.

Brothers Four Pizzeria was crowded. Troy Resnick was there with Min Kessler, the eye doctor's daughter. Jack and Troy slapped loose hands. "How was the trip, man?" Troy asked.

Jack said, "Outrageous, man."

Troy examined the watermelon-colored Kryps on Jack's skateboard, and Jack informed Troy that his haircut was *butt ugly*. I lifted a copy of *Dan's Papers* from a stack on the floor and took the front table. Through the ribbon of mist that divided Newtown Lane, the red neon sign from

Sam's Restaurant seemed milky red and noirish, making me think of detective novels—single-bullet shootings. A pop, a body, some footsteps, a detective.

"Catch you later, man," I heard Jack say.

Troy slurped back cheese. "Meet us at the beach."

"Which one, Wiborg's?" Jack asked.

"Indian Wells."

"Too far," Jack said. "I don't have a car, and I'm not driving with you. You suck."

Other kids starting calling out to Jack. He transmitted a series of apathetic hellos, then declared with annoyance, "Listen, people, I gotta get some fucking food."

At the counter he ordered two slices and stared down Dino and Vinny while he waited. They irritated Jack, the way they thought they were masculine. He liked to say that they must have had some very big hairy dicks beneath those oil-stained pizza aprons. For his part, Jack astounded them, the way he was puny and unkempt but had a girl like me. He seemed to personify for them the trouble with America. Dino would just shake his head when he saw us, which pleased Jack infinitely. Jack liked to take me there; we went about three times a week.

Jack deposited two paper plates on the table, each with its own overhanging slice, and the plates swirled a bit from grease coming through. Jack lowered his chin to the plane of the table and bit his folded slice. "Mooks," he said through his food. He didn't know what a Mook was, he'd just heard it once in a movie called *Mean Streets,* which my dad had taken us to see. Ever since then, everybody who pissed him off was a Mook. I tore the crust from my slice and chewed. Jack wanted to know if the pizza guys had given me a hard time while he was gone.

"This is the first time I've been here since you left," I said.

He knocked his head back to suck the soda from his can. His hair fanned out against his shoulders, and I could see his Adam's apple dip and rise. I don't like to see them, not ever, Adam's apples. I turned away; Dino was staring.

"Let's go, Jack," I said, standing and pulling my sweater around my shoulders, buttoning one button at the neck. "The movie starts in five minutes. We're going to miss the oil globs." Before the beginning of every film, the theater would project wafting oil globs on the screen, kind of like a giant lava lamp.

"Right," he said, jumping up to grab his skateboard. When I tossed the remainder of my pizza into the garbage, he caught it before it hit the can and crammed it into his mouth.

As we started for the theater, he jumped onto his skateboard and whizzed by me in the street. Jack was handsome, in a seedy and purposeful way, the way a barn in disrepair looks so good in the middle of a lush green field. It was true he had changed over the summer, or maybe it was me who had changed. I said, "I can't believe we're finally seniors."

"I was just thinking that," he said as he rode up the curb, then popped back off in front of Tony's Sporting Goods. "Troy's doing whippets tonight. That's why he wants to meet later."

"Isn't it like breathing into a paper bag?"

"Yeah. It's so stupid. That's what makes it fun." He approached Newtown and Main, and at the corner he twirled smoothly on the rear wheels. His arms were bent at the elbows, his right leg extended, his left leg flexed. His hair windmilled lightly. Then he leapt off, flipping the front end of his board into his ready hand, waiting for me to catch up. We met at the light.

"Your leg ever bother you?" I asked.

"Nah," he said. "Sometimes."

Jack was wearing a cast when we met. "The summer of 1978 is a study in bitter irony," he liked to say. "In the midst of the worst period of a particularly shitty life, I met you."

Because of his broken leg Jack had had to cancel his annual Outward Bound trip, which meant he was stuck at home with his family. For weeks he wasn't even able to climb the three flights to his room, so he had to sleep in the den, or, as he said, in the *transverse colon* of the house, *where all the shit sits and ferments before moving through.* Jack was forced to endure the petty mechanics of family life—every dinner and phone conversation, every key jingle and cabinet slam.

Once, he and his dad fought so bad that Mr. Fleming called the police.

"What did you do?" I asked.

"I threatened him with a weapon."

"A gun?"

"No," he confided, "I couldn't reach the gun. A knife."

"A *knife*? Your leg was broken! He couldn't possibly have been scared."

Jack shrugged. "What can I say? I have excellent aim."

I knew Jack from school; everyone did because of Atomic Tangerine. Prior to that he and Kate had had the same piano teacher, Laura Lipton, a songwriter from Sag Harbor whose dog, Max, was a television actor—Ken-L Ration, Chuck Wagon, and so on. Occasionally Kate's lesson would encroach upon Jack's, and she would play with the dog just in order to stick around and listen. She would call me after to say how well Jack Fleming played.

We never actually spoke until the day in early summer when he came with his parents to the Lobster Roll, where his older sister, Elizabeth, was a waitress and I was a busgirl. I watched him from across the room. I'd never seen anyone so uncomfortable in my life. As his father talked without pause, Jack stared through the window out onto Napeague Highway, clanking his spoon against his cast, keeping a secret rhythm. He would lower his face to the table to sip his water. His broken leg was propped onto a second chair.

Elizabeth asked me to carry over the drinks. "Please. I can't deal with them."

The cocktail tray rested on the flat of my left forearm, and I bent to deposit each drink carefully. I couldn't help but notice the way the afternoon sun encountered Jack's face, the glassine glow to his eyes. When I looked into them, I could not look away. They became a beautiful horizon, dominions of clouds and winds of ice and insinuations of birds. I considered sadly the world he saw through those eyes. Probably nothing in real life could match the purity of vision they beheld.

Mr. Fleming asked my name.

I set down his plastic cup of chardonnay. I said, "Eveline."

"Eveline? Fan-*tas*-tic!" He began to sing. *Eveline, Evangeline.*

I delivered Jack's Coke, and my breast accidentally grazed his right arm, a little beneath his shoulder. We both kind of froze.

"Which of your parents reads Longfellow?" Mr. Fleming demanded. Jack shifted protectively as though to block me.

"My mother," I replied, "teaches poetry. Short stories and Shakespeare too. But I think my name is from *Dubliners*."

"Joyce—bah. Overrated," Mr. Fleming barked dismissively. "Let's see, let's see now, Longfellow. It's been quite some time."

"Where does she teach, dear?" Mrs. Fleming interrupted.

"Southampton College," I said. Mr. Fleming cleared his throat and begin to recite. *"Gentle Evangeline*—et cetera, et cetera, something, something, something—*When she had passed it seemed like the ceasing of exquisite music."*

Jack glowered at him and clapped three times very, very slowly.

"Well, now, Eveline-Evangeline," Mr. Fleming said. "What do you intend to do with the great fortune you will have amassed by the end of summer?"

"Oh. I'm not sure. Probably just buy paints and stuff. You know, art stuff," I said.

He was silent—they all were—stunned no doubt by the humorless sincerity of my reply. As I delivered straws and cleared away soiled appetizer plates, I felt for the first of many times the intensity of Jack's gaze and the blood that pooled darkly in my cheeks.

At the waitress station, Elizabeth garnished glasses of iced tea with lemon wheels, and she spoke of Jack. I listened from the far side of the lattice divider. It was funny to see her face after seeing his—his was so much prettier. Her parents had tried everything, she said. She said that Jack had seen psychiatrists since he was seven, that he was a noncompliant patient, that he had been on more medications than there are states, that he was talented in music, and that he had just been enrolled in boarding school near their grandparents' house in Connecticut. He was leaving in September. "He tried to kill my father a few weeks ago, you know," Elizabeth whispered to Sue and Renata.

Renata admitted she'd read about it in *The East Hampton Star.*

"He should be grateful that he's going to school instead of prison." Elizabeth hoisted a tray onto her arm and walked away.

Since I'd never spoken to Jack, I could not really rise to his defense. But I figured that at least I ought to tell him how I felt about what I'd heard. You sort of have an obligation to tell someone that he can trust you more than he can trust his own sister.

No one offered Jack a hand as they prepared to leave. I held his chair for him as he stood, and I followed him to hold open the door.

"Good luck, Lady Evangeline," Mr. Fleming thundered above his wife's head as she crossed the vestibule to join him. "Though I don't expect you'll need it."

Jack swung past with his body hanging far over his crutches. "Thanks," he mumbled, and I went with him into the corridor, which seemed to confuse everyone, including me.

Mr. Fleming winked knowingly. "Meet you outside, son."

"Sorry about that," Jack said when they left. "He's a dick."

"It's okay," I assured him, feeling shy to be the object of his eyes. Inside the enamel blue rings were specks, little stars twinkling. "So when do you get your cast off?"

"Thursday," he said caustically, dragging the word out. He looked to the ground. Without lifting his head, his eyes returned to mine. To say he was handsome was not quite right, not quite enough: the look in his eyes was transcendent. On the restaurant radio was that Wings song "Maybe I'm Amazed."

We watched the cars race down Napeague stretch.

"You should come over sometime," I said.

"What time do you get off?"

I said at five.

"All right," he said, moving off, "see you at six."

"Wait," I called. "You don't know where I live."

He paused at the door. "By the tracks," he said. Then he left, his compact frame ticking gracefully between shiny pale crutches.

People always asked why I went out with him. I just liked him better than anyone else. He didn't have that ballooned chest or stiff-shouldered look other boys had. Jack was skinny, but fluid, loose in the legs, and, though he was careful with me, the chances he took with himself were real. One night when he, Dan, and Smokey Cologne were out of pot, they smoked oregano leaves and drank codeine cough syrup. On a dare, Smokey did a shot of Downy fabric softener and had to get his stomach pumped. After the hospital, they came to my house and dove kamikaze-style off the back of the couch until Dan broke his nose and they had to go back to the hospital. Jack had tried peyote in New Mexico and LSD at the Roxy during a George Thorogood concert—*a rockabilly nightmare,* he'd said. He'd snorted speed and done cocaine. He hated coke. "I end up smiling all fucking night," Jack complained.

It didn't really bother me if he got high. His was like a body without skin, and he had to desensitize himself. I didn't mind the way he predicted his own disappointment, calling everything pointless and existence senseless. I just figured it was a way to protect himself. The only truly threatening thing I ever noticed about Jack was his surplus of confidence—a tremendous ego is a dangerous thing in someone so gloomy. He could not be persuaded away from his blackest convictions, and anyone who disagreed with him was part of the whole fucking problem to begin with. Though I would never ever have told him so, Jack was very much the son of his father.

"We were sleeping in an open field," Jack said as we stepped forward with the movie line. "In Montana. After dawn we heard a weird whooshing sound."

"A UFO!" I said. Jack and I had seen one at Albert's Landing once. It looked like twin pods, like a salt circle pinched at the center.

"No, almost. A hot air balloon," he said. "Hovering. Like a rubber rainbow. We jumped out of our sleeping bags and ran after it, all of us naked." Jack would've made a good Indian. He could make fire with a magnifying glass and sleep naked on mountains in the cold. He could tie knots you could not escape from.

"Girls too?" I asked.

"Two for *Amityville Horror,*" Jack told LizBeth Bennett, who was working in the box office. She tore two pink tickets off a spool. "Yeah," he said, "Girls too."

It didn't bother me that he had seen the girls naked and maybe had sex with them. I was only envious of all the places he'd visited. I'd been to only eight states—mostly with my father. Jack had been to twenty-six—always alone.

He shoved a messy wad of change into his pocket. "I wrote a song about it."

"About the balloon?" I asked.

"About how you weren't there to see it," he said.

We sat in the third row and followed the wafting oil globs on the movie screen. Jack removed his black journal from his coat to show me the stuff he'd collected and recorded and all the songs he'd written for me during his trip. His drawings were compact and obsessively detailed, mathematical almost, like da Vinci's. Most pages had variations of the same landscape—upside down and tilted. Like a vortex, like water down a bathtub drain.

"That's in the Tetons," he explained solemnly. His group had to cross a ridge with tremendous drops on each side, and there was this yellow plastic tag nailed to the point where some guy had fallen off. "It would have been so easy, Evie." Jack used my name for emphasis, and I listened with care. We were low in our seats, so low that people behind probably couldn't see our heads, only our knees propped on the chairs in front of us. I held his bicep with two hands wrapped around his red windbreaker. "The free fall. I would have shattered and spread." His hands pushed out in two opposing directions, "Like, distributed."

"*Re*-distributed," I said. "Like back to raw matter."

"*Re*-distributed," he said, "*Exactly,* yeah."

I liked the idea of marking the place where a life ends as opposed to the place a corpse is buried. And also the idea of leaving remains uncollected. It's bad enough *being* dead, but it's worse to have people *see* you dead, to have living hands feel a dead you, jostle and dress you, push your stiffening arms into clean sleeves and cry over your blood-drained body. At a wake or funeral, people say a dead body is "at rest," but actually, it is working. The corpse assists the living, it stops time. It helps to postpone the reality of loss. It's hard to know which is worse, never seeing a loved one again or seeing them again packed with fixative and formaldehyde, with plastic and whey and alkalis and binders, and hearing people mutter, *She looks so peaceful,* when what they really mean is, *She's stuffed like a glycerol scarecrow.* Probably that mountain climber's spirit was drifting motionlessly like an eagle soaring in place. Flags flap that way, blowing grandly to nowhere.

"I missed you," Jack said.

I'd missed him too. I took a handful of popcorn, then brought my fist to his mouth, pushing some kernels gently in. He ate until he reached my hand, which he bit lightly. The projector jolted on, and his face flashed to blue snow.

"That death marker thing is cool," I whispered to cheer him. Jack could be quick to turn, and suddenly he seemed down. "Instead of cemeteries."

"Ah, forget it. It's a bogus idea. There'd be bodies everywhere."

"Not bodies. *Markers*. Bodies get cremated."

"True," he said with new interest. "Highways would be littered." We hated highways.

"I want my marker to be suspended in midair, only not hitting the mountainside, just like if I died of shock during a fall from a peak. Or maybe projected upward like the Batman logo, if that's even possible."

"Sure it is," Jack speculated, "if you got shot out of a cannon."

"But you'd have to be a clown to die like that."

"That would blow," Jack said. "Dying as a clown."

I asked him where he would like his marker to be.

Jack said, "Right here." He touched the inside of my elbow.

One time after Jack and I met, I mentioned him to my friend Denny. Denny and I were lying on the steps outside the barn. The door behind us was open, and light from inside seeped out to form a pale pond around our reclining bodies. We were like seals on an iceberg.

"Seals are fat," Denny said. "Besides, it's July." He was breaking pieces off of sticks and throwing them at fireflies. "Let's be shipwrecked. On an atoll."

When I had to pee, I went behind the barn. It would have taken too long to go to the front house, and I never knew when Denny might just take off. He was private with his personal life, and he often made plans he did not share.

"Hey, Den," I called, "what do you think of Jack Fleming?"

"Jack Fleming?" Denny called back. "He's cute, if you like the grungy look. Why?"

"I saw him at the restaurant."

"Not *working*, I hope," Denny said. "He's a little hostile for the service industry."

"He came in with his mom and dad," I said when I came back. I lay against Denny's belly, and he began to play with my hair.

"It's so fine," he said of my hair. "Like the white stuff in corn. Those limp fibers inside."

"He gives me a funny feeling," I said, meaning Jack, "like I'm supposed to do something."

"Have you ever heard him sing?" Denny asked. "I was at a party at Dan Lewis's house and their band was playing. The band sucked, but when Jack sang alone, it was pretty incredible."

"What did he play?"

"Normal stuff—covers of other people's songs, I guess."

"I mean, what instrument."

Denny said, "Oh, he played the guitar."

A few weeks later, Jack and I had sex. We were sixteen and we drank rum. It started out when Jack came to find me in the barn. Instead of talking, he leaned against the wall and watched me draw. He had just gotten the cast removed from his leg, and it was the first time I'd seen him without crutches. An orange glow warmed his face; it was from an outdoor light coming through the glass. I wiped my hands on my legs and pushed the loose hair from my eyes with the back of my wrist. When I stood, Jack pulled my face to his, giving me a kiss.

The Fourth of July fireworks erupted over Main Beach as we made our way from my house to his. When you walk at night in East Hampton, the sidewalk goes black before you, and the world pitches left. It's the massive roots of the trees that split the concrete walkways.

"You okay?" he kept asking, and I kept saying, "Yes."

David's Lane is stately and broad. I'd passed Jack's house on my bicycle about a thousand times, but it looked brand-new now that I knew that Jack lived there. An open plaza of grass led to a beige colonial façade. Inside was beige as well, parchment-colored and bland, with furnishings that were measured and moderate.

Things were the opposite at my house. My mother was constantly picking up some moldering armoire or fusty wall-mount ironing board at the dump and hauling it home. I would find her waiting for me on the front lawn, bewitched by some relic. "I practically had to wrestle Dump Keith out of his wheelchair for this one," she'd say.

Somehow we were always alone on those nights; it was possible that she didn't want distraction or interference. "You and I can move furniture better than any two men," Mom would call out proudly as we maneuvered hulking items through doors and up staircases. Every corner of the house became eligible for overhaul. Phones would be moved, drawer contents rotated, bedrooms swapped, bulb wattages finessed, chairs recovered. Surrounded by staple guns and fabric remnants and tools given to her by my father, we would pick at TV dinners of meat loaf and apple cobbler as we rewired old lamps, antiqued the woodwork, anchored mirrors into brick, and outfitted tables with perfectly pleated fabric skirts.

To make space for a new piece, she would give others away. Nargis Lata, her professor friend from the college, took the "electric couch," a bizarre wooden chaise with embedded metal plates for heating the extremities. Big John got the hassock embroidered with black leprechauns, Dad and Marilyn got the Balinese crèche, and for Christmas one year, Walter the mailman got the knee-high copper cannon. He came to collect it on a Sunday in his sagging blue station wagon. My mother said that out of his postal uniform, Walter looked "laid bare and brought to the light of day." His Rottweiler wouldn't let us near his car.

"There's a fine bit of irony, Walter," Powell said. "Usually dogs prevent *your* approach."

I navigated the Fleming house, listening to the pressurized pops of fireworks exploding, counting booms—sixteen, seventeen, twenty. On the kitchen counter, beneath a fawn Princess wall phone was a prescription bottle with his mother's name on it: *Susan Fleming, 500 mg, BID. Refill 3.* Three refills seemed like a lot. Three seemed like a condition. Next to a list for Rita the maid was a neat stack of stamped envelopes— paid bills to mail. A pair of men's leather strap sandals were near the back door on a new straw mat, and hanging from a hook on the white wainscoted laundry room wall was a key chain with a shiny BMW tag. The dryer bounced confidently. I was pretty sure that the Flemings never had checks returned or put locks on the telephone dial to keep people from using it or walked around collecting all the lightbulbs in a straw basket and putting them in the car trunk whenever the Lilco bill got too high. The last time Mom did that, someone rear-ended the Scamp and all the bulbs broke.

I wondered how it felt to be rich, or to have money, or at least to have some sense of sufficiency. At my house we lived in chronic fear of what the next day would bring. The only time that terror got suspended was on a birthday. That's probably the point of birthdays, to give people a break from black unknowns, to indulge the person for a day. You hear it all the time—*For Christ's sake, it's my birthday.*

And yet, despite his family's means, it did not seem wrong to say that Jack's had been a life of deprivation. Except for his record collection and his guitars, all the items in that house belonged to Mr. and Mrs. Fleming exclusively. When we were at my house or in town, it was easy to forget about his relations—he was just Jack. But the more familiar I became with his home, the more inextricably bound to those people I found him to be. His parents maintained control largely through tactics of guilt and fear, through threats of withholding, by calling what they'd accumulated "their own," as though whatever had been earned hadn't been drawn from the bank of family time, against family interest.

Jack patted the kitchen counter, gesturing for me to sit. He reached into a cabinet above the wall oven and got the rum. "One hundred eighty-one proof," he informed me. "My old man picked it up in Jamaica. On a *golf trip*. With his *lady friend.*"

"He has a girlfriend?" It seemed hard to believe. It would have made more sense for Jack's mom to have someone else. She was actually attractive.

"A *lady friend,*" Jack corrected. He hopped up next to me, breathing in through clenched teeth because his leg was still sore. "He's had several that I know of. He loads them up on gimlets and recounts his sob story of white male supremacy—prep school, Ivy League, two cars, Madison Avenue apartment, house in the Hamptons, condo in Bermuda, spoiled kids, spendthrift wife. Women feel sympathetic, thinking he's devoted but misunderstood. Then he drags them back to his lair—our place in

New York—and he pops them. The family is his script. He gets his *money's worth* for supporting us."

Jack took a few belts from the bottle, drinking expertly, but when it was my turn to take a mouthful, I held my breath, knocking the liquid down like screwing a cap on a jar with the heel of my hand.

I said, "That's really gross."

"The rum?"

"Your dad." Though the rum was gross too. "Does your mother know?" I didn't like to know something about her life that she didn't know. If there was a code, that would surely be breaking it. Sometimes life is irreverent, and you accidentally discover you are a party to irreverence, and it's hard to know what to do.

Jack shrugged. "His most recent conquest is the receptionist from Ogilvy. She's not the sexy type of receptionist assholes snag in movies," he related in his darkest drawl, "but the terrifying type they end up with in real life."

"You saw her?"

"I walked in on them screwing in the maid's room. I came into the city on a Tuesday to go to the frigging orthodontist. He must not have gotten the message, but what else is new? Elizabeth was in a coma once for two days after a bike accident before we found him—he'd called in sick to work, then took off for a 'midweek getaway,' neglecting to mention it to my mother. Anyway, I got to the apartment and heard gagging from near the kitchen. I thought someone was choking. I figured the super had come up to fix a leak, maybe, then swallowed a chicken bone during his lunch break. Unfortunately, no one was dying."

I took the bottle from his hand and placed it behind me, out of reach. His hands came together in his lap. I hadn't yet heard him talk that much. His delivery was controlled, his voice made richer by the lack of inflection.

"Couple years ago, I found a stash of creepy love letters in the basement ceiling rafters. I run to my mother, thinking, *She's free*. But she refused to read them, saying that I was *mistaken,* that I was out to demean my father, that I needed more therapy. Even if I could have gotten her to admit the affairs were true, she probably would have taken the blame for the failed relationship, for her *frigidity*—that's his descriptor of choice. *Frigidity?* More like common sense. Who knows who he's been with?

"I admire his *originality*," Jack said sarcastically. "Instead of being grateful that my mother and sister give him the fucking time of day, that worthless piece of shit wakes up and says, 'I have an empty apartment, an absent family, a high-paying job, and I live in a city full of desperate women—*What damage can I inflict today?*' It's like a criminal with a loaded gun and a full tank of gas, or a plantation master with a whip and a horse. They're all thinking the same thing: if I don't use these conditions to my advantage, what a waste of weapons."

I put my hand on the back of his neck and swept aside his hair. He had beautiful white-blond hair to his shoulders. He never brushed it—it just twisted and tangled softly.

He looked from his hands to my face. His ice-blue eyes worked in earnest, as though taking in more of me than I could present. The fireworks were still popping, but the finale would soon be coming. "C'mon. Let's go upstairs," he said.

As we mounted the first and second flights of stairs to his room, I felt somewhat like a trespasser, especially after Jack's story. But the third set was thinner and steeper. It had a curious turn at the top and a feeble light at the end, giving it the feel of a tunnel leading from one world to another. With each step we detached ourselves further from everything and everyone we had ever known. The privacy we felt was unlike any other, coming as it did when we needed it most. Ours was a very lucky privacy.

Jack was before me, we were near the bed, we were kissing, we were lying back, descending. The smell of his bed was the smell of him, only multiplied. It confused me to be initiated into his aloneness; it confused me to know such a place existed, such a repository of untried masculinity and pathetic virility, such a site of self-love and self-abuse. The quilt bubbled around my body and the weight of Jack was good, reminding me of the times I have been buried in sand. I pressed my hips into his because it seemed like the right thing to do, although the part that longed for pressure was farther down and deeper in. My muscles raised me, uncertainly at first, in a practicing way, each time squeezing more expertly, each time tightening an invisible tube inside.

I thought we might have been waiting for something. I thought maybe it was me. My hand journeyed from his shoulder, drifting fitfully down, and he lifted himself so I could reach where he seemed to know I was going. He was leaning and supporting his body on his left knee, making room. His head hung to watch, his hair cascading around my face like a paper waterfall. With my finger I traced the teeth of his zipper upward from its base to its flap, and as I started to draw it down, the zipper pushed itself open from pressure. Everyone knows about the parts of a woman, but you never hear about the parts of a man, not in any specific regard. Even in great artwork, men's genitals are under-realized, scribbled or shadowy, as if the artist wanted to be courageous, but only *sort of*. As if there were some incentive to keeping men mythic, as if the part and the man were the same, and preserving the mystique of one meant preserving the power of the other.

But in my hand was a contradiction of skin and muscle, something solid but fragile, potent but meager, something both majestic and vile. Jack seemed helpless to the way it stood parallel to his belly. It occurred to me that grown-up men such as teachers and coaches know but keep secret the way erections make boys defenseless. Maybe women know, but maybe it's late already when they find out. It seems like something girls should know too, and earlier, the way boys are capable of such delicate reversals.

On our way out of the house that night, we passed the piano. Jack faltered, touching it. Though he used to perform for his parents, now he only played when they were out. He tried to deprive them of pleasure whenever possible, he said, but I knew it was because they made him feel hateful, and he couldn't touch something he loved so much with hating hands. He sat on the ebony bench, and just when I thought he'd forgotten I was there, he reached to pull me to his side.

"Eric Satie," he said of the music he played for me. *"Trois Gymnopedies, Number 2."* Then he tried something melodic and easy, something you'd hear on the radio. Over and over he practiced the same few bars with a single hand.

"Whose is that?" I asked. "It's pretty."

"No one's," he answered. "I just made it up."

6

Our bodies lay entwined in a musty navy-blue sleeping bag. The flannel interior had a rodeo pattern with tiny cowboys on bucking chocolate horses, swinging golden ropes against a wan blue sky. I wondered if such places exist. If they did, someday I might like to go there. My head rested in the space between Jack's arm and chest. Above us, night was an absorbent black, like felt.

"You haven't told me anything," he said. "It's been three weeks."

Though I didn't feel like discussing Maman's death, he seemed to *want* me to discuss it, or *need* me to discuss it, and so I agreed, since part of harmonious living is conceding to the wants and needs of others, even if you don't feel like it.

"First you left, then I went to my dad's, then right away Kate called, saying, 'Come home.' I guess it was still June. After that the days merged into one hazy, humid streak."

Kate and I witnessed the moody stillness of summer as if from the backseat of a speeding car, catching only glimpses of sundresses in pink and lime, and shapeless straw bags. Crickets in the morning, the solitary hum of a mower pulsing through grass, the menacing banter of gulls, the whoosh and patter of flapping things at the beach. Kites and towels. It was like a memory of all the summers I've ever had, chopped up and stuck together.

Jack said, "A montage."

"Yes," I said. "Exactly."

On the train from Manhattan back to East Hampton, I placed my head against the mottled graffiti-etched glass. A grime smell from the vent that ran along the lower edge of the window filled my nose. I replayed Kate's phone call in my head until it was like a meditation.

Is it you?
Yes, it's me.
I took my mother to the hospital.
Oh. Is your brother there?
Not until the weekend.
Do you want me to come?
Yes. There's a train at nine.

It was hot when we arrived in East Hampton. The crossing bells rang slowly as the train ambled into the station and landed on its chin like an exhausted bovine. The scene was like a portrait of itself, a preternaturally still landscape of poetic components—a station house, a deli, a dry cleaner, a pickup truck, a mailbox resting squarely on sloped grass, trees in tight rows. I stepped out and moved along the platform, feeling dizzy and vaguely lost, though my house was just a few hundred yards away.

"I don't know why, but I called home," I told Jack.

When I saw my reflection in the pay phone, I could see stains beneath my eyes from crying on the train. I kept making mistakes dialing. My fingers kept slipping from the holes.

Eventually I got through. There were funny rings like gargles, then my mother answered.

I said, "Hi, it's me."

"Hi, *you!*" she said. "Where are you?"

"At the train station."

"Well," she prodded gently, "come home."

"Have you heard from Kate?"

"I have. Kate took Claire in to the hospital this morning."

I wondered what was the difference between taking someone *to* the hospital and taking someone *into* the hospital and taking someone *in to* the hospital. If there was a difference, she seemed to be referring to it.

On the walk home I was confused by the prismatic brightness of the sun. I felt a scalding heaviness, an urging into ground. I stared at my feet, clinging as best I could to each moment. With every step forward, I took two more down, walking heavily in the heat like entering at a diagonal into dirt, weary like a miner, filthy already before the day.

———

"The scariest part was the drip," I explained to Jack, "the knowledge that her body was dehydrated and unable to retain fluid."

Nurses would inject needles into the bag instead of into her arm. The bag was buxom, but Maman's arm was like a broken-off branch. I would watch the liquid bubbles come down the intravenous tube and into her, grateful for the entry of every drop into her starved body.

Once we were watching her sleep, and I asked Kate if she remembered the old *Little Audrey* cartoon about drought, when Audrey's garden dries up in the heat and only one drop escapes from the hose spigot.

"Kate kept saying she didn't remember," I told Jack. "And I kept saying, '*Yes,* you do. Remember the way the flowers had drooping heads and limp leaves and crying faces? And the rivers burned out and the fish sat in the sand, fanning themselves?' She just kept saying 'No, I don't remember, no.' But I know we saw it together. I guess, I guess she just—"

Jack kissed my head, pulling me closer in.

Mornings are best for hospital visits. Uniforms are neat, halls are clean, moods are generally blithe. Pain loses some of its drama in day. In the morning tanned doctors with abstruse test results and breezy manners make you think of all the golf you're missing even if you'd never consider playing. In the morning the newspaper cart comes around and the sunshine plays against the walls, like bouncing balls. There is a collective feeling of hope.

"In the evening," I told Jack, "there's only waiting for day."

And the drone of televisions and uncollected dinner trays and fluorescent light. There is the feeling that something has run down in the world like a tank out of gas and that the great machine is winding into crisis. Beneath you, in the emergency room, great tragedies transpire, night tragedies. And when your visit has ended and it's time to go home, you go fully conscious of leaving your loved one alone with their illness, like leaving a child to sleep with a monster in the closet.

"Kate lost a mother," I said, "but I lost nothing."

"Kate doesn't feel that way," Jack assured me.

"But what about everybody besides Kate? How can I ever explain to anyone what Maman was to me when our relationship had no name? People need names. I wasn't a relative or a friend," I said. "I was just an object of her kindness."

He wiped my cheeks, saying *"Ssshh."* I buried my face in his shoulder.

"Kindness is everything," I went on. "When you receive it and express it, it becomes the whole meaning of things. It's life, demystified. A place out of self. Not a waltz, but the whirls within a waltz."

"You're the one now," Jack said definitively. "That's why you met her. She had something she needed to pass on."

One day I tiptoed past the woman in the first bed and set my things on the chair. It was one of those toffee-colored vinyl hospital-style easy chairs that make you think of germs and bad luck. Usually I leaned against the window ledge or sat on the bed.

"Your mother's not here, dear," the woman called over. "They took her to radiology."

I'd noticed the new name on the doorway—Krieger. There was always a new name—someone coming in, someone transferring out, someone getting well and going home. Maman's turn never came. Things kept happening. The last thing was pneumonia.

"She's not my mother, Mrs. Krieger. But thank you anyway."

"Not your mother? An aunt?"

"My friend's mother."

She examined me, one eye half-closed. "Your parents dead?"

"No," I said, thinking, *Not exactly.* I peeled the newspaper off the wildflowers I'd brought from my garden. "I'd better get these in water."

She waved her hand, excusing me. "Just pull the drape open, will you?" I complied, and Mrs. Krieger rolled to face the hall. "These doctors. They expect you to recover in the dark."

At the nurse's station, a brown arm reached automatically over the counter with scissors. It was Mrs. Eden—Sara's mom—and the scissors were the special kind with the angled blades and rounded tip used for cutting adhesives, sutures, and flaps of skin. The nurses did not lend them out because they were supposed to be sanitary, but they made an exception for me. "You're starting to read my mind, Mrs. Eden."

She continued to tend to business. "Maybe not your mind, but certainly your footsteps."

Nurses have a lot of business to attend to. That's why they do not always get to you right away unless you are irrefutably dying. Marilyn is a surgical nurse at New York Hospital. She calls paperwork *lawsuit avoidance detail.*

I returned and dumped the old flowers in the bathroom. The water in the vase was gray like sodden cardboard, with a putrid smell. I hadn't changed it for two days. A lot can happen in two days, in the organic sense.

"My daughter's bringing bagels Saturday," Mrs. Krieger said loudly.

I poked my head around the door. "Are you allowed to do that?"

"Well, you know what it's like when you're dying for a bagel."

"Actually," I said, "I've never had one."

"Never had a bagel? That's ridiculous. How do you read the Sunday papers?"

"I don't know. I guess I usually just eat toast."

"When my brother worked in Geneva," Mrs. Krieger said, "my late husband and I would pack fresh bagels on dry ice and ship them from the Upper West Side to my niece in Paris, who would take them by train when she visited him."

I placed the vase on the food tray between the beds and stood by her.

"We called it the Bagel Connection," she said sadly. She studied the edge of the sheet, threading it through both sets of fingers. When she spoke again, she spoke quietly, as though the disease might hear. "It's in my lymph nodes, you know," she confided.

In her voice was the gravest echo. In her voice I could hear the place her soul could see. I felt sorry to have to leave her there, detached like a balloon adrift, unbefriended and surely sort of homesick.

"Do you know what lymph nodes are?" she asked. She looked beautiful to me, wide-eyed and shiny, like a ladybug.

"Yes," I said, looking to the ground. "Like glands."

"Oh, so you know about lymph nodes but not bagels. What a world I'm leaving."

———

I called Kate one day near the end. I didn't know it was near the end, it just worked out that way. I said I couldn't make it to the hospital.

"Okay," she said, not even asking why.

If she'd asked, I might have said that I needed time to think or something. But she didn't ask. It was as if she'd been expecting me to defect, like *she* thought *I* thought I needed a break. Like she had discussed it already with her brother, Laurent, or my mother. For some reason, I ended up telling a lie.

A lie you volunteer is no different from one you're forced to tell. Forthrightness does not erase the fact that you intend to deceive, especially when the illusion of candor often works to your advantage. The *truth* was I didn't want Kate to think I was abandoning her, when in fact I *was* abandoning her, and I had no idea why. It's madness, of course, to lie to preserve the perception of your good character.

"I'm filling in for someone," I said for some reason. "I just got home and now I have to go back. I still smell like beer and fries."

"Yuck," Kate said. "Didn't you shower?"

"Nah." I took a bite of an apple. "Too tired." I would have continued, but I didn't because I've noticed that when people lie, they commonly say too much as a way to compensate for all they're not saying. That's why it's a good rule to eat when you lie. Whenever someone tells me something while they're eating, I suspect a lie.

"My sister does that shit all the time," Jack injected.

When I hung up with Kate, I realized that I had to go out for the entire duration of a work shift, from afternoon until midnight, in case she happened to stop by my house on her way home from the hospital to see my mother or something.

"The only place I could think to hide," I told Jack, "was Montauk."

"*Montauk?*" Jack asked. He seemed surprised. "How was it?"

"Okay," I told him.

"That's it?"

"That's it," I said.

Twenty minutes before the train left for Montauk, I called my dad at work and killed time by talking to him about things—his job and politics and all these people in my family I never asked about. He kept saying everyone was fine, and then he'd ask again how I was doing.

I'd say, "Good, good. How's Marilyn?"

"Fine, fine, she's fine. And you? What are you up to today?"

"Not much."

It occurred to me that there was a chance he might talk to Kate. He might call back that evening, and if Kate actually did stop by, she might answer the phone and say I was working a double shift, in which case my father would say that he had spoken with me earlier, and that I hadn't mentioned it. I considered covering myself. I considered telling him the same lie I'd told Kate, or even better—*approximately* the same lie. I could use the opportunity of a conversation with my father to *undo* the lie to Kate. I could have told him that I was *supposed* to fill in for someone at the restaurant but that the waitress called and said she decided to go in after all. That way if he talked to Kate, and Kate found out I *hadn't* worked an extra shift, the original lie would sound super-authentic. But I'd never lied to my father, or to my mother. They'd never given me a reason to.

Lying is a full-time occupation, even if you tell just one, because once you tell it, you're stuck with it. If you want to do it right, you have to visualize it, conjure the graphics, tone, and sequence of action, then relate it purposefully in the midst of seemingly spontaneous dialogue. The more actual the lie becomes to the listener, the more actual it becomes to the teller, which is scariest of all. Some people really get to believing their own lies.

The funeral parlor was air-conditioned and minty. I felt guilty to be relieved to be out of the heat. The walls were lined with flowers that flaunted life, jutting triumphantly into the room.

I asked Jack if he'd ever noticed how arrogant cut flowers can be.

"Actually, yes," he said, on his parents' dining room table they could be very arrogant.

My mother and father, Marilyn, Powell, Aunt Lowie, and I signed the guest book, then we took our seats. I walked unsteadily, feeling a little sick from the flower fragrance. Mom informed me that the original intention of funeral flowers was to mask the scent of the dead.

"When Uncle Billy died," Lowie said, "he was waked on a board in the living room. Remember, Rene? The board was really a door off its hinges propped on a table and a borrowed sawhorse."

"In those days," Mom said, "children had to kiss the corpse."

From my position behind Kate, I was forced to abide the procession of crying faces, crying and advancing for meaningful embraces and European kisses. I felt bad for Kate, sitting and standing, standing and sitting, each time smoothing out the back of her midnight-blue crepe skirt. If there were rules, she seemed to know them—I wondered how. Together with her brother, she acknowledged each person's nearness to the dead and helped the group in its struggle for order—who grieved most, whose pain was most real—because in life there is always hierarchy, and it is frankly not profitable to remain modest and anonymous, not even at a funeral. Kate set aside her own despondency to render gratitude for sympathy received.

There was a lyrical aria, Parisian and melancholy, a woman softly singing. My eyes fixed resolutely on the casket; I admired its workmanship, the hinges, the handles, the cherry veneer, the quilted interior. In the crushingly tiny window of my view, I could see people pass, coming upon the body, looking as if looking were nothing, as if her remains were naturally laid out, naturally speechless. I stood and joined the line, moving slowly forward. At each end of the coffin were thick candles in amber glass, massive pekoe sentinels stationed on twining iron holders. Behind them was a framed photograph of Claire with her late husband and their two children. It was a picture I'd taken.

Maman lay still in her pleats of fluted silk. Physically, little had changed in the days since we'd last spoken. I wouldn't say she looked peaceful, necessarily, but she had the look of self-possession, of satisfied detachment from the relationships that continued to bind survivors to the grind of existence. What I saw was what I'd never seen elsewhere— the look of *being done*. Maman would give a neat swipe of her arm whenever she'd had enough of whatever, of dinner, of an argument, saying, "*Fin.*"

She looked well, I thought, with the slenderest of smiles. I kissed my fingers and touched her cheek, leaving her to rest in kingdom and cradle.

———

The last time we spoke, it was a Friday. July thirteenth. Four thirty-three in the afternoon.

Kate had gone outside to talk to the doctor with Laurent and his wife, Simone. I sat at the bed and held Maman's hand. Her lips were dry; I wet them.

She whispered to me, calling me Babe. *Beb*. I leaned closer.

"Please," she entreated, "she is your mother."

Though we had not been discussing my mother, Maman spoke as if we were concluding a long conversation, which in a way we were. It was a deficit she'd perceived in me from the start because we were a match— what I lacked fit exactly with what she was able to give. Of course I knew my mother loved me. She thought highly of me, automatically, intellectually, by virtue of genetic proximity. Yet, every time we met it was like meeting again, with all I felt compelled to explain and withhold, with all she had forgotten.

Maman's childhood had been far more difficult than mine. She used to tell us stories of France during the war, when German soldiers patrolled the streets after curfew, when behind locked doors people gathered quietly by the light of a single candle. Once, when she mistakenly spoke out during the enforced silence of dinner, her father removed his cap and threw it at her, forgetting the knot of chewing tobacco he'd stored inside. The hat flew across the table and the wad fell into the tureen of soup and it broke apart like tea leaves, spoiling the precious meal. The family had to go to bed hungry. Her mother was extremely angry. *'Stup-eed girl,' elle a dit*, Maman would relate to us, mixing languages in her sorry passion.

Kate's father would nod, corroborating—he'd known his wife since they were children. Maman would sip her Bordeaux and smile, saying of herself, *pauvre petite*. But I would not smile. I did not like to hear of anyone throwing a hat at her or calling her stupid.

And so it was for us—or, so it had been. She believed in me as a woman separate from herself, and she seemed to take pride in our friendship. This made me feel worthy, and on the inside there was a change in me—a finding, a becoming. One day, perhaps, I would be of equal service to someone.

Her hand shifted slightly. It was a signal, a warning—there was no time to drift. She needed something. In speaking to me, I suspected she spoke to herself. *"Tu comprends?"*

"Oui," I said, glad to give something, anything. *"Je comprends."*

Her eyes were clear and wet, lustrous and smooth, and she was more present than I could remember her having been in a long time. Inside, something had shifted; it was as though she had moved on. For some reason, I was permitted the honor of joining her there. I felt my soul approach; I felt myself move several steps in, unforgettable steps—they were to be our last. I felt us walking as we'd always walked, with the inside of my arm supporting the nook of her elbow, with the sound of her good brown shoes rapping, with the sweet region of her powdered cheek grazing mine, with the afflicted melody of her voice, provoking, initiating.

"D'accord, ma petite?" she asked. I laid my face on her bed and nodded into the stiff sheets. She touched my cheek. *"Je t'aime."* That was the last thing she said to me. That and, "Be a friend to Catherine." *Ca-trine.*

There were three rings, despondent and shrill. "It's me," Kate said. "Are you alone?"

I was alone, but it occurred to me that I might not be alone *enough.* I dragged the phone by its cord into the upstairs bathroom. It was like a miniature body being hauled by the hair, slaggard and obedient. I sat on the tub. "Okay," I said.

"She's dead." Kate said, just like that, and just like that, I told her I was on my way.

I hung up and sat for a while, looking out the window, waiting for the 7:15 train to go by. As I sat, I felt myself undergo a partial breaking. It was as though the forces that had been binding me loosened. When I went down the stairs, I went carefully, feeling conscious of these sudden separations, estrangements between me and the things around me. In the living room, a familiar lamplight warmed the delphinium-blue walls, lined from floor to ceiling with books I'd always known, standing upright on the shelves like soldiers at the ready. The irregular margins in front of the bookshelves were lined with fractured pottery and shards of glass, framed drawings, diplomas, and photographs. No matter how familiar the objects were to me, nothing could fill the new absence I felt.

I turned into the kitchen and met a flare of bright light. My mother was standing where she rarely stood, doing something she almost never did—the dishes.

I heard myself say, "Mom?"

"Yes," she answered, and she turned.

"The phone," I said, holding my hand to the light. "It was Kate."

She rinsed the last dish and placed it carefully in the rack. Taking a towel to dry her hands, she crossed to the table, and she sat. I could see a change in her eyes, in the green, and then nothing. I wondered if Kate would harden as my mother had when she was young and her own mother died. Some people exist quite well in injury. It's like having gills to breathe underwater. Some people are clever about not drawing others into their affliction. You could hardly tell by looking at my mother that she was a stranger to providence.

Suddenly she was up again, moving—something big, something eloquent, some business with dash and rush. There was the sound of the phone dialing. She was calling the hospital, calling Kate, calling Kate's brother. The dialing made a spinning sound like the sound of infinity, like the feel of drawing the number eight, your hand just going around and around.

Kate would live with us through her senior year and graduate from East Hampton High School rather than go to Canada with Laurent and his wife. We often had people stay—Magnus Ove, the Swedish exchange student, known to us as the Great Egg, and Washington, the computer programmer from Seattle who slept on the love seat for six months. There was always some teenager "in transition" or visiting college student or wayworn navy sonarman in need of a bed for a week or two.

"She'll be safe and happy here with Eveline," my mother consoled Laurent. "Your mother would have wanted this."

After the cemetery was lunch. Laurent invited us to join them, but Mom respectfully declined, saying she had to head over to her office at the college. As for me, I could not bear to think of food.

Kate said, "See you," and when she and her brother crossed the street, you couldn't tell the difference between them. Both of their bodies were lean and black and their heads were hunched. They appeared headless, as if they could not bear to admit anything new.

"You okay?" Mom asked as she stepped into her car. "Want me to drive you home?"

I rested my arms on the roof and looked in the window, the casual way people do, except I was not so casual. "No, thanks. I'll walk."

I moved as slowly as possible down Cooper Lane, then along Newtown, cutting across to Osborne, staring at the shingled houses, depressed in general by *ongoingness*—the sudden gusts of charcoal smoke emerging from behind garages, and the Big Wheels abandoned at the edges of driveways and the shy twinkling of televisions prematurely on. Everyone was oblivious to the untimely death of Claire Cassirer, leaving me to ponder such imponderable things as the stark brutality of the human condition. So much is made out of an individual life until a life is lost. Then it seems to be quickly forgotten.

At home I undressed carefully, making little contact with the fabric, not wanting to look at what I had worn. I added the clothes to my mother's dry cleaning sack. It would be months before she took the contents to the dry cleaner and months again before she had the money to pick them up.

Mom always joked with Mrs. Burns, the dry cleaner, when we saw her in town. "I'd get my clothes, Rose, but your building might tip."

And when the garments eventually did come back, the funeral things would be on hangers mixed in with normal things, and Mom would just stick the whole plastic-wrapped bundle in her closet, forgetting about it until she needed to wear something nice, which could take another six months.

In the barn I climbed to the loft and lay there, hands on my chest. I was a body lying, and Maman was a body lying, both on the same day, three streets apart. Above me was the roof. Above her, the coppery cold earth pressed sizably, like a sulfur quilt. She was still so close, as unaccustomed to death as newborns are to the breezy world beyond the womb. I wondered were there nursing hands to help her, and singsong voices to console her. I hoped that there were.

I kicked off the covers because my legs itched from the stockings I'd worn. I was hot, so I switched on the fan and moved it close to me, but then I got cold, so I moved it back again. I rubbed my temples. I wished the lawn needed cutting. I wished we had a television. I wished a phone would ring, but there was no phone where I was. I didn't feel well. When I thought of Kate, I felt worse. I had to get out.

The sunlight struck the westerly wall of the barn at a sunken bevel. That was where I went, where the light was brightest and the heat the hottest. I lowered myself onto the bench, and soon Kate was there, walking over, sitting next to me.

"Simone and Laurent are having a baby," she said. "It comes sometime in March."

Kate would be an aunt. I wondered if the baby had hastened Maman to the grave, in the generational sense.

"They asked me again to go with them to Canada," Kate said. "They're leaving tomorrow."

"Tomorrow," I said, "wow." Tomorrow seemed sooner than usual.

"I told them no," she said.

I felt relieved; I sighed and said, "I decided I'm going to be cremated."

"Me too," Kate agreed. "I was thinking that all day."

I recalled the gutless thud and the pebbly, spreading sound the dirt made as it slipped and got trapped in the casket's fittings. I said, "It's tough. The whole thing is tough."

Kate's eyes were fixed on the dampening flame of the sunset. It was the sunset of the last day in which her mother had been a participant. It was the last time she would have to be on time for her mom, get dressed up for her mom, be nice to her mom's friends.

"Things keep happening," I went on. "Every day, new things, awful things. It's hard to think about them, *really* think. But, then, they're the *only* things. You know what I mean?"

"It's true," Kate said. "After this, there's nothing."

Just then we heard the driveway gravel popping, a car door, a gentle whistle. My mother was home, calling the cats. At the sound, Kate covered her face with her hands and crumpled to a heap. I patted her on the back, which was hard for me, comforting a person in that patting way.

Mom brushed apart the hedges. "I thought I'd find you two back here. What a gorgeous sunset."

She squeezed in between us, and our sorrow gave way to hope. Despite her small stature and unconventional habits, my mother was a superhero—arriving infrequently, often late, but repairing chaos nonetheless with her colossal energy and charisma. I was glad to be relieved of the burden of consoling Kate. At least my mother had some idea of how to be. When you lose your parents as a child, you are indoctrinated into a club, you are taken into life's severest confidence. You are undeceived.

"Has everybody eaten?" she asked.

Kate had. I had not. The idea still repulsed me.

"I understand," my mother said, and she patted my knee, "but you're alive."

7

It was the first yearbook meeting of the year, and the editor, Marty Koch was up front, slumped into one of those shiny beige desk-and-chair units. As Marty mumbled about *objectives,* a lock of unwashed hair drooped persistently over one of his eyes. I tried to follow what he was saying, but it was like looking into a pond and trying to trail a swimming frog.

From my seat on the windowsill, I grabbed a chair with my legs. It squawked lamely as I dragged it over to use as a footrest. I stretched and looked through the half-open window behind me. Outside on the field, the football players were practicing tackles against those padded metal rows that are supposed to be the opposing team. If I squinted, the movement of the boys became almost balletic, like rows of rushing swans.

Though my eyesight was fine, I often struggled with aspects of vision. At close range my mind had the habit of animating inanimate articles, such as coats on hangers and ceramic statuettes. Faraway things looked sad and small, destined for defeat. Either way, near or far, it helped me to squint. Periodically my parents would send me to the optometrist for an examination.

Dr. Kessler would look askance as I rubbed my fists into my eye sockets. "Headache?" he would ask, one eyebrow raised. Behind him, all the machinery sat perched in the violet lizard-tank darkness, like stalled robots or expectant marionettes. It's crazy, the way eyeballs require all that equipment—the rolling carts with boxes that blow gusts of air, the slide machines for alphabet projections, and those glass goggles suspended on metal arms that pivot to your face, and which, unlike the telescopes at the top of the Empire State Building, do not magnify the view, but, rather, your eyes.

"No," I would say, "not at all."

As I read the charts, Dr. Kessler would lean over my knees to flip various lenses around, adjusting magnification, checking for some tangible change—I couldn't imagine what. The rim of each ring would inch past the twin windows, *click, click,* threatening to rip my lids off.

"Twenty-twenty," he would conclude, peering at me over the top of his own special glasses, which looked sort of like a View-Master. "Why, then, do you squint?"

"I don't know," I'd say. "To see better."

"But there's no physiological reason for you to have to see better!"

I always felt sorry for him, as sorry as I felt for myself, the two of us stranded in that medieval torture den without hope of resolution. I supposed it was counterintuitive to regard squinting as a way to see better, especially when I had no apparent *need* to see better. But in fact, I did have that need, whether he could see it—that is, *diagnose it*—or not. Maybe he should have asked a better question. Maybe I should have used another word. *Differently.* I needed to see differently.

"Well, that's it for booster sales," Marty was saying. Boosters are those cryptic mini-sentences in the backs of yearbooks—*P.G. dontcha love 2Ramy!!* or *Berry Boy gotta get some tidy shirt?* Marty ran his highlighter across the third line down of a completely filled-up legal pad. "Let's move on to *folio flow.*"

I scanned the bluish and inert faces of the yearbook staff. I was thinking that there was not one guy I would have slept with if we were trapped. When you're bored you can pretend you're trapped, like hostages. You ask yourself where would everyone go to the bathroom and who would hold hands in the dark? Who would you have sex with? And who would be the real heroes? Real heroes are the ones you don't expect. That's the lesson of *Superman* and *Underdog,* the lesson of being patient and maybe someday learning the truth. That's also the lesson of soap operas. In soap operas a bad person will turn good, or a good one will turn bad, or actors will switch roles altogether, becoming neighbors or relatives of themselves. Jack and Dan loved to deride soap operas, with their fake hospital sets, yet they were somehow unfazed by the flimsy scenery of *Star Trek.* And they could argue for hours about whether Juggernaut first appeared in *X-Men 12* or *X-Men 13.*

The football field was warmed by the simmering light of the setting sun. A whistle blew, and the players broke apart, creating a long wall of staggered bodies. I would have liked to have been out there with my camera, capturing them as they cocked their heads and listened intently while Coach Peters paced in front of them. Athletes make the perfect subjects. They ignore the camera; they truly believe they are stars.

Adults are always pushing jocks to become stars. For coaches, the incentive is job security. For parents, it's the possibility of financial assistance. Colleges need to recruit away from other colleges and to sell stuff. Professional clubs need to ensure the ongoing chain of new talent and also to sell stuff, only slightly bigger stuff, like television rights.

But few high school players meet with the success they dream of. Most just get teased out of a valid education. When Mrs. Oliphant, the calculus teacher, complains that the Chinese are beating us in science and math, you have to wonder whether average kids in China spend three or four hours a day on sports. No one mentions how a choice *for* sports is a choice *away* from everything else. And unlike with the Marching Band or the Spanish Language Club, nonparticipants are expected to support the teams or else be accused of lacking *school spirit,* of being *un-American.* Who knows how it happened, but somewhere along the way from Puritan times to modern ones, school spirit and sports spirit and American spirit got totally mixed up. No one even dares question the vapid sports rhetoric you're forced to endure. *It's not whether you win or lose, just don't lose!* Sportsmanship and teamwork are hailed to taxpayers as critical life skills; yet, these lessons frequently escape the players, many of whom extract from their involvement little pertaining to honor or gracious conduct.

My feet bounced against the radiator; my palms drummed my thighs. If it didn't feel so good to be them, those boys might like to think about things. Maybe immunity lifts a weight; but maybe heaviness returns.

In junior year our school was put on an "austerity" budget by the board of education, and team sports were cut. Student energies were diverted to politics and mutual interest societies—theater clubs, chess meets, charity leagues, beach clean-up patrols, and interfaith discussion groups, all of which were funded by flea markets, car washes, and bake sales. We were constantly at school working for causes—there was nothing better to do. People who had never previously spoken were thrust together because needs were great and entry policies liberal. Everyone joked that the school motto changed from *"We are the Champions!"* to *"Beggars can't be choosers!"*

That spring, we entered a statewide competition sponsored by Carefree sugarless gum in which the winning school was the one whose students had written the gum's brand name on the most index cards. All four grades vied against one another, for no particular reason other than boredom and surplus vitality. We held writing vigils. The self-imposed rivalry allowed us to take the state by a titanic margin. As a prize, the rock group Hall and Oates gave a concert in the auditorium. Jack and his friends, irate over the pop music infiltration, took to the aisles during "Rich Girl" and protested by hopping up and down like pistons or gears, screaming, *"Sid Vicious! Sid Vicious!"*

Surprising new heroes emerged that year. Cathy Benjamin, who'd made it through only three grades in four and a half years, organized the biggest moneymaker, a twenty-four-hour dance marathon, and Ginny Warwick, who once cried inconsolably during an argument with the biology teacher about creationism, won best costume design in the class play competition. And Denny got *everyone* to contribute to his old-fashioned Christmas for the holiday hall decorating contest. The home economics department sewed antique-style costumes for baby dolls he borrowed from cheerleaders; the shop department rigged Marcus Payne's miniature mechanical railway to cut through the language lab; the mammoth Parson twins found and chopped down the perfect "pastoral" tree; the typing students created scrolled gift lists; and the art department pieced it all together.

The night before the start of the contest, twenty-three kids gathered at my house, people like Pip Harriman and Kiki Hauser and Daryl Sackler and Sara Eden, people who'd never been there before, all of us wrapping empty boxes, painting ornaments, making soap-flake snow. Alicia Ross came over with platters of cookies made by her housekeeper, Consuela, and Powell ordered six pizzas with extra cheese. Coco Hale and I shared scissors.

"Your snow country landscape collage is nice," she said to me.

I said, "I like your felt sleigh."

Jack and Dan came late, wearing gold paper crowns, and I was happy, the happiest I could remember being. Jack had just dropped out of boarding school in Kent, and his parents had agreed to let him finish junior year in East Hampton. He made his way over the hunched bodies, saying, "It's like a fucking sweatshop in here!"

He moved piles of fabric and Styrofoam globes from the stereo. As he leaned to insert the audiocassette he and Dan had produced for the contest, his key chain swung from his belt loop. It had a leather strap and a seamed bell, the type you find on cat collars and toddler shoes.

"Hey Evie," Dan said as he leaned against the banister and chewed on a slice of pizza. He had a matching set of bells tied to his wrist. "What would you think of us changing the name of the band to the Jesters?"

When the tape began, everyone froze. First came Dan playing the piano solo from Vivaldi's *Four Seasons—Winter;* next was Jack on acoustic guitar, singing "Let It Snow," morosely, sounding like a young Leonard Cohen. If you had seen the faces, you would never forget them—normal faces of normal kids, stripped of rank and status. For one brief moment, I loved them. Later when I told that to Jack, he said he was glad the moment had been brief. Last on the tape was Kate and Coco doing a rendition of "Amazing Grace" on their flutes. The twin whistles wavered bashfully.

Everyone clapped, and some of us cried, and my mother cheered, "Well, all right!"

"Man," Rocky Santiago said, returning to sparkles and glue, "that tape is the *clincher*."

One week later at the holiday assembly, immediately after the choral concert, in the fevered final moments before the start of Christmas vacation, Principal Laughlin ventured to the microphone, awards in hand. After commending the entire student body for its unprecedented display of "esprit" despite the harsh reality of the austerity year, and after thanking Mrs. Quivers and her janitorial staff in advance for the task of dismantling the displays, he explained that the day's winners would receive 250 Spirit Points to add to their Spirit Point account. Spirit Points would one day be transferred into dollars—one day, when there was money. So far the junior class, our class, held the distant lead—1,750 points as compared to 175 for the sophomores, 50 for the freshmen, and none for the seniors.

Laughlin waited for complete silence, then he cleared his throat. "And now, according to a unanimous decision by our distinguished panel of judges composed of administrators, faculty, parents, and local business leaders, *the junior class has won! Again!*"

We flew out of our seats and rushed the aisles, jumping and hugging and screaming so loudly that no one heard the dismissal bell. All the former sports stars joined in too. Mike Stern and L. B. Strickland and Peter Palumbo raised Denny onto their shoulders and carried him around in wild, tipping circles.

But in May of the second term, a budget was approved for the following year. Sports programs were to be restored; austerity was over. Ironically, cuts for the humanities persisted—the board's excuse was that the arts had done *perfectly well without financial support*. To some, the end of austerity meant the potential recovery of former glories and an opportunity to enhance college applications. To others, it meant a return to chronic disappointment and systemic inequity—no more oneness, no more euphoria, no more spirit.

Marty was finishing his yearbook address. Hands clapped flatly, lightly, like damp fins. Marty was okay. Maybe he wouldn't win baseball trophies or volunteer for the Air Force or anything, but he seemed very mannishly determined about his ambivalence, and that counted for something. It takes courage to remain on the periphery, and you had to admire Marty for that, even if you couldn't imagine having sex with him.

I'd joined the yearbook by accident in freshman year. I'd intended to go to a newspaper meeting, but I got lost. By the time I figured out I was in the wrong place, I'd been put in charge of Faculty Fun Facts. I was soon transferred into the photo department. At first I felt embarrassed, since everyone said the Yearbook Club was for losers, but when June arrived and a fragrant wind swept through the open school doors, and kids sat on the floors clutching one another's books, flipping through the pages to see what had been written, I felt okay.

People would rap my arm. "Evie, I can't believe you put that picture of me in there."

When asked for my signature, I always chose the yearbook staff page because there was an unwritten rule that the place you selected had to have meaning, either factual or invented. You could sign the picture of someone you had a crush on, or you could sign near Mr. Schwab if you hated trigonometry. Every year Jack signed Troy's book on the page with Miss Herbst, because once in freshman year Troy got food poisoning and busted out of typing class with a massive diarrhea attack.

Though I'd agreed to join the yearbook, I had not agreed to befriend the staff, yet that's what ended up happening. Suddenly I belonged to a group, which was weird. You couldn't help getting to know people when you worked with them under deadline, when you were stuck together all winter, pasting up copy and developing photos, listening to "Muskrat Love" and "Copacabana," going, *Do you know how much we could be getting paid for this shit?* I would become cognizant of a staffer's acne or excessive weight or hair oil or hand-me-downs only when I happened to be talking to them in the hallway and "popular" kids would pass and stare. This put me in a difficult predicament, because I was fourteen at the time. When you're fourteen, pretty much everything puts you in a difficult predicament.

A worldview is a busy view, engrossed and industrious. To the world you are no more than you appear to be at the moment of appearance, which is frequently unjust. But in fact there are infinite subtleties to identity—that is to say, there is the way that you are, which is the sum of the way you are *becoming* and the way you *have been,* and which does not take into account the way you secretly *wish to be.* Nargis Lata, my mother's friend, calls herself a psychic, though she earns her living teaching accounting to college students. Is she an *accountant* because that's how she spends her days, or a mystic because that's what she feels inside?

"You have tremendous earning potential," Nargis once told me, her eyes fluttering in a type of trance.

Perhaps it's too easy and unofficial to go around stating what you are and expecting people to embrace strictly personal claims. However, it seems equally unfair to be categorized as something simply because you do it every day—ask any "housewife." I like to think that whenever Nargis figures percentages or adds columns, she applies telepathic powers to divine the outcome of the calculations.

"I'm pleased to announce that Eveline will be my partner for the second year in a row as the book's photo editor," Marty said, and everyone clapped again. He gestured for me to join him. I moved to the front of the room, conscious of the fact that people were staring. I sat on the edge of his desk, making myself smaller. The body is supposed to be irrelevant, but frankly, it hardly ever is. "Those of you who are interested in photography can speak to Evie directly," he said. "Just for the record, though austerity year is over, we have no intention of exhausting the entire film allotment on sports. Under Evie's direction, last year's 'austerity budget' book was the most pictorially inclusive in school history, and also the most profitable. Sales were up by more than a third." He looked up to me. "Anything you'd like to add?"

I shrugged. "Not really."

When the meeting ended, everyone said goodbye like there was not going to be a tomorrow.

"*Goodbye!*"

"*See you!*"

"*Yearbook Club rocks!*"

Outside, the parking lot was mostly empty, also the fields. The football team had gone home. No one was in the driveway or on the front steps. There was no movement, not anywhere, no bodies walking, no one laughing, no one lost in thought. There was just light, the last complete light of day. I had the feeling there wasn't much time left. I did not think that feeling; my body just presented it to me, with a new sense of urgency. There was much to do, my body reminded me, though for the life of me, my mind could not conceive of what.

8

Kate and I were in the backyard, both of us curled on a loose nest of blankets. Her sleeping face was next to mine—the fine bones, the milky skin, the fixed music of the features I knew better than my own. And yet, I could not locate us in time—were we years before or beyond? Our friendship seemed a sudden wilderness. There was just this slipping between points.

The cat crossed the lawn and lingered on the corner of the quilt. I stretched to touch its belly, blending my hair into its fur, thinking how grass is a forest when you lie so low. People say the passage of time is the best cure for sorrow. But even when you trudge obediently through the hours, nothing is lessened, nothing is alleviated, not soon enough, not when you need it to be. What good is waiting, if pain is gone only when things no longer hurt? There ought to be a way to get over grief when it is still purple like dahlias and alive.

I wondered if it was death that had eroded the space between us. Had we seen too much, learned too much? Was there nothing left to reveal, no new way to be? Or was the intimacy that had risen up out of childhood meant all along to be only temporary? I knew only that something precious had been deconsecrated and the naturalness that had guided us was gone.

Kate's eyes opened; she checked her watch. "God. We've been out here for hours."

"I know," I said with a stretch. "We're so lazy. Aren't we lazy?"

Kate yawned. "Yes. But *you* are especially lazy. Feel like going to Sag Harbor tonight?"

I said, "Sure." I liked Sag Harbor. It was ghosty there, especially in October. Along the elbowed streets and up around the widows' walks were ghosts of whalers and the women they'd loved. Babies they'd forsaken.

Shortly after Kate went up to shower there was a knock. A stranger, I knew, since friends never knocked. Through the screen door was a guy, maybe in his twenties, well-built, not tall. He was wearing shorts and a *Darkness on the Edge of Town* concert jersey.

"This Irene's house?"

"It is. But she's not home."

"Yeah, well, okay," he said, embarking on an explanation. "I was hitchhiking a couple weeks ago at the college, you know, by the gymnasium, right before the turn onto Route 27." His voice was slightly croaking. I got the feeling he was smart. Croaking voices like that frequently belong to smart people. "Anyway, Rene picked me up, and we got to talking. She told me to stop by next time I came through East Hampton," he concluded, throwing his arms to each side, grinning. A faint mustache drew out like taffy to cap his lips.

"So here you are," I said.

"So here I am," he replied.

"Okay, well, come on in. She'll be back soon." I snapped the latch. The door sprang and he caught it.

"Nice place," he said as he entered. "The way everything's blue. Unusual."

The kitchen was cavelike and cool. I turned on the light and offered him a drink, lobbing a can of club soda from the refrigerator. I lifted myself onto the counter and rested my feet on the edge of the base cabinet door, pushing it open and wedging it closed, going back and forth, playing with it, like wiggling a loose tooth.

"I'm from California," he informed me after taking a sip.

"Oh," I said. "California's far." Three tomatoes lined the windowsill, bright red and radiant at the edges. My aunt Lowie had grown them in her garden. I reached for one and took a bite.

He nodded. "Is Rene your sister?"

"Mother."

"*Mother?*"

"She's thirty-five," I said, anticipating his question. It was always the same question.

I heard Kate's footsteps on the stairs. She came around the hall corner in a curious half-walk, brushing her hair. "Who are you talking to?" she asked with a smile.

"Some guy," I said, locating a single tomato seed and chewing it. "Mom picked him up hitchhiking."

Kate peeked around the wall. "Hello, *Some Guy*."

He smiled brightly. "Hello there!"

"I'm Kate. Do you have a name?"

"Some Guy is fine," he said. "Nice to meet you, Kate."

Kate started to travel around the room as if by conveyer belt. She went first to the refrigerator, where she opened the door smoothly and bent at the knees to ease out a drink, excessively conscious of poise. She looked like one of those old Ziegfeld girls, the kind who shimmies down scenery steps in treacherous heels and sequined breeches, balancing an oafish feather hat. She put the hairbrush down near me and cleaned off the top of the soda can in the sink.

"You two aren't sisters, are you?" the hitchhiker asked.

"Us? *God, no,*" Kate said as she took a seat across from him. "Just friends. Since second grade. I'm staying here for a few months to finish school. My parents passed away."

"Oh," he said. "Sorry." Then he said something else, which I missed. I was wondering what Kate found so offensive about the idea of us being sisters.

Birds were visiting the feeder outside. There was one male cardinal. I like cardinals. They're unimpeachably red. The red bird plus the remaining red tomatoes made a strange pattern. Kate and the hitchhiker were discussing astrology. He was a Leo; she was an Aquarius.

"Aquarius," he said. "*Whoa!* I'm surprised you two are such good friends. Aquarians and Scorpios usually don't get along."

Kate turned to me. "Evie! Did you tell him your sign?" she asked.

He shrugged. "She didn't have to. It's obvious. Scorpios are intense.

They're ruthless and self-contained. No one's worthy of their trust. But Aquarians, they're like silver rainbows." His fingers danced in air. "They're dreamers. Are you a dreamer?"

"Totally," she said. "I'm a total dreamer."

"Well, there you go."

"It is *so* weird that you knew that. It is *so* cool."

I stood and went to the sink, lowering my head in, spraying my hair.

The hitchhiker apologized to me, calling over, "Hey, no offense or anything."

"None taken," I said, waving my left hand up. My voice inside the sink made a hum. Water streamed down my neck when I righted myself, and around my shoulders, and onto my T-shirt. I used Kate's brush, then pulled my hair into a ponytail on top of my head and held it in place while I hunted for a rubber band. There were no rubber bands where they were supposed to be, which was in the drawer for rubber bands and half-burnt candles and paper clips and other weird stuff such as broken sneaker laces and corroded batteries and lamp wicks, so I used a garbage twist thing instead. Every kitchen has a drawer like that—a chaos drawer, filled with everything except the one thing you need. *Chaos,* because chaos is pretty much like having everything but the thing you need.

The Scamp pulled into the driveway, and within minutes my mother was coming through the door, singing out, *"Gir-rls."* Instantly there was lightness. In other houses, "good" houses, where bills are paid and dinner is made from scratch and you get one of those fancy watermelon basket cutouts filled with fruit balls on your birthday, parents walk in and everyone gets sick to their stomach.

She came over the kitchen threshold, struggling dramatically under the weight of her bags. "Hello!" she said, in a British accent, referring to the visitor. "What have we here?"

"Some Guy," Kate said. "A hitchhiker friend of yours."

"Don't tell me," she said. She closed her eyes, tapping her forehead. "Riff. Rug. Bop."

"Biff," he said with a half-grin and a backward jerk of the head, not knowing whether to be insulted. *Biff.* No wonder he preferred "Some Guy."

"Of course," she said with delight, and she sat. "Biff. From Santa Monica."

"San Diego," he replied. "Good memory."

Beyond the window, daylight languished. The shade moved strategically across the grass, advancing the way an army does. I reminded myself that it was Saturday, though I had the Sunday feeling. I wished Jack would come, but he and Dan and Smokey Cologne had gone into the city for a concert at CBGB's. He would show up tomorrow, after the noon train whistle, smelling stale like smoke and rum, his bloodshot eyes an extra bright blue.

"Where you going?" Mom asked me.

"To mow the lawn," I said.

"Don't be silly. It's October. Sit down."

"Yeah," Biff said. "C'mon, sit." He pulled out a chair.

It was nice of them, it really was, but Kate said nothing, so I figured it was best to go.

I pushed the sky-blue mower in diagonal lines over the lawn. Powell had spray-painted it blue because he didn't want me to be outside looking down and seeing nothing of the heavens. Our neighbor Ernie Lever was mowing also. Ernie rode his tractor mower on his postage-stamp yard like a bumper-car cowboy, jerking back and forth, snapping his neck. He'd chopped down every tree on his property to make for easy driving. I waved—I had to, it was a family rule.

"He's a Republican with a colostomy bag," Powell explained. "That makes him twice as eligible for Christian kindness."

The last tree Ernie cut was a giant maple. I cried that day. Everyone gathered around me, patting my knees, rubbing my shoulders, offering icy rags. "It's not about me," I told them. Whenever you're upset, people always think it's about you. "It's about the tree."

No one disputed that what had happened was senseless, yet they defended Ernie's right to tend to his own house. This was no surprise. I'd heard such logic before. Adults accept unacceptable behavior because they secretly don't want anyone criticizing their own actions. Then they encourage kids to tell the truth like it's so easy.

My mother tried to cheer me. "Think of the saplings it sired! The bi-ological work it did!"

"Ernie mowed all the saplings," I stated bleakly.

Trees corroborate the past. Years are chronicled in the rings. The hur-ricane of 1938 pummeled Long Island, but that tree survived, only to be sawed to shreds on an innocuous spring day by Ernie, a retired machin-ist from Astoria, Queens. I wondered how far it might have grown. Maybe it would have broken right through his house, then cut clear across town, making an idle sort of getaway.

"Be reasonable, babe," Powell said, taking my hand. "We can't save every one." His wolf-gray eyes leveled to convey the gravity of his point. His hair was also gray. It swept back around his ears, and his voice was kind. When he came home after months away, he would have a bushy mustache. When he came home, it was always a three-day party with everyone participating, even me.

"But we knew this one," I said.

The night it was cut, I went outside and found the stump. It was stubbornly attached to the arc of the earth, right where the tree used to be. Of course there was no better or more logical place, but the sight of it surprised me nonetheless. There was something harrowing about the untimely tenacity, about the belated show of force. I thought of the cover of *Le Petit Prince*, of the boy standing on the rim of his asteroid with nothing to buffer him from the enormity of the universe. There was sud-denly so much sky. I looked back at the gigantic shadow of wood dumped alongside Ernie's shed. It was more than just a ragged mound of wood awaiting the chipper. There was something about it that was un-deniably offensive to the eyes, something to do with the disharmony of ravaged perfection.

When I finished the lawn, I sat on the front steps, listening to the voices from the kitchen. They'd been talking a long time. Some people can talk incessantly, though nothing of interest or importance is being said. Biff was listing punk bands he'd seen, Patti Smith, Blondie, the Ramones, the Talking Heads. And Kate kept mentioning Jack and all these clubs in downtown Manhattan she'd never even been to, such as CBGB's and Max's Kansas City.

I wondered what the value was, in the Darwinian sense, of making fast friends like that. There must be some scientific significance to being a follower, to allowing yourself to be persuaded by fashion, opinion, doctrine, and personality.

Recently, Marcus Payne had found God. He would come by after school on his moped with a crate full of Good News Bibles. If Jack was there, he would lecture Marcus on the dangers of mind control societies. Jack hated cults; he didn't even like me to do yoga.

"The devil is in the dogma, Payne," Jack would growl. "Don't become susceptible. Those assholes in Jonestown drank cyanide in Kool-Aid and squirted it into the mouths of babies because it dawned on them that Communism might not take off globally. I mean, if Marx and Engels couldn't do it, if Lenin, Stalin, and Trotsky couldn't do it, what chance do nine hundred Moonies from broken military families have? And those Helter Skelter freaks," he would say. Jack *hated* Charles Manson. He said Manson gave a bad name to hippies. "Whoring girls to get into Hollywood houses, hacking people up, then blaming blacks in order to jumpstart a 'racial holocaust' they themselves were predicting. And since it's your lucky day, Marcus, I won't even get into Genesis. Let's just say we've got world economies based on a book that preaches preparedness for an apocalypse. I mean, Noah's Ark—*come on.*"

According to Jack, the philosophy behind any cult is incidental. "It's all about people power. You've got the vocational masses lining up, waiting to be brainwashed. It's like, get a message and make it good, or else lose out to some other cult."

If Jack wasn't there, Marcus and I would just talk about movies. He was a classic film fan as well as an evangelical, and he did his best to forge connections between the two, just in case someone at Church tried to make him give up the movies.

"What about *Harvey,* Evie?" he would ask as he reorganized the Bible sales receipts he kept on a clipboard stuffed in his windbreaker. "The script refers to the rabbit as a pagan spirit, a *pooka,* remember? But I suspect Harvey's actually a Christ figure. Think about it—an *invisible rabbit.* That can only mean one thing as far as I'm concerned."

At last there was the sound of the kitchen chairs pushing back. I heard my mother walking to the sink, saying it was time for her to grade

midterm essays, and Biff throwing his empty soda can into the trash, saying he was on his way to rugby practice at Herrick playground in the village. I thought Kate might mention our plan to go out for a ride to Sag
Harbor, but she didn't.

I moved away before they reached the door, going back to the blankets Kate and I had left behind the house. I sat down, figuring that if no
one came to find me, I'd just wait for night to fall. Night is like an
ocean—in the ocean you cannot be displaced; in darkness it's the same.
Being submerged is like possessing a nationality; it is to *be* a thing completely. I wondered if I would ever know such saturation, or have an
identity that was equivalent inside and out. When I asked myself what I
felt above all else, what moved most freely through the net of me, I could
think only of loss—of things forgotten though never known, of things
sacrificed though never held in hand.

9

After first period history was homeroom. Mrs. Kennedy stood at the
door to her classroom, ushering kids through. Between me and her the
floors were like concrete playing cards. Each slab had thin metal rims and
flecks that were putty-yellow and olive-green.

"Terrazzo," Dad told us the first time he came to help Denny and me
build sets for a play. "In Friuli, Italy, people used to take stones from the
riverbeds to make paths. A couple of guys would stand on opposite sides
of an alley, and saw back and forth, grinding down the high stones with
a rock attached to a wood pole. Eventually Palladio adopted the style for
country houses, using marble remnants in polished cement. Remember
I told you about Palladio and the villas?"

My father was constantly sharing facts with us, telling us for instance
that nutmeg can be a deadly poison, or that there are warts under the tail
of the true descendants of the eighteenth-century Carthusian stallion Es-

clavo, or that Picasso painted "Guernica" in response to the Nazi terror
bombing during the Spanish civil war in 1937. "You can never be sure
what might turn up on a test," he would say, demonstrating an overly
high estimation of the educational system.

My father had been born during the Great Depression, and his
mother had been widowed shortly after. Despite his intelligence, she had
not been able to send him to college. Since getting discharged from the
army, he spent every free minute reading anything he could find, from
manuals on refrigeration to textbooks on the Constitution. "Lincoln was
self-taught," my mother would always say to encourage him. "And look
what he managed to accomplish."

"Lose something, sweetheart?" Mrs. Kennedy asked me.

"Oh, no, Mrs. Kennedy. I'm just looking at the floors. They're beautiful."

She looked down and smiled, which was nice. Smiles suited her. Mine
is not a smiling face. Strangers on the street always say, *Smile!* But my
muscles do not naturally go there.

Stephen Auchard was reading *The New York Review of Books*. Kate was
thumbing through *Glamour*. We said nothing to one another, which was
correct, because no one speaks in homeroom. Homeroom is an alpha-
betic grouping, having nothing to do with compatibility and everything
to do with chance. It's a random civic assignment, like jury duty.

The PA system squawked, and Mr. Martin, the assistant principal,
started the announcements with a garbled Pledge of Allegiance. Before
senior year everyone would stand and recite the Pledge. Those were optimistic times. Optimism is when you're not sure where life is going to
take you, so naturally you anticipate the best possible outcome. But by
the time you are eighteen you have a hint already of what your life is
going to be like, and if that hint is not so wonderful, you might as well
just stretch across radiators and desktops and ignore the announcements,
halfway thinking about the night before, halfway thinking about the day
ahead.

Karen Baker usually slept through the Pledge. Karen was a cashier at
Brooks Discount on Main Street. Every afternoon she wore a name tag
pinned droopily onto a strawberry-red overshirt, the kind with snaps

that ladies in Little Italy call a housecoat. Sometimes Jack and I would see Karen behind Brooks by the dumpster, on cigarette break. She smoked Parliament Lights, which Jack liked to say aren't so much cigarettes as they are expensive toothpicks.

Eddie Anderson worked at Texaco on North Main Street. Eddie definitely could not be bothered with the Pledge. He wore pressed Bad Company T-shirts, though his fingers were stained purple from motor oil. The ratty hair on his head was neatly parted and tamed in such a way as to have the effect of a giant letter *M*. Every day after homeroom he took the bus to Riverhead because he wanted to be a boat mechanic. He went to BOCES—Board of Cooperative Educational Services, a trade school. Jack said Eddie would end up the richest guy in the class. "Better nail him now, Katie," Jack would tease Kate.

Cheryl Bromley, who used homeroom to file her nails, was going to be a hairdresser and a makeup artist, so she also went to BOCES for training in—something, I wasn't exactly sure what—hair and makeup probably, though that seemed an improbable course of study.

If certain people could not be blamed for a lack of enthusiasm in regard to the Pledge, it certainly didn't feel right for the rest of us to leap up and swear allegiance to a nation that was already working out to be more liberal and more fair for some than for others.

I was making a drawing for Jack. *Big Wednesday* was playing at the Old Post Office Theater on Newtown Lane, and we were going to go see it Saturday for, like, the fifth time. It was about surfers, so I was drawing the interior of a wave with a little body riding it—the little body being Jack's—when an object fell to the floor. It sounded like a pen. I checked around my ankles, thinking maybe it'd been mine, though of course mine was in my hand.

A voice said, "Sorry."

It was Dorothy Becker. Her gelatin-soft body was tucked into the seat diagonally across from mine, one row over and up. She hung back to reach the pen but didn't turn. Her arm flopped, and her fingers pinched at the air. She had those white, kind of noodley fingers without defined nail beds.

"I got it," I offered, lowering myself to grab it. I slid the pen into her hand, and I saw the mark on her wrist. My eyes followed the path of the ridge. It was crooked and pale scarlet, a primrose crest longer than an inch, probably shorter than when the incision had been fresh. Her palm clamped limply onto the pen. I kept myself suspended in case she dropped it again. She thanked me, and I straightened, saying, "No problem," which was true.

Scars help you get the point. There's a difference between hearing that someone has tried to commit suicide and then seeing the evidence of work done to achieve that aim. I had a sort of scar. It ran under my left eye and almost parallel to it, though it could hardly be seen. It was not self-inflicted, so it passed on no practical information about me, other than that once I was unlucky and got a burn. When she was feeling affectionate, my mom would call me Apache Princess.

I examined Dorothy's back, her hair, and her clothes. She used shampoo and soap and toothpaste, just like me. The main difference between us was that when she woke up, she knew that a shitty day lay ahead, whereas I could never be sure.

When you're in high school, you're no stranger to death, especially if you live where kids drive and roads are bad and drinking is a way of life. In tenth grade, two couples from school got killed when they hit a telephone pole on Route 114, and the school planted fig trees by the driveway. It was sad, but I was confused by the way girls like Coco and Pip and Breanne got hysterical, though they had never once been nice to those kids.

Coco kept saying, *"Oh, my God. Oh, my God. Oh, my God!"*

Though she did not elaborate, I thought I knew what she meant. I thought she meant, *It could have been us.* She definitely did not mean, *I wish I'd had the chance to know them better.* If those people had popped back to life right in front of her, she still would have been mean to them, same as always.

It's confusing how you're supposed to weep over people who die recklessly, but you're supposed to be disgusted by Dorothy. A calculated decision to die seems less disrespectful than putting yourself in a position to depart accidentally. Was Dorothy weak, or brave like crazy to have sliced herself? And then to survive the damage, *and then* to have to return to school because anything was better than staying home? It was that double failure that moved me the most—the failure of her life and the failure of her attempt to end it.

I wondered if her early end was inevitable but had been temporarily postponed. Maybe a suicidal person is like a lame animal in a healthy pack, dragging a limb, trailing blood. Maybe you cannot stop death from coming to those who have suffered some unseasonable blow or experienced a reversal of instinct, who feel that living is worse than dying.

It must require a massive exertion of consciousness to reach a conclusion that is in such direct opposition to nature. Unless, of course, that conclusion is not oppositional at all. For who can be certain that suicide is not just one particular doorway to death—death being in and of itself irrefutably natural? Why should those who take their lives at once be any more criminal than those who do it tediously, with noxious living, with dope and vodka and nicotine, with junk food and sexual compulsion, with behavior that hurts people other than themselves again and again?

And yet, there are those who endure agony to live. Trapped beneath collapsed buildings or imprisoned in filthy cells, they sing or pray or write microscopic poetry on scraps of paper to sustain themselves. When the will to survive is present, it is so sure, so clear—but what if that determination is not clear? What if a person has been made weary before their time?

I asked Jack about it one night. We were at Georgica Beach. "Do you think suicide is a tragedy?"

"No," he stated. "It's *your* life."

"Aren't you obligated to people who love you?"

"If you love out of obligation, it's not love." He was carving ridges and craters in the sand with a stick. "Besides, you're alone from birth."

"But you're born to your parents. To your mother."

"You don't enter the bond with your mother when you're born; you leave it. Birth is the point of departure from the only real communion you'll ever know. Everything else is invention. Your happiness depends on how well your parents handle that. You know, the fact of separation, the fiction of attachment. *Re*attachment, whatever."

"So you owe your parents nothing?"

He shrugged. "I don't. Maybe you do." He scraped a platform in the sand. "Most parents don't want the kid or each other. They're just carrying out some brain-dead social functions. They marry because it's time, start a family because it's time. They do it for fear of becoming outcasts, fear of acting on an original fucking thought." My name materialized in the sand in large loopy letters. He drew a heart around it. "If abortion had been legal seventeen years ago, I wouldn't exist. That's what my old man told me."

"I can't believe he said that."

Jack said, "Believe it."

"You could have jumped when you were climbing," I said.

"But I didn't."

"Because of me, you said."

"Because of you."

"So you're not alone," I said. "You have me. You owe me something."

"*You*—that's right. By choice, not by obligation. And if that ever changes," he posed gravely, "I'll do whatever I feel like."

"And would that be my fault?"

"*No,*" he drilled. "It would be my choice."

Though I knew he meant what he said, I also wondered if it was possible to isolate a final choice from all the choices that preceded it. Romeo made a choice when he killed himself, but his choice was made meaningful by *prior* choices—Juliet died first, or so he thought.

"How about lost potential?" I said. "The art van Gogh could have continued to make."

Jack shook his head. "Lost potential is irrelevant. How can anyone feel cheated out of something they were never entitled to in the first place? The loneliness van Gogh felt was the loneliness he felt, whether it led to paintings or to suicide. Life may be sacred, but maybe his *wasn't* sacred. In fact, it's well-documented that his life sucked. If people didn't know how to care for him or his art when he was alive, or convey to him the *sacred* sensation of *sacred* living, fuck them after he's dead."

I suppose it is narrow to wish someone had lived longer in order to enrich your life more. Jack had a point—the irony of mourning people who kill themselves is that the rush of love manufactured for the dead did not prevent them from dying in the first place. If suicides result from a longing to be understood, or reached, maybe it's not inappropriate for those who remain alive to feel forsaken, to be forced to endure a somber feast of years.

Jack launched his stick into the ocean and watched it migrate. Moonlight seemed to seek him out. My eye trailed from sand to sea to sky, noticing the way his luminescent form touched down upon each, making me think of the relationship between solitude and infinity.

I knew what he was thinking. I tried to acknowledge the breadth of his despair without judgment. I tried to be moved by the enormity of his vision without feeling small in relation to it. If I could not accompany him to the places he needed to visit, I could at least honor his need, because what Jack said was so, *is* so—love is born of choice. He reminded me of that choice, and he asked me to make it again, despite the risk I took, which was the risk of losing him, and the risk I presented, which was the risk of his losing me.

My face met his shoulder. I wanted to remind him of something—but what? I knew only that at that moment, when he was there and I was there, I loved him more than I'd ever loved anyone.

10

The Pom-Pom Girls changed their name to the Cheerleaders, and the Cheerleaders were not to be confused with the Twirlers, who marched at the front of the band. "It's about time!" declared Cathy Benjamin, who sat next to me in figure drawing. "Can you imagine? Having to call yourself a *Pom-Pom* Girl? I mean, it's 1979!"

The first time I photographed them for the yearbook, they made a body pyramid. It took an hour to use a roll of film because it was raining outside, and there wasn't enough room in the hall to achieve "proper launch." Ultimately they settled on a *finishing pose,* a bewildering conglomerate of kneeling, standing, half-kneeling, half-standing, and a little systematic reclining. The pose had to follow an actual cheer, otherwise it would not appear *natural*. This proved technically arduous since each time they tried it, they would land in a new place.

"Did you get it?" they would huff, cheerfully.

"I think so," I would say. "Let's do a few more just to be safe."

I ended up using a wide-angle lens, which had the unfortunate effect of distorting the image and making the faces look fishy and squished, as if they'd been photographed off a doorknob. The cheerleaders didn't complain when the book came out. In fact, they were good sports in general, always inviting me to join them at their lunch table, telling me how great my hair looked or what a nice sweater.

In the hallway they chanted through lips that were pink and glossy. With hands resting on the square of their hips, they took turns shouting a player's name. *Two, four, six, eight, who do we ap-pre-ci-ate? Kevin! Eddie! Nico! Billy! Mike!*

One rule, either official or good manners, was that each girl got to shout the name of her boyfriend or someone she had a crush on, which was the same as a boyfriend according to the code of girls. If you liked someone, you *called* him, the way you called the front seat of the car when you were a kid. When we were little, we loved the Monkees. Kate called Davy Jones, so I got stuck with Mike Nesmith. Boys have codes also, but the punishment for breaking them is severe. If you hit on someone's girl, you could get beaten or killed. With girls, things are never quite so straightforward.

I once asked Kate why it's considered betrayal on the part of an innocent girl if a boy someone else is interested in approaches *her* instead of the girl who "called" him. "Or take a steady couple," I said, fortifying my point. "If the boyfriend goes after another girl, why does everyone blame the new girl rather than the boyfriend?"

"Because," Kate whined, "the new girl shouldn't have done that."

"Done what? The guy was the one who *did* it," I said.

As each cheerleader called a name, she jumped into the air, making an *X* with her body while the others clapped twice for punctuation. There was something beautifully paradoxical about them. They dressed the way girls are *supposed* to dress, in earrings and ruffles, with blue eye shadow and permanent waves. Yet they were not so ladylike, and the things they did with their bodies were insane. They were powerful and athletic, not like the tennis players whose bodies were of perfectly middling proportions. They were confident, loyal, and optimistic. You have to be that way to fly through air believing someone will catch you. The flying part depressed me. Just how far they would go for their team. How there are no teams in the real world for women like that.

I watched them through my camera lens. Annie Jordan and Elizabeth Hill had just joined the club. Having black girls in the group gave it a visual allure that formerly it had lacked. When the cheer was over, I whistled. They turned and waved, *Hey, Evie!,* and I snapped a picture, which was actually very nice, how they were all standing, modest and tasteful and caught by surprise, pretty and in girlish disarray. I waved too, then walked to the auditorium.

There was a sign on the door: OCTOBER 22, 1979, 3:00–5:00 P.M. FINAL AUDITIONS—EHHS DRAMA CLUB. I pushed the door open, and a round of cheers from the girls rushed in with me. Everyone turned, as Mr. McGintee, the drama adviser who was also the senior guidance counselor, made the announcement that auditions were officially closed.

"That is, unless Miss Auerbach has decided to sacrifice art for the stage. What do you say, Eveline?" Mr. McGintee called.

I drew the door closed and slipped quickly into a seat in the top row. "Oh, no, I'm just waiting for someone." I didn't have to say *Kate,* since everyone knew. Mr. McGintee knew also.

"Do you girls have a moment?" Mr. McGintee had inquired, as Kate and I passed the guidance office on the first day back from summer. "Just for a chat." He had high wiry hair and wiry glasses, and he looked as dry as an old cattail. Like he could use a stiff drink.

While he spoke in private to Kate, I sat in the empty waiting room, trying not to touch anything. The guidance office always made me uncomfortable, maybe because it trafficked in the fate of children, sort of like a doctor's office deals in the fates of the sick. Nothing much happens in either place except waiting of the most agonizing variety. The secretary's clock radio was playing "Sweet Home Alabama." I noticed that it was tuned to WPLR, the local rock station, which must have been an after-hours thing. Usually it was kept tuned to *light favorites*.

The door to Mr. McGintee's glass cube whooshed open, and he invited me to join them. Inside he perched on the edge of his desk and asked questions that were not exactly questions. "So, have you two had an opportunity to review the events of the summer?"

Kate said, "Yes. We have."

And I said, "Yes. We review a lot."

"Very good," said Mr. McGintee, slapping his knee. "Ter-*rif*-ic."

It's not always a crime to lie. Sometimes it's easier to give people the answer they expect than to explain what you really think or feel. No one likes to admit it, but conversation is never truly spontaneous. Everyone works toward a goal, and few people like to be surprised. You can prevent a lot of mutual embarrassment and tedious negotiation simply by pinpointing your partner's aim at the outset.

Mr. McGintee had spent a lot of time and money earning his degree in educational psychology, and you couldn't blame him for trying to get some use out of it. He didn't want honest answers about how Kate was doing, just some key phrases that would allow him to classify her feelings as "normal" and call her case closed. It's like asking someone, "How was your summer?" You don't really want details.

But Kate could not speak of her suffering because words could never convey her specific feelings. I'd *seen* her sorrow. It came in the way she sat motionlessly in her room in our house watching the day skulk from orange to blue. It came in the way time passed twice as slow for her and also around her. We would sit for what felt like hours.

"What time is it?" I'd ask with a yawn.

She'd say, "Ten minutes past the last time you asked."

Invariably she overdressed. And when she cooked or washed dishes, she leaned against the counter with her legs tightly wrapped, one around the other. Her grief expressed itself in trepidation. She was afraid to move, as though movement might draw her irrevocably from the sphere in which her mother had resided.

"Why did you drop French, Catherine?" Mr. McGintee asked the top of her head. Kate's hands played with the fabric of the upholstered guidance chair, which was beady like dehydrated oatmeal.

"She's already fluent," I said. "How much better is she supposed to speak it?"

He shushed me. "The point is, French Five would have raised your class rank, Kate," he said, and his eyelids fluttered. *"The point is,"* he counseled, "we need to consider your future."

He nodded meaningfully to me, asking for backup on that, as if I had any kind of secure future myself, or as if I'd had any experience with the luxury of family outside of what I'd known from Kate's. There was nothing anyone could do, really. Kate had lost an entire way of being—red wine in her water glass, pounded veal for dinner, a platter of cheese and fruit for dessert, strolls around Town Pond with Maman's perfectly pressed skirt crinkling stiffly like tissue paper. On Saturdays there was dancing, Yves Montand or Jacques Brel, and when the song ended, Maman would spin, clapping twice by your eyes like a joyful, brazen someone—*Ha! Ha!*

How could he possibly help? Part of Kate passed when her parents passed. She no longer had proof of herself. She had become a nothing. Not a nothing, but a former something, which is infinitely more complicated.

In the auditorium, I sat on the upright edge of a seat, dropped my knapsack onto the floor, and squinted to find Kate. You could find her by her hair, which in mythology would have been called a *golden mane*. She was in the middle of the second row.

Mr. McGintee complimented the group on the turnout—in addition to the seventeen existing members of the club, there were twenty-six new students who had come to audition. He launched into a clichéd speech about how so few dramatic works can accommodate that many actors, and he ominously extracted a sheet of paper from his briefcase, telling everyone to write down their names and interests, in case they didn't make the cast.

"It's important to remember that the backstage volunteers, the costume designers, the lighting technicians, and the sales crew are just as important as the performers." He shouted up the aisle, again to me. "Isn't that right, Eveline?"

"Sure," I said. I don't know why he always had to rope me into things. He never seemed to listen to what I said. "I mean, I guess." It wasn't really right, not if you wanted to act. I happened to like doing the sets, but Kate would have died if they made her property mistress.

When Kate asked me whether she should join the Drama Club, I said no. She was pretty, and her hair was long, but that didn't make her a stage actress. Carol Channing was a stage actress. Julie Andrews. Ethel Merman. Helen Hayes. Lynn Redgrave. Rita Moreno. I told her my opinion, just not in those words.

I just said, "I don't think it would be good."

Kate would have been fine on film, playing herself or a type of fairy— an equestrian fairy, one that lounged on horse foreheads and sent wand-loads of sparkles into horse ears. One thing is that the plays they pick have to be vehicles for three talented kids and an incompetent mob. If I were in charge, I would have had them act out the newspaper.

"Let's see, *Fiddler on the Roof* was last year," I said as I ate a chicken leg and fell back on the couch. "And *Guys and Dolls* was the year before. It'll probably be *South Pacific*."

"You're so mean!"

"Five bucks," I said. "*The Mikado*. I bet you. *Damn Yankees.*"

Kate felt I was making fun of her hobby, which I was. She wanted to act because she was beautiful, and beautiful people always feel entitled to extra attention. It was the same thing with everyone saying Daryl Sackler should play basketball. It didn't mean he had the necessary stamina or agility or dedication or wits, it just meant he was tall, that his figure would have made sense on the court. People like things at least *to appear to make sense,* even if that visual logic comes at the expense of factual excellence.

There were boys all over the auditorium, sitting against the edges of things. I was surprised to see Jack there. He was on the floor against the wall at the far right with Dan and Troy Resnick, and he was staring at me with a piercing curiosity, as though I were stuffed and encased behind glass. I'd seen him look at me that way before.

"Are the rumors true?" he'd asked.

Twigs were caught on his red plaid lumberjack coat. He'd just re-turned from boarding school for Thanksgiving. His duffel bag was sitting out on the front step, where he'd left it. It was November 1978, five months after we'd met.

It was an uncharacteristic sentence for him to speak. I was confused not by the words but by the tone, the swiftness of delivery. It was as if there were a piece of me he'd lost in a strong wind, and he was frantic to retrieve it. He was staring at me furiously.

"It depends," I said, "on what the rumors say."

"That they slept with you," he countered fearlessly. One thing—Jack could be fearless. He did not ever hesitate to ensure that we were both speaking of the same thing. We were sitting on the couch in the living room. His knees brushed the coffee table.

I looked at the ceiling. "Well, no one really slept."

"You know what I mean."

"It makes a difference, the words you use."

"Did you have *sex* with them?"

"I wouldn't say that either."

Jack took a breath. "What *would* you say?"

"I would say it was the other way around."

"That they had sex with you?"

"Right," I said. "That's right."

Jack looked at his shoes. He looked at his shoes for a long time. He became so still I thought maybe he'd fallen asleep. I tried to think what it would be like to be him, hearing such news for the first time, but that was hard to do when I'd known already for a while. It was possible that he might like to do something about what had happened. Unfortunately, it had happened five weeks before. Though it's not hard to get emotional about the past, it's hard to apply those emotions effectively.

Did the rumors happen to mention the way the guys came into the upstairs bathroom of Mary Brierly's summer house in Napeague while I was peeing, the way they hoisted me against the wall before I could pull my pants up, the way L. B. Strickland covered my mouth with his mouth while Nico twisted the faucet on the sink very hard. Water splattered up from the basin onto my belly in icy slivers. I did not like water to splash up, not ever.

Would Jack feel better or worse knowing that because the back of my neck was pressed against the wall, I could hear but not see Nico's zipper coming undone with one sharp shot. And unwillingly, I memorized the feel of my two wrists fitting into someone's one hand, and the feel of drunken gasps on my neck going in time with strokes that tore me open, and the feel of a stranger's hair against my skin.

"Rapture" by Blondie played. It seemed to play exponentially, with each next verse multiplying out. Surely no one had described that to Jack, or the part about Mary banging on the bathroom door and pushing it open onto the three of us, shrieking, *"Get out of my house!"* and *"You tramp!"* Did people include in the notes they passed a description of her nails going into my arms when she dragged me into the hallway with my pants around my ankles? How when I reached down to dress, there were streams of someone else's fluid running down my inner thighs? How I stumbled down the stairs, how I ran out the front door, how I had hoped against hope that no one had noticed?

The night was moonless but not entirely unkind. Three bodies appeared. Rocky Santiago and his younger brother, Manny, and some underclassman whose name I could not recall. Rocky eased me into the passenger seat of his dented Chevy. My bike fit into his trunk. He drove cautiously toward East Hampton from Amagansett, and Manny followed in his friend's car, cautiously also.

Rocky asked was I okay.

I felt bad not to answer. I could not get past this feeling, this harrowing after-feeling, a feeling beyond grasp or intelligence. Beyond any obvious comparison to having been robbed or cheated, inside I *felt* robbed and cheated. Inside, I felt the physics of injustice, which, as it turns out, has little or nothing to do with the language of injustice. The indisputable wrongness of someone's having taken something that did not belong to them, filthied something that I'd kept clean, made their mark on property that was mine, and contemptibly crossed over into *my* intimacy in defiance of *my* desire, was all distant conjecture compared to the pragmatics of my situation—the pulled muscle in my neck, the cut on my mouth possibly from a watch, the stinging scratches on my arms made by Mary, the dampness in my underwear not from me, the surface abrasions and internal hairline splits that I could not mention to Rocky despite his kind interest because it is hard for people to understand the inside of a girl, the way it is shaped like a conch with filigreed avenues that are spectacular and ornamental. People tend to think it's just a hole.

I asked him to pull over and when he did, I leaned out to vomit. Manny turned off the headlights on the second car to give me privacy.

When we arrived at my house, Rocky shifted the arm of the car into park and asked was I all right to go in on my own. I said that I was. Maybe I was in shock, but I didn't feel embarrassed with him. I had the feeling he'd seen enough of the world to understand the random brutality of instinct and to know I was not to blame for what had happened to me. He'd come from Colombia in 1976, from Pereira. His real name was Raúl. I would have liked to know about his home, about what had made his family leave it for East Hampton of all places, but I didn't want to make him nervous with talk. We both knew that it would have made the story of my assault far more plausible if I'd blamed *him* for what the others had done. It would have made me a more credible victim. It was good of him to take a chance on me.

"Thanks, Raúl," I said, waving my hand weakly.

He ran his fingers through his hair, scratching the back of his scalp. "No problem, Evie."

Rocky walked to the rear of the car, lifted the bike out of the trunk, and waited for me to join him. Then he stood watchfully as I moved down the driveway. The dimmed headlights of the two idling cars poured onto the ground. They were waiting headlights, fraternal and discreet. When I reached the garage door, I turned and waved again, not realizing then that the timing of Rocky's benevolence, the gentlemanly readiness of his heart, had reversed in one elegant gesture the violence I'd experienced. In fact, it saved me. It was poetry, really—the random enmity, the random good.

Jack was saying that I should have done something. That reporting it to the police would have been cathartic. "You know," he said, "like, helpful."

It was a funny suggestion, the part about the police, coming from him. I was sorry for my involvement in an incident that would cause him to betray the basic tenets of his thinking.

Even if he was right, it was easy to say in retrospect what would have been the sensible thing to do. At the time, I did not feel sensible. At the time I was too busy thinking. Should I slice off the top layer of my skin? Should I scrape the lip marks from my neck? Would I use a knife for that, and with that knife could I make a pocket in my belly wide enough for a hand to reach in and remove the contaminated organs? I had the compulsive desire to scrub each fleshy gelatin piece of myself in acid. Periodically throughout the night I would tell myself to get over it, to act practically, to take a shower. Instantly after, I would drop back to the floor of my room, made sick by the thought of my own body, afraid to glimpse even the smallest portion of my undressed self. It didn't seem possible that they'd had ink on their fingers, but somehow I was sure that underneath I looked splotchy like a zebra. Not a zebra, but one of the spotted kinds of animals. I just thought of zebras because of the sorrowful way they hang their heads.

"Have you seen those cops?" I asked Jack, trying to bolster his mood with complaints. My hands made circle motions around my eyes. "Those mirrored aviator glasses they wear?"

"Yeah," Jack muttered. "Fucking assholes."

Maybe the image of me talking to my own bloated reflection in gleaming Ray-Bans would make him understand how pointless it would've been to file a report. Still, if I could have guessed that telling the police would have profited Jack, I might have done it. He seemed to need to know that some manner of justice had occurred. It was like sticking a pin into a bruise, to hear him wish so naïvely for equity.

Jack's body had not yet moved. He was like a jetty rock, obstinate and motionless against the savage force of the sea. I wasn't sure what I was supposed to do or say so I waited, passing time by thinking of things I knew. I knew that he loved me desperately, never more so than at that moment. I knew that he was ready, aroused for once by the honorableness of his emotions, and yet the anger that moved him had no means of expression. How betrayed he must have felt by his belligerent pacifism, by the ambivalence he'd constantly displayed. He was thinking that the attack had not been arbitrary, that it had happened to me for a reason. He was thinking the reason was him.

"Don't you see," I said. "It's like trying to catch a flying bird."

Nothing could have changed what happened. No cop or court would have had the jurisdiction to do what was fair—to vacuum the grizzling glue from my insides and cram it back into the pinhole openings of their penises.

A bleak shaft of carrot-colored light grazed his left eye and a round patch beneath it, making Jack seem one-eyed and invincible like a Cyclops. I wondered if it was three o'clock. Usually things get carroty and bleak and Homeric at three.

"Say the rest," he demanded.

He wanted to hear the part about him—that he should have been different than he was, that he should have been a falsely obedient son who would not have taken a knife to his father and would not have been shipped to boarding school, that he should have been a typical male who walked with his arm around my waist and his hand crammed in my back pocket, who bragged about fucking me to guys he despised, who played a sport and not an instrument. He wanted me to connect it to him.

I shrugged. "There is no rest."

I accepted that things had to happen as they did when I walked back in that night after Rocky left me and I found the kitchen still smelling like food from dinner. The dishes in the drain board were not yet dry, and the radio by the stove that I had turned on earlier was still playing. The time was one-thirty in the morning, on Sunday, October 22nd, 1978. Hours before, it had been the 21st, Powell's thirty-eighth birthday. On Saturday at six, Kate had called to say she couldn't make it to the birthday dinner or to Mary's party, that her mother was too sick to be left alone. They were leaving Sunday at noon for Manhattan. They would stay for two days of tests at Sloan-Kettering. At that time the cancer was just a *suspicious lump*.

I rested my knee on the same chair I'd used at dinner. While we were eating birthday cake, Mom had told the story of a new student who'd ordered a soda at a fast-food place but was given a cup of lye instead. He drank it and permanently lost the use of his voice, but he won four hundred thousand dollars in a lawsuit. He decided to apply the winnings in part to the expense of an education, which he would not otherwise have been able to afford.

"See that?" she'd said, slapping the tabletop lightly with two palms.

"Well now, that really is something," Powell said, brushing down his mustache with his napkin and considering the dark peculiarities of fate.

"I think I'll go to Mary's party," I'd said as I cleared the dishes.

"Need a ride?" Powell had asked.

"No, thanks. I'll take my bike." I hadn't wanted to bother him on his birthday. The bike had affected my destiny; I'd arrived late and alone, and by the time I got there, everyone was very drunk. Like the guy who ordered a soda but got lye instead—had the timing of his day transpired differently, he might have gotten a Coke after all.

I scanned the kitchen hopelessly. Around me lay the gruesome evidence of a seemingly inconsequential chain of events, which, as it turned out, had not been inconsequential after all. I was feeling hysterical. I wanted to laugh, but instinct would not have it. I wanted to move, but there was no place to go.

I threw my ruined underwear into the garbage, then sat in bed and stared at the clock, watching the numbers flap. I timed my headaches.

At 4:09 A.M. it occurred to me that someone might see my underwear in the trash and pull them out, thinking I'd made a mistake. I returned to the kitchen and cut them up with scissors, then shoved them into a cereal box, a Rice Krispies box I emptied. I crammed the package down to the bottom of the can and covered it with other garbage. When I pulled my hands out, they had jiggling flecks of congealed chicken grease on them. I lifted the bag from the can, tied it, and dragged it into my room. Then I returned and put a clean liner in, wondering how people manage to conceal murder. What do they do with their consciousnesses? I could do nothing with my consciousness.

Morning hummed when it came, like a choir of light, and in the clear, I showered. I could not select clothes: I kept trying things until the contents of my dresser were emptied onto the floor. My skin was itching, and there were hives vining up around my neck like ivy. Since I couldn't pick one outfit, I wore several. In the mirror I looked homely, like a straw corn doll with stick-out hair and no neck. I looked like the product of impoverished child artisans.

It was very cold in Powell's car while I waited for the 6:17 train to pass. As soon as it rumbled by, I started the engine and pulled out of the driveway, stopping first at the nature trail, where I fed the leftover Rice Krispies to the ducks. From there I went to the dump, where I had the distinction of being the first customer, if in fact dump users can be considered customers. In Paris, some women are the first customers at the *boulangerie,* where they wait on the dim blue cobblestone *rue* for the doors to open so they can buy bread. I wondered would I ever be one of those women. It hardly seemed possible.

I teetered on the precipice of the sandy mound and swung my arm back to hurl the bag into the abyss. Vulture seagulls swarmed down. I wondered whether they would pick so far through the bag that they would arrive at the cereal box and my underpants, and then would they fly about with shreds of stained cotton hanging from their beaks. I unbuttoned one of the several sweaters I was wearing and listened to the repetitive caws of the gulls. I stood on the edge of the pit of sand feeling like a slave in the Roman Colosseum, with the wind whooshing like a wild opus through the seemingly endless sky above me.

Back at home, Mom and Powell were in the kitchen having breakfast. I considered telling them what had happened, but I couldn't bear the proud way they looked at me to change. Besides, Powell would have ended up going over to everyone's houses, and there would have been confrontations and arrests, more than likely of him.

The telephone rang, awfully. *Bllwanngg!*

"Whoa!" my mother shouted.

"I'll get it," I yelled, diving to prevent a second ring.

Nico Gerardi's voice cracked through the wire. "Hello?"

I took the phone to the staircase, nearly to the top, where I sat, facing up. The carpet felt especially synthetic. Sometimes it hits you, the way a carpet is just weird fake stuff.

He asked was I okay.

"I guess," I said, wondering what would he have done if I'd said no. And, who'd told him to call? His father, his brother? How many people already knew, when I'd told no one?

He kept talking and I kept listening, trying to stay in the present, to keep my mind from receding into recall.

"I think it's gonna rain today," he said. "Do you?"

"Do I—what?"

"Think it's going to rain. Or not rain. You know, get sunny."

Nico and L.B. had families who denied them nothing. Their parents bought them their favorite foods, gave them new cars and nice clothes, intended to pay in full for their college tuition, and dispensed generous allowances without demanding responsibility in return. Such parents are wrong to shelter children so completely, to condone immaturity, to exempt boys from basic social requirements of fair exchange. People can get hurt that way.

"Sun, I think," I said. "Or rain. I'm not sure."

In the end, Nico said nothing of the remotest relevance to me. I really wanted to know if it had had to be me, or could it have been anyone? And did his tendency to commit acts of violence have to do with genetics or environment? The only thing I learned, I learned by supposition— the event had not transformed him or L.B. They were clean. They had no bruises or torn flesh. They had no remorse. There was no larger lesson for them. To them, it was just a night, a *lucky* night. As for me, I'd been critically altered.

Jack examined every inch of my face as if it were unfamiliar to him and yet also very familiar. "You were wrong to keep it to yourself. You let your shame silence you. It's exactly what they were counting on. You protected them."

It was an interesting point, that shame can take your voice away. Maybe it was so. Maybe I thought that if I kept my humiliation to myself, it would go away faster. And if I shared it, then I would have to wait for everyone else to forget also, and them plus me could take a very long time. I tried to recall the half-life of uranium-238. Whatever it was, that seemed about right.

The living room had turned dark. A shroud seemed to cover Jack's head; he seemed to be in mourning. His anger had been replaced by his customary self-analytical brooding, and that was, in fact, progress for the worse. I knew I had to speak to keep him from venturing to a bad place, but I could think of nothing to say. I wanted to lean on his shoulder; instead I lowered my head to my own lap.

Once I had a long conversation with a deaf woman, one of Mom's students named Monica. Afterward I needed to sleep for a while. I knew only the ASL alphabet and very few signs—*dead* and *hungry* and *uncle*—which were not sufficient to convey with any specificity the content of my thoughts. Jack and I were having similar problems. I possessed all this information, but, for whatever reason—survival or shame—my vocabulary was limited. Jack was handicapped as well; he had more space inside than things to fill it. He could only reach forth with his considerable cerebral might to capture and claim my reluctant impressions.

Jack suggested we take a walk up to Georgica Beach, so we did. Though I saw him every waking hour for the remainder of Thanksgiving week, and he even sat alongside me as I slept, those were the last words he spoke to me until the Sunday night his mother took him back to boarding school in Connecticut.

We received a collect phone call that evening. The operator said, "From Jack, for anyone."

My mother said, "Yes, of course, we'll accept," and she handed the receiver to me.

"Where are you?" I asked him. Car horns and a PA system were blaring in the background.

"Port Authority," he said. "I just got off a Greyhound."

"What? What about boarding school?" I asked.

"I'm quitting," he said. "Fuck it."

The next day Jack was back at East Hampton High School, where he remained until we graduated. Once he returned, life became bearable again, though I did not dare tell him. To say things were better would have been to imply that at some point they had been worse. Where would he have gone with his malice if I had confessed how much more painful the public humiliation had been than the private? How might he have treated himself upon learning that people preferred to think poorly of me rather than think of two football players as rapists? I did not tell Jack that after the rape I'd gone to Denny's car at lunchtime every day. That I'd carried all my books all the time so I wouldn't have to stop at my locker. That boys in the hall would cram their hands in the pockets of their jeans and laugh or sigh overloudly, blocking my way if I wanted to pass. That girls jumped on the opportunity to denigrate me, as though they'd been waiting. Not everyone was cruel. Not Denny or Marty Koch or Dan Lewis. Not the yearbook people. Only the popular ones, which is a confounding fact of social science—that is to say, the most-liked people behaving the least likeably.

The only good thing about Maman's illness was that Kate ended up having to stay in New York for the week after the incident. When she returned, she was too despondent over the diagnosis to have been included in any gossip. Possibly I was incorrect; people can be quite heartless.

But once Jack returned to school, and we were together as a couple again, it dawned on people that I had *not* agreed to sex with Nico and L.B., or tried to trap them into dating me, as some girls had suggested. And that actually, I had no interest in them. Suddenly, not only did I possess the practical knowledge of their astounding sexual ineptitude, but my situation showed that they had to steal sex because no one was giving it to them voluntarily.

From then on, all the boys treated me with deference and civility. Possibly they felt bad for me. Possibly they were awed by the fact that I hadn't told on Nico and L.B. By having the boys as allies, daily life became easier than ever. I wasn't proud of this, but I wasn't ashamed either. Things just happened to unfold this way, so I followed the rules of survival—snatching every minor advantage, immodestly seizing help wherever you can find it. The part that bothered me was the girls. Nothing was forgotten or forgiven with them—that is to say, them forgiving *me*.

Jack also never recovered. Periodically he would go on a tirade about how the sacredness of sex had been ruined. He would sink into a penetrating wretchedness marked by a prolonged and seething silence. I never asked what went on in the sulfurous corridors of his mind; I did not care to know. God knows we all have fantasies of retribution.

"You don't understand," he would say once he was able to speak of it again. "I just can't clear it from my mind."

I moved on because I *had* to, because pain gets heavy when you carry it far from its source, like a bucket of water hauled miles from a stream—it acquires a whole new value, which is the sum of *its* primary essence and *your* secondary investment. If I thought about it too much, I would start to forget things, important things, such as meals and homework. Once I found blood on my leg; perhaps I'd been scratching. Another time I was walking; who knows to where. I kept telling myself that it was enough to pity Nico's and L.B.'s criminal lack of kindness, and to feel sorry for all the lies they'd been told—about women and themselves—and for the way they went very fast, like midget dogs, when they had sex. Maybe the cruelest revenge was to say nothing, to inform no one, to satisfy myself with the fact that they'd already hit the limits of their dubious potential, that for them, only stinking crisis lay ahead.

I wasn't sure about the right way to think. I just tried to do my best with the little I had.

"Whom you all know by now," Mr. McGintee was saying, and everyone clapped as a dark figure leaning against the lower left wall of the auditorium gave an abbreviated wave.

I squinted to find Jack, on the opposite side of the room. He was right there, squinting back at me.

Mr. McGintee shouted a few closing remarks as everyone rose. "Roles will be posted. Rehearsals start next Wednesday. Don't forget to sign the paper going around."

Kate lingered near the edge of the stage, and Jack idly ascended the aisle to my left. The lanky muscles of his thighs expressed themselves beneath the paper-thin denim of his jeans. He was wearing a white Oxford shirt over a faded blue Columbia University T-shirt that was the color of his eyes.

"Nice entrance," he said, straddling the arm of the seat by mine, gnawing at his cuticle and kicking at a loose piece of carpet strip.

"What are you doing here?" I asked him.

"I'm like you," he said. "Just waiting for someone."

The group at the base of the auditorium began to thin, passing by us on the way out. Billy Martinson charged up after Troy, saying, "Give it to me, you little shit."

Kate arrived right after. "Hey! You owe me five dollars, Evie."

"Don't tell me—*Oklahoma*." I'd totally forgotten *Oklahoma*.

"*Our Town*."

"Our Town?" I repeated. "That's strange. I'd been figuring musicals."

Jack grabbed my knapsack and followed Kate out. I followed also. As I moved to the door, I glanced over my shoulder. A handful of people were at the bottom. No one I knew, though I felt—I don't know—as if I'd left something behind.

"We had a bet," Kate explained to Jack as she held the auditorium door for us. "About the play. She wasn't very nice."

"She's not a nice girl, Kate," Jack said as we spilled into the lobby. "You ought to know that." He tossed my knapsack to me, thrusting it like a medicine ball. "I'm going to Dan's. See you."

"What's wrong with *him*?" Kate asked.

I wasn't sure. Lots of things probably. I just shrugged.

Kate was combing her hair when we got to her locker, so I opened it for her. I'll never forget the combination, 10–24–8, or the way she looked as she started to collect her stuff. She was smiling to herself. I leaned onto the locker alongside hers and rubbed my eyes with the heels of my palms. I remember feeling sort of tired, sort of electric and free. Like I just didn't care. Like there was nothing in the world that could possibly bind me. Like I belonged nowhere and everywhere.

We headed toward the side exit, our shoulders grazing as we walked. It was five o'clock. One long, low ribbon of sunlight slipped through the parted doors at the far end of the hall, creating a visible channel of dust in the air, and I could smell the rich, ripe aroma of just-cut grass. The school was uninhabited, but there was influence to its stillness. To this day, I believe I can render it, the *feel* of it—the shining, the glowing, the empty. I remember thinking, *Something's coming.* I could feel it coming.

She breathed in. She said, "I think I'm in love."

Then she blushed, and the hollows of her cheeks flushed with pink, like light warming rubies, coming up through them. Her eyes were pleading, as if calling on me to join her somehow. I remember turning. I remember exactly what it was to turn.

I saw a figure, a man. He was several paces behind us along the wall. His presence seemed to consume the entire width of the corridor, cleaving the air like an angry black slash. Never in my life had I seen anything so profoundly extrinsic, so exotic, so mystifying. His eyes were not on

Kate, they were on me. He seemed to know me as I knew him; instantly we entered into confidence. He smiled, one swift and contemptuous smile, as if he'd caught me committing some crime that rendered me eligible for his coercion. And though I could not name what I had done, I felt the accuracy of his instinct. Nothing could conceal the perversion in me that was manifest to his eyes. I turned back. Whoever he was, he was inside—like a bullet, lodged.

The clock on Kate's dresser said 9:05. She came over in a towel and sat next to me on the edge of her bed. The mattress rocked like a motorless boat. I grabbed a *Seventeen* magazine from her table and started flipping through it. She always had all these magazines.

"So, what do you think?" she asked.

I was looking at this article in which Mariel Hemingway was demonstrating her favorite exercises. You had to hang over crossed legs and lay both palms on the floor while straightening your knees.

"Think of what?"

"Of Harrison."

Outside, the railroad crossing bells began to clank, and beyond the window the night blinked red. Within seconds, the whistle blew and the house began to shake, buoyantly, then furiously, then less and less as the train moved west. After a brief buzzing silence, the second set of chimes rang and the gates lifted.

"Is that his name? Harrison?"

"Harrison Rourke," she replied.

Rourke, I thought, not Harrison. Rourke sounded more accurate. "I don't know. He's kind of old." Old wasn't right. Old was the only thing I could think of. That and him filling the hall behind us, a terrifying miracle of engineering, like a jet plowing through an alley.

"He's not *old,*" she said.

I had the feeling I should mention the way he looked at me. If I didn't mention it then, I never could, because Kate would want to know why I hadn't said anything from the start. But often what feels implicitly true seems less true when you put it into words. I didn't want to sound crazy.

"Is he a regular teacher?" I asked. "Or an outside guy coming in?"

Kate got up to put on a record. "An outside guy. The people who donated the money this year for the drama program hired him. They visited one day with Alicia Ross's parents. They had a driver for their car." After the spongy opening lull of the album came the crisp pops of music, and magically, a guitar. It was "Can't Find My Way Home" by Blind Faith.

> *You are the reason I've been waiting all these years—*
> *Somebody holds the key*
> *Well, I'm near the end and I just ain't got the time*
> *And I'm wasted and I can't find my way home*

She sang along in her confectionery soprano and stood at the doors of her closet before a wall of meticulously folded garments coordinated in blocks of evolving color—cobalt to turquoise, coral to red, mocha to black. Kate could hunt for clothes with a transfixing resolve, making you think of Hollywood starlets. The bath towel slipped down the slope of her chest, scraping her nipples before dropping to the floor. I observed her talcum-coated body—I tried but could not imagine it in his arms. Had she said that she was *in love* or that she *thought* she was? Somehow it made a difference.

"Kate, can you do this?" The magazine had a picture of a model with a short haircut.

She returned to the bed. She was buttoning a big shirt with one of those Mandarin collars like the Beatles wore. She frowned. "It's totally layered, you know."

My eyes were closed and she was cutting. When she drew a combful of hair toward her, the rest of me went swayingly with it, which was hypnotic. It took me to the place in the mind where dreams are manufactured, which I pictured to be a hollow shaped like a tiny sea horse.

"It's not so sudden," Kate said, suddenly speaking of Rourke again. "It's been weeks."

I opened my eyes. In the bathroom mirror my eyes looked scared. Sometimes a thinking brain scared me. For the entire time I'd stopped thinking, she'd continued.

"Is that enough," she asked, "or do you want to take off more?"

My hair came to my jaw in a short bob. "More."

Her fingers kept capturing new sections, faster and faster. She would hold them with one hand and with the other she would snip, her head tilting affectedly. Her father had been a barber, and her aunt and uncle owned a salon in France, in a city called Grasse. I closed my eyes again. Kate said hair is dead, but I could feel the scissors cutting. Maybe I only felt the sound.

"Any shorter and you might as well shave it," I heard her say. She tossed the scissors into the sink, and they bridged the drain catch. On the floor I saw my hair, a collection of pitiful commas. My hands moved to touch my head; no strand of hair was longer than two inches.

Kate sat on the toilet. She seemed shocked by what she had done. "I can't believe it," she kept saying. *"I can't believe it."*

I looked in the mirror. I liked how I looked—eyes and bones, my skin so fair. I looked as if I had survived something catastrophic. For the first time in my life, I could see myself.

She was crying. "You look like a war prisoner."

I was probably supposed to tell her not to cry, that it was not her fault. But I felt myself shrink back. I felt mildly insensate, as though the me to whom she addressed her regret was just a façade, and the essential me, the me I was becoming, was safely out of reach, already halfway to vanishing.

There was the roll of the garage door, then two quick raps at the back door to my room. It was late. I came out from deep beneath the safety of my quilt and unlocked the lock.

"The living room lights are out," Jack said, brushing past. "I didn't want to wake Irene." He threw his jacket onto the floor, then he turned and saw me. "Holy shit!" He dropped on the high end of my bed near the pillow. I dropped beside him. Jack took the spoon from a teacup on the bedside table and he whacked it in his hand. Then he began to slap it on his forehead instead. He asked me, "Did it leave a mark?"

"I think you have to do it harder for that. With the other side."

"Fuck it." He tossed the spoon back into the cup and looked to the floor. A long time passed, during which we mostly breathed. Finally, he said, "Your hair is pretty fucking short."

"You said to cut it."

"Cut, not *shave*."

"You said, *'Cut it short.'*"

"Yeah, well, I wasn't counting on short being so incredibly short."

"Let's not say *short* anymore." It sounded weird—*short*—the horsey way you have to drop your jaw. I crawled behind his back, drawing up the covers. I rubbed my legs together.

"Cold?" he asked.

I said that I was.

His eyes remained averted, though he moved closer. His hands reached for the collar of my sweater and he fussed with the top button, then he fastened it, fastening every next one all the way down, jerking me forward each time.

"I—don't—like—people—looking—at—you."

I didn't argue. It only made things worse to argue with Jack. Furniture would break, or glass would shatter, or he would disappear. Once, he took off for days, and when he returned he had a gash on his left forearm. When my mother asked how it had happened, he said, "fishing."

I didn't ask what he meant because I knew what he meant. Rourke had been in the auditorium with us that afternoon and Jack had seen what I had not—Rourke noticing me. Kate had also seen—she'd spoken of Rourke while cutting my hair. It had been a strange day. None of us had been immune to the sweep of its effects, not me, not Kate, not Jack. I felt somewhat like a pet, a little bird, blinking dumbly at the just-opened door of my cage. There was no point in reassuring them, in promising to go nowhere. Evidently they believed otherwise. They seemed to feel it would be asking a lot of me to defy my nature.

"I'm sorry," I said, kissing him. "Sorry for making you angry."

He raised his head, saying, "Okay, so let's see the new face."

11

Cafeteria tables are laid in strategic rows like trenches. That's in case they have to get *to* you fast, or get you *out* fast, or get *away* from you fast. Such are the grim inferences you learn to live with in high school. Madame Murat and Pat Egan, the one-armed shop teacher, circled the room, acting superior as prison guards. I wondered why they acted superior, since they were there just like we were there, only they'd been there longer and we were getting out first.

Jack and I were sitting by the windows in the corner. He was doing calculus, I was studying. Not exactly studying so much as staring at the patterns of text on the page, which were coming together and apart before my eyes like pieces at the bottom of a kaleidoscope. At the table to our left, Peter Palumbo and Daryl Sackler lunged emphatically, playing that football game boys play with the triangular folded paper. To our right, girls with tipped-in shoulders and nodding breasts huddled together over brown bag lunches.

Outside it was raining like crazy. Sheets of water pounded the roof, going straight over the gutters, past the windows, and onto the saturated ground. I could see past the parking lot, and into the sober queues of the potato fields on the opposite side of Long Lane.

The storm had started the night before at two in the morning. Twelve hours is a long time for a hard rain. I suspected it was a special rain, a monumental rain. I wanted to go into it with fanned-out arms, to bow and stomp and dance something similar to an Indian dance. I wanted to be touched by it and changed. It was rain to pray into, rain to save the world.

Jack and I had witnessed the very first drops the night before. The water tapped like rat teeth at my bedroom window. Jack said, "Listen." His head tilted curiously, like an animal's head. The beads of rain stuck to the glass, beached and lonely. We stared in the manner of zombies.

"Time is it?" he asked.

I said, "About two."

"I don't even feel tired. You feel tired?"

My head hurt and my eyes burned. My throat was sore. "A little tired, I guess, yeah." We'd been arguing for hours, though Jack refused to call it that.

"*Disagreeing,*" he said, "is sufficient." Adding, "Strenuously."

"Are we *at odds*?"

"Yes." Jack nodded once. "We are at odds."

I did not like to be at odds with Jack. It was like being in a rowboat with only one person rowing. My oar would be raised, skimming the glassy lake, and Jack's would flail—digging too deep, flying too high, ticking spastically. It would take us forever to go nowhere.

I had certain feelings, I'd told him. "Inside. They need relief."

He peered through me as if to a minuscule spot on the wall.

I asked if he knew what I meant.

"Of course I know what you mean," he snapped. Then he reminded me emphatically that I was not an animal. "You are separated from depravity by a conscience."

Even if it was crazy to consider the activity of a few witless nerve endings as depraved, I did not disagree with him. Other girls hadn't mentioned such feelings, so I knew that I was at the very least abnormal. It was common knowledge that if a girl was assertive in regard to sex, it was because she wanted to keep a boyfriend or steal a boyfriend or act out against her parents and society. Possibly she craved *togetherness*. I'd never heard of a girl who wished to alleviate the tingling sensations along the walls of her vagina, or at the posterior rim of its base, or in a third place, sort of an alcove where the seam of low underwear hits, only on the inside. No girls I knew ever spoke of seeing a boy or seeing a man and *thinking thoughts*.

"The job of the conscience," Jack was saying, "is to marshal urges. Otherwise, any object in your field of vision is eligible for fucking."

I thought he was missing the point.

"I'm *not* missing the point," he said. "It's not a particularly sophisticated point to miss."

Jack stood and did something he never did, which was to tuck in his shirt. His scaly hands crammed the fabric down in bunches, and he began to pace. "Your problem is that you haven't read enough. If you'd done more reading, you'd realize that desire that moves from origin to fulfillment but circumvents the intellect is corrupted by compulsion. It's immoral and untrue—it's *feral*." *Feral* was his new favorite word; he used it cleverly, sometimes three or four times a day without sounding repetitive. "Understand me?"

I said, "Sort of."

"Be specific. What *don't* you understand?" He lifted a scallop shell from my desk and bit at its edge, gnawing at the corrugated reservoir of pink, dragging his lips across the veins that spread in a fan from the squared cap to the sheer, translucent edge. I felt a numb jerk between my legs, and I looked away.

"I'm sorry," I said. I couldn't remember what we'd been saying.

He cast the shell aside. It made a solitary clink when it hit the table, like a fork ringing out on glass. "You were saying you *sort of* understood."

"Oh. Even if longings are immoral, why are they untrue?"

"Because one *arrives* at truth, one cultivates it. Truth doesn't materialize instantaneously. Therefore, how can it be true to go around satisfying impulses?"

"Imagine you're walking," I said, "and you get the urge to run—"

"*Urge* is the operative word," Jack interrupted.

"Okay, fine. It's a *physical* urge or a *feral* urge—whatever. But instead of running, you think of all the things that running entails, like, whether you're wearing the right shoes, and what the neighbors might say, and what if you trip, and so on. If after all that thinking, you decide *not* to run, that decision would be impure. It would have come from fear—fear of judgment or failure. And if, after thinking, you decide *to* run, that choice would also be impure, coming from a wish to defy convention or to take a personal risk. So, you could say that the *first* feeling, the *truest* feeling, the physical, feral urge, is contaminated by secondary things, things coming from thought."

"Yeah," he said. *"So?"*

"I'm just saying, maybe urges start out okay, but it's the thinking afterward that contorts everything."

"Wrong," Jack said. "*Circumstance* contorts everything. Urges are not needs; they are perversions of needs and are inseparable from circumstance. You can't discuss the urge to drive fast without presupposing the circumstance of a car. Or jumping from a plane without presupposing being in air. Or overeating if there's no food. An urge is like not being hungry but anyway you eat. It's like eating cake because cake is there. What if, instead of cake, there's celery sticks. Would your body manufacture the desire to eat celery sticks?"

"I don't know," I said. "Maybe." I happened to like celery.

"To the point that you would actually gorge on it?"

"Probably not." I didn't like celery *that* much.

"So is your urge to eat celery a *true* urge?"

I wasn't sure anymore. It was weird to argue about celery.

"Of course not," Jack answered for me. "An *urge* is relevant only in regard to *urge impetus*. Urges are 'untrue' because they change when circumstances change."

I wasn't sure what it all had to do with sex anyway.

"Simple," he said. "You can't go out fucking every time you get an urge."

"Why do you keep saying 'go out'? This is a conversation about you and me."

"No, Evie. This is a conversation about *you*."

I picked at the carpet.

Jack joined me on the floor and began to gesture with somber hands. "Don't you see? Orgasm is secondary to intimacy. True bliss comes from the union of soul to soul. If you are driven strictly by the will to copulate, you are no more than a beast—unrefined, spiritually bankrupt, devoid of the capacity for distinction. You are *feral*," he concluded triumphantly.

I frowned and exhaled. I knew that the second he left, things would not be as clear as he insisted.

"Okay?" Jack asked, caressing my head. "Silly girl."

———

The falling water formed a curtain on the outside of the cafeteria glass. Birds fluttered behind it, sheltered by the overhang created by the sloped roof.

"I'm gonna take a walk," I said to Jack. "See you later."

"Later," Jack mumbled, going back to his books.

It's always a risk to stand when other people are sitting. It makes you an object of gossip, especially if you are a gossip-worthy person, which I happened to be, and there was no sense trying to change the fact. Some people try to change the fact by being extra nice or helpful to others. Some people depress me.

I was fifteen when my dad's partner, Tony, taught me how to ward off the evil eye. "See that?" he said one day when we were walking through Washington Square Park. "That bitch is giving you the evil eye. Quick, do this." He took my hand and curled all the fingers except the pointer and the pinky. "She don't have to see it," Tony advised. "You don't gotta draw her attention to it—unless of course you want to. Just let your arm hang down, nice and casual. This way you protect yourself." As we passed the woman, he laughed in her face. *"Ha!"* he said. "Comin' right back at cha, babe!"

I moved through a maze of cafeteria tables, with each group going silent as I approached, then snapping to action as I passed, like a baseball wave. I held my hand the way Tony had taught me. When I reached the table with Kiki, Pip, and Coco, there was an outburst of laughter, probably about my hair. When we got to school that morning, Denny said I looked like Mia Farrow in *Rosemary's Baby*. "Big-eyed and sort of eerie."

The doors of the gym were open. I made my way down the right side of the courts, through a corridor of idling boys waiting for the next game or recovering from the last. They nodded, saying, "Hey, Evie." They didn't seem to mind the way I was.

The staccato back and forth of feet trampling the court shook the wooden stands as I climbed the last section of bleachers at the farthest end of the gym. I sat and leaned forward, watching the game, thinking it must feel good to trample and to run undressed without fear of scrutiny, to be the legitimate heirs to such a definitive space as a gym. Sometimes you can feel sorry to be a woman, or at least you can forget why you're supposed to be so glad about it.

There was the piercing squelch of rubber. "Do it! Go! Go!"

The boys signaled with clapping hands or twitching heads, and when the guy with the ball was blocked, you figured he would pass or hand off, but instead his jaw would relax, his eyes would go stony, and he would pivot low to cut past the rangy gate of arms that sought to obstruct him; then he would try the shot anyway, usually missing. In spite of the failed attempt, you had to admire the breakaway risk. Breakaway risk is kind of like the law of the sperm. They'll unify, but only to a point.

The wooden plank depressed alongside me—creaking down, easing up. I looked back, turning almost completely. It was the man Kate had pointed to in the hallway. He moved directly behind me, placing one of his knees on either side of my back. He was soaking wet and his chest was heaving. I figured he'd been running in the rain and that he must have been running a long time, maybe miles. He'd come to give me a message. He wanted me to know he felt entitled. I understood—I felt similarly entitled. He'd come because he had no choice; there was nowhere else to go. I knew that too. I also had nowhere. His soul was not quiet; neither was mine.

The light cotton of his shorts revealed what I had never seen made so legible, a region of tenderness, and it made me both proud and sad, which was strange; to feel proud that way, as if I were connected to his tenderness, and sad because, of course, I was not. His face was like the face of a large animal, kinglike and balanced. The cheekbones were so prominent as nearly to hide the eyes, which were as dark as carbon, but glassy, like lights were shining on them. His hair was black and dripping. Kate had said his name was Harrison, Harrison Rourke.

Someone screamed, "Let's go, asshole, let's go!"

I did not turn back to the court. I knew his nearness was miraculous. It was nothing I could explain; it was an old knowledge. My feelings for him were like memories rising up, dormant things revivified, regaining dimension, spinning to life. To be near him, the world turned alive.

I stayed still, letting him regard me. Unlike Jack, he did not seem to be disgusted by what he saw.

As soon as I was able, I went back down cautiously into the gym. Reaching the end by the doors, I turned back. He had not moved. His elbows were on his knees, his head hanging down, his face turned to me. He was smiling.

12

I was standing at the glass doors in the freezing cold foyer of the school, watching the wind do battle with the objects on the ground outside. In just one more day it would be November, and in six more days it would be my birthday.

Everyone kept asking, "What do you want?"

"Nothing," I would say, because it was true.

I wasn't even sure what the day meant anymore or how it was supposed to commemorate the fact of me or my existence. I could hardly expect anyone to share in that. When I searched for myself among the memories of the sixteen birthdays I'd had, I found no link between the child I'd been, the girl I was, or the woman I might become. Beyond the obvious connection to my having been present when those days actually occurred, I could think of nothing more meaningful for me in the chain than an attachment to the month itself. In November the sun draws back, the sky goes high, and the wind turns bold. Chestnut casings batter cement paths, broken leaves form long and drifting islands in the streets, and there is woeful noise—the music of decay.

I reloaded my camera; twenty minutes left before the Halloween pep rally was to start. There was never a shortage of Halloween pictures for the yearbook, but I'd assigned myself to photograph the day anyway, because it gave me an excuse to wear regular clothes and skip classes. As it turned out I made it through three rolls of film before classes started, so I spent the rest of the day reading *Pride and Prejudice* in Denny's car and drinking coffee at the rear entrance with the cafeteria workers.

According to my mother, Halloween was actually a pagan festival of the dead, a day when the threshold between worlds was considered most permeable, and so the deceased would likely visit. "The point of scary costumes," she said, "was to help the living frighten the dead back to the other side."

Sadly, the holiday had drifted from its more compelling origins. Now it represented an opportunity for everyone to dress in toxic plastic and act like assholes. It was especially disturbing when nondescript adults like Toby Parker, the music teacher, or Mr. O'Donnell, the librarian, went about their normal business, such as teaching trumpet lessons or sorting the Dewey decimal classification while dressed as Coneheads or strangled ogres. The office ladies were all wearing fangs, and Ms. Herbst, the typing teacher, was dressed as a German beer wench.

A blue Mustang reeled expertly into the school parking lot. Ray Trent and Mike Reynolds got out, their doors closing simultaneously— *boom-boom.* Ray and Mike were from Montauk. Like most people from Montauk, they had nice cars. Unlike others from Montauk, they also had nice clothes and lots of money. They were always going on field trips, or into the city to see concerts at Madison Square Garden. Some people said they sold drugs.

Troy Resnick said *no way.* "I never bought drugs from them."

"Yeah, well, who would blow their cover dealing to a douche bag like you?" Jack said.

I didn't really mind what they did—they were polite and you could have a good time with them without getting molested. I knew because Ray had taken me to the junior prom that past spring.

Ray had asked me on Valentine's Day. Jack and I were at lunch, working our way through a bag of heart-shaped cookies Denny had made for us. Denny was an awful cook. He always added stray ingredients— spices, oils, herbs, whatever happened to be around.

"Perfect timing," Jack said when Ray arrived, and he pushed the cookies over. "Help us out here before we puke."

Ray reached into the bag and checked with Jack about asking me to the prom. "Because I know *you're* not going, man."

Jack gnawed at a cookie. "Actually, Ray," he stated, "I'd love to go to the prom, but I can't afford it. Lobotomies are expensive."

"What do you think, Evie?" Ray asked. "You up for it?"

I shrugged. "Okay."

"Cool," Ray said, then he took a bite, gagging instantly. "What's in these things?"

"*Nutmeg,*" we said in unison as Denny came up the aisle with a loaded cafeteria tray.

"So Ray showed up for some cookies too, huh?" he said brightly. "Thank God I got six milks!"

Ray and I ended up having a great prom night, dancing and mingling and driving around in the Mustang. I talked about my dad's sign shop and gypsy moth infestation and films I loved, like Rossellini's *Rome, Open City,* and he spoke of his sister Kerrie, a competitive gymnast, and the giant television set he and Mike had just picked up in Smithtown for Mike's grandmother. Ray did offer me cocaine, but the proposal came more or less as a courtesy, just in case I'd had certain expectations in regard to the evening. He didn't do any himself, not that I could see, and not once did I observe him exchanging packets for cash. After the breakfast party, he returned me safely home and kissed me goodbye, giving me his Grateful Dead *Terrapin Station* tape.

"Thanks for coming out with me, Eveline," Ray said, "and for not being afraid. Most girls in school are—" He broke off and rattled his arms at hip height like he was pretend-spooked, "Whoa, like, weird."

"Yeah," I said. It was true. Most girls in school were *Whoa, like, weird.*

"But you see the beauty in people, so people feel beautiful around you. You don't have any fears or hang-ups," he said.

Tempting as it was to contradict him in regard to fears and hang-ups, I said nothing. It's impolite to refute a compliment. When people need to be nice, you need to let them. Force yourself. Practice.

I hid behind a square brick pillar on the school steps. Through my telephoto, I followed Ray and Mike as they eased around the cars in the lot. They were wearing business suits, I figured the suits were their costumes. Mike banged on the fender of a muddy Dodge Dart, and a girl in an aggregate of shredded purple rayon bounded from the passenger side, Instamatic in hand. It was Laura Migliore, also from Montauk, dressed as Stevie Nicks. Laura passed her half-spent cigarette back through the open window to the invisible driver, and she waved one witchy arm, directing Ray and Mike to come together for a photo. I got a shot of her taking a shot of them and a few more of Ray leaning on the car, bending furtively to talk to the driver, with Mike flanking him protectively, staring into the fields. Mr. Cuneo, the algebra teacher, called the fields *lots*. He was always talking about having grown up in the *potato lots*.

The boys came up the school steps, and autumn leaves whipped their ankles, halfway mounting the lengths of their legs.

"Hey, hey, it's the beach bunny," Mike said, referring to a day I'd spent in Montauk, the day I'd lied to Kate when Maman was dying. The day I'd taken a break from hospital visits.

That day Ray and Mike had found me alone at the beach at the end of Essex Street, in Montauk Village. I seemed down, so they tried to cheer me. They bought me espadrilles and a sundress at the Surf Shop since I'd come by train just in my bathing suit and shorts. We went to the Montauket for sunset, the Yacht Club for dinner, and to Tipperary for darts. Because it's difficult to leave Montauk when the moment for leaving presents itself, Ray and I spent the night together on his boat. In the morning we had breakfast at the Royale Fish in Amagansett. I didn't feel guilty about Ray, since it ended up being a good time when I needed one most. It had been a lonely summer, and I was grateful to the someone somewhere who had taken pity on me and sent relief in the form of friends and fun. *Someone somewhere*— people say that as though it means something other than God.

Ray held the door for me. "Where's your costume, Evie?"

"Don't tell me," Mike said, referring to the camera. "You're a private detective."

"You better go easy on the eye-spy stuff," Ray teased. "I don't want to have to buy you a new camera when Mike busts that one."

A crowd of kids was cramming into the gymnasium, and we joined them. Ray threw one arm around me, and with the other tousled my hair. "That's some chop job," he shouted over the shouting. "Very sexy."

"You working?" Mike shouted too. "Or you wanna sit with us?"

"Working," I yelled. As they waved and walked off, I called out, "What are you guys supposed to be, anyway?"

"Ourselves," Mike hollered, "in a couple years."

I withdrew to the wall beneath the basketball hoops, climbing onto a stack of folded exercise mats. Each grade filled its own section of bleachers, then the cheerleaders burst into the center of the gym, flipping and triple high-kicking. They performed their two best cheers with incomparable gusto, then came that Queen chant—*We will, we will, rock you.* Everyone joined in, stomping their feet, one, then the other, ending with a clap—one-two, *three*, one-two, *three*. I searched for Ray and Mike through my telephoto lens. They were at the base of the senior section, talking nonchalantly, as if they happened to have met on the street. I wondered why I'd chosen Jack instead of Ray, when Ray was good-looking and polite and much better to sleep with than Jack, and he had a car instead of a skateboard.

Next the football players jogged out in full uniform and greasepaint, coming together in bungling formation. After one final gargantuan roar, everyone descended to the gym floor, and soon the whole frenetic assembly was urging itself to the doors. I hopped down and let myself be transported in a swilling back and forth motion, until I was ejected into the lobby.

Kate ran up alongside me. "Did you see him?" Her massive hoop earrings clanked as she spun her head left and right. Kate was a gypsy. Not a gypsy, a "Bohemian."

"See who?"

"Harrison. He was just here. C'mon!" She took off down the hallway, dragging me. "Let's see if he posted the roles. Hurry!" Once the auditorium doors were in sight, Kate squealed. The list was there. She spun and buried her face in my shoulder. "Oh, my God, Evie, I think I got it."

I hugged her. Her eyes were closed, screwed up tight in their sockets, like lavender bottle caps. We were like finalists in a beauty pageant— Kate's breath on my face, the cushiony weight of her breasts against my breasts, the perfumed fragrance of her hair.

"Wait a minute," I said. "I'll go check."

On the door was a sheet of yellow legal paper carelessly taped. It hung tilted to the right as though it had come in forcefully from the left. The letters were blocky and sure; the ink was red. As I dragged my hand down the page, I could feel the architecture of Rourke's handwriting, the reservoirs and alcoves made by the pressure of his pen.

"Did you find it?" Kate asked.

"Not yet," I murmured, reaching again for the top, mesmerized.

"Come *on*." She stomped.

"Oh," I said, "here." I traced the grain of the letters. He had pressed so hard, I didn't need my eyes to read. "Ready?" I asked, stalling once more. "Emily Webb . . . Kate Cassirer."

Her eyes popped open. "I knew it," she whispered, and she leaned back against the wall.

I observed her from across the portal; I was thinking what to say. I was probably supposed to say something. It was weird, but I didn't feel as glad for her as I had at first, when we were hugging. All I could think was that he had written her name.

"You worked hard," I said, striving to sound convincing. "You deserve it."

Then I nodded for no reason, the way people do when they pull their lips slightly into their mouths and set aside the magnitude of their own very exceptional feelings. My fingers remained on the paper, feeling every crease and notch, hunting for the weight of his hand, the breadth of his wrist, the bulk of his forearm, as if I could detect within the marks a message to myself.

13

Jack slid the barn door open, and his left arm in a cherry-red windbreaker jerked the handle right, two times, reminding me of a madman reloading a shotgun. First there was darkness, then the darkness changed to light, and, suddenly, all the faces.

A chorus of voices screamed, "Surprise!" A cold beer made its way into my hand. There was music, the birthday song by the Beatles. Damp lips grazed my face and many hands held me, hugging, touching, kissing.

"*Happy Birthday, Evie!*"

"*Congratulations!*"

Kate tried to steer me into the lurching pack, but I resisted. Denny took my hand. "*I'll* take you around. Okay, honey?"

Lots of people were there—Jack's friends and Kate's and Denny's, and a few who could possibly be classified as mine, like Ray and Mike and Marty from the yearbook and also several cheerleaders. Part of my brain, the thinking part, appreciated everyone's excellent intentions. But the remainder, the loose piles of random brain shavings and brain bits, feared the lazy swag of streamers and the humiliated balloons and the smell of spilled beer on the buckling barn floor. I burrowed under Jack's jacket, hiding there.

After the Beatles came a loud laser beat—*zung, zung, zung.* Then plunging whistles, tripping *bweeps,* manufactured claps, aboriginal whoops, and the deep fishy vociferousness of disco.

"Let's dance!" Denny called from the center of the room, and everyone joined him.

Jack threw his palms over his ears. "Who put this shit on?" he shouted.

"What *is* it?" Dan asked. He raised his head and furrowed his brows as though trying to discern one particular ingredient in a complex stew. He was on the ladder to the loft, rewiring a broken light. He pushed his glasses higher up the bridge of his nose with his wrist.

"It's the fucking Salsoul Orchestra!" Jack complained bitterly.

"Actually," Dan said, "I think it's Parliament."

"Whatever it is," Jack said, heading to the stereo, "it's gotta go."

I grabbed him, saying to wait. "Maybe it will keep them all, you know, occupied."

Jack relented—partly because it was my birthday, partly because it pleased him when I was intolerant of others. He wrapped his arms about me from behind, and together we gazed at the shocking and incongruous sight of disco dancers in the barn. It was somewhat like watching your house burn to the ground from the opposite side of the street. Aunt Lowie always says the two biggest concerns about throwing a party are worrying that no one will come, then worrying that they'll never leave.

Denny kept calling me out to the dance floor. He loved to show off what we'd learned from Uncle Archer. Denny's uncle was a retired Broadway choreographer and dance teacher. We'd been taking lessons for years, ever since *Saturday Night Fever.*

"Maybe later," I suggested.

"Go ahead," Jack insisted, though he was being insincere. He hated me to dance in public. Once he'd gone to Teen Night at a local club with me, and when he saw me and Mike Stern dancing to "Brick House" on a platform, he had some kind of an optic seizure. His left eye stayed bloodshot for days.

"What's an *optic seizure?*" Kate had asked afterward.

"I guess your blood pressure goes up and your veins pop."

"That's a stroke!" she'd exclaimed.

"Yeah," I'd said, "maybe it is."

On the far side of the barn, past the writhing trunks and ticking heads of the dancers, I noticed what appeared to be a cardboard playhouse. "What's that?" I asked Jack, and when he didn't reply, I wiggled past the loose gate of his arms and crossed the room. Against the wall near the door was a refrigerator box with a window cut into the center of its face. Painted above the hole was a message: *To Evie from Jack.* The writing looked like spilled nails.

There was clapping. Voices calling, "Open it, open it."

I lifted the flap. Hanging from a pink ribbon, in the dead center of the box, was a large, uninflated balloon. I looked back to Jack. He stood as I'd left him, leaning a little to his right. I touched the balloon tentatively. Inside was something resistant.

"Pull it off," Denny yelled.

"Don't just stand there," Kate said. "Open it. Aren't you curious?"

I shook my head. I was not curious. I knew exactly what it was.

Earlier that day, we were reclining in the sun on a wooden footbridge in back of the nature trail at the end of Huntting Lane. It was where we always went; once Jack had carved the outline of our joined hands there, chiseling them into wood. We would close our eyes and pretend we were hanging by our backs from the belly of the earth, and we could almost feel the spinning. It was as though we were riding; we felt so light. We weighed a flawless weight, a liquid and inconsequent weight, like cylinders half-filled and lying on their sides. We swore we would never impress too deeply, never demand too much.

"Listen," Jack whispered. "A warbler."

With my eyes closed, I found it: the high stutter, the tiny drill. I could hear it, but also I heard nothing. In my body was a quiescent dizziness, a chiasma of consciousness and unconsciousness. I felt myself float. *Listen,* he'd said, *a warbler.* How beautiful Jack was in my mind, how striking and direct. How good it must have felt to be him, so intellectually capable and morally sure. The way his ideas were clever and his pronunciation clear. The way his integrity was not dormant but volatile. The way his beliefs switched over into language. To know Jack was to know there would never be anyone like him. *I love him,* I thought. *I'll always love him.*

"There it is Evie, look."

Jack nudged me twice and I forced my eyes open. The winter light coming in was burning and bright, like first opening your eyes underwater. He was pointing into the air, his thin arm bobbing wretchedly to chase the able bird. I could see his arm attached to his body, his body connected to the ground, the ground not spinning. I wanted to close my eyes and go back to the place in my mind. Things were better there. *Oh my God,* I thought—*Jack, me—the tragedy of us.*

I turned, saying, "Jack," but before I could say more, he stopped me.

He rolled nearer to me and pressed his forehead to mine. "The way you say my name. I can hear myself in it."

We returned to town with him leading; Main Street seemed particularly immense. I had my hand in his coat pocket and the seam of the pouch cut against my wrist. His jacket smelled waxy; it had that special coating to block the rain. Jack was unusually quiet; I wondered if he could sense the space between us.

As we walked past the window of Rose Jeweler's I noticed an iridescent egg-shaped opal framed by a brocade of gold and attached to a chainlike thread. The necklace rested securely in the cinched center of a sapphirine cushion, like a bug in a palm. I stopped dead, pulling back my hand. It looked just like one of Jack's eyes.

"What is it?" he asked, turning. He came up slowly behind me. The reflection of his eyes joined the jewel in the glass, all three swimming.

I couldn't help myself. I began to cry.

"What's wrong?" he asked again.

I pointed to the opal. "Don't you see? It's the color of your eyes."

I pulled the necklace from the deflated balloon. Jack was behind me, removing the chain from my hands, unclasping it, hanging it about my neck, arranging it on my collarbone. I felt its frail burden. I did not like the bubbling sputters the people made or the thoughts they were surely thinking. They knew nothing about the warbler or the eye, nothing about Rourke.

"*Speech, speech!*"

I said nothing. Jack's lips met mine. His kiss was flat. "Here," he said, handing me something blue and small. I swallowed it.

When quiet came, it came loudly, like an explosion, like an avalanche of nothingness.

Denny laid the gifts on my lap. I looked to see the people, but the people had gone. *Okay, okay,* Denny kept saying to no one in particular. *Hold on,* and, *I'm not ready,* or *I'm coming.*

Kate was there on the floor next to us, with me on the bench, and Jack across the room leaning against a broken dresser. Jack was watching me with the living-dead look of a portrait. I wondered what it was in me that interested him so.

Denny dropped down next to Kate. He was exhausted, he said. I thought he should sleep. I thought we should lie down and I would pull the threads from the hem of his dress shirt and say all the things I'd never said. That I loved him. That it didn't matter to me that he was gay, which I'd never said, which of course I did not have to say. I wanted to tell him he did not need to hide himself from me or from anyone. That he was chivalrous and so very handsome.

Save the ribbon, Denny said with a wink. *I'll make you a hat.*

I pushed my back against the wall and bit at the rubber tag of my tongue. I opened the first gift. Everything felt a little imperious, a little rigid but also light, like a Japanese tea ceremony, though I had never been to one. I wondered when would I get to Japan, how would I ever find the time? Denny and Kate were at my feet, Jack still at the dresser. Packages were coming apart, their innards passing off to the right and the left before I could even see.

Don't worry, Kate said. *I'm making a list.*

Open the heavy one, Denny said. *It's from me.*

It was a *Janson's History of Art.* Between the beige twill covers, the sheets were cool and superior, unlike newspapers which are cheap with leaking ink because their origins are local and insurgent, as if they have been made in basements by the thinking people you know.

I thanked Denny, I thought I did, I definitely did because he nodded several times, and he blew a kind of kiss. He was eating a baked potato. I did not know where it had come from. When he lifted it, it sagged in the center and curled at the edges like a canoe.

Now mine, Kate said, handing me a box with silver wrap. Inside was a rust-red cashmere sweater—Maman's. I drew it to my skin, breathing deeply. I was not trying to recall Maman's smell or how it had felt to hold her. I just liked the shield the sweater made, the way I could hide behind the barrier. When I dropped the sweater down, Denny and Kate were still there. They had not moved; their faces were like moons at my knees. Jack was in the same place too, though surely time had passed. I wondered, did Jack feel what I felt when what I felt was so very high? Did he feel he wanted to move but couldn't, that his legs were sponge? But no, I was wrong, my legs were moving, I could see them rise up like puppets being lifted by hidden hands. And me going up too.

Denny surrounded me with bear arms. *Oh, honey.* Kate's hand light on my shoulder. I thanked them both, for everything. Everything.

Jack and I were alone. I told him I wanted to dance.

He said, *Oh, shit.*

I careened to the stereo and shuffled through the horizontal strip of records. I was flicking them—right, right, right. Going fast to find an album. Something exactly right, I didn't know what, but I knew I wanted it instantly. Not instantly, previously. Instantly was too late. Drugs make you insane over time. Drug time is a window between the moment you feel high and the moment you feel *less* high. I found a record. I pulled it from its jacket.

What did you pick? Jack asked dryly. *Bee Gees?*

The Cars, I said, and I dropped the arm over the turntable. The needle slipped, making a choking parrot sound.

Jesus, Jack said, *take it easy.*

As I danced, I felt the wiggly pressurized feeling of diving to the bottom of a pool, then swimming rapidly to the top. When your hair sweeps back from your skull and your arms are limp like fins that trail the central chesty force of your movement. I felt elastic and wet like a cheerful dolphin. In the water you don't worry about the action of your hands; hands are always engaged in water. I was dancing, making figure eights with my body, using all my muscles, going ever so slightly up and down.

Jack sat at the table, his feet propped on a chair. He was carving a candle with a cake knife. *Evil hips,* he said. *You didn't learn that from me.*

You're all I've got tonight. You're all I've got tonight.
I need you tonight.

Later we were lying in the center of the room, overlapping. I could not tell where I ended and Jack began. We were two halves of something the same, each of us companionless. We were both our essential parts; and yet, for all that we were, we were nothing that we were not. I wished Denny had stayed; his stomach made a nice pillow.

I sighed sadly.

Jack asked what happened to the cheerful dolphin.

I miss Denny, I said.

To make me happy Jack put on the White Album. I'd left it on the dashboard in summer and the vinyl had warped into wide scalloped waves that bubbled hypnotically off the turntable. I liked to watch the record circle lazily, up and down, up and down, like a Hawaiian flower. My head was on Jack's shoulder. If I closed one eye, the zipper tag dangling from the neck of his sweater became like a skyscraper. Pigs were snorting—that meant next came "Rocky Raccoon."

I asked him please to sing. He said I would have to wait for "Julia."

He fed me a piece of my birthday cake, pressing bits into my mouth. It tasted cheap, like box cake with crackled tricks inside; they could have been anything, since Denny made it. Once he filled a cake with Barbie shoes. I spit out the stuff in my mouth. It landed on the floor and I looked at it. My mouth had transformed the cake from black into trenchy brown, and the proof of that internal operation nauseated me. I thought I might vomit.

Don't leave, I said to Jack, dropping back.

Never, he promised.

The floor near my legs creaked eerily. Jack was kneeling over my belly, making a bridge with his groin. His hunched body cast a huge shadow against the wall. When "Julia" came he did not sing. I tried to say this, but nothing came out. I kept moving my head all the way from one side to the other. I was not sure why, except to say that my head was my only mobile part.

What's that, baby, Jack asked, not really asking.

I couldn't remember, though I knew it had been important. I did not like him to call me baby.

I thought I felt him undressing me. I thought I felt the rimy wind pass through the tunnel made by the small of my back arching off the filthy plank floor. I thought I felt his fingertips touch the recesses beneath my hip bones. He may have had sex with me. I thought he did; I wasn't sure.

TRACKS

Winter & Spring 1980

I know another's secret but do not reveal it
and he knows that I know, but does not acknowledge it:
the intensity between us is simply this secret about the secret.

—JEAN BAUDRILLARD

14

am in a room, high up, near some sort of exposed beams. The back of my head smacks the ceiling, and hair that is not my hair hangs around my face, uncoiling stiffly like the tails of chameleons. There is no motion, and time has fallen off its continuum, like gears skipping intervals. I am kept up, pushed up, by what I do not know. On one beam there is writing, code writing, a wicked code, legible to me—legible, and so I am wicked, I think; yes, I must be wicked.

My eyes opened from the nightmare, then immediately closed again, squeezing tight. The twilight seemed robust when I felt so very feeble, so I decided to lay in bed and wait for people to come home and switch on appliances. I wanted all the machines to be on. I did not like the way the appliances were sitting there, arrogant and fat and proving through muteness that everyone was elsewhere, involved with other things, things separate from me.

I switched on the lamp and retrieved the note from Jack that was beneath it. Yellow lamplight soaked the page. Faded gray letters were penciled between the blue rules, strung together and nearly indecipherable. There were words—*love* and *me* and *mystery,* also *key* and *sleep*. I fell back onto the mattress, dropping Jack's note to the floor. My quilt felt soft around my neck, and I nestled into the pillow. Tiny shellfish burrow into the floor of the bay, hiding there. From the safety of their beds of sand they listen to the clamoring of the sea.

That morning I saw him at the record store, through the picture window of Long Island Sound. I was inside; he was walking past. There was no reason for me to turn from what I'd been doing, but when I did, Rourke was there. He stopped and stared incautiously, as though bewildered by me, or provoked. He was wearing a navy-blue down jacket that yielded obediently to his body, and his right hand was crammed halfway inside his jeans pocket. Under his open coat was a pine-green shirt with several unfastened buttons, and the waist of his pants came low around his hips. His black hair was wavy, tousled.

I smiled. He did not smile back.

He reached for the front door. It whooshed open, then clattered to a positive close. I returned to the wall of albums, and experienced that futile feeling of waiting when there's no avoiding the thing you're waiting for. If I tried to leave, he would watch my body on the way out, the way I was bound tight in my jeans. The store was empty except for the two of us, so there was no chance of disappearing among others. I slipped behind a display rack.

He started talking to Eddie, the record store guy. As they spoke, Rourke kept taking pieces of something from his hand, nuts maybe, or candy, and eating them. His jaw moved in even claps, and the muscles at the base of his cheeks flexed into knots. He hadn't shaved.

"It's definitely inferior," Eddie was saying.

"It really is crap," Rourke agreed, and from his coat pocket he withdrew a bottle of lime-green Gatorade, raised it to his lips, and drank.

There was something especially sexy about the random way he was dressed, making it easy to imagine him in bed that morning, thinking thoughts just as I had, jerking off probably, then deciding to alleviate a morning's boredom by going into town for a while. I flipped mechanically through the section of albums marked *S* and imagined that I'd been home with him, wherever it was that his home may have been. I had thoughts of being beneath him, and alongside him, my body to his body, his hands on me, holding me, and his mouth, and his smell. For a moment I felt dizzy. I'd never had such thoughts so vividly: it was like thinking of things we'd already done.

Eddie was much scrawnier next to Rourke than he was beside Jack, practically like a voodoo doll. His badly scarred skin and arched eyebrows were visible to me just above the albums in the wooden aisle dividers as he led Rourke down the row by mine. They drifted to a halt at the *Ps,* facing me. I lowered my head over the record well, pretending to read.

"Petty was influenced by Roger McGuinn of the Byrds," Eddie said. "McGuinn's the one who figured out how to get the long sustains by using a compressor with the Rickenbacker. That's how he got Coltrane's horn sound on 'Eight Miles High.' "

Eddie had an encyclopedic knowledge of music. The store had an "Ask Eddie" lockbox for questions. Answers got posted on a chalkboard by the register. Everyone took the process seriously, especially Jack, who regarded the system as something along the lines of "Ask God."

"Yeah," Rourke said, his voice slipping away from Eddie, moving sinuously, calling to me. Our eyes met. "I know McGuinn," he said softly. "He toured with Dylan."

All the features of the place we inhabited vanished, leaving me alone, with him alone. My heart began to beat rapidly. I adjusted the underwire of my bra beneath my left breast because I did not like to feel my heart against it, the way the blurps felt so miniature, the way the organ strived but failed to be timely. Weeks had elapsed since I'd seen him last, and though I'd thought of him, those thoughts had not affected my mood or disposition. Yet having him before me now, I knew I'd been deprived. I recalled the way he looked at me through the store window. Despite his obvious interest and my real desire, we were impotent with respect to circumstance, and that made me angry, and my anger bound me to him. Rourke understood: he seemed angry as well. In those moments we stepped out equally, we confessed equally, we were rendered equally weak, and as weakened equals we met, victoriously, at some median of daring and possibility.

I was thinking, *I must, oh, you know, say something.*

Eddie pulled out Tom Petty's *Damn the Torpedoes,* then they returned to the front. Rourke's eyes passed over mine once more. I looked away.

Rourke paid, and while he waited for change, he took his wallet between his teeth and yanked his pants up by the belt loops. Eddie inquired about his New Year's plans. I couldn't hear the answer. Probably Rourke's plans involved a girl. When he left, he just left, not looking back, with his head high and his eyes steady on their course, causing me to wonder if perhaps I was wrong. It was possible that he pitied my naïve infatuation.

Right after knocking, Kate burst into my room, her coat still on. "I'm sorry!" she said brightly. "Were you napping?"

"Can you go put the radio on for me?" I asked. "And the lights."

"Sure," she said. She hopped back out to the living room, and within seconds, the lights were on and the radio burst to life. It had been broadcasting all afternoon, transmitting to bodies in kitchens and cars. I had the sickening feeling I'd missed so much.

When Kate returned, she dropped down on the foot of the bed. "I was at the movies," she said. "The matinee. With Harrison Rourke."

I was surprised. I couldn't help it. Sometimes Kate surprised me. I said, "What?"

"Actually," she amended, "he was alone in the theater, so we asked if we could sit with him."

"Who's *we*?" I asked.

"Michelle Sui. Michelle was with me." Kate played with the zipper on her parka. "He said he saw you in the record store. Did you see him?"

"It was pretty crowded in there."

"He said you never say hello."

"I don't really know him."

"Well, he knows you," she said. "You should try to be nice."

I tried to put him out of my mind, the effortless way he had been dressed, the lazy curl of his hair, the hidden influence of his chest beneath his shirt. Unfortunately, the memory proved too powerful to erase. The muscles between my legs squeezed to hold nothing. There was a shiver in my groin, this nagging need to push my hips, and an opposing pull inching up my back.

"Listen," I said, going blank on her name for a second. "*Kate*. Let's just drop it."

"My God," she replied, offended. "What did he ever do to you?"

For a long time we just sat there. I wondered if she was sweating beneath the bulk of her coat. I toyed with Jack's letter, folding it into an origami swan. Kate said Rourke said he'd seen me; he told her I never say hello. Rourke did not exactly lie to her, but he did not exactly tell the truth either. He spoke in code to reach me, or so I thought. I had no proof.

"You're coming to Coco's New Year's party, right?" she asked. "You're invited."

"I feel a little sick," I said, gesturing to my throat. "Thanks anyway."

"Want to come upstairs with me while I get dressed? I don't want to be alone."

Between the twin closets in her room, there was an alcove and, squarely in its center, a window. I sat and propped my feet against the sill and looked into the snowy gray sky, which appeared to be hollow, like it had depth, like you could climb inside if only you could get close enough. I listened to the sounds of Kate dressing: the crinkle of paper-covered hangers, the slippery whisper of plastic bags, the oaky snap of dresser drawers, the clank of miniature buckles, the thin tap of pointed heels against the floor. It was strange to think that I would be home, safe in the ease of my solitude, but Kate would be out. When you set forth, things really do happen.

"What do you think?" she asked. She was wearing light black pants and a silk blouse, ivory and sleeveless. It's weird that people like Kate who normally have strict rules about seasonal dressing, such as no rayon or short sleeves in winter, suspend those rules for New Year's Eve, the one night they probably ought to dress practically.

"What about the blue sweater Lowie gave you?"

She extracted the sweater from the section of her closet devoted to blues, held it to her chest, and pirouetted before the mirror. "It's not too juvenile?" she asked.

The streetlamps switched on; their light reflected up and hit the clouds, turning the front yard into an amphitheater. Flurries were falling faster, toppling like butterflies shot from the sky. In the distance they fell fast, but near the house they scrolled and slowly scrambled, acquiring alarming new dimension. I thought of the line I liked from *The Night Before Christmas*.

> *As dry leaves that before the wild hurricane fly,*
> *When they meet with an obstacle, mount to the sky.*

Jack hated that I liked that poem. He was always telling me to read Rilke's *Sonnets to Orpheus*.

"You're right," Kate said in reference to the sweater. "This *is* better."

The floorboards creaked outside Kate's bedroom door, and Mom came in wearing a crushed velvet bodysuit. It was purplish, the color of pomegranates. She was on her way to a party in Bridgehampton.

"Kate, you look beautiful."

Kate giggled in the self-effacing style of someone who knows she is beautiful, who is always told that she is beautiful, but who, deep down, does not feel very beautiful. She sat at her dressing table and brushed her hair. It was winning hair, populous and blond.

"And you," my mother said to me, referring to my torn long johns and stained sweatshirt. "Miss Appalachia," she joked, touching my cheek. "Remember, I used to call you that?" The pink polish of her thumbnail passed the edge of my eye—once, twice. "Not going out tonight?"

"She's sick," Kate informed her.

"Sick?" Mom asked, then she turned back to Kate. "By the way, your brother called earlier to say Happy New Year. Call him back before you leave, but keep it short." When she reached the door, she said, "Be careful, Kate. Don't get in any cars."

Then the squeaking steps again, and the front door popping open, and outside blowing in. I heard my mother's tread dimming and dulling into the snow-covered path to the driveway. The car engine coughed to a dubious start, and she was gone.

The snow looked nice so I decided to walk to Coco's with Kate. While she waited in the yard for me to grab my coat, the phone rang. It was Jack calling from Dan's house. "You coming?"

I answered but he did not hear. The music was deafening.

"*What?*" he shouted. "Christ, hold on. *Daniel, turn that shit off!*" The music vanished with a flushing *zzzt* sound. "What did you say?"

"I said, I'm not feeling well."

"We-ll," Jack said deliberately, as if stating the obvious to a stubborn child, "come over here. Smokey will make you Irish coffee. He's a master chemist."

"I think I'd better stay home." I untangled the knotted phone cord and poked around my mother's desk, straightening out her papers and reading a few lines from a half-graded essay titled, "Christianity and Salvation in the Works of Flannery O'Connor."

"You think you'd better stay home," he repeated.

I pulled at my bottom lip. It had not been a good day. Not a secure day. I said, "Yeah."

"So then, you're not going out at all."

My coat was in hand. Jack had a way of forcing a lie. I said, "No."

There was a pause. "Fine," he grumbled. "See you later."

"Bye, Jack," I said. Before hanging up, I thanked him. I wasn't sure why I thanked him, except to say that he seemed to be doing me a favor.

I met Kate out on the path. "That was Jack," I said. "He's at Dan's."

"You'd better not go over there or you'll *really* get sick. I bet they're getting totally wasted."

Main Street was silent and lonesome. Blanketed in a carpet of white, and alive with the smoke of small wood fires that joined rooftop to rooftop, East Hampton revealed its colonial heritage. Sometimes a place rises up with a memory of itself, like a company of ghosts trumpeting out from the tops of tombstones. It was nearly impossible not to be transported back to the 1600s, to the time the town was settled.

"It's a miracle, isn't it?"

"What is?" Kate asked.

"The snow," I said. "The way it changes everything." It made the treetops into lace and the branches into panther tails, long and leaning with tiny kinks. On the crooks and twiggy ends of things the snow sat in balls like cotton ready to be picked. The streets were completely carless; it felt as though we were wading through a lake.

"It *is* pretty," Kate agreed.

As we walked, I kept thinking about "The Legend of Sleepy Hollow," wondering what made the story a *legend*. There was one character called Ichabod Crane and another called Brom Bones. Both names were suitable for those living in the post-Revolutionary American countryside, iconoclastic and frightening, calling to mind half-lit lanterns and bitter gusts of wind and leaves that twist inward at the prongs like a witch's fingernails. Neither character was particularly sympathetic; the author seemed to be making a point.

I asked Kate if the Headless Horseman story had a moral.

"What do you mean?"

"Like, what does it stand for?" It wasn't a fable—there were no animals or values.

"It stands for—well, Ichabod Crane was superstitious, and he let himself be run out of town. That's why he lost the girl. I guess the moral is, 'Don't believe in ghosts.' "

"Yeah, but the guy who ran him out of town tricked him. So, there would have to be a second moral, such as 'Don't believe in ghosts—but go ahead and use other people's fear of them to get what you want.' Or maybe just, 'It's okay to be mean.' And the whole survival of the fittest message doesn't hold up, since Ichabod was a teacher and Brom Bones was a thug and a cheat, kind of like a used car salesman. Why should *he* get to marry the girl and make more little Brom Boneses?" It wasn't a very good statement about America—or *was* it?

"I don't know what to tell you, Evie," Kate said. "It's just a story."

I kicked at the snow. "I'm just saying it's weird, that's all." We were standing at the top of David's Lane near the Presbyterian church; Coco lived five houses down. I got the feeling Kate didn't want me to go any farther.

"I told Coco you were sick," Kate said. "What if someone saw you? I'd seem like a liar."

I waved, saying, "No problem, okay," and also, "I understand." Then I watched her slip away, vanishing into white.

The snow in the empty A&P parking lot looked like the uplands of a layer cake. I cut through the drifts, walking without raising my feet. Under the snow was asphalt, and under that, smothered things. It was comforting to think that you could excavate and plow down and begin the world again, though to be perfectly honest, I didn't know who "you" might be, unless "you" was Jack. Jack was always trying to return the earth to its original state. He kept trying to organize a mall-razing party at the shopping plaza in Bridgehampton where the drive-in used to be,

modeled after Amish barn *raisings* in Pennsylvania, the ones where everyone gets together and builds a barn in two days. Only in this case, they'd
tear the shopping center to the ground.

"I have an idea," he would say at Atomic Tangerine concerts, slipping
into his popular imitation of a real estate developer. "Let's destroy the
character of the nation! Let's tear down trees and fill open space! Let's
build cheaply and irresponsibly! Let's increase tax and real estate revenue
by moving shopping off Main Street and into barren roadside plazas!
Let's lease to an endless stream of monster chains that can survive exor-
bitant rents by selling cheap goods at top dollar to ignorant consumers."
Jack's voice would deepen, reverting to his own. "And assholes like you
will burn fossil fuels driving to buy bounceable dinnerware and fireproof
pajamas on credit."

As Jack spoke, Dan would play chords and Smokey would beat the
drums, sometimes playing bongos throughout, and the room would go
wild, with everyone shouting, "Down with the Man!"

As luck would have it, one house they played at was Pip's, and Mr.
Harriman was a school board member and an employee of Tamco, a mall
developer Jack liked to refer to as a "terrorist group." When the guys got
called to Principal Laughlin's office that Monday, Atomic Tangerine was
given a *cease and desist* order.

"It's over with, *Fleming*," the principal said. "No more Hammer and
Sickle Society."

According to Dan, Jack froze back in his chair, with his hands pressing into the armrests. Smokey would add, "Like Lincoln glued to the
Memorial."

"If Mr. Harriman had a legitimate problem, *Laughlin,* he should have
thrown me out himself. And unless there's something you'd like to share,
I don't think the school owns his house," Jack reportedly said. "So why
don't you commit your fascist demands to letterhead, and I'll review
them with an attorney. Or better yet, *the press.* Make sure the letter in-
cludes the part about a public school official pulling students from
classes to harass them on behalf of a private citizen."

I stomped the snow from my Timberlands and looked at my tracks.
They made a twining design, like a maze. It was funny that I'd made it

while thinking of Jack. It looked the way Jack would think, if, in fact, his thinking could have a look. It looked like a meltable wreath. For the rest of the way home I tore through every untouched snowbank, thinking, *Humans ruin everything anyway, so why pretend otherwise?*

The cats converged on my ankles in the driveway, lifting their legs high and prancing like miniature show horses. They shoved past me through the front door and bolted into the living room. I changed into dry clothes and turned on appliances again. I wished we had a dishwasher. Dishwashers can be really noisy.

I built a fire, wondering whether the record store was the last time I'd ever see Rourke. The time before that was the last time for quite a while, for weeks. One day would be the last, I informed myself, perhaps today. The way he looked at me through the window was strange, as though I'd caused a dramatic impasse in his day. Inside he examined me as if for flaws. Maybe he was looking for a way to release himself.

It was odd that we'd never spoken but we understood each other. Sometimes you work hard to understand someone; sometimes you don't work at all. Some people are advocates of shrewd choices. They choose partners more carefully than careers. My mother's college friend Nonnie is a sleep lab technician who ran a classified ad to find a husband. After studying the resumes and photographs of dozens of applicants, she dated all the men from the A pile, and half of the B's, before choosing Brian from the middle of the B's. Within seven years they'd had four children.

"You can never be too careful," Nonnie would caution. "Never."

Mom would smile and say, "Nonnie, you're a brave woman," which, knowing my mother, could have meant any number of things.

At nine-thirty, the front door opened, and Jack and Dan came in. I felt I hadn't seen Jack in so long, though in fact I'd seen him just the night before. Behind him Dan was slender and tall and high-haired, tipped like a pencil engaged in the act of writing. Jack kicked off his boots and scuffed in floppy socks to the fire. He was wearing a blue plaid flannel shirt over a shredded wool sweater. His cheeks were two red circles and the hair that had come loose from his ponytail was frozen in strips. Dan flopped onto the couch, saying "Happy New Year!"

Jack's eyes surveyed the room gloomily. Everything transformed beneath the dismal heft of his regard. He narrowed his eyes to view me. I didn't move. It was like standing still to let a bee buzz past.

"We passed your tracks," he said, leadingly.

I said "oh," and I moved past the couch. "I'm making coffee. You guys want some?"

Dan grabbed at my leg. "Hold on. The ones in the parking lot. You really made them?"

"I guess."

"And Jack figured it out? That's fucked up. You two are totally fucked up."

"It's a small town, Daniel," Jack barked. "A gnat's-ass town."

Jack followed me to the kitchen, opened the refrigerator, and began to hunt around. I jumped onto the counter and waited for the coffee to finish. "So you must be feeling better," he said, plucking olives from a jar, "seeing that you went out."

I ignored his question and turned to watch the coffee bubbles burst through the spout of the pot. "How was rehearsal?" I asked.

"We fucked with the music for that stupid play, and by the time we got to Tangerine, those guys were too wasted to rehearse. Dan puked twice and Smokey passed out on the floor," Jack muttered in disgust. Jack did not like people to pass out or vomit. He said it defeated the whole point of getting high. Why waste money and drugs, he would say, when you could lick raw chicken to achieve a similar effect. "I tied Smokey's ponytail to the drum stand," Jack said, "so he's in for, like, a totally rude awakening."

"I'm glad you came," I told him, which was true; I *was* glad.

That seemed to make him happy. "I came up with a decent melody—want to hear it? *Da-da da-da da-da dum dum da da-ah da.*"

"God, Jack. That's really beautiful."

We listened to Ella Fitzgerald singing "Cow Cow Boogie," and every time the song ended, Jack would lift the needle back to the beginning.

> *That cat was raised on local weed,*
> *He's what they call a swing half-breed*
> *Singin' his Cow Cow Boogie in the strangest way—*

We were staring at this candle we really liked. Each side depicted the same scene in a translucent mosaic of eggshell-white, moon-yellow, lapis-blue: the seashore, with equally spaced planes of sand, sea, and sky, and directly in the center, a flying bird. Because the landscape was collapsed, it was hard to tell whether the bird was flying over the beach or over the ocean.

Dan looked inside. "Are you sure that's the original wax?"

"Positive," I said.

"It's the candle that Jesus blessed," Jack said caustically.

Dan respectfully replaced it. "It's *definitely* over the beach," he declared, referring to the bird. He wiped his wire-rimmed glasses with the hem of his shirt. "If it were over the ocean," Dan speculated, "it'd be closer to the line between sand and sea."

Jack agreed. "If the bird had been positioned at the bottom of the middle instead of at the top, you would think low—small. *Small,* meaning *farther away,* meaning *over the ocean.*"

"But it's high in the middle," Dan went on, "meaning *big* and *near.* It's over the sand."

"Exactly." Jack sucked on a joint as he spoke, his voice constricting with a chestful of smoke. He offered the end of it to Dan, and Dan accepted it gingerly.

It didn't seem exact to me. The candle had no converging lines, no infinite distance, no vanishing point. There was no inferred single light source—after all, it was a candle. There were three flat planes and a bird within a field with no apparent dimension. Comparatively the bird was huge. And it was on the central plane—the water.

Dan screwed his face to one side and coughed. "She doesn't seem convinced, Jack."

Jack squeezed my shoulders. His cheek on my cheek. "No? Why not?"

"The way it looks. I suppose you can apply laws of perspective to something without perspective, but why bother? Meaning can be conveyed perfectly well without math and science. After all, Giotto painted gold rings on the heads of saints—the rings are obviously halos, not sunrises." I pointed to the candle. "There's no reason to think about close or far, over, or under. There's just *on.*"

"You are very fucking high," Jack said to me. "Aren't you?"

Maybe I was. "Where did you get that pot? It's pretty trippy."

"From Frankie," Jack said.

"*Fat* Frankie?" He was always talking about Fat Frankie.

"Yeah, except he's not fat anymore. He lost fifty-five pounds."

"Fifty-five!" Dan exclaimed. "That's almost half my body weight."

"He went on that Moonie thing. That thing Dennis does."

"The *Scarsdale Diet*?" I said. "That's weird."

We were interrupted by a thump at the front door—Kate. We all called out, "Kate!" She stomped her feet on the mat and unwrapped her scarf. Behind her through the glass was a wall of white, like a down quilt. "Oh, no," she moaned, "not the candle, again."

"Katie," Jack said, "who'd you kiss at midnight?"

"No one, Jack," she replied. "Yet."

Dan stood, combing back his hair. "What time is it?"

Kate draped her coat over the banister and checked her watch. "Twenty to twelve."

Dan said, "Shit. I thought it was, like, two in the morning."

"That's because you've been drinking since breakfast," Jack said.

"The roads are really bad," Kate told us. "Coco is having people sleep over. Denny and Michelle are coming here. Did Mom call?"

"She did," I said. "She's staying at Lowie's."

Dan asked if Kate had seen the tracks I'd made in the snow by the A&P.

"Tracks?" she said dismissively. "I didn't see any tracks."

"Maybe they're gone by now," Dan speculated.

Jack peeked to see my face, to see if I was sad, then he held me. Jack was most virile near a hearth fire. If in public he used me—the look of me—to indicate his mannishness, by a fire he was truly invincible.

Kate went upstairs to get undressed, and I followed. From the corner of her bed, I watched her shadow on the floor beneath the partly opened bathroom door. She seemed quiet. I wondered what had happened. Maybe someone had hurt her feelings. Hopefully, it had just been over-bright lighting or cheap cologne or music by Journey or Boston. Coco might have served pigs in a blanket, with blankets made of Bisquick. Or possibly she'd had mismatching cocktail napkins. If the cocktail napkins were Halloween leftovers with pictures of grinning pumpkins and arched black cats, that could be depressing.

"How was the party?" I asked.

"Everyone was drunk. They were acting like complete assholes."

I retied the string on my sweatpants. It embarrassed me when Kate cursed, not because I objected to profanity, but because she was not particularly good at it. Jack swore so effectively and so constantly that he would exercise restraint for emphasis. When Kate said "asshole," she pronounced the *A* like in *aha* or like when you stick out your tongue at the doctor's office. *AAAAhhhhh.*

She unpinned her hair. In the mirror her eyes were like plums. It was strange to reconvene there, in the same spot where earlier she'd been looking forward to the evening. Jack always said the trick to happiness is to expect things to be shitty, then you won't be disappointed. "Just keep a low-level plane of dissatisfaction going," he'd advise.

Dan called up the stairs. "Happy New Year!"

"Oh, gosh," Kate said, shaking herself awake. She came halfway to me, and I came as far to her. Our cheeks met like praying hands. "Happy New Year," we said in unison, sending the words out into the universe beyond the petite round of each other's shoulder.

To commemorate the snow Jack put on Oscar Peterson's version of Cole Porter's "In the Still of the Night." It was the snow song, the anthem to the snow.

We cuddled on the couch, the four of us, eight legs, eight knees and feet, all high and drinking tea, facing the fire, thinking but not believing that it would be our last New Year's together. We had all just sent in our college applications. If everything went as planned, in one year, I would be in Manhattan at NYU and Kate in Montreal at McGill. Jack would probably be in Boston at Berklee for music, if he went anywhere at all, and Dan would either be at Tulane in New Orleans for jazz studies, or at Juilliard, where his dad was a teacher.

"I have some thoughts," Dan said, "on the psychology of perception and the problems of consciousness. Does anyone mind?"

Kate and I did not, but Jack stipulated provisions.

"No talk of functional neuroses or maladjustments. No dream analyses."

"Actually," Dan said, "I was just thinking about qualities that are essentially incommunicable, like color. For instance, take *roses*. Kate and I can both call a rose red, though I might see coral and she might see pink."

"Do you mean color blindness?" Kate asked.

"Not exactly," he guided gently. Dan was always gentle with Kate. At parties he would dedicate songs to her, or he would write compositions called "Kate 9" or "Kate 16." "My point is that it's impossible to know that what *I* see matches what *you* see when we both say *red*. Comparisons of redness aren't possible. Redness is ineffable: it has to be experienced to be known."

"Big deal," Jack said. "Perception is variable. If you perceive a speeding car to be forty feet away when it's really four feet away, and I perceive it to be four feet away, I'll jump, and you'll get hit. Relative perception doesn't change the position of the car, and it doesn't affect the color of a rose. The rose doesn't care what color you think it is."

"I'm not saying that physical absolutes don't exist," Dan said. "You're right—the rose is the color it is. I'm saying *absolute perception* doesn't exist. That no one interpretation is more valid than another. Like redness, or jazz, or—"

"Nationality," I added. "Or race."

"What's your point, Daniel?" Jack wanted to know.

"Well, I'm just thinking about the candle again."

"That's it!" Jack swatted at Dan. "Get rid of that fucking thing!"

"I'm just saying," Dan said, defending himself with crisscrossed hands, "Evie has a point: art doesn't have to be held accountable to accuracy, and there's no one right way to look at things. Clearly, the candle's artist was not looking to 'prove' a bird."

"In terms of the 'ineffable,' we're not talking about the birth experience here," Jack said. "We're talking about a piece of shit candle. Maybe there is no bird, but, for all we know, there was no artist either."

Kate wanted to know what happened to the rose.

Jack said, "Exactly, Kate."

And for a long time we were silent. I felt bad for Dan. It was nice of him to try to defend me, but he should have known better than to argue with Jack.

By three-thirty in the morning a curtain had closed on the house. The snow fit like a second house on the house, or a skin, and inside was bright without lights, snow bright. Shortly before Jack and Dan went home, Denny and Michelle arrived. I gave them my room, which was biggest. Michelle took my bed, and Denny took the floor, as usual, just lying flat on his back with his long legs crossed and his hands behind his head. It was a funny way to sleep, as though staring up at the clouds on a summer's day.

All things through the living room window were pale cinder. My palms and cheeks left cool dripping circles on the frost-covered glass as I measured the frailness of the membrane that shielded me from the universe. I wondered by what accident of chance I'd been blessed with shelter. There were creatures whose only sanctuary was the flat valentine heart of night. If I looked, I believed I could see them, with their nestling necks and heavily lidded eyes, huddling in clusters between twigs and rocks, sharing fur and feathers, breathing in shallow puffs to make heat.

"You're seeking to control your world," my mother speculated when I told her that I always wake up at night to look out the window.

I didn't disagree, because my mother seldom fawns on me. When she does, she does so excessively and briefly, like a toddler mothering a baby doll. But, in fact, control is not a requirement of mine. It's just that I'm in awe of the darkness, and reassured by it—its obstinacy, its unmovability— so many things happen there. Beyond the metropolis of any night is a new day—beyond that, a new night to follow. If you look, you can see them, stacked like panels one behind the other. If you listen, you can hear them move. And you can think about your part to play being so very small.

The phone rang. I lifted the receiver and walked with it from the desk to the front door, pulling until the cord could stretch no farther. I stepped out into the snow, my bare legs vanishing to the knee.

Was I clear from the sky? Was I a speck, a stain, a tiny spot to spoil the white—tiny, so tiny—the eye of a needle, the head of a pin, a nick in the void, aimed like a compass through the inaugural waste to the place I knew Rourke lay? Or did I not appear, was I incapable of being seen, was I nothing to no one? Was I wrong to feel manifest, wrong to feel seeable? Wrong to feel like a giant just to know he was alive?

"Evie," Jack called. "You there?"

"Hey," I said, barely audible.

"They're still there," he informed me, meaning the tracks.

I didn't reply. He was reaching to me. I felt him reaching.

He said, "Do you know what you made? A fleur-de-lis," he said. "It's nearly perfect. One part at the top was fucked up, but I fixed it."

I thanked him for calling. On prairies there are creatures like weasels who live in packs. One stands sentry while the others sleep. The one waits, scrawny and long, perched on hind legs, reading the landscape with coalified eyes, scouting for predators. Its generosity is not without incentive. It gets to run first.

15

The assignment in art class was to render one object from several vantages—the Object Project. I'd chosen an onion; Denny had picked a clock. Miss Lilias Starr from Baton Rouge was handing out a newly mimeographed list of considerations:

> *External—Superficiality! Command.*
> *Surface—Tenderness! Durability! Watertight?*
> *Skeleton—Concretization. Uprightness vs. Decline.*
> *Positive and Negative Space—Yin/Yang.*
> *Center—Viscera/Gut/Breadbasket.*
> *Mood—Disposition/Habits/Dreams and Regrets.*

Denny lifted the damp purple sheet to his nose and sniffed deeply. "My clock looks cheerful, but it's not. Its breadbasket is leaking."

"That's really gross," Alicia Ross said. Alicia was doing a bird's nest.

Denny shivered and pulled his denim jacket tighter. Two metal buttons on his breast pocket read NO NUKES and THE ROCKY HORROR PICTURE SHOW. "It's so cold in here, I should have picked a space heater."

Miss Starr flitted like a fairy about us, materializing at our elbows in aromatic bursts. She smelled like eucalyptus. Her hair was dyed green, the color of Granny Smith apples. Everyone said I was lucky because I'd been to her studio, and she'd been to my barn, and she insisted I call her Lilias. Her studio was a potting shed behind a cottage off Springs Fireplace Road, near the house where Jackson Pollock and Lee Krasner had lived. "It has no plumbing," she explained when I visited, "so I pee in a bottle. But the light's divine."

She appeared at the bench where Denny and I were working, carrying a still life she'd painted—a bowl of flowers, very accomplished, velvety and Dutch. It reminded me of a painting Dad and I had seen at the Met. "I think the artist's name was Brueghel," I said.

Miss Starr flicked her hair back behind her neck. "Oh," she cooed, "do you think so?"

When she left, Denny whispered, "Kiss ass."

Mr. McGintee from the Drama Club sauntered in about halfway through the class. Directly behind him was Rourke. From the moment he came in, he was all that I saw and all that I could see; it was strange, as if the door had opened and water had flooded through. He was wearing a camel hair dress jacket with a crewneck sweater beneath; his hair was windswept, his skin olive-brown. I returned to my work, dipping my head. Why did his name sound Irish when he looked Mediterranean, like the type of person who vacationed on yachts? Sometimes my mother spoke of the "Black Irish"; maybe he was that kind. His eyes settled on my face; I could feel the way they settled. I bit at the top of my turtleneck, hiding my lips and chin.

I breathed a cleansing breath, telling myself, *God, Jack is so much better than Rourke is.* Earlier that week, I'd seen him three times in one day.

The first time there were people, so he ignored me and I ignored him. The second time we were alone and our bodies defied our minds: I felt myself come to a stretching stand in the yearbook office exactly as he loitered at my doorway, hunting through his pockets for elusive items, coins or keys. I didn't say hi, though my body advanced. I stopped on my side of the door frame. He seemed surprised, and he froze, just looking up at me, smiling. Later that afternoon, I was in the main office delivering my letters of recommendation to the guidance office, and he passed by. He leaned on the door frame and smiled at the flank of thoroughly enamored secretaries, saying, "Any of you ladies plan on answering that phone?"

Mr. McGintee walked around and remarked on Miss Starr's still life, saying, "It's *nice*."

"Eveline says it looks Flemish, like a Brueghel. Would you agree?"

He smiled vaguely. "Absolutely!"

Rourke moved to greet Alicia Ross, who was fussing with her bird's nest. Together they looked ravishing and dark, like Spaniards or Arabs conferring. He would speak and she would respond, brisk and sure, with the charismatic self-confidence of a well-bred someone. Alicia had attended Spence in Manhattan until tenth grade, but she transferred out when her dad came to their summerhouse to recuperate from heart surgery. Mrs. Ross didn't want Alicia to graduate from East Hampton, but Alicia didn't care. She adored her father; we all did. He would often take six or seven of us out to O'Malley's for burgers and fried mozzarella sticks.

Alicia would imitate her mom. *"You'll never get into an Ivy League! You'll lose all fashion sense! You'll marry a dentist!"*

"What's wrong with dentists?" Denny asked.

Alicia shrugged. "I guess she thinks they're kind of, you know, *dentisty*."

I liked Alicia. She was overanimated and uncommonly direct, but within her resided a colossal humanity. She made hats and wore them with pious flair, like Southern church ladies. And she always remembered things I said.

"How's your cousin?" she'd ask.

"Which one, the one who's converting?"

"No, not the physicist, the potter."

The only problem with Alicia was that she was always talking about her father's famous clients; he was an entertainment lawyer. You had to steer your way through dialogue with her to avoid irrelevant references.

"Parker and I saw one when we were skiing," she stated on one occasion. We were in art class; she was speaking of bobcats.

"Can you hand me the glue?" I requested.

"Sure," she said, reaching for the bucket. "We were in Aspen and—"

"What do you think of this?" I lifted my decoupage.

"You need a wider margin," she suggested. "Anyway, he's even—"

"*Wider?* Are you sure?"

Alicia crammed in her sentence. "He's more gorgeous in person, if you can imagine."

"*Who?*" I asked.

"Parker!"

"Parker who?"

"Parker Stevenson, silly. From *The Hardy Boys*."

Miss Starr was explaining that the family who had donated money for the drama program had also earmarked funds for the art and music departments to create original works. The senior art class would be responsible for creating backdrops and costumes.

Alicia tugged twice on the lapel of Rourke's jacket, saying something to make him smile. Then she spun on her stool, and her black hair bobbed serenely about her face. I wondered how they knew each other when she was not even in drama.

Cathy Benjamin asked, "When are the drawings due?"

"You're the experts," Mr. McGintee said. "You tell us. A week? Three days? I'm guessing here." He waved a half-erect index finger around the room. "Any suggestions?"

An uncanny quiet descended, as quiets often do. I was about to be called on. Sometimes you just know. I lowered my head, engrossing myself in my task.

"Miss Auerbach," McGintee declared. "Your thoughts?"

I didn't bother to look up. "Is *Our Town* even supposed to have scenery?" In Kate's playbook, I'd read something about no scenery. It was in Thornton Wilder's notes.

Mr. McGintee laughed as though something was funny. "Bravo! If only our actors were as familiar with the script. Isn't that right, Mr. Rourke?"

Rourke was still next to Alicia. He stepped forward, his body soaking emphatically through space like an inky spill. He located without effort the precise center of the room.

"The script calls for no scenery," he said, him looking at me, me looking at him. "That's true." His voice was mossy and opaque; it had this lastingness, this abidingness. "But I think we can get away with some set design without compromising the integrity of the play."

No one moved when he spoke, not even Miss Starr. I bit a tag of flesh on the inside of my cheek and continued with my onion, with the silky feel of it. I'd penciled a luxurious arc that tapered to a flush and narrow run, with feathery stuff at the end. I inclined my head to view my drawing. I supposed it was madness to think I knew him. I knew nothing about him.

"How about, like, a village green?" Dave Meese asked.

I touched the actual onion. Its barrier was no more than a dried membrane, papery brown and tearable. It was ironic that something so potent could have such a fragile shell.

"How about a chapel?" I heard myself say.

McGintee said, "What's that, Eveline?"

Denny answered for me. "She said, 'a chapel.' "

"Wonderful! A chapel. And, Dave, yes—a village green."

Miss Starr told us to set aside the Object Project and see what we could come up with for the play. We all instantly complied. She was a huge fan of spontaneity. Frequently in the middle of class she would call out a challenge. *Two minutes—low tide! Ten seconds—a toe!*

Rourke came toward me, and the room behind him collapsed in the wake of his steps. He touched down at the bench on my left. He was close, his leg brushing my leg, the scent of him captivating me. I could almost hear his blood, the cadence; in my mind I trailed its avenue.

He lifted the rendering of my onion, raising it an inch from the table, tilting it, asking softly, "What is it?"

"Well, it's not an onion," I said, and he smiled. "It's the *feel* of an onion."

He reached for a new piece of paper and slid the sheet to my belly. Beneath the umbrella of his protectorship I took my pencil to paper and began to draw freely. It was not difficult to do with sunlight bearing down on the snow in the courtyard, and the light drenching us, making all things around us chalk and silver. I remembered a place I'd visited with Dad and Marilyn, a town in winter; Amherst. They'd taken me to see the home of Emily Dickinson, where the floors squeaked like slowly stabbed things, and through the purling windows daylight was sterling and merciless. After lunch, my father bought Marilyn a Rookwood vase from an antiques store in a barn near a stone bridge. I waited on the stairs of a clapboard church beneath trees with no leaves.

Rourke's arm moved minimally, signaling for me to stop. I formed two more lines. We studied the paper. It was unifying to share a visual object with him. Until now we had only looked at each other. I imagined what it would be like for us to have a child, the way we would observe it, separately and sometimes together. The steeple of my church extended at a peculiar angle, tipping forward like an antler or horn, and the main body of the building was low like a plank. Rourke took the paper from me.

"I'd like to take this," he said, meaning the drawing. He spoke softly. No one could hear but me. It was strange—the size of his arm, the whiteness of my hand.

He had not moved, not physically, but he was receding. I thought he was brave. I couldn't bear to abandon the solace conceived by our nearness, knowing that as soon as he was gone, I would be left to confront the known range of my own frontiers, the plaintive vacancy there. He had filled it so perfectly.

He was waiting for an answer.

My eyes focused keenly on nothing in particular—a name carved in the art shop bench, *Winn*, a date that followed, '76. I wondered where Winn was. Four years was a long time to be gone.

"You can take it," I said. It was just a thing. What he actually took away was more precious, infinitely so.

16

He came through the door of the darkroom as I was laying out my prints to dry. Betsy Callaghan and Annie Jordan were developing in the back. My drawing was in his hand.

"Okay," Rourke said as he returned it to me.

"Okay," I repeated, taking it from him.

We were face-to-face, almost but not quite, since I hardly came as high as his shoulders. If I were to lie against him, my hand would just reach the recess between his arm and chest.

I did not raise my head, just my eyes. "Is that it?"

He nodded. "That's it."

Reverend Olcott exited the rectory, his belly jiggling ever so slightly as he crossed the driveway. He was dressed as usual in casual black, no silk, no sash.

"Hello there, Eveline," he said. "Long time no see."

I'd been leaning on a tree, regarding the church spire through the rolled-up tube of my sketch. "I'm sorry. I've been, you know—"

He raised a comforting hand. "Any word on college yet?"

"NYU, probably."

The reverend came from Wisconsin. I couldn't recall the name of the town, but it must have been nice if the people in it were like him. He was a man of restless intelligence and limitless energy. Powell always said that the reverend had so much bounce as to make you think privately of fleas. If Kate and I happened to be feeding the ducks in the morning, we'd see him jogging past, or, if you stopped by the church to use the bathroom, you might find him painting the wheelchair ramp. Everyone said he was the best Cajun cook on the East End.

I gestured with my sketch. "I'm designing a chapel. For the Drama Club."

He jerked his neck toward the church. "Let's have a look."

The mammoth white door closed behind him with a tidy click, and the room we entered was stark and still. It made me think of the inside of an egg. We moved in the direction of the front pew. We sat, and Reverend Olcott examined my sketch.

"Yes," he said, and he nodded. "I see."

With a low stroke of one hand, he referred to the body of the church, which was nothing compared to the steeple. "The congregation is minimized," he said. "The architecture is part of the landscape. It has a proportionate relationship to nature."

My eyes ventured to his face. His glasses bridged the base of his nose, and his head was tucked into his neck, adjusting to the near distance of the sheet of paper.

"But the steeple, the *reaching* to God—to godliness—is immense. Symbolic, muscular, like a fist thrust into the air." He tapped the drawing twice and returned it to me. "Very nice."

I considered his remarks. It was strange to have communicated something that I supposed I believed, but didn't think I knew how to relate.

"It's the striving that intrigues you, the theoretical endeavor," he proposed. *"Abstraction."* The reverend cleared his throat. "Do you know it's been nearly thirty years since I joined the church? January 1951. In that time, I've encountered as many devoted worshippers who lack true compassion as"—he paused to search for a word—"*individualists* like you who possess a pious reverence for life."

He pointed to the paper, now in my hands. "I especially like the easy lines, the quickness of hand, the conservation of voice. Spontaneity is too frequently mistaken for immaturity. But we are spontaneous when we are at our genuine best—*childlike* as opposed to *childish*. Standards of goodness and propriety are necessary, of course. They're guideposts for those who stray. But ideally, decency resides in the heart, undiminished from birth." He continued, "One sometimes wonders, though, whether purity of heart is sufficient."

"It does confuse me," I ventured, "the whole idea of God as a man." Reverend Olcott looked toward the altar. I hoped he was not offended. "You know, the beard and the robes. Six days to create the earth."

For a while we sat in silence. I gathered he was thinking what to say. Probably he wanted to choose his words carefully. It did seem like a risky and unofficial way to discuss God, sitting in the first pew with our legs stretched out.

"Some prefer to draw inspiration from the story of Jesus rather than from belief in God." His tone was circumspect. "We can be certain that a man named Jesus existed and that he preached—at great personal sacrifice and without material compensation—the virtues of faith and forgiveness. And from that ancient narrative, we continue to extract messages pertaining to the sacredness of devotion, and we follow its prescriptions for living peaceably. In fact," he added as he gestured to the steeple in my drawing, "such a proposal is in keeping with your notion of ideological enterprise, the expenditure of spiritual energy in working toward actual understanding. That's the reaching part," he said. "Do you see?"

I thought I did. I thought he was saying it was okay to be confused. I thought he was alluding to how he himself had come to terms with confusion.

"It's like, heaven is not an actual destination," I said, "but a conceptual place of peace."

He said nothing, which was okay. I understood that he couldn't. It seemed like the right time for the conversation to end, so I stood. He encouraged me to sit and think.

"Oh, no," I said. "It's hard for me to sit and think." I had to move and think, or sit and do. It was just one of those things. I held up my sketch. "But thank you very much."

As Reverend Olcott and I parted, I thought again of light glowing through an eggshell. I thought of mosaic, geometry, overlap. Maybe I could use texture instead of color and line. Maybe I could use pieces of vanilla canvas to make a collage. If I shined stage lights through the back of a scenery flat, it would make the muslin glow like an incubated egg. I thought of that candle in my house, of light coming through a wall.

17

Nico's book landed on his desk with a *whumpf,* and he straddled his seat, peeling my hands from my face, prying them apart like shutters.

"Happy Valentine's Day," he said. His hands smelled like metal.

I blinked and shook my head. "Is that today?"

"Is that today?" he said, dropping my hands in mock disgust.

I sat up tall and stretched. "I'm just a little—"

"Out of it." Nico gave Mike Stern a wave. He spoke to me, but his eyes darted professionally. *Professionally* because to some people popularity is a business. "You gonna get a rose in homeroom today? Or is your boyfriend anti-flowers?"

I lowered my head. "He's anti-flowers."

Somebody smacked Nico as he passed. His desk knocked into mine and my teeth jolted. "Watch it! Evie's napping." He tousled my hair. "Poor kid."

Mr. Shepard entered, and I propped myself on one arm. I set my pen on my open notebook, and as he began to talk, the pen began to move, transcribing everything.

> *Louis-Napoleon, son of Louis Bonaparte, king of Holland—in the hall a locker slams, a voice says Hey, Farrell, wait up—and nephew of Napoleon Bonaparte, is elected emperor. In 1853 he marries Eugenie de Montijo. By the way, Montijo is not the name of a new Oldsmobile—moans, yawns, desks scraping, erasers whizzing—The Second Empire becomes one of the most productive monarchies in France—whooping howls from English 10 next door—*

I was drifting, so I wrote my name, over and over. *Eveline Aster Auerbach.* I didn't know what it was supposed to mean, my name, how it promised to define me. Jack loved the way Maman used to say *E-vleen*, but he would never copy it because she was French and we were not. Nothing is more annoying than when people randomly insert exotic pronunciations into everyday talk. One thing Americans do best is mispronounce words they know nothing about. It's a confession of sorts. It's like saying, *We may be stupid, but we're not pretentious.*

I wrote the letter *A*, several letter *A*'s, one leading to the next, charging forth like a locomotive, stark and emphatic, the way screams are discharged—*AAAAAAAAA*. Just as the row neared the margin, my wrist dropped sharply to produce a single vertical line; then it retraced that line to the top, unfolding in a curve to the right, making a bubble and collapsing at last in a bar to the finish: *R*. I finished it off—*o-u-r-k-e*. It was true that I was tired, because when I looked at his name, at the way I'd written it, jittery and uncertain, I began to cry.

Stephen gestured to me, shaking one corner of a test paper. The class was going over the exam. I pulled mine from beneath my notebook. Stephen got a hundred. I got an eighty-nine, which was depressing since I hadn't even studied. Being slightly better than average at schoolwork is like being a good soldier or a talented receptionist. Three minutes remained. I tore a corner from a page in my notebook.

> *J—I think I am shrinking. Someone told me that today is Valentine's Day. I am sad because I have no gift for you. I'm sorry. I'm so tired. I love you, promise. E.*

Mr. O'Donnell was at the library counter, performing the sort of grim rituals librarians perform with index cards and stumpy pencils and those rubber stamps with columns of rotating numbers. "Ms. Auerbach! What will it be today? Camus, Cervantes?"

"Actually, I'm looking for a book of poetry by Emily Dickinson."

He paused somberly, toying with the tightly twirled tip of his mustache. No matter how seriously librarians are engaged in their work, they are always glad to be interrupted when the theme is books. It makes no difference to them how simple the search is or how behind on time either of you might be running—they consider all queries scrupulously. They love to have their knowledge tested. They lie in wait; they will not be rushed.

"Let's see," he said as he puttered out, taking to the aisles with a trifling waddle, inching to a halt at the stack near the windows, "poetry. D,
D. Well, here's Baudelaire, Byron, Davies, Drayton. No, no, that's mis-
filed. You see what happens when one sorts poetry helter-skelter? Let's
pull that out and replace it as so, and here we are, Dickinson, Emily."

Next I stopped in the art studio for colored paper and scissors—later
in study hall I would make cutout hearts to stuff inside the envelope. By
the time I got to homeroom, I had just enough time to copy half of a
poem on the bottom of my note to Jack.

> It's all I have to bring to-day.
> This, and my heart beside,
> This, and my heart, and all the fields,
> And all the meadows wide.

E. DICKINSON, C. 1858

After the homeroom announcements, Mrs. Kennedy passed out roses
wrapped in paper, like shiny green wands, strained shut and dirt-red.
They looked like living headaches. Karen Drapier got one, and Missy
Burke, and so did Warren Baxter.

"Mind if I keep it?" Mrs. Kennedy asked when Warren told her just
to trash his.

Jack was not waiting as usual at the door of my English class, so I
went to his locker and crammed the poetry and hearts I'd made through
one of the slots. When he still had not materialized by lunch, I wondered
if he had taken off. I vaguely recalled him saying something about fifty
dollars and a homeopathic dentist in Connecticut. In sixth-period calculus, I observed the advance of the clock hands—three, four, seven minutes, and still no sign of him.

"All right, people," Mrs. Oliphant called, "let's go."

She launched the door from its propped station in sync with the articulate prong of the late bell. The door whooshed, and just as it was
about to click shut, an arm caught it—Jack's. He was wearing a new
sweater and jeans that were clean. Dan was behind him, looking hand-

some as well in a blue blazer, despite unwashed hair shaped in a flat jaunty spray on the left from the pressure of his pillow.

"Glad you could make it, fellows," the teacher said.

"Glad to be here," Jack said sarcastically, and everyone laughed.

He deposited an overstuffed envelope on my desk and sat behind me, his feet punching squeakily into the gap between the base of my seat and the attached book rack. I played with the little package, making lazy orbits with one finger. Sometimes it confused me to see him in school. It's confusing to greet your privacy when access to it is prohibited. It's like going home for lunch when you have to leave again. Mrs. Oliphant made a slanting series of numbers on the board, which joined together into the shape of a torpedo. I pulled the flap of the envelope from Jack, and it eased its way open. Nestled within imperfectly plied sheets of crepe paper was a dried flower, a kind I'd never seen, with elegant petals that faded in hue from tip to base—violet, lavender, white. Mustard anthers had fallen into the folds of paper, staining its crevices. On a second sheet was a meticulous drawing of the same blossom, shivery and crisp. And alongside it there were words.

> *For the girl. It's called a camas. I slept in a meadow full of them*
> *on a mountain in Wyoming. The flower thrives when closest to*
> *the clouds, just like you.—J.*

A shred of paper landed on my desk—a scrawled response to my Valentine's note:

> *You're small because you don't eat. You're too obsessed with your*
> *space needle set design. Dan and I are cutting out early so we*
> *can finish the music for that asinine play. How about some-*
> *thing red for dinner? —J. P.S. Your eyes look bruised.*

My head fell back through the air. My shoulders also flew, moving in reverse. I watched in despair as the halls of my mind blackened and grew cavernous, with rooms and vaults and doorways multiplying exponentially. I labored to stem the epidemic nothingness, to hold my focus, to return to some port or place of safety, but I could not find my beginning.

I awoke in pitch dark. The air was murky and cold. Denny was there, holding me. Behind his shoulders, I recognized the bare yellow bulb of the darkroom. I wondered who had moved the ceiling fixture to the wall.

"I'm going to lift you honey, okay? Ready, here we go." I felt his arms slide under my back, and as he straightened his knees to raise my body, the bulb disappeared upward in a fluid arc.

He eased me onto the stool and asked what had happened.

I said I didn't know. It was not good to sit. My head throbbed. I reached to touch the place that hurt, and it hurt worse. Denny moved my hand away and measured the knot. It seemed to be about the size of a lime.

"I can't tell if it's bleeding. I think it's bleeding," he said.

"It's like a lime," I asked, "isn't it?"

"Okay," he said, searching nervously around the unoccupied dark-room for someone to consult, someone other than me. "I've got to get you out of here." He wagged his hand in front of his nose. "This air is poison. How many times have I told you—*Solvents kill.*"

Denny ducked beneath one of my armpits, and he lifted me. Denny was strong. When he hugged you, it was like entering a whole new room. Once he heaved Nico into the air and smashed his head three times against the lockers—*boom, boom, boom*—saying, "You filthy runt. You're lucky I don't toss you under a fucking car." I didn't see it, I just heard about it, not from Denny but from basically everyone else in school. Denny didn't mention it because he was a gentleman, and it had to do with me. On the same day, L. B. Strickland got two broken fingers and a dislocated shoulder.

We stopped at the main office. Denny leaned me against the door frame while he ran in.

"How can I help you, Mr. Marshall?" one of the secretaries asked as he hustled past her to the nurse's office.

"Just getting an ice pack, Mrs. Miller." He went through the side door of the unattended infirmary and came out right away, blue plastic bag in hand. "No need to exert yourself on behalf of an injured student. Here," he said to me, handing off the pack, sweeping up my body, glancing back over his shoulder and shooting a last look at the women inside. "God forbid they should burn a few calories."

In the car I placed my head on his leg. During the drive home, he talked incessantly but lovingly, the way some dogs bark.

"You shouldn't have been there alone. What if I hadn't come? What if you tried to get up then fell again? You're lucky you don't have a concussion. And the chemicals! Don't you know that every egg you'll ever have is in your ovaries already? That room has no oxygen supply. Tack on your history of low blood pressure and sleep deprivation, and you've got the recipe for disaster!"

Denny was good in science, particularly in regard to the body and how it worked, but you had to be careful not to act impressed or say, *You ought to be a doctor!* Though all his test scores had been nearly perfect, he refused to consider a career in medicine. "I just spent eighteen years pretending to be straight," he said the day we drove to the post office and mailed his application to Fashion Institute of Technology. "Medical school would kill me." He acted like he was happy that day, but I knew he was not.

When he pulled into my driveway, he was explaining the phrase "mad as a hatter." *Something, something,* he was saying, and, *licking mercury.*

"Okay. Time to get up."

"But we just got here," I said, looking up from his leg.

"I know, but now I'm late. I didn't expect to have to stage a rescue this afternoon."

"Late for what?" I asked. "Do you have a date?"

"I do," he said with a nod.

"A Valentine's date?"

"Yes," he said, "a Valentine's date. And you are not invited. Let's go."

I stirred, and the upholstery squeaked. He slipped carefully out, then bounded around to the passenger side to help me out. I tried to recall the last time I'd had as much energy. It seemed like such a long time ago that it must have been never.

"There, there," he said, hugging then releasing me in one motion. He pointed me toward the house and gave me a tiny shove. I hit the hedges, missing the path entirely. "You're breaking my heart," he moaned as I stumbled along to the front porch. "Sneak in back. *In back*," he directed, throwing a loud whisper over the top of the car. He waved his arm in frustration when I reached the steps, and in his normal voice said, "Too late. You'll never sleep now."

Kate was stretched across the couch in the living room, phone in hand. It occurred to me to run back out, but Denny was already gone. He'd tapped his horn before taking off down Osborne Lane. I shut the storm door behind me.

"Got to go," Kate said. "Evie's home."

I waved, signaling to Kate that she shouldn't get off the phone on my account.

She hung up anyway and sat upright. On the shoulder of her sweater was one of the Valentine roses from school. "I got it anonymously," she said, coming to show me. "But I think it's from Harrison Rourke."

The lump in my head throbbed and also vessels in my temples. I wondered if it was possible for the veins behind my eyes to rupture. My scarf got caught in the zipper from my coat. I tugged at it, saying, "Shit."

"I'll do it," she said, rushing over. I raised my chin and she patiently worked the zipper down to the base. Some girls are just good at things. Of course, those same girls are usually bad at other things.

I dropped the coat and made my way to the bathroom, where I ran the water and pretended to pee. Possibly Kate was right. I had no idea of Rourke, what he felt. In the mirror I examined the irregular terrain of my face, the pyramidal zones of shadow and light. Jack had looked handsome in calculus. Maybe there was another girl he liked, one with bruiseless eyes, like Nina Spear, who rode horses, or Joss Mathers, who had signed his cast and given him a blow job two days before he and I had met. I thought of Denny's Valentine's date and of Kate and her rose and how everything was bursting forth from the dormancy of winter. Everyone was falling in love, in real, active love, while I was trussed to my own axis, like some dead meat spinning.

Kate called through the bathroom door. "You hungry?"

I splashed water on my wound and mussed my hair in back to hide the gooey spot. Flakes of blood stuck to my fingers, staining the towel in dots. In the medicine cabinet was an old compact with powder clinging in a kind of deranged ring to its outer edge. I pried off a chunk and dragged it on my face. The edges of the hard powder were sharp.

"Not really," I called. "Jack's bringing food."

"Oh. Maybe he wants to be alone with you. You know, for Valentine's."

I rubbed in the makeup, flinching somewhat. It really was sharp. "Jack? I doubt it."

When I came out, Kate was preparing coffee—laying out cups and spoons, filling the sugar bowl, pouring milk into a little china pitcher.

I cleared my throat, saying tentatively, "So, did you say something?"

"To Jack? About what?"

"No, I mean, you know—about the flower."

She regarded me with curiosity. "Are you wearing makeup?"

"Why?"

"No reason. You look pretty, that's all. You always look pretty."

I leaned up to turn on the light. It was early for lights, but I thought it would be good to move the day along. Just, like, get to night.

"Well, at rehearsal," Kate began, "Harrison said, '*Nice rose.*'" She started peeling an apple over the trash. "And you know when someone is thinking something? Well, he was definitely thinking something." Kate finished with the apple, went to the counter, and cut it. She offered me some. I said no, thanks. She continued. "So, *I* said, 'I wish I had someone to thank, but unfortunately, there was no name on the card.' You know, I sort of hinted around."

The coffee was boiling; she moved to turn off the heat. I felt embarrassed—for her, and also for Rourke. Kate could be very coquettish. I rested my head in the basin of my arms. My chin touched the table; the glass was cold. I thought I might vomit.

"And *he* said, 'I doubt whoever sent it will stay anonymous for long.' "

"And then what?" I asked.

"And then, well, that's it." She handed me a hot mug.

"That's it?" I lifted my head.

"Well, Michelle had a flower, so did Ellie, but he only mentioned mine."

I took a sip of coffee. It was hot but good, and I felt better right away. It was nice, actually, spending time with Kate.

The front door slammed and Jack stormed in. He dumped two pizza boxes on the table and popped the stapled lid of the top one. Inside, the pie was shaped like a heart.

Kate said, "Hey, that's really neat."

Jack gestured to the pies with annoyance as he wiped his nose with his sleeve. "All they had to do was cut the dough to make two lousy hearts, and they wanted an extra buck per pie. Fucking proletariat morons."

"Was it crowded? They were probably just busy," Kate said.

Jack chucked his coat onto the floor in the hall. "Nah. It was empty. They just figured it was for her," he said, referring to me, "so they gave me a hard time." He hopped onto the counter. With his sneaker, he opened the base cabinet door and rested his feet on its rim. "Save the second pie," he directed. "For Irene."

He shot his hand through his hair and examined the room angrily. Kate whistled cheerfully, thoroughly immune to Jack's sullen influence. Her body grazed his as she slid three unmatching glasses from the cabinet behind his head. He pulled back. I considered what was between them. There's always something between people.

Jack glowered in my direction and scratched his jaw. "You haven't slept yet, have you?"

"Oh, I forgot!" Kate interrupted, thrusting her shoulder at Jack. "Did you see my rose?"

Jack contemplated her with extreme disinterest, his hand hanging frozen on his face. "I know all about it."

"What do you mean, *you know*? How do *you* know?"

Jack capitulated, plunging his arm to his lap. "Because Dan's been talking about it for three fucking weeks."

"Dan?"

Jack said, "Yeah, Dan."

Kate set her coffee down and shuddered slightly, repeating "Dan." She stood and padded out of the room, saying "Dan" again. Moments later her bedroom door slammed, and there was the distant sound of sobbing.

"What the hell's wrong with Dan?" Jack demanded. He leapt off the counter and moved to the table and began plucking mushrooms from the pie.

I rubbed my face in circles with both hands, wondering what to do. It felt a little perverse to be in my position. Jack was contemplating me. The longer I remained silent, the greater the opportunity for him to construe that silence as evasion. It was amazing, the work his mind could do. He let the pizza lid float to a close. Stamped in red ink on the cover was a mustached guy in a chef's hat holding a steaming pizza. He looked happy.

Jack raised my coffee cup. "*Caffeine?* Are you *trying* to kill yourself?" The mug smacked the table and coffee looped over the lip. "Dennis called me. He said you fainted."

"I guess I—I fell. Or fainted." I wasn't sure what had happened.

He was behind my chair. "Stay still," he urged, then he tilted my head to examine it. "Christ, Evie, there's blood on it. Where's the first aid kit?"

"Upstairs. In the bathroom."

"Well, I can't go up there. I might slap her," Jack said. "You'd better go."

I headed up slowly. I thought it was contradictory for Jack to get so upset over blood and caffeine, considering the abuses he leveled against himself. Besides, I hadn't caused myself to faint, it just happened. Some people get bloody noses, others sleepwalk. Marilyn can get the hiccups for three days straight and Dad sneezes in series of thirteen—I faint. I've fainted at the Guggenheim, at Woolworth's on 23rd Street, and at an International House of Pancakes in Cape Canaveral. Whenever Dr. Scott checks my blood pressure, he says, "Eighty over fifty. It's a wonder you're alive."

I nudged Kate's door. She was in bed, crying. "You don't understand," she said.

If she meant I didn't know what it felt like to be in love, and in love with Rourke, she was wrong. But if she meant that I didn't understand *her* love for him, she was right. If it was love that she felt, it was the sort of love that conveniently bypassed natural law and practical reality.

I felt a little light-headed, so I moved to her bed. I looked back to the spot I'd been standing in. I tried to imagine what it was like to talk to me. Was it hard or easy? Jack had said the blood was fresh. Maybe it was running down my back like a mane or tail.

"You think you know everything," Kate said.

I thought she was alluding to sex. I wondered if she felt it was time, that to venture further into virginity would be to attach unwanted magnitude to that state. Maybe she hoped to resolve it, just as some people *have* to get their driver's license at sixteen, though they have nowhere to go. It's a perilous business, devising to be taken—the flouncing and cuing, the skittish surrender of reason. Sex demands equality because sex involves the will—someone's will, preferably one's own. Maybe I didn't know everything, but unfortunately, I knew that much.

"One thing's for sure," I said as I moved to get the first aid box from the bathroom. "He's not crying right now. He's not crying over the Valentine you didn't send."

18

I dreamt I was a paper doll. I was one in a row of paper doll cutouts sitting on a swing set. We wore triangular lime-green dresses and had shoulder-length flip hair, like from the sixties.

At lunchtime I tried to draw the dream, but couldn't. Beyond the doll bodies, there had lain a sleepy hint of magic, something astral and sublime that continued to insinuate itself upon me, like an ocular echo. After school I rummaged through my mother's bossa nova records. There were ones by João Gilberto, Stan Getz, Antonio Carlos Jobim. I finally settled on *Getz/Gilberto* because it had Astrud Gilberto singing "Corcovado."

I stripped to my long johns, leaving my clothes in a pile near the hearth, and I listened to the song, closing my eyes to reconstitute the dream's elusive vitality, its lightness and lift. The song was delicate and de-emphasized, melodious and modern, serene and insurgent, similar to the feel of my dream. It was feminine, but also civic and political. The women on the swings had been separate and connected—it would not have been possible to extract one without collapsing the whole. It was the way women used to be in the 1960s, or maybe just the way I imagined them to be. It occurred to me that I shouldn't draw the dream but try to cut it, so I got a stack of paper from the basement and some sewing scissors from Kate's room, then returned to the fireplace.

By the time I heard the rain, it was after six o'clock. Frozen drops were making a spreading sound on the roof, like nickels on a tent. I once proposed a study of the water cycle for a science fair. I wanted to draw attention to the beauty of the rain. Everyone always just complains about it.

Nick Kraft, the earth science teacher, said, "*No way*. Do not try to make rain." He recommended a tidal wave or a volcano. "Tragedy is more fun," Nick told me. "You buy some glue and plastic doodads at the five-and-ten, and create a theater of disaster."

I wasn't surprised by his response. In high school, the study of the earth is pretty much the study of maps and catastrophe, as though the only possible points of interest are border wars and devastation. It's similar in other subjects—history is the history of battle, language is the study of English, and science is an excuse to play with acid and cut frogs. If you're waiting for some creative digression into the rhetoric of math or the zoology of conquest, you will be waiting a long time.

I spread my legs as wide as possible and folded another sheet of paper in rectangular strips. I'd been having trouble with the hairstyles. They weren't flipping properly. In my dream the hair had been weightless, curling up and in, with party kinks. I often dreamt of long hair now that my own hair was so short, though never before of happy, bouncing hair.

Suddenly the room darkened freakishly; the sky turned to ash. Wind discharged against the picture window in erratic gusts, and there was an itinerant commotion—sounds of people running through rain, of voices caught in pockets. The front door blew open with a slam, and Kate came through, her body huddled against the water. Her acting partner Tim Storey followed, urging her in, going, "C'mon, c'mon." Tim stomped his feet and shook his head like a two-legged dog. It was funny to think of him that way, as though he were standing upright with difficulty, as though he would have been better served on all fours. He removed his shoes and crossed directly to the fire and stepped over me. I drew my papers into the pocket of my legs.

The door did not close. It was braced by a hand—Rourke's. In one giant stride, he moved from the porch to the plank floor. When he passed through the door frame, he had to lower his head. His eyes found mine easily, as if he had expected me to be exactly where I was.

"Hey," he said, and I replied, "Hey."

He dried his feet and smiled shyly. I saw the edge of his perfect teeth and the dimple on the right side of his face, which was a furrow like a pen puncture. I returned to my work, though I continued to regard him from beneath the hood of my head. He unzipped his jacket, and there he was, in my tiny house. It was like having a constellation down from the sky.

"It was raining too hard for me to walk," Kate explained. "Now it's raining too hard for them to drive. You can just put your coat there," she told Rourke, referring to the couch back, as she turned on the desk lamp. The incandescence blanched the firelight; I flinched. "Sorry," she said, smiling tightly, rolling her eyes, adding, "Evie hates lights."

Rourke scrutinized my mother's bookshelves, the exhausted textbooks and frayed novels, the thumbtacked newspaper clippings and the loose nudes on cocktail napkins. How small the house seemed with him in it, how steeped with color and congested with effects. It was like a feast or a carnival; the ceiling seemed to swag. His eyes lingered on a white wooden sailboat I'd built in my dad's shop when I was five, and he lifted it—feeling the canvas triangle crisp with paint, running one finger across the name painted on the block bottom. *Eveline.* It was nice that he looked for me there; no one had ever looked for me there.

Kate invited them into the kitchen. Tim hopped right off the hearth, but Rourke remained, continuing to scan the shelves in silence. When she called him once again, he moved to join them, first turning off the desk lamp that Kate had put on. His hand lingering on the switch, his back to me.

I looked for new music. I'd lost interest in bossa nova. The woman Rourke awakened in me was not gifted with delicacy or political cause;

she came in an atomic rush, possessing nothing more than instinct and courage. I chose Al Green's "Here I Am (Come and Take Me)." The song played the way I felt—knowing, but new, secretive, but open.

> *I can't believe that it's real, the way that you make me feel*
> *A burning deep down inside, a love that I cannot hide*

Rourke's jacket was across the room. I resisted as long as I could, and then I crawled to the couch. My hand felt the leather. In the kitchen they chatted capably, as though they'd been brought together by choice rather than chance.

"Actually," Rourke was saying, "I took a costume design course in college."

"You're kidding!" Kate giggled.

Tim said, "Why not, Kate? It was probably an easy A."

"Not quite. I almost failed."

"Oh, shit," Tim groaned. "There goes the GPA."

"I asked the teacher if there was anything I could do to bring up the grade. She said, 'As a matter of fact, Mr. Rourke, there is. I'll give you the weekend to make a wedding dress.' "

There was an explosion of laughter. "No!" Tim said. "The *bitch*."

"What did you do?" Kate asked.

"I made a wedding dress."

"And did your grade go up?"

"I got an A," Rourke said, "and several marriage proposals."

They laughed again and then moved into a discussion of politics and sports and classic cars. Rourke talked about the upcoming election and President Carter and the Soviet Union and Afghanistan and the boycott of the winter Olympics. Coming from his voice, with its rich cadence, worldly things did not seem petrifying. It intrigued me, the way he excelled socially, the way he spoke that language but also mine. If I was sorry not to know more about current events, I was consoled by the fact that I could mold a finch from clay and recount in detail the aroma of a half-dead oak leaf. But possibly that all counted for nothing.

One by one, I burned my cutout attempts. The dolls made a contorted lattice on the logs, leaping eerily to puppet-like existence, contracting to pitiful cinders. It was like a breath—like breathing life *into*, like sucking it out again. There was a place in the middle where they looked best. It was the place of my dream.

A single sheet of paper remained. I folded it, then cut without penciling, my body reaching for each new inch, going by sense of feeling, and as I went, I kept thinking, *It's not the chime of the bell, it's the echo of the chime.*

To make the inner openings around the bodies and swings, I used an X-Acto knife, unfocusing my eyes, steering through resistant folds. Just as I made the final incision, and the curious remains dropped to the floor, the glow of the firelight darkened.

"What are you making?" he asked. Rourke spoke with care, as though aware in advance of the difficulties he might face. He wanted me to know he regretted using words on me so soon after using words on them and that the words reserved for me were different words. His caution was not inappropriate: somehow I felt I'd been lied to.

He squatted, his knees coming to the height of my shoulders. He allowed me to examine him, letting my eyes go slowly over. In his willingness to be searched and to be seen, in his conscious quietude I perceived his resolve. I had the feeling of being a cat to catch. Once Powell taught me how to catch cats. We were at the tracks, crouching to lure a stray kitten. "Build trust," he instructed, hardly moving his lips. "Gesture slowly."

Rourke's forearms ventured off his legs. They reached into my vicinity then paused. When I did not pull back, they came farther. He took the paper from me, and I let him.

"I had a dream," I said, speaking because he willed me to. "I was a cutout. On a swing."

From each end of the chain, he grasped a doll's hand, a fist really—there were no fingers—and, gently, he pulled. The hair was perfect. He smiled. "Which one are you?"

I stared widely. "Which side is the front?"

"This side," he said. The side facing him.

I pointed to the third from the right. "This is me."

Dishes clattered in the kitchen. I startled, but he did not move, except to reassign his weight to the opposite leg. He seemed disinclined to give my dolls back. Maybe he was going to take them away, like he took the chapel. But instead, he released them reluctantly into my reluctantly receiving hands. There was a single second during which we each held one end of the dolls, and, in that second, I felt a riveting and arduous bliss.

"No more hail," he said, looking out the window. Then he stood. Though I was sitting, I felt I might topple without him there. My hand grabbed the floor.

"See you soon," he pledged confidentially as his arms entered the sleeves of his jacket.

"Yes," I said, pledging too. "Soon."

"What were you two talking about?" Kate asked as we watched Rourke's car pull out onto the street. The headlights scanned her face through the window, and implications of raindrops slithered across her cheeks, skulking left to right like legions of obedient insects. I thought of an old detective movie, *The Big Sleep* or *The Maltese Falcon*. Kate and I had come to inhabit a menacing realm of extremes—shadows and light, desire and aversion, faith and betrayal, wins and losses; in that realm, we were liars, each of us.

"Nothing," I said. "The rain."

Kate hoped I was friendly, at least.

I told her I thought that I was.

She fell back onto the couch. "I can't believe he was actually here."

"Neither can I," I said, agreeing. It felt good to agree with Kate. It had been a long time.

19

There was a strip of casement windows painted olive-green that separated my bedroom from the backyard. I taped my cutouts to the glass. Thirteen hours earlier, Rourke had held them. His fingerprints were there, though I couldn't see them.

At eight-thirty the phone rang. I rushed to the living room, sliding in my socks to stop the second ring so no one would wake up. I liked to wake up first, before everyone else, with all the colliding needs and pop-up hair, the talk over cold cereal of nightmares and tooth grinding. The cats clustered at my ankles, sticking to my feet like a crazy beard, like from one of those make-a-face magnet shavings games.

"It's me," Denny said. "Did I wake you?"

I whispered, "No."

"Good," he said, whispering too. "I stopped at Guild Hall on the way back from Woolco last night to get out of the hail. Did you see the hail?"

"Yeah, it was beautiful."

"Not really," he said. "It practically cracked my windshield. Anyway, rehearsal was cut short, so the place was empty except for Richie—the lighting guy, you know Richie—and Paul Z., and that new kid Jason from AP Lit. They said the scenery had just arrived, so I went to check. The flats were completely wet. Someone drove them over in the rain."

"Well, that was stupid."

"I guess they borrowed a flatbed before the rain started. Richie helped me pull everything apart so it can all dry. There's some damage, but nothing too bad. I'm getting Dave Meese at ten. Want me to get you too?"

"No, I'll ride my bike over."

"Okay. I'll see you around ten-thirty," he said, and he hung up.

I left right away, though it wasn't nine. I wanted to be outside. I wanted to be cold. First I stopped at Dreesen's to get old bread from Rudy, then I rode to the nature trail, passing Jack's house on the way. The light in his attic room was on—maybe he was practicing guitar, or maybe he had fallen asleep that way. Sometimes he got scared.

The ducks were hungry. They got out of the water and came to me, climbing rocks and waddling briskly. They ate the bread as fast as I could supply it, and when it was gone, they left. Jack despised waterfowl. He said he did not feel obliged to creatures with liquid feces. "Give me another piece," he would urge when he went there with me; then he would squeeze the Wonder Bread into pellets to chuck at them.

I rode fast down Main Street, like a rocket. Right before the offices of

The East Hampton Star, I leaned into the vacant oncoming lane and bounced onto the sidewalk in front of the white brick theater, where I came to a skidding halt.

Guild Hall is a community arts center, though the community didn't use it much, at least not like they did the VFW on Main Street or Ashawagh Hall in Springs, where they held pancake breakfasts and potluck weddings. Sometimes plays were held there, sometimes art shows or classes, lectures or films. It was good that the Drama Club was having its play there. The high school auditorium didn't even have a curtain.

The theater was empty and hardly lit. Cast call wasn't until noon; I knew from Kate's schedule on the refrigerator. And I still had forty-five minutes before Denny got there—an hour if you factored in his certain lateness. From the top of the auditorium the sets looked okay; actually, they looked great. They were monochrome collages of geometric shapes—the "chapel" was a huge vertical ivory diamond jutting from a horizontal polygon, and the "village green" was a trapezoid in smoky rust, like fox fur, because Dave Meese had decided that in the village it was autumn.

At the end of the far left aisle, there was an archway leading backstage. I went through and immediately ran into Rourke. We collided in the boxy shaft between two doorways. He retreated, so did I, each just a step. Scarcely two feet of air divided us—I had to tilt my head to see his face. Burgundy drapes cloaked the door behind him, and the dreamy glow from a safety bulb gave the vestibule the appearance of a tasteful coffin.

"I was just coming to get you," he said. "I saw you from backstage."

"Oh. I came to fix the flats."

Rourke shoved a hand into his pocket, debilitating himself, neutralizing something. I'd seen him do it before. In the record store. In the art room. "Sorry," he said. "I shouldn't have left so early last night."

"It was raining pretty bad," I said. I was glad he'd left, since, after all, he'd come to my house.

"Yeah. It was bad."

I didn't mind my work getting damaged; it's the nature of art to yield. When you're an artist, you possess a drive, you clear yourself of it, you relinquish the outcome. Susan at the laundry by Dad's house gets crazy.

Once, Chihuahua Man draped the shirts she'd ironed for him over his forearm. Chihuahua Man has four Chihuahuas and nothing else—no family, no car, no phone. His dogs run loose, crapping up the sidewalks, and all the old ladies with buckets yell and throw bleach. That day, Susan raised the hinged countertop that sequestered her from the rest of the world, and she ran out front. I'd never seen her legs before. "Take the hanger! Take the hanger!" She was within her rights to yell, since it's rude to demean someone else's labor, but, for all she knew, he was going to take the shirts home and let the dogs sleep on them. Sometimes the best you can do is your small part, perfectly. For months after, it was the talk of the neighborhood—*What could Chihuahua Man have been doing with those nice shirts?* "I don't get it," Tony Abbruscato kept saying. "He don't even own leashes."

Rourke asked how long did I think it would take.

It was hard to think clearly with him standing there. "I haven't seen them yet."

"Let's take a look," he said, leading me back through the stage door, holding it for me. At the light board he paused to survey the bank of switches and levers. There was a crack and the stage was illuminated. A sultry pressure cosseted the back of my neck as I crossed to the rear, him behind me. I felt strangely three-dimensional walking with him; I was conscious of the back of me, the sides and the top. Even my feet felt like new feet. I wiped the palms of my hands on my legs. They felt active, buzzing kind of.

I loosened a bent shingle from the chapel. He was alongside me. "The glue will have to dry before I can paint. It might take a few hours," I said. "Will I be in your way?"

His breath, my ear. "You won't be in my way."

In his shadow everything felt right. If it was wrong to be close, I didn't care. I didn't care if we were seen, and I didn't care by whom. It was a feeling of being outside the world. By providing me with what I'd been seeking, he proved not only that I had been seeking, but that I'd been correct to seek.

"I'll be back," he said, and I felt myself list. I felt him tend as well, then stop, then straighten. Him whispering, "That okay with you?"

I emptied my knapsack, and tubes of paint spilled onto the floor. While waiting for Denny, I paced the stage. Walking onstage is the same as walking in life, only the lights make you feel like a star, and when you reach the edge, you have to turn back to center. Maybe that's why the English excel in theater, because Britain is insular. People there can venture only so far before hitting an end, before having to fold in. America is a wasteland; here we ramble without modesty or restraint, leaving things behind, just picking up and going when things get complicated. Actually, America *was* a wasteland; now it's all built up.

It was almost eleven, and still no Denny. I stretched out on the floor, lying there, and I drifted, going in and out. I wondered if I'd chosen the wrong talent, if in fact talent can ever be a matter of choice. The theater was the first place I'd ever felt happy.

Within several minutes, I felt light pressure on my chest, like a cat's paw. I raised my head and found a lily. "A peace offering," Denny's voice said. "Sorry I'm late." He was standing over me, wearing the purple velvet newsboy hat Alicia had made for him. He looked like a dyed mushroom. "Don't ask me what took so long." He tossed his coat near mine and launched into a rambling explanation anyway.

The lily was exquisite. Six petals burst from a tubular casing, proud and electrifying like fireworks inscribing the sky. I touched one. It was bumpy, with a lone blaze of yellow crimping it down the center. The fragrance was combative: a gluish, maudlin aroma. I would have liked to draw the smell. It reminded me of Maman's funeral.

"Then," Denny concluded, "we couldn't find green tape for the Village Green." He plucked three softening coffee cups from a paper bag, handing one to me. "I tried Vetault's Florist. Jen Miller was working and I bummed the tape from her. The flower too."

I sat up and popped the lid off my cup.

"The ham sandwich is yours, the chips are for Dave, and the soda's for me. I'm back on Tab. I need to lose ten pounds by Wednesday."

"What's Wednesday?" Dave Meese asked as he hopped up onstage.

"Day after Tuesday, Dave," Denny said. He took off his hat and set free a mop of black hair. Denny had gorgeous hair. His cheekbones were high under his eyes and his teeth were perfect. Everyone said he looked like Elvis, which really upset him. "They don't mean Memphis Elvis or Elvis at Sun Records," he'd complain. "They mean Elvis in Hawaii. 'Caught in a Trap' Elvis. Fat sweaty Elvis. Elvis on dope."

"What's up, Evie," Dave greeted me as he set down his tool kit and dropped his maroon snorkel jacket on the pile Denny and I'd started. Dave was a good artist, but his gift was rigging. He'd been making booby traps since first grade. By sophomore year he'd figured out how to get from one part of the high school to another without touching ground, just by going through ceiling ducts and roof accesses. Dave was the only one allowed to touch Jack's guitars besides Dan and me. "When the shit hits the fan, you're gonna need a guy like that," Jack would say. "Rigging is a practical art, like growing crops or skinning deer."

From the figureless murk of the theater came the springy gong of a seat bottom folding up and smacking its frame. I squinted to see Rourke heading up the aisle to the lobby. I wondered how long he'd been there. It occurred to me that he hadn't left at all, that he'd been there the entire time.

While waiting for the glue to dry, Denny, Dave, and I watched rehearsal from the audience. We sat about ten rows back, across the aisle from Mr. McGintee and Toby Parker, the music teacher, who were observing, though they had not removed their coats.

"Oh, gee, look who's pretending to earn their paychecks," Denny said. "This is the first time I've seen them in weeks. And the show opens in five days."

Rourke dictated cues to Richie, who was backstage at the lighting board, and to Paul Z., who was operating the spot from the top of the auditorium. First the lights would blacken, then they'd rise to a uniform faintness. That was the cue for Peter Reeves to step out from the wings to deliver his monologue as he arranged furniture.

Peter had the part of the Stage Manager. In *Our Town,* the Stage Manager remains on the periphery during the entire play, conversant both with performers and the audience but allied to neither, leading me to wonder if loneliness is the price you pay for omniscience. Peter was a good actor; I'd heard Rourke had helped him with his monologue for NYU Drama. If Peter got accepted to NYU and if Denny got accepted to FIT, they planned to get an apartment together in the city. And if I got accepted to NYU, they wanted me to be their roommate too. "And *if*," Jack said sarcastically at the time of the offer, "Denny's mom marries Peter's dad, they could adopt you, and you three could be triplets."

"Good job, Peter. Take a break," Rourke said. "Let's skip to the flashback."

Kate and Tim came out, and Tim growled and playfully chased Peter offstage. There was an awkward pause. Rourke filled it. "Whenever you're ready."

Tim began. "Can I carry your books home, Emily?"

"Why, uh, thank you. It isn't far."

The two moved stiffly across the stage. Tim was lousy. Kate wasn't great, but she wished so strenuously to please that she semi-succeeded. It was like real life—she could be exceptional at anything, as long as her vanity found some incentive in it. Unfortunately, her vanity found so many *dis*incentives to being exceptional that she ended up doing very little, or giving up bored halfway through. My mother often used Shakespeare to caution her, saying, *Lilies that fester smell far worse than weeds.*

Rourke stood near us, one hand gripping his jaw. I could read his body through his sweater—he appeared ready to spring. He snapped at Richie and the lights changed fast. The actors faltered and stared out. "Go on," Rourke insisted.

"He seems pissed," Denny whispered. "Probably because those goons are watching."

"They're not stopping on their marks," Dave said, meaning Kate and Tim. "They're out of sync with the lights. They keep delivering lines in the dark."

Kate and Tim began again, and again the lights ended up trailing them rather than moving with them. Richie cursed, and Rourke suddenly bolted, jogging to the front and vaulting onto the stage.

"Holy shit!" Denny said.

Rourke startled when he faced the performers, as if surprised to find them there, or himself there—in the center, in the light. He gripped his temples with two fingers, sucked in one cheek, then exhaled. He faced Kate and smiled an introductory smile, then he took a step, a meaningful step, a transforming step. There was no frame; yet he seemed to have crossed a threshold. He dug his hands into his pockets and inclined his chest when she spoke, listening closely as he shepherded her as if down a country lane. He was leading her powerfully, but invisibly. I could tell because as the two moved through shadow and glare, I understood their lines for the first time, though I'd been listening repeatedly. I heard the threat of consequence. The lighting plan kind of linked courtship and tragedy: you couldn't help but think, *It's because Emily marries George that she dies.*

I didn't feel jealous, but I felt, I don't know, somewhat sick about the logical look of him with a girl.

Rourke withdrew abruptly, turning to Tim. "Got it?"

Tim nodded, and they shook hands, and everyone clapped, except me, and Denny, who whistled, and McGintee, who yelled, "Bravo!"

Rourke jumped down and took to the aisle. A shock of hair fell forward. He ran a hand through it, and his eyes passed uncomfortably over mine. "Okay," he called. "Again, guys."

I stood and left. I went backstage, going as far as I could from the front, far from where he was, all the way to the last dressing room. Rourke's voice trailed my steps. I squatted in the corner and wrote on my arm with a pen I found there.

Sorry for my eyes, sorry to have seen you so.

The dressing room door opened; it was Denny. He knelt behind me and played with my hair. "You know, I was thinking that maybe you should go home and get some sleep. I'll drive you, then I'll come back to finish the scenery with Dave."

"I have my bike."

"I know. I'll put it in the trunk. I'll drop you and come back."

He helped me to a stand, and when I stood, he rolled down my sleeve to cover the writing on my arm. He led me through the auditorium, and he retrieved my stuff. Rourke was busy so I didn't say goodbye. Denny loaded my bike into his car, and he took me home, where I slept straight through to Sunday morning, except for one brief exchange with Jack.

"Actually," Jack said, "I sat with you for three hours."

20

When we got to the dressing room, Kate told me to stay. Michelle Sui and Adrienne Parker were there, hunched over a cracked console, somberly applying makeup. Adrienne was the music teacher's daughter, and a very good cello player. Sometimes she played with Jack and Atomic Tangerine. The mirror was fingerprinty. Uncapped tubes and jars were everywhere. Clothes and shoes and stockings had been thrown all over. Two gray wigs rested freakishly on Styrofoam heads—the wigs were skewed, making me think of drunken monsters. I said I'd wait up front.

"You sure?" Adrienne said, her lips not moving a millimeter, her chin jutted out. She stroked each eyelid repeatedly with turquoise shadow until the glaze was thick and round like bakery cookies. None of them seemed to be terrified by the zombie mannequin heads.

"I'm sure." I waved. "Good luck."

Kate lingered in the doorway. Behind her, boys dressed as villagers held a karate match.

"Thanks for practicing my lines with me, Evie."

"Oh," I said, "it was fun. You know, I guess." I stepped back, and back again.

My words sounded insincere, though they were not. I wished she hadn't thanked me. Sometimes it's better to suppress gratitude. Sometimes it puts the person you are thanking into a tiny crisis of cognizance. I told myself just to say nothing the next time I found myself over-whelmed with appreciation.

"See you," she said, and I waved again.

The auditorium was still dim. At the top was a pile of programs. I took one. I walked to the ninth row from the stage on the right, draped my coat over my shoulders, and snuggled into the third seat over. In the booklet I found the paragraph devoted to Rourke. He'd acted professionally as a teenager, earned a BFA in drama from UCLA, and done small parts in film and television in Los Angeles for a year and a half before moving back East. The epigrammatic brief contained more information than I wanted to know. I did not like to think what a minor part of his history East Hampton represented, when it was all I knew of him.

California—I'd discerned no evidence of that place in him, which just shows that people can see only as far as the eyes can see and that no one can know your story unless you broadcast it, which is not seemly. I wondered if his work on *Our Town* would amount to a sentence in his next bio or just a name on a list. More than likely it would not appear at all, and like some sharp pain once preoccupying but since resolved, I would be forgotten. In a few hours we would be divested of common topics and shared episodes. We would have no reason to talk. I tried to devise a notable thing to say in parting. *Good luck!* Or, *It's been nice.* Neither sounded particularly right.

There was a rush of cold. It did not come in a single draft but in a multiplicity of gusts, scrupulous and exacting. If the feeling had been a sound, it would have been the sound of bird wings flapping or guns discharging. And a fragrance—favorable, alien. Rourke took the seat alongside mine. I did not close the program; I did not care if he noticed the page.

We sat for several minutes, mute and unmoving, the staring-ahead way you sit when you go to the movies with someone you know very well and you're waiting for the picture to begin, but you don't feel like talking. Time tarried, as though there were nothing of relevance to mark or chronicle. I had one knee propped on the back of the seat in front of mine, and I was low, with my head coming only as high as his shoulder. He slouched a little too, but he was too big to do so with any sense of purpose. The effect was that he looked weary, which was perhaps the case. I thought of the way Jack slouched. No one could slouch quite as well as Jack.

I sighed in my mind, thinking, *Los Angeles,* as if things suddenly made sense, though they did not. I could not imagine Rourke spending all those years in the artificial pink glow, where people tour by bus the locked deco gates of stucco mansions, or him hanging out on the prairie-like boulevards beneath the looming and incongruous Hollywood sign.

I felt a forward lurching. I thought he was getting ready to go. I wondered what did it mean when I'd been fine before he came, but then he came and then he was leaving and I was not fine.

But Rourke did not rise. And this gave me confidence. Just when I believed that nothing short of contrivance would make him stay, he stayed. Despite my silence, he stayed, proving there was a confluence of need between us. He rested his forearms on the back of the seat in front of him, his head on his wrists. His tie hung perpendicular to his body, his dress shirt stretched across his back. Through the taut fabric, I could see his shoulder blades protruding.

"How are you?" I asked in a voice I'd never heard myself use before. It was a voice of invitation and daring, deep and devoid of inflection. It was the voice of a woman. Sometimes in movies when enemies meet, they greet each other with deference and civility, acknowledging affiliations more profound than the competition itself, acknowledging a parity, an evenness of match. At the end of *The Hustler,* Minnesota Fats and Fast Eddie say goodbye, and it's sad, sadder even than when Eddie's girlfriend dies, because life is full of tenderness where you would not think to find it.

Rourke tilted his head to his right and he regarded me. His face was square from forehead to jaw and graded mildly to the chin. His eyes were black; it was true. Eyes can be called black, but I didn't think eyes could actually be black. Rourke's were a reverberant black, a blackness of conviction, as if they had forfeited subordinate hues by decision, as if they were that way by will. They were the eyes of someone who reads the world in terms of opposition. And yet there was light. I could see where they were susceptible. I could see blind pools where the light hit and bounced back. Then, quick as it came, the light was gone, replaced by a cataract of grave insights.

"Looking forward to the end of this," he replied. In the natureless dusk of the theater, he shamelessly memorized my face. I memorized his as well.

Suddenly the houselights went up. We discerned a milling gurgle, and Rourke stood. He walked to the basin of the auditorium, then disappeared into the vestibule where we had collided a week earlier.

I felt elated; I'd never felt that way before. I thought to go out to the lobby. I wanted to be where there were people; I wanted to mingle, to be one among many. I liked the idea of everyone crowded together, sheltered from the frigid March night by the walls of the theater. As I stood to go, Dan appeared at the base of stage left, sheet music under his arm. Jack stepped next from the obscurity of the corridor, grim, hunched, and scowling. He looked like the vampire in *Nosferatu*. I was surprised to see him, though of course I should not have been. Their instruments were right there, waiting for them.

"Hey, Evie," Dan called softly up to me, taking a seat at the bench of the keyboard, adjusting the light, setting out sheet music.

Jack wouldn't look at me; I knew he'd seen me with Rourke. He plied the brown felt keyboard cover with painstaking precision, pulling and folding, pulling and folding, reminding me of my crime with each gesture, challenging my conscience to profit from his misery. Behind the stage drapery, someone said, "Five minutes!" and the lobby doors swung apart.

All I recalled of the play after it ended was intermission. While everyone stretched their legs, Jack and Dan stayed bent over the keyboard, toying like alchemists. The music discharged from the corner of the auditorium as if from a void, radiating like steam from a crevice in the earth. The first piece was lush with nuance, busy with conversing chords—Dan's. Jack's song was less sophisticated, leaving nothing to chance, but far more beautiful. Its complexity came from layering, from a nagging superimposition of the central refrain, which had been written in a minor key, evoking heavyheartedness. Despite Jack's tortured prophecies, people were enticed back from the lobby to hear him play. They listened attentively with their crisscross peanut butter cookies and warping paper mugs of cider. I felt pride for Jack, but also a sick, forward-moving fear. It was strange to experience in one night the difference between wanting something you cannot have and having something you cannot want. I wished it wasn't my time to learn it. No one else seemed to be learning much of anything.

When the curtain call came, the audience stood, and Jack and Dan played again. I went backstage to find Kate. Kids scrambled to sign programs and solidify romances. Parents obstructed staircases and dressing room doors, kissing greased faces, bestowing obligatory bouquets. Paul Z. pushed a towering stack of chairs past me, and Richie adjusted the lamps behind the chapel. An increasing sense of unease came over me. The evening's incidents kept playing out in my mind—Kate thanking me, Rourke and Los Angeles and the flickering in his eyes, the rush of the crowd, and Jack's song. In my head and my heart, it rang and rang again. *Jack is my hero,* I told myself, *with all his messages and abilities.* And yet I had a troubling sense, a visionary sense. I felt like I was holding hands with myself, guiding my shell through an evening previously lived.

Rourke's back blocked the door of the girls' dressing room. Seeing it moved me—just the idea of him possessed the clarity that everything else lacked. I took two steps closer through the crowded hall. I could hear the sound of his words through the back of his chest, the vibrations. He was talking to them about the show. He must have sensed me because he turned to look, then he quickly stepped left, making room. He leaned against the side wall and folded his arms; I stood next to him. My left breast pressed lightly into his right arm, behind the elbow. I didn't move; neither did he. All the talk drifted down to nothing.

"Congratulations," I said to no one in particular.

"Are you coming to the cast party, Evie?" Adrienne asked.

"C'mon, Evie, everyone's going," Cathy Benjamin said.

Michelle said, "You're coming, right, Harrison?"

"Only going if *she's* going," Rourke said, jerking his head slightly, referring to me. The girls giggled, except for Kate. He looked at the ground thoughtfully, taking a minute, nodding twice. "Well, thanks again for good work," he told them. When he turned and stepped sideways to pass through the door frame, his body brushed flat against mine, his head bowing down, his face looking to my face. *It's a treacherous world,* his eyes seemed to say. Unlike everyone else, he did not deny the treachery.

I staggered lazily up the theater aisle toward a group of people waiting for Jack and Dan. Dan's father, Dr. Lewis, and his girlfriend, Micah, were there with Jim Peterson, the sax player from Dr. Lewis's band. Smokey Cologne was there too, with Troy Resnick, Kathy Hanfling, Joss Mathers, and Nina Spear.

Dr. Lewis hugged me. "Fabulous sets! Where's Irene?"

"A lecture, I think. She's coming tomorrow. To the matinee."

"What's she teaching this semester, Evie," Jim inquired. "Poetry?"

"Short stories."

He nodded and they all nodded, saying to say hi.

Micah caressed my cheek with one finger. Her wrist bangles clattered lightly, reminding me of distant porch chimes. "Coming to our house for the party, Eveline?"

"Of course she is," Dr. Lewis said emphatically.

Smokey stood, which meant Jack was coming. He crammed his hands into the pockets of his tattered herringbone coat and shook his purple hair from his face to little practical effect. Beneath Smokey's bangs, his eyes were chronically claret and watery, making it appear as though he'd reached us by way of a channel. "Smokey is one strange dude," Jack would say, "but a great fucking drummer."

Jack swung an open hand to Smokey in greeting. "Marvin," Jack said, using Smokey's real name. "What's up?"

"Nice job, men." Dr. Lewis launched a new round of applause. "Glad to know my gear is being put to good use." His hand rested on Jack's arm. Discreetly he asked, "Did your parents come?"

"He didn't even tell them about it, Dad," Dan informed his father, and we all headed for the door in a funny bundle.

On the brick path that led from the doors of Guild Hall to the street, we dispersed. Dan climbed into Smokey's black Nova, and Jack and I headed east on Main Street, walking in the direction of the village. Jack unfolded his collar and pulled his Chinese Red Army cap to his eyes. I tucked my hands into my sleeves. He offered his gloves to me. As he wriggled one onto my left hand, the other slipped from under his arm and fell to the ground. We knocked shoulders as we both bent to retrieve it.

"What a load of shit!" he proclaimed, meaning the play. "What a criminal waste."

"Your song was good."

"That's hardly an endorsement for the play. The acting sucked."

"People have to start somewhere. You weren't born a musician."

"The difference is I've been playing every day since I was four. This is like handing out thirty guitars to people who've never played before, who'll never play again, and trying to get something coherent in three months. And for what, five lame performances?"

"At least it's not football."

"No, no. It's exactly like football. Half-assed recreation, a distraction for the kiddies. It's about deceiving taxpayers into thinking juveniles are being kept off the streets, that they're being offered concrete opportunities. It's about college résumés."

I tried to remember my point. I wasn't sure I had one. "Kate worked hard, and—"

"And *you* worked hard," he said, though I hadn't even considered myself. "That crap was a waste of your time. Your church will be in the trash on Monday."

I hadn't considered that—the trash. I said, "You know what I mean."

"*I* know what you mean, Ev-e-line." Jack stretched my name to fully fill its three syllables. He faced me. "But do *you* know what you mean?" His blue eyes were bleached and even, making a strike through his face like the crossbar of the letter *T*. "Listen to yourself."

Kids from the play closed in on us from behind. Jack slipped into the garden of the Huntting Inn, and I followed. He sat on an enormous rock, took a joint from his pocket, and lit it. Our eyes met above the embers. I wished to be drained; I wanted him to drain me.

"The whole thing got me down. The whole fucking night." Jack was referring to Rourke, though he would not introduce that name into our dialogue. He would not risk making it more real than he guessed it to be, as real as it was. I kicked the ground. He kicked the ground as well, setting a piece of ice to fly. "You're headed down a bad road, Evie. I won't be able to see you through this."

The wooden porch of the Lewis house creaked under our weight. It was a moldy cedar-shake colonial on Pantigo Road, held together primarily by its odor—a composite of curry and candle drippings. Micah refused to live there, choosing instead to remain at their apartment on West End Avenue and Eighty-second. She visited East Hampton rarely, almost exclusively in summer. "The heat burns off the negative ions," she once told me.

Inside was a sequence of rooms lined with instruments, dubious art, obsolete electronics, stacks of flaking scores, and mountains of damp books. Inside, you never knew exactly where you were or how to get out. The wainscoted hallways were papered in framed photographs of Dan's father with greats such as Oscar Peterson, John Coltrane, Dexter Gordon, and Sonny Rollins. Besides being a musician and composer, Dr. Lewis was also a professor of music theory at Juilliard, which he called his *day gig*. He and the band traveled to places such as Newport, Hamburg, Edinburgh, Paris, and São Paolo. When in town, they would sit around discussing the evolution of jazz, debating East and West Coast composing signatures, and lamenting the loss of quality clubs and the declining musical interest among young people. My mother would sometimes be with them. She and Dr. Lewis had dated when Dan and I were in grade school, the winter before she met Powell. This was a big deal to Jack. Unlike his revulsion to the idea of me, Denny, and Peter as college roommates, he liked the idea of Dan and me as siblings and his coming to live with us and Mom and Dr. Lewis in one big jazzy, literary house with everyone being cared for by Bitsy, Dr. Lewis's housekeeper from the Philippines. Bitsy wore ill-fitting sweat socks and threw down paper plates of muddy lasagna and yelled uniquely when Dan put his feet on the table. After yelling, she would squish his cheeks together and slap the side of his head. Bitsy was seventy-one and an avid golfer.

Jack joined Dan and Smokey in the living room, going straight to the piano, bowing over, his powdery white hair splaying in a fan. There was a guitar on the couch. I wished he would have selected the guitar instead. He was less sure of himself on guitar, and his vulnerability plus his refusal to relent was beautiful. I wished he would be beautiful.

Denny and Kate were at the base of the stairs, laughing. Kate's face was flushed. I could see they'd been drinking. Denny caught me and reeled me in, squeezing like toothpaste. The smell of cheap Chablis mixed with the smell of his deodorant depressed me.

A flurry at the front door was accompanied by shouting and whistling. The teachers had arrived. Dr. Lewis, Micah, and Jim Peterson came in first, then Mr. McGintee, Toby Parker, and Lilias Starr. Rourke came last, shedding ounces of midnight cold as he filled the foyer.

McGintee complimented everyone. "Terrific job! Top shelf all the way! And that meeting house," he said, giving me a firm wink. "The sets were the finest we've ever had."

"Thank you," Denny said, patting me on the back, using my arm to pat him on the back. He thrust my hand into the crowd. It stuck out like a little clock arm. "Her hand is like ice!"

"Maybe she's anemic," Lilias said.

"You do look pale, Eveline," Micah agreed.

"My God," Denny said to me, "don't faint again." And then to the crowd, "Last week I found her passed out on the darkroom floor."

There were general expressions of concern for my health. Rourke reached for my hand, forgoing false propriety. He collected it as though taking up a baby, baby homeless something. In his hands my bones felt like bird bones, like crayons or small pencils. I demurred with a smile, and I pulled away. Not a smile, but a vague flickering. It was nice for a moment to have him, and sad to have to lose him.

I burrowed my hand into my jeans pocket, and looking down, I moved obediently to the living room, where I found Jack, leafing through a songbook, getting ready to sing. He appeared wafer-thin, wraithlike, there, but not there. My body moved about the perimeter of the grand piano which was already crowded with people who had come to listen.

Dr. Lewis joined Jack on the bench. A cigarette hung precariously from the corner of his mouth as he slapped his legs establishing a light rhythm prior to Jack's playing. Then real banging—Smokey, whipping the lid of the piano with the heels of his hands. And Jack's fingers hitting the keys, *thump-thump, thump-thump-thump.* And him singing Muddy Waters:

> *Who's that yonder come walkin' down the street?*
> *She's the most beautiful girl any man would want to meet.*
> *I wonder who's gonna be your sweet man when I'm gone?*
> *I wonder who you're gonna have to love you.*

In his voice there was new weight, masculine weight. Jack had never been hurt by me before. At least I'd given him *something,* even if only just a passport into sorrow. When the last chord came, he jammed the piano one final time—*bwomp*—and he smiled mordantly into the crowd, his eyes latching on to no one and nothing. His rejection of me was correct; I understood it had to be that way. If in life there is flow, a current or a course, I had the feeling I'd found it. They began a second song, Leonard Cohen's *Suzanne,* my favorite, he knew. He sang it so beautifully.

Past the piano on the southern side of the room, a wall of windows overlooking the porch extended from floor to ceiling. I moved behind the frayed drapes and went to the farthermost window, the top half of which was open. Pantigo Road lay ahead. The oily gloss of the street and the sound of passing cars suggested it was raining. Wheels on wet pavement make a very particular going-home sound, serene and conclusive. I wondered what Marilyn was doing. Maybe she was making tea, scooping stray leaves from a wrinkled paper sack with Golden Assam stamped in withering red. Maybe she and Dad were reading. If she was looking out the window at the rain, perhaps she was thinking of me.

"I'm leaving," Rourke said, his voice coming practically from within my mind.

I was not surprised. Lots of things were in there—him too. My eyes didn't leave the street. I was in some unattended place, some dangerously unattended place. He was on the porch, on the other side of the wall, leaning against my open window. I did not look to see him, but I could feel him, the way you can close your eyes and feel a hand above your skin. He emitted something electrical, and I responded, electrically.

"I want you to know," he said, "that you're very talented." Quieter, down an octave. "I think you're going to go far."

A car passed. I traced its lights eastward. It was a curious thing to mention talent. He seemed to want to persuade me of something. I might have told him not to bother trying. Though I could not name the choice, it had been made the first time I saw him. My preference for him was unconditional, absolute—*feral,* as Jack would have said, the type of choice animals make. Jack was mistaken about the ability of conscience and moral reciprocity being the best means to move humanity. In the end it's just natural will that inspires us to action. Love, hatred, hunger, desire, indigence—things that find no home in logic. What I felt for Rourke was a partiality that situated me. It defined and animated me.

He moved suddenly, his shadow changing radically from a lean vertical strip visible only from the corner of my eye to a carbon shield that obliterated the view, like a door swinging decidedly shut. His mouth came down on my cheek, the one farthest from him. With his jaw he pushed my face into the hard pocket of his inclined chest, and with loose lips he softly held it there. I was breathing, my breath wetting his chest, going down the tendons of his neck. Beneath the membrane of his lips lay the complete and threatening remainder of his body. I could feel the way he held himself in check. Just when he might have retreated, he lingered, noticing perhaps as I did the way his mouth had been shaped by God to fit the hollow beneath my cheekbone.

"I have to go," he breathed in apologetically. When he withdrew, the skin of his lips and the skin of my face resisted separation. I wondered when we'd reached a place of apologies.

"Yes," I said. "Go."

Rourke leapt from the porch. He seemed dauntless, satisfied with himself, and with me. He reached his car—a 1967 cameo-white GTO with a parchment interior. I knew the details because I heard him talk about them the night he came to my house in the hailstorm. He opened the door, and his body vanished into what looked like a tank full of moonglow. I wished to vanish also, but I was bound by the things that professed to designate me—family, friends, school, culture, country. How had I fallen under their influence, when these things referred to something other than what I felt myself to be, when the care I received was diluted by their self-interest?

I was no prisoner, and yet, when faced with an occasion for determination, I was not to follow the lead of my will, but to endure in tedious familiarity. What is freedom when you're too beholden to act spontaneously? What is desire that is absolute but untimely? Or obligation when you have ignored your soul's conviction? Is sacrifice really a virtue when in your heart you feel not a shred of devotion? I knew all this and more, but for all that I knew, knowing did not bring him back, and knowing did not move me. Only he could have brought himself back, only he might have moved me. And that is just slavery of another kind— which was something to consider.

I listened to the push of his car in reverse—a steady, hard push, tail-lights coming back. I nestled into the glow, and then he cut out to the right, in the direction of Amagansett and Montauk. I was to go back and face Jack and Kate, my parents, school on Monday. I was to gather away the monster I'd become, and, in the meantime, count on Rourke for nothing. He had acquainted me with the next place, but he would not take me there. I felt slightly doubtful, the way caterpillars must feel in the instant they are awakened to become butterflies.

That was the promise I'd made to Rourke—to fly.

The piano was unattended, though the room was still packed with peo-ple. I moved to the kitchen at the rear of the house, where I found Jack and his friends, an androgynous, invertebrate puddle of flannel and denim, sitting in a sooty cloud of pot smoke. Jack was slumped so low in a ladderback chair that his head met the middle rung. One foot jutted across the dining table, and he was rubbing the gummy label from a beer bottle with a nail-bitten thumb. His friends looked smug. They didn't like Jack with me; they thought I wanted something from him, who knew what, since Jack had nothing to give. "Unless it's the flu," Jack would speculate. "Or a hangover," Denny would add.

One time Trish Lawton called me a *calculating bitch*.

"Who's Trish Lawton?" I asked Jack.

"Troy's sister's friend from Michigan. From Flint."

"Has Trish even met Eveline?" Dan inquired mildly.

Jack thought for a minute. "I guess not, no. Pretty sure she hasn't."

I didn't care what they thought of me, but I didn't like how little they knew of Jack. If they insisted on remaining blind to his capacity for ma-nipulation, his hunger for intellectual ascendance and moral leverage, his aptitude for dealing abuse, then without me, he would be as good as friendless.

"I'm going," I announced, and there were a few mumbled good nights.

Jack thrust back his chair, standing before the legs were square, so that it marched and threatened to topple. He stormed up behind me and tossed his coat over his shoulders. One limp sleeve skimmed my back.

The screen door slammed behind us, hitting twice. I left, and Jack followed. His feet punched the porch steps as he descended, and when our bodies were aligned, he zipped his jacket and handed me his gloves again. The cold was not the same tranquil cold as when we'd left the theater, but a sharp chill. Jack and I walked as we'd always walked, on the streets we knew so perfectly well, and as we did, the drama of the evening began to dwindle into distant nonsense.

At my house I washed and put on long underwear and socks, and I felt more like myself again, whatever that was. Or *who*ever. I joined Jack on the floor. He was picking threads from the torn knee of his jeans.

"I know what's happening," he said into his hands.

I didn't ask what he meant. If I forced him to put his thoughts to words, they would appear to lack foundation. He could only say, *I saw you two sitting together, not talking,* or, *I saw him take your hand after Denny offered it to the crowd.* I could defend myself against accusations, but that was a lawyerly way to waste time, assailing an argument's logic rather than conceding to its probability. Something *was* happening, it was true.

"I'm really upset," he said.

I was also upset. "I don't want to lose you."

"You're not losing me," he said. "You're forsaking me."

Forsaking implied choice. I had no choice with Rourke. I said, "Jack, I love you."

He tilted his head back and fell silent, for a long time, saying nothing. He was heartless to retain his grief, to inflict me with the knowledge that for once I was the cause of his torment, not the remedy. For purposes unknown I had been entrusted with the care of his soul, and so it was the most vile type of treason for me to have enriched his self-loathing. His existence suddenly seemed so tenuous to me, his figure so fragile. He was just one body, leading one life.

He breathed in, and three lines appeared in the middle of his forehead. He reached for me, and I folded into his arms, happy to give him the thing that I lacked—the object of his desire. I wondered if he'd felt happy when I'd told him I loved him, and was he relieved that I did not say different things—or worse, nothing at all. Through his sweater I assessed his breathing. I knew it by heart. It was shallow, like water you can hardly wade in, and unsynchronized, as if he could not match with the atmosphere.

"You're shivering," he said. He took the comforter from my bed and wrapped it around my shoulders and then his, making a nest. Jack stroked my hair and I kissed him. And we listened reverently to the night—to the chronic buzz of the refrigerator, to the occasional lurch and jerk of the boiler, to the dainty *tink* of the metallic numbers on my digital clock, flapping scrupulously. At three-thirty, he said that he should go home.

"Not yet," I begged, "please." I couldn't be alone, not yet.

21

I knew what to do. I would renounce my feelings. I would resume early loyalties. I would reduce my needs. I would disappear. The dispossession of Rourke would become for me a symbol of life's divine impermanence.

My days began and ended the same as anyone's—with light, with dark. The difference was that mine were stripped of the routine that generally divided the middle. I forfeited the comfort of habit. I wandered unpredictably, leaving school early or staying late. I began to accept offers. If Lisa Tobias or Dave Meese or Rocky Santiago asked if I needed a ride home, I said okay, even if I wanted to walk. When Alicia Ross invited me to O'Malley's for Sara Eden's birthday dinner, I brought balloons. When my mother invited me to watch her friend Francis Holland do his Dylan Thomas impersonation at the college, I accepted. When Denny needed me to drive with him and his mother to her pulmonologist in Stony Brook, I did. And when Dad was building frames for my final watercolors, Jack and I went into the city one weekend to help.

Though everyone was grateful for the congenial way I was acting, I did not particularly enjoy doing the things I kept agreeing to do. My only aim was to avoid Rourke until April. Kate said April was the last drama class. In science fiction movies, women in suit dresses and men in skinny ties stand at plate glass windows, waiting for the invading things, ants or birds or pods, to finish whatever they're doing, breeding or eating, and to leave. Home became that way for me: a place infected with risk.

All time became my own time, regulated by a mysterious inner mechanism, superior to the clock. I understood time; clocks merely measured it. I would rise to leave one place and move to the next. I did not need to know that it was Tuesday or Thursday afternoon to detect his occupancy in the building. I could feel the changes Rourke rendered—in the halls, in the rooms, in a track that drew in the school like a belt. When I sensed that he had engaged with whatever it was that he had come to engage with, usually with drama class in the auditorium, I knew I could safely slip away. Weeks went by this way.

"I'm totally confused by this new schedule," Jack grumbled one day. He came into the yearbook office and hopped onto Marty's desk.

"You always seem to find me," I said.

"Yeah, well, I don't want to make a profession out of it," he complained. "What do you do in here, anyway?"

I shrugged. "Make lists. Sort."

"Sounds pressing," he said. "C'mon, let's go."

"A few more minutes."

He reached for Kate's flute case. "What's this doing here?"

"She asked me to take it home for her."

"Take it home for her?" Jack asked sarcastically. "Why, did she sprain her wrist?"

"She has drama. She didn't want to carry it there."

He opened the box. Inside was a peculiar bed of opaque sapphire fabric, that crushed velvety instrument case stuff. He peered inside the joints of the flute, then pieced it together obligingly, the way mothers brush newborn hair. When he blew into it, it cooed sweetly. Jack could play anything. He paused. "I was accepted at Berklee," he said.

Berklee was a music college like Juilliard, only in Boston. Jack could have gone to Juilliard with Dan, which would've been logical with me at NYU, but he refused to live at his parents'. "No contest," he'd said from the start. "I'd take up hairdressing to avoid living at home."

We both began to talk at once. "What did you say?" we asked, simultaneously also.

"Go ahead," I offered.

Jack insisted, "No, no. You first."

I'd forgotten what I'd been thinking, and he seemed to forget also. His leg started to swing, slow then fast, even and hard, like a carpenter's hammer, with the toe of his blue suede Puma kicking the metal garbage can and the heel bouncing against the side of the desk. In one jolt, he banished the canister into the defenseless center of the room. It pirouetted on its rim in the suspenseful manner of a rolling coin. "We're driving up this weekend," he said. "My old man hasn't been there yet."

So it was final. Jack would be in Boston and Kate in Montreal. I would be in Manhattan at NYU. None of us within walking distance of the others. One thing about friends is that they have to be within walking distance. That's why mothers with kids in parks and guys in the military and people who work in offices become friends even if they have nothing in common.

Jack started to speak, but his words were consumed by a change in pressure, a nearly inaudible sound that passed as it appeared, like the light nick of a record skipping. Rourke—engaged in class.

I raised my chin and cocked my head. "Let's go."

"Excellent," he said, somewhat surprised. "Cool."

Kate started to make me nauseous. One night I was reading in the living room, and she came in and answered the phone. She spoke so loudly that I thought I might get sick. When I tried to get up, I fell back down in a queasy cyclone of confusion. My stomach pitched. I lowered my head to my knees.

My mother's hand touched my neck. "Let's get you to bed."

She tucked the edges of my blanket around me, trimming the perimeter of my body. Probably I resembled one of those homicide outlines, marked indelibly in the position of my collapse. My mother sat. I was consoled by the depression made by her body in the mattress. I drew her hand between my palm and cheek. Maybe I would sleep. There was a chemical coming in, dripping in. I felt microscopic pulses of something, diminutive gates opening.

"When was the last time you ate?" she asked.

My eyes opened—how much time had passed? It seemed she'd been sitting only seconds, yet it had been long enough for me to dream a dream. Something about lost passports and missing luggage and foreign customs officials in a makeshift room set up on the tarmac.

"Be right back," my mother said. She took back her hand and left me, stepping into the kitchen. A ruthless dusk replaced her, hitting quick, like a prison cell door shutting.

Kate popped in, her hair rippling like a flag. "Sick again?" she said, and I felt another wave of nausea. I pulled the quilt over my face. "Well, excuse me!" she said.

I stopped sleeping almost altogether. The malignancy of night and lust and loneliness made me shift restlessly. All that I'd struggled to suppress during the day would erupt into the dark at night, flooding the silence of my room, and I would call for him. If I slept at all, I would find him behind closed eyes, like an object through bright water, a shivering richness. We would convene—*reconvene*—in some substitute district, at some alternate age, with him not speaking and me not speaking. In those false regions, at his false side, I found my first peace.

It was then that I began to write. Writing helps when you can't talk to your friends; it wasn't that my friends were untrustworthy, it's just that I would never discuss something that was hardly real as though it were really real. Often people do this, forcing friends into authenticating an imaginary life. I composed a list for myself. One column for all the times I'd seen him, another for each time I'd discussed him. Mom's accountant friend Nargis would have called this a *table*. I liked the idea of a table, of providing a frame for runaway numbers or dodgy ideas. I noted peripheral details such as conversation, clothes, and weather. I used a code for names, which was somewhat pointless since the list was in my room in my handwriting, and there were not enough characters in my life to outwit a motivated intruder. For Rourke's name, I substituted the letter *S*, which followed *R* in the alphabet. Kate was *B*, which preceded *C* for Catherine, and Jack was *G*, the last letter of Fleming.

> *Last night at the play S and I sat next to each other in the dark. He has eyes that are black. When you mix paint, black is like all color, but his black is no color. I spoke to him and my voice was strange. Later he kissed me through a window at Dan's. When he left I wanted to go with him, only I didn't, though there was a beautiful rain. At home G and I sat all night like we were waiting for something. He said my chapel would be trash by Monday. B & Den came in drunk at 1:30 A.M. and we made vanilla pudding. The pot bottom cooked off and there were Teflon flakes inside, but the four of us ate it anyway. Today B made me sick. She was on the phone between the matinee and evening performances, saying how "in love with Harrison" she is. Mom measured my temperature at one hundred two and put me to bed with tomato soup that tasted like scalding ketchup water. Mom's hand felt bony and mortal. It's still raining. It's been raining since Saturday. Even after five days it's a beautiful rain.*

Seventeen encounters in six months, and eleven conversations. I thought maybe I should burn the document, but I liked the compact and illegible blocks of handwriting. The dense and inky look of the pages seemed official and purposefully slanted, urgently conceived and textured to the touch, like the original Constitution.

22

Someone called my name from the pay phone area. "Hey, Eveline."

I froze, though I knew it could not possibly be Rourke. I went slowly to the alcove across the hall from the main office and peeked around the edge of the wall. Ray Trent was there, picking through a handful of change. He wore a black turtleneck and blue jeans, and his blond hair was feathered back. He looked like a handsome Tom Petty. Under his arm was a worn, liver-brown phone book held together by a rubber band. It seemed urbane, the need to make calls from school. I wondered was my number inside.

"Did I scare you?" He smiled. "I didn't mean to scare you."

"No, I just, no—you didn't."

"That's a nice sweater."

"Thanks, it's Kate's."

"I'm sure it's nicer on you," Ray said, then he held up one finger to me as he told the person he was calling to hang on. He covered the mouthpiece with his hand. "What are you doing Sunday?"

Jack would be in Boston with his dad. I said, "Nothing."

"Ever been to the St. Patrick's Day parade in Montauk?"

"No," I said. I hadn't.

"Great," he said. "I'll pick you up at nine."

At eight fifty-five on Sunday morning there was a knock, and my mom answered the door. Steam was rising from her coffee mug, fanning her face. "Hi, Ray," she said. They'd met before—the first time was when he took me to the junior prom.

"Happy St. Paddy's, Irene." Ray kissed her cheek.

My mother raised her cup. "I made coffee. Want some?"

"A quick cup, sure." He stepped into the house and followed Mom to the kitchen.

I had no idea why I'd said yes to the parade, except to say that the invitation had taken me by surprise. Though I knew Ray well, I felt nervous about widening some circle I didn't intend to widen. Now that I'd experienced being a woman to a man I was in love with, I'd become self-conscious about being a woman to the world in general. Of course, being female is always indelicate and extreme, like operating heavy machinery. Every woman knows the feeling of being a stack of roving flesh. Sometimes all you've accomplished by the end of the day is to have maneuvered your body through space without grave incident.

Ray felt my coat. "Have anything warmer? It's pretty cold out there."

My mother reached into the closet. "Take this, Eveline."

"Cool jacket!" Ray said.

"United States Navy," Mom informed him as I put it on. The coat was black and straight with a blunt collar and a zip pocket on the left breast. If Jack had been there, he would've told us to *Put that fucking thing away.*

The coat had belonged to Arlo Strickley, Powell's navy friend from Tennessee. Once during a stopover in Montauk, Arlo got leave and paid a visit, raging drunk. Jack and I were home alone. "Carolyn'd be just about your age now, Evie," Arlo cried when he saw me. Carolyn was his daughter.

"Where is she?" Jack demanded testily. He did not like drunks to cry. "Is she *dead?*"

"No," Arlo sobbed. "She's in Far Rockaway." He then launched into the maudlin story of his luckless life—three failed marriages, two episodes of financial ruin, the loss of his parents in a charter bus accident, and a sinus infection that had plagued him for years.

Jack tried to piece together elusive details. "Hold on, Arlo," he'd say peevishly, "are you talking about *Gloria* or *Louise?*" Then Jack would turn to me. "Are we back in '74? Didn't Louise run off with the Cuban chef?"

"Did I say Louise?" Arlo belched. "I meant to say *Lois.*"

When he had finished talking, Arlo stumbled to a stand and began to divest himself of his jacket, tearing his arms from the sleeves and turning them inside out as he did. "You hang on to this," he insisted, blindly passed it over, missing me entirely. "Carolyn won't want it."

It was no use explaining about the coat to Ray. One fact of life is that it's hard to explain old things to new people. "That coat will keep you warm," my mother assured me as Ray and I stepped into the frost-beaten yard. I paused to kiss her goodbye, and her fingers drifted uncertainly to the spot on her face where my lips had lain.

"Oh," she said, surprised. "Bye, Eveline."

Ray tapped the horn of his Mustang as he backed out. She waved through the hedges. "Your mom's pretty. She looks like the actress from *Dr. Zhivago*. Julie Christie."

I told him thanks. "Lots of people say that."

Ray's car was clean and lush: it rolled like mercury onto Route 27. I wondered if *lush* was right. Maybe *lush* meant *drunk*. If *lush* meant *drunk* and *lush* also meant *luxurious,* that would be strange. The Allman Brothers' *Eat a Peach* was playing and it was perfect for the wintry world streaking past. Driving in the morning is like having wings, like today is connected to yesterday.

> *Meanwhile I ain't wasting time no more*
> *'Cause time goes by like pouring rain and much faster things—*

The village of Montauk is largely horizontal: it has the appearance of being deflated, like something dropped from the sky. There was nothing pompous or false about it. As we descended into the town, I got the same feeling I always got when I visited, that there was no place in the world I would rather be.

"You like pancakes?" Ray asked.

"Not really."

"Eggs?"

"No, not eggs." Chickens inside.

He parked halfway up Main Street. "I know what you need," he said. "Coffee."

"Coffee would be good."

John's Pancake House was full of people and fogged up with sausagey smoke and smells. We unbuttoned our coats at the door, and several conversations lapsed. "Must be your hair," he whispered. We squished through to a table in the far corner, and I picked the seat facing the wall. Ray collected the dirty dishes and carried the pile to the counter, where he greeted someone he called "Captain."

"What do you want, Evie?" Ray called back to me.

"She'll have pancakes, of course," the captain said, as if Ray were missing the obvious. He tucked his neck into his chest and bellowed, "Stack of blueberry! And you, Raymond?"

"Sorry about that," Ray said when he sat. "I ordered eggs so you can have the toast."

"It's okay." I assured him. "Maybe they'll like me better if I eat the pancakes."

A harried waitress appeared over our tiny table. She wiped it roughly and deposited two worn mugs of coffee with cheap spoons sticking out. She withdrew a mass of napkins from her apron and plopped it between us.

"Busy, Deirdre?" Ray asked.

She blew out some air. "It's just me today. And town is packed for the parade."

"Guess you're buying tonight," Ray joked.

As she walked away, she said, "Don't hold your breath."

He tore the tops off of two sugars. I took the packets from his hand and tipped them at an angle above his cup. We watched the boxy grains cascade and disappear.

"When we walked in," Ray said, "it reminded me of that Bob Seger song 'Turn the Page.'"

"Yeah, me too." I leaned forward and began to sing.

When you walk into a restaurant, strung out from the road,
And you feel the eyes upon you, as you're shaking off the cold—

"You have a nice voice," he said.

"It's an easy song for me to sing." Jack always made me sing that song, even though he didn't like Bob Seger.

"You in chorus?" Ray asked.

"No. I hate that chorusy singing style."

"With the parts that are supposed to come together."

"But they never do."

"And the shitty songs they give you," Ray added heatedly. "When my sister was in chorus, she had to sing the theme from *Oklahoma!*"

"I quit with 'Eleanor Rigby.' "

" 'Eleanor Rigby,' " Ray said. "Jesus. It's depressing enough when the Beatles do it."

Deirdre was back with hot plates, and so Ray and I leaned back, the partly reluctant way you do when your food arrives and you've been leaning in having a good time. Being in Montauk was like being on vacation in America. Nothing looked the same as it did at home, though nothing was very different either, except there were no phones to answer, and you weren't sure where your next meal was coming from.

"I'm glad you came," he said, trading his toast for pancakes off my stack.

"Me too," I said. It was true, I was glad.

"It's called Massacre Valley." Ray pointed west over the top of the parade route. We had parked on a slight bluff behind the crowd. "It was the last battle site of the Montaukett Indians. Fort Hill is there to the right, and behind us is Montauk Manor."

Mike Reynolds tapped the keg that he'd been setting up in the back of his van. Two sleepy German shepherds were inside curled on scraps of shag carpet. After breakfast, we'd met Mike and the dogs at his grandmother's house near the golf course at Montauk Downs, where it would have been hard to argue that you were not in Ireland. Generally when people speak of natural beauty, they are referring on the one hand to livingness and on the other to masterlessness. In Montauk nature was not indifferent, nor was it servile. It was as if every blade of grass, every tree and hedge, was clinging to existence. Whether emboldened by the proximity of the ocean or by the blunt beginning of the nation, the landscape had a vitality that things elsewhere seemed to lack.

"Across the street is Fort Pond," Mike said, handing out cups of beer, "and above it—"

"America," I said, and together Mike and Ray said, "Right."

We toasted and stared out. I didn't really see America, or, for that matter, much of anything through the mist, but I squinted and imagined I did. I asked myself what would it be like to head blindly into it, blindly west? Would it be easy to vanish? I hadn't even begun, and yet the instinct was in me to start over.

There was the sound of motorcycles; three bikes drove up and stopped to our left. They made a row when they parked, like they were poised to race off the edge of the hill. Mike walked over, and Ray and I followed. It was nice, the way they got excited to see people. They introduced me to their friends—Ralph LaSusa, a fish counter for the National Marine Fisheries Service, and Will and Jane, from England, husband and wife pub owners who'd lost their place outside London in a fire.

"They took the insurance money and came here," Ray said. "We're going to open a bar together. My father's backing us."

Will was well-spoken despite his scrappy looks, and Jane was a tall, chesty blonde with a pie-shaped face. Ralph was lame. His left shoe had one of those shoe-shaped blocks on it.

"How about a ride, Eveline?" Will offered. "Before the parade kicks in." People with motorcycles always assume that everyone without one wants a ride. I didn't want to offend him, so I said sure. "Be a love, Janey, lend us a helmet." He snapped his fingers at her.

Jane cocked her head. "Lend a helmet? What, so she can ride with you?" Her leather jacket emphasized the curve of her hips and the gentle roll of her buckled belly.

"S'right," he responded.

"Do you think I'll allow you to nick up that face," she asked, referring to me, "or those legs?" She threw an arm around me. "*I'll* take her out." Jane thrust her hand at him, and Will surrendered his helmet with a grin, seeming to cherish her all the more for her minor victories.

"Suit yourself," he said. "More beer for me."

I followed Jane to her bike. It was shimmering crimson. "What kind is it?" I asked.

"A Ducati," she said. "It's the only thing I carried over from home— besides Will." Jane offered her own helmet to me and she kept her husband's, which I took to be a display of biker etiquette. The helmet wobbled on my head like a globe of ice cream on the tip of a pin. "Have any gloves? You'll need them."

"Just one," I said. I'd lost the other. Maybe at breakfast.

She started the engine with two powerful thrusts of her right leg.

"Don't be nervous. Will's reckless, but I'm not." I climbed on. "How about you?"

I looked to locate the foot pegs and I wrapped my arms around her waist. "About half."

"Half-reckless," she said, and laughed. "Yes, I can see that."

Jane flexed her wrist, and we took off. The drive off the hilltop made a slight corkscrew, and when we leaned into it, we went low, maybe forty-five degrees off the road. Angels must have seen us, drilling into the earth, wending our way, rotating conchoidally. We emerged along-side the parade, which was just beginning, then we cut behind the crowd, heading north toward the docks. She opened up the engine, and the bike accelerated in shifts, winding out to the full capacity of each gear. It felt good, like purging yourself of pent-up feelings. I didn't think I'd had pent-up feelings until I experienced the sensation of purging them. It's true what people say about the way bikes vibrate be-tween your legs. Jane's hip bones met the pale backs of my forearms, and my clenched hands burrowed into the pillow of her middle. I won-dered what it's like to love a woman. I wondered—*Is it nice, like this?*

She downshifted at the entrance to the wharf, and the air began to slacken. We coasted into a spot by the fishing boats. She hit the kick-stand, and I removed my helmet, reacquainting myself with the planet's peculiar serenity. It's humbling to travel by motorcycle, to suffer the cost of time travel, to earn the distance covered. We crossed over to the dock and began to walk.

Jane drew a vivid breath. It seemed like she might sing a song. "Will's good enough," she said. "Good enough."

I shoved my hands into my jeans pockets. They were frozen.

"Are you in love, Eveline?" she asked.

I said that I was.

"Not with Ray, though."

The ships squeaked resignedly against the wooden pier. "No, not with Ray."

"*I* am in love," she proclaimed, unperturbed by the aches and grunts of the boats. "With Martin. He lives in Devon, England." *Ma-tin,* she said, without the *R*. The first syllable sounded maternal, almost bored. The *tin* was crisp and close; it barely escaped her mouth. At the end of the dock, near Gosman's, she turned a quarter-turn to the right, east-ward. "I come to look," she said. "You understand, toward England."

Her resilience fell away as she conjured her loss, and the loss animated her. It was a delicacy she revealed, that she'd been longing to reveal. I wondered how she had recognized me as a pitiful equal. *Will's good enough,* she'd said, reminding me of the savage enormity of the world, the interminable length of life.

"And yours?" Jane asked. Her face was serene, immune to the stiff bite of the wind. "Where does he live?"

I did not think of Rourke as mine, though I supposed Martin was not Jane's, not really. I liked that she reserved for him the best of herself—her imagination. That's like a work of art. She slept with her husband, but, in giving her body, she gave nothing of consequence, not when secretly holding the rest in check. I wondered if Will knew but didn't care, and if she despised him for that, or if secretly he despised himself.

"I'm not really sure where he lives."

"Ah," she responded, seeming to absorb in full the meaning of pretty much everything. "It's not an easy one then, is it?"

I shook my head.

"Find out where he lives," Jane solemnly advised, "so you'll know which way to face when you lose him."

We returned to the weaselly and gaunt pitch of bagpipes. The notes shot into the air, the sound at once both solitary and allegiant. Will was wait-ing alone by his bike. He folded Jane into his arms, and I slipped off to find Ray and Mike, with the two dogs following me.

I stopped to look down at the parade. The avenue was packed: a long stream of green bodies and floats slithered past. I came alongside a man with a child on his shoulders, and both the boy and his father had waxy kelly clovers painted on their cheeks. I wondered why I felt no will to ex-press myself that way. Maybe it was because other than my parents, I have no known ancestors. In fact, my ancestry is just the span of my par-ents' lives plus the span of mine—about fifty years.

There was a piercing whistle, and I turned to see the dogs bolt back to the van, where Ray was waiting. Directly behind me, only feet from where I stood, was Rourke.

How mysterious to see him, mysterious and gothic—with the wind and the water, the bluff and the bagpipes. The space between us was precarious, like a ropeway between two landforms. Sixteen days had passed since I'd seen him last, since I'd begun to avoid him. And yet, by his eyes I could see that nothing had changed.

There was a car behind him, cherry-red; the paint looked new. A guy appeared from the periphery, wiry with a handsome haggard face. He looked like maybe he was from Brooklyn originally. He wore a green baseball shirt that read Katie O'T—O'Toole's, maybe. The last letters fell beneath his unzipped sweatshirt. He placed a bottle of Beck's in Rourke's left hand.

"Better watch out," he warned me. "Your boyfriend's gettin' nervous."

I thought he might have meant Ray. I wasn't sure. I said, "My name's Eveline."

He leaned back onto the hood of the car. "Yeah, I know who you are," he said. His accent was concentrated and compressed, and somehow familiar to me; I liked him instantly. He took a pull off his beer and minimized his eyes. He extended the bottle in my direction. I stepped forward, taking a mouthful and handing the bottle back.

"This is Rob," Rourke said unceremoniously, as though stating the obvious, the way a wildlife guide might say, *This is a lion.* He kicked at the sandy ground. "Cirillo."

"Hi," I said. "Where are you from? Brooklyn?"

"*Brooklyn,*" he said with a grimace. "Jersey." He flipped his chewing gum between his teeth. "I came out to see Harrison. He lives across the street." Rob turned to Rourke. "She doesn't know that?"

"Guess not," Rourke said.

"Oh," Rob said, "and I figured you were a smart girl."

"Guess you figured wrong," I said.

Rourke moved to the passenger side of the car, and he paused chillingly before stepping in. The door slammed shut.

"Guess I did," Rob said, with a pause. "Figure wrong."

Rourke's anger was new to me. It was not slow and corrosive like Jack's, but fast and volatile. I didn't know Rob well, but it was clear he understood Rourke's state of mind. I looked to him for an explanation, and he looked to me, withholding one. I was glad Rourke had him as a friend. I would've given anything for a friend like that.

Rob slipped from the hood, popping the latch of the driver's door. On the red fender was the chrome head of a running cougar. Rob rolled down his window before getting in, and he looked at me. "See you," he proposed with a cautious wink.

"See you," I said, walking off before they pulled out. It was nice of Rob to let me go first.

By the time we got to the Tattler, I'd lost the spirit of the day. "I'm sorry," I told Ray. "I think I'd better go home."

"Don't worry about it," Ray hollered over the noise of the bar. "I'm glad you came."

"Can you give me a ride to the train?"

"I'll drive you home," he insisted. "I'm totally sober."

"It's okay. The train goes right to my house."

In order to make the train, I had to say goodbye quickly. Everyone was disappointed to see me go, though no one seemed surprised. I wondered if I seemed like the type who would just head out.

"Don't be a stranger to Montauk," Mike said as I kissed his cheek.

Will patted my shoulder. "Take it easy there, Evie."

"Don't worry, Will," Ray said, "she'll take it easy *everywhere*."

Jane gave me a hug and whispered, "I saw you with your beau."

"Oh," I said, "not the skinny guy."

"I know, I'm not blind," she snapped amiably. "Remember—find out where he lives."

The Montauk train station is like a toy train depot. Alongside the station house and platform, there is a fanning spray of track lines where overflow cars get emptied, repaired, or cleaned. It was nearly dark. I wondered if Montauk got dark first in all of America because it's so far east.

"Almost," Ray said, checking his watch. "The New England coastline is farther east than we are. The most eastern spot is in Maine."

"Still," I said, "coming almost first in nightfall. And in dawn."

"That's right," he said. "You'll have to come back sometime when it's less chaotic."

By chaotic, I knew Ray was referring to Rourke, not to the parade. Though they hadn't spoken, it would have been impossible for him not to have noticed Rourke appearing out of no place. If he had been a drawing, he would have been a scribbled hive or an inky twister approaching at a treacherous incline from the corner of an otherwise unpopulated page.

The doors of the waiting train opened all down the line. A uniformed man emerged and toddled unsteadily toward us. He looked like Oz—not the Magnificent Oz at the end of the movie, but the roadside fortune-teller at the beginning.

"And what can I do for you young revelers?"

Ray put his hand on my shoulder. "How much for one passenger, to East Hampton?"

The little man peered at me. "Well, now, that depends on whether or not you're Irish."

Ray said, "Everyone's Irish on St. Patrick's Day!"

The conductor mounted a set of steps to the last car. "You've a fine head, son. No charge!" He scanned the empty platform and cried out, "All aboard!" Silence filled the wake. "Looks like you're the only passenger," the man said. "Either you're a rebel or you know something no one else does."

"A rebel," Ray said admiringly.

The trainman told Ray to check again. "This one has a secret."

Ray gave me a kiss. "See you tomorrow in calculus," he said.

"Okay," I said, climbing up. "Bye."

The train rocked back, readying itself, then it jolted westward. It was strange that I'd never said goodbye to Rourke, and yet, despite the odds against seeing him again, there was always another time. It was risky, like gambling. One day I would miscalculate, and there would be no next time. I looked through the scraped window at America's nearly first night sky, thinking, *Once, Jane boarded a plane bound for the States.*

Cars were parked askew all down my street, like porcupine needles, and from the head of the driveway, I could hear strains of "Danny Boy." Through the front window there was a sea of heads lit by candlelight, filtered by the gauze of smoke. I slipped past into the kitchen.

Lowie and her boyfriend, David Hill, were at the table, and Mom was getting a refill from a pitcher of beer for Lewis, her disabled friend. Lewis referred to himself as a crippled dwarf or a twisted midget. "Anything but a *small man*," he'd say. "Small is relative."

When they saw me, they all shouted, *"Evie!"*

Lowie was first to kiss me. "Kate just called." Kate was in Montreal; her brother's baby had arrived—a boy named Jean-Claude. For months the plan was that I would fly up with her, but when the time came, I couldn't leave. I don't know, just, Rourke, the nearness of him. "I didn't realize the baby was a C-section," Lowie said. "Isn't that a shame?"

"You can't deliver every baby yourself, Low," Mom said.

"It was just seven pounds, Irene. It's abuse of women by the medical establishment."

"And the insurance providers," Lewis added as he climbed up the chair onto the seat.

"Let me get you the phone book, Lewis," Mom suggested.

"The chair's fine, Irene. Thank you."

There was food on the counter, edible food. "Let me fix something for you, Eveline," David said. He was a cook at the American Hotel in Sag Harbor. Occasionally, on a night off, he and Lowie would stop by with the sort of food I never saw, not even on holidays—roasted lamb with rosemary sauce and Yukon gold potatoes au gratin and brussels sprouts sautéed in fresh ginger. "I'd cook for you here, Evie," he would say, as we'd unload pans and trays from his car, "but your mother's got no knives, no pots, no silverware, and no ingredients. The few plates she has that aren't chipped are covered in cigarette ash, and half the time she's surrounded by a starving multitude. I'm not a rich man!"

David handed me a paper plate, and I sat. Lowie asked how the parade was.

"Montauk was okay," I said. "I went on a motorcycle ride."

"Who with?" my mother wanted to know.

"A girl I met. Jane."

"Jane *what*? What was her last name?"

I shrugged. "I didn't ask."

"That wasn't smart," Lewis said sternly. "What if you got into an accident?"

Lowie said, "Who would've given the hospital your blood type?"

"*I* don't even know her blood type," my mother admitted.

"How can you not know her blood type?" Lowie reprimanded. "You're her *mother*."

In the sanctity of my room, I lay in bed, and the fluid in my horizontal body compressed. I felt half-full, like the tide in me was lowering. I found a sheet of good paper and I drew a tornado. The hard part of drawing a tornado is the frenzy of contradictory motion—lightness and leadenness, a thing there and not there, heaving and still, cruel and oscillating.

There was music coming from the living room—slow clapping, a harmonica, a guitar. I opened my door. Through the crowd, I saw my mother on the Eskimo dogsled chair she'd gotten at the dump. She was low to the ground, elbows on knees, harmonica in her hands. Jack was next to her on the enamel blue hearth, playing guitar. The room was silent except for her humming and the squeak of Jack's fingers moving along the strings. He began to sing "Jesus Met the Woman at the Well," which, according to Jack, had been recorded by Canadian folksingers Ian and Sylvia, and also by Peter, Paul and Mary.

> *He said, woman, woman, you've got five husbands*
> *And the one you have now, he's not your own.*

Soon Mom joined in—

> *She said, this man, this man, he must be a prophet*
> *He done told me everything I've ever done.*

At the end came applause, and my mother hugged Jack, and he smiled. He loved her, everyone did, and she loved him with a special love she reserved for things so flawed. Jack especially admired the way she played harmonica. "The only thing my mother can play," he'd say, "is bridge." Right before his Outward Bound trip that summer, my mother loaned him her best harmonica, the kind with a button on the side so you can change keys.

Jack revolved it reverently in his hands. "I can't take this, Rene."

"Sure you can," she said. "I insist."

Jack thanked her and inquired as to whether she knew that Ben Franklin had invented an instrument called an *armonica,* an upright glass harmonica. Jack adored Ben Franklin.

"Yes, Jack," my mother said, "Franklin was a wizard."

Jack climbed in bed next to me, both of us facing the wall. He reached back to take my hand and place it over his waist. I was happy he was back from Boston. I'd missed him. Just the uncomplicated way things could be.

"I want to take off with you," he suggested. "I want to go where they'll never find us. Italy, maybe. We'll hang out in olive groves and drink Chianti."

It would not be good with Jack in Italy. I said, "How about someplace north?"

He lifted his head. "North? Where?"

"Someplace with ghosts. Someplace white and cold. Norway."

"Norway has no ghosts," he said dejectedly, going back down.

"Yes, it does. They're silvery and tall. They have capes with shredded edges like icicles."

We stayed that way for hours, drawing off love and affection from one to the other, my face nuzzling into his baby fine hair, his back pressing into my chest. If I am left with the regret of having been so blinded by the new fierceness of life in me that I neglected to see him—substantially lighter, wasted and debased following a weekend with his father at a college, I am grateful that I have in my heart that solitary piece of nearness, the warmth of his body, his clean, firm hands holding mine, calming me, comforting me, passing off his remaining shreds of courage. Passing off generously, like he knew what lay ahead for me. I moved on in my mind that night; I received the imprint of his release.

23

Debris from Sunday night was still all over the house when I got back from school—leprechaun hats and empty whiskey bottles, and on the kitchen counter the remainder of David's ham was covered in flies. I didn't think flies came in the cold. I thought they were warmish bugs. One by one I killed them, then I cleaned the kitchen, as quietly as possible. Typically I longed for noise to drown out my thoughts, but for once I wanted quiet. I was trying to *listen*. The unusual thing about quiet is that when you seek it, it's difficult to attain. With each next sound extinguished, another rises up, finer and more entrapping, until you arrive right back in the infinite attitude of your own riotous mind.

I turned down the lights and slipped into the living room, where I swept the cold hearth, taking up the silent ash that had once been wood, but before that trees, and before that other things, living things, moss and leaves and hares. My eyes stared into the soot, the way eyes sometimes do, numb when you are nothing to no one. The room was so silent I could hear the falling snow.

After cleaning, I showered—slowly, mindfully, and with gratitude. When I turned the knobs to stop the sound of the water, the sound stopped, and I remember feeling grateful for the simplicity of that enterprise.

There was sound from downstairs, though no one was around but me—not Kate, not my mother, not Powell or Jack. I stepped out of the tub and moved to the top of the landing, where I could hear the throaty crack of a new fire. I leaned against the door and grabbed my jeans, wrenching them up around my wet hips. I pulled on a T-shirt and started down the stairs. As I walked, I went slow, then slower, because, just because. It was as if I'd never felt the plush of the carpet, the pocked plaster walls, the wormy surface of the banister.

Rourke was at the hearth, his hand against the mantel, his head hanging. He seemed quiet also. The fire jumped irritably, carping and stuttering before hurling itself into an empire of nothingness—if ever you have dreamt of flying at night, that is what you have dreamt. When he turned his eyes assessed me, as if by accident, as if he had not expected me, though of course he had. I shoved my shirt into my jeans and zipped them. He stepped right. I went left, taking his spot at the hearth. I shook the water from my hair. I noticed that his mouth appeared swollen, as if stung by bees. I longed to kiss it, to be kissed by it.

He reached to pry something from his back pocket, and he tossed it onto the coffee table. It was my glove, the one I'd lost in Montauk. Though he said nothing, I understood. He'd seen me at breakfast with Ray. It was strange, the way the glove hit the table with a knock instead of a slap. I wondered was it frozen.

Immediately, he left, and the door closed after him with a punitive click. I looked at the glove. It lay very still, palm up, fingers serene, as though caught in a gesture of divine meditation. Not in any gesture, but in *my* gesture because the glove possessed the shape of my hand. Though it was compelling to think of myself in terms of such things as absence and presence, me and not me, I was drawn more to themes of Rourke. I could not help but view the glove as his, insofar as it had fallen into his custody, insofar as in his trust it had achieved dynamic new meaning. I thought he was telling me he could not be provoked. Asking me not to provoke him. It was a confession of sorts.

I turned down the lights and moved to the window, letting the fire languish. I passed through the quiet night with quiet thoughts. I left off thinking that something must have hurt him very much for him to have traveled so far.

24

Jack was kissing me by the barn, and I was wondering about all this stuff, such as school and Kate and where sod is farmed and how to spell *ankh* and how I'd never seen a single episode of *Saturday Night Live* or *Eight Is Enough*. Our lips pressed together lifelessly. I wondered about the lifeless quality to Jack's kisses. It occurred to me that they'd always been that way. Kissing him was like kissing a heel of bread, if in fact there was bread that tasted like Blistex.

Kate ran down to the base of the stairs, her hair in a series of elaborate pigtails, and she was wearing silk pajamas. She pressed her hands onto the screen door, talking through to us. "Coco just called. There's a party tonight at Mark Ashby's house."

"And there are rings around Saturn," Jack said. "That doesn't mean we're going."

As usual, we got high, and for a change, we played dice, the three of us sitting on the kitchen floor, listening to *Let's Cha Cha with Puente* with the volume up to ten. "What's your favorite?" Jack shouted as he jiggled the dice. " 'Cha Cha Fiesta,' 'Lindo Cha Cha,' or 'Let's Cha Cha'?"

" 'Cha Cha Mungo,' " Kate yelled back. "Hurry up and roll."

This made them laugh, and they laughed and laughed, and, as they did, I could see into their heads. I could see Kate's teeth and Jack's teeth, base to base archways, like propped-open coon traps. Teeth ought to be clandestine, like spies meeting down alleys. Jack stuck his head into the refrigerator because he became asthmatic, and Kate smacked the oven door repeatedly with the back of her head saying "Ouch" every time. Her silk shirt caught the light the way pearls do, the way pearls in light look like milk on fire.

When Jack peed, he did not close the door to the bathroom all the way. His pee made a bright bursting sound before the toilet flush concealed it. I switched from the floor up to a chair, and with a pen I found I played a dumb game, which was taking one finger and skittering it around the center of the pen, making a windmill on the table. Then I drew on the bottom of my sneaker, trailing the rubber passageways until I got frustrated. Kate just stayed on the floor, pinching and sucking a wooly strand of hair. Her shoulders sloped downward. With her right hand she scraped at the tile grout with a giant safety pin. It bothered me; everything bothered me. It was like I was standing in the center of a cube that was collapsing—*phoom, phoom, phoom.* I was feeling three sides down—one more coming.

Jack came out. I said, "I'm going for a walk."

He said, "Where to?"

I said, "The tracks."

They followed me to the living room. Jack offered me his Dartmouth sweatshirt that Elizabeth had given to him. It was pine-green. It slid past my head and hips to my thighs. Kate knelt for a moment to pet the cat, then started up the stairs.

"See you, Kate," I said, wishing there was some way to make her happy, knowing there was not, wondering if she felt the same. Yes, I thought, she *did* feel the same, and *had* felt the same, only she'd felt it sooner. I supposed an end was as simple as contradictory wishes. Baby birds abandon the only world known to them: the treasure is flight.

The door creaked when I opened it, and the cat bolted. I plunged down the porch steps and was rushed by night. It carried me the way wind carries a hat. I looked back to Jack. He was gripping the banister and paused at the bottom step. The pallid light from the landing upstairs broke through the bars of the stair rails, slitting his features.

"Good night, Katie," I heard him say, then he followed.

Our house was shielded from the railroad by a massive barrier of gnarled vines on the south side of the driveway. When the train went past, the beacons of light would flood the property before fading away. At the end of the driveway on the other side of Osborne Lane, there is a street-lamp; its light made a spacious pool at the base. Jack had already reached the outer rim of that light and was turning onto the tracks. I wondered was he moving very fast, or was I going very slow. One of us was out of time.

I kept my eye on him as I walked the length of rail between us. When I sat, he sat with me. My hands stroked the rail. It was blistered from the load of the train, and yet improved by the blisters, by the inference of endurance. I asked Jack where the rails run to and why.

He reached to tie his shoelace. His jaw was lightly bearded and red, and it drew his concave cheeks down. His hair spilled forward. "They run the train's distance. They go where the train needs them."

His voice was near, so near that it seemed to originate in my own head, and it reminded me—mostly that I had to be reminded. And me, did I remind him, or anyone, of anything? I felt sad. "No," I said, "they run their own distance. Separate from the train. It's the thing they do. They have their own purpose."

He poked at the tar with a stick, his chest low by his feet.

"Jack," I said, regretting the sound of my voice. Its sheerness, its vicinity. He did not lift his head but rotated it obligingly, leaning to rest his chin on the back of my hand. His face came into the ring of lamplight. His eyes were there—a very conspicuous blue.

There was a flicker. Jack did not move exactly, but his figure conveyed new poise. He turned stable as he shut down against me, and the self-protection completed him, leaving me to wonder if I'd ever really seen him, known him. I was made mindful of my sacrifice. I imagined the places he would go, the people he would meet. I thought of his music, of me listening anonymously and in vain for my residence in his songs, of his offering to others the words that had once passed from his lips to my ears. I thought back on the dreams we'd shared, and on how our lives had not been actual—we'd never once felt entitled or precious about the fact of ourselves. We'd never once taken for granted the smallness of our place, or the magnitude of our liberty. Though it could be a consolation to no one, I would regret the loss of him for the rest of my life. Almost as painful as the loss would be the inevitable public impression that I'd loved him less than I'd been loved by him. This was not so; I'd loved him truly.

"Sometimes I feel myself falling," I confessed, "then I see it, as if the falling thing is not me anymore. When I reach to grab myself, my hands catch nothing."

He frowned. "*You'll* never have to worry about being caught, Eveline," he said. "It's all there for you, the whole world, waiting."

I looked past his eyes, to the stars. The millions of stars, joined into one avenue that draped over his head like a cowl. A terrible premonition seized me; I began to cry.

"Did you ever think how pointless it is to cherish the stars," he said, taking up the object of my focus, "when they've all extinguished by the time the light reaches us?"

"Jack," I said. "Don't."

He continued anyway. "Love is exactly like starlight. Just a signal, a flare, diminishing in brilliance from the point of origin, dead by the time you receive it."

"I'm sorry, I'm so sorry."

"Don't be sorry. I fucked up," he said lifelessly. "It was my fault, not yours."

I lowered my head between my knees, and for a long time we sat. We did not hurry, in case it was to be one of the last times sitting. When he stood, I stood as well, and at the street we parted. He walked to the corner, his figure bouncing down and away like a ball shooting out of reach.

I stumbled down the driveway as if drugged, kicking gravel, wasting time. I lifted my ear to the sky and listened for the wail of the train. Sometimes you can hear it, even if it's not there—sonorous and low, riveting and heroic, dejected and alone.

I began to spin, rolling along the row of privet that divided the front and side lawns from the driveway. At the farthest end, I spun off, singing the words to a song I'd never heard, something about *trees, trees, trees,* and *lights out.* When I came to a stop, there was the sound of the train— mournful and clear. I wished I knew enough about music to name the note. In it I heard a calling, a cry to life.

Rourke was there, standing and waiting. He said, "Hi."

I swayed slightly, saying hi. "I didn't see your car." I glanced back. It was definitely there—on the street near the top of the driveway. I could see the white body in pieces through the leaves. It looked like a horse, waiting knowingly, chewing grass. Twigs were on my sweatshirt—*Jack's* sweatshirt. I brushed them off. It was funny, I hadn't thought of Rourke all night. Actually, that wasn't true; I'd thought of him constantly. I wondered if he was still angry. He didn't seem to be. He was just leaning against the side of the barn near the forsythia. Forsythia is first to bloom, first to vanish. Every year it flowers without my noticing. Every year I vow to catch it next time. I moved closer and pulled at some petals.

"I just got back from Jersey," he said. "I was driving by."

If there was something to say, I could not think of it. I might have asked about driving past my house when it wasn't on his way, or how long he'd been in Jersey and when he was going back, or how much older was he than I, and did he love me too.

"Forsythia," I said, opening my hands to show the yellow. "It always blooms without me." I nudged the torn flowers in my hand. I was sorry for what I'd done. I could not refasten the petals to the stem, I could only cast them off, and I did, watching them spin down like lemony propellers. It was true that I was still a little high. You know that leaning kind of reasoning, like a glass on one side and all the contents tipped against an edge.

I was walking, he was also walking, and sometimes our hands would touch. We stopped near the back door to my bedroom. His face was close to mine, and his eyes. To stand before him was to stand before a body of natural consequence, an orchid, a stallion, something maverick and elemental, something too exquisite to be sustainable and so you feel strange pain. I tore a splinter of cedar from a shingle. I wondered if he knew about Jack and me breaking up. Probably—he seemed to know everything. If he were normal and I were normal, I might have solicited his sympathetic regard and allowed myself to be persuaded by it. But it was not tenderness I wanted, and it was not tenderness he would have expressed, only self-interest. Maybe all tenderness is self-interest anyway.

He looked at me like he was comparing me to surrounding things, to the trees, to the dark, like he was seeing me as he would have had me seen, as he would have had me see myself, and then he smiled, coldly, professionally, expressing himself in his heat and his prime, making my grief over losing Jack into the nothing it surely was.

I twisted the doorknob and entered my room, half-hoping he would follow. *Half*-hoping because no matter what I wanted for me, I wanted more for him. I wanted him to be superior to my need. We stood on opposing sides of the threshold. Behind my back, my little room, velvety and moonlit, a jewel box—at the end of the driveway, his car, grazing.

I closed my door. I rested my forehead against it. A long time passed before I heard his footsteps and the muffled thump of his car door and the churn of the engine, and, when finally he had gone, I spent the remainder of my night in cardinal desolation, comforted only by the knowledge that his was spent in the same way.

25

When I entered the classroom, Mr. Shepard was discussing the upcoming Advanced Placement exam, explaining what was the lowest possible score we could get and still earn college credit for the course, which didn't say much for his teaching. I was late, but I cut past him, not even caring. Nico cleared his throat and Stephen Auchard raised one eyebrow.

I turned myself to face the window. Past the cinder-block walls was the courtyard garden. No one ever used it. Denny once tried to organize a garden club. He had the idea to grow produce for the cafeteria and flowers for the art class to draw. Science students could study mulching, he said, and shop students could make benches. Denny hoped it would be a model for public schools across America.

"They refused to look at the blueprints," he told Mom and me after his presentation to the school board. "They said there's no money in the budget for maintenance. And I said, 'Well, that's the whole point of a club—*free maintenance*.'" He shrugged. "I didn't even get to mention the poetry teas."

It seemed the most the garden would ever be was some kind of teenage mind control thing, some remedy for the psychosis of confinement, like a mural or an indoor waterfall. If necessary, it would distract us from the fact that we were not being trained or inspired, we were being held in custody until it could be proven to at least 65 percent of some dubious national standard that our ingenuity had been assimilated into the tastes of our comatose generation. Then you're ready for college. People say, *You have to go to college. This is America. In Russia, they don't even have tampons.* And yet, how often had I heard my mother complain, "I'm not teaching Shakespeare. I'm teaching phonics."

The real truth behind college for every American is that high school graduates would cripple the job market and drain social services if their dependency was not extended.

We'd just found out that Nico had been accepted to the University of Vermont.

"Cool," Jack said when he heard the news. "Is he going to major in Physical Molestation?"

"Actually, he's on the payroll," Denny said. "They're going to study him in bio lab."

In America, college is not simply a privilege, it is an industry. It begins early in high school, where there are people on staff whose job it is to feed the machine. Sexless, pink-faced men like Mr. McGintee help students *evaluate qualities* and *calculate options.* Ladies with long dry hair and "degrees-in-progress," like Lydia Kilty, let you know whether or not you have *the right stuff.*

At seminars in creepy, carpeted guidance rooms, cultish recruitment officers draw looping arrows on glossy easels with bizarre-smelling Vis-à-Vis markers, while you sit in a cataleptic stupor, tracing dust pyramids in the air and making planes out of pamphlets until the sales pitch slithers to a suspicious semi-halt. You are roused in the midst of a damp handshake with some guy named Stu from Ithaca, and you wonder, "Good God, have I just been initiated?"

If you take time off after high school, you are thought to be a pariah. Former friends ignore you on the streets, and their parents freak out like you are a dope addict. Parents cannot really be blamed for their paranoia, when all they ever hear about from the time their kids are in kindergarten are tests and essays, scores and tours, deadlines and fees. At money management assemblies, they are reassured that what they cannot pro-

vide through savings and second mortgages, the government will generously supplement with low-interest loans.

"What a racket," my father would say while sorting through the
brochures that flooded the mailbox. "Jimmy the Onion never had it so
good."

One thing they make sure to teach in high school is how to drive.
Well-meaning people, such as Mr. O'Donnell, the librarian, believe that
driver's education contributes to public safety. What they fail to see is that
in order to accommodate additional drivers, families need *more* automo-
biles and *more* insurance. Teaching and insuring teens is not a social service, it's good business—otherwise companies wouldn't bother to do it,
no matter how many lives might be saved. The problem is, when you give
cars to people with no responsibilities, no destinations, and no privacy,
they will most likely use them for things other than driving. Two weeks
after Troy had won the school's coveted Driving Ace Award, he and Jack
got so stoned off homegrown pot in their shampoo bottle bong that Troy
drove his Vista Cruiser home from Indian Wells beach in reverse.

Lots of programs make sense in theory but go awry in practice. It's
similar to when town planners bring in one species to lower the popula-
tion of another, and then the town is overrun by the predator. Sometimes
you interfere with nature, and its ferocity emerges in new ways, in perverse extremes of attitude or number. Sometimes it happens quickly;
other times, you can't see the effects until it's too late. Sometimes you
can't help but feel you are part of a giant out-of-control science experiment.

Dad said that when they introduced rabbits to Australia, the rabbits
had no natural predators, so they evolved into a crazy kind of super-
rabbit. They decided to poison the rabbits, only the poison was the
wrong poison, and all the rabbits died an exceptionally cruel death. "I
can't even think about it," he said, and he shuddered.

If you ask, "Who are *they?*" he'll say, "*They.* Those college bastards."
According to my mom, "*They* are the ones who killed Kennedy." Jack
would say, "*They* are the pharmaceutical companies."

Mr. Shepard finished the lesson. I heard notebooks flapping shut. Too
bad about the courtyard. The grass looked nice. I would have liked to
spend some time outside.

———

Miss Panetta sighed hard. "This is basic science, Miss Palumbo." She repeated the question, enunciating peevishly. "The function of water in photosynthesis is—*what?*"

Arms shot up, sleeves lightly whipping.

"Thank you, everyone, but Miss Palumbo is going to impress us with the truth."

Mike Stern took advantage of the delay to talk to Billy Martinson. "We went to Tick Pete's last night." Tick Pete sold beer from the back of a shut-up diner in Amagansett. He slept behind the counter on a cot and watched TV, living off Slim Jims and Trix, Jack claimed, though Dan swore he once saw Pete eating Chinese takeout. "We still have half a case left," Mike told Billy. "Meet us at Sammi's Beach before Donkey Basketball."

Jodie Palumbo stirred in her chair, her chin glued to the palm of one hand, the other hand playing lethargically with her practice AP Bio exam. She selected a random multiple choice answer and began reading lamely. "B? To absorb light energy?"

Ms. Panetta shuffled the test papers and shot a glance at the clock. She seemed upset. Sometimes you could really get to feeling bad for the teachers. "I—think—we—should—call—it—a—day."

My locker closed, and all down the hall they slammed shut in succession, clacking like dominoes. Inside I'd found three bundles of paper. The first was from Denny.

> *Guess what. This is so unbelievably stupid you will die. Today in chemistry The Walrus was substitute and Dave Meese and Nico took one of Stephen Auchard's chess pieces, a horse, and they hand-drilled a hole in its face and attached the bottom of the horse onto a gas hose and lit its mouth and fire shot out and burned Marty Koch's legal pad with all his yearbook notes. Marty threatened to sue and Principal Laughlin had to come down. All I kept thinking was, I am so glad Evie is not here to see this. You would have been disgusted. Here's a drawing—*

The second was from Kate.

> *Do not show this to anyone under penalty of death. I thought*
> *essay was spelled S.A. I kept thinking what is an S.A.? Do you*
> *still refuse to come to Donkey Basketball? Michelle and Tim are*
> *going so I can go with them if it's okay. I think it's funny to see*
> *teachers on donkeys. Mr. Myers keeps scratching his back*
> *against the edge of the door. So gross. Don't forget the spring*
> *concert Saturday. C.C. P.S. News bulletin: Kip and Paul Z.?!?*
> *P.P.S. Check out Lisa T.'s elephant ankles!!!!*

The third was from Jack. The third I couldn't open.

I skipped lunch to finish a lab report for Ms. Panetta, and while I was in the bio room, I heard a piano start to play Cole Porter's "I Get a Kick Out of You." I knew it was Dan because no one else in school was good enough to play it except Jack, and Dan played differently from Jack. Jack steadied the keys and smoothed them, hunching fretfully as though they might bark or bite or turn on him. Dan played with exuberance.

I crossed the hall to the choral studio. Dan brightened when he saw me. He slid on the bench as his right hand tapped out melodies and his left tested rhythms, one song leading to another—"The Shadow of Your Smile" to "Rhapsody in Blue" to "Stormy Weather" to "Summertime." I sat on the lowermost carpeted step of the choral risers, and then I lay down, still clutching my dirty scalpel. It had been submerged in formaldehyde; it had poked through bobbing corpses to locate the aurora pink tissue of a fetal pig, my very own pig. I knew which pig was mine because around the right eye was a gray wheel, cracked here and there at the outer edge like a pineapple ring. As Dan played, I was thinking that jazz works the way the mind does—something occurs to you and you think it, or, in the case of jazz, you play it.

People who passed peered in at me, as though I were kaleidoscopic, as though I were at the end of a long tube but could not materialize. I closed my eyes and started lapsing, receding like a discrete entity into its constitutional whole, like a gem to its mine, a drop to its sea. I wondered

if Dan had heard the news from Jack about our breakup. It was nice of
him to play for me regardless. Would I miss Dan, I wondered, or just the
time we'd shared, his connection to the original meaning of me? I would
miss him, I thought. Definitely, I would miss him.

Gym was last. I considered skipping, but frankly I didn't want to be anywhere else. Wherever I was depressed me, but wherever I was not depressed me also, sometimes even more. In the locker room girls laughed
as they changed. Girls have a giggling way of bending forward when they
laugh. When boys laugh they present their chests proudly to the city of
God.

My lock would not open. I yanked the round base but nothing happened. I tried the combination again, concentrating on the spinning
black dial. I started to black out so I pressed my forehead into the damp
bones of my left hand and with the right, I covered my nose and mouth
to block the stench of the metal locker. It smelled like blood. Why did
blood smell like metal? I could hear the bending laughter of the girls and
the squeaks of sneakers slapping the ground and the flatulent squirts
from near-empty bottles of body lotion. Later there would be water—
toilets retching, sinks spewing. I could feel myself weave back, and back,
into a writhing meadow of sound, with all that I saw and all that I could
not see vanishing equally, though that could not have been so. Probably
things had remained in place.

Caroline Boylan was above me, offering her hand. She was standing
in the center of a group of girls; I'd obviously fainted again. Caroline
wasn't wearing a shirt or bra, so I couldn't help but notice that her breasts
were strange, sort of like cabinet knobs. In eleventh grade, the television
show *The $10,000 Pyramid* had chosen her to play in its national teen
tournament, making her into a lesser sort of celebrity. As I lay there, the
memory of her on television returned to me, her giving clues to her partner from Appleton, Wisconsin, for "Things That Have Sauce." Biting
her lower lip, nodding, leaning forward, like a hood ornament, saying,
Pizza, spaghetti, spaghetti, pizza, pizza, pizza.

"Thanks," I said, coming up to sit. "I'm all right."

The crowd disbanded in the sulky way crowds disband, like they haven't quite gotten their money's worth. I made my way onto the bench beneath the wall of lockers and lowered my head and squeezed the muscles in my thighs to send blood back up, because that was what Dr. Scott said to do whenever I felt faint. My parents kept sending me to him for tests, but everything kept being normal. He would just say that I was blessed with unusually low blood pressure, which should not be a problem "for anyone who actually eats and sleeps."

"You okay?" Someone must have told Coach because it was her voice I heard, and when I lifted my head, it was the myriad surfaces of her body that came into complex focus through a mist of puckered stars. Her dimpled knees and distended belly were known to me and I was comforted by the sight of them. Perhaps there was nothing wrong with her; perhaps she was just straightforward about the inescapable fact of herself. "Need the nurse?" she asked.

The nurse would just give me a place to rest. But it's impossible to rest when everything smells like the sweet of Band-Aids, and when the kidney pan she puts near your mouth is covered in those crazy black finger smudges, and there are depressing posters about alcohol abuse and car wrecks. You just sit and wait for an appropriate amount of time to pass before you can leave, hoping nobody you know comes in for some really gross and graphic problem. If they do, the nurse puts up a screen that you can totally see through. Before you leave, you have to thank her like she actually did something to heal you.

"Can I just stay with you?" I asked.

Coach gazed widely, blankly. She nodded once, and her oaky brown button eyes folded back into the confectionery flab of her face. "Let's go out to the tennis courts." She did not help me up, but she did get me a cup of cold water and a bag of salted cashews from her desk while I pulled on my shorts and sneakers. Together we crossed the deserted gymnasium, which was a queer sort of distinction.

The cyclone fence around the courts was cloaked in green tarps with cutout flaps—I sat and rested and waited for things to end, things such as the day and the tired way I felt. The sun beat against my lids, creating geometry underneath, wandering and upraised like swimming braille. The tennis balls smacked the rackets and hit the spongy ground to create a succession of hollow pops.

In the cavern of my room, after Rourke had left the night before, I was stricken with an incompetent longing, a clumsy physical loneliness. I was not clever with that lonely feeling, with its drift and wicked magnitude. I caressed my own body, seeking heat, seeking relief and restitution, seeking rewards withheld; and in the end I felt I had transgressed. It was not me I wanted but him, and that was a sorrowful offense, sorrowful because I was an animal and he was an animal, yet we lay separately in the gaping obscurity of one anonymous night on earth.

I did not change from my gym shorts or bother to go in to get my books. After the final bell rang, I just walked from the court, cutting through the side yard to the street. I was about to head home when I noticed the GTO parked in the front lot, and without even thinking I turned back to the building. I quickly navigated the crammed halls by minimizing myself—everyone else had grown so much bigger during the day that if you just stayed low and tight, you could cut through pretty easily.

In the crowded lobby, by the guidance office, Rourke was talking to Mr. McGintee. They shook hands amiably, saying "Good luck" and "Take care," and when McGintee slipped into the auditorium where janitors were setting up for the spring concert, Rourke cut directly through the pack to meet me where I stood.

He said hi. I said hi. He seemed younger, or maybe just tired like me. There were lines beneath his eyes. "How are you?" he asked. I got the feeling he was referring to the previous night with Jack.

"I'm okay," I said, and together we walked, him behind me. I was aware of my thighs in my shorts, the bareness of them, the way I knew he was looking.

"I have to pick up a check," he said. "I'll meet you at the car."

I sat on the entrance steps and watched everyone leave. *The* car, he'd said, not *my* car. As the last yellow bus took the bend going from the school lot to Long Lane, a set of shoes appeared on the sidewalk before me—caramel-colored loafers with tassels. It was Mr. Shepard, finishing bus duty.

"*Miss* Auerbach," he said definitively, as though he'd come upon me in the thick of the jungle.

I blocked the sun from my eyes and looked up at him.

He smiled tightly, and his chin gathered into his neck in that skepti-cal way that older men have, which they use on you when no one else is looking, and which is frankly just a patronizing manner of flirting. Skep-ticism suggests they know more than you do, and a superior intelligence is the only seductive power that remains to them at older ages, or so they think. Lowie once dated an alligator handler from the Florida Keys who was very handsome at forty-five. And firemen are always sexy, no matter how old, as are men who work at sea, like Powell. In general older men can be attractive as long as they use their accumulated experience to bully things other than you, such as reptiles, fire, and the ocean.

"Late to come, late to leave," Mr. Shepard remarked as he started for the lobby. "Your timing is off today." I actually thought my timing had been good. At the main entrance, he encountered Rourke, who was on his way out. Rourke drew in his chest and swept his arm like an awning to hold the door from inside. Shepard looked from Rourke to me and from me to Rourke—figuring, figuring darkly.

Rourke jogged down the steps. "Let's go."

In the car, we sat, and the leather was warm. Traces of him were everywhere—the confidential fragrance that had incubated beneath the roof, the microscopic shed of skin, the fingerprints on the vinyl dash. I felt an uneasy resolution—like everything was finally right, and yet noth-ing was very right at all. He had his last check; I had six more weeks of school. When I considered his keys, the slick conviction of his hand as it forced them into the ignition, I felt envious of the vehicle, of its promi-nence in his life. I squeezed into the gap between the bucket seat and the door, and the car moved from its spot. As he swerved left from the lot onto the main driveway, the car leaned against its two right wheels, against my side, and I heard a giant swish of wind—my door, flying open.

Tentacles of air pulled at my chest, suctioning me, summoning me. I felt wind on my face, and my knees pulling right as if inside there were pieces of metal and outside there were magnets. I began to slide, and I thought, *I am going to die. I am going to plunge through the air and smash down and spill out across the asphalt.* For some reason I thought of my fetal pig from bio lab—its starch-white face, the sock on its left rear leg.

It was stiff and narrow like a wooden pull toy. I should have objected to dissecting it.

The whole thing took long, so long, seconds ticking and unticking, space transforming telescopically between the status of my body and that of the ground, until at last it came, not the fall, but Rourke's hand, curling like a whip around my ribs. I actually thought to break his grip, to continue my fall—I'd been so tired lately. But he would never relent. Though I didn't know if he loved me, I knew that he would not allow himself to be defeated in action. My right arm reached left, my fist clutched his sleeve, the car straightened, and my door slammed shut.

I collapsed in a ball against him, and he held me, shifting gears over the bridge of my ribs, his forearm jerking up and back, his hand returning each time to my body. Other than that, Rourke did not move, and I did not move, but we were breathing, both of us, our chests rising, falling, rising. We made our way slowly through East Hampton Village and eventually around to my street, at which point each muscle of his hand eased as if coming loose one at a time, and my body peeled itself from the electrifying shelter of his.

The screen door shot open like a slap. Kate leapt from the front porch and skipped across the slate walkway. She leaned on the passenger window, looking in. "This is a funny surprise," she said with an inquisitive frown.

I popped the door, shoving her a little and slipping past; I didn't want her to change the way I felt. I proceeded to the garage entrance and into my bedroom, where I stripped before the mirror and examined my naked body to see what it was that I felt, when what I felt was ever mortal, ever viable and real. I looked like a girl, and I looked like a woman, and in my eyes was a consecrated knowledge.

Suddenly there were so many things to think about. On the one hand, it had been very mechanical: a door opened, and I nearly fell. On the other, I'd confessed a willingness to die, and he'd confessed an unwillingness to let me. And his instant concern elicited in me instant trust. I'd never felt trust that way before.

The near miss provided a reminder about the fugitive constitution of life. Perhaps death is always so proximate; perhaps life and its loss are two opposing states—life as suspension, death as the reverse, as a dissolution of structure. Reverend Olcott says hell is simply a place outside the society of God, and that God is what you conceive Him to be. Maybe hell is an absence of presence, a wall down—loneliness. That was the part Jack went out of his way to confront—the ease of loneliness, each time telling himself that an end could be simple and near, simpler and nearer than living and its requisite effort, when no one hears the things you say, when everyone has their own ideas of you, when everything you want is impossible to achieve, and every day you're dying anyhow. I thought I understood. If I'd melted through the divide, if I'd passed from one side to the other, it would have been better to leave Rourke then, at the exact moment his body had confessed a need for my body, than to prevail and endure the inevitable anguish of the inevitable loss of him.

Jack had felt the same, only for me. On the tracks the night before, he'd said, *I fucked up*. By that he meant that he'd waited too long, that our time had gone by, that all that had been good was gone, that he should have had the courage to end it first. *Love is exactly like starlight,* he'd said. By that he meant that love has *its* time, which is not necessarily *your* time. You have to be big, I think, or old or brave or rich or mad, or something other than what I knew myself and Jack to be, to make love's time your own.

The front door slammed and I grabbed a blanket, covering myself. Kate ran into my room, breathless, saying something about Harrison and Friday night, something about going out, two friends in town.

"Will you come?" she said. "He said to ask."

Beneath the blanket my fingers jammed the welt on my rib cage that he'd made when he grabbed my side in the car. The pain radiated in an imperfect circle. I liked that he had caused it.

"He's outside waiting," Kate urged. "He leaves for good on Monday."

She didn't want me to go because she wanted my company. She didn't want me to go because he'd asked. She wanted me to go because she was afraid to go alone. I thought she had reason to be afraid. It would have frightened me too, to be her, to be beautiful but deaf and blind to incentive, to have the world venture no farther than my immaculate façade.

In her words I heard him speak. I heard him remind me that I am alive, and therefore, forgivable. That I cannot despise myself for my failings when it is those failings that make me desirable. That love has its time. That nature does not favor those who would resist its hour and its course.

"Okay," I said. "I'll go."

26

The row of budding wildflowers ran like tiny tombstones alongside the barn. Delphiniums and phlox will come first, then irises and astilbes. Tiger lilies are always last. It's usually not until July that they ascend and promptly collapse, their overlong necks buckling beneath the heft of their blossoms. There's a lesson in that, I'm not sure what, but I liked tiger lilies least.

I wiped my hands on my jeans and regarded my painting. The canvas was five inches square, depicting celery-green shoots with darjeeling-purple tips, little *V*s that had lost the logic of perspective. *V* as a shape is piercing and effective—the head of an arrow, the edge of a blade, a plow, a beak, the tip of a plant that creaks up through soil, the cooperative formation of migratory birds and schools of diligent fish.

My mother walked over, coffee cup in hand. "Eveline, that's beautiful," she said. "Is it for me?"

"Sure," I said. "You can have it if you want."

"What a gorgeous day!" she exclaimed, as though it were the first she'd ever lived. She breathed deeply. At thirty-eight, her skin was clear and firm and her body was slender. She'd had the good fortune of exacting revenge on the standards of beauty popular during her adolescence. In the 1950s, she was considered scrawny, but in the sixties and seventies, she was an ideal, perfect for fashions that did not work on shapelier women—wide link belts and paisley A-line dresses and bodysuits with twin bear-ear cutouts around the abdomen. Even poverty became her. It enhanced the atmosphere of liberty and luck you felt in her company. When she entered a room, people stood, recalling like a crisis all the hopes they had.

It *was* a gorgeous day; all the colors had come alive. The sky was candy-orange, the color of those spongy Easter treats—not Duck Peeps, but the melony ones called Circus Peanuts that taste like bananas. Why are they shaped like peanuts when they taste like bananas, and what did the circus have to do with it? It was a strange set of falsifications. Jack and I placed some on the tracks once to see if they would widen, but instead they disappeared, possibly sticking to the train wheels. "Well," Jack said that day as we watched the last car vanish around the bend, "I hope at least we slowed the fucker down."

My mother sat alongside me, and she took a sip from her mug. "Can you believe I was married at your age?" she asked out of nowhere. Her observation was largely scientific, making the fact that I was the product of that union into something only slightly more than extraneous. "You'll have so much fun at the Talkhouse tonight," she continued. "Kate's excitement is infectious. Don't forget to say hi to Kevin Fitzgerald, if he's tending bar."

I pressed my palms into my eyes. If I pressed hard, maybe I could erase myself.

"What's wrong?" she asked uncomfortably. "Is it Jack?"

"Jack?" I said, surprised. "Kate maybe, but not Jack."

"*Kate?*" She seemed surprised too. "What about Kate?"

"I don't know. We're just—not clicking."

"What do you mean *not clicking?*"

"It's like, we're going at different speeds," I said, striving for clarity, though to hear myself, I didn't sound very clear. "We're, like, not close anymore, you know, *spatially.*" I amended that. "Not spatially—I don't know." I gestured with my hands. "She's not moving."

Unfortunately, my mother thought she understood. Things were usually better between us when she didn't have the faintest idea what I was talking about. "The first thing you need to do," she said, "is to get over the idea of growth as measurable by speed and distance."

As she spoke, I began to gather the paintbrushes that I'd strewn on the grass. It was difficult to see them in the twilight, and I felt bad about that, about them maybe feeling lost.

"Linearity and progress are completely male notions," she counseled. "Evolution is not necessarily linear. You can't think in terms of you girls having been shot from the same pistol. You come from entirely different guns. One has bullets, the other has—"

"A flag," I said.

"Exactly," she said. "A flag."

I counted slowly to ten, then stood. She stood also, and she hugged me, whistling as she returned to the house. She seemed satisfied with herself for having been there for me.

Kate's door would not open. "Watch the ironing board!" she called.

I squeaked through the gap and discovered her testing shoes of various heights. The light from a candle flirted against her, throwing her shadow upon the wall. I sat for a while and watched as she dressed. I wondered if being loyal meant being honest or being kind. If there had been a cohesive truth to tell Kate about Rourke and me, it would have felt cruel to relate it, and yet it didn't feel right to say nothing either. It was hard to see her employ her best strategies to win—something. She wasn't even sure what.

"What do you think," she inquired. "Collar up or collar down?"

"Down," I replied. "I guess."

"You *guess,* or you're *sure?*"

"I'm sure."

"Sure *down,* or sure *up?*"

Neither was good, actually. "Up."

"Ugh," she said, ripping off the shirt. "What is *wrong?*"

Maybe something *was* wrong, since my mother had asked the same question. The change in our friendship didn't seem to bother Kate in the least. She didn't seem to care that we were forging ahead blind and dumb, relying on habit in the absence of devotion. Maybe such breaches are obligatory in the biological sense. Maybe it would not do for girls to evolve beyond pubescent attachments, to exceed basic constancy.

"Can you at least try to be friendly tonight?" Kate was saying.

I said yes, that I would try, though I was so convinced of the meaninglessness of my own will in relation to the night that I wasn't even planning on participating actively. Free will is an illusion. People like to believe their choices are singular and circumspect, when in fact they are completely trifling. Despite the odds, we had all strayed into the night—Kate and me and Rourke and however many others—our fates assigned, our histories synchronized.

"Why don't you go take some aspirin?" Kate said. "That will make you feel better."

Alongside the oven there was a cabinet where the liquor was kept. I didn't realize it was my destination until I found myself filling a coffee mug with brown stuff—Jim Beam, whatever, whatever. Bourbon, whiskey, rye. Label, proof. I didn't comprehend any of it. All I knew for certain was that no one would notice the loss of alcohol, except Jack, and he wouldn't be coming by so much anymore. It was amusing, actually, the idea of his visiting sometime in the distant future and right away going, "Hey, who polished off all the whiskey?" Jack was amusing, unlike most everyone else.

My arm reached to the shelf where the medicine and spices were kept. The unopened spices had been a wedding present to my parents, which made the jars and the contents older than me. I did not like to touch them: it was as if they measured me or my life. I plucked the aspirin bottle from a field of caps, popped the lid, and shook out two pills, thinking how medicine and spices are similar since both are concentrates. Savory, cumin, marjoram, and mace are totally weird substances that probably even the greatest chefs don't know how to use.

When I passed back through the living room, Mom was talking on the telephone to Lowie. "Yeah, but then," Mom said, "I had to rewrite the entire curriculum."

I drank some whiskey and listened. My mother is talented on the phone. She always sounds connected. I never even feel that connected in person. I wondered if the connectedness she finds there is real or imaginary. *There.* People say "there" as though it means something. Where is

There? Maybe There is where *They* live. I swallowed the aspirin with a giant gulp of liquor. Aspirin or *aspirins*. I wasn't sure.

In my closet I had just one dress. I'd bought it at a thrift shop in the city on Greenwich Avenue near Charles Street. I grabbed the dress, refilled my mug with whiskey, and went back upstairs to get showered, this time avoiding Kate. I did not want to be influenced by her monstrous good cheer. Not monstrous. What was the word my mother had used? *Infectious*.

I locked the bathroom door and turned the radio loud, because I kept hearing Kate through the door, bouncing around like a loose balloon. *Shuffle-shuffle-skid-shuffle*. I sat on the sink edge, taking several swigs. Pieces were repositioning inside, jockeying about, here and there. I figured I might as well finish the mug of whiskey because, well, *just because*. The liquor started to move down easily, going into my throat instead of through my sinuses. I wiped my chin with the back of my hand, and I hiccupped, once, then twice. I said, "Shit!" since *shit* is the thing to say when you get the hiccups. To get rid of them, I employed a method invented by my aunt.

"Close your eyes," Lowie would coach, "point at your forehead, and gradually move in to touch a pretend spot. Breathe." Because she was a midwife, Lowie was always coaching you as though you were in the middle of giving birth, whether you were backing out of the driveway or making an omelet. "You can do it. Just focus. Breathe. *Breathe*."

"The principle," she would explain academically after she had rid you of the offending problem, "is to concentrate electrical energy above the neck, thereby depriving the diaphragm of the means required to spasm."

I hiccupped again and closed my eyes. My finger journeyed to a hypothetical spot, which my mind made into a pinwheel, lightly spinning. My forehead sensed the erotic nearness of my finger. *Erotic* because there was fighting back. As soon as I thought to double-check, the hiccups were gone. Too bad Kate wasn't with me. If Kate were there, she'd be sitting on the edge of the tub and she'd say something funny, and we'd laugh. When I tried to think of the funny thing Kate might say, my mind drew a blank. When I tried to think of a funny thing Kate had ever said, my mind still drew a blank.

Alcohol crept through my veins, pooling in areas. It was hard to distinguish what I was feeling, something vague but clear, crooked but straight, like a beach blanket in the wind. I wondered why no one ever listed patience as characteristic of wild animals; I felt patient, the wild animal way. In the medicine cabinet mirror I looked for the woman Rourke saw. If I looked with his eyes, I could see her. It was good to trust his vision since I could not trust anyone else's. He had no preconception of me, no idea at all beyond the fact that we fit. Rourke would never call me feral. I was a package in his eyes, the best and the worst I could be— a cowgirl, a jaguar, a soul to cleave.

I found a lipstick the color of brown shoes and applied some, then I leaned into the mirror, close and closer, observing my green eyes through half-closed lids. I didn't like the oblong way I looked if you were kissing me. Jack had neglected ever to mention that. *Jack,* I thought, with an awful sorrow. This sorrow grieved me, and grief made me thirsty. I raised my mug. "To Jack," I said, "my very special regret."

"Here's David Essex and 'Rock On,' " the deejay said, and when the song started, it gushed from the radio onto the floor and over to my feet, boiling up my legs like liquid rubber. I began to move, dancing, peaceful, unburdened.

Hey kids, rock and roll. Rock on! Ooh, my soul!

I inched a pair of stockings over my legs. Then I put on shoes, last the dress. The dress had cost three dollars. It was plain and tight and short— no longer than a skirted bathing suit. It had long sleeves and a crew collar and darts at the breasts. The fabric was a complicated green—not trees, not grass—turtles possibly. I reached back and tugged the zipper up in portions. The girl in the thrift shop had said that the dress was "a de la Renta, for a fact, circa '66 or '73, and for a fact it was worn to Studio 54 by Bianca Jagger." I did not bother to ask the girl how she had managed to establish such facts, since, if the facts were not facts but fictions, they were affable fictions with the effect of contributing positively to my state of mind and undoubtedly to hers. When I tried it on, she peeked into the bathroom. Her pumpkin hair formed a cone on her head, like one of those Halloween corn candies. I wondered if she could receive signals. "I'll be your mirror," she said, as there was none. Softly adding, "Oh, my, it's celestial."

From the top of the stairs I heard voices. I wondered how long they'd been waiting—I had no sense of public time. I walked down the stairs slowly. I wished I'd been born to a better staircase, to a sophisticated flight of marble with a wrought iron handrail and a quarter turn at the bottom. I wanted to step into a portrait-lined receiving hall with black and white square floor tile, a gilded mirror, a grandfather clock, and a table adorned by a single wax-sealed envelope.

As I turned the corner into the kitchen, I saw Rourke and he saw me. There was a change in his face. It did not liven or lift so much as it latched squarely on. By the rigor in his eyes, he tried to guide me. I labored to sustain my way.

Sitting at the table was Rourke's friend from the parade, the one who looked like a bookie or a short-order cook, and another guy, and Kate, who was dressed all in yellow. The kitchen was crowded with those big bodies in it.

Kate said to me, "This is Rob and this is Mark. These guys all went to UCLA together."

Mark was well-dressed and collegiate, and Rob was the same as the first time—shifty, like he was looking for a fight. Rob didn't mention to Kate that we'd met before; neither did I.

"I'm sorry," Mark said, and he stood. "I didn't catch your name."

"That's because no one said it," I replied. "I'm Eveline."

Rourke was leaning on the counter, leaning massively, his waist hard and flat, like a safe place to encamp. I wanted to feel him. I *needed* to feel him. It was frustrating that his body belonged to him and what belonged to him was not mine. I set my cup on the peak of undone dishes, then turned away from the sink, facing out. The guys at the table looked away, flinching a little, like I was swinging a sharp object. My arm brushed Rourke's sleeve, and I was mindful of the impact, of the way the spectacle of us reduced the room to silence.

I bit my tongue in a fine line between my front teeth. "So, are we going?" I felt ready, loose in the limbs, tight in the trunk. If I were to play ball right then, I would not miss a catch.

"Impatient?" Rourke said, speaking quietly.

"Hardly," I answered, thinking of big cats. "Just the opposite."

"We were ripping down Bruckner Boulevard at four in the morning," Rob said as I slid over to the place behind the driver's seat. "We passed some cops, but they didn't budge. Ten seconds later, Bobby G. cracks up. He was doing sixty-something when he hit. He flew up like a friggin' rag doll."

"Harrison told me his spine is destroyed," Mark said.

"Legs too. One leg. Yeah, he got busted up pretty bad."

"I'll take the middle," Mark offered as Rob began to climb in back.

Rob ignored him, continuing over, coming next to me. "Nah," he said. "I like the hump."

Behind us, Rourke paused on the driveway—I knew because my body was keeping his body in range, tracking it. "Better put that in here," I heard him say to Kate. The car bounced as he opened the trunk, put her pocketbook in, then shut it again.

"Anything you need to put in the trunk, Countess?" Rob asked me.

"Yeah," I said, "a corpse."

"That's funny," he said, elbowing me. "A corpse."

Mark squeezed in next to Rob, and Kate won by default the seat next to Rourke up front. There were sounds—a door, another door, a cassette, the men talking, the engine starting, the mincing snitch of leather against vinyl. Rourke hit the tape deck; Pink Floyd's "Wish You Were Here" came on. In the rearview mirror, Rourke's reflection consulted with mine. Our images floated like we were co-conspirators passing in a crowd, like we were acting on plan. I closed my eyes to preserve the image—it was like saving a fallen leaf.

On the way to Amagansett, Mark said he couldn't remember the last time he'd had a tetanus shot. "I practically get one a year," Rob stated, adding something about a flooring nail that recently went through his fist.

"You're an idiot," Mark said. "You only need one like every ten years."

He shifted, and Rob shifted in turn, moving closer to me. Mark leaned to see me. "Got enough room?"

I said I did. I felt bad about having so many people embroiled in the business of my destiny. I wondered if they felt bad too, or if they felt at all peculiar, like parts or materials.

Rob folded a piece of gum into his mouth, then flicked the pack in my direction. I took a stick. The oblique flare of the streetlights plunged rhythmically across his jaw. I could see him chewing, sucking his cheek to his molars. His eyes were obscured by the blind of the roof. "What's up with that Porsche?" he asked Mark.

"Working on it," Mark said with a sigh, plowing his fingers through his hair. "I should have it by the end of this month." He was not necessarily being untruthful, he just seemed it. Some people are unfortunate that way.

"Good, because it's been, like, three years already."

Next came talk of Syd Barrett of the original Pink Floyd going crazy from too much LSD, Mark said, but Rob said no, it was from photo-epilepsy brought on by stage light displays. Then they moved on to a '68 Challenger being sold by a guy from Jersey named Pat, and also various engine options—a 426 hemi, a 440 with a six-pack, a 383 magnum. It's strange that cars and guns and liquor share terminology. Somehow it's indicative of something. According to Rob, the two biggest sports upsets were the Mets against Baltimore in the '69 series and something to do with Sonny Liston. This was followed by a discussion of classic fights— Marciano KO's Louis, Robinson beats Basilio, Jersey Joe gives bad count, Frazier wins Olympic Gold in '64, Rumble in the Jungle, Thrilla in Manila—and some obscure questions Rob had for Rourke about Sam Langford's blindness and Stanley Ketchel's murder. I stared out the window, letting everything that was said turn otherworldly, like a foreign language. I leaned onto Rob's shoulder, and he leaned back, giving me a little more. It was nice, him knowing I needed a little more.

The Stephen Talkhouse is a roadside bar named after a Montaukett Indian who walked all over Long Island. According to legend, Talkhouse could walk to Brooklyn and back in a day.

"I believe his name was Pharaoh," Powell told us one time when we were fishing for fluke in Shinnecock Bay. Actually, *Powell* was fishing; Jack and Denny and I were tying knots and spearing sand eels, or just hanging quietly over the side, trying to spot the large fluke Powell called "doormats." "Or maybe Faro, with an *F,*" he speculated as he cut the engine, and we drifted into the shallows. Powell liked *skinny water.* He said it gave fish the chance to ambush the bait.

"Not much was recorded back then, and what *was* recorded was not *carefully* recorded, seeing as how we were experts in the language of record but they weren't. The only time we adopted native words and ways was when it came time to buy *their* land. A couple blankets and a dog for thousands of acres. We liked those terms fine."

Powell cast out, hipping smoothly up into one shoulder, the hook touching down like the soft cluck of a tongue. In his wallet was an Indian Status card. Though he has Nanticoke blood on his mother's side, on his father's side he's white. He's the first to admit that the crimes of his paternal ancestors afforded him advantages for which many of his mother's ancestors are ineligible. "Plumbing, for starters," he'll say.

The Nanticokes were tidewater people who believed all things possess a unique spirit. The Nanticokes *are.* They still exist. I wrote about the tribe for seventh-grade social studies. I'd interviewed Powell's sister Esme on the phone from her home in Salamanca, New York. She's married to Jim, an Iroquois. Coach Peters, who was teaching history that year, gave me a B for improper sourcing—which he spelled *sorecing.* When my mother saw the graded paper, she called a meeting.

"The purpose of the assignment, *Mrs.* Ruane," said Mrs. Schmidt, the middle-school principal, "was to encourage encyclopedia use."

"The purpose of an encyclopedia, *Ms.* Schmidt," my mother said, "is to assist those who have limited access to reputable information. Encyclopedias are hugely reductive. Their scope is confined to the interests of the publisher and its constituents. They should be used as supplemental, not primary references, which is exactly how my daughter has used them—that is, *pursuant to point of view.*" In her most serious tone, my mother added, "I want it to be a matter of record that I consider that gym teacher to be as qualified to teach academics as he would consider *me* to teach football. If you intend to promote white supremacy, I suggest that you go out and find some whites who are, in fact, supreme."

The next day Coach Peters sent a note saying that my grade on the paper had been changed to an A. Mom sent a note back. *Your lesson has proved invaluable. Let the B stand.*

Two bouncers sat slumped like vultures on the wooden ramp that led to the Talkhouse. I wondered if I would have a problem getting in—Kate was eighteen, but I had six months to go. Rob placed his hand on my lower back and escorted me up the ramp. Rourke came next, then Kate and Mark, lagging behind. "What are the damages?" Rob asked, spreading his wallet.

"Five bucks a head," one guy said. The lump in his neck journeyed unevenly. The second bouncer leaned to get a better view of me. Rob threw a shoulder to block him.

"Relax, man," the guy told Rob, and then he said, "Hey, Scorpio!"

I peered over Rob's shoulder.

"It's me." He swatted his chest. "Biff."

"Oh," I said. The hitchhiker. "Hi."

He seemed glad to see me, which was nice. No one ever seemed that glad to see me. Three other people squeezed past, paid the cover, and went in. Sounds of the bar swelled out in a dull ruff, then night silence again.

"I didn't recognize you," he said. "You know, with the legs."

"How's rugby?"

"I just got back from San Diego. I played all winter. Where's your friend?"

I pointed behind me, calling Kate. "Oh, my God!" she said. "Biff! I can't believe it."

Rob returned to his wallet. Biff waved his hand, and the second guy opened the door to motion us through. Biff winked at me. "See you later."

Inside was woodsy and damp with the moldy stench of saturated alcohol. We entered in single file, inching through a yeasty shaft of bodies wedged between the bar and a partition separating the tables. I kept moving in, my body caressing unfamiliar bodies, the curves of me conforming to the curves of them. I waved to Mom's friend Kevin Fitzgerald, who used to swing me in the yard when I was little. He waved back from behind the bar, blowing kisses, making a big deal over seeing me.

Rob muttered into the back of my ear, "Nice going, Countess."

"Don't thank me. Kate's the friendly one."

"She might be friendly," he said, as we paused to let someone with drinks pass, "but she'd never get five through the door."

I turned back to Rourke. He was behind Rob, just a body away. When my eyes found his, he looked away. I understood. I didn't like getting in for free. It appeared as though the hitchhiker was repaying a favor. Probably he had not done so with foresight or malice, but by letting us in that way he had staked a piece of me, and the piece he'd staked already belonged to the men I'd come with—or so *they* thought. Biff had been to my house to visit my mother, obliging him to protect me—or so *he* thought. The free entry was not a favor but a signal, a warning, a message between men. It's tiring, keeping track of them—the posturing and the egos, the private worlds of their private minds, the strengths so directly compensating for weaknesses. In public they feign leniency and affect simplicity, but in private they want you to know how very damaged they are.

My mood was lapsing. I'd lost the sensation of being connected to Rourke, and that loss dispossessed me of motive and prudence. I forgot who I was and what I was doing and what was the point of everything anyhow. I had the idea of walking through to the rear exit and then out. It would have been funny to go without telling him, except for the part about no car. I felt unhinged: if things couldn't get better, I wanted to make them worse. I felt myself become acquainted with my capacity for extremes. I had the idea I could be completed by risk. I began to like the bodies touching mine.

Rob handed me a beer over my shoulder and gestured with his chin to a vacant booth on the far side of the partition. Together we cut around, and when I inched across the seat on my knees to the farthest end, he followed. Then came Kate, and last Rourke on the end opposite me. Mark swung a chair to the outside of the table and he straddled it. Rob arranged the clutter left by previous occupants, building a meticulous mountain of plastic, paper, and glass.

"So, Monday's D-day," I heard Mark say to Rourke. "*Departure* day."

Rourke said, "Yeah, Monday's the day." I wondered if Rourke was happy when he talked or not. He didn't seem happy.

"Too bad. We could have all been out here together this summer."

"We still *can* be, Mark," Rob said. "We'll just stay at your parents' house—for free."

Mark laughed. "Anytime you need a place, you have one."

I was peeling the foil from the neck of my beer bottle. Rob nudged me. "You know what they say about people who do that?"

"What's that?" I asked.

"That they're sexually frustrated." He winked and took a swig of his own drink.

"I haven't found that to be true," I told him. "But I'll take your word for it."

"*Ha!*" Mark said. "She got you!"

Kate whispered to Rourke. He inclined his head obligingly. A slender lock of hair fell by his face, skimming with caution the lashes of his right eye. With her he seemed easy, approachable—a boy, a brother, a son, a friend. It pained me to see him that way. I could not evoke that in him. I smiled despite my epic disgust, because it was impossible not to admire the handsome look of him. Kate said he was nice. Maybe that was true, maybe to her and to all the world he was.

Hips moved across the dance floor exactly at the height of my eyes. The hips belonged to normal people having normal fun. I wished I were one of those people. I wished I'd left the building when we'd first arrived, when I'd had the chance. I wished there was a way to leave but stay. That's the appeal of drinking and drugs—leaving but staying. It was good that I didn't have anything more than a beer. Sometimes you see some girl slooped up against a wall, half-unconscious. Basically she felt the way I did, only she'd gotten her hands on liquor and drugs. I looked around for Mick Jagger. He'd been to the Talkhouse several times. That would be good, to see Mick Jagger—you know, like, not a totally wasted night.

Mark stood. "I'm gonna take a walk," he said. "Be right back."

The table felt different without him, uneven, as if missing a critical component. I didn't know Mark well enough to name the missing part, but I suspected I'd lost an ally.

I stood, saying I was going to take a walk too.

Rob shifted. His instinct was to accompany me, but he had Rourke to consider. Rob would never disappear with me, especially if it meant leaving Kate and Rourke alone together. They could all get up, but Rob would never give up a good table.

Mark was at the jukebox. I walked toward him and looked down into the meadow of luminous tags.

"I knew you'd come," he said.

I believed him, though I didn't even know I'd come. Having exercised my freedom, my freedom felt good.

"Pick some songs," he suggested.

My finger floated above the glass. "M-Five. A-Seven."

He inserted the quarters, pushed the buttons, then faced out, watching the dancers, not really watching. "That's quite a dress," he said, his lips hardly moving.

"It cost three dollars," I confided, still reading the tags.

"That works out to about a dollar an inch," he said, looking at me for just as long as he thought I could bear. There was a slippery quality to him, like if you set down an object it would slide. "Next time I see you, I hope you'll be wearing a two dollar dress."

He was no more than a foot away, in the near darkness. I looked away.

"He can't see," Mark said, cutting straight through to the place I was. "Don't worry."

"I'm not worried."

"Oh, you *want* him to see."

Actually, I didn't want that.

"If you're uncomfortable," Mark said, "let's go back."

I didn't want to go back. I wanted to go farther into the crowd; I wanted to embed myself. There was a post between the jukebox and the bathrooms, and I moved to it. I leaned back and the wood pushed between my shoulder blades. Mark propped his arm on the post alongside my neck, facing me, making a barricade between me and all the rest. I liked the wall he made.

The jukebox finished a song, then whirred to a new start. It was the Four Tops.

> *Bernadette. People are searching for—*
> *the kind of love that we possessed.*
> *Some go on searchin' their whole life through*
> *And never find the love I've found in you.*

"Do you know the lead singer's name?"

"Levi Stubbs," Mark said matter-of-factly.

I reached for his sleeve. "Listen," I said, adding his name, "Mark. I love this part. The false ending. The way he screams her name. *Bern— a—dette.*"

Mark nodded as we listened.

"I'll never be loved like that."

He shook his drink, looking into it. "I doubt that."

I wondered why he was there. There must have been a reason. I asked, "Why are you here?"

"In East Hampton? My parents have a house here."

"That's not what I mean."

"You mean—tonight."

"Yes, tonight."

"To see you," he said. "To find you." That's when I first saw the eyes. They were gunmetal gray and speckled like the underside of certain fish. His hair was straight and sand colored, long around his face. I eased the glass from his hands and swallowed some of what was inside, coughing up a little cranberry. "Would you like one?" he asked.

"No, thank you," I told him. "I'll just share yours."

The song changed and he drew me to the center of the blackened floor. Before pulling me in, he said something, I wasn't sure what, but I smiled and held him, laying my head on his shoulder, grateful that he had stepped up and given me shelter when I needed it. Being in a bar is somewhat like being homeless if you cannot be with your friends. You wander and linger and land wherever there's room and heat, sometimes getting in trouble, sometimes not.

Tell me somethin' good, tell me that you love me, yeah.

Mark was good, better than Denny. Maybe it just felt better to dance with Mark than with Denny. He wrapped one hand around my waist, bracing my back, and our hips affixed, bone to pelvic bone.

Your problem is you ain't been loved like you should
What I've got to give will sure enough do you good.

We oscillated, bending and rising in controlled, compact arcs, our torsos hanging slightly back. My left arm dangled loosely, my right arm held him. There was resistance in my abdomen and a tautness in my legs, and our shadows trespassed long against the tables, transfixing the crowd, restoring Rourke's customarily heavy countenance. I was glad. It hadn't been good to see him happy, knowing for certain he was not.

By the time we returned, Kate had moved into Rourke's seat and Rob had slid into mine. Rourke had taken Mark's chair and turned it away from the dance floor. Rob was bending over a plate, halfway finished with a burger. There was the broad smell of onions.

Mark gestured to the dance floor. "Kate?"

She waved her hand dismissively. "*Please,* no."

"Thank God," Mark said, pretending to collapse back against Kate, nudging her farther in.

"What's wrong? Need a *bed*?" Rob said derisively, not meaning Mark, but me and Mark.

Mark ignored the comment. He reached across for Rob's plate, lifted the bun, and said, "Brave man." I could see that Mark was not the type of person who would waste time with innuendo and sarcasm or who would let anything work at cross-purposes to determination. I'd never thought of sarcasm as a waste of time, but it's true—it is. And Mark was fast. He'd reached me quickly, quicker than anyone. I hadn't even noticed him coming.

I set my left knee on the edge of the banquette, and my right thigh pressed into the rim of the table near where Rourke was seated. The waitress delivered a drink to Mark, which he pushed in my direction, and I pulled out a few pieces of ice to eat. My stomach swelled in tandem with my chest. Rourke leaned back in his chair and stared into the middle distance. I thought I knew what he felt. He felt what I'd felt the day I'd seen him in the gym. The time his legs came on either side of me and the lip of his underwear was visible beneath his shorts. When he was wet and there was the smell of sweat. I'd wanted to leave, but I couldn't move.

"You know," Kate said in a sarcastic voice, "there's a hole in your stockings."

Everyone looked. I raised the hem to see—the dress didn't have far to go. Kate was right, though I didn't like the way she'd called attention to me. I took the stirrer from Mark's glass and inserted it into the hole, jerking my wrist. The crossed edge of the stick scratched my leg, and the nylon shredded like a limited web.

Kate said, "Christ, Evie!" and Mark said, "Shit," and Rob muttered something I couldn't hear.

Rourke managed to express gross disinterest. I didn't care what he thought or what anyone thought. If he wanted to leave me free, he could not exactly object to the applications of my freedom. I was no more than the shameless thing they'd made of me—a woman, a fiend, my own lowest form. There was a trippingness to it that I liked, a capability I'd been missing. Why remain polite but powerless, in love but a beggar?

"You take the front," Rourke directed Mark over the roof of the car, then he propped the driver's seat forward and took my arm, guiding me in behind him.

"Hey, no complaints from me," Mark said. "It's cramped as hell back there."

He sped back through the fog. We were going so fast I wondered if we would crash and disintegrate into mist. Kate was on the other side of Rob, sleeping lightly. Rob remained serious and silent, staring ahead through the windshield from his place in the back as though he might have to grab the wheel and take over at any instant. Mark just kept chatting professionally with Rourke, who kept replying, professionally as well.

I wished it was winter. In winter you can scrape ice on the inside of your window. I wanted to scrape ice. I wanted my window to be coated in that shattery type of window frost. I breathed onto the glass and with my finger spelled out my name—*Eveline*. Was I still me when I did not feel like me? Was I the girl my mother bore, my father adored, the one Jack loved? *Jack*. I thought an unthinkable thought, something about asking for mercy, about going back in time, back to him.

The car thrust to a laborious and inexact stop at the intersection by the post office in East Hampton. The placid mechanical hum and puckered clicks from the streetlight slit the air, and the bloody electric haze it made warmed Rourke's face as he looked left into the dead May night. Though he was in profile, I could see his eyes. I could see his fear, and in it, the place where I resided.

Rob's voice came, soft under his breath, breaking through to Rourke, "Green light."

When we pulled into the driveway, Mark and Rob stepped out of the car, with Mark helping Kate, asking when she thought she would be heading to college.

Rourke leaned down and gave me his hand, lifting me out. In the slender murk produced by our bodies, his hair touched my hair and his breath mixed with mine. When I turned to go, his left hand caught my waist, cupping it, his body pushing up behind me. Bending slightly, his right hand came down around my front to grab my right inner thigh. I was lifted slightly as his fingers found the run in my stockings, and through the shreds he found my skin, clutching up into obscurity.

27

The families of graduating seniors emptied out of cars, sheepish in uncommon splendor, like milling clans at the origin of a parade. There is something spent about the families of teenagers; possibly it's the look of exhausted loyalties. Perhaps it's only right that we grow overbig in someone else's space. Perhaps we need to tire and differentiate, leave and adapt.

"Hey, Evie," people kept saying, and I kept saying, "Hey."

Sara Eden joined me on the curb in front of the school, where I was sitting, waiting for the ceremony to begin. Sara looked especially pretty all dressed up. Her eyes sloped at the farthest edges, like the opened wings of a tropical bird. Her skin was rich dark brown like a friar's robes, her teeth perfectly even. A car engine quit alongside us. Sara waved. I listened to the tinkling fuss of her bracelets. "That's my cousin. Marika."

"What a pretty name," I said. "Marika—like a spice."

Sara pulled her braids back incompletely on the side nearest me in the disarming way that some girls have. Though I had not felt sad before, with Sara there I felt sad. She was going to Georgetown, in Washington, D.C., and D.C. is one of those places people never come back from. They don't necessarily stay, but they almost always go from there to elsewhere. Sara was asking me about Alicia's graduation party. I'd already said no, to Alicia and also to her, but it occurred to me that I might not see either of them so much anymore.

"So what do you think? I'll pick you up at five, okay?"

Sure, I said, five is fine.

I'd remained in place for fifteen days after Rourke moved away, not leaving my house, moving only to touch the things I knew he'd touched—the door frame, the bookshelves, the couch, the paper dolls and the sailboat I'd made, the section of the kitchen counter on which he'd leaned. I kept my schoolbooks on a windowsill in my mother's bedroom upstairs, where I labored to observe beyond the greening leaves the street his car had traveled. There was a chair, petite with a round swirling mauve seat and painted black wood. It was not a comfortable chair, but it was there that I sat every day until dark, except for brief hours at school, briefer hours in bed. Everyone was good to me and kind, deferring, always deferring. They seemed afraid for me, though it wasn't necessary. They didn't know me. They didn't know that my path had been decided, that when I moved through the present, it was as if through a paraffin corridor. I would have spoken of such things, but it was likely that I would not have been heard. When anyone asked what I was doing, I would say, *studying*. If no one answered the ringing phone before I got to it, I would lift the receiver and drop it. It was always just someone calling, just a person, not Rourke.

From a quilted, sequined sack, Kate withdrew a tangle of bobby pins. She secured her graduation cap, tilting her head into the light at funny mannequin angles, contemplating space beyond the cafeteria window. An impeccable razor line separated the two halves of her hair. How long ago had the strands at the bottom been by the scalp? Maybe the ones on the bottom were there last time Maman cooked veal for dinner. I'd never thought of hair length as a measure of time. It's sickening actually, the way hair sprouts from pores, squeezing up like famished worms even after a body is dead.

"Still in a bad mood?" Kate asked.

On my hand I was drawing a cup. I had no idea why a cup. I was looking down, trying to avoid the last circus of my peers. A red construction paper sign on one of the doors had been changed from PICK UP GOWNS HERE to PICK UP GIRLS HERE. Paulie Schaeffer and Mike Stern were wrestling by the kitchen, Dana Anderson was applying a second coat of nail polish, and Regina Morris was crying because her school ring had dropped behind a radiator—janitors were on the way. Marty Koch was drinking an orange soda. Dressed in his gown he looked like the nebbish cousin of a vampire. Others milled wistfully—Kiki Hauser and Min Kessler, Adam Sargent and Lynn Hyne—each borne down with memories, and yet each preparing to step experimentally into the half-light of a new life.

Cameras were flashing—*zic-zhing, zic-zhing*.

Have a great summer!

Good luck out there!

See you next life!

Jack appeared. I didn't see from where. He thrust his gown at Kate. "Fix this piece of shit. The snap's busted."

"I can't believe you broke it already," she said.

"The snap sucks. All snaps suck. Snaps are for fags," Jack said blackly.

As Kate hunted for a safety pin, he turned to face me. It was like meeting a puppy I'd given away. I found myself searching for signs of neglect. Wine-colored sacs hugged the undersides of his eyes, attaching like nesting cocoons, like bloody slings. The knuckles of his right hand were badly scraped. Skin flapped over in certain parts and was missing entirely in others. The blood looked dry but not old. His T-shirt said, *It's cool to love Jesus*. I was surprised to see him. I had not expected to see him.

"How are you?" he wanted to know.

"I'm okay." I extracted a strand of hair from the corner of his mouth. "You? You okay?"

"Me? Oh, yeah, sure. I'm okay."

He'd come before dawn, just six hours before graduation. I was sleeping lightly. I heard the barn door creak. He climbed the ladder, and from halfway up he tossed a bottle of liquor onto the bed. I could feel it hit the mattress; I could hear the cramped slosh of fluid. It sounded one-third empty.

"What time is it?" I asked, sitting up.

He said, "Night." His legs swung off the ledge of the loft. I had the idea he might jump, though he would not have gone far. If I could have taken his pain, I would have, because my love for him was undiminished. You hear of paralyzed people who send signals to sleeping limbs. Or amputees who feel phantom tingling in parts that no longer exist. Despite his violent removal, all the space around me that he had occupied still belonged to Jack. Not a day passed without me sending signals to missing pieces.

"I could cut my wrists," he said, "put a bullet through my skull. If I thought I could reach you. But nothing can reach you."

I guided his head to the basin of my lap. I brushed back his hair, and unraveled the many knots. If I was cruel, I did not feel cruel. I felt new. I'd met the darker side of life; I'd met its animal. The animal came to me because it knew me. Jack understood what I'd become. I could tell by the wonder and the disgust in his eyes.

"Every time I see a flower," he said as he wept, "it's your favorite."

———

Kate fanned the air as she fastened his robe. "You reek of alcohol."

Jack lifted his chin. "Quick," he said sarcastically, "hand me a mint."

"Where's your cap?" she asked him as we stood to take our places in line.

"Daniel!" he bellowed. Dan's head emerged from the crowd. Jack clapped, going, "Chuck it." Dan snapped his wrist, and the hat came gliding over like a square Frisbee from line L-Z to line A-K.

The band began to play the school song, and we all inched through the halls in two lines. Andie Anderson and Brett Lawler were each the head of a line, and the first to reach the auditorium doors. They stopped, and we all stopped in succession, crashing somewhat. Andie's legs were jiggling beneath her gown as she waited for her cue—her knees were poking like horse noses running a race in tandem. At the first note of "Pomp and Circumstance," Andie and Brett received the signal to go, while every next person was held by the shoulders for a count of two, then released with a solemn press to the small of the back.

Inside, the auditorium was inky and stifling. Parents and extended families filled the seats, and teachers papered the walls, craning their necks, fanning themselves with programs—all eagerly bearing witness to our indoctrination. We were being given over, who knows to what. The sad truth is that there is no original future. From my chair on the platform, I had an unobstructed view of Denny's mother, Elaine, who was weeping in the front row. The shank of doughy flesh under her arm wagged as she leaned down to hunt through her pocketbook for a tissue. To prevent Denny from being late, she had changed all the clocks in the house, and she got him to the school two hours early. Unfortunately, it was so early that Denny went downstairs to sleep in the wrestling room and nearly missed the whole thing anyway.

In his valedictory speech, Stephen Auchard spoke of promises and responsibilities while everyone was thinking primarily of the rewards of lunch. He could not say what he really thought, whatever it was that that may have been, if in fact his real thoughts were even known to him. But he had not been singled out for the inventiveness of his sentiments. He'd been chosen as the one most brilliantly weaned of idiosyncrasy. Stephen returned to the seat next to mine, and I bumped against him, giving him a small thumbs-up. Poor guy. He wanted to be a surgeon. One day we would meet again, one day in the distant future, one day when I required surgery, though at the time it was hard to imagine what part of me might need to be cut.

Principal Laughlin beamed and shook my hand like he meant it when he presented my diploma. On it, my name had been carefully written in veering script: *Eveline Aster Auerbach*. People shouted that name exactly as I read it—people I knew and others I did not know, all clapping loudly. Clapping is bizarre. Powell says in certain places people do not do it. In certain places they call out in repetitive hoots, going, *loo, loo, loo*.

Afterward, my parents were in the lobby, Marilyn and Powell too. It was strange to see them there, representing me. From a distance they seemed credible, semi-sociable, and nicely dressed, making it hard to tell strictly by the look of them that they knew nothing about me. They were standing with Coco's parents, discussing college acceptances as though they'd played some part in the process, as though they'd helped with applications or offered money. Mr. and Mrs. Hale had visited ten schools with Coco, often staying at four-star hotels, where Coco got *massages*.

"I can't believe Coco's going to Amherst," Denny said one day during finals when he came to see me at my window in my house. He pulled his chair closer to mine. "For political science. Bitch."

He came every day to keep me company, bringing presents— chocolates and hyacinths and rocks he'd painted, these portraits in gouache. I had eleven, all propped against the window screen: Alicia, Sara, Kate, Stephen Auchard, Lilias Starr, Mom and Powell and Denny's mother—all on one rock, Eddie from the record store, Marty Koch holding the new yearbook, Coach Slater, the new logo Denny had designed for Atomic Tangerine, and of course, Elvis. "Which is your favorite?" he asked.

I pointed to Elvis. It looked exactly like Denny.

"Really? I happen to like Coach Slater. I mean, I know she's not your favorite person, but the workmanship is by far the best. Do you know she sat for three hours? Did I tell you?"

He reached into the pocket of his windbreaker and removed the latest. There wasn't much room left on the window. I'd have to start a second row.

"Your father mailed me a photo," he said as he placed it in front of me. On the irregular saucer-sized rock was a masterful replica of Chihuahua Man. He was wearing a starched yellow dress shirt, and all four dog heads were floating around him like alter egos. "I used a toothbrush to do the fur," he said. "I cut off all but ten bristles then melted back the toothbrush wall with a blowtorch."

I thanked him, and together we looked out the window.

"I forgot to tell you," he remarked soberly. "L.B. got off the waiting list at Tulane. He's going for pre-med. I mean, can you imagine getting him as your gynecologist? Or Coco as a lobbyist for the lumber or sugar industry? It terrifies me to think of these people with checking accounts and voting rights. They'll reverse the progress of the entire preceding generation! We're doomed."

I pressed my Chihuahua rock against my cheek. It was warm. Denny must have had it on the dashboard in his car. It *was* strange how much things had changed since we were kids, or since we'd started high school. No one was liberated, not the way my mother and her friends had been—free from consensus and imitation. No one wore homemade clothes or marched on Washington anymore. The closest we'd come to history was Jack and Smokey getting arrested at Shoreham power plant for climbing the fence during an anti-nuke demonstration.

Record store Eddie hadn't received a single inquiry in the "Ask Eddie" box for months. Everyone just read *Rolling Stone* as if there were nothing to learn about music beyond what magazine editors saw fit to present, as if published information could ever truly be free of advertiser influence. "It's not that they don't care about answers; they don't even know how to ask questions anymore," Eddie told me and Kate.

Even feminism had been stripped of its legitimacy and relegated to tasteless jokes about women picking up dinner date checks or carrying their own luggage or standing on buses while men sit. There'd been some collapse, some shattering of invisible walls, some backlash from liberalism, some conservative revival. And yet, no matter where you stood idealistically, your involvement couldn't be willed away: everyone bore some responsibility. If Denny, Jack, Kate, Dan, and I represented one extreme, and Coco, L.B., Pip, and Nico represented the opposite, we were still relatives of the hour. Society had never felt more like a bizarre arrangement.

"Have you ever seen something normal magnified that ends up looking like tubes?" I asked.

"Yes," Denny said right away. "Bark."

"Once I saw something," I said, "possibly bark. It was a gnarled mass of tunnels. Maybe there's similar architecture to society, only more fragile, like a nest of twisted glass that gives us shape but that can shatter at any instant from the slightest stress." Jack's absence was conspicuous; I felt the trauma of not having him to complete me, to interpret for me. I added, "I imagine they look like glass canals."

"Neat," Denny said, encouragingly, obviously relieved that I was talking. "Like an ant colony, only positive space, not negative."

Denny seemed to understand, so I continued. "It's like, we work and work to construct these systems for the good—civil rights, the environment, mind expansion—then they all shatter, like fragile avenues, like they were too delicate to sustain weight. Maybe there's a limit to human tolerance for idealism."

"It's true. For a while we were doing well," Denny said. "But no change is ever secure so long as someone else has the incentive to blow it off. Look at reconstruction in the South. You get the tragedy of the Civil War, the beauty of the Gettysburg Address, the death of Lincoln, and racists *still* figure out how to segregate the South—through legislation!" Denny adjusted his chair. "Then again, difference is essential to freedom. And to adaptation. No one wants a fascist state."

"Maybe everything that gets built *has* to fall apart," I said.

"Maybe. The process shakes us from complacency, and inspires us to build new avenues. In fact, it might not even be *mechanically* possible to have acts of liberalism without conservatism, or heroism without cowardice, or revolution without tyranny—"

"Or love without loss," I said, and I don't know, with Denny there, I just started to cry.

He reached to hold me. "Don't worry, honey. He'll be back."

———

"Eveline is going to NYU," my mother was telling Coco's parents, "to study art history."

I stood a little behind them. Coco was there too, with shiny coral lips and newly frosted hair, sipping cola from a clear plastic glass.

My father looked confused. He turned to Powell. "What happened to art?"

Powell just shrugged. "Or photography?"

I did not wish my parents any harm; however, I didn't know why I should have wished them well either, beyond the obvious fact that they were nice people. I didn't even think I had anything good to inherit. The dictionary says a parent is any animal, organism, or plant in relation to its offspring, and so of course, in that explicit regard, I was their child. Yet they'd set my soul adrift, tending to themselves with the urgency due me, believing me capable because they needed me to be capable, never guessing that their faith in my strength would not make it fact, or that I might grow dangerously weary of sufficiency. Maman had seen through my mask of adequacy. She'd loved without hope for profit the girl she'd found, but Maman was dead. Rourke had not insisted upon my competence either. He had not even seemed to notice it. There was something else in me he wanted, something small and discrete—the frailty in me, and my frailty adored him.

My father tugged his jacket cuffs. His hands were beautifully proportioned. My hands were the same, and it depressed me somewhat to be faced with my DNA like that. Maybe everything was hopelessly predetermined, them to me, me to the next.

"Thanks for coming," I said to the four of them, and they said that I was very welcome.

Sometimes a day is a symbolic day, and you behave symbolically. Sometimes you search inside for a feeling, and, finding none, you remember that no feeling is frequently the most possible feeling.

At Spring Close House for graduation lunch, it was me; Mom; Dad; Marilyn; Powell; Kate and her brother, Laurent, and sister-in-law, Simone, with their baby, Jean-Claude. Jean-Claude was cute except for the

way his head came together at the temples like he'd been plucked out
with cob tongs. Laurent also had a head shaped that way, sort of like a
guitar. Looking out the window, I felt mostly lonely. It was the kind of
loneliness that cannot see past itself, a skulking suspicion that the world
was not mine to inherit. I listened as they spoke, laughed when they
laughed, raised my glass as such moments presented themselves, all the
while marking time. I was sorry for the way everyone imagined my life
to be my own, for the way they really did seem to like me, asking did my
fish still have bones, and how pretty I looked. I wished I could give something back. But yet, I knew that all that they wanted from me was all that
they *needed* from me, and that is a treacherous path to consent to travel,
in the sense of suppressing things sought for the self. That is to say, you
being solely what others want you to be.

After appetizers, Dad neatened the table, scraping crumbs with the
flat of a knife, and Jean-Claude gnawed his mother's necklace. When the
strand snapped, everyone dove and hunted on their knees for scattered
pearls, which was a strange and spirited sort of family happening.

Marilyn brushed her skirt and sat again. "When do you leave for
Montreal?"

Laurent deposited a handful of beads into the ashtray. "In an hour or
two. We're hoping the baby will sleep before we stop for dinner."

"Have you finished packing, Catherine?" Simone asked.

Kate shrugged. "Except for what I'll pick up in August."

"And what about you, Powell," Marilyn asked. "Your next job's in
South America?"

"Brazil," he said, putting his arm around my mother. "I actually leave
this evening."

My lips paused over the rim of my drinking glass, which smelled the
dusty way water smells if you stop to let it. A smell like a long thin te-
dium, listless like an elderly neighbor's kitchen with cracked linoleum
and spilled prescriptions and overpainted cabinets that do not suffi-
ciently shut. Like the knowledge of passing things.

"What was that man saying to you?" my mother whispered audibly to
my father when he returned from paying the check.

"Which man was that?" Dad wanted to know.

"The tall one with the fish tie."

"Fish tie," he pondered, looking around. "I think I would have remembered a fish tie."

Back at home, Kate flitted in loose circles, gathering up the last of her things. I sat on a wicker hamper stuffed with all her fabric scraps and sewing notions and waited while she zipped and tied the last of her luggage. Beneath me the basket bent and squeaked with that slightly bending wicker sound. I wondered how Kate would do. I wondered whether a femininity so refined is not ominously reliant upon the beneficence of circumstance. I guessed she would do fine. Lots of women are out there, doing fine.

"Isn't this pretty?" she said of her dress. "It's chambray."

When she finished packing, we took Mom's car for a drive down Three Mile Harbor Road to the bay. Darts of sun pierced the trees, breaking up the retiring darkness with pools of apricot. We listened to "You've Got to Hide Your Love Away" by The Beatles, hitting rewind on the tape deck whenever it ended. First I did it once, then twice, then she did it. And when she did it, it was different. It was like pouring bronze over a bird's nest, casting the moment in metal. There was this understanding that of all the songs we'd heard together, that one would be the last. The beach was empty, despite the early June heat. She parked near the fishing station, by the channel, where the strip of sand was curved and rocky.

"Careful," she said to me. "There's a broken bottle."

We lay on the stony sand and watched the boats return to harbor. The water was twinkling and distinguished. In the theater you can make water by waving bolts of silk from one end of the stage to the other, and sometimes real water looks that way.

Kate began to cry; I thought about the song. But instead she said, "I keep thinking about Harrison." Her tears congealed in her eyes like pudding. I was thinking what a simple creature she was—we were. Maybe I would take her hand and lay it on my neck, make her say his name again, have her feel my throat convulse. Feel the acid echo, the disease in me.

"Here," I said, stretching my shirt to wipe her eyes. Above us the birds soared triumphantly, arcing, diving, chasing each last swoop.

"I'm sorry," she apologized, "for ruining our last afternoon."

I rested my head on her middle. Her babies would come from there. How sad, not to know them. "Don't be sorry. Don't ever be sorry."

Sara asked if I was okay. She was driving. I said I was fine. If I said it uncertainly, it was because the armrest was pressing into my spine. I was facing her, not the street—I could not bear to face the street. The street was like a plank shooting off into nothing. There's this cartoon where the main character drops black vinyl circles onto the ground behind him for his pursuer to fall into. It's a scary concept—circles being holes, and strange to explain, but in fact that was exactly how I was doing.

"I'm sorry I missed Kate," she said. "Was it hard to say goodbye?"

"Not really. The baby was crying."

There were no more places to park by Alicia's, so we drove to Apaquogue Road and walked back. The Ross house was shaped like a sideways barn, only it was a mansion. On the right was a screened terrace room, and on the left was the driveway, which, like the walkway, was lined with paper bags filled with sand and burning candles.

"Look at this tree," I said, pointing up as we passed it. "Isn't it beautiful?"

"Is it a maple?"

"No," I said, "it's a copper beech."

Though we could see that guests were gathered on the lawn behind the house, we went through the main entrance. The porch was gracious and white with pink geraniums. Sara put her pocketbook in the front hall closet, and she handed a graduation gift for Alicia to a uniformed woman. I offered a bunch of wildflowers I'd picked from the garden near the barn.

The woman said, *"Sí, sí, gracias."*

"Gracias, Consuela," Sara said, introducing me in Spanish.

Consuela replied in English, "Yes, hello. Yes, hello. Yes, this way."

We were escorted through an impeccable hallway and down two stone steps into a living room with an ivory carpet and furniture that was snowy and low as if it had settled in a frost. Wooden stairs without risers went up to our right, and, on the far wall, single-pane glass doors faced the eastern end of a crowded brick terrace. Consuela led us through the formal dining room, which was attached to an enormous kitchen by a skylighted butler's pantry. Here, the doors to the patio were open: a reggae band was playing on the other side. Consuela set my flowers on the kitchen table and looked for a vase. She made a fuss over how beautiful they were, but I couldn't help feeling the gift was not right, that it was primitive, and me too, that I was also primitive.

Her eyes twinkled at me; I remember that, her eyes twinkling.

Sara and I made our way out, pausing for hellos and introductions. People we knew from school were in ties and skirts and freshly ironed clothes. Past the terrace, there was an open lawn that was decorated with giant paper ball lanterns suspended from bamboo poles, and in the center of the expanse was a fountain, with a bronze sculpture of a cube standing on one corner, and a stone bench wrapping around. A pool the gray-blue color of goslings sat alongside a gardener's cottage and connected garage that ran perpendicular to the main house. The structure was at least three times the size of my mother's house.

"Do you mind if I go out to see the sculpture?" I asked Sara.

"Not at all," she said. "I'll find Alicia and let her know we're here."

I took a seat on the concrete ring of the fountain. I raised my head and breathed deeply, giving in to the celestial gardens and lurking servers, the smells of grilled meat and freshly baked goods, the chinks of genuine glass. My back straightened; my head found center. Feeling heartened, feeling sure, feeling finally more than meek, I took my place in that robust utopia. I imitated the want of humility of my hosts, and in my mind I became a *guest*—someone special, chosen.

At the edge of the packed terrace I spotted Mark, Rourke's friend from the Talkhouse. He was moving toward me as though swimming with necessity. The graphic reminder of Rourke filled me with a barbarian sort of hope.

He crossed the lawn, calling, "Eveline!" Then he gestured to himself, saying, Mark, as though I'd forgotten. He was actually very handsome. By the dark of the night we'd met, with Rourke there, I hadn't noticed.

"Hi," I said. "What are you doing here?"

"This is my house," he said, and he smiled. "Alicia's my sister."

I instantly recalled the day in art class last winter when Rourke came in to talk about the sets for the play. The way Alicia was laughing and touching his jacket. *That's how they knew each other—through Mark.*

"Mind if I sit?" Mark asked. The fountain surged brightly as he came down next to me. "Alicia and Sara told me you haven't been going out. I was worried you might not make it."

I looked at the house. It was strange that my name had been mentioned there. Was it in the hallway or on the stairs or in the butler's pantry? I considered asking. I had the feeling I could ask him anything.

"Is it true that you haven't left your room?"

"Not exactly," I said. "My *mother's* room."

"Oh, your *mother's* room," he repeated with a nod.

And then Mark began to speak; he spoke for a long time. He'd attended UCLA, then he'd gone to Harvard for his MBA. Crew was his sport. He'd biked across Nova Scotia and golfed in Scotland. He'd been hired by a Wall Street firm named Drexel Burnham to work on mergers and acquisitions, something about asset valuation, vertical integration, four in the morning, activity in Japan. He would be moving into his own apartment on West Sixtieth Street, twenty-five stories up, with a terrace overlooking the river.

"The trick to marinating bluefish," he said, "is milk. It kills the fishy flavor."

The tone of his voice was artificial and intensely sure, pungent and dry as the inside of flowers. It was as if he spoke without allowing his vocal cords to vibrate excessively. The sound was controlled and hypnotic, and I felt subdued by it. I felt a faraway feeling, a night and a dead feeling. Through the sliverish gap formed by our bodies, I trailed the crystal swirl of water. When I looked up, Mark was staring. I perceived the ignition of his desire. I wasn't sure what to do about that. Probably it was too late to do anything. My own desire for Rourke, for all things indirectly related to him, including Mark, surely only made matters worse.

"If you need a shot of culture this summer, come visit me," he proposed as the sun began to set, its phosphorescence slinking unevenly off, like the thin straps of a dress from a woman's shoulders. "We'll hit the Met. Get lunch. Have you ever been to the Stanhope?"

I didn't reply. I didn't have to. I had the feeling he preferred my indifference. I was not offended. He was cunning and agreeable and so obviously without ethics that he aroused me—perversely.

"So, Kate leaves today. Alicia told me."

"She left already."

"Canada. Is that right?"

"Yes, her brother lives there."

"And in September, she's going to McGill."

I nodded once. "McGill."

"Montreal is beautiful. You'd love it there," he stated with certainty— already certain that I'd never been, certain as well of the things I'd love. "The old city is an island in the St. Lawrence named after Mount Royal, the mountain at its center. The French say, 'Mont Ray-al.' In America, we say 'Mon-tree-all,' which, of course, is misleading. We'll have to visit her sometime."

Sara stepped off the patio, moving toward us. Mark stood to greet her. Their voices coupled warmly, turning festive, buoyant, ruffling like emancipated doves. It was clear that they'd known each other for a while. Mark relieved Sara of glasses and napkins, and he extracted a plate from the crook of her forearm. I wondered why they were not in love when they were so beautiful together, when the world they inhabited was legitimate with manageable particulars, when their mindfulness seemed to extend no further than the moment they occupied. They would have had a normal love, a confiding union felt to the core, not the desperation I'd known with Rourke, the panic I felt when he was gone. Mark spoke amiably, though the pressure from his mind to mine was serious and unceasing. His was an exceptional power—he was blessed, he had no doubt. I wondered how he had gotten Sara to get me to come to the party. She seemed like the type who would be immune to influence.

They were talking about collections. Sara kept keys.

"Nonsense," Mark teased. "Keys. I keep cars."

"Oh, well, cars," she said and shrugged. "Naturally."

Mark turned to me. "And you, Eveline?"

I had none that I could recall except the rock portrait collection, which technically Denny had started, so it probably didn't count. I was not interested in keys, though I agreed that they were collectible, with the way they clink and cleverly hang.

"What do you think about cars?" Mark asked.

"I don't know much about cars."

Sara laughed at Mark, "Ha!"

"Not so fast," Mark said. "She hasn't seen it yet."

"It *is* nice," Sara conceded. "Actually, Evie, you might like it."

"It's so nice, the previous owner didn't want to sell it," Mark said. "He finally gave in to persuasion." *Persuasion* is the type of word only certain people can use. I'd never *persuaded* anyone of anything. Mark took my hand and drew me to my feet. "Let's see what you think."

As we descended the mild grade to the gardener's cottage, he said, "This is my place. And this," he announced as we made the turn onto an opened garage door, framed on both sides by a fan of wild roses, "is my new car."

We faced off with a gorgeous gunmetal-gray Porsche with an elliptical body. I touched it, bending prudently, as if to pet a sleeping animal, my fingers skimming the semi-scripted chrome lettering that flickered and repeated in the light.

"1967," he said, leading me deeper into the impeccable garage, popping the door handle, taking me by the elbow, helping me sit. My legs drew up involuntarily, and when he shut the door, it made a solid seal like the lid of a coffin. The leather interior was supple and medicinal, the color of coffee ice cream. The glove box was at my knees. I was thinking, *Once it held gloves.*

Mark joined me, bringing himself behind the wheel. Though it felt wrong to be with him, I did not feel responsible for my loneliness or for his desire to violate it. People had been speaking to me for weeks, and yet only Mark had gotten through. I waited for him to refer to Rourke; it was exactly the right time to refer to Rourke. If he didn't, it was clear that he had a plan.

"So," he said, "NYU. We will both be in New York."

"Yes," I said, feeling something sinking. "It's strange."

He started the engine. "Not strange, Eveline. Fate."

The rest until the end was fast. Frequently there is more time to think than there are things to think about, and you sit around contemplating the most trifling details. Other times it feels you live your life in a minute. Not in the sense of things racing past, though there is that, but of things spilling out in an undulating twist, simultaneous and unoriented, flat and circular, present and future, like a Möbius strip. Because although I was surprised to see Rourke, I'd also been expecting to see him. And though I knew not to trust Mark, I'd been unable to break away.

The Porsche coasted past Georgica Beach, but then Mark hit the brakes and popped the car into reverse. We swung into the parking lot. Many cars were there, including Rob's and Rourke's. As we pulled past the GTO, I saw the ghost of my name still etched on the little window in back. *Eveline.* From the night at the Talkhouse.

Let's go back, I said. I thought I said.

Mark killed the engine anyway, and we coasted like an arrowhead into the heart of the lot.

Three figures appeared at the crest of sand—a guy in a Red Hook Fire Department T-shirt and two girls in sundresses. Mark pulled the emergency brake and hopped out. He kissed the girls and shook hands enthusiastically with the man, both of them pumping until their palms swung down. Something was coming up from the direction of the water, from behind the girls. I saw Mark's face stiffen.

Through the planes of twilight came Rourke, a silhouette ascending the slope of sand from the west. He passed Mark and the others, moving silently and directly to the car, which was not even as tall as his waist. He stopped at my door, staring down.

I heard Mark say, *Eveline. This is Lorraine, and this is Anna, and this is Anna's husband, Joey, Joey Cirillo—Rob's brother.* Mark pointed loosely from me to Rourke, from Rourke to me, and with an uncharacteristic trace of sarcasm or maybe pity, he said, *And of course, you two know each other.*

Rourke continued to look at me. If I had not been sickeningly aware of my compromise, I would have found proof of it in his eyes. His left hand entered the pocket of his Levi's and his white dress shirt hung like paper from his shoulders. The wind blew back his hair and his body blocked the sky—no, skies. The one over him and me, and the other one.

What brings you all out here? Mark asked.

Harrison dragged us, Joey said. *We had lunch in Montauk and a day at the beach. The girls did a little shopping in East Hampton. We just passed your house—looks like you're having a party.*

For my sister, Mark said. *She graduated today. Why don't you come by?*

How about it, girls, you up for it?

Heads! A voice. Rob's. A football appeared from the direction of the water, boring cylindrically up to us. Rourke reached above my head to catch it. I could feel the breeze made by his arm.

Watch yourself, there, Mark said to Rob.

Well, well. Look at the new toy, Rob said. *And the car's nice too.*

Everyone laughed and Rob clapped once for the ball. Rourke threw it back. I observed his arm—the lengthening, the retracting, the feverish white of his shirt against his dark skin.

Let's go girls, Rob said, *let's go. Harrison. C'mon.*

See you in a few, Joey said.

Mark said, *See you in five.*

Rob turned back and snapped, *Harrison. Now.*

Rourke jerked imperceptibly, then he moved, saying *Later.* I did not know to whom, maybe to me, probably to me.

Probably all three cars arrived at the same time. Probably when Mark and I went through the crowd down the driveway to the garage, Rob and Rourke went to park on the street. I was thinking about where to find him. *Inside,* I thought. I'd begun to shiver.

Mark automatically led me to the screened porch on the side of the house. The roof was low and flat like a tarp, and through the walls the night moved like gentle water. People were lounging on rattan sofas, and there was music. He chose the porch because he knew I wouldn't go to where I could not easily be found. I began to perceive the scope of his project—it involved not simply a win, but an eventual, strategic win. It was as if he was helping me with Rourke, feeding an addiction, making me dependent on him.

Alicia knelt at my chair. *Is she okay?*

She's cold. I was driving with the top down. Very foolish of me.

Is that true, Evie? Alicia asked, glaring at him. *Are you just cold?*

My eyes found Mark's. *Yes,* I said, *it's true.*

She said, *Mark, I could kill you.*

Kill me, please, Alicia dear, he said playfully, smiling. Then slower, to me alone. Not smiling, mouthing the words again. *Kill me.* And then, aloud again, *I'll get some cognac.*

Honestly Evie, he drove us crazy for weeks to get you here, then he gives you pneumonia. Alicia gave me her sweater, pulling it off, one side, the other. There was an extra hole in her left ear, and in it a diamond that flared in the light, like a miniature exploding thing.

Sara came in from outside. *Why don't I just take you home,* she offered.

Let's try the cognac first, Mark suggested and Sara retired to the window to check on the status of the night, her gauzy slacks undulating. *I'll be right back,* he promised me, and as soon as he left the room, I wanted him to come back.

Within moments, Rourke filled the doorway between the porch and the living room. A luminous band etched the perimeter of his body, giving him the aspect of hanging forward. There was a precision about him. I didn't need to guess his purpose. I felt surrounded; I felt myself at his center.

Sara said hello to him, and they spoke briefly. I wondered what she felt. Did she feel what I felt? Did she feel an anthem in her heart? Did she see the lines of his face and think they were beautiful? Did she think if she could not hold him, she would die? Was she sorry for everything she'd ever done?

Mark returned, passing through, saying *hi* to Rourke, and *excuse me,* then coming to me, blocking my view of Rourke, giving me a glass. *This is for you.* Mark's voice originated from elsewhere; it was detached from his body. Exactly as he handed me the tumbler, I stretched to see Rourke, but he was gone. The glass slipped through my hand, smacked the table-top and broke. There was a fanning slosh of liquid.

Sara pulled back the throw rug. Someone crammed a newspaper against the side of the table to catch the widening stream. I slapped my hand down to catch the pieces of glass.

Mark shouted, *Evie, no! Consuela!*

It was too late. A fragment cut into my palm. Blood mixed with the liquor along the slice and it stung. Sara took me through the crowd to the bathroom, and she left me.

The door clicked shut; the dim tiled room; in the mirror, my face, so pale. And Rourke. His likeness behind my own, swelling like smoke to encircle me. I did not wonder where he'd come from, nor did I think as he lifted me onto the counter and attended to my wound. When it was clean, he pressed his lips to my hand, then to my mouth. The kiss, the first, penetrating and inquisitive, with each of us trying to capture all that had become active, the mysterious traits of a mysterious desire, now miraculously, and perhaps just tentatively, in hand.

I need to get out of here for a couple days, he said. *I thought I could leave you. I can't.* With my mouth I could feel him speak. His voice was like underwater vibrations, like the inky scuffs and thuds you hear in a submarine. He held my chin. *Understand?*

Yes, I said, nodding.

All right, he said, *let's go.*

There was a place near a pond where the trees divided to accommodate the belly of the night. It was there that we stopped. The moonlight was like a body dropped to earth, a luminous stellar wreck. Rourke eased the car forward to where the issue from the moon was widest, and he jerked the brake to park. Beyond the windshield, day was making minor gains on the night, coming and retreating in whispers like the pull and the push of his breath. By his hands, I was carefully considered, as if it were not me he wanted but something I possessed. I could feel the burden of his eyes upon me, a hunter's eyes, keen and suspicious, as if I were the keeper of some conclusion that he had intuited but of which he had no evidence.

Say it, he said, the words caught at the base of his throat. *No one.*

No one, I said, I swore, *but you.*

I said it because it was true. There was no one but him, and there never would be. I loved him with pain and with something greater than pain, with a barren ache that pealed not in the heart but in the desert dry alongside it. I knew it was so even then: if in his arms I was a woman, beyond them I was nothing.

MONTAUK

Summer 1980

At first, one is struck by his peculiarity—those eyes, those lips,
those cheekbones . . . that face reveals . . . what any face should
reveal to a careful glance: the nonexistence of
banality in human beings.

—JULIA KRISTEVA

28

Rourke drove through the last remaining darkness. The preliminary azure cool of morning was coming up full around us, clear as the whistles birds make. The ground ascended like a platform into day, and across it we shot, passing from one highway to the next—rolling west, rolling south, with the sun rising and the ellipse of the planet beneath. I felt defiant and alive, like a criminal in the midst of a crime—visionary and dissolute and removed from the world about me. I felt I had entered the tempo of my era. When you study explorers such as Magellan or Cortés, you follow lines across oceans and continents. The miles and the perils, the forfeiture of lives and hearts, the years lost and monies disbursed, are all reduced to trails of dots and arrows. Rourke and I were that way—no more than the eye could see, paving paths through the universe, the look of us amounting to the entirety of our story.

He said to sleep if I wanted to; I didn't want to.

At the end of an exit ramp, a Volkswagen Beetle waited to turn. The GTO cruised down and closed in on it. We turned as well, left then right, going up a hump into a gas station. Rourke's wrist flipped, and the engine shut, and you could hear a ring through the silence.

"Better use the bathroom," he said.

Our doors closed simultaneously, *whump, whump*. As Rourke reached for the pump, a graying man in a windbreaker approached from the garage office. *Al* was stitched on his jacket opposite the Texaco logo.

"Good morning, there," Al said, setting his hand on the pump. "You're out early."

Rourke said something I couldn't hear, and Al laughed, answering, "You bet."

My head was hanging as I stepped over oil stains and embedded chips of glass in the asphalt. There were patterns, and in the patterns, gleaming variations—tiger likenesses and fighter pilots. If you looked, you could find them. Also I saw my legs, my knees and calves, and beneath them the carob dirt unpacking, smoking up as I walked, adhering in a film to my bare feet and ankles. In my hand were my shoes from the graduation party the night before. I put them on before going into the bathroom.

The dented steel door creaked mightily. I rinsed my hands and face with cold water and combed down my hair with my fingers. I wondered what Rourke felt like to wait for me. He'd never been mindful of my needs before. I hoped he wouldn't think less of me for them. Being in love is like leaning on a broken reed. It is to be precariously balanced, to teeter between the vertical and the horizontal. It's like war: it's to demand of one's sensibilities the impossible—to expect paranoia to coexist with faith, chance with design, to enlist suspicion insensibly in certain regards and suppress it blindly in others.

He was inclined against the hood on the driver's side. His arms were folded, and his legs were stretched out and crossed at the ankle. His feet were on the oval island that housed the pumps. My stomach felt weak to see him again, the fullness of his shoulders, the gesture of his body. When I neared, he looked over, turning because he knew to turn, because of messages sent between the sex of us. Al spoke, and Rourke answered, not taking his eyes off me. I knew what he experienced when he watched me walk, because I felt my body's response. I felt myself become at once everything I was originally and everything he had taken and touched. I felt my skin assume the burden of the sunrise. I felt the luxury of flesh beneath my dress. My lips were chapped and my hair damp and un-brushed, and when I stepped, my foot touched down with the benefi-cence of angels. In my heart dwelt a primitive kindness. Mostly what I felt was relieved to live for his regard.

"I don't know which is prettier, young lady," Al said, "daybreak, or you."

Rourke stretched back across the hood to hand me a Coke. He must have gotten it from the soda machine while I was in the bathroom. I cracked open the can and drank. The sugar was shocking.

"That's no breakfast," Al chided as we climbed into the car. He rested one arm on Rourke's open window. The other waved in some unseen direction over the roof. "Try Adrienne's—it's a truck stop up the road." The hand on the window was mottled and chapped, with the thumb splaying stiffly. I found myself hoping that Al had been in love once, that when he was in his prime, he fulfilled it.

Rourke thanked him, and as we turned onto the service road, he asked if I was hungry.

I told him no, not really.

No one had been awake when we'd stopped at my mother's house after Alicia's party. Rourke parked at the head of the driveway, and our feet made even sounds on the gravel as we walked, though his sounds were heavier than mine. I hadn't asked him to accompany me, and he hadn't offered. It was just that when I got out of the car, he got out also, and when we met at the hood, he took my hand. Of course we would not encounter resistance on the inside. In my mind it was not a possibility or even a consideration. My entire life had led to that moment of autonomy, and I was grateful for the authority I'd been given over myself.

Rourke opened the back door to my bedroom for me, propping it with his arm and drawing me through. He looked around sweepingly, assessing everything. As the things he viewed came to life, these things as I had known them turned dead. I knew without question that I would never again live at home. If I was mistaken, if, in fact, I would be driven back, it would be because I had failed or because I had brought failure upon myself. I would not fail. He stood with me by my dresser, him leaning on the wall and me opening drawers. I emptied out the art supplies from a small canvas tool bag, and in it I packed two T-shirts, a pair of jeans, a pair of shorts and a dress, my favorite sweater, one pair of shoes, a bathing suit.

"Anything else you need," he said, "we'll pick it up."

Highways narrowed as we shot down the New Jersey coast, taking the Garden State past Asbury Park, Ocean Grove, Sea Girt, and then numbered routes that turned to single-lane stretches flanked by hilly embankments with painted houses. At the shore we trailed the flight of the boardwalk, and a hot wind caressed my face. I wondered if I climbed through the window, would I float. It seemed like the air out there formed a belt of heat and salt, a parallel place to crawl upon.

"This one's for Leeanne out in Mountainside," the deejay said. Then came "Bennie and the Jets."

> *She's got electric boots, a mohair suit,*
> *You know I read it in a magazine.*

I was changing my clothes. He was driving, and he'd told me to.

I reached through my bag for my bathing suit, and when I found it, I put it on, sliding my dress above my hips and pulling up the bottoms, and slipping the shoulder straps off my shoulders and tying the top piece around my chest. In the side-view mirror I could see the elongated hollow at the base of my neck, the downward pools of my collarbone, the rules of my chest, and above that ladder, my face. New lines marked the skin beneath my eyes, preclusive new lines. I pushed back my hair. Somewhere were my barrettes, in the seat or on the floor.

We pulled into a parking lot at Point Pleasant and stepped out onto the already steaming tar. I could smell the unctuous glue of it. We walked up the ramp, and at the top I shaded my eyes from the glare. The boardwalk spilled out in either direction like a carpet, like a platform that made you spectator to the sea. It seemed to extend along the entire coast. I imagined it dipping intermittently—tucking underground, coming back up, like sewing stitches. It was awful, yet somehow democratic, with all the people there talking and reading, walking and running. There were old people strolling with cups of coffee. You hardly ever saw old people at the beach in East Hampton.

Near the water he dropped the towels he'd carried from the car. The sand was not like the sand at home; it was flatter and darker. I pulled off my dress and waded into the ocean, going until my feet didn't touch. Rourke was sitting contemplatively in the morning light; the ice-blue dress shirt he'd worn since the party was half-open and wrinkled. Behind him the arcades and game galleries were creaking uniformly to life, forming a low-rising headland of noise and neon, despite the early hour. The sky ride and the photo booth, the Ferris wheel and the merry-go-round, the batting cage, the signs for strollers and umbrellas for rent—the antediluvian relics all securely fastened, looking as though nothing short of a flood could remove them. He undressed and entered the water also, and soon his arms were around my waist. I wrapped myself around him. He carried me farther out, just the two of us, and water, water all around.

When I opened my eyes from sleep, I knew where I was but not how long it had been. It had gotten very hot. I could hear a common whirr, a public rustle. My head was heavy from the heat; I could hardly raise it. Through the glare I saw that hundreds of people had settled around us while we slept. I reached for Rourke, but he was gone; alongside me in the sand was the impression left by his body. He must have been waiting for me to wake up, because exactly when I wished for him to reappear, he did, coming from the direction of the water, blocking light and noise like a spread cape or carbon overlay. Moisture traveled from his skin, and cold.

He kissed me. I could taste salt from the sea. He said, "Let's get out of here."

I stood and went to the water to cool off. I was glad it was still June. In June, nothing bad happens; old songs sound new again and all of summer remains. Only hours had passed since we'd started, I reminded myself, and hours is not so far in. When I got back, he was in his jeans and shirt, and the towels were draped over his shoulder.

The way we walked was smooth, two of us moving as one. His arm cut across my back, high to low, and his fingers gripped the handle of my hip bone. I observed the things around me—the Mechanical Gypsy Fortune Teller, Jenkinson's Aquarium, the Daytona Driving Game, and those stuffed cats you knock down with softballs—*Three down wins choice. Dolls must be flat.* There were the rides that once you died for— the Whip, the Ski Bob, the Swings. There were fat ladies in skirted bathing suits and peddlers hawking baby hats with names in Day-Glo toothpaste script, racks of flexible sunglasses, and raffles—*Ten chances to win a red Corvette.* And that game with the gun that shoots water into the clown's mouth with the bell that screeches long and hard and forever-seeming. Through the waves of heat came the nauseating gum smell of honey-roasted peanuts and the greasy snap of sausage and the crack of frying zeppole. Children waving beehives of cotton candy and picking carameled apple from their teeth, going, "Let's go to the bumpa cauz."

At a storefront with the sign "Psychic Readings by Diana," a girl in a tangerine miniskirt and a bikini top leaned in the arch of the curtained door and called to us. "Come, come." Rourke ignored her, and I felt relieved, though I wasn't sure what I was afraid she'd say.

It was a Sunday, so adults were everywhere—leather-skinned women squinched into belly shirts and stripped-down guys with chains and nesty chests and meandering scars. All of them occupying the top of the food chain, all of them immune, impermeable, oblivious—the cutting edge of evolution.

We slowed when we approached a low brick corner building with no marking other than faded red letters at the top that were modern and straight and missing in part. *C-R-I-T-E-R——N*. As we neared the entrance, we saw a couple of guys with gym bags go in. One stopped when he saw us, and he waited at the unmarked door. He was overbuilt so his head appeared smaller than it actually was, and his hands did too, perhaps because of the thickness of his wrists. His eyes were bloodshot. He had red hair and red freckles beneath random bruises, and his ears were knuckled up like knotty growths. His jaw was enormous on the left. It looked as though it had just been broken.

Rourke said, "Looking good, Tommy."

Tommy ignored Rourke, confining his gaze to me. He checked me out like I was meat and he was shopping. I wasn't afraid with Rourke there, but still, I didn't like to think of those freckled hands.

Rourke pulled out an envelope and handed it to Tommy. "Give it to Jimmy."

"Not goin' in?" Tommy mumbled. It sounded like gargling.

"Not today," Rourke said.

Tommy shook the envelope near one weird ear. "What is it," he chuckled, "a *Dear John*?"

Rourke stepped forward twice, coming close to Tommy, dangerously close. He inspected Tommy's jaw, first the good side, then the bad.

Tommy stood frozen. He reminded me of a dog getting sniffed by another dog: it was in his best interest to be polite, but he might decide to bite anyway.

"Not a chance," Rourke said, and he took my waist, pulling me away.

On the way back to the car, Rourke bought two ice-cream cones, and we sat in the shade of the carousel house to eat them. I wasn't hungry, so I gave what I couldn't finish to Rourke, and we watched the ride go round. Something about it made me sad—the riderless horses, the exhausted wheeze of the calliope, and the greasy flicker of the mirror pendants.

He pulled me close. There was a space between his arm and his chest that seemed to have been made just for me. It was warm and I could feel his heart beat. "What is it?" he wanted to know, his voice soft and unobstructed, free from the burden of other listeners.

"It was such a long time ago," I said, "when I was little."

We walked along the water's edge the rest of the way, silently collecting pieces of beach glass that we found in the sand, jagged peppermint treasures. I gave them to him, and he put them into his shirt pocket, saving them for me, for later, which was nice. Nice to think there would be a later. Back at the car, he kissed me, and a breeze picked up out of nowhere. A wish, I thought, granted.

The house was the color of silver wheat. It was upright and immaculate, Victorian but modest. Some of the houses we'd passed really drew attention to themselves, but not this one. Its face was guarded by mammoth rhododendrons, with clusters of pink flowers set high and low, quivering like choirs of butterflies on the bendable ends of branches. I wondered about his parents, and as I did, Rourke became clearer to me: it obviously had taken special talent on their parts to manage something so wild.

The car idled at the front of the driveway while he emptied the mailbox. He walked back over, sifting through papers, extracting certain pieces and examining one envelope in particular before getting in, wedging the pile on the dashboard, and easing the car to a stop at the driveway's end. He turned off the engine, and we sat. And it was nice, and it was strange, because though it was not home, it was as good as home, and in fact, it was better—it interested me more.

A brick walkway led from the car to the backyard, passing through a wooden gateway. On the other side was a garden in full bloom, enclosed on three sides by a high wall of yew. There were birds, their calls colliding, creating a miniature symphony of sound. Rourke reached into the iron frame of an outdoor light fixture and withdrew a key, then he unlocked the door to a ground-floor apartment.

I followed him into a sun-filled studio. The mottled plaster walls were off-white and bare, and the woodwork was charcoal-gray. It smelled like recent construction, as though it had just been renovated. To our left, two glass-paned doors opened onto a brick patio, and in the corner opposite the entry, there was a modest kitchen with new appliances.

He set my bag on top of a stack of packed cardboard boxes that lined the entry. I figured they were from when he moved out of his house in Montauk the previous month, though I supposed it was possible he had not unpacked because he was leaving again to go somewhere else. Rourke moved to the kitchen counter and rifled through the remainder of his letters, popping a few apart. The room was hot, so I stepped around the couch and unbolted the doors to the yard, splitting them for air.

"I'll be right back," he said, and he disappeared down the hall.

When he left, a certain heaviness in me was alleviated; I felt my consciousness seep back into my body. Sometimes you see people on television get awakened from hypnosis. There's a dumb blink followed by an apish inner inquiry as to how long they've been witless and what degradations might have occurred. If it is a cartoon or a comic, there are stars about the eyes.

I just remained in place at the patio doors, waiting for him to return. Watching the day lower like the curtain on a play you wished would never end. I could hear the summertime nothingness, the haunting children's voices, advancing, then waning. And yet, I did not slip beyond Rourke's field of influence. It was as if we were sharing the same web or net: no matter what position he occupied, I would be moved.

His voice called my name; I met him in the corridor outside the bathroom. He was wet with a towel around his waist. On his hips and on his sides, the muscles were like cords and knots. There were drops remaining on his chest; I touched one, and the water parted. The shower was still running, so I passed Rourke, undressed, and stepped in. The heat of sunset warmed the bathroom window, and also the stall.

When I came out, he was there, dressed in jeans, holding a towel. He dried my neck and shoulders, then wrapped me up and drew me in, leaning his face on the top of my head, and I began to cry. When the tears came, we did not speak of them, either of us. Maybe it was the closeness of him, the excruciating nearness. Maybe as a vessel I was too delicate for a love so whole: it felt beyond my capacity to keep. Hanging limp over the doorknob was a dress that we'd bought on the way home from the beach—rayon red and moody, with a high waist and a halter top. He held it for me to step into. The zipper tugged at the curve of my back. In the mirror we were enigmatic, my eyes so tragic, my dress so low, and Rourke, a triumph of masculinity. He drew on a navy sweater with a short zipper at the neck, and he watched as I combed back my hair with my hands, put on lipstick, and fastened my shoes. I felt no shame before him. Shame was a luxury. We had no time for shame.

Everyone stopped and stared when we walked into Mineo's. Waiters made way, flattening their chests and inclining their heads. Rourke escorted me through the cramped space, the broad heat of his palm making an impression on the small of my back. People were waving from a booth in the rear. They seemed to be expecting us. Rourke introduced me to a woman named Lee who was pretty like a doll, and her husband, Chris, who was twice her size and who had skin like polished metal. I'd never seen skin like that. Later Rourke told me it was that way from taking steroids. The other guy was Joey, Rob's brother, whom I'd met the night before in East Hampton.

"At the beach," Joey told Lee and Chris with a jerk of his head. It seemed as though they'd been talking about it. I wondered if they'd mentioned Mark. Joey kissed me, then told Rourke he was sorry his wife, Anna, couldn't make it, but she had to stay home with the kids. "We tried to get a sitter but *nothing doing* on a Sunday. And my mother was at church all day, so she's wiped out."

"What are you talking about? How can anyone get 'wiped out' at church?" Chris snapped derisively. "She just has to sit there."

"Who knows what she does. I think they got her cleaning. She comes home and naps."

The three of them sat on one side of the booth, and I slid sideways across the bench opposite them with my back to the dining room, gripping the table to steady myself. I wasn't very steady. I tried to copy the others; they seemed more or less sure of distances and weights. I left a place for Rourke but he just stayed standing at the end of the table.

"Where's Rob?" he asked.

"Good question," Chris said.

Everyone looked to Joey, who shrugged. "I'm not his keeper."

Rourke scanned the restaurant, then excused himself. When he was gone, I felt self-conscious of my body in that dress—my breasts beneath the halter top and my thighs under the skirt, the bare way they were touching.

"So you're an artist," Lee said, leaning sweetly over. "I wanted to be an artist," she confided. "But my parents didn't think it was—not that there's anything wrong with—actually, I mean, I think they were afraid I'd marry a—well, you know. It's just—it takes confidence. You must be confident." Lee's eyes were millimeters too big for her head, and when she talked, she talked fast, captivating you with insecurities. She and Chris picked at the antipasto simultaneously; they had matching wedding bands. "Do you eat meat?" she asked. "I don't. But there are these stuffed pork chops that everybody gets that look really good."

When Rourke returned, he came up behind the waiter, who was reciting specials. As soon as the waiter realized everyone was looking behind him, rather than at him, he turned and said, "Oh, sorry, Harrison."

Rourke slid in next to me, and our two bodies notched together like pieces of a puzzle. He seemed better, lighter: I figured he'd found Rob. As soon as the waiter started talking again, Rourke cut him off, saying, "We'll take two swordfish."

Chris collected his menu and Lee's menu and tapped them on the tabletop before handing them over to the waiter. "Make that four."

And Joey said, "Five."

"So, what happened?" Chris asked Rourke. "You find him?"

Rourke said, "I just saw his car in the lot. He's parking."

I pressed lightly into him, and beneath the table, he touched the top of my thigh. My hand drifted shyly into the complicated space between his legs.

"So you went to the Jersey beach today," Lee said. "It's different from East Hampton, right?"

"Very different," I said, and nodded.

"Hey, Evie," Chris said, "did Harrison tell you he used to run Skee-Ball at Coin Castle?"

I looked at Rourke. "No, he didn't."

Rourke smiled. "Must have slipped my mind."

"That's where he met Rob," Lee said. "How old were you guys, thirteen?"

"Thirteen," Rourke said. "That's right."

"And it was love at first sight," Chris joked.

"Not quite," Joey said. "Rob always tried to hustle him."

Rourke said, "*Tried to* is right."

Rob stood at the head of the table and hunted through his pockets for something, withdrawing nothing. He'd come with Lorraine, the redhead from the day before. She said hello and distributed kisses, but Rob said nothing, not to me or anyone, though his eyes frequently darted to Rourke's. Though he was in a bad mood, I felt better with him there. Everyone did. You could tell by the way they shifted in their seats, coming up higher and adjusting the bands of their watches. Rob gave you the feeling that everything was going to be okay, that there was nothing going on in the world that he did not already know about and have an opinion on.

Rob pulled a chair to the head of the table, and bumped up next to Lorraine. I figured she was his girl. She acted bored like she was. "I had rust comin' out of my pipes all day," he reported with miserable enthusiasm. "It was like clay."

"You gotta call," Chris said.

"I *did* call," Rob said, leaning back in his chair. "I go, 'I'm supposed to shower in this shit?' " His left shoulder wrenched up. "I go, 'What, am I supposed to make coffee outta this crap?' "

As the waiter delivered two pitchers of wine and checked on Rob's and Lorraine's orders, I wondered who in Jersey took such calls.

Rob scanned the table and said, "What did you guys get, the swordfish?"

Everybody said yeah, yeah, swordfish, yeah.

Rob flipped his hand. "G'head, Ronnie, make it two more."

"They must've been working on a main line," Joey speculated about the water pipes. "They probably stirred up sediment. Give it a day."

Lorraine rearranged her bag and laid a pack of Larks near her plate. She looked like the kind of girl with brothers, the kind with a knowledge of pistons, lures, and end zones. The frayed tips of her ginger hair reached in a fan of kinky curls as if to capture creatures. It was like underwater hair. "I keep telling him—*use bottled.*"

Rob clicked his tongue. "It's the pipes, Lorraine, not the water."

"Lemme tell you something," Chris informed all of us, "that bottled water thing is *bull.* New York State tap is best. Studies show."

"Lot of good that does us here in Jersey," Rob said.

Chris said, "Yeah, well. I'm just saying."

Lee cut in, leaning toward Lorraine and asking how was Mark Ross's house in the Hamptons.

Lorraine swiped her hands through the air and said, "Unbelievable. Gorgeous." *Gaw-jus.*

Rob shook his head with disgust and shot back the first of several glasses of wine, going, "Fuckin' guy."

After dinner Lee and Lorraine went home. Lorraine didn't feel well. At least, that's what she said, though it was obvious she and Rob were fighting, probably about his drinking too much because she took the car.

"Leave me stranded," Rob called after the taillights. "G'head. I don't give a shit. I'll make new friends."

Lee said she had to work in the morning. She was a market analyst for Lehman Brothers on Wall Street. It sounded like a big job, in terms of responsibility, somewhat like being a surgeon or a bus driver. I wondered how somebody so little gets a job so big, and what she'd been doing out with us, drinking pitchers of sangria. She slid behind the wheel of their

new white Cherokee, her head rising inches above its northern arc. "It is
Sunday, isn't it?" she checked with Chris. "I have work tomorrow, right?"

Chris kissed her through the open driver's window. "Yes, babe. It's
Sunday. Go home."

"Keep an eye on him," she requested of me with a wink.

"Okay," I said, though it seemed like a major obligation. I watched
her pull out and wondered at her husband's iron constitution. I would
not have been able to let my wife go like that, into the night like a lame
firefly, buzzing off sideways into an immeasurable wood.

"Let's get outta here," he said, climbing into Rourke's car. "Let's head
over to Vinny's."

Vinny-O's was the kind of place my dad would have called a beer garden.
It was booze-logged and corrosive and lit primarily by backward neon.
How we ended up there I wasn't sure, except to say that Rob had to meet
somebody, and nobody was very happy about it. I didn't ask about the
names of the establishments—Mineo's and Vinny-O's. I got the feeling
it was a Jersey thing.

We walked into the clatter of pinball and the *ching* of the bowling
game and "Two Tickets to Paradise" by Eddie Money. I went straight to
the bathroom, which was filthy and poorly rigged. There were convoluted instructions on how to flush posted over the toilet, and they were
yellowed, not necessarily from age.

LIFT TANK TOP [CROSSED OUT] TOP OF TANK TO SINK. PULL
STRING, HOLD OR TIE TO HOOK BY LITE AND REPLACE TOP.
TAKE OUT STRING TO EXIT.

I looked, but there was no sink and no hook. There *was* a string—but
it was wet. Needless to say, the toilet had not been flushed for some time.
Voices came through the wall from the men's room, low and intermittent. When I came out, Rourke was near the front door, deep in conversation with Joey, so I went to the bar and bought myself a beer.

"Bottle or tap?" the bartender asked.

"Tap," I said. It seemed like the thing to say.

The louvers to the bathroom corridor flagged again on their spent hinges; I turned to see Rob and Chris coming out with a third guy, who cut through the front and disappeared. Theirs had been the voices I'd heard. At first I suspected they'd been buying coke, though they didn't look high. Maybe it had to do with gambling. Chris breezed past to join Joey and Rourke by the window, but Rob came to me, tossing his arms slightly out, grinning as though he hadn't seen me for so long.

"Holdin' up the bar, gorgeous?" He landed at my side and shifted in half circles, like a cat getting ready to lie down. Eventually he settled, lit a cigarette, and examined me. Each of his features looked as if it had been broken twice, yet there was something irresistible about the urgent way they all pieced together, like a skyline. He took a sip of my beer and grimaced. "What the fuck is that?"

I thought it might be Schlitz.

"Schlitz?" He looked over his shoulder to the bartender. "Hey, Marty." Marty didn't move. His arms were folded across his chest, his eyes fluttered back. "Jesus," Rob mumbled to me, then he shouted, *"Marty!* You alive?"

Marty roused himself and hitched lamely over. "Sure, Robbie. I'm alive. Unless you happen to be a bill collector."

"You're startin' to worry me over there," Rob said. "I seen more blood run through a goalpost." He lifted my glass and gestured with it, saying, "Gimme something to rinse the taste of this outta my mouth."

"How about a shot of Red?"

Rob pulled a wad of bills from his pocket. "Nah, I'll take a screwdriver." *Sh-crew-driva.* "Want something else?" he asked me. "A little brake fluid, maybe? Some rubbing alcohol?"

I told Marty I'd take Courvoisier if he had it.

"That's a giant leap," Rob said, "from Schlitz on tap."

"That's because you're paying," I told him.

We got the drinks and toasted. "So, whaddaya think of Jersey?"

"It's all right," I said. The cognac burned my throat.

He said, "First time?"

Actually I'd been a few times. My dad and Marilyn had taken me on vacations to visit things such as underground railroad sites and revolutionary war battlefields. I said, "Not technically."

"Not technically," Rob repeated with a smile, and he signaled for another drink. He looked off, as if distracted by something, maybe just something in his head. He bit the inside of his cheek and jiggled the leftover ice in his glass, making a sound like a beaded instrument. I waited and watched, because that's the thing to do with someone who is complicated and drinking heavily. I'd had lots of practice with Jack. Frequently, people try to act screwed up, but Jack really was. Sometimes you hear, *He was as strong as ten men!* Jack was not strong that way; he was screwed-up that way.

"So, you made it through," Rob said. "You and Harrison. I'm surprised." He took a drink, and his eyes skimmed the ceiling, lingering before returning to me. "So now what?" he asked.

I hadn't thought about it; I hadn't thought about much of anything. I glanced over my shoulder to Rourke; he didn't look back. Music started, mournful music, making me feel kind of lost. I set down my glass and pushed it away.

Rob watched me for a minute, then said, "You like to dance. Come dance with me." He took my hand and led me to a place between the bar and the empty dining room next to unused tables. His wiry arms held me square and polite.

Sometimes when I'm feelin' lonely and beat,
I drift back in time, and I find my feet, down on Main Street.

"Remember you and Mark danced at the Talkhouse?"
I said that I did.
"I called you Countess," he said, and I asked him why.
"Because," he said, "you have rank." He leaned close, whispering, "Just be careful."

His words gathered at my ear. I felt something surge through his body, ragged and incongruous, frustrated in its effort to transfer smoothly. Then I felt myself traveling back—it was Rourke, pulling me away. Though he stood naturally, you could tell he was not happy. Rourke didn't need to posture to intimidate, he just had to be within reasonable range of his object. His fingers closed tight on my wrist.

"Let's go," he said, taking a step, pulling me closer, my back to his front, like a hostage.

The road home was not the same as the one we'd taken on the way there. It was a local road, leafy and closing in, top-lit and wet. We made it back in minutes. The light in the third-floor room was lit; I liked seeing it. It made me feel safe. Rourke leaned over and popped my door. "You know where the key is?"

I nodded, getting out. "In the box."

The car squealed in reverse, swung around, then shot forward. How able he was to exist in the misfortune of night. How afflicted he must have been, by ritual, by rivalry, by things mannish and abstruse, to go back out. I reached for the key, wondering how long it would take him to return, and whether he was going to have to drive those guys. It was strange to think that whatever safety home provided was inadequate compared to the riddling principles that moved him.

I stepped through into the dark, remembering a small iron lamp on the bookshelves. I searched for it and turned it on. On a low table in front of the couch was a dish filled with the beach glass we'd collected. I went into the kitchen and looked in the cabinets. They were empty except for a new set of dishes.

Just be careful, Rob had said, and also, *So now what?* I wondered what else Rob might have said if Rourke hadn't stopped him? Though I had no reason to mistrust Rourke, for some reason I trusted Rob completely.

I placed my palms against the bedroom door and pushed slowly. It was empty in there except for a bed and an antique metal table with a vintage work light and a black telephone. I took up the phone cautiously and listened for a dial tone. The closet was empty, but then, he'd just come back from months in Montauk. There were boxes in the hall. Like the rest of the apartment, the room smelled of cut wood. Possibly his parents had fixed it up because they intended to rent the place, though perhaps it had been done for Rourke. It was nice to think of him as loved, as the recipient of feelings that were worthy and true.

When I heard the car, I went to the door and waited. Rourke seemed as relieved to see me as I was to see him. He pulled off his sweater before tossing it onto the couch. As he unbuttoned his shirt, his hand moved in practiced jerks. The thoughtful way he cast his gaze into space was lonely.

"He okay?" I asked.

Rourke nodded, saying, "Yeah, he's okay."

"I'm sorry," I said. "If I—"

Rourke pulled me near. I leaned against his chest and felt his head on mine, his hand on my lower back. "Forget it," he said. "It's complicated."

What followed was less a kiss, less an embrace, than a precise exchange, a diving in from opposite ends and a rolling, gliding lull at center, like mammals swimming expertly beneath the sea. I felt known, I felt assimilated. I felt a gift from life that I hardly merited. He didn't have to say that he loved me, not when I could see the gentle cast to his eyes and feel the puerile softness of his lips, not when I could sense the solitude in his hands resolved by touching me. If I didn't know what he was risking to be with me, I could feel when he held me the consequence of his choice.

The next morning we stopped at Eddie M.'s house in Red Bank. They said that we were there to see a car and that Eddie M. was a friend from high school. Rob was there already when we arrived, taking a leisurely walk around a '71 Corvette—yellow. It made me think of Mark's Porsche, with the way it was sitting in the driveway like a lost shoe, like a princess slipper. The GTO and Rob's Cougar looked like giant slabs of beef in the street. One day in Jersey, and I'd never look at cars the same.

"They didn't do too bad a job on the paint," Rob said to Eddie M. "The problem you're gonna have with the Vette is the heat coming through the floorboards."

"Tell him what happened to Jimmy Landes," Rourke said, joining the conversation without ceremony. The two showed no sign of having argued in the bar the night before, if, in fact, it had even been an argument. There was a newspaper at the end of the driveway. I sat on the corner of the lawn, flipping through the pages, taking care not to look too hard. I didn't want to know anything.

"My wife's at her mother's," Eddie M. informed me, strolling over, gawky like a farmhand. His eyes were electric and clear blue, like a husky's. "Otherwise she'd make coffee."

"Why can't you make it yourself?" Rob called over, in disgust.

"Because I don't know how to work the thing."

"It's a coffeemaker, not a backhoe."

"It doesn't matter," Rourke said to Rob. "We're going out."

"Where to," Rob wanted to know. "Pat's?"

Rourke said, "Yeah."

"I'll go with you," Rob said. "He owes me fifty bucks."

"I'll come too," said Eddie M. "I can't sit around all day waiting for Karen."

After Eddie M. put the Corvette in the garage, we took off in two cars, driving past the weeping willows, cyclone fences, and idle flags of the residential area onto the backstreets, where there were forlorn sidewalks and dwarfish brick buildings and the funereal reflection of ourselves as we proceeded in a long loose wave past the plate glass storefronts.

At a red light, Rob pulled up alongside us, his window inches from mine. The music from his car was deafening. He was singing, *"Be my love!"* When the light changed, he turned down the volume and shouted, "Hey, Contessa, what do you think of Mario Lanza?"

Morocco's was a spherical diner, like a space station or an automotive air filter, set on the side of a four-lane roadway. The steaming hot air and the diesel exhaust from all the traffic going by formed a plane of smog to walk through. The men fell into a quiet line, with me in the middle. Rob and Eddie M. were thinking how Rourke and I had just had sex. I could feel on my skin the tread of instinct and imagination.

The waitress came to our booth. Rob asked, "Where's Pat?"

"Which Pat's that, doll?" she volleyed in a gravelly voice.

"What do you mean, 'which Pat'?"

"It's a big place. We got a lot of Pats—Pat Wolf, Cellar Pat, Patty G., Kitchen Pat."

"Kitchen Pat?" Rob repeated incredulously. Eddie M. bit his cuticles and smirked. "What do I look like, a bread salesman?"

"No offense, honey, but I didn't bother to check."

"You new here, or what?" Rob inquired.

"Yeah," she said. "I just started about—sixteen years ago."

"Sixteen years, and you don't know Pat Webb—*Spider* Pat?"

"Night shift," she informed him. "If you wanna talk to someone on night shift, you might wanna come at night. We don't got dorms in back." She lifted her pad to her chest. "Now, what'll yas have?"

Rob ordered a turkey club with fries, Eddie M. got pancakes with sunny-side eggs on top, I asked for a grilled cheese, and Rourke pushed the menu toward the table rim. "Burger, medium rare."

"Coffees?" she inquired, taking up menus.

Rourke said, "Yeah, for everybody."

Rob pushed some quarters to the little jukebox suspended at the end of the table. He told Rourke to find something decent.

Eddie M. chuckled. "Find him 'Stayin' Alive.' "

"Fuck you, Eddie M."

Eddie M. said, "You jellyfish. You love the Bee Gees."

"You jerk off to Gordon Lightfoot."

"Lightfoot's a genius."

"Genius!" Rob snorted. "Let me ask you something. 'The Wreck of the Edmund Fitzgerald'—*what is that?*" Rourke and I laughed, and Rob stated dryly, "I'm totally serious. What *is* that?"

"I'm telling you, he's a poet," Eddie M. muttered.

Rourke flipped the jukebox pages. He had the inside seat across from mine, so I couldn't help but notice how his forehead was square and his cheekbones were prominent. His eyes had a black and avaricious clarity. The diner's windows were coated with enormous transparencies to mitigate the view of the highway and to tenderize the inclement glare. The sapphire cellophane light gave the impression of things Mediterranean, of him where he naturally belonged, southern France, northern Italy, a village with battered streets along the coast of Spain—with me, in white, by his side.

"Want some?" Rob asked, gesturing to me with the ketchup.

I said no, thanks.

Eddie M. popped his eggs. "Seen Tommy, Harrison?"

Rourke said, "Yesterday."

"At the gym?"

"Outside it."

"I heard he got a fracture."

Rob laughed. "A *fracture*? Some fracture. He looks like he got hit by a wrecking ball."

"That's right, and he's still standing," Eddie M. said. "Better watch your back, Harrison."

Rob chucked a napkin at Eddie M. "You know what, Eddie M., shut up. And wipe the yolk off your mouth, for Chrissakes."

Rourke put the money in the jukebox and Marvin Gaye came on. When the music started, we retreated, each of us, picking through the wilty last halves of fries and gazing into the theatrical stillness of the diner.

Mother, mother, there's too many of you crying.
Brother, brother, brother, there's far too many of you dying.

The dessert carousel stood sentry at the door. It was like a phosphorescent obelisk, twirling sleepily. The pastries marched around in a demented parade—towering meringues, tilting cakes, mammoth pies and puddings, balloon-like jelly rolls, surreal mousses. An older couple loitered at the register as they paid, satisfied and distracted. He was cleaning his teeth with a matchbox; she was straightening the vest of her peach summer suit. Past the window on the other side of the highway was another mall.

Everything looked different to me; everything *was* different. I felt an acuteness of being, a lonely fury of connectedness. It was as if I'd set off from home and its false promise of security and accidentally found sanctuary in the arms of my generation. Though I hadn't gone far, I was worlds away. And being there was like occupying a place you have long feared, but in which you suddenly find yourself, and you think, *This is okay, this is really okay.*

C'mon, talk to me, so you can see
What's goin' on. Yeah, what's goin' on.

Rob's fingers drummed the tabletop. He and Rourke looked at each other. Something passed between them, something dark but not newly dark. It was as if they were each privately thinking the same thoughts, sharing the same concerns.

"You headin' out?" Rob asked.

Rourke reached for his wallet. "Yeah, right now."

Rob lifted his hand. "I got it."

"Me too?" Eddie M. asked, somewhat surprised.

"No, you bastard," Rob said. "You pay for yourself." Then he reached over and slid my sunglasses from the top of my head. He cleaned them carefully, using the soft corner of his sweatshirt. "I'm gonna have to teach you how to take care of these things."

"I spent a weekend in Jersey once too," my mother reminisced as she filled two coffee mugs with cold Chablis. Rourke had dropped me off just hours prior, though the two had not met. I'd called her the day before to say that I was safe and with friends. "At Princeton. Very memorable." She handed me a cup. "Sorry about the mugs. I'll do the dishes tonight." She joined me at the table. "It feels like you've been gone for weeks. Susan Parsons finally moved in," she said.

"*Here?*" I hadn't figured Kate's room would be so quickly filled.

My mother furrowed her brows. "Not *here*. Into an apartment in town. You remember Susan. She was in the car accident by the bowling alley."

"David and Lowie's friend?" I asked. "The caterer?"

"No. That's *Suzanne*. Susan's the astronomer. Oh, I forgot to tell you," she said, changing the subject. "Since Powell's in Brazil through September, you can use his car for the summer. It's gotten too dangerous for the bike. The city people are insane."

I thanked her, saying that it would be great to use Powell's car.

"I'm going to an art opening tonight at Ashawagh Hall, for an artist named Ortega. He mounts bowling balls on wedges. They look like giant olives on giant cheeses. Very *geometric*. Feel like coming?"

"I'm pretty tired. Maybe next time." She smiled, but I knew she was down. It would have been easy to tell myself that my leaving home would mean nothing to her, but I kind of felt bad to take my-self away.

On the mail table there were two phone messages from Kate and sev-eral from Denny and Sara Eden and one from Dad. There were en-velopes from the NYU bursar's office and the NYU School of the Arts and a single tattered card from Jack, postmarked the day before gradua-tion. It was a vintage photograph of East Hampton, with cows in the middle of Main Street, and, huge on the right, the tree we loved. Jack had written a long note that I didn't really want to read, so I set the card writing-side out on the windowsill by the kitchen sink. I stepped back to regard it, noticing that his writing reeled and lurched to form the shape of an owl. From where I stood it looked like a relief or woodcut. It did not inspire sadness exactly, but something that moved in the mask of sadness, influenced as it was by the infancy of summer and the recent in-vincibility of my heart.

In the basement, damp towels from the weekend were piled on the dusty, cold concrete floor. I sat against the washing machine, removing from my bag the pieces of clothing I'd worn to Jersey, pressing each one to my face, deep and close like an oxygen mask, smelling my sweat and his, soaking in each kiss, and the last—especially the last, the one in the driveway with his palm taking the ladder of my neck, drawing me in.

"You know where to find me?" Rourke had asked.

I didn't really, but I said that I did, then I released myself from his grip, slipping out. He would be in the same cottage in Montauk he'd stayed at all winter. Before we'd left Jersey that morning, I'd heard him call the owner and arrange to take back the house and keep it through the end of August. I'd never been there, but I remembered the St. Patrick's Day parade when Rob said Rourke lived across the street from where we'd been standing.

The night that followed was a long one. Through the length of it, I felt many contradictory things—I felt alive, but I felt also and intensely the part of me that was dead. If I was unattended, I was not lonely. I was kept tranquil through the hours by the memory of the tenderness of his hands, by the devotion in his eyes, by the glorious opposition between us that could never be lost to me, not even if he was lost to me.

29

After my waitressing shift at the Lobster Roll, I changed in the bathroom, put on lipstick, and had a Beck's out back with the lunch staff, all of us listening to Neil Young. It had been a long time since we'd seen one another. We didn't talk much; we looked out onto Napeague stretch, the two-lane highway that ran alongside the restaurant, and we watched the cars pass. The sunset spilled down the road from west to east, returning to us slow, like honey from an overturned jar.

I drove Powell's steel-blue Dodge Charger toward Montauk, whipping around the treacherous curves of Old Montauk Highway, ducking oncoming Jaguars, speeding over peaks, sending my stomach flying. I knew I was not going to die—not then, not that way.

In Montauk, the giant lamps of the ballpark illuminated the northern arc of the traffic circle, so I headed in that direction. Rourke's car was parked at the field, so I swung into the lot next to Trail's End Restaurant, left my shoes in the car, and walked across the street to the field. There were bleachers with friends and family mixed from both sides. It seemed like a nice group. I climbed a few rows up and sat, pulling my skirt tighter around my thighs.

Rourke was at first base. Though he wore a uniform that matched the other uniforms, he looked unlike the others. I located him through the cloth. I saw him differently now; I saw his limbs, and I knew their weight, their strength. Buttons were missing from the base of his shirt, and just past the split was his abdomen, the pale brown of his skin and black of his hair. He didn't acknowledge me, though he knew I was there.

An old man paced on the rim of the field. He turned to those of us in the stands and chastised, "Shout it up out there, Montauk. You sound like a bunch of mutes!"

When the last batter of the last inning hit a foul that popped past first

base, Rourke ran backward, then leapt to catch it. For a moment he pre-
vailed in air; there was a collective breath, the slap of the ball against the
hide of his glove, and raucous cheers. He headed in with his teammates,
his stride long, his head modestly inclined. Before home plate he split
off, coming to me, straddling the bench I was on. His face lowered to
mine, our foreheads grazed, our hair intertwined.

"I missed you," he said, breathing out. "C'mon." He gave me his
hand, the two of us rising. "Let's take a walk."

I followed his lead. It felt out of control to be in love with someone so
masculine. It was like being an amateur with your own supernatural ca-
pacities. Both teams had collected informally around the second set of
bleachers, and, as we passed, Rourke was handed two bottles of beer,
which he took in his free hand, the one not holding mine. The guys
spoke to Rourke warmly.

"Glad you showed up, man."

"Nice catch."

*"Hey, next time you move, let a few weeks pass before you come back. We'd
like to have the girls to ourselves for a while."*

At his car Rourke put the bottles on the hood and he bent to kiss me,
wrapping one arm around my waist, pulling me in and up, bearing
down. I remember the cool metal against my shoulders, the wet grass beneath my feet, and around us, the curious imperative of cricket noise
swelling to near crescendo.

"How did you get here?" he wanted to know.

I pointed across the street. "Car."

"Car?" he said, like that was funny. "C'mon. Get in. I'll drive you over."

Before joining me, he removed his wet shirt, tossing it into the backseat, asking me to hand him a clean one, which I did, holding it out to
the part of his abdomen that obstructed the open driver's window. As we
were about to leave, there were two knocks on the trunk. Some guy
leaned in the window. On his kelly-green jersey there were numbers, and
a name, Roger.

Roger nodded to me politely, saying hi. "You guys coming to the Tattler?"

Rourke just said, "Not tonight, but thanks. We're heading home."

———

My first impression was of the darkness, the way it was dappled. The moonlight entered the cottage from various angles and settled in irregular patches like it does on the floor of a forest. There were earthy odors and the thrill of encampment. I thought of his winter alone, and about the applications of his privacy. I wondered how he'd stayed warm. I thought of the nights we'd missed—an entire year.

Besides the random pools of moonlight, the room was featureless in the near pitch. A cast-iron stove materialized at the distant right. He knelt before it, matches in hand. One triangular tip of paper swelled to life within the elliptical swing gate, then the flame progressed down the edge before catching entirely and illuminating in a fan the shallow range around him, his upraised hand, his bent leg, several inches of floor. The kindling caught, brightening more—a couch, a chair, a stretch of old windows above the kitchen fixtures, the suitcases, boxes, and stereo he'd taken back from Jersey. I knew because I'd helped him load the car.

I knelt in front of the fire while he went in back to change. There was nothing in my mind while I waited, nothing other than the vanes of firelight tripping erratically and the rising temperature of my skin. It was as if I were becoming the fire and the fire were becoming me. Rourke returned wearing a frayed blue sweater and a pair of jeans that were soft with holes. He was tall until he came down, sitting alongside me on the floor, looking at the fire too. He seemed less complicated than usual, his masculinity more authentic. I thought maybe I was seeing not what he chose to show but what he chose not to conceal, which was different. Though physically we were opposites, emotionally I felt strangely similar; I felt almost as I'd felt with the fire, as though being with him was like being with me.

I heard him take a breath. He asked if I felt like staying. He went no further, but I knew what he meant. He meant the whole summer, week to month, night to day—he was asking me to suffer the transformations in his arms. Yes, I said. I would stay.

30

The he anonymous green-and-white cottage sat at the crest of a hill over-looking the bay on a street called Fleming Road. The reminder of Jack was unfortunate, but the connection ended with the name. The house was unlike any other I'd been in. The constant currents of light and air it received made it seem invulnerable to misfortune; and yet, it was mod-est, like a tent or teepee. Each day there was a new day, with nothing car-rying over from the previous one—when morning came through the window, it came as if by surprise. The sun would advance upon my skin, reminding me to be grateful, and his arms would take me tighter.

It was there that I met myself, there that I discovered my soul's in-vention, the feminine genius of me. I often thought about life beyond the summer, acknowledging that an end was imminent, that I needed to prepare. The world sloped against our door like a barren belly—I could feel it. Had I been sentenced to death, I could not have interpreted time with a fiercer consciousness—every twilight seemed to be the last, every rain the final rain, every kiss the conclusive aroma of a rose, gliding just once past your lips.

If he loved me, love wrought no change in him. He did not speak of such things, and neither did I, because words and promises are false, re-solving nothing. I was an American girl; I possessed what our culture val-ued most—independence and blind courage. From the beginning he had been attracted to the savagery in me that matched the savagery in him, and yet, what bound us was the prospect of that soundness unrav-eled. I began to unlearn things I'd been taught. Often I was afraid, but my fear was a natural fear, a living fear, a fear of the unknown. I would not have exchanged it for a wasteland of security. It kept me vigilant through the night.

No matter what was to happen between us in the end, he would not be to blame. If I were to be wounded, it would not be because he wanted to wound me. His battles lay elsewhere, with things of which I was reluctant to conceive—time and obligations, ambition and money. I wished it didn't have to be that way. I wished there were no place in life to go. I wished for his sake that I were older, stronger, better, that I might have sheltered him.

Sometimes when I lay in the cradle of his arms, he would draw me closer, squeezing as if to concede something. Sometimes when his exhausted weight landed against my breasts, and his hair invaded my parted lips, and all I could hear was silence, a palisade so sullen and arid that nothing could possibly breach it, I would say, "Rourke."

The days were simple, numb, and narrow. My impressions collected in layers like generations of rock beneath earth, impacted to form a single idea—that I was happy. I didn't write; I didn't draw; I kept no record of conversations or clothes, places passed or inhabited. Each moment that expired was a butterfly escaping, imperial in hue and contour, membranous and sheer, fluttering magically, slipping off to the gaping enormity of liberty and oblivion. Like whispers through grasslands or heath entwined with dew, in my mind and in my memory, what remains of that summer is an overriding sense of completeness.

Though my body's demands for nature were met by days spent outdoors and evenings working in a roadside restaurant, by expressions of flesh and trials of desire, I found no end to my interest in the wild. Wherever I looked, I wanted to lie, though that was not always possible. It was like being hungry for blood and smelling it everywhere around, hearing it drive, and you do not mind it touching you when you are it and it is you. If, at night, I would have dared to leave his side, I would have walked into the velvet stealth, knowing that nothing would ever hurt me there. That summer I felt the casing of my skin dissolve. I felt myself connect as pools connect.

In the mornings, I would sit on the step beneath the chipped front door after a shower, waiting for the sun to dry the water from my skin. I would push my heels into the grass and warm dirt, thinking, *God really is everywhere.* Rourke would join me, coming to the porch with a pot of coffee and a cup for us to share. A space between the houses across the road revealed the smoky blue bay, and through that slender break we would look to the west. And him reaching, his hands touching my hair. And pain, a knowledge of the advance of time, an instinct that luck does not last, a feeling of modesty in regard to the opulence of my circumstances. And a sense that we had to hurry.

"Is it time?" I would ask.

"Yeah," he would say. "I bet you're hungry."

The GTO would barely drop speed before veering to the shoulder at Four Oaks, where we bought breakfast—either there or at Herb's in town. Our doors would pound in unison, and I would walk a little behind, watching the even force of his legs as they hit the street. Sometimes Doreen, the cashier, would wave before we reached the door, and Rourke would toss up his arm. If you didn't know already that Doreen drank Jack Daniel's, you could tell by the purple swell of her face. Once at Tipperary, Rourke bought her a drink. She thanked him, and when she lit a cigarette, the hand gripping the match trembled. The bartender brought a rocks glass filled with rust-colored stuff, not bothering to ask what she'd like, and she sat back in her chair and sipped like she was comfortable, more comfortable there than at home.

Inside the deli, the floor tiles felt stark under my bare feet, and the air was so cold it seemed to come from my bones. Near the coffeemaker was a platter of collapsed and sorry Danish. I would dig through for a few free of flies while "Piano Man" played on the radio. If people were talking to Rourke, as often they did, I would wait by the creaking novelty rack, spinning it to see the latest yo-yos and water pistols, and the guys behind the counter would stare, calculating the circumference of my ass. My eyes would pass over theirs, as if to say, *Do you honestly think you could do to me the things he does?*

Sometimes he would scan the headlines while we waited for sandwiches, other times he avoided them, in either case striving to follow his way. He would run a hand through his hair, then turn to find me, as if afraid that I might have vanished. Upon seeing me he would return to summer, seduced again, despite some sounder verdict of which I remained unaware. It was as if everyone had been evacuated, but by some miracle of stupidity we remained.

"That everything?" Rourke would ask, pulling bottled water and peaches from my arms, and tossing knots of cash on the counter.

At the beach, we would eat. He would run several miles and swim several miles, and I would read and sleep, and if he thought I was getting too much sun, he would lay a shirt on my back—the cotton dropping down like a parachute. When he stood or walked, women would adjust their glasses and arch the bridges of their ribs. If they lay on their bellies, they would tug the strings of their suits higher around their lifted bottoms and spy him through the fragrant triangles between arms and blankets. Jealousy was not possible; no one could love him better or more. I would just turn away and face the sun, feeling it heal the flesh he'd used. The women didn't know what I knew. They knew nothing of unconditional discretion or singleness of heart, or femininity, when femininity is madness and uncertainty and vertigo in his arms. By two o'clock he would pull his jeans over his shorts, fastening them. During our procession to the car, everyone would watch solemnly, even children and dogs.

He would knock the front door open with his thigh because his hands would be full, and after shaking the blanket and hanging the towels to dry, we would meet by the side of the bed. The influence of his body would weigh down the mattress, and for a moment we would sit. Tenderly, we would touch, each striking lightly against the skin of the other. Sex in the day can be sad. It is to risk in light, to reach for things there and not there, to confess that you are searching, despite what you have found. In day, his face was a reflection of my own, his features flushed with innocence and a reassuring lack of sufficiency. At times, I could not bear the monuments there. At times, I felt sick from the sight of the child I'd been, lost until found in his eyes—and him, a child too. I often thought to say something. It was possible that he wished to talk.

I never once felt the way I'd felt with Jack—baffled and agitated, unable to articulate some grave humiliation, some feeling that I'd been wrongly used, despite Jack's maudlin concerns and conceited timidity. Jack's tenderness was like a barrier, a reef you dared not swim through. He expressed care because he saw cause for anxiety; if you responded to it, it would prove his anxiety correct. But with Rourke there was dignity in indifference and grace in separateness. As I'd suspected, Jack had been wrong—desire is not deviant. To seek resolution through intimacy and to achieve it is to rise with your feelings confirmed, and not as if things have been unclosed and will remain that way until they are unclosed some more, each time a little wider. After sex with Rourke, the nerves in me would be stilled. Afterward he did not disgust me with tenderness. Afterward I said nothing, and he said nothing, and the look of my underwear on the floor did not depress me.

While I showered and dressed for work, he would make phone calls; I didn't know to whom. I didn't think about where his money came from. I never asked what he did while I worked at night. I never looked through his belongings. His discreteness was sacred to me; inside, I preferred it. It's hard to explain, except to say that when Jack and I used to walk, we would crash into each other, listlessly, lazily. But Rourke and I never bumped into each other. If ever we intersected, it had meaning, new meaning, not mine, not his, but a *third* meaning. The only thing that changed noticeably was that every Tuesday was more difficult than the one that preceded it. Tuesday was my day off, but not his. He would get up before sunrise, throw on some clothes, and before leaving the room, he would turn his head incompletely, saying, *See you later.* And when, late on a Tuesday evening, he returned, I would not go to him; I could not even necessarily move. I would just watch him, overwhelmed by the need to vow something, secure something.

Montauk was the Vegas of my imagination, a dwarfish Vegas, with garish toylike motels and two-story arcades bright as airfields, and tourists in unscrupulous attire. Men in black socks played miniature golf at Puff 'n Putt with beet-skinned ladies in extra-large T-shirts, while teenagers secreted off to the muddy seclusion of paddleboats. Chesty guys from the boroughs named Sisto and Vic who ate three- and four-pound lobsters but never got a drop of lung on their shirts swatted at their kids' heads, and checked me out through my sweater, while their wives bought miniature lighthouses and driftwood seagulls and boats inside bottles. Locals I never saw but read about in the paper grew pot in their gardens and kept arsenals in their basements, and celebrities hid like game in the cliffs. Steps away from the midget scrub pines of the village was the ocean. Not a tranquil ocean, like the lagoonish satin-lit backdrops of

Florida or the Caribbean, but a northern one that coerced you into the confidence of its fury. When you swam at midnight in Montauk, you waived everything—you surrendered. Montauk was not pretty; it was something else entirely.

Sometimes we'd go to the Tattler, or to the Montauket for sunsets. The Dock was the place to get coffee after midnight, black or with Baileys. At the Dock, the tables would fill up with people Rourke knew from slow-pitch or the beach and occasionally with people I knew, like Lisa Tobias or Sam the Dominican waiter from the Lobster Roll, and his girlfriend, Lou, from the Surf Shop. The first time we went, Ray Trent and Mike Reynolds walked in, and they were surprised to see me. I introduced them to Rourke, and the three of them sat around until closing, talking about rugby, the start of the Olympic Games in Moscow, and whether or not Ali stood a chance against Holmes in Nevada in October. I left them alone, like leaving three toddlers in a room with toys, and when Rourke pushed back his chair that night to go home, I pushed back mine as well, kissing those guys goodbye. Rourke didn't seem to mind them anymore, not like he had the day of the St. Patrick's parade.

If Rob was in town, we would go to Gosman's for dinner and wait for an outdoor table even if it took twice as long, because Rob didn't come all the way from Jersey to sit indoors. "If I wanted to sit inside," he'd snap at the hostess who'd make the obligatory inquiry: *inside or out?* "I coulda stayed in Jersey watchin' *Love Boat* with my grandmother."

From the cocktail patio near the docks, we would observe the eerie cortege of yachts slinking to berth after a day of lusty immoderation, the strings of spotlights on deck shining into the sable wax of water. You couldn't help but wonder what it would be like to be those people on the yachts, with arrowhead jaws and matted hair and wrinkled whites, flesh alive with the stink of coconut oil and vodka. The luxuriant smell of tar would blend with the grasping stench of fish, and hostile gulls on pylons would face off with you. When the hostess would call out—"Cirillo party"—we would leave our daiquiris and go slow, the three of us, like we were somewhere else in the world, somewhere with stepped streets, cob-bled and precariously narrowed, where bread is wrapped in paper and wine in wax and string, someplace where it does not hurt to be happy, where there are no necessary ends, where it's not humiliating to end up exactly where you start out.

Rob stayed on the couch. He would wake up first because he didn't sleep well except in his own bed, which was a Sealy Posturepedic. He would rap on our door two times fast, and Rourke would sit up, throwing his legs over the side of the mattress, tossing a piece of the sheet over my hips, though he didn't have to do that. It didn't matter if Rob saw me. There was nothing I needed to hide from him.

"Yeah," Rourke would say.

The door would creak open, and Rob would hop up onto the door frame and hang from his fingertips to do a few chin-ups, saying, "C'mon, let's go get some eggs."

On the walls of Salivar's, there were fish carcasses of an affecting diamond blueness, befitting equally the subterranean depths of seas and the paneled walls of saloons. Rob would make fast friends with strangers at the counters, talking about how much weight DeNiro gained for *Raging Bull,* and the Islanders winning the Stanley Cup, and bizarre marginalia from the papers such as streaking or Texaco making gasoline from corn or the surgical detachment of Siamese twins.

"Leave 'em," was his solution to the Iranian hostage crisis. "Anyone dumb enough to go to Iran in the first place is up to no good. Either they're missionaries or monkeys for industry."

Rob never sat at the beach. He paced restlessly, talking to everyone. He organized volleyball games with burly guys in True Value towels wrapped high on waists, and he played paddleball with every adolescent like it was his personal duty. He threw balls to lonely dogs, he built castles with kids, and he always only faced the sun. "Why should I bother getting a tan on my back? If I'm walkin' away from you, I don't care what you think."

When Rourke was gone, it was Rob's hand on my waist or his coat on my shoulders, Rob's voice suggesting we get a cup of coffee or a couple of sandwiches and go do laundry.

"We'll be right back," he told Rourke one morning after fishing out on the *Viking Star,* a charter boat Rob liked to go on. Rourke was hosing off bluefish in a plastic tub. Rob ran me across the street to Zorba's Inn, a dilapidated motel near Gosman's that looked like a lean-to. He pulled an Instamatic from his sweatshirt pocket. "Get a shot of me in front of Zorba's. I'm gonna tell Jimmy Landes this is where Harrison is living."

Sometimes when I was at work, they would go over to the OTB in Southampton and then to the Woodshed by the Bridgehampton drive-in to see some waitress Rob had a thing for. I met her one night at the carnival in North Sea; her name was Laura Lasser. Laura wore blue eyeliner and stonewashed jeans with an eyelet T-shirt and skinny white skip sneakers from Caldor. She was pretty but heavy, which was okay by Rob, who frankly liked a big ass.

When Rob took her on the rickety old Ferris wheel that night, Rourke told him, "Jesus, be careful up there."

Like wayward objects from the sky, the guys would just show up at one of the picnic tables behind the Lobster Roll, usually around ten, straddling the benches and talking shit about Johnny Rutherford doing 142 miles per hour to win the Indianapolis 500 or Ottis Anderson's 1600-yard rushing season or the Steelers or the Lakers or Evel Knievel's Snake River Canyon jump, or just old times in Rob's '68 Challenger or on the boardwalk with Daisy and Pongo and the Chinaman.

When Rob's friend Bobby G. died that August from complications following the motorcycle accident he'd had in March, Rourke met Rob in the Bronx one Sunday for the service. They showed up in Montauk after midnight with Rob hanging limp off of Rourke's shoulder, both of them wearing navy pinstripe suits. Rourke jerked his head for me to leave the room, but Rob said no. "Don't make her go, Harrison. I don't want her to go."

Rob halfway undressed, and he straddled the arm of the sofa in his sleeveless undershirt and his suit pants, clutching a bottle of Cuervo. Rourke made egg sandwiches, and I watched the topography of Rob's skinny tattooed arm flicker as he folded and unfolded a matchbook from Ruggerio's Funeral Home. It was a beautiful arm, tapered and muscular, like a junkie's arm. When the deejay on WPLR said, "This is Dana Blue. The request line is open," Rob waved the bottle left and right, going, "Get me the phone, get me the phone." As if by some supernatural occurrence, he got through to the station, and we three drew together in a memorable trinity—Rourke holding a plate of eggs and hovering over Rob, Rob on the sofa, legs apart, knees high, holding the receiver, and me kneeling on the floor with the phone like an offering, all of us still except for the manic push of Rob, the life and guts of him.

"I just lost a friend," he said. "You know what I'm saying—he's dead." Dana Blue must have said sorry and asked what could she do, because he thanked her, then cleared his throat. "Can you send out Dylan's 'Knockin' on Heaven's Door' to Bobby G.? Tell him it's from Robbie and the Chinaman."

If they came to pick me up before my shift ended, I would bring them beers and fries, which made Rob happy. Rob liked to get a deal, it was a matter of pride, it made him feel less cheated by life. His was in a tough predicament. It's tough when the things that make you proud—family, heritage, home—are the same things that shame you. One reason Rourke meant so much to Rob was that Rourke was like one foot in and one foot out. And Rourke was conscious of that line. Whenever Rob was around, Rourke tightened up, like trying not to stumble or risk hurting Rob in any way. Sometimes they would talk quietly, and when I'd pass by, they'd get quieter still. I'd pick up the empty fries baskets and the beer bottles and wipe down the table, and Rourke would unfold his arms and reach for me, taking me by the hips into his lap or running a hand up the inside of one thigh and down the other.

Sometimes Rob would manufacture fake conversations when I would come by to hide the fact that they'd actually been speaking of Mark Ross. "So, this girl Rudy married, right, she's a born-again. They're over there in Stuyvesant Town now."

Once in August, Alicia came into the Lobster Roll to see me, and she told me they'd all had dinner together the previous night at the Driver's Seat in Southampton—Mark, Rob, Rourke, Alicia, and her boyfriend, Jonathan, and some other people I didn't know, friends of Mark's probably. I realized they'd probably been seeing one another all along. I wanted to ask her how Mark was doing, how was his new job and apartment in Manhattan, but I didn't want to open any closed avenues. I wondered if Mark had heard I'd been living with Rourke, and what he thought about that. For a long time I'd forgotten to remember Mark, then it all started returning to me—this knowledge that he was waiting. That's how you know summer's almost over, when things start returning to you.

Last time I saw Rob that summer was a Tuesday, near the end—at least it seemed near the end. Possibly there had been a previous end, another day that I hadn't noticed.

After Rourke left that morning, I rode my bike to the beach, stopping first at Whites Drug Store for gum. The air was still, and the tide was low, so I placed my towel near the waves, and I opened my book—Hemingway's *The Sun Also Rises*. Two white-haired babies ran around a sand castle, and a boom box played Pink Floyd.

> *Hey you, out there in the cold, getting lonely, getting old.*
> *Can you feel me?*
> *Hey you, out there on your own, sitting naked by the phone.*
> *Would you touch me?*

"You waltzed right past me." It was Rob, bending for a kiss. "I'm playing volleyball."

"What are you doing here? It's Tuesday. Don't you have work?"

"I came out this morning. I told everybody I had jury duty. Come on over."

I shaded my eyes. There were a lot of people. "I'll just wait here."

"Come *over*." He gestured with my book as we walked, slapping it twice in his palm. "Good book," he said. "Brett Ashley, that's you." He spread my towel near his, by the net.

"Hey, Rob," one of the guys called. "Sometime this century."

"Keep your shorts on," he barked back, then he put his cap on my head, adjusting it until it was low near the bridge of my sunglasses. "Red Sox," he said. "Don't lose it."

My bike just about fit into the trunk of the Cougar, and Rob threaded his tank top through the metal coupling and tied a knot to hold it in. He had white surgical tape around his wrist. I could not see his tattoo from where I sat because it was on his left bicep and he was driving. It was a lightning bolt through the word *Zeus*. At the carnival that time, Rob told

Laura Lasser that Zeus came down to fertilize the earth. He peered into her blushing face. "You know what I'm talking about, *to fertilize,* right?"

We dropped the bike at the house and left a note for Rourke to meet us, then we grabbed some pizza and ate it on the hood of the car, watching the mellow defervescence of day. In the waning heat, the village seemed a place of endless possibilities. Everyone waved like they knew us.

"That's because they do," Rob said. "Everybody knows you."

On the way down Old Montauk Highway to Surfside, I was thinking that life is like being born into a prison that is you, and there comes one opportunity to escape, one second when everything coalesces into something like perfect timing, and you dash, or you don't. Maybe everyone gets a chance to run, but not everyone goes for it. That summer I had the feeling of being on the outside, of having crossed over. I was thinking about that, and about bravery and identities that are original, about my grandparents getting on boats alone when they were fourteen and coming to America from Europe. I was thinking of opportunities my father never had because of risks taken by his own parents, and whether my mother had wanted me. If my mother hadn't wanted me, she must have felt bad about that, over time, through the years. And I was thinking of Rourke, how he could not be possessed, how I loved him for it, but at the same time I knew I couldn't ever let go. I wanted to ask Rob. I had the feeling Rob would have something to say about releasing things you love.

"Today's my birthday," he said as I reached for the door handle.

"Oh," I said, turning back in. "Happy birthday, Rob." I reached to kiss him, leaning far because he was still at the wheel. It was nice that he wanted to spend it with me.

Surfside was in that peculiar state of restaurant nothingness before the full staff arrives, when the kitchen and bar are the only points of activity, and the main room is set but sleepy and unpeopled. When I was little, my mother used to waitress part-time at Bobby Van's in Bridgehampton, and sometimes she'd take me to work with her. Between jobs such as polishing spots off silverware or folding napkins, I would eat pan-fried hamburgers and do homework and draw on Guest Check pads. Before closing, I would get chocolate ice cream in the overbright kitchen, then fall asleep in a back booth until my mother was done. She would put her feet up and count cash.

"What are you thinkin' about?" Rob asked. We were in the doorway, white ocean light behind us. Probably we looked cool like thieves or ranchers.

"Nothing," I said. "My mother."

The bathroom was frilly, like a man's idea of a ladies' room. I brushed the sand from my skin and washed my hair under the faucet. It had gotten longer and lighter over the summer; it went straight below my jaw, and I had bangs. I removed my bathing suit. Two white triangles marked my breasts, and one marked my bottom. I threw on khakis and a white top I'd taken up to the beach with me so I could go shopping before riding my bike home. My breasts had gotten bigger. I wondered how long had they been that way. Maybe from birth control pills.

Rob was at the bar. I walked over, and the bartender stopped cutting limes. He smiled, saying his name was Val. I returned the Red Sox hat to Rob, and I said my name was Eveline. Val was a curious name for a man, I thought, without obvious origin. Rob and I drank two mint juleps each, and when Val started to make us another, Rob said, "Just one. No more for her."

"Why, what's the problem?" Val wanted to know.

"With the Contessa over here? I gotta keep my eye on her," Rob stated matter-of-factly. "She's very loosely wrapped."

Before the dinner shift started, Val went on break. Rob and I joined him out back behind the building, cutting through the kitchen. We headed through a screen door so covered in gunk that it didn't even bang when it slammed shut. It made a sound like a donkey—*hee haw*. Then—nothing. Right away Val lit a joint. It had been months since I'd gotten high, the last time was the night I broke up with Jack. I didn't really feel like it, but I didn't want to say no since it was Rob's birthday. It hit me quickly. I'd forgotten the way everything leapt to life: the smell of creosote from the retaining wall, the growl of the walk-in refrigerator, the insects sawing noisily, the uneven clamor from the kitchen, the waitresses calling early orders, the newly sizzling things, the clinking racks of last night's glasses exiting the dishwasher. I felt myself shiver. My skin felt sunburned, which is to say both cold and warm at the same time. Rob removed my sunglasses to clean them, and I thought about Val's name, whether it was Valery or Valentin.

"*Vallejo*—it's my last name. My first name's Rick," he said. "My grandfather was *Juan Vallejo,* a matador from Pamplona who got pinned in the ring. The bull's horns came on either side of his chest. He survived, but he had scars here and here." Val opened his shirt and pointed to the pockets beneath his arms. His body was like his name, sleek and curiosity-inspiring.

"Funny coincidence," Rob said. "Evie's reading Hemingway—the bullfighting book."

The cook came up to the kitchen door. He pulled a navy bandana from his pants pocket and tied it ceremoniously around his head. "You guys feel like eating?" he asked.

Rob said, "Absolutely!"

Within the half hour, three plates of grilled tuna hit the bar. The tuna steaks were shaped like triangles with charcoal stripes, and the vegetables were twigs stacked like teepees. There was a little ball of wild rice. I couldn't imagine eating; it made me sick just to look.

"I'm gonna take a walk," I proposed.

"What are you talking about?" Rob asked incredulously. "The food just got here."

I didn't know what to say, so I said nothing, which seemed to make him nervous. Instead of arguing, he gazed into his plate like it was a far-off horizon. "Where to?" he asked, taking a bite, chewing, not looking up.

"The bathroom."

"The bathroom," he repeated, processing. "You planning to use it, or are you just going sightseeing?"

I said, "Sightseeing."

"At least she's honest," Val said.

"Let me tell you something," Rob said, "I'd rather watch somebody's dog than their girlfriend." He tapped my plate with his knife. "C'mon, eat first, babe," he advised. "It's on the house."

Montauk Daisies are sturdy low bushes that grow in sand, and out by the road where Rob parked there were several, a few beginning to bloom. It was early for flowers. Usually they don't flower until mid-September.

One of the bushes was by the rear fender of Rob's car, so I propped open the driver's door and sat sideways in the seat, facing the plant, facing south over the ocean, kicking my feet through the renegade sand that had made its way to the roadside. The ground had begun to turn cold, the way it does on late summer evenings. I brushed my hair and put on lipstick and played around with Rob's eight-tracks—the Four Seasons, the Stones, the Del Vikings, Stevie Wonder, Frank Sinatra. Though it was totally outdated, he kept an eight-track in his car so nobody would steal his tapes. The floor was littered with empty Chinese take-out containers and flaccid newspapers, and there was a box of Wash'n Dris on the dashboard. Rob was a fanatic about clean hands.

On the back of a cocktail napkin, I drew the daisy for Rob and I composed a birthday note, which contained the usual sort of wishes, *Happy Returns* and so on, except that at the end, right before my name, I wrote *I love you.* I set it under the steering wheel on the glass pane in front of the meters and indicators. For a long time I stared at the words, positive of meaning and sure of fact but uncertain as to why that love was suddenly so emphatic, and I began to cry. In the mirror I saw my tears. They were like little missives, tiny flags and trumpets, announcing messages from the inside of me to the world beyond, though I could not think of what the messages were because at that moment Rourke appeared. Through the passenger window I saw him jog onto the restaurant's porch, and my tears disintegrated, everything vanishing upward. I heard myself say, "Oh."

Rob stepped out of the front door before Rourke stepped in, and Rob gestured to me in the car: Rourke must have asked where I was. It was nice to think that he had come for me. If Rourke did not exist, then maybe I would have ended up with someone like Val, who would have been nice to kiss, though it would not have been love or anything like it. It would have been something lonely and fascinating, like occupying someone else's house for a night or two, if it happened to be a particularly nice house.

Rourke propped his shoulder firmly against a porch post and began to talk. From where I sat it looked as if he were keeping the building from folding in upon itself. Rob turned and leaned on the rail. I could only see his back, but I could tell by the uncharacteristic way he slumped, with his arms hanging lifelessly, that he was upset. Rourke I could not read; his body was organized as usual by an economy of action and emotion. I assumed they were arguing. Soon Rob stood and walked back into the bar. Rourke remained in place, staring out, no doubt deciding what to do— wait for me or go in after Rob. He turned and went in.

I locked the car and took the path back to the restaurant, walking slow. I had the impression I'd forgotten something. I felt for Rob's keys in my hand, making sure they were there. I looked to my shoes. They were there too. Behind me was nothing. Just Rob's car and Old Montauk Highway and the ocean, far down.

The bar had become crowded, but it wasn't hard to find them. A room changed wholly when Rourke was in it—energy tagged about him in a sort of helix. They observed my approach as I squeezed through the pack to reach them. Rourke put out his arms, jerked me to his chest, and lifted me onto a stool. He touched my halter top, saying, "This is a little revealing to wear in public, isn't it?"

"Leave her alone, Harrison," Rob said dismally. "I picked her up at the beach. She wasn't there with a suitcase."

For the remainder of the night the two of them hardly spoke, though Rob made sure to get one more free meal for Rourke. No matter how angry Rob was, it wouldn't have been in him to cut Rourke out of a deal. While Rourke ate, Rob kept drinking whatever Val put in front of him. The more Rob drank, the more he kept reaching out to others, greeting old friends, making new ones, until eventually we'd become a sizable crowd. Rob commandeered the pool table and hustled six players before turning to Rourke and challenging him to "a serious game." Rourke consented, standing without a word, as though he'd expected the invitation. It occurred to me that Rob had intended to play Rourke from the start; that all the other games had been leading to this one.

They each laid down two twenty-dollar bills. Though the bar was noisy, there was the impression of silence in our area. The men concentrated on the table, moving around it like it was theirs and theirs alone. As one would shoot, the eyes of the other would lock on the ball pattern, memorizing the layout. The game had a different quality than the preceding ones; not only was it an even match, but Rob and Rourke had obviously played together thousands of times. In the end, Rob won, but it was unclear whether Rourke had simply let him.

"C'mon," Rob said. "I'll give you a chance to win your money back."

Rourke handed Rob the twenties and said, "Happy birthday."

I stood off my stool and gave it up to Rourke, who sat and pulled me onto his lap. I felt his thigh between my legs. Next up against Rob was Roger, the captain from the slow-pitch team, but by then I'd stopped paying attention. I was distracted by Rourke; he was distracted too. I could tell by the death-like tranquility of his hands. Through my stupor, I could only register the knock and split of the balls, the slugs of color whizzing across the verdant felt, the thuckish gulps of the pockets swallowing balls, the ups and downs of drunken conversation.

"He's doing really good," I said to Rourke. "Too bad there's no girl to impress."

"There is," Rourke said. "You."

We were outside—midnight, a little after, walking to the cars. Ahead was the sea, and behind, the chime of Rob's keys kicking up irregularly, which gave us an indication of how he was walking.

Roger and the guys were taking him to meet some girls.

"You're not driving," Rourke turned and said. "Remember?"

Rob took his time answering, as if relishing the messy power he had, as if he could not be completely perceived, as if his drunkenness concealed him.

He made his way around the rear of Rourke's car, moving with the confidence of a heavily armed man. "We're going dancing," Rob slurred as headlights appeared behind him—a car approaching from Montauk. "She loves to dance," he said of me, his eyes gazing inches beyond my face, somewhere to the left. And then to me, Rob said, "Come dance with us."

Rourke grabbed Rob by the shoulders and lifted him forcefully onto the fender just as the car shot past. The rush of wind blew their jackets open.

Rob tried to shake Rourke off. "I'm all right. I'm all right."

Rourke gripped him tighter, shoving him farther. Rob's gaze trawled upward from Rourke's chest, its focus continuously adjusting until arriving at Rourke's face. Rob's mouth split into a solemn smile of recognition, and when another car came, the headlights glinted off his teeth, and his eyes looked like dry tobacco rings. He threw his arm around Rourke, falling into him, and for a time they were speechless. Rourke slid the keys from Rob's hand.

Roger and his friends jogged down the restaurant steps to meet us. "C'mon, birthday boy, let's go get laid."

Rob lurched away with the pack of guys and settled into the front seat of the first car, which was Roger's Camaro. Roger was a student at Brooklyn Law who made three grand a summer waiting tables at Gosman's. He flashed his lights and leaned on the horn as they pulled away, and all the passengers screamed out the windows—"*Yahhhhhhhh!*"

Rourke seemed lost in thought on the ride home, so I didn't speak. Back at the cottage I cleaned up a little, then showered while he washed dishes, and when the water turned hotter, I knew he was done. I was cold so I dressed in one of his sweaters, and I knelt alongside him in the living room. He was deconstructing a camera. I had never seen the camera before. I didn't know where it had come from or what was broken about it. In the action of his hands I tried to follow the action of his mind. He was studying the blown-out mess like it was a chessboard midgame, like he had looked at the pool table with Rob. His hand hovered in studious benediction over the parts before settling on the pieces to replace. I was thinking a fire would be nice.

Later we went to the bedroom and he undressed me before the mirror. His chest was a block of copper; my skin was copper too, both of us dark from sun. His head was inclined and his lips moved down my neck from ear to shoulder. In bed he drew me onto his chest, not letting go, just holding me, and it was there I remained through to morning. I slept very little, him not at all. Anytime I stirred, he would rock me back to sleep.

The next day was normal. I showered like normal, and after Rourke picked up Rob at some house on West Lake Drive, and they got the

Cougar from Surfside, he and Rourke acted normal, whatever normal was for them—broken bones and film trivia, plates of eggs and engine options and sisters in trouble. One thing was different—when Rob got into his car to leave for Jersey, he kissed me and said, "I love you too."

Later that afternoon, when Rourke was driving me to work, he swung the car off Montauk Highway and onto the overlook. He downshifted to the edge of the lot, rolling dangerously close before pulling the brake. It occurred to me with a degree of fascination that maybe he intended to just, like, fly off. It made me happy to think of dying with him; in fact, of all possible ends for us, it was the one I would have preferred. I recalled the guy Jack had told me about when he'd come back from Outward Bound the previous summer, the one who had fallen off the ridge while hiking. I remembered how Jack and I imagined him floating in space, suspended, like a flag flapping to nowhere.

Together Rourke and I confronted sundown, and I collapsed into the shadow of his lap, facing him, tracing my name into the parchment of his abdomen. And he sighed, laying his hand upon my bare back, fingering the straps of my shirt.

31

When I came out of my room and into the kitchen, my mother set down her book and slid it to the center of the table. She was sitting exactly where I'd left her when I moved out in June. I wondered if that was a good omen or a bad one. She leaned back in her chair. The milk in her coffee pooled to caramel streaks at the top.

"How's the packing going?"

I said, "Almost done."

"Feel like going shopping tomorrow?"

"For what?"

She thought for a moment, pulling back her lips. "Shampoo. Do you have shampoo?"

"I figured I'd just take some from upstairs."

"Do you still have things in Montauk?"

"Not really. Anything left will fit into a bag."

I visited her once a week to do laundry, mow the lawn, call my father. It wasn't necessary, but it kept my parents from having to ask questions, which they preferred not to do. As far as they were concerned, I was miles ahead of where they'd been at my age—I was working, going to college, and paying my own way. My father had left home at seventeen to join the army, and when my mother turned seventeen, she married my father. They had no means to help me financially, and no intention of *finding* the means—they were not about to take out loans or find second jobs. So whatever right they might have had to inquire into my affairs had been relinquished.

She rotated her feet at the ankles and stretched her legs, then reached for her book. She caught herself and put it down again.

"Well," I said. "I'd better go finish."

"What time does Lowie get here?"

"Four, I think."

"Okay," she said. "Try to hurry."

Lowie and David were going to Bucks County, Pennsylvania, for Labor Day weekend, so they'd offered to take my things into Manhattan to the NYU dorm. All I really had was one suitcase and some art supplies. I went out to the barn with an empty wooden milk crate. I draped brushes in fabric and placed charcoals in plastic bags and paints in old coffee and cookie tins with lids that did not exactly fit. I tied pencils into logs with rubber bands. Once the box was full, I reviewed the contents. It was strange—I could remember touching them, using them, speaking shyly through them, but I could not recall what I thought I'd needed to say. The girl I'd been seemed far off, vaporous, like a cloud. There was a purity that was gone, a purity of essence—in its place stood something else, something I did not know how to name.

Mom and I left that night at the same time. As I turned at the end of the lane, she drove off toward the college with a merry wave. Rourke had asked me to meet him at Herrick playground; he was filling in for someone on the Montauk Rugby Club.

I walked to the far corner of the field and stood next to Mike Stern, from high school, who was in a neck brace. He'd been injured on a construction site.

Mike turned stiffly and glanced at me. "How you doing, Evie?"

I said, "Hey, Mike."

Rourke was in center field. His hair cleaved and spindled softly against his forehead. His thighs were a smutty green; his knees were black. He looked young, eighteen maybe; though I knew he was closer to twenty-five.

In rugby, there's shouting. There's the accumulation of bodies like an unlit pyre, then all of them treading as one before a rapid and unaccountable break—a *maul*. And in the moments preceding penalties and free kicks, there are slack hands on hips and aimless walks, and heads tossed to the sky, or stretched in jerks to either side, or dropped, chins to chests. It's a very particular sport, sometimes less like a sport than a brotherhood. At the end comes the departure from the field, the resounding emancipation, like every creature on earth freed at once from its cage. There is the adrenaline-fueled backslapping and hip-slapping and the ritual approach to losers. When you say hello to one of them, there is a pause followed by a vague sharpening as they reconnect with the world around them. Sometimes you get not quite a coherent response—"Hey, how you doing?"

"Thanks again for filling in, man," Mike said to Rourke. "See you down at my place, right?"

Rourke wiped his forehead with the tattered sleeve of his shirt, shoving up, so the dirt mixed with sweat into a streak. "We'll try to stop in on our way home."

The car was on Newtown Lane, facing the village. "You can shower at my mother's if you want," I said. "The house is empty."

It was a queer feeling that came from being with him again in that house; the dimensions of everything had changed. We had become larger, and home hideously reduced. We were like giants, colossi, Apollo at Rhodes, or Alice in the Rabbit's house, limbs poking through casements, heads cramming through chimneys.

The only shower was in the upstairs bathroom. I led him up the narrow stairs and through Kate's former room to reach it. Her bedroom was bare except for the bed she'd used. Rourke removed his dirty clothes and laid them on the sink. Kate and I had stood at the sink on the night she cut my hair. That was the first day I'd seen Rourke. It was also where I'd stood drinking whiskey the night we all went to the Talkhouse.

I waited while he showered, feeling heavy, feeling blue, not feeling pain, exactly, but a universal sort of weakness. I sat backward on the toilet seat, straddling it, and I looked out a miniature window into the enclosed front yard. I'd been looking through that little window for years; I knew the view well. Earlier that day my mother had spoken of the possibility of having to move because the rent was going to be increased. It would be sad if she lost the house—so many things had happened there. I wondered where she would go, and from where her new memories might come.

When drops of water began to tap my shoulders I knew Rourke was behind and above me; he was bending and looking out too. I leaned back lightly against his hips. One of his hands came around my throat and caressed my neck—his fingertips flattening the muscles, petting the trachea, measuring the fragile cervix, calibrating the breaths, as he seemed to consider the enormous burden of loving me.

On the way back to Montauk we stopped at Mike's house in Springs. Trucks and cars lined both sides of the street, so Rourke pulled onto the front lawn. Before we got out, we could hear the thud of Led Zeppelin's "Kashmir." *Da na na na nat. Da na na na nat.*

As we approached the porch, a shredded screen door flew open. It had no spring, so it cracked against the side of the shingled house, sounding like gunfire. Rourke instinctively grabbed my arm and pulled me behind him. Mike shoved some kid through the door, saying, "Jesus, do it outside," and the kid flew down to the bushes to vomit.

"Sorry about that, Harrison," Mike said, and he adjusted his neck brace. "I just don't wanna get one of those chain reactions going. Next thing you know it's a big mess of puke to clean."

Rourke said not to worry about it, though the sound of the kid in the bushes was hideous. I loosened my grip on Rourke in case I was next to go. Rourke steered me through the door.

"It's a little crazy in there already," Mike warned. "You two might not want to stick around too long."

Mike was right: the house was packed. Inside the first room, we hit a wall of about twenty guys, and just a few girls. I tugged the hem of my shorts down lower on my thighs and straightened my shirt to conceal my breasts, which were perceptible through the cotton. I should have thought to change at my mother's when Rourke showered. I should have known better. Men are free, but women are not. Men cannot be held accountable for their reactions to your negligence. Sometimes you're just too busy leading your own life to remember theirs.

Rourke had vanished into the crowd. There were people he knew from somewhere, Jersey, maybe, or college. I walked toward the back of the house to find him, making a turn into a dining room that was empty except for two bicycles propped beneath a regulation dart board. The board was surrounded by a ring of hole pokes, and wider beyond that ring the sheetrock walls were scuffed and torn. To my right was an open kitchen with avocado-colored appliances. Rourke was there, leaning on the counter, talking to a huge man with red hair and a hulking back. It was that guy we'd seen outside the gym that day in Jersey, that guy Tommy, with the strange ears. Between them there were two pretty girls. Maybe they weren't pretty, maybe they just seemed that way with long hair to toss, hair that probably smelled of florid shampoo, hair he could not help but inhale. Rourke looked different, his face a sort of mask. Maybe it was the smile, with his top and bottom teeth meeting and his dimple cutting in like fire. He didn't see me, so I moved on.

Past the bikes, through a slit in the side of an almost closed door, came the insubstantial flickering of a television. I looked through and saw five bodies sitting around a coffee table. The sound was turned down on the set; by the light I could see that they were doing coke. Suddenly cocaine was everywhere. It had trickled down from rich people to all the rest of us. Jack blamed corrupt foreign policies; in one of his last rants before we broke up, he said, "Cheap blow is U.S. government issue, just like bulk cheese."

I walked into the room anyway; I had nowhere else to go. The walls were covered with warped paneling, probably from the sixties, and two lamp shades were draped with yellow towels. The room was dreary. I straddled the arm of an empty vinyl recliner, and just sort of sat there.

"Hey," a voice said. It was that guy Biff again. "Eveline. How you doing?"

"Hey, Biff. I'm okay."

"You hang with a pretty rough crowd," he said and laughed.

"Yeah, well, how else would I ever get to see you?"

Biff was quick to talk, which meant that he had no drugs. As a rule, the one with drugs is not so quick to talk. Across the way, perched on the rim of the couch and focusing on nothing in particular, was a skinny guy with ruddy skin and tame blond hair that grazed the shoulders of his Jimmy Buffet concert shirt. "This is Chet," Biff said. "Chet comes up to Montauk from Florida for summers."

He nodded; I did too. I wondered was Chet short for Chester. "Florida is hot," I said.

"Not hot enough for me," he stated, averting his eyes as he drove a heap of powder to the center of a plate and began to chop. The muscle beneath his right eye shuddered. Chet nudged the results in my direction.

"Oh," I said, "no thanks." I didn't want to seem ungrateful, so I came closer, kneeling on the floor.

His eyes met mine; he wore thick glasses. "Go ahead. It's okay."

"No, I just—I feel a little—dizzy, I guess."

Biff quickly took up the plate in my place. He said, "That's too bad."

Two of the other guys, one still in a muddy rugby shirt, were talking about weather—forecasters, maps, advancements in accuracy. Somehow this led to a heated disquisition on world wars and political scandals, with Biff joining in. I wondered how they could sit still even though they were so high. You must just hit a critical point of intoxication, a mortal sort of limit, and your body goes into shock, becoming indisposed to motion. I waited until they had done another round before I stood to leave, which was on my part an excruciating gesture of propriety.

"Taking off?" Chet said.

"Yeah, I guess. Nice to meet you, though. Good luck in Florida."

"Come on back," Chet said. "We'll be here."

On my way out, I heard a voice say, "Harrison Rourke."

Rourke hadn't moved from where I'd left him; he was still in the kitchen, leaning on the counter, holding two beers. No one seemed to notice that he was disconnected from everything about him, that his smile was a lie, that he hated Heineken. No one noticed his eyes furiously fixed on the door I'd just exited. Rob would have seen, but Rob wasn't there. Maybe it was because he was mad, but he looked sexier than ever. His eyes were narrow, impervious as marbles, tilted slightly down at the outer rims. The tousled heaviness of his hair, the conceited set to his jaw, the form beneath the clothes. I thought of how lucky I'd been to fuck him, how vicious would be my physical loss. I became conscious of my breasts, of their desirability. I wanted his hands on them, his mouth. He beheld me stiffly, inertly, as if staring at a compelling design on the wall. I moved on.

I passed through a set of sliding doors onto a deteriorating deck that faced a wall of scrubby adolescent oaks. There was a dented sweating keg surrounded by bodies. To the right were voices. To the left, past a cluster of taken chairs, an empty stretch of rail. I went over and looked down. It was a short drop to the ground. It was not impossible to jump and run— Springs Fireplace was the nearest road, but then I might never see him again. If I waited, at least I would see him again. I considered going back to Biff and Chet, but it would not have been good. It wasn't worth making Rourke upset.

After Rob and I had finished eating at Surfside on the night of Rob's birthday, Val and Rob and I took another stroll out back to the walk-in. The kitchen staff just glanced up as we passed, then went casually back to work. They seemed accustomed to people cutting through. Once inside the cooler, Val removed from his silk shirt pocket a brown glass vial with a baby spoon attached by chain. He stuffed the spoon full and offered it to me.

"No thanks, man," Rob said. "I've been off that stuff for a while. And, as for her, she stays clean."

"Jesus," Val said. "No liquor, no coke. What kind of asshole is this boyfriend, anyway?"

"Not the kind you want to swap punches with," Rob said, adding, "He fights."

"So what? Everybody fights. What do you mean *fights*?"

"Fights, fights, you know, *bing, bing*," Rob jabbed at a gigantic mayonnaise jar on a shelf. "He's a light heavyweight. One seventy-eight," Rob said. "Exact." *Eggzact.*

"Professional?"

"Amateur so far. This past winter would have been his first Olympics."

"Oh, shit," Val said. "Then the U.S. boycott happened. What's he gonna do now?"

"He'll turn, probably. Maybe. We'll see. He has offers."

"More money to be made in professional."

"There's money to be made in everything," Rob said. "If you know what I mean."

Later that same night we were lying in bed, Rourke and me; around us things were strangely quiet. The lupine night came through the windows, haggard, sinuous, haunting, hunting.

I asked him, "Do you fight?"

He did not seem surprised by the question. He said yes.

"Is that why you have scars?" He had several.

He pointed to his chest above his heart. There was a three-inch line. "That I got when I was fourteen. In a fight over my father. After he died." He pointed to his left arm. "This one on my arm like a star is from a dog. A pit bull. See, it puckers."

"This one?" It was on his thigh. I touched it.

"You don't want to know about this one."

"How come you don't do drugs?"

He breathed out thoughtfully. "Because they involve debts to people not worth repaying. Because they show up in blood and urine. Because they destroy the body and the character." He yanked me higher up on the flat of his chest by the swell of my ass. He aligned us, naturally, perfectly. In an undertone he added, "Because I don't like to paralyze myself."

"What did you win? Prizes?"

"Prizes, sure," he told me. "And bets."

———

Someone grabbed my shoulders. It was Mark Ross. He was behind me on the deck, bending to kiss me. The beginnings of a beard sprouted from his chin. I reached to touch his face. "How *are* you?" he inquired with diligent concern, as though I'd survived an ordeal, which possibly I had.

I didn't bother to ask what he was doing down there in Springs at a rugby party, since somehow I'd ended up there too. He must have guessed my thoughts. He slipped a hand into his khakis and said, "I'm here with Tommy. Tommy Lydell. He's out for the weekend."

"The big guy?" I asked. "From Jersey?"

"That's right."

I didn't understand how Mark would have known him. "Did he go to college with you guys too?"

"Tommy? I doubt he made it past the eighth grade. I met him at UCLA several times. He would visit us, mostly for fights. We kept in touch. He's actually staying at my house tonight with his girlfriend and her sister."

I had the feeling there were things he was leaving out. Rourke and Rob had left them out too.

"You should get out of here," Mark said. "This isn't the place for you."

"I've seen worse."

"Trust me. You haven't. The night is young."

I stepped away, and he followed, closing in on me, parting a fan of leaves above my head that was obstructing his view. When they flopped back, he snapped off the shoot, twisting it crudely, throwing the piece down. I looked at it on the deck, uncurling slightly, as if in a final sigh. I leaned on the rail. Mark leaned as well, his forearm skimming mine. The stars were far—I pointed.

"Look how far they are," I said. "September's coming."

"No, Eveline," Mark said. "September's here."

At the driver's door, Rourke paused. "Mind driving?"

I knew he hadn't been drinking. Anyway, I said sure. When we changed places, our bodies brushed at the front of the car, which was

unsettling. Behind the wheel, the view was his view; this was also unsettling.

"Ever driven standard?" he asked.

I pressed back into the seat to stop shivering. "No."

"Take the stick." He covered my hand with his own and jiggled it.
"This is neutral. Now turn the key."

I started the engine, and the car came alive. Though I'd often heard
talk of the car's specifications—a 400 cubic V-8 engine with 335 horse-
power and a 4-barrel Rochester carb—I hadn't until then understood
their meaning. It sort of lifted and hovered.

"Step on the clutch," Rourke said, "and put it into first." With his
help I guided the bar to first, where it nuzzled into a nook. There was no
need to ask if I was in gear—nothing feels so right as an exact fit. "Come
off slowly, as you press the accelerator."

The car churned down and pulled forward, making me think of sled
dogs. It seemed to want to go faster, farther. It was as if I was holding it
back. He told me to hit the clutch again, and he drew down my hand,
helping me pop it up into second, and next third.

We went to the ocean, to one of the private beaches in Napeague. It
was where he wanted to go. Despite the mildness of the night, the deserted beach seemed inhospitable, practically haunted, like the ruins of a
building following a raging fire. I didn't feel well. I started to shiver.

"Still cold?" he asked, looking to the shore. There was a blanket in
back that smelled of sweat and wilted grass, and when he wrapped it
around me, sand from the morning trickled down.

He asked about my family.

I said I didn't have one.

"You have a mother," he said. "I've met her."

Strange that he had, strange that he'd kept it to himself. Probably he'd
met her with Kate. Maybe Kate had called her *Mom*, saying, *Harrison,
this is my Mom*, and maybe Rourke shook my mother's hand and told her
what a great girl Kate was, all the while searching in my mother for traces
of me.

"And a father too," he added.

I didn't know what he was getting at, but I was convinced of my parents' irrelevance regardless. I thought of his house in Spring Lake, his apartment, those giant rhododendrons. And his chest, disfigured in a fight over his dead father. You didn't need to know his parents to *feel* them; they were incorporated into the boy they'd raised. Whatever it was that had attracted him to me was the result of absence, not presence.

"It's not what you might think," I said, though it was too late, really, to speak of myself. "It's like something else, like never having been heard."

He laid his hand on my thigh, and for a moment we froze, immobilized by the insinuation of sex, by its promise to restore us to conditions of denial, to get us past the putrid business of relating. I focused on the dashboard.

Rourke withdrew his hand with excessive caution, as if from a house of cards, and he lifted my face—reverently, like a chalice. "Something," he said, kissing me, "about you."

His mouth, that mouth, nearing, advancing, seeking in vain to capture all that I did not have and could not give. His wrists joined beneath my chin, supporting my head. His thumbs pressed my cheeks.

"Do you know what I feel?"

I said yes, yes I did. I knew a kiss was not enough and sex was not enough and living with him was not enough. I knew the irony of having failed despite the extremes of our consummation, that it was not conceivable to reach the place we needed to go. Around his eyes were beautiful creases. His knuckle dug into my jawbone, forcing my head sideways, my ear to his lips.

"And you," he said. "You would do anything."

"Anything," I said.

I began to cry. I thought to wipe my eyes, but I liked looking as I felt, a thing half-dead. He covered my mouth with his palm, and he waited, breathing, driving himself back. "Then I'll ask for what you can't give," he said. "Nothing."

The light from the moon off the ocean beat against the car like a stationary rain, bathing us in a pool of white, turning everything the color of bones. In such light I could see: I could see he was alive, extraordinarily alive, and I could see his will to persevere. I could see that he had abandoned that will when he'd met me, and that he needed to return to it. I could see the hatred that followed from his need, the rage at his defeat in wanting me. It was the fiend he believed himself to be that expressed itself in the light.

We remained in the car until daybreak, and we had sex for so long that inside I hurt. I thought I understood. We had to go until there was no going back, until it was certain that we could not meet again without recalling the degradation of our final night, until all that we'd shared had turned irreclaimable. His eyes never stopped staring. They seemed to shed their own color, like casting off black. The wry malice in his face, the animosity, the challenge to his successor—could he see him? It seemed that he could see him. Rourke seemed to be leaving in me some message or a sign, changing me for good.

In the end, the car was moving, and I was receding, every second thinning more. Through my mouth, my breaths sounded like those of a felled animal. I could hear the hydraulic thunder of the engine, like a sound from some contiguous time, and the fizz of the wind through glass. I raised one hand to my window. My hand was heavy like lead reaching into the dead sunrise.

I dreamt I was hauling boxes through tides of sand. I was alone, and the terrain was rugged. I passed a figure suspended in the cliffs, red and robed and supported by string, warning me. Ahead of me was my destination, a camp—snakelike, ophidian, like a low, slinking train of lantern lights. From the camp I knew I could be seen walking alone. On the way, I met a woman. She was crying, and on her face were burnt braids. *These have not disappeared,* she said, *since coming to America. Disappeared* is a beautiful word, I thought—*appeared, dis-appeared.* I also met an eagle, decrepit and drooling. It said, *Your mother was luxurious and your father was luxurious.* I asked the eagle what I must be, and he said, *What you were meant to be.* The last part of the dream was about a figure, several figures melded to one. They lifted me; they pulled away; I levitated. There was an imposing wetness on my legs and around my neck. And hands, sure and soft, there but hardly there.

I felt for my head—my hand couldn't find it; it hurt to think where it had gone. I did not move from my back. I could not. Slowly and by degrees, questions formed in my mind, not many, only so many as my intellect could tolerate. I felt pressure in my pelvis. I wondered if I needed to pee.

"What happened?" I asked, or tried to ask.

A cup met my lips. "You had a fever," he said.

My eyes, they opened, and my hand drifted up to stop the sunshine. Rourke raised my shoulders inches from the pillow and shifted me to face away from the window. Beneath the sheets I was naked.

"How long—"

He said two days.

Two days. I remembered speaking. "What did I say?"

He moved to where I could see him easily. "You just slept."

I met his eyes; they had grown small. He'd spent two days alone with his trespass and his lust. Two days to think what it meant to abandon me, betray me. I wondered did he fuck me while I was sleeping.

"What did I say?" I repeated.

"You apologized," he said, cautious not to tender his voice. "You said you were sorry."

He carried me to the bath, and set me down in the water, feet first, then his hands on my arms, helping me to sit. He sat too, on the rim of the tub. I straightened my legs and shivered as he trickled water from his hands onto my head, my back, my chest, and he helped me wash. I looked up, and he looked down, and there was an admission in his eyes that matched the feeling of admission in my own. It was not supposed to have ended this way, with him clinging so kindly to the shell of me and our eyes meeting. Had we left each other after the car, we would have had only the worst to sustain us. But the accident of my illness had ruined everything. His presence by the bed, the remedial caress of his hands, the way he'd nursed me like a dressless doll through an anxious sleep, the pouring of water, the pouring of water—I couldn't think anymore. My heart was thoroughly broken.

"I thought—I guess I thought you would go someplace close."

He looked at me carefully, so there could be no doubt, and he said, "It won't be close."

TROPICS

Random Seasons 1982–1984

Reason does not move in the circle of natural life.

—SIEGFRIED KRACAUER

We have lost naïveté.
We can achieve nothing that will transcend
the fatal games of appearances.

—ALBERT CAMUS

32

This is where I falter, where I lose myself. This is where ideas of what is good and right upend, and time is dispersed, thrown down like leaves to be read. It's difficult to say what happened. I know that my heartache was indescribable, the depth of my loneliness astonishing. I know that I worked very hard, and I never intended to hurt anyone.

I cannot describe a life dispossessed of happiness. Episodes and events stand out as happy, though that happiness was the sort of euphoria you feel at a party you throw for yourself, when you say how much fun you're having, but you're sick inside with self-loathing, wretched all the more for having come so close. What I missed was something lost. What I'd lost was my very self. Perhaps I was resilient: perhaps if called upon by God, I might have survived fire or famine. But who is so able as to endure heartbreak? Heartbreak is a puzzle apart—pieces missing, pieces mutilated. It is to be consumed by the wait, and I was.

I became someone new. She was a mystery. She was striking, like the frayed end of a live wire. She was reckless, because in order to drown, you need to hang by the degenerate edge of the sea. I remember her, pleading into the faces of friends, but for nothing. Who did they see when it was not herself that she showed? What was it they wanted when her lack outweighed her capacity, her desperation exceeded her gifts, her competence eluded her? If she was loved, it was because it's easier to be lovable than to be honest. If she loved in return, and it's not impossible that she did, it was a thin sort of love, emaciated and apt to vary, a love that would not alter his design or fracture his standing. Often I regretted the confusion I caused.

Of course there were angels—there are always angels—people with the soul capacity to see beyond your mask, who come forward to say something *meaningful to the purity in you. But no one possessed the power or the will to move me from my circle of sorrow.*

If there are rules for finding your way through darkness, I tried to follow them. I tried to behave my way out of pain. I gave away the little I had, unencumbered by a desire for reciprocation. I had no reason to lie, no agenda to keep me from listening. My small assurances were trusted, and it gave me a numb sort of gladness that those closest to me valued my attention. And yet that attentiveness was not without flaw; it was limited and erratic, governed by arbitrary factors such as dreams and the seasons, cars and passing shadows. I would be moved suddenly to sadness and detached from the requirements of time. A color or noise, a texture or smell. A reflection or a trivial wind, or sunlight receding menially against a building. Sometimes I would get almost to where I was going, only to turn home again. Back home, wherever it was that home happened to be, I would sit in the gentle coma of my affliction, thinking of Rourke.

This is not easy. This is when my youth escapes me, when I age, with everything shutting down. These are years without accident or incident, when the end of each day is determined before it begins—when there is no possibility of seeing him.

There are people you hear about, laborers who knead the guts of the earth for poor reward, people too indigent, too cowed by cold and hunger and lightlessness to object to the conditions of their existence. They drink themselves to sleep, and why not? Certain conditions are not meant to be tolerated, certain states are so deprived of tenderness that you discover the meaning of hell. Hell is only loneliness, a place without play for the soul, a place without God. How could there be God in loneliness when God is presence?

33

"You can't bring that bird in here."

The bird twitches lamely in my scarf. Mark approaches from the couch, dropping his *Wall Street Journal*, crossing over.

I don't understand. I say, "It's already here."

"You can't keep it here. It's full of disease." He ushers me onto the terrace. "Set it free."

I look down twenty-five floors. I say, "It can't fly."

"It's a bird," he says. "It'll figure it out."

Mark doesn't know about birds. We once saw a documentary about condor eggs stolen from their nests and hatched in captivity. The narrator said that those eggs were the last, and the risk of them being eaten by predators was very great. In the movie, puppet bird heads nursed chicks through rubber gaskets in incubators, and wildlife technicians scaled mountains to set fattened chicks in place of the eggs they'd stolen. The camera remained on the babies as they sat blinking and shivering, awaiting the likely rejection of their mother.

"Why are you crying?" Mark had asked. "They're being rescued."

He could not conceive of the depth of the mess. He could not see the calamity of a genetic last chance, of having your offspring stolen because you cannot be depended upon to provide. In his way, he tried to help.

"Let's fly to Washington, D.C.," he suggested soon after, "to see the cherry blossoms. And the zoo."

On the airplane the stewardess in first class catered to us. Her tag said *Jana*. When Jana bent, she bent low. She served us croissants and fruit salad with real silverware and mimosas in real glass, and when we dropped things like sunglasses or sugar cubes, she retrieved them. Jana seemed to think she could get something from us, or anyway, from Mark, like maybe he would leave me on board and take her instead. Humans are remarkable in terms of need. We all have plans like maps in the mind.

"Here y'all go," Jana said, leaning down to hand me aspirin, revealing exquisite cleavage. The saturated color of her eyes bled into the white, making a subordinate color, which was spooky. If I had eyes like that, I might have become a stewardess too.

In our room at the Hay-Adams, I played with the curtains, opening and closing them—White House. No White House. When Mark went for a run, I ended up in the lounge. The bartender seemed to think I needed a margarita, and after I finished it, I thought I needed another.

There was a stack of cocktail napkins, and I had the urge to draw—not so much to draw as to feel the pen squish into the cushion of paper. I drew intertwining things—feathers and patchwork quilts, corncobs and tatters of burlap.

Eventually Mark rushed in. "I've been looking everywhere for you." He talked overloud as if to a dog he'd left tied to a parking meter. Mark doesn't like people to think he is not tending to things. He over-tipped the bartender, then steered me toward the door. "So you've been draw-ing!" he said, loudly. He was always trying to get me to draw.

In the early morning before the zoo, we went to the cherry blossoms. We were the first there, and it was nice to circle beneath the continu-ous, low, and protective parasol of flowers. The Washington Monument appeared unexpectedly here and there through the branches like a sty-lus referring to the infinitude of heaven. Actually *zoo* is incorrect. Zoos are *conservation societies* now, which is why there are pie charts and bar graphs in the doorways of every exhibit. But visitors who do not want to read about the importance of environmental equilibrium can still enjoy the sight of submission. They can see primal needs confront civility.

Mark told me the animals have no memory of home. And yet I could see traces of savagery and pride. In order to persevere, they assign home to a position within themselves; they store it, safeguard it. By their eyes they say—*We will return*. Look into the eyes of anyone who has suffered diaspora and you will find a home, implicit and original, glinting like specks of starlight. You will envy them. You will wish their home were your home. You will know irony because you have nothing as substantial to assist your identity.

Maybe home is elusive to so many because it is not a place we should be seeking, but a zone of self-determination. In order to arrive there, you must first relinquish false knowledge of a false self. You must allow your learned rendition of reality to turn back to conjecture, allow your life to grow small again, like someone beloved left at a railway station, growing narrower and shallower as the train pulls away, a hugeness waning. And then when it's far gone, you can actually see it. Your home. Yourself.

"There's one there." Mark pointed to a tiger. "Blanche."

She was high in the grass, the fake zoo grass. I saw her eyes and chocolate flame markings. I saw her panting at rest. It seemed to me that she was missing the moonlight. I wondered if she missed the moonlight as much as I missed drunken walls of cattails by the bay and barefoot walks across parking lots coated with the frailest layer of sand, blown like glitter from the palm of a giant hand. Could she still hear the thudding bluster of wind against the night the way I could still hear the roaring fortress of the sea? Did she too hate her hunger—when her appetite stirred, did a plate appear? The most awful hunger is the type that is satisfied too soon, before it moves you, before you are moved by it, before it becomes protracted and superior, a motivating business, making you honorable, graceful, clever—a hunter.

I turn in from the terrace. The broken bird jerks and trembles. "I'll keep it someplace small," I say. "I won't catch a disease."

Mark sees we have reached an impasse. On certain subjects I cannot be moved. "Let's get Manny," he declares brightly.

Manuel the super is in his office in the swill-green subbasement, pouring black wax coffee from a thermos. He drinks ten cups a day. He is diabetic. When I said that to Mark, he asked how would I have come to know such a thing. I said I assumed that anyone who drinks that much coffee is not drinking it for caffeine but for milk and sugar. The next time Mark saw Manny, he asked him directly, and Manny confirmed my guess, only he didn't use the word *diabetic*. He said, "Technically, yes. I have a *litty* touch of *The Sugar*."

On an otherwise vacant metal desk is a miniature TV showing *The Dukes of Hazzard*. While Mark explains the situation with the bird, Manny glides evenly to the cradle of my arms, steaming cup in hand. "Twisted wing," he surmises, using one pinky to check. His voice dips beneath Mark's, speaking only to me. "Don't worry," he says with a wink. "She's not broken."

There is a cardboard box in a cove behind the service elevator, and when Manny kicks it out, a thousand keys jounce like sleigh bells against his uniformed navy thigh. Manny builds a bed of rags. "We'll keep it in the boiler room. I'll tell Frank to lock the cats."

It takes four days for the bird to heal. Manny constructs a Popsicle-stick splint, though we never actually use it, and Frank, the assistant super, buys it a seed ball. It isn't a very pretty bird, just a sparrow.

"Technically," Manny says, when we finally release it into the court-yard, "we could have freed her sooner."

Everything with Manny is always *technically* this and *technically* that. We watch the bird skip and flutter. Spring is here. There are crocuses. It scares me to see them poking out like little green horns. How did spring come again so quickly? It seems just to have passed. It's strange, but I've lost track of birthdays and seasons; in my memory there are islands that have turned dark.

"But it was happy," Manny concludes. "Maybe it needed a vacation. It's gotta be tough, being a bird like that in a place like this."

We drink Stolichnaya at Café Luxembourg, and we lament the decline of America. We blame groups. Blaming groups shows that you yourself are not involved but that you are intellectually connected, especially if the group you blame appeared in Sunday's *New York Times*. When I say "we" I do not mean *me*, though I cannot exempt myself insofar as I am pres-ent. When a pack of wolves mangles a carcass, it doesn't matter which one's not eating *that much*.

"You and Mark are so cute!" Naomi exclaims in the bathroom. Every-thing happens in the bathroom. The clock stops. There is a kink in the spin of the world. She comes out of the stall sniffing, pinching her nos-trils. "It must be wonderful to be in love."

I don't think I'm in love. I don't know, maybe I am. I smile, sort of. I think I smile.

We return to the table, me behind her, her ravishing ass ticking like a metronome set high. She hits shoulders, practically, of men in chairs on the way. We sit side by side. Naomi is a model. Sitting next to Naomi is like sitting next to a Kleenex. When you ask a question, she tilts her head and flits her eyes and asks you to repeat yourself, which you don't bother to do, because whatever you asked the first time was already so abridged for her benefit that it does not bear repeating. We order the same meals. That is to say, she copies mine.

"Yeah, that," Naomi simpers on the heels of my order, handing back an unopened menu. It occurs to me that she cannot read.

Mark and Richard Spencer switch to Chivas Regal Royal Paisley, and they discuss supply-side economics, the $235 price of Hanson Citation ski boots, fluctuations in the index, and fishing in Argentina, which is *the* place to buy land. Richard is Mark's boss; he is the one with the dent in his head that makes him appear cleavable. "Mia and I are going in September. Why don't you join us?" Richard says of Argentina, adding discreetly, "Everyone there is *white*. It's not what you'd think."

Richard's girlfriend Mia's name is not pronounced *Mee-a*, but *My-a*. This you must know without being told. If you cannot intuit this, it confirms your lack of sophistication. Then you will be ostracized and Mark will never make partner at work.

Mia loves September. "All the new fashion!"

Mark looks at me, his eyes wide, his manner encouraging. I'm supposed to reply. His head makes miniature downward jerks as if he's watching me struggle to tap out a dance he's already perfected.

"Fashion—and—September," I say. "Yes, I think so too." This is a lie. To me September is watermelon rinds with panes of ants, monarch butterflies migrating to Mexico, chestnut leaves like shriveled stars fallen to the ground, luminescent dragonflies catching the sun off the cliffs in Montauk, cranberries on the bogs out in Napeague, sweet autumn clematis hanging over fences in Sag Harbor.

Brett snaps a match and lights a clove cigarette. Brett is Mark's best friend. They met in kindergarten at Collegiate. Brett is sort of a 50-percent man—not 50-percent like left or right, but 50-percent like partial or deformed. Brett is into bonds; he says bonds are *the thing*. Naomi is Brett's date. Brett dates only models. The men are talking, cataloging the ravages of nature—earthquakes, fires, floods, tornadoes, hurricanes, mud slides, plagues, killer bees. I wonder, why do they expect the earth to remain passive as we pave it?

"Let's head to Xenon after chow," Brett brays like an old quarter horse.

A few tables down, a girl cries into her drink. I feel bad about that. I think I know how she feels.

———

At the curb I announce that I am not going. The curb is the place for such announcements, especially when everyone is half in a waiting cab. That way it's too late for objections.

Mark's grip on my elbow tightens. He turns to me; his brows are furrowed. "What is it?"

"I have some reading to do, you know, for school." I wave lightly into the taxi, into the frosty aggregate of heads. "Good night." They do not wave back.

Mark has Brett and Naomi hold the first cab, then hails me a second one. He pays in advance. It's not that he doesn't trust me with cash; it's his way of controlling outcomes. If ever there are ways to control outcomes, Mark discovers them. "Things tend to happen to you," he always says. "You're like a magnet that way."

"Drive safely," Mark tells the driver. "*Very* safely. Keep the change."

He adjusts the collar on his cashmere overcoat and kisses me, lingeringly. He wants to come, but it would not look right. It would seem like something it should not. You can always count on Mark to conform, which is good. A girl has to be able to count on something.

The cab pulls out, and I submerge myself into the duct-taped vinyl seat. It feels good to sink into a taxi seat after you've been drinking. It's like settling into a steamy bath or removing tight shoes. I'm happy to be relieved of having to socialize, or more accurately, to appear, somewhat like a logo. There is that flowery smell in the cab, that peculiar taxi smell, lazy and reliable and without obvious origin—not aerosol, not incense, not those little hanging pine trees. Denny says the glass crowns on dashboards contain magic tinctures and essences—vanilla and vetiver and frankincense—but tonight there is no crown. I remind myself to call Denny. Tonight, I'll call. Possibly tonight. Or maybe tomorrow.

The city snakes past—*very safely past,* and I pretend to fly. Sometimes in a taxi you can pretend you are flying. I blur my eyesight like I am swooping, skimming the surface of the planet.

When we turn off Tenth Avenue onto West Sixtieth Street, Carlo jogs out to the curb and waits. It's like a relay race, and I am the baton passed palm to palm, Mark to Carlo. Carlo is the night doorman. I wonder

what he does with his days. His children are at school and his wife is at
work at a blood lab on Lexington Avenue. Does he sleep past noon, eat
cold pork chops, go to the barber or the bank? Sometimes I see him
walking to work from the subway in a dress shirt and jacket. The toes of
his good shoes are woven like kitchen chair caning. Invariably there is a
storm of aftershave.

He grips the handle and assists me, steering me clear of the vehicle
while closing the door and nodding professionally to the driver.

"Thank you, Carlo," I say. The alcohol on my breath vines up about
us. I wonder if he pities me. Sometimes you can't help but pity the people you meet.

He whisks me through the entry and gestures to a hideaway by the
mailboxes. "There's cleaning." He looks me over and reconsiders. "No
problem. I wait for Mr. Ross."

"It's okay, Carlo. I'll take it." He hands it over, and I topple. "Wow,"
I smile. "Heavy!" Mark sends everything out; even jeans get cleaned and
pressed. Carlo tries to get the stuff back from me. There's a minor tussle.
"I'm fine," I say, spinning the load behind me and involuntarily going
half-around again to face the wall. I right myself. "I need something in
here. A nightgown."

He's unconvinced but too circumspect to confront me on the subject
of lingerie. Anyway, the Solomons are at the curb. He taps the elevator
button and backs cautiously away. "You sure you're okay, Evie?" I nod
through the hangers, and he says, "Okay, then. Good night!"

Sandalwood candles line the black Lucite and chrome console that
runs beneath the picture window in the bedroom. I light them. Sandalwood is an aphrodisiac, Mark says. Mark says some men wear it for
potency. I don't like the smell, but they're the only candles in the apartment. Near the candles there is an antique mirror Mark bought for me,
hand-beveled from Czechoslovakia with sterling corner clips. In it I see a
reflection of a reflection, something cubist and delusory.

"You get more beautiful every day," Mark often tells me.

I don't know why he says that, why he bothers. He doesn't have to
work so hard; nothing matters to me. One night I saw myself in another
woman, a redhead with dark eye circles and orchid lips. She seemed luck-

less and afflicted, damaged and indifferent. I could see how a man would want to possess a woman like that. I wondered how she'd made it to that state—breakable with secrets. Did she start out in high school too—just a girl, like me?

I sleep, I wake. I toss, I turn, I brood and flip, and flip, concentrating just to breathe. The ultra-fine texture of my pillow, the detergent smell of the sheets, the genteel tangle of my nightgown. On the bedside table is a bouquet of drying tulips. Every time a petal falls, it cracks when it hits. I reach for my journal but I can't think of what to write. I wonder how long Mark will stay out. Sometimes you depend upon the sight of yourself in someone else's eyes. Babies bat at toys to confirm their existence; touch proves that they are. Mark is my proof. I play with the telephone, dialing, dialing, dropping it, dialing. The receiver is extra heavy when no one is listening.

Mrs. Ross arranges a job for me at Mary Boone Gallery, where she buys art. I work four days a week year-round, making ten dollars an hour. I never had so much money. I don't really need it for living, so it sits in the bank. My mother went on welfare and worked as a waitress to put herself through night school, and my grandmother sent her children away when her husband died so she could work two full shifts a day. They each refused to remarry; they would not allow themselves to live off the beneficence of a man. There's a difference, I think, between a woman who would do that and a woman who wouldn't.

"Women must make themselves financially self-sufficient," Mrs. Ross says one day at the Ross's New York apartment. She rifles through her closet, handing her unwanted clothes to me. "It's never too soon to start."

"Mom, you don't work," Alicia flatly states. "You never have."

"For *money*," she says dismissively. "A *technicality*." Mrs. Ross is a volunteer for the National Organization for Women. She is an ardent feminist, a soldier in the fight for the ERA, Title IX, and right-to-choose legislation, counting such women as Gloria Steinem, Bella Abzug, Marilyn French, Marlo Thomas, and Frances Lear among her closest friends.

The art Mrs. Ross buys is experimental, but she claims it will be worth something someday, and she really does know art. She was an early collector of Andy Warhol's and Robert Rauschenberg's. In her latest

Hamptons collection there are canvases with broken plates and electronic readout signs and photographs of headless baby dolls. The entire house was painted white last summer to feature it all.

"It looks like a Yugoslavian burn ward," Mr. Ross complained when he saw it.

In the New York apartment the art is much nicer, though there is no Goya in the living room. One of Mr. Ross's clients has a Goya in the living room of a Fifth Avenue apartment where maids wear black-ruffle French uniforms with sheer aprons like in porno films. We went there once for an event. Those people must have felt very important to have purchased that painting, to possess something of such historic value, to control its destiny. There is a buzz, sort of, to mix your tiny fate with the great fate of antiquity. All around the city, all around the world, there is a buzz.

Mark held me the first time I saw the Goya and stood admiring it. "Someday we'll have money like that. Someday soon."

Rob contrives reasons to see me. He brings poorly folded newspaper clippings about things like the MoMA reopening and van Gogh at the Met and current events articles about artificial hearts and test-tube babies. He asks for help filling out Lotto slips, then he makes plans for the things we're going to do with the winnings. He teaches me *creative accounting*—game theory and magic tricks and hand signals for cheating at cards. Also how to decipher market data and racing forms and the science behind the daily number and the sucker schemes behind the boardwalk games, like the wood blocks placed behind the cats—those stiff flip-down dolls you throw hardballs at. They don't even look like cats.

"She's quick," Rob says approvingly to Mark. "*Very* quick. I think she's ready for under/overs and *the vig*."

One day Rob came and talked excitedly about construction in Atlantic City, Harrah's, and how great it was gonna be, and also all the action down at the Criterion. He talked about the Holmes-Cooney TKO the previous week, and when Mark said, "Let me tell you something, old-timers like Joe Louis and Jack Johnson could pummel today's boxers," Rob didn't engage. He just glowered and said, "Fuck you, Mark."

When Rob left that day, he seemed particularly torn. I walked him to the door of the apartment, and he faced me squarely with his hands on my arms to say goodbye. The look on his face was aggrieved, like the look of a healthy person leaving a hospital patient alone with their terminal disease. He glanced up at Mark, as though he was considering grabbing me and making a break for it. He started to speak, but Mark interrupted.

"Hold on. Let's ask the boss," Mark was saying to someone on the other end of the phone, Brett probably. He set the receiver on his shoulder, asking, "Sushi, baby, or Thai?"

I turned back and Rob had gone. The door *ka-thunked* against the vacuum of the hallway. I touched myself, feeling for effects. There ought to have been effects. I searched for signs of him—the cup he'd used, the newspaper he'd carried. There was a football on the coffee table that he'd rolled in his hands. He'd been wearing a tank top, and he had a new tattoo—a cobra on his right shoulder. Every time the ball spun, the cobra flickered.

"Ev says sushi," Mark reported falsely. "We'll meet you at Japonica at eight."

A kiss at the beach, salt on my lips. I open my eyes to see but the sky is slit by a streak of bobbing pentacles, a blinding row of asterisks that cascade from the sun to me. I wonder if the sun can blind me.

Mark says no. "It cannot."

He met some Harvard graduate school friends by the lifeguard station, Lisa and Tim Connelly. The Connellys are architects "talking to the Hilton" in Atlanta. If you ask what is the meaning of that, of "talking to the Hilton," you will be told, *negotiating a major contract.* If you ask, "Doesn't Atlanta have its own architects?" you will be told of the Connellys, "They're hot. They just did Avon."

There is logic to business, just don't expect to find it. It's really nonlogic masquerading as logic, and it depends upon the fact that you, and people like you, are too stupid or too busy to make inquiries. When considering the convoluted principles of business deals, look for nepotism, cronyism, extortion, insider trading, ordinance evasion, or bulk airline fares.

"We're meeting them at the Lobster Roll later."

"No," I say, squinting up. "Not the Lobster Roll." I will never go back.

Mark stiffens, the hand at his jaw clutching a tiny peak of towel. He pats his face, drying it, and he smiles. "No problem. The Clam Bar."

He goes no further. There is nothing to fix when he finds what he wants in the wreckage of me. Like a missionary, he is called upon to save—saving is atonement for his ascendancy. And like missionaries who marry natives, he is inspired to emancipate deeply, down to the level of the DNA. It doesn't matter that I feel nothing, say nothing; it matters simply that I am docile. He is resolved and he is apt, and if he suffers from my apathy, he shows no sign of it. There is much at stake in the rescue of me—I cannot begin to guess what.

I feel his shadow growing over my body. He kisses me again, saying, "I love you."

I believe that that is true. He truly loves the lie that is me.

"I'll go tell Lisa and Tim that there's been a change. It might take me awhile. You want something to eat before we go, an apple, a peach?"

I don't answer. I don't eat fruit anymore. He knows I don't. I can't bear the idea of seeds or pods. I close my eyes again and lift my hips to straighten my towel. In my mind there is a place to hide, padded and small like a cell. No one gets in. No one dares to try.

In my dream, we are together again. There are three separate locations. The first is at his sister's house, though he doesn't even have a sister.

"Come in," she says, inviting me into her kitchen. I can still see it perfectly; it will never leave me—the orientation, the light, the furnishings. The counters are the color of putty, the walls are stone-yellow. From someplace close there is the faint sound of children, like the crackle of fire or the sotto voce gurgle of sewer water.

Her husband comes in directly behind me, tossing down his keys and patting her waist. He calls the kids, nodding to me as he passes. He is a good husband, I think. My eyes trail him as he disappears down the corridor.

At the end of the hall is Rourke. It's been so long since I've seen him. He smiles. I smile too; I'm happy. I feel distinctly that this happiness is wholly new. He is going to take a shower. He asks, "Do you mind waiting?"

When he goes, his sister hands me a letter he's written. In it he confesses so much. I hold it in my hand, gripping it tightly.

He and I begin to walk through a deserted village. There is a soft wind, like shrouds blowing softly. As we walk, we pass houses and churches and graveyards, and we decide things, though for me there is nothing to decide.

In the hallway of an apartment on Manhattan's Upper West Side, I attend the future. Rourke is there—but only visiting. This I know because his feet do not touch ground. Children chase children throughout the apartment. It is a party, a birthday party. He and I speak to each other with undivided attention. There is the knowledge that I have withdrawn my feelings from a strictly guarded place, like jewels from a box.

The children burrow in a train under the bridge of his legs, and one stops, the one that is mine. I know it is mine by the way Rourke pauses to admire him, and the boy peers up with peculiar tilted brown eyes. In my dream there is a perceptivity about the boy. He seems to see what we are unable to see, though we have been powerfully seeking. I see the tiny hands hold the giant leg. And Rourke touching him, raising him up.

Mrs. Ross gets four tickets to see Betty Comden and Adolph Green perform excerpts of their work at Guild Hall in East Hampton. "And then we'll go to The Palm after the show."

"Great!" Mark says. Mark says great, though he knows I don't want to go. I don't ever want to go back to Guild Hall, where the play was held in high school, but I can't decline. That would require discussion. It's pointless to discuss anything with anyone.

The theater has a musty and untrafficked smell. It's as though nothing has moved here in the intervening time, or as though I'm not visiting an actual place but some sort of eyeless pit inside myself. Everything has been strangely preserved. There are things I once touched—walls and chairs and scenery items—that probably have not been thoroughly cleaned of my prints, and that is sad, like I was here in fact, but, in fact, it doesn't matter. I have ceased somehow, yet only in portion. To have ceased completely, well that would be something.

Rourke is present all around, clear in my memory and in my mind. All the areas where I remember him to have been are brought into focus. There are the seats we sat in on the night of that play, the night he said he was *looking forward to the end of all this,* the night he kissed me on the cheek at Dan's house. And, though it is not cold, I feel cold, and I recall the way that I loved him, and the blind faith of seventeen. I was never afraid then, though I'm always afraid now, which is incorrect, since the worst has already happened. Perhaps at first he did not love me, perhaps he never loved me. But if he wanted me only for sex and readiness, at least that's better than being with a man like Mark who wants you for reasons you cannot even fathom. Without the knowledge of why you are desired, you are powerless, an object. Love is not reciprocal.

At The Palm we will eat meat, and I will be made to speak. Not much, maybe just what did I think of the show and is my food okay. "They're going to mention Christmas at the Breakers," Mark warned. "Try not to say anything negative about Florida. Or about being afraid to fly."

From the moment we arrive at the restaurant, Mrs. Richard Ross—Theo—will capture the attention of every decent gentleman, as she is breathtaking and ageless, with cascading blond hair and a sea-salted, rose-hip-oiled body, and silk blouses skimming skirts that go narrow to her knees. Over a succession of chilled vodkas, Mr. Ross will tell stories of celebrities and money, because that is what is expected of him, but when he digresses inevitably into tales of his youth, he will address me to the exclusion of the others. Unlike the others, I know what it is to have nothing and to lose everything. Unlike the others, I am not imperiled by my need or his nostalgia. He was just a man once, unprivileged, a fighter of sorts, much like Rourke, and I see that—that is to say, I *grasp* that, and he senses my grasp. He senses what I truly feel—that few things in life are more beautiful than the bareness of a man.

In any event, he is kind, as is his wife. It's kind of them to take care of me and to treat me like family when I am not. It is right to respect your children's choices. And the Ross family is a nice family to have if you have no other.

I stop by to visit my mother on a Sunday morning one weekend in East Hampton. I hear her through the screen door before I see her.

"Well, the apple and the fly symbolize sin and evil," she is saying speculatively. "And the cucumber and the goldfinch are redemption."

"I need seven letters," my aunt says. "Symbol of Christian sway—how about *cypress?*"

"Cypress is longevity," Powell replies.

"Try *crosier,*" my mother says. "The bishop's staff, the shepherd's crook."

"That fits," Lowie says. "With an *S* or a *Z?*"

I step in past the door, saying hi.

Mom leaps to greet me. *"Eveline!"* Right away her face darkens. "Have you been sick?"

Powell also stands. He kisses me and steps back, squinting as he regards me. "She looks good to me, Babe. Same as always."

"She just grew," Lowie insists quietly, drawing her cane in front of her, but not getting up. "Come over here, honey. Sure you did."

"She has at least four inches on me, Low," my mother remarks indignantly. "And she's no heavier. She needs at least ten pounds."

Powell tips his head. "Maybe your mother's right. *Maybe.*"

Mom lectures me on the perils of health foods. She is biased against health foods. She thinks if you use them, you belong to a giant mind-control society. As if consumers of cigarettes, alcohol, sugar, and soda do not belong to a giant mind-control society.

"You don't have to work in the city this summer, Eveline," she suggests. "Stay at home. We'll install a bathroom in the barn. You can work at the Lobster Roll again."

It's nice of her to think of me, but sometimes even the nicest plans are unbearable. "The gallery is fine," I reassure them. "I answer phones and file slides and design invitations to openings. And New York is nice in summer with no one there." In the mornings SoHo is like Paris, damp and hueless blue. "I've been thinking of calling Dad and Marilyn soon. Maybe we'll go to the movies. Or try one of those walking tours they take, like through Harlem or Brooklyn Heights."

My mother's brow contracts. She and Powell seem unmoved. But if she is contemplating my dishonesty, she's also calculating the effort required to engage with it. She decides to let it go, and frankly, who can blame her? I wouldn't want to try to talk to me.

After catching up with all the stories over several cups of coffee, I walk the two miles back to the Ross's Georgica house, depressed to leave but

comforted somewhat for having been vigorously treated. I'm always han-
dled so delicately by Mark and his family. Sometimes I find him staring
at me the way you might stare at a fish you keep, like he's convinced I
don't see him back. How ironic—Mark thinks he's so considerate, so cultured, such a gentleman, and yet, I'm apparently so adversely altered by
his company that people who have never worried about me before, not
even when I was in really bad shape, suddenly worry.

The city glints amiably beneath a mannerly drizzle, so I go slow, taking
the long way from the Varick Street station to the East Village, pausing
to read the plaques on brownstones, stopping at the record store on
Carmine Street and the chess shop on Thompson. In the chess section of
the newspaper, you read of *cornering* and *abducting, lunging* and *captur-*
ing, yet here players sit face-to-face, inert and imperturbable, insou-
ciantly grazing knees and sharing breath. The combination of mental
vigor and physical inertia is weird, like the glacial way reptiles hunt. And
the little chessmen are regal and fiendish, like from gory visions you
might have had. I buy myself a knight.

"A replacement?" the man asks.

"Yes," I say. "A replacement."

McSorley's is so packed there's not enough room to choke if you had
to. Whenever a girl walks past the sign shop in tight clothes, Tony Abbruscato says to my dad, "Hey, Anton, take a look at this. There's not
enough room to choke in there if you had to."

Mark and his crowd are in back, half-sitting, half-standing at a table.
There is the attorney they've all slept with, Marguerite, who's been engaged unsuccessfully four times. Brett's with his new girlfriend, Rachel,
who is not a model but a *former* model. There's a difference: a former
model is just as vain as a working model, only a former model is *just so*
happy to be out of the industry. Mark's friend Anselm is with his fiancée,
Helene de Zwart. They're all calooshing their mugs like it's Oktoberfest
in Germantown. Mark's tie is flapped over his shoulder as if blown by a
strong wind. I know exactly the kind of night it's going to be.

They see me and wave. I unzip my coat. Brett leaps to his feet and
croons loudly; he used to be in a band.

"There she was just a-walkin' down the street, singin' . . ."

The bar joins in,

"Do wah diddy diddy dum diddy do."

Right off, a couple of guys step in front of me, blocking my way, asking would I like to stop at their table instead of where I'm headed. Mark and Brett bust over, and there is nonsense shouting and miscellaneous intimidation, culminating in a few clapped backs and an upturned chair or two. As our group gets escorted out, Marguerite stands, fashionably posed, toe-deep in sawdust, clutching the milky top to her Chanel Pierrot suit, paying the tab. Marguerite always manages to be fashionable, even in the midst of picking up the bill during a bar fight. Shopping is her life. She will tell you all about the three *Bs*—Bendel's, Barneys, Bergdorf's—and how she never wears underpants because they corrupt the clean line of slacks. She rarely speaks to me, though she does stare an awful lot, and once I caught her in Mark's bedroom, going through my drawers.

The first time we met, she looked me over and exclaimed to Mark, "Au naturel!"

Mark always apologizes for her, which is unnecessary. She's one of those women who make you sad, no matter how scrupulously they dress or how much money they claim to make or what fabulous event they supposedly attended the previous evening. Of course there are women who have the opposite effect, inspiring complete admiration and awe. They wear blue jeans but no makeup and they have gorgeous eleven-year-old sons. All the best women have good skin and gorgeous eleven-year-old sons.

Outside on a murky unlit Fifth Street, the group straightens their ruffled jackets and calculates what to hit next—Odeon for burgers or Chinatown for pork fried rice. Brett pees in a doorway. The urine makes the shape of a lizard on the ground.

Marguerite takes my hand. "Oooh, how short your nails are! So easy to manage!"

Mark picks me up at the gallery after lunch on Fridays and we go to East Hampton. Other employees stay until six, and some work through the weekend. I never asked for the abbreviated schedule; Mark arranged it. It doesn't make me tremendously popular with the staff, though the sales-people are careful to remain friendly in case I have any power over Mrs. Ross.

"You're there to build a résumé," Mark says, "not to make friends."

Each week he pulls onto the curb and bounds up to retrieve me be-cause I don't always recognize the car. There's always a different car—he is perpetually testing, borrowing, buying, trading vehicles. The beloved 356B Porsche remains in East Hampton, except for those special occa-sions when he needs to make a *dramatic impression*. Whenever I hear that, I think of the first time he showed it to me—and how, yes, I was dramatically impressed.

Today Sara Eden is there. She has just arrived from Washington, D.C., for a family reunion, so she is driving out with us. As Mark escorts me to the car, Sara steps out and moves toward me. I'd forgotten how beautiful she is. I hang my head slightly, feeling ashamed.

She kisses me hello and her fingers make a circle around my wrist bone. "You're white as a sheet. When was the last time you saw a doctor?" she whispers sharply once Mark is out of earshot.

Mark drives south down the cobblestoned Mercer Street; he likes to take the Manhattan Bridge straight off of Canal. The architecture in SoHo deceives. Loading docks and freight elevators allude to industry, though there no longer is any. Behind the cast-iron façades, abandoned factories have been gutted and sterilized to make loft apartments. No one cares to think too long or hard about the long-term consequences of the loss of American manufacturing. Except my father, whose first job was at Shuttleworth Carton Company, a die-cutter on West Broadway, and who complains that moving industry to where it can't be seen isn't stop-ping industry. He always says that we're still polluting the same god-damned planet.

"Every idiot thinks they're entitled to flushing toilets and a space sta-tion future, but nobody can make a cardboard box anymore," he would lament when he and Marilyn walked west to SoHo to see me. "If we keep sending the dirty work overseas, what happens in the next depression?"

My father is always talking about the next depression like you can set your clock to it, though if it's coming, no one in New York seems concerned. They're there to get what they can for themselves for as long as possible before cutting out to *follow their dream*. Chiseled blondes in Agnès B. miniskirts, hip Asian girls in obtuse shoes from Tootsi Plohound, and gray-haired gallery directors in tortoiseshell eyewear sell transparencies of Jesus and close-up photos of genitalia and elysian landscapes in oil copied off of overhead projections. At openings, girls with body-painted breasts serve drinks but fail to hold anyone's attention. Faces whoosh at you as though ejected from fireplace bellows saying, *What a fabulous show!* During lunch, people swarm the pay phones like flies on fruit, waiting peevishly to call their answering machines, the latest *must-have* devices. They bang in numbers with lightning-fast accuracy, desperate for messages, for recognition, for distinction among the masses.

Lately I've been thinking of Cuba. I imagine it to be the last original place. All you ever hear of Cuba is, *There is no freedom there! Television is state-controlled!* Yet for all the supposed freedom in America, there is a confounding deficit of ingenuity in terms of thought and taste. Style is dictated by the controlling influences and concerns of a mass marketplace. People are trained to be dutiful consumers—we all want the same stuff, not because it's good or useful, necessary or lasting, but because we allow ourselves to be convinced that we can't live without it. We forgo all logic of quality and durability.

If you travel internationally, you will feel shocked by contemptuous talk of America. To hear your fellow citizens characterized as barbarian shoppers who know nothing of love, food, health, and religion, but everything of lawsuits, fast food, and guns, is to experience a national fidelity of which you may not have thought yourself capable. And yet, you're at a loss for a convincing defense. It's difficult to refute the accusation of misapplied liberties when rifles are sanctioned but public breastfeeding is not.

At least in Cuba, television doesn't pretend *not* to be state-controlled, and supermarkets don't stock pre-decorated cakes. In the United States, supermarkets carry pre-decorated cakes, walls and racks of them viewable through specially molded plastic flip lids. There are probably factories where women and children labor without protection and bathroom

breaks to make lids for those cakes, and that place is undoubtedly governed by exactly the sort of despots Americans vilify. It's impossible that
all the supermarket cakes are purchased and eaten—where do they go
when they expire? *Do* they expire? Why do we need so many? What is so
psychologically valuable to the American public about the idea of excess
and its obvious corollary—waste?

Sara has been to Cuba through an international program. She says I
would love it.

"Don't say such things," Mark says as he pulls onto the Manhattan
Bridge. "You might not realize it, Sara, but Castro makes prostitutes of
his women."

"*Most* men make prostitutes of their women, Mark," Sara says point-
edly.

Mark might not be wrong about inequity in Cuba, because Cuba is a
dictatorship. Then again, Sara cares about equity and Mark doesn't. So,
his attack on Cuba is insincere but valid, and her defense is sincere but
incomplete. Talk is funny; it's like a volley with no one getting anywhere;
it's better not to bother trying. If it's blasphemous to imagine running
away to someplace different, I remind myself that we are a nation of
refugees, and so it would not be so very un-American to reject one or-
thodoxy for another in pursuit of more pertinent freedoms.

"It's beautiful, Evie," Sara says fearlessly. Was she always so unafraid of
him; I can't recall. "It seems untouched by time. Everybody sings."

Quite often in summer, Mr. and Mrs. Ross will go out to Los Angeles to
conduct business. During those weekends, the East Hampton house
loads up with chic yuppie strays. Consuela loses dominion of the kitchen
to heavyset debutantes with sweaters wrapped around undulating waists,
and perfect Bordeaux-colored toenails poking out of high-heeled mules.
They assemble tuna shish kebabs, chug Chardonnay, discuss diaphragm
sizes, and play house to the combed-down boys on the patio. There's always this squall of perfumes and constant talk of fat. I never knew until
then that cherries were so fattening.

"Everything has a fat content," Mark's cousin Luce says with a wink.
"Everything."

Mark knows they don't like me. He misses no opportunity to force them to endure public displays of affection. He defers to my judgment on the most mundane matters and calls me his *better half.* Frequently he will grab me and break into an impromptu slow dance. The girls flick mascara-crusted eyes over pink drinks with paper umbrellas that perforate rows of fattening fruits, and they watch us scornfully, thinking foul thoughts of what it is I must do to make him condescend to want me. At the lavishly set patio table, outfitted with Mrs. Ross's best crystal, linen, and sterling, Mark interrupts any prolonged conversations I might be having with other men, saying things like, "I worked too hard to catch her, Aaron. I'm not about to lose her." If it's suggested that we join the others for the nightly skinny-dipping, Mark laughs loud. "Forget it," he'll say. "I'm not sharing."

Despite annual overhauls, the Ross house is essentially the same as the first time I saw it, big and breezy with bound copies of entertainment and fashion magazines in the bookshelves along with the complete works of great authors such as Dickens and Twain and Austen, which are not really books but trompe l'oeil containers for stowing valuables. Of course, classic law texts and journals line the coniferous-green walls of Mr. Ross's office, but they are of little interest to me as that room is too dismal to visit. Even when Mr. Ross uses it for private phone calls, he drags his armchair out into the hallway. It is the only fixed space in an ever-changing décor.

"What the hell happened here?" Mr. Ross demanded of his wife after one particular renovation. He'd just returned from L.A. to find vines stenciled and painted on all the walls, connecting room to room. "Are those supposed to be leaves?"

"Blakely calls it Byronic," Mrs. Ross replied matter-of-factly. Blakely is the decorator.

"Byronic!" Mr. Ross removed his jacket at the entrance and stepped tentatively into the living room, looking skyward into bogus foliage. "It looks like Pan might skip through!" He loosened his tie. "Now you listen to me, Theo. An East Hampton home is a country home, and a country home should have a country atmosphere. This place looks like a Lily Pulitzer whorehouse!"

Mark won't let Blakely near the cottage. He knows I like it as it is, serene as an attic in Europe, with the lambent tread of light coming everywhere at once like little footprints of little animals. He turns off the central air and we lie in front of fans, and through the parted shutters pieces of the beyond blow in—rushes of pollen and random butterflies and flower petals like baby bonnets. At night when the moon is high, I see them skate down the stray prongs of light, and I pretend they are fairies, dancing.

It's the Friday before Washington's birthday. The art studio is empty; I am alone. To my right is a pile of contorted tubes, and fresh paint dots line the tray I use as my palette. Today's paint looks pulpy and alive alongside the scraped and raked stains of old paint. I light candles and turn up the volume on the music, Puccini's *Madame Butterfly*.

Come una mosca prigioniera—l'ali batte il piccolo cuor!

On the canvas is a female figure, a face and bare shoulders. She first arrived before Christmas, and I examined her as though I'd discovered a dead bird in the house—I tilted my head, wondering where she'd come from, and how to get rid of her. Her body is like living resistance; it cuts across the canvas in two directions and in multiple fields, like stop-motion photography or time-lapse film. The muscles of her chest and shoulders are pronounced as she leans to escape the frame, though her face contradicts her body by addressing the foreground. She connects with the observer despite risk; that is, the risk of exposing her leap as a leap to nowhere. After all, she is trapped in paint.

Yet she has lessons. In revealing intention, she admits the possibility of failure, so she is courageous. Despite her imprisonment, she clings to the idea of freedom, so she is faithful. She reminds me that faith is better than hope. Hope is blind expectation; faith awaits nothing. It is a means of preserving the self, regardless of outcome. With faith, every day of constancy is itself a good day.

In the first review of the new term, Don Matthews, my teacher, told the class that my figure's story was one of "entrapment and emancipation, a discrepancy not unlike that of Jesus on the cross—wood and flesh, bondage and deliverance, defeat and triumph." It made me think of how Jack used to call the crucifix *the perfect corporate logo*. Don was an older version of Jack, if Jack happened to be an irritable art theorist from Dublin with round gold-wire eyeglasses and a full-time job teaching at NYU. It would be good if Jack had a teaching job and glasses. Apparently he didn't even have five dollars. The most recent news I'd heard about Jack was him hitting up Denny for cash on St. Mark's Place. When I asked Denny if he knew how to find Jack, he looked at me and said, "It wouldn't be a good idea right now, Evie."

I look at my painting once more before preparing to leave the studio. Though I rendered what I thought I saw, the image bears no resemblance to the model used by the class, or, for that matter, to the paintings of the others. For a while it looked like stacks of color until it looked like a woman; then you couldn't see it the first way anymore. Sometimes you perceive a secondary figure in an image, like the etching of a cube that changes orientation when you blink or the goblet that is obviously a goblet until it is two faces kissing. Sometimes you get stuck in the subordinate state, and that is stranger still, because you recall most clearly that there was an original way of seeing, yet you can't return to it. When people talk about *seeing like a child,* they are referring to a state in which the eye and mind are fluid, and can pass easily from specificity to ambiguity. Like when strings of letters look like shapes, not just words.

From a dented El Pico coffee can, I select the black handle of a putty knife and drag it through the wet paint. "I'm sorry," I say to the figure, saying the words to her that no one ever says to me. And my knife moves. Horizontally, one side, the other, dissecting with new oil the meringue cliffs and ponds of paint that have comprised her image. My hand makes olive lines, repeating, crossing over, bars, and between these, I use a rust color, integrating the two tones, corrupting them, marrying them. Yes, marriage—a corruption—a gain, a loss, a twisted sort of balance.

The room blackens; two hands mask my eyes. The hands are scented like soap from a recent washing. "Don't move," Mark whispers into my ear, holding for a minute, kissing the back of my neck. He pulls away and hits the light switch. The fluorescents creak and yaw in their casings, then surge to life. Mark always sneaks up on me. Don Matthews calls him "the ferret." Don didn't tell me this directly; I overheard him.

Mark gasps. "Evie! You ruined her!"

I like how she looks. She seems to have satisfied some pressing desire. She adjourns contentedly into paint, defenseless to the very nature of herself, as if only that which made her unique and which gave her substance has the genius to deprive her of continuance. She'd just been so— locked in.

"Consider the importance of process," Don once said to me. "There is no end greater than the means. Buddhist monks spend days and weeks making sand mandalas, grain by grain. They drop streams of colored sand through the tapered ends of these minuscule funnels to create magnificent patterns intended to graph the order of the universe. At the end, the mandalas are just swept away."

The painting was nothing. Just paint, just canvas, just work in time. And the time, in turn, is a fragment of my existence. If I had not been living with Mark or taken that class or gotten to know Mr. Matthews, the image would not have materialized—at least not through me. And of course, if she did begin in me, then she hadn't vanished at all. She'd simply withdrawn, the way turtles' heads squirm back into shells.

Farewell, I say. In my mind I say it, then my wrist arcs to obscure her entirely.

Mark sighs, exasperated. I wonder what he could possibly think he's lost. She seems so exclusive to me. I would not want to hang her at his home. Or at Brett's. Brett bought two other paintings of mine, one of rooftops and one of a bird's nest. Whenever we go to Brett's loft, I avoid the bedroom. If Mark forces me to go in, I see the paintings and I end up thinking, *Oh, babies, poor babies.*

Denny and I are on Bleecker Street under the awning at Figaro's, and it's raining. Rain falls, it disappears, more comes. There is a beautiful sizzling sound it makes, like bacon frying. People huddle in doorways. A man in a saturated white parachute suit and Birkenstocks passes. His toes are black.

Denny takes a forkful of deep-dish apple pie. "Know what my mother calls this?" he asks, then answers his own question. "Pandowdy. Want some?"

I shake my head.

"So you'll do it?" he asks. Denny got money to produce the clothes for a music video one of his friends is shooting. He wants me to design the sets.

"I don't know. I've just been so busy. I really don't know where the time goes," I say.

"What are you talking about? You have too *much* time. You have no life outside Mark or the gallery. And you still look exhausted."

I *am* exhausted. It's exhausting to give up the past as I do, as I have done. It's like having an autoimmune disease. I fight against myself, against everything that is natural: love, memory, autonomy, desire. I don't want to breathe. There's this balance I need to maintain that breathing upsets. I don't know what it means not to breathe, but I heard Lowie say that everything you have ever done is *written into your respiration*.

"It's just, the seasons," I try to explain to Denny. "And time. I can't tell if it's spring, fall, winter. Days of the week run together. I lose track. I don't even—"

There is a cloudburst, then a downpour. The rain is torrential, a co-valent, sticking rain. The building across the street has scaffolding, and the raindrops cascade like marbles through a maze of planks and pipes. It reminds me of that game Mouse Trap. Scaffolding is awful. The other day I was thinking how nice the city will look when all the construction is done. Then I remembered: it will never be done.

Denny sets his knapsack on an adjacent chair, where his cane is hanging. An air conditioner fell out of a fifth-story window on Christopher Street awhile ago and smashed to the ground in front of him. A piece of metal flew into his leg and he had to have surgery. He ended up winning a twenty-four-thousand-dollar settlement.

"If I'd been one step forward," he'd confided with shock and horror at the time, "it would have killed me. It just wasn't my time."

If Denny *had* been killed by a falling air conditioner, everyone would have said that it was *destiny*. People would have to say that, just to give meaning to something seemingly meaningless. But he didn't die, and so the incident becomes irrelevant and remains largely undiscussed, which is regrettable, because of all the remarkable things about life, the most re-markable are the near misses.

When he arrived, he said he's almost ready to get back to dancing and that we should sign up for instruction soon. He'd bought us a series of lessons for Christmas last year, or possibly the year before. Mark kept telling me it was too dangerous to go, that those dance studios are really just money-laundering fronts.

"Getting any sleep at all?" he asks.

"Sort of. Not really. A little, I've been dreaming."

"Well—*good!* Dreaming is good. It's brain work. It's a sign of health. You know, I read somewhere that death row inmates have disproportionately fewer dreams than the rest of us," Denny says as he pays the check. "And that a majority of them choose Dr Pepper as their last drink. Wouldn't that make a great ad campaign?—*'The last word in soda—Dr Pepper.'*"

The weight of the rain lifts; the sun presses through. The street dries rapidly, making me think of those hooded rollers in car washes. Denny and I make eye contact through the picturesque vapor, which is awkward—awkward because I want something from him, which feels like asking for money to buy pills. I want him to remind me of where we started, since where he started and where I started is the same. I wonder if he retains the impression of me and of Rourke like keys to a former house.

I ask Denny, "Do you remember me then?"

"Very well," he says. "You were happy."

"You need some rest."

"Rest is all I get," I tell the doctor.

She says, "Obviously not the right kind."

I didn't even know there *were* different kinds.

Dr. Mitchell replies, "Well, first of all, rest at home is cheating. You still have the phone and bills and mail and shopping and cooking to deal with. You know, cleaning and laundry."

I do not bother to tell her I do nothing, pay for nothing. It's too embarrassing.

She prescribes Halcion and an extended vacation.

"Don't you have a school break coming up in February?"

"Yes," I say, thinking, *Mark has put her up to this.*

Jamaica is hot, hot like you will need emergency services. It is a lonesome and detestable heat, a broad, blinding heat, like being tied to a post at a crossroad. Like there is no shelter, no friend. No help in sight. Just you, left to burn.

In the tropics I think without reprieve; maybe it's the heat or maybe it's the medicine, with outside sounds that grow softer and inside ones growing louder. There is a long dock with a thatch-roofed awning at the end; in the morning I go out there to where the world is orderly, where it is arranged in plates of color—white and blue and blue. Like the candle we used to look at in high school, discussing whether the bird was flying on the plane of the sea or on the sky. I wonder about that conversation, about why we kept having it, and about *all* the probing conversations of our adolescence. There was a simultaneous coming to consciousness. It was like a circle of ladders wide at the base and tapered at the top—with each of us stepping up together, testing in tiny rises the ideal of a single-ness of perspective, gaining by rungs new things to swear by, going as far as we could possibly go before forsaking the ascent altogether.

What is it that we were hoping to obtain? Did we speak in the pursuit of unity because we could not speak in the pursuit of power? Is that why early allegiances are discontinued, because eventually you must demand of friendships some advantage? I certainly don't need to become more politically liberal or artistically aware or socially open-minded to survive; as a matter of fact, my opinions often cripple me. Was it that we had nothing pertinent to give one another anymore, such as sound invest-ment advice or better career credentials? All Mark's associates just make one another richer. It feels incredible, how hard I tried, how much I lost—the luxury of time and friends and poetic aptitude, the modest op-ulence of home, where definitions of success extended no further than the pleasant close of the day you were in, where dreams of paradise were enough to sustain you.

Through these thoughts, thoughts of Rourke appear. Is this soul preservation I am feeling, or the vanity of sorrow returning? I don't mean to go back to grief. It's just, there are memories of days when I did not have to do, but only to be, when I was desired for the little grace I was. I tell myself, *We all lose such days. Why should I be any different?*

Mark helps me to advance, despite my own aversion to my *better-ment*. It hardly seems just with so many going untended in their despair, but somehow I feel cheated. I feel dispossessed of leverage. The fact of my living a life of privilege precludes me from *reflecting* on privilege—there are rules about thinking or saying too much about your place if your place is an especially comfortable one, even if you arrived there by accident. Though I'm conscious of the comparative ease of my position, I can't access it in my head—it's like pushing peas through molasses. If privileged is not how I feel, it is how I look, and how I look is how I am viewed, and view is everything. It's irrelevant that I myself possess nothing, that I am more destitute than ever. If I am dependent, if I am subjected to views with which I disagree, if I live a life of compromise, it's a life I've chosen. I am wholly responsible.

My mind turns naturally to my parents: to my mother's struggle to support us while she attended college and graduate school, though she could have married anyone she wanted and attained financial security; to my father in his Ray-Bans and khakis, ready for a drive in his Plymouth station wagon to Gaslight Village in Lake George or the Danbury Fair in Connecticut, grateful for the inglorious luxury of a two-day vacation and a full tank of gas. Stuffed into the visor there would be maps and site brochures to caverns and motel recommendations and a leather pouch filled with change for the tolls. In a cooler would be the lunch he and Marilyn had made when they'd gotten up at five in the morning.

The day Mark and I pulled up to the sign shop in the Porsche, Dad came out with Tony. When I introduced my father as an artist, he shook Mark's hand and said, "Actually, son, I'm a sign-painter."

And me, not an adult, but a sick shell, void of fury, purpose, instinct. Not even a sellout, since *sellout* implies that there is some superior identity I've left behind.

Mark is coming. I feel the bob and creak of the dock with every step he takes—forty-seven steps. It's time for breakfast. At breakfast, the tables are immaculately set upon a curved concrete lagoon beneath huge tracts of cranberry-red bougainvillea where middle-aged Teutonic couples who do not touch in the night suck back poached eggs from thick silver spoons like sucking back oysters off of shells, and where the silence is uncanny until the arrival of our party—we are twelve. When we arrive, we create chaos. There is turbulent chair-switching and table-shifting and off-menu ordering. There is the flamboyant tying of slipped bikini straps and the indecent cross-table sharing of food and the rummaging through beach bags for cameras and aspirin, lotion and sunglasses.

Mark kneels behind me on the dock and puts his arms around my waist. "What are you looking at?"

"Home," I say, because as a couple, we are not without our virtues. I speak the truth when asked, and I never care to hear what he chooses not to tell. He doesn't mind that in my heart I betray him. I steal because I've been stolen from. It would take forever to replace all that has been taken from me. He knows that.

"Did you take your pill this morning?" Mark asks. I tell him yes, I took two.

Ocho Rios is about an hour's drive from the Half Moon Hotel, where we are staying. To get there, we rent motorcycles. Brett found six Triumph Bonnevilles through a British expatriate in Montego Bay. We take off east down the road—steep and angry highlands to the right, tranquil Caribbean to the left. We stop for beer at a place called the Famous Lovely Lynn's, a roadside shanty made of sundry timber and corrugated tin painted a caustic berberine-yellow.

A Jamaican man with an elongated head and spooling facial hair observes us from an aluminum folding chair. Lynn opens twelve tepid bottles of Red Stripe—there is the limp *chzzt, chzzt* of bottle caps snapping off. She sets the beers next to piles of bananas and neat rows of pineapples and peeled-back coconuts. I know she's Lynn because right away Brett asked, "Are you the famous Lovely Lynn?"

The man in the chair wants to know my birth date, which I give. He tells me my number. "Eight."

I turn my bottle in my hands and think of the number eight—stacked *O*s, a pair of glasses, segments of an earthworm, bubbles fused.

Mark takes a swig and makes a gratified sound. Lynn smiles at him. He inquires about her bracelets. Her arms are loaded with them—silver, gold, colored plastic.

"Fifty-two," she says, dangling her wrists in air. "One for each week."

"These three are identical," Mark says. "They only count as one."

The man continues to inspect me. "Whatever happened to you happened through *eight*."

"We started going out when she was eighteen," Mark chimes in.

"No. Not eighteen," he reports flatly to Mark, all the while his eyes boring into me. "Seventeen—one plus seven—*eight*. She knows what I'm saying."

Yes, I know what he is saying. Rourke.

Mark stiffens. He pays for the beers, then gives the guy twenty bucks. "Buy your lady another couple of bracelets."

At a local happy hour club named Bloody Mary's Jerk Pork BBQ, we all dance on a stage that cuts through the tables like a runway. For some reason, it's dressed on the sides in drooping velvet. It looks like a fancy coffin—a catafalque, a draped casket for presidents and kings. I remind myself to smile and to be pretty. It's hard to remember anything when I have the heavy feeling that Rourke is looking, that he's coming, though it's not likely that he will find me, since it's dark where I am. I wonder— when Rourke left, did he give me up to Mark consciously, like laying a baby on the steps of one particular house?

We dance until dark, moving the way the Jamaicans do. The men press their penises against the women's thrust-back asses, and the whole place is a party. From outside you could probably see the little shack shaking, going side to side.

Back at the hotel there is the sanitized rendition of Jamaican culture. We reenter the walled and gated property, return the motorcycles, and end the evening with a civilized stroll by the water's edge. We stop at the bulletin board to sign up for upcoming activities. The next day we take the glass-bottom boat tour at ten, and in the afternoon I rest by the pool while Mark goes with Richard to work on his swing. I don't ask if *swing* means tennis swing or golf swing. In New York, it means squash swing. Dinner that night is followed by a rum punch festival in front of a calypso show with steel drums, limbo dancing, and crab racing. The crabs get soaked in beer. I don't like the crabs part. It makes me sick, but I stay anyway, because, *just because*.

Dudley arrives with a cup of Blue Mountain Coffee for me. His grandmother drinks several cups a day, he told me one afternoon, and she is ninety-six. Dudley is our waiter; every day and night we get him. He is soft-spoken, clear and proud, with prominent cheekbones upcurving like stripes beneath his eyes. He is a king from another time. Now he clears tables and rectifies silverware, making all things parallel and perpendicular. When he puts down the china cup, the act is delicate, though if he wanted, he could crush it. I look at Dudley and am overcome by shame. I honestly don't know what to do about the nauseating fact of myself. He understands, I think. He nods to me, knowingly, quietly, pushing the coffee cup closer.

The world beyond our suite is silent. The sea is not far beyond our terrace, but I can't hear it because the sea doesn't move where we are. There is just the sound of the ceiling fan over the bed blowing my hair and the ribbons of my dress. *Tick, tick, tick.*

Mark tosses down a box, and the bed rocks. It is long like a pen box, only heavier. Unless it's a very nice pen. I try to remember the weight of a nice pen, but my mind is a mess from rum and Halcions. I can't remember how many pills I've had. Nothing can eradicate the images of the flat sea and stifling air, the coarse sand and ever-present air-conditioning, the walled hotels and unhappy island inhabitants.

"Open it," Mark says.

I roll from my back to my side, my head coming last. The hinges on the box snap to bite. Like crocodile jaws. Inside I find a diamond bracelet, a queue of ivy leaves or linked arrowheads. It seems to move, so I pull away. Mark unfastens it and lays it flat on the starched sheet. It looks like a procession of angelfish. Once clasped, the fish will swim nowhere, just in a perpetual ring about my lame wrist. How sad, my wrist, a universe.

"That was funny today," he says, "that woman and her bracelets."

I touch each link, count each fish. There are eight—oh, *eight,* my number, another coincidence, one to leave unmentioned. It will be my secret, my secret way to wear the bracelet, something to think about as I am forced to tolerate the talk it will generate. Everyone will say how lucky I am, how lucky we are. *Mark is so generous, so kind, so faithful— I've never seen him look at another woman!* It's true. He works hard to keep me, since we are joined by nothing of substance—just filament and fiber; it would take so little to set me adrift. Everyone believes he is nice, which he is unless you happen to be sleeping with him, in which case he is not, with the things he wants to do to you. It doesn't even matter to me what he does, and that is worse. When you don't care what a man does, he comes up with new things until you do. I feel bad that he cannot get through, that my tolerance is high, that my indifference exposes him for what he is—contemptible in the dark. Perhaps all men fall under the spell of their perversions when given the chance.

He drops onto the bed, first his knees, then his hip and thigh, then his elbow by my ribs. My wrist goes up; the cold metal slaps around. I feel him fasten it once, then again, hitting a special lock. I lie back, floating, my body in free fall, and yet some determined piece of my mind keeps jerking me back. It is as if I am on the brink of discovery, but of what? My mother calls the feeling *presque vu,* the almost seen, a lost word or phrase that rests on the tip of the tongue, the nagging feeling that there is something you have forgotten to remember. It has to do with Jack, and the night a long time ago when he gave me the opal necklace and a pill to drug me. But I am looking for something more elusive than that connection, a deeper realization having to do with the incentive to give such a thing. Jack was terrified of losing me then, and it was the appearance of Rourke that terrified him. Maybe Mark is terrified too. My eyes pop open. Suddenly I think, *Rourke.*

He has a flu. He smells like illness, and the bedroom in the apartment stinks like a teenage boy room, like semen and budding funk. I wash his tanned back and legs with cool water, then I go to the bathroom and flush my prescription pills, and also all the aspirin. I tell Mark we are out of aspirin, and that I have to go buy some. Without lifting his head he waves. He knows I'm lying. He also knows I'll be back. I have nowhere else to go.

Carlo is at the front door. "Where you going, Miss Eveline?"

"For aspirin. He's sick." I don't bother to say "Mark."

"I have aspirin downstairs. It's too late to walk alone."

"It's okay," I say. "He needs other things too. From the pharmacy."

"What pharmacy? No pharmacy's open this late."

"On the East Side. There's an all-night pharmacy."

I take Broadway to Columbus Circle, and as I walk I watch my reflection in the store windows—my hair swept back, my lips the color of lilacs. Beneath my eyes the bones make a *V*. I behold something imposing but tragic, resistant but capitulating, something like the flag of a poor but proud nation. I cut east on Fifty-ninth Street at Central Park South. And then at the Plaza, I head south for a few blocks, though the pharmacy is north.

When people say time heals, they are wrong. Time simply extinguishes hope. New mothers are told to let infants cry at night to learn to sleep alone—*Just a week, and you're free!* Yes, it takes one week of hysteria for the child to learn it can count on no one. It takes one week of abject misery to break the spirit, to inure it to abandonment and betrayal. Maybe it took longer with me, but by then I was grown. If I've devoted myself to Mark's happiness it's because I can't see well or perceive well. If he laughs or is happy, then I know things are okay. If he feels cold, I take a sweater. In the absence of true love and true joy, maybe it's best to treat happiness like any other need—hunger, exhaustion, thirst—factually recognized, functionally resolved.

Rain finally comes. I want it to rain hard. When I hit Madison Avenue and turn uptown, it begins to fall swiftly, and I swallow drops. I walk until I am drenched, until there is a feeling in me that is clear, shining like the street, slick like the slush of a city bus.

CITATION

Fall 1980

It was in the fall of 1915 that I decided not to use any color until I couldn't get along without it and I believe it was June until I needed blue.

—GEORGIA O'KEEFFE

34

The first thing I heard was someone say the date. I thought I heard October, though that didn't seem right. The next was how fortunate I was, which was funny. I didn't feel fortunate.

"You're a lucky young lady. You got a good bump."

It was a woman. My eyes tried to fix her. Her lines were out of register, like she'd been drawn by a broom. She was inserting a needle into the top of my hand. "I'm a nurse," she explained. "My name's Tilly. Do you remember what happened?"

A pig getting its throat cut. A swirling world like dancing. Faces in a ring.

Did I think I could manage a few questions, Tilly wanted to know. My age and name she got from my driver's license, but there was no insurance card.

"Do you have insurance?"

My feet were bare. I wondered who had my shoes.

A man in greens entered. "Hello there. I'm Dr. Tollman." He felt my head, manipulating it. My hand reached up. There was gauze and tape in a line above the eye bone. "Minor injury, no big deal. We'll get some film anyway, just to be sure. I'm mainly concerned about your blood pressure—70 over 50. You're completely dehydrated. I've ordered a bag of fluids."

He shined a penlight in my eyes, panning it from side to side like they do in the movies. His eyes were brown, his hair sandy and straight. "You're in the ER at St. Vincent's," he explained. "You passed out on the subway. Lucky you didn't hit the tracks. Ever fainted before?"

"A couple times," I said.

"When you get your period? Tilly says your underclothes were bloody."

I did not respond. He waited a moment, then leaned back, slapping the side of his legs twice. "We'll run some blood just in case. Anyone we can call?" He waved loosely. "Parents, anyone?"

"I can bring a phone over if you want," the nurse prodded. "There are jacks everywhere."

"Take your time," Dr. Tollman said. "We're not throwing you out." There was a commotion nearby, and he popped to attention, long-necked and perky alert. "Be right back," he promised as he passed through the curtains. Then ducking in again he said, "Hey Tilly, get some urine on her." Tilly didn't laugh despite the unfortunate choice of words.

"Excuse me," I said.

"Yes?" Tilly lifted her face from her work.

"I do have someone to call."

Dr. Mitchell wrote illegibly on my chart. I wondered what she was writing. She seemed to be writing more than I was saying.

"Of course, it's rare for a pregnancy to occur while using birth control, but not impossible. You probably missed a pill or two. Miscarriages, however, are not uncommon. We used to think they were late periods. In terms of the fainting episodes in the past, you *must* take better care of yourself. You can't go very far using more energy than your body manufactures."

"How far was—*it?*"

"Judging by the lab work, I'd say ten to twelve weeks."

The end of July. I wondered what we'd been doing then, what he'd been wearing, did it rain that day. I remembered one rainy day in particular.

I dressed and we met in Dr. Mitchell's office. On her desk was a latex mold of female genitalia and a laminated flip-book depicting ailments—tumors, warts, cysts. There were also photographs of her children.

"You'll need a D and C," she stated. "Do you know what that is?"

I said like a vacuum.

She said, a vacuum, yes, or a scraping. "You might still have tissue inside. You don't want an infection. I've made arrangements for tomorrow. They'll squeeze us in at nine."

I touched my belly as I walked down the hall. A scraping. How absolutely Rourke would be removed. There would be no trace. A little tissue, a little infection, at least that was something to hold on to. Maybe a scraping would be best. Yes, a scraping.

The feeling after leaving Montauk that summer was the one that persisted, which was that I wanted to die. I would have killed myself as soon as Rourke dropped me at home, but then I'd never see him again, and true love is devious. I remembered Jack once saying to me, *I could cut my wrists, put a bullet through my skull. If I thought I could reach you. But nothing can reach you.* My God, I thought, Jack.

There was no narrative completeness to the last day. It transpired in sick and silent fragments, like snapshots deadly passing, with no story to fill the places in between. Rourke's grim shadow in the bitter predawn light, sitting vigil over me on the edge of the bed as I passed fitfully through a fevered sleep, his eyes boring holes through open space as though his will could forge the future. Clean clothes for me at the foot of the bed. The Montauk cottage, a broom-swept shell, cleared of almost all our belongings. The car, idling and meticulously packed; the brightness of the sun, the whiteness of the sky; the neighbor's three-legged dog, blocking the end of the driveway and Rourke leading the dog home by the collar. Us on opposite ends of the moving car, not speaking, my face against the padded vinyl door. My mother's house, completely empty of people; him carrying my bags directly to my room, leaving them there, turning to go. Me alone on my knees surrounded by thrown clothes and overturned drawers, with the dresser sitting hideously dismantled like a mouth missing teeth. Me again, somewhere else entirely, the barn maybe, leaning upright against the wall, clutching it, as though I were on one of those carnival gyroscope rides, erect and perpendicular and holding hard because real life is centrifugal, because in the middle of everything is nothing.

And intermittently, sound. Cars rolling blithely up the street; the pernicious rap of the kitchen clock; the agitated whisk of my breath; my voice, hoarse from sobbing. I spoke to myself; there was no one else to speak to. *Be brave,* I kept saying. *Be brave.* Maybe there was something else I needed to be, but I couldn't think of the word for it.

On my bed there were messages. Labor Day weekend—I'd missed the entire thing. Kate had come from Canada to get the rest of her stuff. *Where are you? I'm with Marie-Helene. Meet us later!* I didn't know anyone named Marie-Helene. Why had Kate written the name as though I knew it? Sue from the Lobster Roll had called twice, the first time asking where I was, the second time asking if I felt better. Rourke must have called to tell them I was unwell and could not work. The thought of him calling on my behalf was overwhelming. I ran to the bathroom and vomited twice. Not much, just the food he'd given me that morning before driving me home. A banana and some toast. The phone messages in my hand accidentally got wet, and the papers attached to one another, the ink soaking and swirling. The stack flipped into the toilet, landing in a muffled *plock.* The bottom note I read backward. In my mother's handwriting it said, something, something, *taob,* which was *boat* in reverse. A message from Mark Ross.

At NYU, I did not unpack, just in case—in case of what, I wasn't sure. I kept my suitcase packed at the bottom of the closet, a few shirts and coats hanging. I never missed a single class. Classes were the only way to move forward: they marked time. I kept thinking, *December. I only have to make it until December.* If it was a good day, I might think, *May.*

I wrote a letter to Rourke—four times, ten times, copying, recopying, my words gaining greater distance from their original meaning with each draft until they became just a string of shapes, like operating instructions in another language, strokes and little arches, buckled bridges and circles with proud sashes. I wanted to tell him that since he left there was this absence. I did not send the letter. I did not want to trespass.

My dorm room was in Brittany Hall on the corner of Tenth Street and Broadway. It was a spacious room on the fourteenth floor with casement windows overlooking the gothic spire of Grace Church. It was bigger than Denny and Peter Reeves's whole apartment on East Fifth Street. My roommate, Ellen, was big and agreeable like a barmaid from a Dickens novel, though that could not have been accurate since she was Greek and Jewish, and Dickens never wrote about big Greek Jewish barmaids, not memorably anyway. Ellen's family lived in a just-built mansion in Rye.

Her dad was the chief heart surgeon at Albert Einstein Hospital in the Bronx, which amused my father immensely since he was a sign-painter and Dr. Christopolos was a cardiologist, but their kids wound up in the same goddamned place anyway. I didn't bother to elucidate the more salient differences—upon graduation I would be forty thousand dollars in debt and Ellen would be loan-free, settled into an investment condo, a guaranteed job, and the white leather seat of a brand-new BMW.

Ellen had the highest standards for personal care of anyone I'd ever met. She was entirely devoted to her own comfort. Thursdays to Mondays she anxiously returned to her parents' house in Rye weighed down with homework and laundry because it was *just so nice up there*. Besides, it's common knowledge that dormitory washing machines spread disease.

"Be careful," she warned the first time I used the laundry room. "My cousin Ruth at Tulane found a used condom stuck to the drum."

Instead of a stereo or typewriter, Ellen brought spa supplies to college. She had rolling wooden massage devices and fleecy slippers and velour bathrobes and giant plush Egyptian towels. There were vanilla balms for night and peppermint splashes for day and a constant supply of homemade brownies and 3-percent milk in her Permafrost mini-fridge. In the bathroom there were plaque picks and callus shavers and orthopedic shower shoes and super-cushiony toilet paper. Her goose-down quilt added five inches to her bed, and beneath her mattress her brother Stefan had laid three-quarter-inch plywood for added lumbar support.

I never heard her mention boys, not once. She was far too cunning to allow sex to endanger her lavish lifestyle. And since I did not infringe upon her sufficiency, we got along well. She treated me with benevolent indifference, and I found it admirable, actually, that she was so extremely disinclined to be idle, motivated as she was to get out of the city and return to the comforts of home. She went to bed at ten, got up at seven, and was in classes or the library all the hours in between. She wasn't unsociable; she simply had no time for anything other than an hour or two of television every night, *Dallas* or *Knot's Landing*. Invariably she shifted the TV set toward my bed so I could see too.

Ellen was a busy girl; you couldn't blame her for not noticing.

——

"You okay?" she asked. "You've been sitting for, like, three days."

Ellen poked at the desk lamp near my bed, turning it on, and the yellow light broke the blue of morning, which was a relief. The room had been like a pond with me at the bottom. Ellen took an involuntary step back, an instinctive step, thinking quick, in case I was contagious. On her shoulder was a duffel bag full of laundry. She was on her way home, which meant it was Thursday. I was pretty sure I'd lain down on Tuesday.

"Are you feverish?"

Maybe I had a fever, I wasn't sure. There were cramps in my abdomen, like mice squinching through narrow tubes.

"It's food poisoning," she said definitively. "That cafeteria is shameful. I keep telling you not to eat there." She thought for a moment, then asked if I wanted her to wake up the RA.

I shook my head. That would just be the beginning of a chain with every next person passing off responsibility, right through to my parents, who'd end up handing all decision-making back to me anyway. "You should go," I said. "You'll miss your train."

Ellen considered my advice, but some fundamental sense of ethics prevented her from taking it. She dropped her bag, opened my closet, and dug through my suitcase for clothes. She helped me slip on a pair of sweatpants and replace my T-shirt. When it came time for feet, she knelt on one knee and sucked back her lips with determination, manipulating the shoes, never once checking her watch, though surely she was thinking she might miss her train.

The transaction was extraordinary, not because we were strangers, but because the business of helping was obviously new to her. If I regretted having to inconvenience her with private problems, I appreciated the changes in her as she condescended to assist me. There was a give to her stiffness, an elongating of her cheeks, a paling of her complexion. She looked smaller when not so confident, and genteel, like a lady from a mannerist portrait. I thought to tell her, but it would not have come out right.

"Okay, let's get up," she said, taking my elbow. "One, two, three."

There was blood on the sheets. I tried to cover it, but my hand skimmed the blanket ineffectually. She could not have missed it, though she said nothing. Despite my obvious abnormality and her absorbing fear of contagion, she conducted herself graciously, which I decided had to do with good breeding.

There happened to be two available cabs rolling down Tenth Street. Ellen hailed both at once with a superhuman whistle and a mighty wave of a mighty arm. She put me in the first. "You gonna be all right?" she asked.

I managed to say yes. "Sorry about your train."

"There's another one in fifteen minutes." She handed me a twenty-dollar bill. I declined but she insisted. "If anything happens to you, who knows who they'll stick me with."

She got into the car behind mine, and the two cabs waited side by side at the red light on the corner. I sat, she sat, each of us awkwardly chauffeured. I imagined what it was to be Ellen Christopolos of the ubiquitous E.S.C. monogram, charging up to Grand Central to catch the 7:55 to Rye, popping into Zaro's Bread Basket and ordering with a certainty that was enviable and supreme a toasted raisin bagel and a coffee before buying magazines to breeze through on the train as she anticipated the luxuries that awaited her at home—Jacuzzis and tuna salad with fresh dill and a full-time housekeeper. On Friday night, there would be a movie and Chinese food with her grandparents. On Saturday, a few hours at Saks. No one would have guessed at her association with a hemorrhaging girl. I would have liked to make it up to her somehow, find a way to erase the knowledge she'd received prematurely concerning the dizzying and rancid phenomenon of carnal life.

The light changed, and her cab flew east across Tenth, while mine made the right down Broadway. I could see by the ponderous set of her jaw that she'd been making a picture of me as well. She'd been envisioning the squalid uncertainty of modern disease and remedy, the putrid working back to probable cause, the foul business of changing and cleaning bloodstained linen, the dismal occupation of a life without guardians, without ethnic net or religious shield, without refuge or resource. How unnecessarily expanded her mind must have been to review a life as luckless as mine. How relieved she surely was not to be me, poor and parentless, desired but defiled by the opposite sex.

The cab left me at University Place near Health Services, which of course was closed at seven-thirty in the morning, since any respectable student illness occurs during business hours. The walk to the Astor Place subway was macabre, with chained storefronts and cyclones of trash whisking down the Eighth Street corridor. I would have taken a cab, but I thought to save Ellen's leftover money for later. I must have thought things might get worse later. I recall being cold except for the parts of me that were hot. I recall the sheer slope of subway stairs going from street level down to the train platform. I know the train arrived: there's an image of the owlish face of the Number 6 implanted in my head. And the train's crippled dynamics, the labored jerk and groan of the brakes, the spitting inside-out puff of the doors, the garbled declarations by some recently paroled conductor, the porpoise-gray benches, the scattered souls.

Who knows where I was headed. I seemed to have had an East Side hospital in mind. Lenox Hill maybe. I was born at Lenox Hill.

The streets between Fifth and Madison Avenues on the Upper East Side are like halls of windows reflecting infinitely onto themselves, canals of pink-gold boxes repeating across the narrow streets. I sat on the stoop of a brownstone near Mount Sinai waiting for nine to come so I could go and meet Dr. Mitchell. Maybe that's not right. Maybe time does not come. Maybe you come to time, or through it. Or maybe you are a wheel and it is a wheel and periodically you line up.

July made sense. Hadn't I felt unwell in August? I'd been nauseous all the time. And then in September there was this tenderness, an ache disentombed like being bruised all over. What I'd felt were messages, weaving and unweaving, a new thing: half me, half Rourke. I would have guessed such a mix would survive, but how could it when those who brought it into being could not find the purpose to carry on? How was a baby to be strong when everyone else was weak? As a child I'd wondered such things too, and often.

There are those who would claim that I'd done nothing wrong, that it had been an accident, that nothing was killed, but rather, something had ceased to live. But the same people who say things such as, *It wasn't a baby; it was a zygote,* also say, *It's cruel to wear fur.* Then again, those who advocate killing animals for sport or fashion are equally hypocritical to speak of the sanctity of life. Maybe a deer has feelings, maybe the origin of a child is in the protoplasm; frankly, it's impossible to know. And yet, people keep trying to assign logic to sensation and consciousness in beings and entities other than themselves.

No one can say for certain that the grief of failed life does *not* enchase the walls of a woman. God knows you see so much sadness out there. There's proof enough of peculiar transmissions if you choose to seek it. I've heard that cows release adrenaline into their flesh as they're slaughtered, which in turn can alter you when you eat it, and organ transplant recipients can develop the dead donor's habits.

I did not have to envision a dead infant to make myself sad; I had only to think of what had happened *in fact* to what *in fact* had been: a minuscule cluster of cells artlessly awaiting the assistance of its life system, its world and its home, seeking sustenance—whether hormonal, electrical, or food-like in nature—but receiving nothing—nothing consistent, nothing adequate. I had only to think of atrophy in me, and my heart broke again, and worse.

The very brevity of the thing's existence was sacred to me—fine force and gossamer essence. In its economy there was a lesson I needed to learn having to do with windows of opportunity being fantastically small, with powers I had that were hidden. It had never occurred to me that I possessed such aptitude for damage. For several days I cried for Rourke and I cried for me and I cried most especially for the soul that had come and gone like a solitary flicker of the tiniest light. When I thought of the fluttering quills of an angel, consecrated and divine, flapping, flapping, slower and slower to sleep, I cried until the water in me dried; then I did not cry again. For years I did not cry.

"Date of last menstrual period?"

I did not know.

"Form of birth control?"

"The pill."

The nurse was preparing a needle. She wore a plastic heart pin that leaned to one side. Like a heart blowing. "Did you eat today?"

"She's not getting general," another nurse said. "She's getting Demerol."

"You're Dr. Mitchell's patient?"

"Yes."

"Dr. Mitchell's nice." The nurse drew blood, her head bent. Her hair was dense and coarse, like chocolate wisteria, twining like woody vines into a twist. Her skin was caramel with acne scars that were blackish by comparison. I asked her name. She said Lourdes.

"Are you Puerto Rican?"

"I am," she answered as she snapped the rubber tourniquet off my arm. Her eyes drooped lazily. "Open your fist for me, baby."

The syringe filled rib-red and she withdrew the needle, pressing cotton to the prick. I wondered if her life was nice. Maybe there were bridal showers and dowager aunts. A mother with hypertension and a cherished dog. "It's a hard decision, honey," she said. "I've had to make it myself."

"I didn't make the decision," I confided. "The baby made it for me."

In the procedure room I lay with my legs strapped in and spread apart, knees over padded stirrups, blue plastic sheeting over knees, green foam slippers imprinted with smiley faces flipping halfway off my feet, and a needle with a tube shooting out of the back of one hand—a far cry from his arms in the dark. There were strangers in scrubs, monitoring, arranging. Faceless nurses tearing plastic corners from sterilized utensil packs, laying instruments on metal rolling trays. Their hands were professional hands, like the hands of casino dealers, making your game their business, making your condition real, making it impossible for you to pretend otherwise. Eyes modestly lowered, eyes that know your truth. You think your story is original—it's not.

"I'm here to help Dr. Mitchell," a voice said. "I'm Dr. Burstein, the anesthesiologist." Dr. Burstein was tall. He seemed to teeter, or perhaps it was me, teetering beneath. "I'm going to give you something to help you relax," he drawled. He lowered himself onto a stool by my shoulder, then shot a filled needle into the top of the IV bag. I wondered if the feeling in his fingers was the same one you get from pulling the trigger on a pistol—the swift push, the mellow thrust. How omnipotent, to narcotize a body with such a small gesture. My arm went cold, my wrist and shoulder went cold. I could smell it behind my sinuses, and taste it. Was it possible to smell and taste it? There was a noise, a papery slap, then a growing whoosh like crickets.

Do people call you Eveline? I opened my eyes. I could not recall having closed them. Dr. Burstein was watching me. It occurred to me to ask how much time had passed. He appeared connected to time and reliable that way. *Or do they call you Eve?*

Evie, I answered, carefully. I couldn't tell if I was speaking very loud or very soft.

Evie, how sweet. Can you tell me how you feel, Evie?

I feel really good.

He laughed, and everyone laughed. *You might feel a little pressure.* Another voice, Dr. Mitchell's. I looked to see her. She was sitting on a stool or standing low at the base of the bed to my right and people were handing things to her from opposite sides.

Dr. Burstein patted my arm. *Good girl,* he said. *You're doing fine.*

It was nice of him to call me *good girl,* nice of them all; they were all very kind. It had been a long time since anyone had been kind that way. And then I fell back, and I began to waltz through the wonder of my own sensation, daring to tour regions ordinarily avoided, hunting despite the promise of pain for the wound he'd made. I discovered a lesion of such fury that it was positively viral, like an envenomed entirety, like daylight showing inside a blown balloon.

"You okay to walk?"

Mark met me at the door they admit and release you through. He led me past the girls who had not yet gone in, and he took my bag.

"Here, let me get that for you."

In his hand my pocketbook looked like all the other girls' pocketbooks, lilting and suspicious and possibly filled with germy sanitary supplies and other female stuff. In my pocket was a tissue full of Oreos. You get cookies at the end, and Dixie cups of juice like in nursery school. At the end you lie in recliners and watch game shows on a television bolted to the ceiling.

Mark grabbed the tissue before I could throw it away. "What's this?"

he inquired. "Are you supposed to eat these?" He placed them in his pocket. "You'll eat them in the car."

He protected me from an anemic flank of abortion protesters on the curb. They shuffled around rattling oak-tag posters with photos of mutilated babies, and they wore ankle-length down coats, though it wasn't even cold out. The guard said they came every day.

When I was little, my mother and her friends took me with them on a trip to march on Washington, D.C. There was the dieselized rumble of the Greyhound engine and the stench of cheap beer and costly marijuana and the low glandular singing of Janis Joplin's "Summertime." Periodically, the driver would pull off the highway and release the passengers onto the shoulder, and everyone would urinate. When hungry they would descend into diners, plunging into booths, terrifying humorless customers, provoking beefy truckers, and confounding nest-headed waitresses by making substitutions, switching seats, paying with penny rolls, and tipping with love poems and pocket contents—jawbreakers and torn snapshots and half-used Chapsticks. If they believed it was the function of the American youth to topple the old guard, to acquaint it with its inequities, to demand that everyone be compassionate and accepting of differences, they neglected to set a good example.

My mother said the march was for women's rights, for the rights she herself had not had. She'd had to have an abortion in an apartment on East 110th Street shortly after I was born. My parents were too poor for two children. I didn't even have a crib, just a dresser drawer. When I first learned the story, it made me sad, not for my mother, who recounted it without any desire for sympathy, but for myself. It would have been good to have had a sibling.

That was all I'd been told. But there had been more. Prior to the legalization of abortion in 1973, there was no anesthesia. There were no medics in hygienic disguise, and the equipment that had been used to penetrate a woman's cervix and pop her amniotic sac might well have been the same object employed to probe slits in car windows when you lock your keys inside. I once heard Aunt Lowie mention this substance they used to spray up there, like a lacquer or an ammonia. Did they use a flashlight to find their way? Did they give you aspirin, or was there whiskey, like in movies about cowboys and soldiers who get limbs amputated? Everyone knows about cowboys and soldiers who've had their limbs amputated—these comparatively rare events are frequently memorialized in film and on television. But it's distasteful to discuss abortions, safe or unsafe, though millions of women have had them, and continue to have them.

At Union Square, Park Avenue turns into Broadway. From the sky you would see not an *S* exactly, but the limber coil of a pried-apart paper clip. I felt weary. I felt I could not be alone anymore. I'd been staring at dogs lately, each time thinking, *A dog would be good.*

"Almost home," Mark said, glancing over.

I had no home. My dorm was not home. There was no home now that I was grown. Being grown means living among strangers. I did not say this to Mark. When you are grown, you can't speak foolishly. It is not profitable, not wise. You don't want to offend. You never know who you might need. "Are you going to leave me there?"

"Of course not," he said. "I took the day off."

I looked out the window again. In the shelter of his presence, I dared to touch my belly.

35

On the streets of Greenwich Village juvenile trees shaped like lollipops sat spaced like in collectible railroad towns, and when the wind went through them, it did not blow but hiss. Through the casement windows of the dormitory, I could hear the sound like the sound of suffering.

In classrooms and lecture halls, in the gym and the cafeterias, people stared as though they could see on my skin the stain of disgrace. Whenever possible, I avoided interaction; I led a solitary life. Days would pass when I didn't even speak. For meals, I went to eat alone at Loeb Student Center, the commuter café on Washington Square Park, instead of the dorm cafeterias, where boys would invariably come to my table, saying, "Is this seat taken?" or "Aren't you the girl from the gym?" At Loeb, everybody paid cash for lunch because they weren't on the housing or meal plan. People there were grateful for college. They dressed nicely. They let you cut in line. They would sit for hours, Korean guys from Kew Gardens and Greek girls from Astoria, waiting safely between classes, ten or twelve at a table, reading the news.

I was obsessed with the news. I read papers everywhere, sometimes twice, snatching up any rag from counters, garbage pails, exercise bikes, asking strangers, "Is this your paper?" I was constantly thinking, *Rourke's out there, somewhere.*

Just as he had been during the most difficult moments in high school, Jack was invisibly present during those months. Thoughts of him carried me. Having been loved by Jack I did not think that I could love Rourke better or more than Jack did me, or that my own heartbreak could sur-pass Jack's. It was the single equivalency I could find; in fact, it was per-fect. By my honest wish to make amends to Jack, I survived the loss of Rourke. I chose an ascetic life and dedicated my efforts to Jack and his well-being. I found contentment in conducting a private reconciliation with him. Sometimes I thought to try to find him, but I suspected there are some doors that are better off remaining closed, locked from both sides.

I had to pay Mark what I owed him.

Five hundred dollars for the private operation and the shot of De-merol, which was worth about four of the five. Lowie once said that a shot of Demerol is like a week in Bermuda.

"Forget about it," Mark said. He preferred to erase the debt, to pick up after Rourke and own a piece of me, only he didn't push because he was smart. He knew I would never allow anyone to lessen Rourke. If you ever saw Mark's eyes, you would always see them figuring.

"I'll pay you back anyway."

"Take your time," he said, fast. Mark spoke fast, giving the impres-sion that nothing was new to him, putting you at a rhetorical disadvan-tage, giving his remarks the illusion of having been born of experience. "The longer it takes, the longer you stick around."

On November 4th, 1980, the night of the Reagan-Carter presidential election, I got a job. I was out because Ellen had turned off the television.

"It doesn't make a damn bit of difference to my life who wins," she'd said. Her face was obscured by a layer of chamomile face cream, which made her mouth stand out, like the Joker's mouth from *Batman,* or like Pagliacci's. I was sitting on my bed in half darkness, fully dressed, and feeling weirdly ungoverned, kind of solo. "You can watch the results with the sound off if you want," she offered.

I started out looking for a coffee shop or some place with a radio. I ended up downtown, on the vast and virtually deserted Varick Street below Houston, in the printing district, where the only bodies I encountered were three men in the blackened doorway of a nightclub. I knew it was a club by the way the music thrashed against the doors from the inside, pleading like a prisoner.

One guy looked south into lower Manhattan toward the Twin Towers. "Where you headed, doll?" He had white hair and a crew cut, which had the effect of making his head appear shiny and thick, like a nickel. "Hate to tell you, but there ain't nothin' down there."

A second guy said, "Better watch out you don't get chucked in the backa some van."

The guy with the nickel-head asked where I lived.

I said, "The Village."

"Aureole's on MacDougal, right, Phil?" he confirmed. "She can cab up with Aureole."

Phil was boss—he had a clipboard. Anytime you saw a bouncer with a clipboard, he was boss. He jerked his head. "C'mon inside."

I stepped forward to the door and looked up to Phil. "Are they looking for help?"

"Ask for Arthur," Phil advised. With one bloated, I.D.-braceleted wrist, he waved me past the cashier and the second set of bouncers.

Inside was purple, like a black-light basement or creepy fish tank. The main room was huge and hardly filled. The place must have been a cafeteria during the day, because breakfast special menus hung near the ceilings, and the deejay was set up on a grill. The decorations were vintage neon diner signs. Ten or twenty customers stood at the perimeter of the cement dance floor, shuffling experimentally to Patti Smith's "Because the Night." Another fifteen or so hung off the ledge of a mammoth bar like there was nothing happening in the nation of greater consequence than vodka and cocaine.

"Where's Arthur?" I asked a girl at the service bar.

She gestured over a tattooed collarbone. "Try the kitchen." The tattoo looked like a banana and a dot. "Algerian flag," she said, noticing my interest. "It didn't come out right."

"Are you Aureole?"

"Frankie," she replied. "Aureole's around somewhere."

The enormous kitchen was spotless, as if it hadn't been used for cooking in years, and vacant except for a guy leaning against one of several counters reading a folded newspaper. I could make out the granular sound of election results on his AM radio. The count was in: Reagan had won. I couldn't help but think of Jack, where he was, what he was thinking. And my mother, and Powell, even Kate. I longed for the intellectual security of home. It felt wrong but somehow symbolic to find myself among strangers on such a night.

"Arthur?"

"Mike," he said, swinging up, extending a hand. "Arthur's the manager. I'm a bar-back."

"I'm here for a job," I said.

"Sure. I'll get him." Mike handed me his paper as he passed. It was the *New York Times'* crossword puzzle. "Do me a favor. Help me out here. I'm too freaked out to finish."

I answered as many as I could in the time it took for him to return from the rear of the kitchen with a case of Heineken on one shoulder. In his back pocket was an application. "Fill it out while you're waiting. Use my pen."

I marked Thursday through Saturday as my available days and gave the application to the elusive Arthur, a towering, sour-looking man in black leather and tinted glasses who appeared from nowhere and gave the impression of being dead or guilty.

Arthur scanned it impassively. "References?"

"None I feel like listing." Our eyes met over the sheet. I couldn't imagine him calling the Lobster Roll, which anyway was closed for the

season. Besides, there is a trick to getting a job, which is not really needing it and only half-wanting it.

"Fine," he said. "Start Thursday. Stick around and have a drink if you
want. It's been a rough night." Without another word he left as he'd arrived, vanishing into concrete and neon.

I finished the crossword with Mike and had a Beck's while we listened
to Reagan's acceptance speech. Reagan said he was "not frightened of
what lies ahead."

Mike chucked my empty bottle into a trash can, where it smacked the
rim and broke. "Great. In a country of two hundred million, that makes
one of us. He'll reinstitute the draft. He'll ban abortion. He'll clear-cut
forests. He'll set us back thirty years. I mean, he's *nostalgic* for the 1940s.
We were at war in the 1940s! We were dropping atom bombs in the
1940s! I'm getting the hell out," he confided, and he pulled out an accordion strip of wallet photos. "I'm taking my wife and kids to Australia."

The club filled considerably after the results were in. I couldn't imagine where all the people were coming from. Mike dropped me at the deejay booth while he restocked the bar.

A sign on the glass grill barrier said, D.J. JEROME. "*Jim* Jerome," he
clarified, extending a hand. He sounded Midwestern and sincere, like
Mr. Rogers. "The sign is supposed to say 'D.J. *Jim* Jerome,' but they
printed it wrong. Now everybody calls me Jerry."

I introduced myself, and he said my name twice. "Eveline, Eveline,"
he mused thoughtfully, as if imagining a place, trying to recall if he'd ever
been there.

Mike returned with Aureole. He'd found her locked in the basement
bathroom drinking Dewar's. "I'm sick," she said, regarding the election.
"I don't know what to do except drink." Aureole blew her nose hard. Her
hair was a swervy bob the color of Darjeeling tea, situated wiggishly over
a pair of violet doe eyes ringed red from tears. On her left cheek was a
mole. She looked like a young Liz Taylor, only not such an absolute
knockout. "Sure, I'll share a cab with you. I'd leave now, but I don't feel
like being alone."

Jim pulled a new album and tucked one headphone cup between his ear and shoulder. He engrossed himself in the mix, fingering the album back and forth. Underneath the song that was already playing came the Rolling Stones' "Beast of Burden." The absence of interruption in music as he went from one song to the next was nice; it was symbolic of cohesion in rough and fast times. It was as if no one could bear a second of silence.

As soon as the song became recognizable to the crowd, people peeled away from the bar. Their faces were familiar to me; they belonged to people my mother might have befriended, rebels and outcasts. Only I noticed a new lameness about them, an increased lack of relevance. They looked *off message*. It was as if within a matter of minutes, the avant-garde had become the periphery. The bodies crept to the edge of the dance floor, sitting on tables or standing next to them, swaying, nodding, soothed for the moment by the injection of the Stones' familiar antiestablishment voices, though, as Jack would have said, *The moment was bound to be brief.*

"How'd it go?" Phil inquired when I left. He was alone outside, just standing there, staring thoughtfully toward the street.

"Okay, I guess. I start Thursday."

He nodded. "Work out all right with Aureole?"

"Yeah," I said. "She's getting her stuff."

Phil had bad skin and bulky wrists. I suspected that he was self-conscious about that, that he was sort of a lost gentleman, so when he offered a cigarette, I took it. I didn't smoke, but Phil didn't deserve a *no,* and sometimes that's all a *yes* needs to be. We stood there for a while—actually, I leaned. Cigarettes make me dizzy.

"So, Reagan won," I said.

"Yeah." Phil evacuated the smoke from his lungs and flicked his butt to the curb. "The actor."

Heartbreak was not a great club, it was an okay club, a dive actually, but an enduring sort of dive popular among idiosyncratic losers and peripheral celebrities, iffy brokers and borderline musicians, those haggard, nicotine-types in creased leather and reedy denim who sleep all day but somehow manage to earn livings. I worked three nights, eleven to four, earning shift plus tips. I did more dancing than drink-serving, but no one seemed to care.

The atmosphere was remarkably wholesome. Dad and Marilyn stopped by sometimes to see me. Like everyone working there—gentlemanly bouncers, family-minded bar-backs, timid deejays, law school waitresses—I was in it for the money. And like everyone else, I had a complicated past that made me insusceptible to entanglements and indifferent to wild times. If only the loneliness there could have alleviated the loneliness in me, if only a nightclub were not such an institute of longing, maybe I would have gotten better.

At two-thirty in the morning one Friday in December, Mark came in. I hadn't seen him since the procedure in October. Every week I mailed him a money order for twenty-five dollars, which he always acknowledged with a phone call, and when he called, we would speak at length. I didn't have to force myself—I liked talking to him. It was like a window open, small as a needle's eye. But I never called him, no matter how reckless I felt.

"I can't stay," he reported. "I have a car waiting."

I was holding a freshly loaded tray. "Okay. Let me get rid of this."

I crossed the suddenly packed dance floor to deliver drinks to the guy who'd ordered them. He wiggled his blubbery ass and sang along as he fished leisurely through his pocket for a wallet.

He kept trying to dance with me, and I almost spilled the drinks before he finally handed me a twenty. It wasn't good to think of where his hands had been, such as shaking himself over a urinal. When people say, *Don't put that money in your mouth,* they basically mean someone like him had been holding it. Denny was always telling me to be careful because guys masturbate in bathroom stalls. *And worse.* The guy waited until I got the change together, then just told me to keep it. Six bucks, which was a lot, but somehow still inadequate compensation for having to deal with him. Good tippers are frequently the most despicable citizens—they pay you for tolerating them.

It'd been a nice night before Mark had arrived. Maybe it wasn't fair to blame him, but nightclubs are places of explicit laws. It takes just one body to transform a benign gathering into an intolerable mob.

"Who's the suit?" Mike shouted, meaning Mark. I was waiting for an opening to cross the floor.

"Just a guy I know," I shouted back.

Aureole joined us. "He's cute. Like, totally undone. It looks like he ran here."

It was true. Mark's tie was loose and his jacket unbuttoned and his hair made Caesar bangs on his brow. He'd obviously been drinking.

Mike leaned forward. "What the fuck's he doing?"

"Is he busing tables?" Aureole asked, leaning as well, squinting. "Oh, my God, he is."

Mark was emptying ashtrays into a gray plastic bucket, wiping them with cocktail napkins. All the tables around him had been cleared.

When I got over to him, I said, "What are you doing?"

He said, "I hate to have you touch filth."

"We have a busboy," I informed him.

"Obviously not a competent one. There's shit everywhere."

"Anyway," I yelled. "What's up?"

"I want to borrow you. For New Year's Eve."

"I'm working New Year's Eve."

"Take off," he declared emphatically. "How much will you make?"

I didn't know. I'd never worked on New Year's before.

"Take a guess—a hundred, a hundred fifty?"

I shrugged. I'd never made more than fifty a night. "I don't know, maybe."

"I'll double it," he proposed. "I'll give you three hundred."

"That's prostitution."

"It's not if we don't have sex." He kissed me and ran out.

36

The dorm on New Year's Eve had a cinematic emptiness that called to my mind the evacuated ministries in European wartime movies or the hospital where they put Don Corleone in *The Godfather*. Most everyone had gone home for the holiday break; only a handful of students remained—me, some resident advisers, a few internationals.

Anselm from Berlin was on my bed. He and Mark had met at Harvard, though he was at Columbia now, earning his doctorate in American history. His burgundy shirt was unbuttoned beneath an orangutan-orange leather coat, and his chest was bare. He was not so much a man as a symbol of one, like a dictionary illustration or a figure on a lavatory door. He was a gorgeous unfortunate, one of those people in whom vanity overwhelms sexuality to become a preoccupying sort of project. He was a little tragic overall, a little east-west, a little male-female, childishly divided, like the city he'd come from.

We made a champagne toast. "To 1981," Mark said.

"1981," Anselm repeated with a nod.

I told him that I liked his jacket. "You look good."

"Looking good is what he does best," Mark said, taking out his credit card to cut a pile of coke.

I pulled on a pair of gray jeans and a peach T-shirt with a lazy ruffled neckline. I dressed in front of them because modesty seemed solemn and unnecessary, because sometimes a night has a natural drive, and you are transported past the conceit of your despair. Sometimes you can't help it—your constitution is strong despite yourself.

The three of us stayed in my room for a few hours, with them talking and me dancing, half-listening, always agreeing. It didn't matter what they were saying, or what anyone said anymore—everyone kept conversation light. Days were different without people like Jack in them. No one was smart enough to take exception, no one dared to object or go too deep; if you tried, you would encounter walls in the faces of your friends. And anyway, life moved faster than expostulation would allow.

Earlier that day, I'd picked up some classic Motown albums at Bleecker Street Records. We were listening to "Love Child" by the Supremes.

"Psychedelic soul," Anselm remarked above the music, examining the album cover—it was a picture of Diana Ross, Mary Wilson, and Cindy Birdsong waltzing in flowing pink caftans.

"Not exactly Parliament," Mark said, "but an attempt at a social statement nonetheless."

"C'mon," Anselm said. "'Love Child' knocked 'Hey Jude' off the number one spot on the charts. Parliament couldn't have done that. The masses move in baby steps."

"Okay, since you're the expert on American culture, what's your prediction for the eighties?" Mark asked.

"Disempowerment of youth, dismantling of liberalism," Anselm said without hesitation. "In order to restore the right, which has suffered repeated blows since the fifties, Reagan has to destroy the legitimacy of the left. Alternative thinking and living will become synonymous with failure. It is a big ideology."

"I guess it worked for Hitler," Mark said.

Anselm said, "Precisely."

"Luckily, Reagan's no mastermind."

"*Un*luckily, it's all too simple. Look at any totalitarian regime. They succeed by feeding greed, inspiring terror, rewarding complicity. By eradicating shades of gray, by promoting contrasts—black-white, good-evil, in-out, us-them. For those who play, there is wealth, security, respect. For those who do not, there is the pathetic echo of their own enlightened but impoverished voices. It's all theater, which is why there's no better messenger for the moment than an actor."

"No uprisings?"

Anselm shrugged. "Drugs will silence us."

"In the sixties," Mark said, "drugs provided impetus for change."

Anselm toyed casually with the radio. With his right wrist he spun the receiver dial while his body leaned left. I was not sure if he knew what he was saying, but it sounded good when he said it. In all the gum and whoosh of his German accent, everything he said sounded jurisdictional.

"I would not say *change*. I'd say *review*. Nothing changed, per se, otherwise, how could we find ourselves *here*, at the mercy of a conservative regime? The difference is that drugs were once in the service of creating common ground. Now they are in the service of narcissism. In the sixties people were emboldened by the draft—not drugs. Reagan would have to reinstate the draft," Anselm said, adding, "which is why it's nonsense to think that he will. He won't risk activating people. He wants us to sleep."

Mark noticed I had stopped dancing. He spoke my name abruptly, as though I were a child eavesdropping on an adult conversation. "Eveline. Put on some lipstick; it's a holiday."

I looked to him, startled, for an instant unable to recall how we'd met, how he'd come to know me. I felt myself on unfamiliar ground. And yet, I knew that in order to come through, I needed to conform, regardless of the calling of my heart to the contrary.

I applied lipstick. Mark was behind me, sharing my mirror. "Good girl," he said.

There were no cars in SoHo. We walked down the middle of the street, and Mark greeted everyone—huddled couples, dog walkers, lost and rambling revelers—saying "Happy New Year" with great congeniality. Mark was congenial. It was hard to despise him for it when affability is a skill of survival. He took my hand, I took Anselm's, and we walked, united by darkness and dope. If you tried, you could almost feel the newness; you could turn susceptible, the way you can relax and sense a phone about to ring. It truly was the eve of an almost something, something not yours perhaps, but connected to you nonetheless. If what Anselm said was correct, and change was inevitable, I wished it would come already, even if it meant change for the worse.

Snowflakes together with the wind blinded me, leaving me dependent upon the mercy of the men. It had been just one year before that I'd seen Rourke in the record store. I told myself to set the thought aside; it was a dead thought. And yet, one year ago was easy to recall—if I was remembering, I realized, so was he. Wherever he was, he was thinking of me. My step quickened.

"You seem happy all of a sudden," Mark said. "I'm glad."

We turned from Prince onto Thompson and raced to where we were going. In the yellowed stairwell leading up to the fifth floor, the pathetic odor of currently cooking things mixed with years upon years of long-ago cooked things, packing up the passage like a dam. Each landing was dressed for the season with a paper snowman head and a sorry bit of garland tacked beneath a feeble hall light. Where the linoleum was peeling away there were those little black and white floor tiles. It was exactly like the building my father lived in.

"No kidding," Mark said. "Where does he live?"

"On Elizabeth Street. And Spring."

Two apartments on the top floor joined in front to form one large living area. Through strings of lights that made *X*s across the windows, you could look north over the roofline of the tenement buildings on the opposite side of the street. The floors were painted glossy white, and the furniture was pale wood. There were glass tube lights with chrome caps that looked like devices from old science movies. A red-and-yellow tapestry was hanging on the wall above a pumpkinish burl sofa. I was not sure about the word *burl*. It was all I could think of.

"So," a voice said, "this is the little girl I've been hearing about."

The voice was like cellophane melting. It belonged to a man with close-cropped hair, and brown eyes with pupils like leaping fish. He had sunken cheeks with razor stubble. The drooping contour of his hairline was like the shadow of a suspension bridge. He looked, I don't know, *Carpathian*. He took my coat and passed it to unseen hands.

"I am Dara," he said, and his words emerged as if spaced by slender blocks. Dara led me into the gathering, and Mark waved an encouraging farewell. I felt like a social experiment along the lines of Eliza Doolittle. We made our way toward the cryptic posterior of the apartment, where fashionable people fashionably gathered—Italians, Jordanians, French. "As an American," Dara said, with a condescending sneer, "you will find you are among the minority."

If he was somewhat racist and sexist, I excused him. I told myself he was cultured and European, and practiced as a gentleman, and practiced

European gentlemen think of women differently than American women are accustomed to being thought of. I told myself that it's not reasonable to expect uniformity of perception, that it's actually nice to be held to lesser standards, to be kept unaccountable, to listen until being called upon to reply—so long as the reply is brief. It was a relief to be asked to contribute only the gift of grace—the lips, the ankles, the fragrance of the hair. Such are the marks of worth when you have no others. These were the things I told myself.

Anselm joined us with three glasses of champagne. We raised them to the New Year.

"Father gave me an excellent New Year's resolution," Dara told us. "He said, 'Take taxis. Your time is too precious to waste.' "

"I hope *Father* gave you an excellent bank account with that advice," Anselm replied.

"Well, not everyone is born into a dynasty, my friend."

Anselm laughed, Dara laughed, and our glasses clinked as their laughter joined other laughter, all galvanizing in a raucous eruption. I also laughed, at them and at me, and at the hilarious fact of my own misery. I would have left the party, but I had no better place to be, and for whatever reason, they had extended themselves to me, though I was underfed with substandard shoes and cheap eye makeup. Besides, I couldn't possibly spend another night alone, cultivating the company of my own American mind. So I resolved to endure the night, the company, the talk of easy fortune as though I were on a plane half-listening to flight instructions that I knew could never possibly save me.

> *Advertising was up 25% by the third issue—The stock split twice in the first year—The Moral Morel, organic mushrooms, maybe you've seen our trucks—She comes right to the office with a portable table—My sister sells hats to Barneys—We just bought a flat on the Left Bank.*

Periodically I remembered Mark, periodically I located him, rustling in corners, other heads and his head hunched together, whispering, planning, selling—always selling.

"Money talk," Dara whispered. "And people say art is dead."

Anselm took me by the hand and led me away to the bathroom. I acquiesced. Who cared—more coke, less coke. I was glad for the diversion, for anything that would alleviate my anxiety to get started, to catch up, to figure some gimmick to win. Everyone I'd met was robust, vivacious, already chic, already traveled, on track to fame and fortune, or at the very least, to paying jobs. By comparison I was common, provincial—it probably seemed as though it was I who was interested in Mark for his money. It was amusing to consider that their disparaging opinions of Americans and elevated ideas of Europeans related directly to the fact that our ancestors had courageously escaped Europe, whether by choice or necessity, due to some disadvantage, while theirs had remained, hogging up all the wealth and privilege. Or perhaps theirs had simply been too fearful to make a break.

Anselm tapped cocaine from a brown glass vial onto the finlike membrane between his thumb and forefinger, the place where you make ballpoint pen puppet faces. He offered it to me, and I accepted a little, just a little. I'd already had a lot. I'd never had so much before, and my body was small and my metabolism rapid and my heart still so terribly unsound. Dara's medicine cabinet was full of stately apothecary bottles. There was a horsehair brush.

I asked Anselm to brush my hair the way Denny used to.

"Of course," he sputtered, as if it had been his intention from the start, and he returned the coke to his breast pocket, fingering it down like men finger down sunglasses or theater tickets. He rinsed the brush in steaming water then shook it, which was a precaution I would not have taken for myself, particularly since it implied I was superior to Dara in *something*, and I thanked Anselm, and he made a noise not unlike a hum.

I sat on the toilet and he sat on the tub, with our thighs lining up, parallel, touching. I watched us in the mirror, wondering if perhaps we were related. We looked alike in coloring and also in bones. My father's father had come from Germany, from Kiel, in the north. Kiel was a port city that had traded with St. Petersburg, which is why I looked Russian, my mother always said. I closed my eyes; Anselm's touch was gentle. I could feel the strands of my hair separate between the bristles.

"Thank you for not asking who Denny is."

"I try to be sensitive," he said.

I liked hiding in there with him, and he liked hiding with me. It was obvious that though he had money—a *dynasty,* Dara had said—he wanted something he couldn't get from other women at the party, the seductress accountants in unitards and models in shiny leather boots like Diana Rigg wore in *The Avengers.* If I had to guess his pain, if indeed it was pain that he felt, I would have thought it involved a Swiss girl or fashion muse, some Imperial China blonde in a chinchilla-trimmed jacket, some cognac, and three days in Biarritz.

He placed the brush on the sink ledge—just *so*—and accidentally touched my neck. Though our bodies were close, there was no chance of drifting into intimacy. Anselm needed only the woman with whom he was in love, or some qualified replacement capable of satisfying his family's demands for status and affluence. And as for my part, I could never settle for anything less than a renegade and a runaway, a descendant of greatness capable of voluntary disinheritance. Someone who would choose self-governance or death. An American.

When the music got good, we stood simultaneously, and went to the living room where we were first to dance, and that was triumphant but lonesome, like being the first of your group to swim.

Fire. The way you walk and talk really sets me off—

The floor filled soon after we arrived, and for a while things were manageable, until someone started to bump, then everyone started to bump, bones and bits of flesh tipping bits of flesh and bones and a forest of arms overhead, wintry and erect, like limbs attached to bodies begging to be exhumed. Something about the bareness of the arms plus the unity of the bodies made me feel claustrophobic and terrified.

I withdrew to the window and looked at the snow-covered streets. The stormy sky was pretty, a white-pink city haze. I wished someone would come get me, but there was no one. That might have been a common thought to have on New Year's Eve; in all the world I was surely not the only one thinking that way. The trick, I supposed, is never to have that thought, never to stray far from those who would give anything to rescue you. Such people are *friends* and typically they reside at *home*. One year before, I'd been in my living room with Jack, Dan, and Kate.

That night, for the first time, I began to understand the graphics of hardship, which I saw as a fraction with failure on bottom and time on top. It's close to impossible to carve even a moderate fortune from a society that is locked; the math of the fraction is the impermeability of the culture divided by your desire to make it permeable.

Mark appeared, like an emissary or ambassador, just as I was discovering a whole new low.

"My God," he said, petting my jaw in upstrokes with the back of his hand, like I was catlike, like I was cunning, "I am so in love with you."

It was past dawn when Mark and I headed back to the dorm. He stayed several yards in front, facing back. He wanted to watch me walk, he said. At my door he held me, but I did not kiss him. I did not have to. I'd already compromised so much.

He brushed his cheek against mine, keeping it there just for a moment. "It wasn't so bad, was it?"

The bad part was to come. The bad part was going inside alone, lying alone, waking alone. He must have known how it would end for me because in fact he did not leave me alone. He'd left an envelope when he was in the room earlier with me and Anselm. Beneath my pillow. Inside was three hundred dollars cash.

"Listen to me. You can't get a word in edgewise."

We were at Le Bernardin. It was two days before Valentine's Day. Mark was too clever for Valentine's Day. Though had he asked, I would have accepted. I didn't mind being with Mark. Time with him was public time. There was no need to do anything but project outward from the sphere we occupied. He knew Rourke; he knew Rourke's effect. He was not repulsed by my heartache or impeded by my devotion. He searched for Rourke in me the way an archaeologist might crawl through caves, feeling for gouges, testing for oxides and ochres. When I was with Mark, I could feel Rourke alive.

"Jesus, what did he do to you?" Mark said.

I liked that he said that—*Jesus, what did he do to you?*—and erotic thoughts of Rourke became intertwined with erotic thoughts of Mark, and I had to work to keep the two separate. The effect of the remark was such that I wondered whether he had anticipated my response. It was possible that he had given it as a gift, but more along the lines of a degenerate gift, not to please but to test. He wanted to measure the profundity of my need, as if by exacting those dimensions he could gain some advantage against Rourke.

For the remainder of the night we ate sculpted nouveau meals in fancy clothes, and Mark talked without abeyance—of sailing his boss's boat to Anguilla, of a '66 Mustang GT 350 he was thinking of picking up, of someone he knew who'd gotten murdered by the Jewish Mafia. I'd never heard of a Jewish Mafia. My dad had spoken of the *Russian* Mafia; maybe Mark meant that. He talked about his former girlfriend Diane, a journalist in Los Angeles who'd had breast reduction surgery.

"She had to go out every night," he said as he worked through a crème brûlée. "In New York it was Xenon, Studio 54, Danceteria. And in L.A., well, you wouldn't know the clubs in L.A., but she burned through them. Beautiful like Rita Hayworth in the old classic movie *Gilda*—but shallow. In all the years I dated her, she never once looked at the stars."

"Why did you stay with her?"

He shrugged. "Everyone wanted her, but only I could get her."

At the end there was a gift for me—a book on Giotto he'd purchased while we were at the Met that afternoon.

"There's a chapel in Padua where the walls are covered with Giottos," Mark said.

"Scrovegni Chapel," I confirmed.

I noticed for the first time that he appeared unrelated to his sister. Alicia was dark and exotic, like an Egyptian. Mark was neutral in color, with skin that was pale and hair without any particular accent or modulation. He wore it long and back off his face. The color of his suit was the color of his eyes, a grief-stricken gray, like shark hide, and light licked off his eyes, making him appear shrewd, diligent, making him seem to work twice: once for effect and then again for the pleasure of it. His lips were straight and his nose was straight; yet, for all that directness of line, he was obtuse. Everything he said came out as though in code. I was moved by the ease with which he could manipulate me; he held keys to doors I didn't know I had.

"I'd like to take you there so you can see them in person," he suggested softly, staring back at me.

Mark became attractive when he referred to money. Money meant attractive things to him—freedom and fulfillment—and a girl cannot be blamed for taking a man as he prefers to be found, for giving in to self-confidence when it makes itself manifest like lightning before your eyes. It's like being hypnotized.

He assisted me as I stood, placing a hand on my lower back. I didn't flinch. No one could touch the place that was Rourke's. No one would ever get through.

"What are you thinking of?" he whispered to my neck.

"Hypnosis," I said. "I'm thinking of hypnosis."

37

Rob wanted to know what I was doing that night, did I have plans. It was late April.

"Not really," I said.

"Fine," Rob said. "I'll be over in twenty minutes."

I came down to sign him in and found him sitting on the security desk, sweet-talking Juanita the guard. Under one arm was a record album, and in his hand was a paper bag.

"Right outside Bedford," Juanita was saying.

Rob repeated like he didn't hear right, *"Bedford?"*

Juanita's walkie-talkie hissed at her hip. "That's right."

"Bedford Falls, like in the Jimmy Stewart movie? The Christmas movie?"

"Actually, just plain Bedford."

He creaked his neck around. "You had me goin' for a minute there. Bedford Falls. That'd be like meeting somebody from Mayberry."

I signed Rob in. Beyond him, through the doors to the street, there was a pull to the night. Like a puppet being lifted to a stand, the earth was coming alive to spring.

I asked Juanita if Rob was giving her a hard time.

"Not at all, honey," she said.

"Me?" Rob exclaimed. "She's the one telling me she's from Bedford Falls!" I pulled him off the desk by his sleeve. He leaned down to her. "You wanna know something? I've seen *It's a Wonderful Life* a dozen times, but I've never made it through *Miracle on 34th Street* once."

We boarded the elevator, and the heavy doors knocked closed. It was the first time I'd seen Rob since the previous summer in Montauk. Though I had changed and he had changed, there was a place we shared that was enduring. In that region, we observed the need for caution. In that region was Rourke.

"Ever chew tobacco?" he inquired, staring ahead.

I said that I hadn't, staring ahead too.

"You're in for a night." He shook the suspicious-looking paper bag, dangling it like a mouse he'd caught. "Elephant Butts, it's a type of chew you can't get down here. Charlie Cutlass drove it down from Oswego. I ever tell you about Charlie Cutlass?"

I shook my head.

"Sad story. Tell you later, over a good stiff drink. Remind me."

We were sitting on the floor by my bed, chewing tobacco, listening to a Richard Pryor album. Rob had obviously come to tell me something or ask me something, and that something had to do with Rourke. Behind every situation is a picture, and I got the picture as best I could: Rob felt bad for me but Rob stood by Rourke's decision to take off. I could not speak of what had happened without seeming to blame Rourke, and Rob could not speak without seeming to betray him. I would not compromise their friendship by speaking of feelings, yet my silence had the very effect I'd hoped to avoid. Maybe there was more; I really wasn't sure.

From the moment he arrived, Rob's eyes would not rest long on me. I thought he would have kissed me hello. He couldn't even kiss me. Every day I dealt with the business of my handicap, I'd become used to it, but it was new to him. I was sorry for the shock of seeing me changed. Denny had recently given me a photograph he'd taken of me from my birthday party senior year, to show me how different I looked now. The change was unsettling. My face was still my face, and yet it seemed like all the life had gone out.

"Where's your friend tonight?" Rob asked.

"Which friend is that?"

"*Which* friend," Rob repeated flatly. He spit into a paper cup, the tobacco juice shooting in a streak between his top and bottom teeth.

I stood to flip the album. I was incredibly high from tobacco. I felt like someone was tossing me sideways into the wall, only there was no someone and no tossing, just the wall. "He's away. Somewhere."

"Somewhere my ass. He's golfing in Palm Beach with his parents. Tough life."

"I don't know. I don't like Florida."

"You'd change your tune fast enough. That family travels in style. Five stars all the way. For breakfast there's oatmeal, fruit cups, trays of bacon, the papers, a swim. Then sun. Later it's shopping, tennis, a massage, another swim. You pop a button off your slacks or spill hollandaise on your dinner jacket, and they got a Polish laundry lady and a tailor in the closet of your suite. Waiting, like elves. They come out when you're gone and pick lint."

I dropped back down to the floor, crashing shoulders. "I wouldn't trade places with them."

Rob looked at me and smiled. He slapped his thighs. "Right. Who needs margaritas and white sands when we've got everything right here—chewing tobacco, Richard Pryor, industrial carpet, and a couple cans of—what is this crap we're drinking?" He hunted for his soda.

"Tab." I'd taken it from Ellen's refrigerator.

He shook his head. "Jesus. *Tab*. I'm happy as a clam."

"Don't forget the girl," I reminded him.

"No," he said. "Who could forget the girl." This was followed by a hapless interlude. Rob kept looking around, nodding serially like one of those hard dogs in the rear windows of cars from the boroughs. "So," he said, "who does this roommate think she is anyway, one of the Gabors?"

———

The main thing to do at Gulf Coast is drink jalapeño martinis. Rob ordered two and he removed his hooded gray sweatshirt. Underneath was a denim vest, and under that, a T-shirt: *Fantini Brothers Construction. If I had my way, I'd tear this fucking building down.*

The bartender said, "Seven bucks."

Rob gave him a withering look, then paid. "I gotta get you to Pinky's out in Brooklyn, in Williamsburg," he proposed to me. "My cousin owns it, so I drink cheap. It's worth the trip. None of this three-dollar-and-fifty-cent pepper water served by actors. When's your birthday?"

"November."

He shook his head. "Too far. What's the next holiday?"

"Easter?"

"Nah, Easter passed." *Easta.* "Tell you what, though, next year we'll get a couple bunnies and go to Pinky's. My mother makes up baskets for the Sunday School kids. I'll get her to make you a basket. With that shredded crap, that nest crap. Girls like that. What do you call it?"

I shrugged. "Shredded nest crap."

He eyed me. "You think I'm kiddin'."

"I don't," I said, laughing.

"You're gonna back out on me, aren't you? I'll be sittin' there alone with a beer and a bunny basket, and I'll be lucky to leave Pinky's with my nose on straight."

Denny was late as usual. We'd called him before leaving the dorm. He and Rob had not yet met, though they'd heard about each other. Just in case, I prepared them. I told Denny that Rob was not a bigot despite the fact that he might look like one, and I told Rob that Denny was *gay-ish.*

"What's that mean, *gay-ish*?" Rob wanted to know. "Don't he know by now?"

"It's probably better if you don't mention it."

"Oh, yeah, yeah. Sure, I getcha." Rob nodded and pointed. I wasn't exactly sure what it was he got, and got so vividly, but I decided to let it go. Apparently Rob forgot his promise because the second Denny walked in, Rob said, "Hey'ya, kid, how's curtain-making going?"

"Just fine, sweetheart," Denny snapped back without missing a beat. "I'm knitting you a Speedo for summer." He folded his new blue trench coat over a stool. It was the same coat John Lennon used to have. Denny was still in mourning from Lennon's death. He kissed me and sized up Rob's outfit. "What happened? Did you have to change a few tires on the way over?"

Denny gestured for a new round by snapping his fingers in the air then making a lasso with his left index finger. Denny was a lefty. Every now and then he would fly into a panic. "Lefties die sooner than righties. No wonder! It's the stress!"

He acted slightly more gay since moving to New York, which may have been belated self-expression, or something more formulated and political, or just a time-saving transmission of preference. I was confused about whether to be glad for him because he was finally able to express himself, or concerned that he was losing his individuality and imitating others. He had a lot of new friends. "FIT is filthy with fags," he'd say.

Rob couldn't deal with the cost of drinks at Gulf Coast, and Denny couldn't deal with the "film crew" atmosphere, so we walked west across Twelfth Street, then turned up Tenth Avenue to head to some dive in Chelsea called Stecky's. On the way, Denny said he had started dating someone named Jeff. Denny wasn't with John anymore, which was too bad because I liked John. They'd been together for two years.

"John gave me cooking lessons for Christmas," Denny complained. "Can you believe it? How sexist is that?"

I shrugged. "Cooking's okay." I didn't see anything wrong with cooking lessons. Denny was actually a lousy cook.

"I hope you used the lessons before you split up. That would be a tremendous waste," Rob said.

At Stecky's, we each grabbed a stool and pulled up to the bar. The minute we sat down, Rob started asking the bartender about his handlebar mustache.

"How long's that thing?" Rob inquired. "You know, after a shower? Is it down to your chin, or what?" He flipped up his hands. "Just curious."

Simultaneously Denny started in on the trivia question written in blue wax on the bar mirror—*Who was the Triple Crown winner before Secretariat?*"

"It's a tough one," the bartender said. His name was Billy. "It's been up for a couple days."

"Call your dad about the trivia question," Denny suggested to me.

"That's right. Get him on the horn," Rob said. He asked Billy for a phone, then he nudged me. "You never mentioned parents. I figured you came from swans."

"You mean storks," I said as I began to dial.

"No, baby, I mean *swans.*"

Dad picked up.

"Hi, Dad. It's me."

"Yeah, hi!" he called out excitedly. My father always calls out on the phone, like he's talking into one of those candlestick jobs. It's a wartime habit, like hoarding canned foods. The basement of the shop is full of canned foods. "What's up?" he asked.

"I'm at a bar with Denny and Rob. What's up with you?"

"We just got back from dinner with Ralph Russo. He's got neck cancer."

"Neck cancer?"

"That's no name for a horse," Rob said into my ear.

"First, he had polyps," Dad was saying. "They biopsied them. Now he has to get that operation. You know, the hole and the battery-operated thing. The wand. Poor bastard."

It didn't feel right to mention the trivia question considering Ralph Russo's condition, but the whole crowd at the bar was kind of hanging over the counter, watching.

Dad didn't have to think. He just said, "Citation, 1948."

I asked Billy, "Is it Citation?"

Billy said, "Bingo!"

Denny took the phone to say hello, then Rob took a turn, saying, "You've got one hell of a trap brain and one sweetheart of a daughter." A few more people grabbed the receiver to ask Dad if he had any tips on tomorrow's races. When I finally said goodbye, my father sounded cheerful. I was glad we'd called. "Bye, Dad. Say hi to Marilyn."

"All right, then," he shouted. "Have a good time."

Billy gave us a round of highballs even though the prize was for one free drink. "Technically, soliciting recruits isn't legal, but I'll let you slide. I was just about to wipe the board anyway."

When Johnny Mathis came on the jukebox and Denny heard the slow beginning notes of "Chances Are," he grabbed me. "C'mon, honey, let's go dance."

Denny was big, but he wafted when he moved, and when he held me close, it was like flying—my feet hardly touched the ground. His Uncle Archer had taught us all the dances from *Saturday Night Fever*. We must have seen the movie about fifteen times.

"Seventeen," Denny corrected, and we dipped. The bar and the liquor bottles drifted obliquely. "I still have the stubs."

I'd forgotten how confusing it is to touch a body that is an attractive body to which you are not necessarily attracted, to be near your opposite but not your match. All the things that click on in your head have to click off. My breasts were bearing into his chest, my hands were holding his biceps, and I could feel his penis through his pants, which was a nice feeling and not intimidating, because his body was his own and not something he hoped to share with me. Denny finished up, singing sweetly through the end, then we kissed and bowed and the people at the bar applauded.

Rob whistled from his tilted-back chair, saying, "Man. I gotta get you down to the Criterion."

Denny wiped his brow. "What's that?"

"A club down in Jersey, for fighters. What are you, six-one?"

"Six-two." He squeezed the skin around his wrist. "But I'm fat. I need to lose ten pounds."

"Nah. You just need to make muscle. Somebody light on his feet like you would make good money as a sparring partner. A lot of guys are powerful, but they're dead weight. Fighters need to practice moving. So long as you don't cry or anything."

"Denny wouldn't cry," I said.

"Let me tell you something, angel, they *all* cry," Rob said. "Right at weigh-in. You'd be surprised what the thought of a ruptured spleen'll do to a guy."

It was about two in the morning when Denny decided to take off, which was a record for him. I'd never known him to stay in one place for so long. Before he left, he and Rob exchanged numbers. When Rob wrote, he hung over the table, parallel to it, focusing his might on the task at hand. It was beautiful, his aliveness, his connectedness, his focus. Like he really wanted to make a friend. And Denny, looking on with a tender fascination, watching the careful letters take shape. I remember thinking, if anything ever happened to damage either one of them, it would destroy my faith in living. As I formed the thought, I realized that's exactly how they felt for me.

At the Empire Diner, Rob and I sat at the counter.

"I was driving over tonight," he said, "and I heard some crackpot on the radio saying how she broke her back and the doctors told her she wouldn't walk for a year. She prayed to God to get well so she could pay the mortgage on her house. A couple weeks later, she's walking. 'God granted my wish,' she says." Rob shook his head. "When did everything get so literal? Where I come from, you pray for hard times to get better and they do, not because God pays the mortgage, but because your family and friends lend you money."

He took a bite of cheeseburger, buckling the splayed wedge into his mouth. "When my mother prays, you can hardly hear. It's like a slow leak in the faucet. She would never pray for anything specific. She asks for help becoming *a better person*—more compassionate, more patient, whatever. Every day she stops in church. The priest comes by the house—dinner, coffee, holidays. My grandmother makes him *pasta e fagioli* to take back to the rectory. If I go over to pick up the used Tupperware, he comes out with a shopping bag full to the top with containers. God isn't supernatural— God is like, the street, the neighborhood, the way things are. If you've got pressing questions about it, you don't go *talk* to the priest. You become one."

The waitress collected our plates. She was pretty with bangs and short black braids. Rob stopped her, and picked the remainder of my tuna sandwich from the plate.

"Growing boy," he explained with a wink, then he ordered coffee and cake for us.

The door opened and three guys walked in. Rob looked over his shoulder and shifted instinctively to block me. Lots of people say, *Over my dead body,* but with Rob, it was true. And unlike with Denny when we were dancing, Rob *was* my opposite. I couldn't help but wonder if my perfume distracted him as much as the way he chewed his ice distracted me.

He set his elbows on the counter. "You believe in God?" he asked.

"I don't know," I said. "I'm not sure."

"When we were in college in L.A., we heard shit like, *I don't believe in God, I believe in an all-powerful, all-loving being.* All-powerful, all-loving being? What is that? Same as God, only no rules!"

The waitress returned with dessert and coffee. The cake was circle-shaped and flat like a soggy disc.

Rob threw up his hands. "What happened?"

"Pineapple cheesecake," she said. "It gets wilty."

"It looks like you dropped it onto the saucer from midair."

"It happens to be very popular. You guys got the last two pieces. I can take them back and resell them."

"Nah. I'm just giving you a hard time because I like those braids." But as soon as she turned, he stopped me from taking a bite. "Watch it with creams," he warned under his breath, "They go rancid very easy." He tested the cake and gave it his reluctant approval. "You remember my brother Joey?"

"The firefighter."

"Yeah, right. The firefighter. He recently dragged a couple kids out of a fire. Dead." Rob sucked back a sip of coffee and gestured to the side of his skull like he was screwing in something invisible. "He's all fucked up now," he said. "My father thinks he needs counseling. *Counseling*— I mean, you gotta know my father. Not exactly the therapy type. But Joey can't sleep, can't eat; he sits up all night staring at his sons. So tonight I'm listening to this lunatic on the radio, thinking of my brother running into a burning building. Where was God for those kids? Or for their parents? Or my brother? And—"

Rob glanced up and noticed the clock. It was almost 4:30 in the morning. "Shit!" He half-stood and polished off his coffee, going, "Shit, shit, shit." He looked at the check, threw down some cash, and waved. "C'mon, c'mon. Gotta go see Uncle Tudi."

Rob had a tight bouncy walk. He leaned forward as if his torso were connected in a line to his legs, and he walked with purpose, though it was rare that he had one. He pulled me by the wrist down Tenth Avenue into the meat district, past the hookers and queens and the stalled and steamed Impalas. Girls in sheer baby doll dresses and boys like girls in zipper-back shorts and vinyl boots riding up brawny thighs. At the loading dock for Falco's Meats, Rob pulled something folded from his back pocket, opened it up, and checked it over.

I took another look at the prostitutes. They were like lost sentinels, flecking the concrete horizon with bioluminescence, leaning to solicit the occasional passing car just like they do on *Starsky and Hutch*. At first you are not sure they're there, they go so slow, but if you wait, they appear, like decorative fish caught in a choke of algae, bobbing out with omnidirectional eyes.

Rob crammed the paper back into his jeans pocket, and we entered the building. Remembering himself, he stopped to hold the door for me.

"How ya doin', Tommy?" he said to the guy at the counter.

Tommy flipped a wilted page of yesterday's news. "Hey, Robbie, *que pasa?*"

"My uncle leave yet?"

"Nah, he's still in the back."

Rob parted a row of foggy plastic strips, then turned and stopped me. "You're not gonna get sick, are you?"

"Not in front of Uncle Tudi," I said.

Rob said, "That's all I wanted to hear."

Curtains of animals lined two sides of the sawdust aisle, and I held my breath as we walked toward a room in back of the warehouse. I noticed that the pigs had no conspicuous necks. Pig necks are not so noticeable when pigs are standing in a barn or at a state fair, but when they are pendant and dead, you can see how their backs slope directly up into quadrangular heads, which are kind of boxy, like dice.

At the end of the bright run was a filthy glass wall and, behind it, the hunched torsos of men playing cards. We walked into the office to see four men with eyeglasses and caps tipped rakishly over long faces habituated to a world of flesh for sale. There was a tar-coated Mr. Coffee machine and a half-eaten Entenmann's cheese strudel. Three of the men wore smocks streaked with brown stains, where they'd dragged their freezer-swollen fingers dry of blood and guts and marrow. The fourth man's meticulous street clothes were an obvious expression of superiority—a dress shirt, a sweater, a quilted corduroy hunting jacket. Rob kissed him on the cheek, so I figured that was Uncle Tudi. He was huge. I wouldn't normally stare, but his massive anatomy coupled with his shameless self-confidence was mesmerizing. Like one of those giant pumpkins you see in October at country stores, he was squat and sideways-tilted. You couldn't help but try to guess his weight—three hundred and seven pounds.

The guys nodded.

"How ya doin', kid?"

"Hey, Robbie. What's up?"

Uncle Tudi breathed thickly and finessed the cards beneath the bulk of his manicured fingers. Just past the knuckle of his left pinky was a solid gold ring set with a flat face and diamond chip. His cologne was a jungle about him. "Who's the lady friend?" he wanted to know.

"This is Eveline," Rob said, jiggling nervously, picking an end-slice of cake off the table.

"Eveline. What kinda name is that?"

Rob motioned with his head in the direction of his uncle.

"I don't know," I said. "Just a name, I guess."

"What kinda name? Irish, English, what?"

"I think my mother just made it up."

Tudi creaked back unevenly in his chair. "I thought so. I never hearda that name before. Sounds modern."

"I fold," the guy across from him said, laying down his hand and checking his watch.

"Me too," another said.

The one next to Rob said he was in, and he threw a five-dollar bill on top of the pool. Tudi matched him, and they showed their hands. The guy had three jacks; Tudi had three tens and a pair of sixes. He scooped his winnings.

"Maybe it's an old-fashioned name, Tudi, like Ernestine or Lily," the guy with the watch speculated. He swept the cards into a pile and shuffled expertly.

Tudi clicked his tongue. "If it was *old-fashion,* we woulda heard it before. Especially you, Tony. You're older than dead dog shit. That's why it's gotta be modern. Am I right?" he asked me, peering intensely and expectantly into my face like a seaman gauging a swelling cloud. One eye was millimeters larger than the other.

"I guess—"

He interrupted me. "Where'd youse meet?"

"Montauk," Rob answered.

Somebody said, "Montauk! She fishes?"

"I ever tell you, Pat," one of the guys said to another, "the transmission in my car has five settings—park, drive, neutral, reverse, and 'Montauk.' I adjust the arm and it goes." His flattened palm cut into the air, *Bzjump*.

Through his teeth, Rob said to his uncle, "At Harrison's place."

"At Harrison's place," Tudi repeated as he organized his money, lining up bills by denomination, then folding the packed knot into his shirt pocket. He coughed a little, repeating, "Harrison," then he coughed more, and the room got quiet. He picked up a napkin and held it over his mouth, and he stayed still and everybody stayed still. I had the feeling Rob was going to get hit.

Tudi shouted, "What the hell's the matter with you, walking around with a girl this time of night? It's meat packing out there, you moron, not the boardwalk!"

"Which one's Harrison?" Pat murmured. "The fighter?"

The others nodded.

Tudi stood and adjusted his collar. "You got some numbers for me?"

Rob said, "Yeah."

"Gentlemen," Tudi stated formally. "If you don't mind."

We followed him to the door, and he just squeaked through by making a slight corkscrew motion with his belly. Outside, Rob exchanged the contents of his pocket for ten fifties.

His uncle perused the sheets. They were photocopies, lined and filled in neatly with numbers in Rob's writing. "How'd it work out?"

"Good," Rob said, sounding normal again, which is to say, confident. He always sounded confident when referring to numbers.

Uncle Tudi must've felt bad about yelling or good about the papers because he slapped Rob tenderly on the cheek then laid a barrel-size arm around my shoulders. "Listen," he said. "You seem like a nice girl with a modern name. Don't get me wrong, but don't come down here again, understand?" His face was inches from mine; it was like kissing the moon. "I hate to think what Harrison would do if he knew Rob had you here at five in the morning."

I promised I wouldn't come back, and Uncle Tudi seemed satisfied.

He jerked his head to me, asking Rob, "She met your mother?"

"Not yet," Rob sputtered, and his uncle shot him a look. Rob threw up his hands. *"Whaaat?"*

"Lemme tell you something," Tudi said to me. "My sister, Fortuna, is a lady. Rob was raised decent, with manners. But he was a change-of-life baby for her. That's why he's spoiled." He lifted a finger to Rob but said nothing. Rob also said nothing, then he nodded and kissed his uncle again.

Before we got to the door, Uncle Tudi called out. He was waddling to catch us. "Boneless pork," he said breathlessly, handing me a package the size of a shoe box. "It's nice."

"She doesn't have a stove, Uncle."

"Whaddaya mean *no stov*e?"

"She lives in a dormitory." Rob backed away, taking me along. "You know. College."

"Next time I see you two," he warned as he withdrew the pork, "it's in daylight!"

We spent what remained of the night on a stoop on Horatio Street. A jaundiced glow from the inside filled a second-story window across the way, and we watched it like a movie. Something had come over Rob, something not unfamiliar to me. A constitutional shift, sort of a shut-down. Sometimes he just stopped, like a machine idling.

"How long have we known each other?" I asked.

"One year," he said. "St. Patrick's Day."

"That's funny," I said. "Seems like longer than a year." That meant that eight months had passed since I'd seen Rourke.

He lit a cigarette. "Seems like a year."

"I liked you as soon as I saw you," I confided.

"Oh, yeah?" he said. He jiggled his knee lightly.

"What did you think when you saw me?"

"I thought you were good-looking."

"Did you tell that to Rourke?"

"Not in those exact words."

"You don't remember?"

"I remember."

I had the feeling that I owed him an apology. I thought to say sorry. I thought to thank him for coming. Only I couldn't thank him, or say sorry, or say anything really, not when I would have had to look at him with gratitude in my eyes and still let him know he'd failed. He was the closest thing to Rourke, but he was not Rourke.

"How you been?" he wanted to know.

"Good," I said. "I've been good."

"You been all right?"

"I've been all right."

I lied because Rob didn't need to know details. He didn't need to hear how Rourke stalked the periphery of my nights, stealthy as a feline in my dreams, mad as a dream cat. How my heartbreak kept me alive, keeping me whole the way your skin keeps your pieces in. You cannot live without skin. You don't think to manufacture it, but absently you do. Every seven days it's new again. I didn't tell the truth because Rob might say, *Try to be happy*. People often say that. But it's difficult to move beyond certain losses. Fire, for instance, as Rob had said, and death. It gets to where you can't even talk to people who haven't suffered as you have. I lied because I didn't want him to know what it means to be sick. All the time, sick. I lied because he knew the truth anyway.

"I haven't slept with Mark, you know."

Rob drew in for the last time from his cigarette. "Not yet," he said. "You will."

TREES

Spring 1984

Try always, whenever you look at a form,
to see the lines in it which have had power over its past fate
and will have power over its futurity. Those are its awful *lines;*
see that you seize on those, whatever else you miss.

—JOHN RUSKIN

38

The Water Club is near the heliport on the East River. If you're careful about where you sit, you can avoid the sorry sight of dormant helicopters, which look like women with wet hats. That is where Alicia and Jonathan announce their engagement, over dinner, the four of us alone. The announcement is no surprise. Mrs. Ross had told us weeks before; she'd wanted to prepare Mark.

"He's a pansy," Mark had said bitterly. "The asthma, the Mercury Zephyr, the backgammon. He's allergic to mesquite. How can anyone be allergic to mesquite?"

"Jonathan treats her well," Mrs. Ross said. "She'll be deprived of nothing."

"Except in the bedroom," Mark mumbled.

His mother smacked him on the shoulder. "Oh, stop it."

Mr. Ross shrugged. He tries to think of the big picture. His children are nice-looking, well-off, and connected, and that's going to have to be enough since he's dying and will soon be dead. He doesn't have the stamina for the minutiae of survival; as far as he's concerned, no one is going to go shoeless.

I know because he tells me things. I always come early for dinner—family dinners are on Thursdays—and I meet him at one of the cocktail tables at 21 or in the Oak Room or at Tavern on the Green. Every now and then we eat at Doubles, a club in the Sherry-Netherland. He lays down his cigarette before he stands to greet me. Then he grabs the waiter's sleeve to order me a Tanqueray and tonic, which I accept even if I don't feel like having it, because I made the mistake of ordering one once, and from that point on, Mr. Ross thought it was my preference. One law of being a gentleman is to know a lady's preference, and it's not good manners for her to keep switching on him. When my drink arrives, we eat nuts with brown husks, the kind that look like pussy willow buds.

Sometimes I find him smoking across the street from his house, on a bench by Central Park. If it's somewhat depressing to see Mr. Ross huddled on a bench like a bum—especially one of those broken benches without back slats to connect the exposed cement posts—it's a clever place for him to hide, because no one would ever think to look for him there. He's not supposed to smoke because of his health. Everyone always yells at him, but it never does much good. I usually try to take his mind off death for a few minutes.

He's been talking about dying since I met him, and according to all reports, for some time before that. But since he returned to work following his heart surgery five years ago, no one seems particularly alarmed by his fears. Maybe he talks about dying to try to get people to take better care of him. Or maybe he secretly wishes to be done.

"The soul seeks equilibrium," my father speculated when I asked why a man who loves his family and his job would smoke and drink in defiance of medical advice. "People who are responsible and successful often act recklessly to counterbalance all that selflessness. If you're ninety percent accountable for others, chances are you'll fill up the remaining ten with unaccountable behaviors."

On one unseasonably warm day in March, after he put out his cigarette under the broken bench, Mr. Ross and I walked south toward the park entrance across from the Beresford, where the Ross family lived. We climbed to the top of one of those mammoth rocks with sides that look like the flaky Italian pastries Dad loves, the ones shaped like seashells, with all the layers, called *sfogliatelle*.

"Look at the sunset, Mr. Ross." It was beautiful, like standing inside a purple pillow. "Those clouds aren't *really* purple," I said. "It's the orange that makes them seem so."

He set his briefcase between his knees and sat carefully. I put my hand out behind him. He was a big man, almost twice my size. Still, I felt compelled to catch him should he lose his footing.

"Do you think *all* animals notice color changes the way we do?" I asked. "I mean, even if they aren't conscious of changes in the same way, they still *experience* sunset, the serenity of it, the purple-sky feeling. It's like a certain vibration. And of course, there are variations infinitely subtler than color which people know nothing about. Cats see in the dark. Pelicans catch fish you can't imagine are there."

Mr. Ross did not speak for several minutes. I thought he might actually have been unwell after all. Usually he was talkative like the rest of his family. He just lifted his face and squinted like Robert Mitchum into the still point of sundown as if fire-gazing.

" *'The vision is for he who will see it, and he who has seen it knows what I say,'* " Mr. Ross recited, adding, "Plotinus, third century A.D. Plotinus spoke of *'The flight of the alone to the alone.'*"

I wasn't exactly sure what he meant, though he'd obviously moved beyond pelicans and cats. *The flight of the alone to the alone*—what a pretty thing to say at the close of a day, and an appropriate thing, and I was grateful as ever for his company. It's interesting to think that in order to see, you must be *willing* to see, and that you can share what you have seen only with those who have also seen it, or with those who are similarly willing. Probably the best you can hope for in life is to journey as an individual and to share your vision with whomever you happen to meet along the way. *The flight of the alone to the alone*. I wondered if Mr. Ross meant to refer to me and him, or to me and Mark, or not to me at all, but simply to himself. Jack would often talk that way, to himself, through me, conducting a test of his most inward thoughts.

I shivered; he patted my leg. "C'mon, sweetheart. Let's head back."

We give congratulatory kisses and handshakes to Alicia and Jonathan. Mark coughs artificially into his napkin. "So," he says, "when's the big day?"

"In June," Alicia replies. "After all the graduation ceremonies."

"*June!* Are you pregnant?"

"Oh, stop it, Mark. Evie, when do you graduate?"

"May. Mid-May, I think."

"Mine's the twenty-sixth," Alicia says.

"The timing on this is ridiculous, Alicia. It's April. That gives you three months to plan a wedding." Mark finishes off his wine.

"Jonathan's parents are moving back to London in June. Besides, Mark," she injects meaningfully, "Daddy's health."

"He's lasted this long, Alicia," Mark assures her.

"You never know. Sylvie's father died in the hospital—while holding the baby." She turns to Jonathan. "Did I ever tell you? His first grand-child."

"Alicia," Jonathan chides. "That's hardly dinner conversation."

"If you're so worried about Dad dropping dead," Mark says, "think what the bill for this thing is going to do to him."

"I've already thought of that," Alicia says. "I'm having it in East Hampton, at the house."

Mark is silenced. Alicia has beat him again. She beats him at every-thing, even golf. She sets her empty champagne glass carefully near her plate. "Need the bathroom, Evie?"

I don't, only I say I do.

"Great. Let's go," Alicia says, and she saunters elegantly away.

As soon as I enter the bathroom, she shoves the door closed behind me. "I'm dying for a cigarette," she says. She leans her crocheted purse against her belly, then bends over it like she might dive in. "Please don't say anything," she implores as she fiddles first with the clasp and then with the matches. "I told Jonathan I quit, which I will, just—after the wedding."

Her hands shake. It's awful to see. She's like a cartoon character vi-brating after an electric shock, like Wile E. Coyote. "Here," I say, taking the match. "Let me help."

She relaxes into the initial surge of nicotine. "Okay, so tell me. What do you think?"

I'm not sure what she means.

"About Jonathan," she adds. "Does he *really* love me?"

I think for a minute. Real love is tricky. It's like an extremely subtle flavor that most people can't even discern. All I *can* say is that *whatever* Jonathan feels, he feels for her alone. "I don't think he loves anyone more."

She shoots smoke through her nose. "Well, that's diplomatic."

I figure I'd better pee. It looks like we're going to be awhile. Through the split in the stall, I observe her as she completes her cigarette. It takes me a long time to finish. Maybe not. When you pee when someone you know is listening, it just feels like so much more than normal comes out.

I rejoin her, and as I wash my hands, she brushes her teeth. I watch her reflection. Her eyes are set apart, and floating on the outer corners are microscopic ruffles, like lines on a lake, or faraway birds. She dries her toothbrush and returns it to her bag.

With some difficulty she says my name, *"Evie."* She is staring at her shoes. I look to see if she's dropped something. "Jonathan—is—you know—"

The paper towel in my hand is wet, and the garbage pail is behind her. I would have to lean past her to reach it, but I don't want to appear rude. I continue to dry my hands with the damp towel.

"Do you think I'm—I mean, I know you—" She leaves off again. "I'm sorry. I've embarrassed you."

"Not at all," I say, which is true. I'm not embarrassed in the least.

With the back of a hand, she sweeps at the atmosphere as if fatigued by the noise of herself, and she smiles, charmingly. "Let's just head back." Her gold earring catches on the neck of her sweater as she turns. I unlatch it, and we stand, face-to-face. Her hair is parted down the middle and drawn into a thick twist like good bread. Her nose is Roman; her lips naturally red. She is beautiful, like a Spanish princess, like someone who comes with a dowry of Andalusian horses. "I know about Harrison," she says. "About what happened."

There is a funny delay, like dropping an egg that doesn't land right away. I don't feel myself wince, but possibly I do, because she jerks forward, as if trying to catch something that's flown from my mouth.

"I'm sorry. It's just, the way Mark tells it, Harrison *ruined* you. Of course, Mark's ridiculous. I've known Harrison since I was twelve, since they started at UCLA. He would never hurt anyone." Softer then, "You two must have been completely in love."

She's waiting. She wants me to describe being in love with Rourke, which is like being asked to discuss a murder committed in a prior lifetime—it's hard to say why it was so particularly important at the moment, though you have no doubt that it was. I can think only of fog, of being consumed by fog, so much so that it appears as though nothing is out there, but *everything* is out there, brushing by, inches off. You're powerless to correct your restricted perception, so you surrender to blindness. You survive by touch. You reach to know, reach to feel. You learn to live by sensation, and as soon as you become adept, you are released. Just like that, let go. And everything turns very explicit, and the explicitness is worse than the blindness. There's no poetry there. Not there—*here*. I mean *here*.

"My God, listen to me," she says. The faucet drips behind her. "I don't mean to be nosy. I was just asking what you thought about Jonathan and me."

"I think you're very—passionate—about things. I hope Jonathan will give you the security you need to stay that way."

"Is that what Mark does for you?" she asks.

I consider a lie, but what good is a lie? A lie will not affect her fate, and she's been lied to enough. As for the truth, I prefer to spare her.

She raises a finger to her lips, *Ssshh,* and with those lips she kisses me. I feel the waxy double arc on my cheek, and I am incorporated into a plushy cloud of Chanel and into the society of those whom she adores. It is a fine society. With her thumb, she wipes lipstick from my face, then she nods and breaks into a gracious smile.

As we approach the table, the boys stand. "What happened?" Mark asks. "Did some pipes break?"

"Yeah, did pipes break?" Jonathan repeats.

Alicia takes up her napkin. "Girl talk, gentlemen."

"That's exactly what we're afraid of," Jonathan says. "We're afraid you two might decide to make it a double wedding."

After *Tristan und Isolde* we stop at Fellini's for dinner. Mark feels like having a plate of fresh spinach pasta with pheasant sauce. The restaurant is practically empty because it is late, and the few remaining waiters leap to life. "Hello, hello. Good evening signore, signorina." They seat us in the same place they always seat us—five tables back, against the southern windows. The table looks out over West Sixty-eighth Street, which is ghastly still like a scene from an Edward Hopper painting. I don't know what makes us deserving of this particular table, but each time they escort us to it with a smug sort of pride, as though surely they've pleased us immensely.

The waiter recommends Aglianico del Vulture, from the Basilicata region, a young wine, 1981—*delizioso*. When the bottle comes, Mark caresses it approvingly, after which he tastes the wine and nods, thanking the waiter, who pours obsequiously as Mark adjusts his cuff links, fluted platinum with onyx inserts. A gift from me with money he provided.

"That fucking soprano gave me an intense headache," he says.

I knew the opera had been difficult for him—the rich king versus the dragon slayer, the estranged lovers devoted unto death. It didn't help that the king's name was Mark.

"So," he says, drinking, and then pulling back his lips in a businesslike manner. "Let's talk about what to do after you graduate. I don't want you jumping into anything."

I don't answer; he seems relieved. I wonder, does he think if I get a job, I'll leave him? How could I leave? I have no place to go. I have no friends or resources that are not his. How could I go when I have come to value things and have faith in them? Things mean distance between me and everything else. Diamonds mean I don't have to talk to shopgirls with thumbtack eyes and perpetually suntanned cleavage who want to know where I got *those shoes*. Cars mean I don't have to take subways that smell of vomit and urine, or cabs where drivers ask into the rearview mirror, *Have you been baptized?*

Sex with Mark means I don't have to wait tables and talk to drunks who say I look like one of the girls in the Robert Palmer video, or go home to my mother's in the summer where memories of life and of living are everywhere. And sex with him is perverse. In the absence of desire, it's good to be set upon without expectations of affection. At the end, when I'm overtaken by the same abject longing for things I will never have, I can get up and walk away, clinging to that loss without interference.

I will not leave Mark, because when I wander through the house at daybreak, repelled by the sight of the bed, by the wet circle in the center, by the place on the mattress I leave unoccupied, there is some small consolation in a refrigerator filled with thirty-dollar-per-pound smoked Scottish salmon and organic strawberries and fresh-squeezed orange juice, and the fact that the mess in the sink can be left for someone else to clean. In the garage is a car I can drive to anywhere; in the top dresser drawer is all the cash I could ever need. If being in love is consolation when you are poor, money is consolation when you are not. Life is a trap not because I can't leave Mark, but because there's no reason to.

"The workplace is such a scene," he's saying. "The politics, the bull-shit incompetence. I don't want you ending up as the subordinate to some asshole who thinks he can coerce you into—situations."

When the plates are cleared, the waiter brings two glasses of grappa. I don't like grappa; Mark knows I don't. He pulls my chair to his, grabbing a leg. He plays with my hair. "You can do anything—photography, painting, drawing. My mother will help. She'll get your work out there."

The coke snakes round and round on a framed picture Mark removed from the wall. I cannot say what the picture is; it's covered with clumps. The caviar, like the cognac and the cocaine, is exceptional—hand-selected Tsar Imperial Beluga. If you want to know about *hand-selected* caviar, you can inquire, but you'll be judged by your ignorance—and forced to endure an exhaustive account of the size of sturgeon, the shape of eggs, the cost per gram, the temperature of the Caspian, and the vulgar habits of the Slavs. You don't inquire; you prefer not to learn.

Ignorance is as good as intelligence in this contradictory world, this dream landscape, where the sun shines at night and creatures mingle wrongly and seasons are without circumference—no beginning, no end. We are voracious, we are clever, we are the victors, which is the same as being victims because everything here is inversion. Like the bored members of a royal court, we are insular and divine. No one told me about this place; I arrived unprepared.

Mark's friend Dara turns to me, apologizing for *shoptalk*. He has been discussing credit derivatives.

I don't mind. It's better than other things they discuss—the size of bonuses, breasts versus legs, all the Mexicans "crossing over."

"Don't apologize," Mark tells Dara. "It's about time Eveline learned some of the principles of economics. In fact, let's give her a little tutorial."

His friends settle into Eames armchairs with their chilled vodka and smuggled Montecristos and cashmere pullovers with suede elbow patches, and they listen solemnly beyond moribund undertones of the English Beat and the Psychedelic Furs as Mark describes *debt-to-equity ratios* and *supply-side economics* in the simplest possible terms, which is sexy. I know that inside he wants very much to be sexy, so I smile, and he smiles back, appreciative that I've given him the opportunity.

"Rule of Seventy-two," he instructs as he licks black-light bubbles off a mother-of-pearl spoon, "is the formula used to calculate how long it will take for an investment to double. So at eight percent, your investment would be doubled in nine years."

Maybe I'm experiencing a type of dark adaptation; maybe my eyes have grown accustomed to him. Suddenly Mark is attractive to me—at least, tonight he is, as he sits there, twinkling isochronally like a movie of himself or a crystal catching light, losing it, catching it again. His delivery is artfully uninterrupted, gluey smooth as the siphon of a clam. His eyes are ringed with fatigue from achievement—they are gray like the cinders of volcanoes, like ash. There is a richness to the remains; lives have been lost to form the dust. Somehow I've never seen him so clearly— the inclemency in his features, the cohesion of his skin, like living marble, like he'll last forever, like he will prevail. He forges time to fit his will, like bending iron; timing is everything to him. This is what he knows that I need to learn. For the first time I think, *I love him.*

If I've never said it to him before, it's because I've never felt it. If it's fair to say "I love you" only when you mean it, then it's wrong, perhaps, to withhold it when it occurs to you. I lean off my stool, coming to kiss him. *I love you,* I am about to say, but he stops me. He has been viewing me watchfully; it is as if he noted the change in me before I perceived it myself, as if he'd been observing me stir to life after a protracted sleep.

"I want to marry you," he says, holding my shoulders. "Will you marry me?"

"Okay," I say, and the room is reeling.

There is applause and the bright bullish sound of Sinatra's "Summer Wind" followed by champagne pops and high fives and jokes about the broken hearts Mark will leave behind. This is a surprise—have there been hearts to break? I'm passed from hand to hand, lap to lap, squeezed and kissed. Alicia is on the phone; she loves me; she has never been happier. "Can you imagine?" she says, her voice so small, so far. *"Sisters!"*

I wonder where she is, where we have reached her. Possibly at Yale, ignoring her studies, making hats. She is always making hats. We all wear them—Denny, Sara Eden, Jonathan, even Mark. He is good that way, never forgetting where his loyalties lie.

Brett knocks on the bathroom door. "The cars are waiting."

The cars will take us to Odeon to celebrate. We always travel in cars. There are so many of us that one is never enough. People are suddenly anxious to place themselves in relation to me. Already everyone is acting more, more *something*, I don't even know what.

"Make yourself decent," Brett calls out. "I'm coming in."

The bathroom door opens. Perhaps I've been in for a long time. At the mirror, he rights his suspenders. I don't see him do it, but I hear the elastic snaps. The water comes on hard, and he combs back his hair. I feel the flying drops.

"What are you doing?" he asks, his voice like a croupy cough. "Listening to neighbors?"

My hand is on the wall. My forehead on my hand. If you rest your forehead on the back of your hand, you'll notice how many protruding and breakable bones your hand has, like a chicken foot. It's a disgusting feeling, the feeling of your own skeleton.

"Yes," I say. "Listening to neighbors."

Mark has a confession. He opens the closet door and reaches into the breast pocket of a gray Armani suit. He withdraws a ring box.

"I've been waiting for the right moment."

Yes, I think. *A public moment. Witnesses.*

The ring is a square diamond, a rare chameleon, he says. Looking into it is like looking into a well of infinite angles. He tilts the box, and light hits the jewel, casting kaleidoscopic prisms on the wall. I strain my neck to see, awed like a peasant beholding an act of sorcery. It is not wrong to compare Mark to a magician when he is so clever, when he turns my methods against me, obliterating the natural with equal doses of artifice. Like a true master, he leaves nothing to chance. Like a true connoisseur of ruin, he does not destroy me directly but lures me to my own destruction. He hands me champagne.

He bought the diamond first, then had the ring made to specification—*built* is the word he uses—by Ronnie Armeil, a West Coast jeweler who is a client of his father's. Armeil builds for television stars like Victoria Principal and Stefanie Powers. The diamond has characteristics. Talk of characteristics is code for talk of cost, and I don't want to know cost. I'm sure it cost at least five thousand more than Alicia's, and everyone knows the cost of Alicia's. It's a sanctioned topic of conversation. Mark would never be outdone by Jonathan.

He sits at the foot of the bed, facing me. He moves to put it on my finger. I stop him. He takes hold of my waist. "What is it?"

I look into his eyes. I remind myself that I know him, that I've always known him, from the first night we met. That is something—something important. "I want you to know that I said yes because every day I pray that the worst has passed. Every day I think I can't possibly feel as bad as I did the day before, but every day I'm wrong. I said yes because he's not coming back."

The ring remains suspended near my finger; I wonder if it can drive off the terrors of the night. I hope it can. "Now you can put it on," I say. "If you still want to."

39

He sent one letter, on yellow legal paper, carefully folded. I opened it on an April afternoon as I cut through Central Park in a taxicab, going past dogwoods in full bloom. Every time I see dogwoods in bloom, I go back to the day of the letter, back to being in love, back to Rourke.

It was eight months after he left, back when Rob visited my dorm room, back when I still had hope. I remember thinking, isn't life amazing—the letter flew on an airplane; the plane touched down. The paper was carried in a canvas sack, delivered to me by anonymous hands. At the end, his name; at the beginning, my own. My name, tenderly rendered. Clear, perfect—*Eveline*. Proof.

I have one photograph. This came to me much later. In it Rourke is young, maybe seventeen. I keep it with his letter in a box on Mark's dresser, where my things are kept. I don't fear discovery; discovery would change nothing. I would never hide evidence of Rourke or lie about him.

I remove the photograph to touch it—sometimes, when I can't help myself. First it's strange, like looking at a picture of fire, feeling no heat. Then I fall into the false dimension, and I feel him, warm like flesh, and soft.

He stands on the boardwalk and faces the water at an angle; the sun sets behind him. There are no lines in his face; his skin is clear, his cheeks are mesmerizing hollows. He is lean and solid and tall, self-conscious of his separateness from the crowd around him. I draw my fingertips along the line of his jaw. I want to know him then, kiss him then.

"That's the Criterion," Rob told me the first time I saw the photo in his wallet. Rob pointed to the second story of a yellow brick building in back, the one Rourke took me to that day on the boardwalk. "Harrison was 34–2 at the time. Just regional matches, but still, it was an awesome record. He was untouchable." Rob lifted the wallet closer to my face. "That's Eddie M. in back there, yanking up his pants. Remember Eddie M.? And over in the corner is Tommy Lydell—that big redheaded asshole. And that's Chris DeMarco. You had dinner with Chris and his wife, Lee, in Jersey that time. Remember? Take it out," Rob prodded gently. "G'head, take it."

I held the photo, thinking, *Time is so important. Time is everything.* It's a mystery, the way time for us was wrong when time is right for so many useless things, when things that should be impossible are in fact possible. There are machines that divide atoms, jets that fly at the speed of sound. Flags on the moon. And yet, we could not be together.

"You keep it," Rob said, folding his wallet back up. "I've got the negative somewhere."

——

The rest is intangible. Events unfolded quickly and unexpectedly, like things exhaled and evaporated, so lacking in exactness and effect, it's hard to say they even happened.

The phone would ring and I would run. I would know it was him, feel it was him. He would speak, and I could see him sprawled across his couch, lit by the lapis light of his stereo, in his underfurnished living room, wherever that room might have been. I never asked; he would not have answered. If he did say where he was, I would have left, going until I found him. I would hear his loneliness—it was all he would give. Still, I wanted him to be happy, but I wanted him to say that he was not, that like me, he was incapable. *Why did you have to go away?* I'd want to ask. *Why are you back?*

But I could say no more than "I dreamt of you last night."

"I dreamt of you too," he says. "You were beautiful."

Over time I came to grasp the nature of my position among women. I came to see that despite what I knew to be the rarity of my bond with Rourke, my feelings of uniqueness were not unlike other women's feelings of uniqueness. At bridal showers, at picnic tables, in dressing rooms and hair salons and kitchen gardens, I listened with compassion—if every woman has made herself available or has given herself over despite some better knowledge, isn't that the same as faith, and aren't women so faithful?

I began to pay attention when women talked; I learned to interpret the language of grief. Women who have suffered use talk as a way of addressing the baffling sea at their feet. They talk to make the abstract real. Like men who name flowers, viruses, and boulevards, women talk to stake ownership. They talk to reclaim the pride they feel they've lost.

In December of my sophomore year, after Mark and I had begun to see each other, Mark and Rob arranged for their friends from Jersey to come to an art show I was in. It was Rob and Lorraine, Chris and Lee, Joey and Anna, and Mark. Everything of mine was city rooftops. Chris and Lee bought a charcoal of Madison Avenue rooftops, and Mark bought an acrylic of a black bird sweeping over Murray Hill rooftops. Afterward we all walked through the snow to Patisserie Lanciani in the

West Village for coffee and dessert. Halfway through pastries Lorraine ran out because of something Rob said; I didn't hear what. It must have been bad, because the men looked down and shook their heads and Anna and Lee followed Lorraine, taking their coats to the bench in front of the café. Through the glass Lorraine's hair fanned against the picture window like a corona of hooks and coils. It looked like a squid sucking up against the side of a tank.

"Fucking guy," Chris said. "What's the matter with you?"

"I don't know how you expect to keep a woman," Mark said.

Rob said, "I don't want a woman to keep, just one to fuck."

"Yeah, well," Mark replied, "any woman worth fucking is a woman worth keeping."

"*Yeah, well,*" Rob said, copying Mark's voice, "exactly my point."

I figured I'd better leave. Lorraine and I weren't exactly friends, but it wasn't right to listen to the men discussing her. I joined the girls on the bench. It was cold but pleasant. West Fourth Street is beautiful in snow, with flesh-colored lamplight seeping through branches and everybody with dogs and packages, going slow. Lorraine was relieved that I'd come, though I couldn't say precisely how that relief was communicated.

Lee was striving to boost Lorraine's self-esteem, but Lorraine's head was junked up with crazy information. By the pool at the Ross house one day when they visited us there, she saw an article in *Cosmopolitan* called "Keeping Your Man Satisfied—10 Tips to Great Sex." Just as I thought, *What a profitless bit of journalism—a damp cushion could satisfy a man,* Lorraine tore out the article, folded it, and placed it in the back flap of her date book. I couldn't help but wonder whether the woman who's afraid that she isn't satisfying her man is being satisfied herself. Is anyone giving *him* tips?

Lorraine kept blowing her nose and shaking her head, saying she lives in constant fear of Rob getting arrested or busted-up or "worse," but when she asks him things, she's told to mind her own business.

"*Mind your own business?*" Lee repeated indignantly.

Lee could become very indignant. She was not the average Jersey girl; she was going places. You could tell by the impeccable way she dressed.

"If only he would talk to me," Lorraine sobbed, guilty suddenly to have impeached Rob's character. "It's just, he won't even talk to me."

"Don't defend him!" Lee snapped. "His behavior is inexcusable."

I thought it was okay for Lorraine to feel guilty. Life is complicated, and she and Rob were complicated, and it's often difficult to render in language the dynamics of the heart.

After the café we walked around the Village in twos and threes, looking into the parlor windows of brownstones, saying how great it would be to live in this or that house. Just as we were about to turn the corner from Bleecker onto Eleventh, Lorraine stopped me.

"Thanks a lot for listening back there," she said. "It helped me out. You know, us girls sticking together."

Something about the skittish look in her eyes and the freckles around her nose and her plump hand lying mildly on my wrist made me wonder if there's a formula to humanity—such as all anyone wants is to be loved, even the employees at the Department of Motor Vehicles. Lorraine wasn't necessarily hateful. It was her frustrated love for Rob that made her seem that way. When they first met, that love had likely been an agreeable love, but at some point it changed. Maybe he'd been too opaque, maybe she'd pressed too hard for answers. Maybe she should have quit back at the best time, while feeling capable and desired.

Just as I started thinking that Lorraine should have kept custody of that first love, I could see myself—cinched behind a screen of heartache, committed to the legend of my own sorrow, clinging to something spent, holding out for something hopeless, contributing to the disintegration of whatever Rourke and I had once shared that was good and true and private.

I remember that moment. I remember setting it all to drift like a stick in a river. I remember telling myself, *Just let go.*

"No problem, Lorraine," I said. "I hope things work out for you guys."

The bottommost item in the box was a scrap of paper with phone messages taken the week after that art show by my roommate, Corrine. Corrine became my roommate in sophomore year, when Ellen got an apartment, a hygienic duplex on East Twenty-first Street with a terrace facing the Empire State Building. Sometimes I would go to Ellen's for dinner, sometimes with Mark. He felt she was my one respectable friend, and she felt he was equally respectable and unquestionably clean, and they were both happy for me and happy over the stalwart and prosperous fact of each other. Once Ellen had a cocktail party and asked me to come early to help set up, and she introduced me to guests as her *best friend from school,* which depressed me. I felt she deserved better.

Corrine was an economics major who danced to the Go-Go's and Cyndi Lauper and Katrina and the Waves in orange shirts with cutoff collars and turquoise leg warmers. She would do splits and backflips in the room. That's all I knew of her, since I never slept in the dorm again after freshman year. Beginning in sophomore year and going through to graduation, I stayed at Mark's. We didn't make a big deal out of it, it just sort of happened that way. I only stopped by the room to shower and dress on busy days or after using the gym if Mark wanted to go out some- place downtown like Il Cantinori or Chanterelle. But by my junior year, Mark kept telling me, *Go off of housing, for God's sake.*

When Corrine called me at Mark's apartment about the calls from Rourke, I jumped on the subway, got off at Sheridan Square, then ran fast to East Tenth Street to pick up the message.

> *12/18/81. 7:50 pm. Harrison Rourke*
> *Harrison again, 10:30 pm.*
> *HR 1:15 am. Meet him at the Mayflower Hotel, Room 112.*

I gripped the list of messages, turning it over—it was pale green, ac- countant's green, torn from one of Corrine's graph books. As I turned it, I wondered if Corrine had written while on the phone with him, or if she'd written after she'd hung up. For some reason it mattered. She told me that she'd tried calling me until 2:00 A.M., but there was no answer. Mark and I were at his company's holiday party.

Instead of going to class after getting the messages, I went back up- town to Mark's, walking the whole sixty blocks. Once inside the apart- ment, I stared at the phone and thought about calling. Possibly Rourke had not yet checked out. Possibly he was sitting there by the phone, waiting for it to ring. I stared and thought, thought and stared, and one complete day transpired that way, with me not leaving the apartment. Tuesday became Friday, and by then I thought it had become too late to call.

"You must be getting home after dinner," Mark said when he arrived home from work that Friday night. Typically Mark left the apartment before me in the morning and returned after I did. "Manny told me he hasn't seen you all week."

"Actually, I've been staying in," I told him. "Headaches."

A few days later, the phone rang at Mark's. It was Christmas Eve.

I was quick to pick up. I knew it was Rourke.

"I got in to the East Coast a week ago," he said. "I left six messages at your dorm. Then there was no answer. I guess your roommate went home for the holiday."

"I'm sorry," I said, slipping the phone around the corner into the hall. That wasn't a lie. I was sorry. For everything.

"I'm flying into Boston the day after tomorrow."

"What for?"

"A fight."

"Oh," I said, "a fight." Him getting hit. Him bleeding. Him being watched. Imaginations laying claim. "Are *you* fighting?"

"Not me," he said. "A friend of mine. Jerry Page. I can get you a plane ticket."

I thought of—I don't know what. Nothing good. Lorraine, waiting, "minding her own business." My parents, how they had loved each other and still loved each other but it wasn't enough. And Jack. I thought of Jack. Everything damaged, everything broken, everything lost. No effort, it seemed, could ever be good enough.

"I'm sorry," I said again. "I can't."

When he hung up, I hung up. I sat numbly, like I'd just received news of death. To get out of it, I kept telling myself that I was not some possession that he had lent, that he could not appear out of nowhere to reclaim me, that I'd already done the work of losing him. But the words in my head sounded stilted, like when you memorize a phrase in a foreign language or a phone number when you have no pen.

"Who was that?" Mark asked. He was half-wrapped in a towel at his dresser, holding a glass of Cabernet, looking for collar stays.

I said, "Harrison."

Mark froze. "Harrison? What did *he* want?"

"He wants me to meet him in Boston for the weekend."

Mark set down the glass he was holding and it teetered and nearly fell. He caught it, then sighed with annoyance because wine splashed out.

"Don't worry," I said. "I told him I couldn't."

And then that was it. After that, there was nothing. No more calls. No messages. No letters or visits. I got what I wanted, something to hold, to control. Something dead—a memory.

40

With the shower off, I hear a bottle pop and voices.

"So, what's up with Lorraine?"

"Same old shit."

"*Same old shit,*" Mark repeats. "I mean, where is she?"

"She couldn't make it," Rob says.

"What do you mean, *couldn't make it*? It's a Friday night. Didn't you say we have something to celebrate?"

"She had plans."

"You didn't even tell her about the engagement, you prick, did you? And why are you dressed like that? You look like a manager at the movies. I have clients coming tonight."

Mark stops talking when I come out of the bathroom, and Rob stands. Rob looks great, actually. His vintage jacket is tan and black plaid, and his Western shirt is tan also, with snap buttons and a pearl-white collar with white stitching on the edge.

"Congratulations," he says, kissing me spiritlessly. "Lorraine couldn't make it. She has a virus."

I try to think of what to say. I'm speechless. It never occurred to me that Mark would tell everyone so fast.

Rob helps me despite his disgust. He takes up my hand. "So where's this rock I had to hear about?"

Area is the hot new club downtown. It has themes. Tonight the theme is *night,* so the place is practically black. I am left dancing with Dara while Mark and Rob step outside to argue. At least I think they stepped outside; I can't see through the darkness.

Mark returns alone. He walks past me, going straight to the bar, where he orders a drink and confers with his clients, Miles, who works for the State Department, and Paige, a pharmaceutical heiress and an equestrian. Miles and Paige are up from their estate in Arlington to attend a reelection fund-raiser for Reagan. They are very high; they are frequently high, injection-high. If it's hard to notice, it's because they are professional about concealing. Miles has this way of locking down, of stiffening and leaning like plywood against a wall, only there is no wall. Except for an occasional Buddy Holly–type spasm of his left leg that comes so fast and hard you think his knee has buckled backward, you might believe him to be musing and meditative. Paige adjusts— constantly. She flicks her feathered rabbit-brown hair and reapplies lipstick and tweaks nonexistent particles from her shoulders and straightens her skirt even if she is wearing pants. When she takes up the fabric on the thigh of her pants to descend a flight of stairs, she is the picture of Southern refinement.

We don't call them *drug addicts,* though Paige has been in rehab twice, and last month Miles drove his car through their garage door. We say, *They like to party,* even though the word *party* implies sharing euphoria, whereas they conceal it. They get giddy off stealth, as if what they crave is not the substance but the subversion.

At least Jack had cohesive ideas about the political significance of mind-expansion. It's sad to think that the survival of people like Miles and Paige is more secure than the survival of someone like Jack. They're *chic;* Jack is a junkie.

That winter I ran into Smokey Cologne at Canal Jeans. Smokey told me that he didn't play drums for Jack anymore, that Jack had basically "blipped off the radar." For a while Jack had been doing fine—they had a new band, Piss Pot, dates at CBGB's and at Continental Divide, an album's worth of recorded songs that were ready to be mixed—until all of a sudden Jack pulled out and hit the streets. I told Smokey to call me if he thought I could help. Smokey said sure, but he doubted I could.

I wait for Rob to come back; he never does. I excuse myself from Dara, leaving him to dance alone, and I approach Mark and Paige. I wait politely. Mark is concentrating on her face as if watching an ant farm. Even he has difficulty viewing her in her spasmodic entirety. It's too nerve-racking; it's like watching in dread as a speeding car veers between lanes on a highway. Mark wants to protect Paige's interests, he says. Frankly, he's worried about unscrupulous operators trying to get their hands on her trust fund and her pharmaceutical inheritance—*especially now with the whole AIDS thing*.

"Ever heard of *churning*?" he inquires, meaning the constant buying and selling by a broker from a client's account in order to earn commissions.

Paige shimmies out of time to the music. "I'm doing it right now, honey," she drawls.

I tap Mark on the arm. "I'm going to the bathroom," I say.

"Fine," he says. "Watch yourself with that ring."

Rob is alone by the back bar, pounding Chivas. I can just make out the caramel color of the alcohol through the dim. An attractive girl in black is alongside him. She is catlike with liquid mascara, a body leotard, and lace-up leather boots. Rob doesn't even notice her. I watch as he clears two tumblers and signals for a third, then pushes the hair off his forehead like he just received bad news. I like to see him this way; it speaks to the bond between us. We each admire in the other the tendency to travel great distances. Neither wants the other to be hurt, but covertly, we push; both of us long to behold true audacity, modern heroism. But it's like watching a movie star cowboy. You forget sometimes that beneath the skin the blood is real.

Rob sees me coming. He stands straight, shoving his latest glass to the rear rim of the bar and rolling his head in its socket. "Shit," he says, "you got some fucking legs."

"You okay?"

He pulls back to make eye contact. "Who, *me*?"

"You seem upset."

"I'm fine. I'm not sleeping much," he says. "That could be it. You know, my back." He bends to pluck something off the floor—a five-dollar bill. "Look at this. Must be our lucky night." He looks around and says, "C'mon, let's split a beer."

We walk a few blocks north to a photographer's party in a loft on Varick Street, Mark and Miles and Paige and Dara, me and Rob. We pass Heartbreak on the way. There is a crowd lined up—all the people who'd been rejected at the door at Area. You can tell because they're overdressed for Heartbreak. I see Phil the bouncer, but he's busy and doesn't see me. I wonder how Aureole is doing and D.J. Jim Jerome and Mike the barback. It's been three years—maybe they don't work there anymore. Maybe Aureole finally made it to L.A. Maybe Mike finally brought his family to Australia. I hope everybody got out to go pursue their dreams. That's funny to think about, me having gotten out, me and my dreams.

The building we enter has morgue-like lighting and industrial halls, and a filthy cement smell, like behind the Sheetrock is wet concrete, like you can bite the air and eat mortar. We ride up the elevator with fabulous strangers, all of us brushing shoulders, someone giggling. The guy having the party is one of Dara's investor clients; Mark says he shoots editorials for *Vogue*.

The music gets louder as we go up, like a temperature rising, and when the doors open, we're hit by a wall of sound. The place is packed; there are hundreds of people. There are motorcycles parked on the dance floor. We follow Dara to the host's bedroom; by the time we get there, Rob is gone. Miles and Paige pull out their alligator skin kit bag full of pills and foil and pipes and rocks of powder. That's their community kit; there's another that you never see.

Women immediately rush in, beautiful mannequin women with breasts like teacups and washboard abdomens and narrow hips. Brett and Mark's boss, Richard, are behind them. Their fiancées are out of town, so they invited a few model *friends* along. The models are hardly friends, though it's true that the guys often pay for their meals and car service, and do things at the girls' apartments that they would never do at their own, such as kill mice or scare off stalkers or haul furniture up four flights of stairs. Richard's fiancée, Mia, said she wouldn't mind having the "girls" around as long as we start to use more appropriate descriptors for them, such as *freeloaders, social climbers,* or *usurpers.*

My dad once told me about a parasitic bird that air-drops its own egg into another bird's egg-laden nest when the mother bird is out. The nest mother then returns to unwittingly hatch *all* the eggs. The invader chick emerges first, grows disproportionately, evicts the mother's babies, and monopolizes her resources. In the end you have a tiny mother bird struggling to meet the demands of a gargantuan baby. Something about laying eggs in a nest *already built,* something about family work being *largely done* reminded me of women who prefer attached men. It is as if they can't trust themselves to determine on their own the worthiness of a partner.

With all the commotion, Mark doesn't notice me slip away. I pass through the loft, finding a hallway, a door, a staircase, the roof. There are other guests up here, dancing and playing children's games.

"Mother says, 'Take six wondrous city pigeon steps!' "

"Mother May I?"

"Yes! You may."

Some of them are so fucked up I'm concerned they might try to fly. When I was a kid, you always heard about dope fiends trying to fly. Nobody tries to fly anymore. There is something to that, I think.

I walk to the roof rail. I look to see if there are balconies or ledges, but it's just a straight shot down. The cars in the street look like gribble, lonely like bugs in paths on rotting wood.

"Don't go getting any crazy ideas," a voice says from behind me.

Rob. His elbows line up next to mine on the rail, and for a while we just stand there, staring. It's like we're looking off a ship. The music from the loft below is like the pounding of the boat on the water, and our faces press into the night wind as if seeking relief from some indwelling nausea. Unlike our fellow passengers, we are disappointed with where the ship is headed, yet we assigned ourselves to its course long ago. No asylum ahead can approximate the one we once imagined reaching.

"I figured you were downstairs," I say. "With the rest of them."

"Me? Nah. You know I've been off blow for years, and I'd never touch smack. And forget about ecstasy. Look at those free-love lunatics." He gestures to the people across the roof, skipping in pairs. "They were playing Duck, Duck, Goose before, very nice, then all of a sudden one of the ducks starts holding hands with a goose and that's it—*chaos*." Rob finds my eyes. "Listen."

I look back down at the street. Whenever people start sentences with *Listen,* you know that no matter what comes next, it's not going to be good.

"I'm heading out," he says. "I don't want to tell you what to do or anything—I know it's not my place—but you should probably let me take you home."

Rob asks if I understand. I do. He's telling me that things downstairs are bad. But I know that. They were bad already at Area when Mark picked a fight with Rob, and then bad again when Miles and Paige arrived. Rob is saying that my commitment to Mark is for the present nullified—that Rob is under a prevailing obligation to see me safely home, that obligation being to me, and also to Rourke. I understand that by agreeing to honor forgoing loyalties, I betray Mark, and in turn condemn myself for my movable allegiance.

I say okay.

"Okay," he repeats, *okay*. He is surprised and also relieved, not exactly happy, but lighter. "Let's do this fast. What do you have downstairs, a pocketbook?"

"A sweater."

He nods, calculating. "Fine. A sweater. I'll wait by the elevator. I won't leave alone unless you walk out and tell me you're okay. But I'm warning you, you're gonna have to be pretty fucking convincing." He takes my hand. "Let's go."

Going down the roof stairs and back into that party sickens me. Everyone in the loft is dancing, or rather, staggering like zombies. It's like their knees won't hold them. I recall the roof. If not for Rob, I think in fact I would try to fly.

Rob points over the tops of heads to the entrance. "I'll be right there."

The door to the bedroom where I left Mark and everyone is open about eighteen inches. Through the opening I see Mark, reclining on a chaise in the center of an encampment of people, king of a wax tribe. He shifts when I come. As I look around for my sweater, he says, "C'mon people. Let's dance."

Two of the girls flanking him lend him their arms and aid him to his feet, and he laughs, at himself, I suppose, at the way he imagines himself to be. He uses them like canes to right himself across the path to me, where he stops, shaking them off with a burst of manly animation. The girls saunter insolently past as if to imply that he slept with them while I was gone. Obviously they know nothing of his revulsion to disease, or of his obsessive fear of being cheated on by me in return. Or how Mark figures himself to be a man of ideals; he would not want a woman whose attraction to him is defiled by a lust for assets. Anyway, I feel no jealousy where Mark is concerned. There is simply an emptiness in the place where such emotions might reside.

The room has cleared; his friends have gone to the dance floor. He and I are alone. Mark comes closer. He smiles a false smile. His eyes are wild and unable to focus; they look off slightly to the side. The veneer of his skin is white as birch. His upper lip is a band of sweat, his nose is running, and his breath smells like steel getting cut, like when Dad and Tony cut steel with a chop saw for some sign they're making. I wonder what he's been doing, snorting coke or snorting heroin, or both. I've seen him do it before. The last time Miles and Paige were here. It's not a big deal, Mark told me—*strictly business, purely recreational.* Probably I should have seen this coming. That's my job, I think, to see things coming.

"I think we should go," I say.

He pulls my sweater from my hands. "I think we should stay."

I reach for the sweater. "I think I'm going."

"I think you're staying," Mark snaps, and he flings my sweater across the bedroom. His body plows into mine and he pins me against the opened door. He yanks the fabric of my skirt toward my waist with his left hand, and he grabs my ass with his right, taking up the flesh and groping it, driving me back, writhing, worming.

"Mark!" I am able to lean far enough left to see across the dance floor. Rob is not in the appointed spot, which can mean just one thing: he's on his way over. Within seconds, I see him; he is about ten feet away.

Through the leather of his jacket, I can make out fists in the pockets. Mark casts a lethal gaze in Rob's direction, then he turns me completely outward, exposing my bare back to the crowd. Mark pulls me into the bedroom and kicks the door shut. Rob's foot and shoulder jam it. There is powerful shoving.

"*Mark!*" I shout again, thinking, *Rob is going to end up in jail. Shit, Rob is going to end up in jail.*

Immediately, people come out of the bathroom behind us, taking Mark and me by surprise. Dara and Brett emerge with two of the models, one of whom is swaying feverishly to the blaring music—"The Age of Aquarius." It's at the horn part, at its most hallucinatory and cultish.

Let the sun shine! Let the sun shine in! The sun shine in!

With Mark's attention diverted, he loses his hold on the door and Rob smacks it open. Dara throws out his arms to protect the girls as Rob lurches at Mark and Mark lurches at Rob and Brett cuts over, forcing his way into the middle.

Dara yells, "*Everyone freeze,*" and they all comply, I guess because I'm so obviously caught in the mass. I don't kid myself into thinking Dara cares. As far as he's concerned, I'm Mark's property, and under any other circumstances, it would be my place to acquiesce to Mark's will. But Dara is looking at Rob, and he's thinking, *For all I know, that barbarian is carrying a gun.* Furthermore, we are guests in Dara's client's apartment, and Mark's clients have drugs. Everyone is equally compromised, which is somehow a sign of the times. Dara retrieves my sweater from the floor, then slides over. He extends his arm, helping me to disembark as though assisting me off a high-speed amusement ride. I try to withdraw but can't. I don't know who has my hand. Someone has it tightly. Oh, Rob—I can feel the leather cuff of his jacket.

As soon as I am extracted, Mark and Rob press back at each other, but Brett firmly holds the center, saying, "Break it up! Break it up!"

"Sorry your fiancée is unwell, Ross," Dara states to Mark, loudly and clearly. "You are wise to send her home. Unless, of course," he adds with contempt as he opens the bedroom door, "you have a little headache also?"

Mark does not reply. The three men stay immobilized, congealed into one dynamic solid, like one of Michelangelo's unfinished sculptures of slaves breaking from rock.

"Let's take a walk," Dara insists, "together." He takes the lead step, and we cross the central room as one. "Does the future Mrs. Ross have a car, or does she need a taxi?"

"Taxi," I answer.

At the elevator bay, Mark reaches for his wallet. The force of his own hand entering into his breast pocket throws him off balance. He finds two twenties, pinches them ineptly, then thrusts them at me. I join Rob on the elevator, and everyone looks at one another like factions facing off. I press the button fast.

As the doors begin to creak closed, Mark tosses out an arm, blocking them, and Rob pushes me behind his back. Brett grabs Mark's shoulders. There's that irregular thucking that elevator doors do. Mark manages to break free just enough to dump the remaining contents of his wallet onto the elevator floor.

"Here," Mark says to Rob. "Go buy yourself a matching outfit."

Rob kicks it all back, rapid fire, cramming the toe of his shoe into each piece, not missing a single bill or coin. "Save it for psychotherapy, you sadistic motherfucker."

"I'd warn you to keep your hands off her," Mark says, "but I won't bother. You've always been too afraid to try."

I look up Varick Street for a cab, but Rob snaps his head to one side. "C'mon, I got the Cougar."

The ride home passes in withering silence. I consider telling Rob that what he saw was not typical, that Mark was not himself, but even if Mark were worthy of defense, I would not have insulted Rob by lying to him.

Rob glares through the windshield, head down, eyes up, as if checking for broken bulbs in the streetlamps. He chews furiously—a toothpick, I think. We take Sixth Avenue up past all the silver towers. I'd always been pure to Rob, from the beginning, a palace in his mind. He had erected me and tended to me. I wonder if we'll ever recover, if we can ever find a way around disgrace.

At the entrance to my building, he hits the hazards and comes around to my door. He hands Carlo a five-dollar bill and tells him to keep an eye on the car. Rob takes me up to the apartment; he has to do *something*. Leaving me at the curb is not an option. In both our minds is the meaninglessness of his prudence. Mark has keys, just like me.

I will not say that Mark and I have sex when he eventually comes home. I will say that somehow he manages to ejaculate inside me despite the stubborn flaccidness of his penis, and right away he passes out and right away I bathe, allowing gravity and soap and near-boiling water to purge the tapioca clots of stinking debris he deposited in me. And men make fun of the way women taste and smell. If only women had voices.

41

I throw my legs over the side of the bed. My head is pounding, though I had nothing toxic the previous night. Mark is on the phone in the living room. When he hangs up, he comes in carrying juice, and he sits, facing me. His face looks stiff like a shield.

"If you're not too disgusted, I'd like to apologize."

I shrug. "Whatever."

"No, not whatever. Don't say *whatever*. Say what you feel. I behaved shamefully."

I say nothing. He can't handle what I feel. I feel released. "It was embarrassing, that's all."

"I'm sorry you were embarrassed. What else?"

I have nothing to add. "That's it," I say.

He reaches over and pets my hair. "I was drinking gin. You know I can't drink gin." He follows me to the bathroom and watches me wash and dress. "It's not like I was with another woman. C'mon, I'm a wreck about this."

This is only a partial lie. Obviously he's a wreck about something. "Forget it, Mark."

"Oh, no," he states with sudden menacing rectitude, "just the opposite. I won't forget it. In fact, I've called everyone. I just got off the phone with Rob. I took all the blame."

I brush my teeth. I wonder if there's a difference between *taking* the blame and *being* to blame. If there's a difference, he's referring to it. At the door, I grab a coat and my knapsack.

"Where are you headed?"

"School."

"The gym?"

Mark doesn't like me to go to the gym. He says it's a pickup scene. If I promise to avoid the basketball courts and the weight room, and just go to the pool and sauna, he'll say that's worse because of the lesbians. Once I said, "What are you talking about? I've never noticed any lesbians," and he said, "That's *precisely* the problem."

"The library. I have to finish my papers."

"I thought you finished your papers. Aren't they due Tuesday? You should have told me. If I'd known, I wouldn't have dragged you out last night and we could have avoided this entire mess." At the elevator, he kisses me on the forehead, speaking into my temple. "I have your graduation present. I spoke to the travel agent this morning. We're going away the day after Alicia's wedding. I wanted to surprise you, but we'll need to have your passport ready. What would you say to Italy?"

Italy, I think as I board the elevator. It's the least he can do.

I spend the day walking around the city, and when it starts to rain I take a twelve-dollar cab ride to Pinky's, Rob's cousin's bar in Brooklyn. Rob's over there at least once a week, though he lives in Jersey. It has something to do with gambling. The driver takes Third Avenue to the Queensboro Bridge because there's been an accident on the Williamsburg and the Manhattan is closed for repairs.

The streets glisten from an evening rain. Outside is warm, even for May. Through my window I hear the tick of tires against wet pavement, and on the radio, I listen to a lecture about relationships.

"Consider, for example, what happens when we walk," the speaker explains. "Our intrinsic reality is, quite simply, that we are moving in a given direction toward a given destination. Extrinsically, however, we are reliant upon the earth beneath our feet. If the earth were as absent in reality as in our perception of reality, our legs would swing in air.

"People seek equity in love as though love is a business. They look for equitable investments and gains. But relationships," he continues, "can possess equities separate from those that can be easily named or known. Equity can exist, independent of *interpretation* of equity, which, of course, is variable. By seeking *quantifiables,* we lose sight of mystery—the real binding power."

The taxi slows to a stop at Fifty-eighth Street and Third Avenue, near Alexander's department store, before making the turn onto the bridge ramp. Creaking up to consume my entire field of vision is that bizarre mural of globular buttons over Alexander's corner doorway, like a collection of random hemi-sected eyeballs, like some insane manifestation of things urging me to see. And so I see.

If it never occurred to me to move beyond the idea of having been abandoned by Rourke, it's not because I'd been victimized, but because in my mind one is a victim when one does not triumph. The parts of me that came to life with Rourke were parts I could not have conceived of alone; naturally I believed that if the best I could be was with him, then *without* him I was nothing.

When he left, I told myself that I was not good enough, that he wanted someone better. My anguish rendered me insensible. At the time, I forgot that life is strange and long and beautiful, and that something so extraordinary in its success could hardly be ordinary in its failure. I persuaded myself that he did not love me, that he never had; and yet, not once when we were together did I need to tell myself he did. It should have been enough to love and be loved, but there was more, I thought— I must have thought—because at some point everything changed from my simply wanting more of him to my wanting more of something else—something substantive, something *normal*—all the while denying the egocentricity of my aspirations, and forgetting the universe we'd made.

The cab is on the lower roadway; the cables and girders are *thoomping* past, animating the steel beam windows of the bridge.

I feel shame to have doubted him, especially when I recall his absence of artifice, the way he knew me when he met me, the way he worked to move us despite obstacles of age and position, the way he trusted that I would feel as he felt, the way he was patient and true. And so, the way he let me go—let *us* go—surely must have been just as deliberate.

Since he knew things at the beginning, maybe at the end he knew things too. That we had gone as far as chance would take us. That nothing is more sacred than youth or more hopeful than turning yourself over to someone and saying, *I have this time, it is not a long time, but it is my best time and my best gift, and I give it to you. When I revisit my youth, I revisit you.*

I had not been walking on air. Rourke had been there, pressure, earth beneath my feet, always.

At Pinky's everybody's watching a game on television. Rob is down at the end of the bar, in his usual place, by the telephone. His mood has not improved since fighting with Mark—the stiff hunch to his back, the shaking leg. He does not smile when he sees me; he just kicks out a stool. I drop my book bag and climb up. Something happens in the game, and the men shout in unison—"Ho, shit!" Rob's voice joins the chorus. He concentrates on the set, pretending to ignore me. Eventually he turns, his eyes drifting toward my lap. My legs are crossed, and with the pants I'm wearing, the crevice between my thighs is revealing. I slide my hands to cover myself.

Rob grabs a couple of bar napkins and blows his nose hard. "I'm allergic to something in here." He looks over each shoulder. "Must be somebody's cologne." He gestures to my knapsack. "More school? It seems like you've been in school longer than anyone ever—why is that?"

"I don't know."

"You don't, huh?" he says. "Well, when are you done?"

"I have three papers due Tuesday."

"And that's it?"

"And a presentation."

"A *presentation,* oh, excuse me. What's that, like Darrin Stephens?"

"Kind of. Only no witches."

He faces the bar, puts his elbows up, and wipes his nose one more time. "Where's the ring?" he asks, talking into his napkin.

"I left it at home."

"Home," he repeats facetiously. "That's not fair play. Some poor slob might get the idea you're available. Unless of course you weren't *allowed* to wear it. Did he tell you I'm gonna steal it and hock it?"

"He doesn't—"

"The future Mrs. Ross," Rob says, repeating Dara's remark from the previous night. "I should have popped that vampire asshole. He was asking for it. Tell you the truth, I'd rather you were gonna marry that queer friend of yours. Dennis. He's actually a good guy."

"Mark's okay."

"Yeah, sure. Okay. Capital *O*."

"Do you hate him because he's rich?" I ask.

"Do you sleep with him because he's rich?" Rob snaps back. "Oh, no, I'm sorry," he taunts, "you sleep with him because you *love* him."

"No, I—"

"*No?* Then why do you sleep with him?"

"I—I'm not sure. He was there—"

"Lots of people were *there*. I was there." He slaps his chest. "How come you never fucked me?" His fingers come together. "I'll tell you why. Because I know the code." He clenches his jaw, leans back, pulls out his wallet, and drops a fresh ten on the bar. Rob's wallet is full of cash. Rob's wallet is always full of cash. The bartender draws two tap beers and pushes them to us. Rob says, "Thanks, Pink."

Pinky leaves the money untouched. "How you doing, sweetheart? Long time no see." Pinky's an albino. They call him Pinky because he looks like the inside of a conch. I had a cat like that once, like Pinky, with two different-colored eyes, only my cat was deaf. Pinky can hear just fine except for a vague ringing sometimes. He keeps thinking there's a break-in at the pork factory across the street.

"Sorry, Pinky," I say. "I've been busy with school."

"She graduates next week," Rob reports. "A 4.0 average, dean's list. She got a certificate. One of these rolled-up parchment jobs."

"If she's so smart, what's she doing with you?" Pinky cackles as he chugs off, sideways and slow, like a failing tug.

Rob lifts his mug and polishes off a third of the contents in one swallow, then bends in like he's got a secret. "You wanna know what I think? I think you're with him because he doesn't care that you don't love him. Any other guy, any *normal* guy, shit like that matters. But you don't want anything normal. You're holding on to the past. He knows it. That bastard worked your . . . your—situation to his advantage. Just like a crook, he saw an open window, and he climbed in." Rob's eyes screw up tight like the lens of a camera. "Lemme tell you something about Mark—he don't come through. You know what I mean, *come through*? Principles, ethics, the code. He knows the code. He knows it and ignores it."

"What difference does it make?"

"It makes a difference," Rob says. "Certain things you don't do."

"Nobody owns me, Rob. And anyway, Rourke left."

"He had no choice."

"He had a choice."

"Don't tell me. I was there." Rob wipes the bar around our mugs with another napkin. "The reason Harrison took that job in East Hampton with those kids in the first place was Diane backed out."

"Diane *who?*"

"Diane who," he repeats.

"I'm serious. I've never even heard of her."

"Nobody over there ever mentioned Diane *Gelbart*? A Mr. and Mrs. Gelbart? Does Mark open your mail too? Take your calls?"

"Do you mean Mark's old girlfriend?"

"Oh, so you *have* heard of her."

"I guess I just forgot."

"I'd like to forget her myself. All the bad luck started with her. Let's just say she's overaccustomed to getting what she wants. And what she wanted at the time was—well, you can imagine."

He doesn't have to say. I *can* imagine. She wanted Rourke.

Rob stares into his mug. "I'm surprised you two haven't run into each other. She's always flying back and forth from California—like a carrier pigeon. Her parents are friendly with Mark's parents. They have one of those places in Southampton. Between the ocean and the pond."

"Gin Lane," I say, sounding outside myself.

"Yeah, that's it, Gin Lane. Very swank. She tried to persuade Harrison to live there that winter, but forget about it. He'd rather live in a cold-water shack and have his freedom, if you know what I mean."

I shift on my chair, lifting my ribs roof-ward, breathing deep. I try to remember what I've heard about Diane, something about Rita Hayworth and nightclubs and never looking at stars. Surely she's beautiful and glamorous. Probably she visited Rourke's house in Montauk, telling him it was *quaint*. Maybe the plans he'd had that first New Year's Eve were with her. And during the summer we spent together, Rourke probably went to Gin Lane when I was working at the Lobster Roll, going to play tennis or eat dinner by the pool house, and when he left that September, he probably— No, Rob is right. Unlike me, Rourke had integrity. He would rather live in a shack and have his freedom. *You know what I mean,* Rob said. Unfortunately, I know all too well.

Oh, I remember what Mark had said about Diane. *Everyone wanted her, but only I could get her.* I suddenly feel sick to my stomach. I rest my head in my hands.

Rob's hand touches my shoulder. "You okay?"

"It's—hot in here."

"That's because Pinky's a cheap bastard. He hates to put the air on before, like, August. I keep telling him it's gonna kill business, but he has the brilliant philosophy that heat makes people drink more. I go, 'Yeah, Einstein, at the bar down the street.'" Rob whistles. "Hey, Pink! Spend a couple dimes and hit the AC! She faints easy!"

Without removing his chin from the saddle of his hand, Pinky breaks from the television to acknowledge Rob, then heads out from behind the bar to flip the toggle by the front door. The machine in the transom sputters to life and starts to spit through its grubby vents.

Rob makes a squeaking noise with the side of his mouth, and stares at the ceiling. He looks like Reverend Olcott the time we talked about God. Like he has a whole reserve of information but is afraid to release it too fast in case it overwhelms me. And yet, he knows I want the truth, and he wants to be truthful. I see him take a walk through the conversation a couple of times, weighing the dangers of honesty against the opportunity for personal gain. He hates Mark. There may not be another chance like this one.

"Okay. So, Diane's two years younger than the rest of us. When we graduate back in '77, me and Harrison stick around L.A., doing our thing. He fights, I do grad school for accounting, Chris DeMarco comes back east to NYU Law, and Mark heads to Harvard, not breaking off with Diane. He doesn't want to keep her, but he doesn't want to lose her. He prefers to string her along. It's one of those things assholes do. He met his match in her, though. There's no bigger asshole than Diane. Right off she demands attention from a distance; she doesn't waste a minute. She hooks up with a bad crowd—booze and coke mostly but, like, a lot of coke. Several grams per week is my gentlemanly estimate. UCLA puts her on probation, her parents threaten to cut off the cash and ship her off to some Minnesota rehab—but she just keeps going. Finally she ends up at some party in the Hills where her girlfriend drowns. *Very* big deal. Diane paid for the drugs. Mark is worthless, of course. He flies out with her folks for one day—*one day*—the day she makes the declaration to the cops. That's it. Her parents offer to send them on a vacation. A couple weeks in Europe, the Caribbean. But Mark's too busy with school, he claims, he can't spare the time, et cetera, et cetera. Basically, she's a total fucking liability, and he's worried about his reputation. You know, he wants to run for office someday, have a seat on the Exchange, whatever— that's why he hangs around with those addicts from Washington."

"Because they have money?"

"*Lots* of people have money. They have connections. Anyway, Mark backs out; Diane calls Harrison. She's alone, she's scared, but basically, she's vindictive. Of course Harrison steps in—me, I wouldn't have bothered—and one, two, three, she's clean. Nobody knows what he did to get through, but he got through."

Oh, but I know. Just his eyes alone, looking at you.

"Naturally her parents are grateful. They pull some strings to get him a big shot agent who right off the bat hits him with decent stuff. Bit parts, but decent—commercials, voice-overs, print, extra work in TV, in a couple of movies—but it turns out to be a deal with the devil. Harrison is under obligation now to Diane *and* this agent—Eliot something, from William Morris. Of course, the agent wants him to quit fighting, and behind Harrison's back goes head-to-head a couple times with the trainer out there, Charles Lopez, Chucho Lopez, who happens to be connected himself, and who's counter-pressuring Harrison to get serious, get management, and start the climb for a title. He'd been fighting for years by then, and he'd established an unbelievable record. But it's a tough climb; it takes focus. Maybe Harrison has it in him, maybe not. I don't know if you realize the kind of money that's at stake."

I shake my head.

"Could be millions. Could be many millions. I've been to houses that would make that Gin Lane place look like a trailer. And the owner will be some twenty-five-year-old living with twelve friends, eight Mercedes, and a basketball court off the kitchen. Harrison is smart, mature, and—whatever." Rob tosses up his hand like it's a lost cause. "Anyway, that agent Eliot gets his tires slashed and other unsavory shit I don't care to get into, and in the middle of it all, we can't shake Diane. She's showing up at the fights, hanging around the gym. Every day she's at the fucking gym. Once she got her teeth in, she infected everything, like a rabid dog."

"Were you guys planning to stay in L.A.?"

"We had no plan."

"Did he want to turn professional?"

"Yes and no. Yes, because of money. No, because of interference. Let's just say he's got a problem with management. I could take on some small stuff, but as far as cutting title deals, I was twenty-four. Just one guy. Obviously I've got access to organizations through my uncle, and I could work for whoever. But signing on to anything separate from Harrison would've meant a break. I wasn't interested in repping other fighters. On top of it, with the acting thing a distinct possibility, he's suddenly not so keen on ruining his face. He's been lucky so far. Luck like that doesn't last.

"So," Rob continues, "spring rolls along—it's 1979 now—and Diane graduates. Her parents want her in New York so they can keep an eye on

her. She's not saying nothing, but you can see the writing on the wall—
she's gonna stick to Harrison like shit on a shoe. Her folks give her a trip
to Europe for the summer and then set up that cozy job on Long Island
for September, dressing it up into a "career opportunity" by making a
couple anonymous donations here and there, figuring it's East Hampton
in winter—if she goes berserk on dope again, nobody's gonna be the
wiser. Meanwhile, did anybody think for a second about those kids stuck
with that freak? Well, surprise, surprise, she refuses to leave him in L.A.

"That's when Harrison decides to go for the Olympics. It's the honorable way out all around. Jimmy Landes, the trainer he's had in Jersey
since he was a kid, was working in Brooklyn with two other guys for the
Games, and to top it off, the Olympics is just about the only organization big enough to intimidate Diane. Harrison commits to moving back
east, in order to convince her to come back too. Diane agrees, but fate
steps in and a big television job opens up for her—she's some kind of entertainment reporter now. With a little added incentive from her folks—
new house, new car—she falls for it. The whole package was too good to
pass up. Even a cokehead like her could see that.

"Then Harrison offered to take her spot in that school job to help her
parents save face and to throw Diane off the scent, so to speak. It boiled
down to, like, ten hours a week for him, but it was worth it to make
Diane think he's on board so she stays out of trouble in L.A. until she set-
tles into the new life. He figured she'd settle. Nobody else believed it. But
he was right. Her parents owe him big-time. Very smart maneuvering on
his part."

Rob breaks to drink some of his beer. I remember Alicia asking about
Rourke. *You two must have been completely in love,* she'd said. She must
have known about what he'd done on Diane's behalf. *He would never hurt
anyone,* Alicia had said.

"Now you see why Mark hates him. Harrison saves the day and looks
like a prince, whereas Mark dumps his nightmare on the rest of us, runs
for cover, and comes across like the rat he actually is. Mark's father almost disowned him for it, but he had a massive coronary instead. I'd like
to say it was related, but I know you love the old man, so I won't. Let's
just say that Mark being in the spotlight looking like a dick didn't exactly

lower the household stress levels. Mr. Ross had open-heart surgery, but he can't take a day off because he's afraid of the damage his son will do. And he's counting on you to make Mark a better man. Good fucking luck."

"Were you upset to leave California?" I ask.

"Me, nah—I hit bottom out there. That's another story for another day. Anyway, Harrison was better off coming home. It got Diane's claws out of him. You know me, I'm superstitious. Last thing I wanted was her bad blood hanging over his head or *mine*."

Rob clears his throat. "Long Island turned out to be a good deal. Harrison was ready to focus on the Games, get his mind off—*things*. And Jersey full-time was out of the question. The temptation would've been too great to make money. Between his talent and mine, it's like sitting on a gold mine. Montauk was perfect, not just because of the kind of shape he got into physically, but mentally. After L.A. he needed a *wash*. He was running, biking, swimming, coming into Brooklyn on the days he wasn't teaching at the school, four, maybe five a week, to train with Jimmy—doing qualifiers, the Pan Am Games, the Eastern Trials, the whole bit. Next thing you know, the Soviets invade Afghanistan that December, President Carter starts talking boycott in January, and by the end of March, it's official. *Poof,* that's that. No more Olympics."

He takes a minute to reflect. We both look at the television set. There's an ad on for Michelob Light Beer. It shows a couple of white guys with headbands playing racquetball. The men in the ad seem worlds away from the guys at the bar.

"Remember the night in the meat district?" Rob asks. "You asked what I said the first time I saw you."

"And you didn't tell me."

"And I'm not going to now." He sucks back his cheek again, and his head twitches right. "Something dumb, not bad, just the kind of thing guys say to each other. Well, it practically got me killed. I was like, *Jesus*." He returns his gaze momentarily to the television. He drags a finger around the top inside of his glass. I wonder what he's thinking about.

"I never told you this," Rob says, "but if I hadn't been there that day, I think that blond kid you were with would've taken a short walk off that cliff. Like joined the parade from top down." His hand makes a diving motion.

"Ray Trent. He's a nice guy."

"Nice *alive* guy," Rob adds. "With nice *operative* legs."

"He wasn't my boyfriend."

"Yeah, well, he wasn't just a *friend* either. That was clear to Harrison at least. Was he wrong?"

"No," I said. "He wasn't wrong."

Rob holds his jaw with one hand and smiles, shaking his head. "That's funny," he says of Rourke. "Fucking guy."

I feel something peculiar on my face, something cold. A tear. Strange, I thought all the tears had dried. Like bouquets of upside-down flowers. Rob reaches to catch it.

"I know what you're thinking," Rob says, handing me one of his cocktail napkins. "You're thinking, *He left her, he left me; he lied to her, he lied to me.* You're making a comparison, only there's no comparison. First off, with Diane he was dealing with a hysteric and a cheat. The thing about cheats is, they don't just cheat *you,* they make you cheat. That's their objective—the failure of your character." His voice deepens. "With you, it was different. You would never cheat to hang on to someone. You did Harrison a favor. You let go."

That's not what I'm thinking, but it's sweet of him to feel this way and to have been feeling this way all along. As if I *hadn't* become hysterical, *hadn't* lied, *hadn't* cheated Rourke, Mark, myself. Perhaps a stronger woman, a better woman, one with a good family, a house, a car, and a job—an entertainment reporter, for instance—would have fought for her rights. Mrs. Ross calls them *go-getters.* "*Go-getters!*" my mother said in disgust when I once mentioned the term. "Every woman is a go-getter. *Go get* me a cup of coffee! *Go get* the groceries! *Go get* the kids! *Go get* undressed."

The bar phone rings. "Take a number, Pink," Rob says, not even looking.

"Did he—did they—"

"He never touched her, if that's what you're asking. Not that I know of. Even if she'd been halfway sane, he wouldn't have touched her."

"Because of Mark."

"Because of the *code*. Because Harrison doesn't just *follow* the code. He wrote it." Rob is so close I can feel the downward stamp of his breath. "He wasn't gonna stay in Montauk that summer, Evie. After the Olympics fiasco, he was just gonna come back to Jersey to fight for cash. He was in shape, he had the apartment in Spring Lake, contacts in Atlantic City. The idea was to stay strong, make money, figure things out. A gym, maybe. We always said we'd open a gym, a chain—Jersey, L.A., Miami, Vegas, the Bronx. Maybe we'd reach out to kids in trouble. Give back what we got."

I consider all that Rob has lost. It's there in his face—a grasping sadness, a lonely frenzy. No one likes to surrender the best place to be. It's like forfeiting riches. It's not *like* that; it's *exactly* that.

"But that shit wasn't happening once he met you. Especially once Ross got into the picture. What a fucking judgment lapse. I think about the night we all went to that place in Amagansett. What could Harrison have been thinking? My guess is he introduced Mark for a reason. He wanted to force his own hand, force himself to come back. And he did. What did he last in Jersey, like, two *weeks* before turning back to get you?"

"Fifteen days," I say.

"*Fifteen* days," Rob says with a smile. "Well, he trained hard for fourteen of them, sparring every night, wiping out the entire local roster. Everybody's going crazy—radio, newspapers, the whole boardwalk is coming to life. On the fourteenth day, we set up a fight—very casual. He kicks the shit out of Chester Honey Walker, who hasn't missed a day in the ring since he was born. Harrison cracks his jaw, right in the second round. You could hear the snap through the auditorium, and we had a couple hundred people there, then he lays him out with a body shot—Rourke's impeccable on the inside.

"Next day he says to me, 'Let's take a drive.' I'll never forget it. '*Let's take a drive*. Two cars.' Okay, I say. We go to Montauk, East Hampton, we show the girls around—the beach, the town, shopping. We go to your house. Just me and Harrison. You're not home. Your mother is— nice lady, by the way. She sits on the back of the little couch there and folds her arms. She says to Harrison, 'Eveline hasn't left the house for two weeks. Are you the one she's been waiting for?' Harrison just goes, 'Yeah, I'm the one.' "

You have a mother, Rourke said to me the last night in Montauk, *I've met her.*

"She tells us where she thinks you are, at Alicia Ross's party, that some girl from school drove you over. Harrison realizes Mark's involved and he shuts down. Before we go find you, I make him stop at the beach. You know, toss a ball, cool off. I figure with the way he's been fighting, he might take lives. What happens? You pull up with Mark—in that freakin' car." Rob looks at me. "I will tell you what I was thinking at *that* moment. I was thinking, *This girl's dangerous.*"

"I never would have—"

"That was obvious. How you felt was obvious. Obvious as how Harrison felt. Obvious as what Mark was doing. The whole situation was painfully fucking clear. Remember I told you that night in Jersey—*Be careful*"? He points to the counter. "This is what I was talking about. This very day. Mark made his decision the first time he laid eyes on you. He *mastered* the obvious. Here we are. Four years later."

Pinky hands me a half-empty soft pack of tissues. I thank him.

"The rest is history. You come to Jersey for a couple days. Harrison goes to Montauk for the summer. And who could blame him? No sense rushing out to get hammered when you got a thing—a girl—you know, whatever." He nudges me with his shoulder. "We had a lot of fun that summer, didn't we?" His voice darkens. "Sooner or later, a man's mind turns back to money, usually from *some* money to *big* money. Harrison had to get back to reality. What was he supposed to do that would've been better or faster than fighting? Maybe he didn't want you watching him get beat up—it's not pretty stuff. Maybe he thought you should focus on your own life, school, what have you. Maybe he didn't do the right thing. Maybe he didn't know *what* to do. He just figured you'd be okay. I guess he had more faith in you than he did in himself. That's what I mean by saying he had no choice."

He takes a tissue from me, "Fucking allergies." He blows his nose hard. "The part that threw *me* was him going alone. At first I was pissed.

You were there—on my birthday, out at Surfside in Montauk. He told me that night he'd bought a ticket to Miami, that Jimmy Landes hooked him up for four months with some killer Cuban coach. Right off with the way he was talking, I knew I wasn't part of the plan. 'We'll meet up later,' he said. 'A couple months.' I wanted to fuckin' kill him." Rob shakes his head. "Miami."

He tears open a pack of Halls and tilts it in my direction. I decline. He pops one out, unwraps it, sets it in his mouth. "Eventually I chalked it up to a misunderstanding. I mean, no promises were exchanged. I never asked anything; he never said anything. He's not exactly chatty— as you know." The cough drop flips around between his teeth. I hear it click; I smell eucalyptus. "But I checked out on him for a long time. Eight months went by, the longest we ever went without talking."

Eight months. April of my freshman year. When Rourke sent me the letter; when Rob came to see me in my dorm.

"Harrison called in April. We hadn't spoken since that night in Montauk. He was coming to New York. He wanted to see you. He figured you and I'd kept in touch. I set him straight, but said, no problem, I'd find you. There was no listing in Manhattan. NYU had your dorm, the one on East Tenth, but no student phone number—I figured your roommate got the phone. I would have tried your mother, but her name is different from yours. Like an idiot, I called Mark, thinking he could get your number through Alicia. Well he'd been *waiting* for that."

Rob stammers into a burdensome silence. Suddenly it hits me. I know what he's referring to. Mark told *Rob* what happened to me. *Rob* told Rourke.

"Mark said you didn't want anything to do with Harrison, then he explained why in no uncertain terms. How you were found practically dead in the street, how he had had to deal with the hospital, how he paid the doctor, how he cleaned up after that animal, how he was the only thing standing between you and a nervous breakdown."

I must be in shock, because the first thing I think of isn't Rourke. The first thing I think of is Mr. Ross. I can almost hear Mark say, *Dad, I need to have a private conversation.* How like Mark to use the tragedy of my private circumstances to elevate his image and dismantle Rourke's. I can't believe I'd allowed it. No wonder they'd all tiptoed around me. Next I think of Rourke, how I'd hurt him. Last is Mark. How Mark hurt him.

"First of all," I say, "Mark *loaned* me money. I paid him back."

Rob lays his elbows on the bar and rubs the inside of his eyes with his fingertips. "Sure, sure. Mark blew it out of proportion. The fact is, you could've called me. You *should've* called me. You gotta understand, men are funny about—well, you can't have another guy stepping in like that—I mean—well, you know what I mean. It's a big decision."

"It wasn't a decision. It was an accident." He turns to me; our faces are practically grazing. "You know, like, a loss," I explain. "I woke up in E.R. I didn't know what happened until after it was over. Did Mark tell you that I—" I leave off with the question; I already know the answer. Mark had told Rob I'd been found *practically dead in the street.* Didn't that imply I'd done it to myself, like with a coat hanger?

Beneath Rob's eyes are the hard lines of misfortune. You cannot read him through his eyes. They defy, they oppose. Rob's eyes are not how you see in, but how he sees out. He's in shock, like me, only my shock is less and his is more. I live with Mark. I belong to a circle of people who are duplicitous, to a world in which friends are disposable. Rob's is a world in which blood ties extend beyond blood. It's difficult to see him forced to confront questions of betrayal among friends. It's like he's got rats in the house. It's a shitty lesson, that of all the reckless ways to live, the most reckless of all is an absence of influence over your own affairs.

"What was I supposed to do?" he says. "Everybody knowing Harrison's business but him, it wasn't right. I had to tell him. If he ever found out that I knew too, it would be bad. Ever since his father died, it's like he's got this pressure. Everything goes back to that." Rob shakes his head. "It's bad luck all around. Except for Ross. He scored a triple win— retribution for Diane, a shot at you—which, I mean, he never stood a chance—and Harrison—he never fought again. Mark called him an animal, and he believed it."

Rob shakes his head. "You know, it's taken me a while to figure it out. I can't believe I've been so stupid. Harrison left without me twice, not because he didn't want me to come, but because he wanted me to stay. He wanted me to look out for you, once in Montauk and then later, after finding out about this. And I failed—*twice*." He drums his hands on the bar and cracks his back to the right. I wonder what he's going to do. He looks like he's going to do something. "Do me a favor," he says to me. "Don't say anything yet. Just think. Think back on everything. And remember what I told you in the beginning—*be careful*."

42

Rob said to think, so I do, though it is difficult to find in myself what happened. Though the memories are there, my mind has transformed them, remaking them over the years into a thing finally crippled, finally deformed, abbreviated, in measure like bones missing from a body.

The first thing is the letter from Rourke, just checking in. The next is the night in the meat district, when Rob came to my dorm room. That was in April 1981, months after Rourke, but still before me and Mark. I'd seen Mark three or four times, never seriously. There was Rob's sudden phone call—*I'll be over in twenty minutes*—and then the delicate way he acted when he saw me, like he was picking up petals that had fallen off a flower. Obviously Mark had told him by then.

After that is a Sunday, one week later. Rob and Mark showing up at my dorm. They were going to play football. "It's a beautiful day," Mark said, swinging open my closet door, "you should get out."

I can still see them standing there looking in at the empty hangers, then down to the ground at my suitcase, realizing that I'd never even unpacked from the start of the year. Rob turned away like he didn't want to see, but Mark kneeled and went through my stuff like a surgeon, careful not to disrupt the piles that were folded and belted.

"This is perfect," he said, withdrawing something white. He placed it on my shoulders. "C'mon, let's head to Central Park!"

Rob's Cougar was double-parked on Tenth Street. I sat up front next to Rob and we pulled out, turning down Broadway. There was a deli on the northeast corner of Ninth Street. Mark ran in for coffees and sandwiches and a pack of Wrigley's for Rob. While Mark was in the store, Rob combed back his hair with his fingers, then threw a lithe muscular arm over the back of the seat. I could feel the electricity behind my neck.

"He's coming back," Rob said, clearing his throat as though he wanted to be very precise. "For a couple days. He'd like to see you. You gonna be okay about this," Rob inquired gravely, "or what?"

I said I'd be fine.

According to Rob, Rourke had been fighting full-time down in Miami with a world-class trainer, but was coming up north because he had agreed to help a friend on a job in Rahway, in Jersey. The trainer in Miami was that guy Jimmy Landes; the friend in Jersey was the Chinaman, and the Chinaman needed Rourke because Rourke knew martial arts and could defend himself, and Rahway was dangerous. No one told me any of this direct or outright; I learned in pieces that day. They must have thought it was the best way to tell me, in pieces.

"What's Rahway?" I asked Rob later. We were sitting in the grass, on the Great Lawn.

"It's a prison," he said. "Maximum security."

Three days after that I saw Rourke.

We all met at a restaurant at a marina in Jersey. There were sail masts towering disproportionately from the low, flat ground as if to tear night from the sky. And stars like shattered dishware, recklessly strewn. And the excruciating clarity of the vast beyond; the clinking, chiming ropes; the welted slap of the water against the wharf; the *flap-flap-flap* of plastic grand-opening flags that draped the raised butts of dry-docked boats. I had to walk on my toes to keep my heels from sinking into the sandlot.

"Rob ever take you here in summer?" Joey asked Mark.

"Couple of times," Mark answered.

"Nice sunsets, right?"

"Gorgeous," Mark agreed. "I was here with you guys for Eddie's wedding."

"That's right," Joey said. "Eddie M. That bastard."

Under his breath, Rob said, "He *is* a bastard."

Mark palmed Lorraine's back as we walked up the stairs. "What do you think, Lorraine? Nice place for a wedding."

Rob stopped at the landing, facing us. "I've often thought about marriage. But it always ends up being just that—*a thought*." He busted out laughing. Lorraine gave him a whack and walked on.

"Why you gotta say such stupid shit?" Joey wanted to know, he and Rob walking abreast. "I swear."

We approached a round candlelit table in a room to the left of the restaurant's entrance, and right away, before sitting, Rob excused himself. He had to make a couple calls. He looked at me before he left, and he winked like everything was gonna be okay. I watched him fold into the crowd at the bar. Then I couldn't see him anymore, but I stayed staring into that same spot just in case he might return to fill it.

"Sit down, Eveline, sit down," a voice was saying. The voice belonged to Lee, the same Lee from the year before, who was there with Chris, her husband. That was the first time I'd seen them since the previous summer, when she said she'd wanted to be an artist. I sat and pulled my chair all the way in.

"You have your driver," Mark was saying, "your mid-iron, your putter, and your spoon."

"There's also a brassie, a mashie, and a niblick," Brett added.

"A niblick!" Joey's wife, Anna, said. "You guys have got to be joking!"

Brett had driven out with Mark and me. I'd never met him before that night. They picked me up at school after eighteen holes in Eastchester. On the way down to Jersey they spoke of peaches. *Open-heart peaches, open-rock, open-seed.* "Freestones are the ones from which the pits are easily removed." Mark drummed the syllables on the dashboard for my edification—*Free-stone.* "Get it?"

But from the moment we arrived at the restaurant, Mark didn't talk to me. He just watched, as if eventually I was going to fall, and he was going to have to catch me.

"Lobsters all around," Joey said to the waiter. "Three two-pound, lemme see, five three-pound."

When Rob returned to the table, Joey started in on him, asking what he was up to and who was he calling. Rob picked sesame seeds off of bread sticks and ate them one at a time. As he chewed, his jaw flexed, making two dark creases that arced parenthetically from his cheekbones.

"From running fights to running numbers. And my mother had big hopes for him," Joey said. "Her *baby*."

"Yeah, well, I'm not dead yet."

"*Yet* is right," Chris said. "You don't have a bodyguard anymore."

Rob tilted back his chair. His arms hung straight off his sides and his thighs were apart. "My mother wants me to be an accountant. I go, 'Ma, think of me as an accountant with a mobile office.' "

"Very funny," Joey said. "Four years of college, then grad school, and he's standing on street corners. My parents had to take out a second mortgage to pay tuition."

"I don't stand on corners."

"Run slips, whatever. You're in the wheel. You're a spoke."

"I don't run slips either. You know what, Joey, you don't know what the fuck I do. *Wheel. Spoke.* Where do you get this shit from—*Baretta*?" Rob's chair slapped down; Lorraine shifted an inch to the right. "First of all, if there *was* a wheel, I'd be at the hub. Number two, I paid back Mom and Pop three times over. And while we're at it, do you think major brokerages recruit guys like me? Harvard Mark and his buddy Brett over here'll each make partner at Goldman in a couple years, but I'd be walled up in some cubicle, crunching numbers, making fifty grand, thinking up scams. You know how easy it is for me to think up scams?" Rob mashed his teeth together. "There's a big difference between a prison-bound entrepreneur and a prison-bound clerk."

"True," Chris said. "Only one can afford a good lawyer."

"Besides," Rob added, "Lorraine over here is very high maintenance. Very Park Avenue." His hand slipped up from her shoulders into the uncivilized nest of her hair. She rolled her eyes. If Lorraine had been a cat, she'd have been a calico—pretty but peculiar. She carried a huge pocketbook, which always contained the thing Rob needed most. "Hey, Rainy," he'd say, flicking his fingers into his palm, "got a deck a cards?"

"How come your father can't get Rob a job at some corporation?" Joey asked Mark. "Something honest."

"Corporations honest?" Rob mocked. "*Ha!* Go back to pissin' on fires, Joey."

"No problem," Mark said convincingly. "My father loves Rob."

Lee leaned over to me. "So, how's everything with you? School?"

"Yeah, how's it going, Eveline?" Chris inquired.

"It's going okay."

"She's all A's," Rob said. "Forget about it."

"And it happens to be a very rigid curriculum," Mark added.

Rob said, "It's not like she sits around drawing pictures all day."

I wondered why they felt they had to defend me. I wondered if I seemed dumb.

Past the heads of Lee and Chris was a plastered archway leading to the packed central dining area, and on the far side of that, another archway going to the kitchen. Red-vested waiters passed from the back arch into the main dining room, one on top of the other like out of a musical, each carrying sweltering aluminum platters, and one time through the steam came Rourke.

I remember thinking, *How did he get into the back? Did he get there before us, or did he come in through the kitchen?*

The seven months had left him altered, heavier, harder. His skin was dark; he was letting his hair grow. Above his left eye, a whole new scar. I noticed a mechanical efficiency, a half-human impassivity. It was like having an animal enter the room, and the animal is also a machine—if you can picture the way animals occasionally simulate machines, if you can picture a fascinating confluence of aspiration and design. I would not have thought it possible for him to be sexier, but he was. If he were a killer, I would not have known whether to run or stay and be killed— I would not have wanted to miss a moment of him.

If it's sad to reflect upon the wrongness of that particular impression, of him as capable of killing, it is germane, I think, to the history of my failure. Because, in fact, I've never known anyone with such a reverence for the sanctity of the body and the independence of the spirit. It's easy to speak in favor of freedom and strength, but grueling to live a life of emotional economy and physical reserve as Rourke did. His capacity to cause real harm obliged him to exist mindfully. Ironically, it was his sober self-containment, his refusal to equivocate, that threatened and hurt people most. I know because nothing has ever threatened or hurt me more than the moderation of his heart.

I felt conspicuous in my need; I felt wrong to be there. Before he even reached the table, I wanted to leave. I reminded myself that I was not very smart and not very pretty. That my eyes had dark circles and my skin was pale like potter's clay. That I did not have a nice haircut like Lee did or good makeup from Saks like Anna or gold hoop earrings like Lorraine. Surely everyone noticed my five-dollar haircut. Five dollars because at Astor Place Haircutters, Dominic charged me the men's rate since I hardly had hair. Probably they could guess that beneath my clothes my underwear had lost its original elasticity and in my pocket was all I possessed—a work-study paycheck for sixty-six dollars. Rourke must have recognized me to be the pathetic liability that I was. That was my feeling. Sometimes a feeling is all you get.

"Hey, hey, it's the grifter!" Joey said, rising first to greet him.

The women rushed Rourke, and the men stood, and the waiters came too, gathering around. He greeted them all, then he looked in my direction, and nodded, smiling, softly saying, "Hi."

I said hi, and after that everything went slowly. I remember the twist of my shoes against the floor.

Chris squeezed Rourke's shoulders. "You ready, or what? Look at this!"

"He's training to go one-on-one with me," Joey said.

"I'd pay big money to see that," Mark said sarcastically, reaching and shaking hands with Rourke. "Harrison, you remember my friend, Brett."

"Good to see you again," Brett sputtered with a deluge of respect.

Rourke shook hands and moved on to Rob. The two embraced. Rourke's arm locked onto Rob's back, and his face inched over Rob's shoulder, his black eyes cutting through space.

Rob patted him genially. "How you doin', man?"

"I've been good. You?"

Rob pulled back and his head tilted modestly. "Same old shit."

"Oh, yeah?"

"It's been a long fucking time," Rob said, shaking his head.

Rourke nodded, saying, "Longest ever."

"I've been following things," Rob said. "You know, checking in."

Rourke took the chair across from mine. "I know," he said. "Jimmy tells me. My mother says you stop over every week. Thanks."

When the food arrived, Joey proposed a toast, lifting his lobster seriously and ceremoniously. It looked like a heave offering, like some kind of tithe or religious gift. "Welcome home to Harrison, the next light heavyweight champion of—"

"The neighborhood," Rourke said, and everyone laughed.

Others took turns toasting him, and the lobster hung there, horizontal in the air, wilting ground-ward at its two ends. Rourke reacted to the compliments as if in response to narrowing roominess. His friends didn't seem to notice his discomfort. One fact of life is that it's simpler to live vicariously than to live free. They singled him out because he'd gotten away and they hadn't, and obviously that would reflect badly on them unless he happened to be specially endowed.

He looked at me. I looked away. Despite Rourke's attentiveness—his voice as it petitioned my ears, the tenderness I saw in his eyes—I couldn't act as I felt. Though I longed to assure him of what he already knew, that nothing had changed, that I loved him all the more the less he tried, my head was reeling. I had the sick sense that I was facing another confrontation, another loss. I could not bear another loss.

Rob broke into talk about St. Patrick's Day in Montauk, about the day he and I met. "Evie gets off a red Ducati driven by this big blonde and she walks away like she doesn't even know the girl. She passes off her helmet to some guy with a club foot, and two huge dogs start following her. German shepherds. And in the background they're playin' that accordion thing, the thing the fire department plays. What is that thing? Jesus, I'm drawing a blank. C'mon, help me out here."

Lorraine poked her stirrer through her drink like she had a job to do, which was to perforate the bottom of the glass. "The bagpipes."

"That's it," Rob said. "The bagpipes. I was thinking, *This girl is different. Very different.* Right, Harrison?"

Rourke nodded, once. "Very different."

After dinner, they decided to stop off and get dessert at a fancy pastry place. In the parking lot there came the usual figuring out of who was going in which car. Lee, Mark, Brett, and Chris went in Mark's new Saab because Chris was thinking of buying one. Joey and Anna rode with Rourke in the GTO because there was a *thunking* noise in the rear on hard acceleration that Joey was pretty sure could be cleared by re-routing the parking brake cables. Rob didn't give me a choice. He just said, "C'mon, you ride with us in the Cougar. It'll give me an excuse in case Lorraine gets any ideas."

All three of us sat up front, with Lorraine in the middle. She kept putting lotion on her hands. Whenever it vanished, she would begin again. Rob was singing.

> *You're just too good to be true. Can't take my eyes off you.*
> *You'd be like Heaven to touch. I want to hold you so much.*

As he sang, Lorraine looked out the windshield at nothing. The perfumey heat of her against my left side and the cold of the door on my right combining with the smell of Jergens was nice, but bittersweet. I figured Rob didn't want me to ride with Rourke because Rourke didn't want to ride with me.

We had to stop at Rob's house to walk the dog. Rob was the only one who could walk it because it was a Doberman he'd rescued from a gas station. *Rescued* meant *stolen,* but Rob had no problem with that, since the dog had been abused and the stinking fuck owed him money. The idea of Rob having to rush home a couple times a day to walk the dog was funny. He was always shooting off to deal with something urgent and unexplained—picking up the cake for his nephew's communion, catching the end of a Little League game of some troubled kid, getting his grandmother at the hairdresser's, shoveling snow at a neighbor's house, dropping off a deposit at the bank for his father.

The place where Rob was living at the time was cramped, and with all of us inside it felt like a Winnebago or the cabin of a boat. We barged in on his roommate, a guy they called Uncle Milty, who was lying on the floor watching the Rangers play Edmonton. He leapt to his feet and tucked in his shirt when we came in, and he made us a snack platter.

"You should've told me you were coming," Uncle Milty said from the kitchen. "I woulda bought sodas for the girls." He was short; just his chest and head were visible over the island that divided the two rooms. He loaded up a cutting board with olives and leftover tuna and a couple of tubes of Ritz crackers still in wax paper.

"Damn, Uncle Milty," Joey said, grabbing some cheese cubes. "You're hospitable."

He and Chris were on the sofa, checking out the end of the game. Mark too. Brett was using the phone. Rourke was in the kitchen leaning on the counter. I was near him, leaning too. Neither of us spoke. I was ashamed to stand so close to him, but I didn't know where else to be.

Rob walked in. "What's wrong with you *cafones*? You just ate."

"What do you care?" Uncle Milty asked. "It's my food. You last the week on a jar of peanut butter."

"I'm just sayin'," Rob huffed. The muzzled dog sniffed at the bare platter. "You coulda saved a couple olives for the dog, that's all." Rob gave the chain collar a jerk. "C'mon, Cujo. They don't give a shit about you."

By the time we reached the dessert place, I'd lost all sense of direction. While the guys went up to the counter to pick out pastries, I sat with the women and played with packets of sugar, trying to figure out where I was geographically.

Rourke was leaning against the coffee bar in his midnight-blue cotton bomber jacket, and he was telling a story about golf. I could tell because at one point he had simulated a golf swing, tossing up an arm, waving flat into the horizon as if to hail an imaginary party onward. His hair swept about his face. With one hand he righted it, then said something to make everyone laugh. To watch him was to feel again what I'd felt exclusively with him—like a woman, feminine and frail, light and in love. I remembered how with Jack, I'd always felt we were intrinsically the same, and though there was refuge in that, there was also a forfeiture of individuality. With Rourke, I experienced opposition, like the simple reflex of a knee when you knock it—legitimate and artless and completely beyond your control.

Mark came to the table first, saying good night. "We're gonna take off before dessert," he told us as he distributed kisses. He and Brett had each had a double espresso at the bar, he said, and they were ready to *shoot back to the Big Apple*. They had to work in the morning.

When he bent to my ear, he whispered, "Why don't you catch a ride with us?"

Though I felt ashamed of his familiarity, I knew I should not be. I reminded myself that he had been generous. I'd been clear, but he'd been clear too. It was not impossible that I'd misjudged things, and in the process, that I'd misled him. Often, I misjudged things.

I pulled away, saying, "Good night."

Mark moved closer. He took my hand and shoved cash into it. Forty dollars. "It's a long walk back to New York," he warned. Then he turned and passed through our little crowd like a mayor, smiling and shaking hands. Was it possible that Mark knew something I didn't? Could he see what I couldn't see? Maybe Rourke had been standing there all along, saying of me, *What's with her?*

I kicked out my chair, grabbed my coat, and started to run after him. But before I reached the closing door, Rob casually stepped out and stopped me, saying, "Where to, Countess? This is Jersey." There is a sensation, lifelike in me still, of Rob holding me, inducing me gently back from the door, steering and stepping like a competent dance partner, delivering me to the haven of Rourke's arms.

And then Rourke's mouth on the base of my neck, the mouth I'd waited for, like for proof of God. We kissed, lightly—the first new kiss, and I wondered at the taste, like a willowy almond after-flavor. I had to stretch to reach him, and he had to bend, lifting me a little.

"Did you get my letter?" he asked.

"Yes, I got it."

And hours later in the car, outside Rob's place again, the two of us clinging tightly to the heat and pulse of the other.

Are you really here?

Yes, I'm here. Are you? Are you here?

Then when it was nearly dawn, I remember him looking at his watch. It was thick stainless steel with a marine-green face, and the silken hairs of his arms were pressed beneath it. It was five minutes after four.

"I have to be in Rahway," he said, "at the prison, in an hour. Rob is going to take you back to the city. That okay?"

"Yes," I said. "It's okay."

He pulled me closer. "I'm done on Friday morning. When's your last class this week?"

"Thursday afternoon."

"Feel like taking off for a few days?"

"I would like that," I said.

"I'll call in a little while, as soon as I'm done." Rourke kissed me on both eyes, and I remember thinking, *He seems happy.* I wanted to be happy too. We kissed once again before I left with Rob, and it was nice, like home again, or anyway, as close as you can come.

Ear Bar is on Spring Street, and by the time I arrived that Thursday night, everyone was there. Everyone except Mark; his absence was conspicuous. Rob was near the door, with Eddie M. and Lorraine and Lorraine's friend Tracy Hollis, a dental hygienist. The elastic cast of rum stretched like a girdle about them. One of Eddie M.'s hands was cupped on the base of Tracy's ass. No wonder they called him a bastard. I wondered about his wife, Karen, whether she was over at her mother's. Karen was always over at her mother's. I'd never met her. "Me neither," Rob liked to say, "except that time at the wedding."

Rob kissed me distractedly, without breaking from his story. It was unlike him. He was criticizing Lorraine—something derogatory about bowling. "First off, she's got her own ball, some designer thing. She gets it up over her head, see, like this, but she can't insert her fingers all the way because of the nails—so the ball isn't too secure—and she starts toward the pins. And I'm just sittin' there thinking, *If anybody so much as sneezes, she's gonna break her back.*"

Rourke was halfway up the bar, flushed and tilting forward on his stool. He wore a sweater. He looked heavy and broken. He looked exactly like what he was *not*—a drunken Irish boxer. It was awful to see him that way. I glanced back at Rob, who remained emphatically preoccupied. He wouldn't even look to check. Normally he was always looking to check.

I approached Rourke slowly. He watched me approach, lifting his beer bottle to his mouth, dipping his head, swallowing hard.

He said, "Hey."

I said, "Hey."

"How was school?" he asked. I could hardly hear him.

I said that it was fine.

"What classes did you have?" he asked.

"Sociology. Drawing from life."

"Drawing, that's right. You said you're drawing rooftops."

"Rooftops, yes."

His eyes searched my face. "Did you bring any with you?"

I said no, I didn't.

"Oh. Too bad." Rourke seemed to wait, or prepare, or gather something stray. "I talked to Black Jack today—did I tell you about Black Jack?"

"No," I said.

"One of the inmates I worked with this week. A former fighter. There are a couple boxers in there. He ran guns through Jersey in the fifties." Rourke slurred when he spoke, and struggled to find the right words. "He took the fall for a murder he didn't commit. That's what he told me. A trooper. No witnesses." Rourke looked at me, and then beyond, eyes darting around table legs, over floor tiles. "He's been in twenty-six years. His wife remarried. He's never seen his son."

It was a strange story to tell. It was as if he were entrusting me with something important, as if there were more that he wanted to say. I suppose I should have inquired further, but as it happened, the moment of his openness coincided exactly with the moment I resolved to defend myself against it. I'd contented myself for so long with his opaqueness that I actually preferred it. I trusted it more.

"Sorry I couldn't call you earlier," he said. "You got the note, right?"

He'd left a note at the front desk in my dorm saying he couldn't pick me up as planned, but that I should meet them tonight at Ear Bar. I'd almost missed the note. I'd been waiting in my room for his call when Juanita the guard had called up instead.

The bar was cold; I drew my sweatshirt tighter. Rourke whistled to Rob, gesturing for him to close the front door, then Rourke took my hands in his own. I remembered the night in high school after the play at Dan Lewis's house when he'd done the same thing.

The bartender came by with two shot glasses. "Here you go, Harrison. Rob sent them over. One's for your girlfriend," he said, meaning me.

Rourke reached for a shot glass and offered it to me, but I declined. He emptied one, then another. "I'm celebrating," he stated. "I took a job—a regular job."

I didn't understand. "When?" *When* wasn't right.

"Six hours ago."

"Where?"

"Out West. Colorado Springs," he said. "Training. Other fighters." His jaw ticked left.

"No more fights?"

"No more fights. A few fights. A couple commitments. Then I'm done."

Colorado seemed far, farther than the last place he went. Florida. And before Florida, California. He had also lived in New Jersey and New York. Five states, maybe more; Rourke made me think what a big country America is. You could really get lost out there. *Training other fighters.* I didn't like the sound of that. I didn't bother to say I was happy for him; he wouldn't have wanted me to lie. What I felt primarily was an acquiescent and moving sorrow, like seeing a bird flying very far in the sky or a tiny cortege passing in the rain.

"I won't be able to get away this weekend after all. I head out first thing Saturday morning, at about five." He came forward, his head tapping my head. His neck stretching, his lips touching mine softly, once, twice. "You wouldn't consider taking a ride cross-country with me, would you?"

I remember his drunken breath on my neck was warm, and the fragrant smell of the alcohol plus the smell of him was dizzying. I remember listening and hearing, like when you listen to a shell and hear the sea. There was remorse, but also unspeakable things—ambition, surely. Cruelty, perhaps. Did he hear me too? Did he hear that I could never go back to waiting, could never become another of his faithful friends, preserved in time, occupying the cherished but forsaken asylum of his youth? Did he hear that I would sooner move on than allow myself to be aligned with things in his heart that were dead?

Whether or not he was sincere about the drive cross-country, I answered as if he was, because, in fact, he should have been, because, in fact, he wished to be. Sometimes men hate themselves for not being heroes, and they need to know they can be forgiven. Sometimes when you love someone, you need to pass their tests.

"I don't think it would be good—for me, you know, to go—like, not such a great idea." I imagined the flight home alone, the sight of this great nation moving in reverse, west to east, me leaving him behind. It would have been impossible. He knew that. "It's just—I haven't been well."

Rourke pulled my hands deep into his lap and manipulated them thoughtfully, tracing the veins. I was free to regard him—exposed and illogical and lame and drunk, and so very *sorry*. Was he crying? I thought he was crying. If only I'd thought to ask about what, but I was too moved by the completeness of my feelings—compassion, fury, desire, tenderness, fear, love.

"You don't understand," he slurred, nodding downward. "You'll never be what I am." I asked what that was, and he said, "Exactly what you see in front of you. A failure."

"Do you remember," he asked, "how to drive shift?"

His legs were parted and his knees skimmed the dashboard. His head drifted back onto the seat, and he closed his eyes. I started his car, keeping to my side, though I was small. Being next to him right then was like being a Lilliputian, like stepping with due caution about a slumbering giant—by his size you knew that the setback was only temporary. I drove him back to Jersey because he'd asked me to, because I loved him, because I trusted no one else. I remember moving through the quills of highway light that seemed like a forest. And the music on the radio, the music like a watcher, like it had intellect, like the box had eyes.

> *Juliet, when we made love you used to cry*
> *You said I love you like the stars above, I'll love you 'til I die*

A precise halo of clove-pink light marked out the room on the top floor of his house—the same room I'd noticed the first time I visited—

his mother's. From the street I could just make out the wallpaper, indigo with ropes of yellow rising like blossom ladders. She must have been waiting for him. In the driveway was a white Oldsmobile; I pulled up alongside it. I did not have to wake him. He had been roused instinctively by the impression of the streets near his home. For some time he had been staring ahead, grim in the grim richness of his thoughts, and this consoled me, ironically.

I accompanied him to the door of his studio. I retrieved the key from the grass when he dropped it, and though I did not help him undress, I laid his clothes on the chair. When I turned, he was curled like a deserted boy on his left side, which was peculiar since I'd known him always to sleep facing up. He was in his underwear. It was true he was bigger since I'd seen him last, but his weight was decisive, controlled. Once Rob told me and Lorraine that when Rourke hit fighting weight, he had to maintain it to the quarter pound. Rob had said, "He sucks the water out of lettuce and spits green."

It was awful to see him drunk, to see him give up. Gently I journeyed like a pilgrim to the wall of his back, close enough without touching to reclaim some of the life of which I had been dispossessed. I kept watch over him through the night. I could be forgiven for seeking out memories of Montauk—of being sunburned, of being in love. After passing one last time through these halls of memory, I sealed them off like rooms locked from the inside. I would not go back. I would ask no more of life than that it allow me in all fairness to hold the perfect knowledge of perfect things. I told myself maybe love can be love regardless of the absence of its object—and devotion, devotion—so long as you are willing to be captive to it, and you stow it secretly, like a mad relative in the attic. Maybe there was an invisible way to love him, like a radio frequency. Maybe if I listened at night, I could draw it.

He stirred, raising himself onto one elbow, the muscles of his infolding abdomen making a miniature city, and he drank from the glass of water I'd set by the bed. He was not surprised to see me, which was bittersweet. It was as though I had infringed upon his nights as often as he had upon mine. His arms went around my hips and his fingers slipped through the empty belt loops of my jeans, and I drew my fingertips across his jaw, and he breathed softly, coming closer.

From where I sat, I could see the bathroom door. Once we showered there, and I had cried, and he'd been good about that, not asking questions. Next to the bathroom was another door to an interior staircase, leading to the first floor, and the second, and at the very top, the indigo room. If I climbed those stairs, I would find her, still awake, reading in her robe. Mothers who wait up read and wear robes; I knew because I'd never had such a mother, so she existed perfectly in my imagination. If I went to her, would she be the sort to solve everything, or possibly the sort to say nothing—to let you make your own mistakes and to hope for the best.

I wondered when as a man Rourke had been proved. After the fight over his father, the one that had given him his scar? I wondered would we die without meeting again, or would we meet and smile in the slightly embarrassed manner of former lovers, with all the intervening seasons of regret coming to life in our eyes. And if I died, would he come to my funeral, and who would call to notify him, and would he grieve—yes, he would grieve; but would he know that if I could be given one day, one hour, one minute more to live, that I would accept only if I could spend that time with him? I thought how a baby conceived in July would have been born in April. That would have been a biological coincidence, to have been brought together for conception and then again for the delivery. People like to say babies come for a reason. If so, was ours taken away for one?

As I watched the ascension of day, with every ripple of light coming like drops to fill a bucket, I held him, and I persuaded myself to come to terms. How strange that I felt most gloriously alive just as I prepared to withdraw from the hazards of sensation. Like some animal gazing into the wondrous world through the door of its dank cave before bowing off to voluntary sleep, I breathed greedily as if each trapped ounce of his vitality could be called upon to sustain me through hibernation. And I became seized by a whole new sorrow, a loving sorrow. Although once again it was Rourke who was leaving me, this time I knew I would bear the burden of the sacrifice. I was turning him over—to soul corruption, to the inclemency of survival.

I said, "Mark Ross is not going to give up."

Rourke answered, "I know." His breath on my wrist.

I left as he slept, the worst and hardest thing I'd ever done. I knew that if I stayed, it would have made everything worse. I knew also that by leaving I was giving up every possibility of coming to some understanding. At daybreak, I walked to the main road, then I hitchhiked as far as the highway, where I hitched again. Feeling forlorn as I did, and lacking a destination, I might have traveled on as far as the road would have taken me, Albany or Boston, Canada maybe, except that I got a ride directly into the West Village from two co-workers, a Polish guy and a diabetic woman, best friends, they said, who left me safely at the corner of Hudson and Morton.

At a Mexican restaurant on Columbus Avenue, Lee and Chris held a goodbye dinner for Rourke. Lee had called me that day from her office on Wall Street.

"I initially planned this for Sunday, since he said you two were going to Atlantic City, but I just found out he's leaving tomorrow. It's been crazy getting organized."

I didn't want to go; yet, I couldn't stay away. I arrived on time, but instead of going in I walked around—north, west, south, then east again, making a fifteen-block square. By the time I climbed the restaurant's staircase to its balcony and joined the party—there were nine people, including Mark—they were finishing dessert—dishes of flan and fried ice cream were scattered around the table.

"You're here," Lee said, rising to give me a kiss. "I'm so glad."

Rourke didn't speak or move to greet me. Everyone else mumbled hellos but fidgeted uncomfortably, not knowing what to do or expect. They were even more ignorant of the goings-on between Rourke and me than we were ourselves, and that uncertainty, mingled with his disappointment, was like a critically elevated temperature. As Rob would say, *Things were pretty dicey.*

Lee called over the balcony to the waiter for another espresso and an ice water, and she drew out a chair at the table's head, which I dragged to Rourke's side, so I did not have to see him, though I could sense him, everything about him. He was in the room with me, I was thinking morbidly. Soon he would not be in the room with me anymore.

Mark raised his café con leche. "Well, best of luck, Harrison."

No one else raised their glasses or cups because Rourke did not accept Mark's toast; he just stared, then stood. He had to get going, he said to Lee; he wanted to spend time with his mother. There was squelching chair scraping, but he lifted his hands, telling everyone to stay put, and giving Lee a quick kiss before walking out.

I remember wanting nothing more than to get up and leave with him, to apologize for having left him that morning, to figure out what had to be figured, to go and meet his mother, to help him pack, to have a private goodbye, and that moment of all moments is most maddeningly vivid to me; it was the last honest need I experienced for years. In a heartbeat, he was gone. I knew I'd never see him again.

Chris paid the check, and we finished in silence. They all stood and grabbed their jackets. Mark thanked Lee and Chris.

Rob lifted my sweater off the back of the chair. He said, "Let's go. I'll give you a ride."

I told him no. Looking down.

"C'mon," he said darkly. "I'm taking the Holland. I'll go straight down Ninth Avenue, take Bleecker to Tenth, drop you there, and then shoot west to Seventh on Ninth Street." *Boom, boom, boom.*

I'd be okay.

Rob swung his chair closer, then glanced over his shoulder at the others. "Look at me."

My eyes looked at his, facing off.

"Once you do this," he said, "there's no going back."

"There's already no going back."

"Would you like to walk a bit?" Mark asked as the cars pulled away.

"Thanks," I said. "Home just seems like—" I waved one arm.

"Like home," Mark said. "Say no more."

The night was magnificent, as such things go, and we infringed upon it mildly, strolling up one side of Columbus Avenue and down the other, gazing into store windows. We passed many of the same places I'd walked by when I was alone earlier in the evening.

"You look like an Italian movie star," he said to our reflection. "With your sweater over your shoulders and just the top button done."

I tried to remember if I'd ever told Mark about Marilyn and Dad comparing me to Monica Vitti. But then again, it was just the type of guy Mark was, the kind who makes you think he's gotten hold of your file.

We turned east on Seventy-sixth Street and headed toward Central Park. I climbed onto a low wall and reached for his shoulder as I walked. When he helped me off, I slid through the shaft of his arms.

"Like an angel," he said, "just descended."

"Fallen, you mean."

"No," he said. "That's not what I mean."

He guided my face back and he kissed me, and I let him because my lips were deserving lips wishing to be kissed and my body was a deserving body wishing to be touched and because there is a moment in every life when you hit the lowest possible point. In that moment you are not you but a monster of you, a creature stalking the cloisters of your own despair. The monster urges you on—*come, come*—and so you do. In fact, you feel better in there, crazed and incautious, capable and free. You feel you have reached the other side, that you have passed through the pain, though you have only capitulated to it. And you are lucky you do not have a gun. If you had a gun, you'd shoot yourself.

"This is where I live." We are at the Beresford on Central Park West. "Actually, my parents live here." He escorted me through the set of doors facing the American Museum of Natural History.

"Good evening, Mr. Ross," the doorman said.

Mark shook the doorman's gloved hand. "Ralph, this is Miss Auerbach."

Ralph greeted me warmly and walked us to the elevator. I wondered what he was thinking. Men are always thinking things, doormen in particular.

The Ross apartment was august and sublime, a quintessential New York prewar apartment. If ever Manhattan could be smelted and poured, it would take the shape of an apartment like that. The difference between it and the house in East Hampton was dramatic—the plaster walls, the original detailing, the chain of elegant rooms connected by high-ceilinged corridors. A Steinway grand was situated near a bank of windows overlooking the park. My thoughts turned to Jack. I wondered where he was and how I had managed to stray so far. I saw the art—a de Kooning, a Stella, a Diebenkorn, several Picasso etchings. Mark had bought the Diebenkorn at a gallery in California, he told me, and had given it to his parents for their twenty-fifth wedding anniversary. In the bedrooms were lithographs by Miró, a charcoal by O'Keeffe, a series of photographs by Stieglitz.

White cabinets towered from floor to ceiling in the main cooking area, but there were also cabinets in the hall that was a sort of larder. The floor was made of those classic black and white square ceramic tiles, and near the maid's room, a door with dead bolts led to a service elevator. Garbage was placed there; invisible hands retrieved it.

Mark rummaged through the refrigerator. "You didn't eat tonight. Let me make you something."

When the kettle whistled, Mark transferred boiling water for tea into a beautiful china pot. It was light turquoise with handpainted geese in flight and gold foliage and a gold border. He showed me the black stamps on the bottoms of the matching cup and saucer. The set was Japanese, from the turn of the century.

"Nippon," he said, referring to the mark. "It simply means 'Japan' and refers to the country of origin. In the 1920s, U.S. Customs law changed and demanded the marks read: 'Made in Japan,' which doesn't sound as nice as 'Nippon,' does it?"

I said no, that it didn't. By the kitchen clock, it was nearly three-thirty. Mark and I had walked for hours. Rourke was finished packing. He was alone in his apartment, thinking of me. Just a day ago, I'd been there too.

"Where are your parents?" I asked Mark, banishing thoughts of Rourke. There was the seedy smell of rye bread toasting.

"Milan," he answered. "On vacation. Then it's up to Monte Carlo for a little gambling, then they shoot through Nice over to Cannes for the film festival."

I was sorry I'd asked; somehow, it made everything hurt worse.

"C'mon," he said. "Let me show you around." We left the dishes on the table for someone else to clean and soon we were moving through hallways. It was strange, but I could see us—moving. One room we passed had window seats and long boxes of flowers—pansies. I hesitated; it was so pretty there.

"Alicia's," he said.

Mark's former room was at the very end. It was smaller and darker than his sister's but nicer. There were built-in cherry bookshelves and a cherry rolltop desk and hanging things such as photographs, pennants, diplomas—Collegiate, UCLA, Harvard. The room was like one of those hidden coin pockets in your Levi's, the perfect place if you happen to have the perfect thing to fit inside.

I understood that Mark had taken me there instead of to his new apartment because there was a chance I would have declined. The visit to his parents' house felt accidental and edifying, and I did not mind being there; in fact, I felt safe, unfindable, like deep in the tail of a snake.

It seemed that Mark was always right—anyway, his instincts were, and fortune was with him, and these are superior traits in a man when you can find no others.

At the edge of his bed, he kissed me again and he unbuttoned my blouse slowly, methodically. It was cotton, a doeskin color with pearl buttons—I still have it. Next Mark lowered the straps of my bra, thumbing down the lace.

"Am I dreaming?" he murmured to himself. "I must be dreaming."

I did not bother to stop him. I did not bother to say no, not when the sun would soon be rising, not when he had walked me through the labyrinth of the night, not when he had worked so hard for so long, and he had waited—one whole year.

Rourke was no god, no king—he was a solitary, solitary man. I had no reason to wait for him. If it was true that Rourke wanted me, perhaps it was also true that he needed to forsake me. Perhaps his sacrifice helped him to proceed; there are men like that, men who need loss to exempt them, who feel unconsecrated without forfeiture.

In any event, did it really matter, days alone or days with Mark, when his eyes had seen Rourke's eyes and my eyes and the exchanges between them? When his loathing of Rourke was so vital as to move him to claim me? Those were the things I told myself.

Mark, kissing my neck, his hands slipping to my waist and my pants.

When he followed the line beneath the elastic of my underwear with one finger, his lips hung apart and he caught his breath. He steered me back onto the bed and removed the rest of my clothes, though not his own— for a long time he did not remove his own. He went very slowly, staring the entire time. I did not dare move. I'd read somewhere that power takes as ingratitude the writhing of its victims. I did not want him to think I was ungrateful.

When he tossed my jeans onto the floor, there was the sound of coins rolling. My money, falling out. He said not to worry. "I have all the money you'll ever need."

43

I meet Rob at a garage, and we are happy, both of us, and free. I follow him to the back, where it smells of incubated diesel and desiccated oil—safe, a world of men. Beneath one of the cars is Rourke. He rolls out. It's been a long time since I've seen him. I want to touch his face, but I cannot reach it. Rob says to try, so I try, and when I do, I feel him, his skin, and things begin to grow—the light and the warmth and my sense of myself, growing from the bottom up, like plants.

Rourke and I are in a room. It's brightly lit without windows; the door is ajar. He leans over a suitcase. Being close to him feels provisional or proba-tionary, like being reunited with someone dead. Like soon he will go again. Like time is marked.

He kisses me, saying he will be back in a few hours. I will wait, though I know he will not come back. He doesn't mean to be untruthful. He simply doesn't know what I know.

I'm not sure about time passing, if any has. But Mark has come, and the room Rourke and I shared is in Mark's apartment. Someone called for you, Mark says. Some guy, calling your name—Eveline. Eveline. From the bed-room, Mark says. Go on in.

*Beneath the covers is a shape. Is it Rourke? I go under the blankets. It's
dark; he is naked. He brushes back the hair from my face. We lie, close and
broken apart, known, unknown.*

Baby, he says. I missed you, baby.

*I am wearing a slip with buttons. He unbuttons, expertly. One hand
holds me still while the other— Now he is in me. I feel him. We lie on our
sides, hardly moving. I find his pulse. I strive to be an organ to him, sightless,
mindless, attached. Is it true, could it be true, has he come back?*

I'm sorry, I say. For doubting you. I love you. I tell him I love him.

Yes, he says, starting to push faster now. I love you too.

*And I—my eyes—they squeeze shut, they will not open, they know not to
open. The sight of Mark would kill me. It kills me.*

Before Mark gets up I take cash from the dresser and I go get the BMW
from the garage. I'm going to see Rob at church. It's his family church,
where he goes every Sunday at nine, by his parents' house, in Rumson. I
know the way because I've been there a few times, twice for Easter, once
for Christmas Eve, and once for Charlie's communion. Charlie is Rob's
nephew and godson, Joey and Anna's son. I would have called to say I
was coming, but I didn't want to take the chance of Mark hearing me
and waking up. After I got home from being at Pinky's last night with
Rob, Mark was out and he didn't come home until after I'd gone to bed.

I wait on the church steps in the drizzle and listen to the end of Mass.
The priest is talking about the *Knack*. He says the Knack is the ability to
live in the present, which is something God has and Lucifer wants. I'm
not sure about that, about the Knack. Priests have a way of extrapolating
a lot, then neglecting to explain themselves. I guess he's implying that
God—or, the goodness in people—is satisfied with the gifts of each ordinary moment, and that Lucifer—or the maleficence in people—is obsessed with the shadowy and elusive things lying ahead and behind—like
dreams and regrets.

Rob dips out with both Mrs. Cirillos, his mother and his grandmother on his father's side. Coincidentally, they share the same first
name too—Fortuna. He opens their collapsible umbrellas, one, then the
other. They hook on to him at the elbows so when he walks he has to

stretch his neck above the fabric arch they make. When he sees me, he stops in his tracks, they all do, in a line. The elder Mrs. Cirillo loses her balance. He steadies her.

"What happened?" he demands of me.

"Nothing."

"You're okay?"

"I'm okay," I say. "I'm fine."

"Jesus, give me a friggin' heart attack, why don't you?"

Both women slap him in sync. "What is *wrong* with you?" his mother says quickly, like this happens all the time. "You just walked out of church."

"He's gonna get struck dead," his grandmother warns. "It happened to my cousin." She makes a hatchet move with her hand. "Dead."

I kiss the ladies hello. Rob's mom is dressed in a union-blue shirtdress with a Peter Pan collar and darts beneath the breasts. Nonna Cirillo is wearing a pressed housecoat with a black crocheted sweater around her shoulders, and with her free hand she clings to her bag, tight, like somebody might snatch it. She doesn't remember me, but that's okay since she never remembers anything other than obscure details from her past such as the shoe sizes of dead sisters and the price of tomatoes from the grocery store the family used to operate on First Avenue.

"You're soaking wet, Eveline," Mrs. Cirillo says, taking out a tissue from her sleeve, wiping my face. "How come you didn't come inside?" She turns to Rob. "How come she didn't come inside?"

Rob looks around. "How did you get here?"

I point to the BMW.

"Which one. The 3.0 CS? Whose car is that?"

Mark bought it. For me. Only I don't say that. I say, "Mark's."

"That's a nice car. He never told me about that car." Rob shakes his head in queasy disbelief. "Follow me back to the house. My father's making lunch."

At Vinny-O's they added a partial wall to make a dining area. Otherwise the place looks the same as it did four years ago, except for a maximum occupancy sign and a Heimlich Maneuver poster.

"You like those signs, huh?" Rob says. "All they need now is a chef and a kitchen. A couple customers. Some food. Maybe a menu."

He takes over like he owns the place, like he's back at the dining room table of his parents' house. He leans on the bar and grabs the phone and pops off a few calls. There's a bandage on his right palm that wasn't there the night before when we were at Pinky's. He fingers the tape as he talks on the phone, saying something complicated to somebody about the under/over being 100/80, so he lighteninged the over 200, and there he was, 8,200 down, and how he swears he would get the rest next week because he's got something big about to break, bigger than big, which you can get a piece of if you want.

I gesture for money to play the bowling game. He tucks the phone in between his neck and his shoulder, reaches into his front pocket with his good hand, and gives me a fistful of change. I cross the room and drop a quarter in the slot and the lights flash slow. *Left-right, left-right.* They haven't upgraded the design of the game since the sixties. The cartoon boy is wearing pegged-leg pants with two-inch cuffs, and the cartoon girl has teased hair and a headband and a linguini-thin belt around the waist of her dress. They seem carefree. I whoosh the shooting disc around and get that feeling of the metal platter swilling back and forth over the sawdusty alley. I take it to my belly and shoot it. *Bee-Baw. Tough luck! A split!*

"Not enough force," Rob says, coming up to me from behind. "You get that from height. Try again." He lifts me. I draw the disc to the far left and shoot it diagonally right where it slides under one pin, meets two points of the corner, and ricochets left, sliding to a standstill right under the second pin—*Chick-ching. Aces! A spare!*

"Nice job," he says, lowering me slow, straightening out his pants around his penis.

At our table, I stack the leftover quarters in front of Rob. He flicks one up and spins it on the tabletop. He blurs his gaze into the twirling coin. "You didn't say anything last night, did you?"

"I was asleep when he got home."

"Does he know where you are right now?" Rob asks.

I say no; Rob says good.

"Watch yourself," Rob advises. "He's snapping."

"Rob," I say, "sometimes when we—when he and I—sometimes in my sleep—I make a mistake and I think Mark is Rourke."

Rob slaps down the coin. He looks up. "Does Mark know?"

"I think so," I say. "Yes."

Rob nods, small nods, minor nods, his head tilted somewhat right. In the light his hazel eyes are green. Most days they are like cork. "C'mon," he says. "Let's take a ride."

When we leave, he swings the front door open and props it for me to go past, forgetting his bad hand. "Shit," he says, shaking it. I ask what happened, and he says, "Nothing glamorous. I was eating salted peanuts out of a can."

In Spring Lake people have the Knack. They wash cars and clip hedges and there is this feeling that the worst is over, that there is nothing going on in the world besides you and the miniature sliver of action in your immediate vicinity. We pass a ball game in the street and Rob brings the car to a crawl. "Hey, who taught you to hold a bat?" he asks a kid. "The vacuum salesman?"

As we approach Rourke's house, I get the sensation of coming home after a war or a long stay in a psychiatric institution. Everything looks the same—the butterfly rhododendrons, the flickering of the asphalt driveway, the carbonated green of the garden hose. I wonder if everything looking the same is worse than everything looking changed, since of course nothing is the same; three years have passed since the morning I was last here, the morning I walked out on Rourke and hitchhiked back to New York. I'd been thinking of it so much lately; it all seemed recent to me.

A figure in khakis and a denim blouse kneels in the front garden, and at the throaty sound of Rob's car, she turns and squints. I wonder if she thought it was Rourke. When she stands she is not small or big—my size, no, a little bigger.

Rob turns down the driveway; he hesitates before cutting the engine. "Listen," he says, "there's something you should know. There's gonna be a fight."

"What kind of a fight?"

"The comeback kind, with long fucking odds. The kind where Harrison beats the shit out of somebody and we make a lot of money." Rob flips the key. "Frankly, I'm in a bit of a situation. I asked your fiancé there to lend me some money, but nothing doing. Meanwhile the *vig* is killing me. You remember what that is?"

"Yes," I say. "Interest." Thinking, *Rourke's coming back.*

"Exactly," he says. "I would've told you about it, only Mark told me not to say anything. And until Pinky's last night, I wasn't sure where you stood with things."

"When will it be?"

"Soon as I can swing it," he says as he turns the ignition off. "Just be careful." He nods toward the figure approaching on the grass. "She's pretty touchy about fights."

"She's not going to mention fights to *me*—is she?"

"Hard to say." He leans to open his door. "She's got, like, ESP. It's weird." He swings around to my side, snap-jangling his keys and stretching a bit. He helps me to a stand, then tosses an arm over my shoulder, bending down into me. "Ready?"

Our footsteps clap on the crisscross brick. There is the *thsst-thsst-thsst* of a sprinkler and the *thwock* of a ball and a voice—*"Gloria-aaa."* And again, birds. Maybe the same birds as the other times I came, maybe different ones. I've forgotten the life span of a bird. Kate once had an African finch that lived for five years, but that is not the right type of bird. Funny to think of Kate's bird, but not Kate.

Rob says hi. She offers her cheek. He kisses it. "This is Eveline. Evie, this is Mrs. Rourke."

She plucks off her gardening gloves and extends a hand. "Eveline. Happy to meet you."

Her skin is the softest I've felt not on a baby. Her smile, her hair, her eyes—it's really very hard. I bite the bottom skin of my lip, inside my mouth where no one can see. Like her son, she projects an aura of radiant health. Her manner of speaking is faintly aristocratic. She married beneath herself, I think—she married for love. Rourke has that kind of beauty, the kind that comes from people in love.

"How are your parents, Rob?" she inquires.

"They're at each other's throats, so they must be okay."

"That's right. It's when they stop scrutinizing each other that you have to worry," she says with regal detachment.

Rob reaches for a cigarette, then recalls his hand. I've never seen him so edgy, except the time with Uncle Tudi. "Listen, Mrs. R., I gotta grab some stuff from the basement."

"Help yourself," she says. "When you're finished, I'd like you to carry down some boxes from the attic. They're stacked beneath the street-side window." She turns to me. "I'm giving everything away. You'd be shocked by what accumulates over a lifetime."

"A lifetime," Rob chides. "From the look of it, you've got at least two more of those to come, Mrs. Rourke."

"Careful with the compliments, Rob. You're liable to make me suspicious. Eveline and I will be inside. Come find us when you're finished."

He falters as he backs away, nearly tripping over a row of boxwoods. He straddles it, asking me, "You gonna be all right?"

"I won't rough her up, Rob," Mrs. Rourke says. "Promise."

She takes my arm to climb the porch. Each broad step of the five we mount is one upon which Rourke sat or walked, as a child, as an adolescent. Surely, at some point, the outline of my foot fills the melted-away outline of his foot.

Inside is cool. The corridor walls are papered with frail caramel pinstripes and columns of cyan. Tucked behind the curve in the base of the mahogany banister is an oval writing table with a silver-and-white pitcher full of purple irises.

The kitchen is airy and brightly lit, and what is wood is a pallid milk-ice blue. It is a cook's kitchen, spacious and fully implemented, with inflections of red—the clock, the dish towels, the moiré swirls in platters. I am seated at a table for eating, and in the corner to my right is another for working, which has a cherry-checked vinyl cloth. It is covered with an assortment of split-open cookbooks and textbooks with frayed paper page markers. She puts heat under the kettle and busies herself, withdrawing cups and plates from the china cabinet and a beer glass for Rob. Although I would not have expected her to be lonely, I'm amazed by how busy she is—the pile of mail, the ringing telephone. The world whirls about her.

I watch for signs of Rourke. They have a physical resemblance, but the bond between them is clearest to me in the subtleties of environment. There is nothing arduous or sentimental about her domesticity. Like his masculinity, her femininity is uncontrived. She moves too fast and too well to be false. Like her son, she's good because no one else is better. The house is charming, and yet I don't feel covetous. It's easy to be seduced at the Ross houses, or at the houses of their acquaintances, to become desirous of things you don't even want, such as Baccarat dolphins and inlaid walnut humidors. Here, instead, I feel pressured to comply with her independence of vision—though I barely know her, I don't want to disappoint. I feel she has faith in me, simply because she shares her time. I begin to count the minutes before I have to leave, before her influence will be lost. That too is familiar.

"This one's on pies." She's talking about cookbooks; she has written three. "I've baked and tasted just about every pie you can imagine—from apple to quince crumb to mincemeat." Mrs. Rourke rests back on the counter, facing me. Her eyes are like the dark of sky between stars. "I despise spice pies," she says. "Do you despise spice pies?"

"I don't know," I say softly. "I've never tasted one."

"Well, in this case, I'd say you're better off for your ignorance."

I think of Maman. If I am reminded of Kate's mother rather than my own it's not just because I loved her more, but because I have a limited inventory of imagery to draw upon when it comes to the business of the kitchen. But the comparison extends beyond food, beyond admiration and wonder; Mrs. Rourke has reached the same empty place in me that Maman filled. It makes me think how lucky I was to meet Maman when I was a girl. How auspicious for a woman with an abundance of resources to come upon a child with a surplus of lack. And, of course, how inauspicious to have died in the midst of that. I recall our awareness of the barter—it was like a tutorial. Next, in an unwelcome leap, I recall the germinating deadness of Maman's home, the picturesque dryness, the claiming-back process of nature.

I feel Mrs. Rourke's hand on my shoulder.

"Why don't you make a trip to the pantry while I pour the tea. There are cookie tins on the left. I'm giving my niece a baby shower. No one will notice if any are missing."

The right side of the slope-ceilinged room is lined with shelves, and to the left is an old meat safe or pie safe, which is where I find the canisters. There are three full ones; I take the one with children dancing. I turn to leave; the pantry door has drifted partly closed. On its back I see marks in the wood—a growth chart, his. My parents never measured my growth, not once, though that is nothing to me now. Now I see only Rourke, metamorphosing downward through the years. I kneel, touching each strike, knowing that he was there every time one was carved. I arrive at last at the first—twenty-nine inches, not much higher than my knee. I feel heart-stricken and regretful, as if flicking in reverse through a photo album of a child I gave away, at once jealous of and beholden to the woman who kept this simple study of him, this careful anthropology.

"This last one is Thanksgiving 1978." She is above me, on the other side of the door jamb. Through the narrow gap I see the cherry-printed dish towel in her hand. "Six-four. Although he might actually be taller now. He refuses to stand for me anymore."

No, I think, *he is six-four exactly.*

"Would you like to see the rest of the house?" she inquires. She finds in the gruesome clarity of my eyes what she surmised from the moment we met. She does not look away. Most people look away, unable to bear the sight of him there.

I say yes, and we go, leaving the tea untouched.

The tour she gives is not merely a tour of his childhood—where he smashed his head, where he carved his initials, where he took his first steps—but a scholarly sort of assessment, as if we are in professional accord as to the relevance of the obscurest technicalities of our shared passion.

She leads me to her room, the one I have seen from the street. An IBM Selectric rests on a table between stuffed barrister bookshelves, and there is a chintz chair with a cashmere blanket folded over one arm. Photographs of Rourke are everywhere—him upside down at two; him swinging a bat at eleven, his muscles already standing out; him brown at the beach, grown-up, hugging her, by a palm tree.

"Hawaii," she says. "We went for Christmas once. When he was still at UCLA."

There are old black-and-white photos, the square kind with scalloped edges, and bleached ones, in color, of a man—her husband. There is the boy on his father's knee in green; the two emerging from underwater in a pool, two faces the same; the infant tucked in the crease of his father's arm. Her fingers stutter over the photos.

"My husband and I eloped," she explains. "My mother refused to help us financially, though she was capable. My grandmother left this place to me, and soon after we moved in we had Harrison. Of course my mother fell in love with the baby and had an immediate change of heart. Every week new furniture would arrive, or silverware, or china. Bill's colleagues from the police department would visit and accuse him of accepting graft."

On a shelf with iron brackets, there is a row of random items. "Trinkets," she says, lifting one, tilting it. "Things I find in the garden— thimbles and buttons—rocks Harrison gave me when he was a boy. Beach glass. He was forever giving me beach glass."

I follow her to the end of the hall. Her left arm lengthens against a door and she pushes it, flattening back, allowing me to pass.

Rourke's room. There are trophies and ribbons and fight posters from the Olympic stadium in L.A., the Municipal Stadium in Philadelphia, and Madison Square Garden—Palomino vs. Muniz, Jersey Joe Walcott vs. Rocky Marciano, Ali vs. Frazier, and also ones from the Criterion— Harrison Rourke vs. Little Tommy Lydell, vs. Johnny Amato, vs. Piggy Harding, vs. Chester Honey Walker.

To the right is a dresser, a mirror, the keeper of his image, the bank of his appearances. It is not neutral; it seems to undulate. I can see him standing before it at various stages through the years, contemplating the twinness of self—the real and the reflected—coming up against the riddle of being. I think of him at twenty-four, when we first met, with me just seventeen, hardly anything really, negligible and slight and completely unable to help him comprehend the mysteries he surely must have been facing.

"He was born here," she says, looking at the bed. It is a double bed, perfectly made, as if she expects him home this very evening. On the bedpost is an autographed glove—Ray Mancini's. I sit and lift the glove, holding it in my lap.

"My husband was a detective assigned to lower Manhattan, to the First Precinct. He raced home, but Harrison was already halfway out." She gestures with a short toss of the head to the memorabilia. "Some of these belonged to Bill. He was a fighter in Ireland originally, in Belfast. I don't know how much you know."

"Only that he died."

"Fifteen years ago April." She lowers her eyes, then raises them. The charm of her eyes is accentuated by black bangs and prominent cheekbones. The remainder of her shoulder-length hair is pulled into a twist. I wonder about her ancestry. She is beautiful in the locked-off, genetically undiluted way of a Senegalese or a Norwegian. Perhaps she is Russian. "I gave this room to Harrison after he got into a knife fight. The doctor said he was fighting because he needed space. As if it's not in his blood."

She tours the room, adjusting artifacts like a museum proprietor. "After Bill died, it was like having a bull in the house. My sister suggested acting. For years I shuttled Harrison to and from New York for commercials, auditions, lessons. The idea was that if he was making money with his face, he would have some incentive to keep it presentable. Well, he tolerated acting, but he didn't stop fighting. He just became more selective about it."

There is a leonine clarity to her voice as she speaks of her son, as she visits the place her devotion is kept. She says to me, "They would bet, you know."

I did not know. Maybe I did. Maybe he told me. Yes, and Rob told me too. *There's gonna be a fight. The comeback kind.*

"He and Rob made a fortune when they were teenagers before I found out and threatened to have them arrested. Those were trying times. Thankfully, they met an elderly Chinese gentleman who taught them martial arts and introduced them to a trainer from the Criterion, Jimmy Landes."

I nodded. "I've heard of them."

"Despite my reservations, Harrison turned into a fine fighter. I don't know whether his father would have been proud or horrified." She looks up. "Have you ever seen him fight?"

I shake my head.

There is a flicker, a smile, instantly disappearing. "Naturally, everyone wanted him to turn professional. Naturally, I wanted him to go to college, and since his father would have wanted it as well, he consented. The boys were accepted to UCLA, which was the best of both worlds—they would be together, Harrison could pursue his interest in acting, and L.A. is full of gyms." Mrs. Rourke sits alongside me on the bed. "Rob majored in economics and went on for a second degree—he has an uncanny competence for numbers. Harrison stuck around and did some acting and some fighting, mostly fighting. He intended to get through the Olympics and then use the credential to get investors. He and Rob wanted to develop an athletic club, a few clubs. Somehow, it fell apart. Even before the Olympic boycott, it fell apart.

"When Rob received his master's degree, we all flew to California. Rob had a black eye—completely hemorrhaged, swollen shut. He was lucky his cheekbone hadn't been broken. We all knew that Harrison had done it. I felt awful for Mr. and Mrs. Cirillo. Their whole family was there. Fortuna's parents had flown from Bologna. I took Rob aside. I said, 'Robert, your eye.' 'Don't worry about it, Mrs. Rourke,' he assured me, 'It was all my fault. I said something stupid.' 'What could you possibly have said to deserve this?' I asked. And he said, *The wrong thing.*' Do you know, I still wonder what the *wrong thing* could have been."

I pour the reboiled water; she sets cookies on plates. Rob makes the last of several trips to the attic. There is the machine gun stomping of footsteps. She likes the noise; it's been a long time. We lift our steaming cups, eyes connecting above china.

"I'm glad you came," she says. "I hope it won't be the last time." Her eyes search my face. She reaches across the table, touching my hair. "It's longer now. It used to be very short."

"I'm sorry," I say. "I don't understand."

"There's a picture he carries. You were in the high school when he took it, he said. In a gymnasium."

———

On our way down the porch steps, she calls out for us to wait. She returns with a letter for Rourke, asking Rob to mail it. Rob is farther than I am, so I reach, taking it in my hands.

"Goodbye again," she says, grasping my hands. I feel something pass from her to me: courage, confidence, soundness.

If you think it's impossible to feel worse than the worst you've ever felt, you're wrong. Worse than numb, worse than solitude and despair, is to possess one particle of hope, to feel the feel of fate brushing so close you think you will die. I say goodbye as well.

Rob honks twice, and we back out and drive away. He pulls up at the first mailbox.

"Not this one," I tell him. "The next." I hold the letter tightly—his name, knowingly printed.

He leans on the accelerator.

"How did his father die?"

Rob reaches to smack down his visor. We must have turned west. The sun, going down.

"He was murdered. By the brother of a guy he killed. He was on duty; he threw a punch and killed a guy. A fluke. A robbery on Chambers Street. The kid's brother came down from Detroit to settle. He got killed too. Billy Rourke's partner shot him. In the face. It was bad. It was a fucking mess."

"How old were you?"

"Fourteen. We were fourteen."

44

Mr. and Mrs. Ross are in Los Angeles, so Mark throws an impromptu party at their glamorous apartment with their glamorous things—food, wine, staff. Mark is careful not to call it an *engagement party;* after the disastrous night with Rob, he knows better. He keeps asking to pick a time to tell my parents "the news," and I keep suggesting that we wait until we see them in person.

The guests look like pigs. Like pigs in suits. All the eyes look dead and round in faces that are compilations of parts—teeth and noses and millions of hairs blown and combed, and lips that liberate opinions through tangles of smoke, sideways disclosures about mentions in *Variety* and the luminescence of diamonds. I stay by my seat. I know it is mine because there is a card with my name. The card is the color of spoiled cream, and the ink is a sort of ochre.

Through the window behind my upholstered dining chair, the city churns, an ocean of catastrophe and chance. A red light windmills and swipes across the treetops of Central Park; an ambulance retrieves a body and delivers it to the aid of strangers. We are high in the air, but we cannot escape the violence of the streets. We content ourselves not to see— it is not the fact of indigence that distresses us, just the spectacle. I remind myself that the red lights are a sign. Every night is the worst night of someone's life. It's easy to forget that.

It is time to turn; I turn. Arms come together like branches of a star rising over the center of the table. Jeweled fingers and gold-cuffed wrists grip clear tulips. Candlelight inhabits the champagne, making it like effervescent caramel.

"Hear, hear," they say, and we drink—to Mark, his promotion, his engagement. His *success*.

There is epic meaning in the erect and stately circle we form, in the alliance of ready arms, in the fists clutching the brittle glass. A toast is a ritual aside, a communal departure, a type of prayer. We step out of time because we have vanquished it. We are superior to the things of which we speak. I think of valorous knights and courageous kings, of notable deeds forgotten, great heroes dead and gone.

"A second toast," Mark says, his voice fashioning tenderness. "To Eveline." He gestures to me, they gesture to me, and I bow to straighten my perfect dress, which hangs against me perfectly. In the glimmering moon of my china plate, I discover a watery likeness of my face. Mindful of the way I hang my head, I right myself to confront the sea of eyes. "May the rest of our lives be as happy as these three years have been."

"*Salud,*" they murmur kindly, though they are not kind. To them I begin and end with Mark. He is my origin and objective. To them I am no more than what I appear to be. They go to lengths to keep me in the prison of their view.

"Hurry up and drink," Alicia says. "Dinner in twenty minutes."

Bodies cleave from the table, forming genial clusters. I wait for an opening, which is like waiting to be picked for a team.

"Three years," a voice thunders from behind my back. The voice belongs to Brett. "A long time, Eveline. A damn long time."

I'm uncertain whether this is true. Sometimes a year is lavish and profuse, riotous as a gale. Sometimes it goes breath by breath by breath. Minutes can be critical, decades without meaning, and so I might say, but he is done with me. My reticence is proof to him of my stupidity. To Brett I am useless unless seen. He scans the crowd hoping we've been noticed. He feels manly when he stands with me, just as some people feel learned when they carry books. His gaze returns to my body. His eyes are mean and his skin prematurely wrinkled, and a shock of brittle hair marks the center of his skull. His nails are manicured, and beneath his cashmere turtleneck his breasts droop. The proposition he makes with his eyes is stealthy and simple—money, power, and comfort in exchange for sex. I wonder by what error of nature he has come to feel so virile. And yet his audacity is not without weight. Brett is a man of business, of wealth and renown. No opportunity is to be left unexplored, no friend so dear that he cannot be betrayed.

Maybe I will take him with me into the kitchen, where appliances gleam harshly in kitchen light, sending back warped ideas of yourself. In the kitchen, I will let him touch me—he would like that. His greedy fingers kneading my flesh, cramming into scars—scars are everywhere, no matter where you touch, you cannot miss. "Yes," I will say to Brett, through the icy kitchen glare. "Three years is a very long time."

My glass is empty. I hold it by its stem, considering the delicacy of the marks I make. My fingerprints are specific and small, like baby bridges. I think of fossils, fishy and particular, weary cadavers in khaki rock— proving, proving something.

Brett and I are joined by Dara and a man named Swoosey Schicks, whose name sounds like a drunk with castanets. They discuss treasury bonds and Reagan's Star Wars missile plan, cycling in Bali, and the price of Brett's 14-carat-gold octagon Rolex—$1,950. Across the room Mark begins to dance with Amy, a redhead who appeared in *Amadeus*. Or maybe *A Passage to India*.

"Uh-oh," Brett says, nudging me. "Things are beginning to get interesting."

I excuse myself. I go to the bathroom. It is the one place to hide. Men want to know what women do in bathrooms. They *hide*.

I sit on the edge of the bathtub. It is a round-edged prewar New York tub. I don't need to pee, but anyway I lift my dress and lower my stockings to my knees. The division is strange, black to white. I touch each side of the division, one side and the other, jumping the line, my finger popping—nylon to skin, skin to nylon. From the elastic of my bra, I remove a small pen, and on my thigh I draw some fossils, rose fossils, which are petrified rose remains. Last time I saw my dad we ate gelato and he gave me a newspaper article about rose fossils dating back thirty-two million years. Also on my leg I write my name. My dad—I haven't seen him in a long time. Gelato means summer.

Behind the shower curtain above the tub is a tall window set deep in a tiled rectangular cubby. It looks onto a sheet of brick, which is the neighboring building. Outside is music from an adjacent apartment. The song comes from a time when music used to say who you were, not how to look, and life was like a dream you dreamt streaking by like you're staring out of a speeding vehicle. Nights were dark then, black, like mother of coal.

I climb into the tub. I push the shampoo bottles to one side of the sill and crank the window open. Some dust blows in, a little ash.

> *Do you say your prayers little darlin',*
> *Do you go to bed at night*
> *Prayin' that tomorrow, everything will be alright.*

The song curls in the air shaft between buildings before getting drawn out through the duct. I follow its route. Sometimes you see a balloon going that way, bobbing in jerks against nothing, like a toy retracted by

God. It's sad to see a balloon disappear that way; it makes you nostalgic. It is seeing the child you once were and conceding that more are coming—you are not the last.

Quiet now; not quiet, just the whimper and rumor of voices skulking through the fissure between door and floor. At the sink I wash my hands. I unravel a strip of toilet paper to wipe my footprints from the bottom of the tub. It's not that I'm neat; it's just that I have so much time to kill.

When the guests have gone, we go back to bed in his childhood room, where we first had sex. I wonder if the last time will be in this bed too. That would be good, a last time.

Mark's body approaches mine. His hands tow across my skin like damp mitts. I feel without feeling, which is nothing, which is easy, like sterile mechanics. I am thankful he does not insist upon cognizance. There are certain things a girl cannot tolerate.

There is a place to go, a place no one can access—a barrier. I do not know what it blocks, but I move to it, journeying, further and deeper, to reach—I don't know, just a place.

"You okay?" Mark asks when it is over. He always asks.

"I'm okay," I say as I sit up, "just thirsty." This is not a lie. The thirst is supreme, as though inside I have shriveled. I stand at his parents' refrigerator, drinking everything, one container at a time, moving left to right so I can keep track of those that I have emptied. I hate to raise an empty container as if it is full—the way your hand flies up, deceived.

In the living room window, I see myself, white from blue moonlight or blue from white moonlight. My arms look like dead arms, clipped to my shoulders by pins, dangling; I watch as my image detaches from my silhouette, stepping away.

I see her. She touches her cheek; my arm remains hanging. She pivots, winding one quarter around, though I am still. Her hands draw behind her back and rest airily on the rise beneath it. *I know this girl,* I think. She may be the one I once was. She is driven. I too was driven.

I wish to speak, to say something. But things that are legible to the senses are often captive to language, such as the dizzying faraway feeling you get from the way daylight pools on the kitchen floor, mesmerizing you in the midst of sudden misfortune, making you think of the frailty of life—and the beauty. Or the shimmery persistence of a perfume that lingers in the air, filling you with longing when you pass through it. No words can describe what it means to lose someone you love, or tell what it is to grieve.

And loneliness. I should say something of loneliness. The panic, the sweeping hysteria that comes not when you are without others, but when you are without yourself, adrift. I should describe the filthy province of mind, the blighted district inside, the place so crowded you cannot raise the lids of your eyes, and your chest is bruised by the constant assault of your heart. I want to convey the burden of despair, the ruin of compromise. *Be brave,* I should say to the girl in the glass, the way brave used to be—desperate to live and to love. I want her to prepare for the curse of perseverance. She may not know about resiliency. That she will last.

My belly still hums from coming. I wonder—can she see me? I hope not. I don't want her to know that sex here is loveless, that here I achieve a goal, an end, like reaching for a ring. But no—she sees nothing. She recedes, slipping back to the chamber of my heart where I reserve the essence of her, and of him. Secretly I keep us, a rustling quilt of madness unfolding like pealing chapel bells that go gradually softer and further, twining in and around, extending beneath and beyond anything anyone can perceive. I cannot say that I loved him—it wouldn't be enough. I can say that I've watched myself die, and that I've seen my lips form his name with my final breath.

45

There are those who attempt to manipulate fate. There are those who gamble for purposes of self-deception. They are stranded on their paths but want to feel otherwise. They want to feel the thrill of determination. They play with chance. They live a reality in which the potential of any single win pales in comparison to the game. This sort of risk is not for the faint of heart. This is Rob.

There are those who leave nothing to chance. They will not be seduced. They connive and hoard to distend the aggregate of what they are, all the while straining down the world to something small, like a stone to clench. The refusal to be enticed is a means of control, a way to guarantee they are not violated, a way to exploit the business about them. It is a matter of determining truth before it determines you. Mark.

There are those who risk to ascertain that they have nothing, that they need nothing. They are open to prospect and blind to hazard because they've been hurt, which is just another way of saying *informed.* They are bodies moving through space, inviolate and impermeable. They are full on the inside; nothing beyond can speak on their behalf. They require no validation; they are owners of themselves. That is Rourke. At one time, it was me too.

I don't know whether life is pre-decided. Perhaps it can be better conceived of as a series of hallways, growing wider or growing narrower, depending upon your receptivity to chance. The trick is to stand always at the crest of fate, to become proficient at response. Never get stuck thinking small, thinking slow, thinking any one state a finality; otherwise, life turns stagnant—the hallways narrow. This is an abuse of the gift of mobility.

When I lost Rourke, I shut down to chance. I risked nothing. I left the table. Once out, you do not get invited back. You have to charm your way, muscle your way.

I look like a whore. On the way downtown everyone stares at the way I'm dressed. At home I tried on several outfits, but no matter what I chose, I looked like a whore. The problem is, I don't know how to be. I don't know whether to be the girl I was, the one who came alive through his eyes, or the other one, the one I've become, proof of the mistake he made in leaving me. Anyway, I won't go back to the girl. I'm afraid to go back. That's why I look like a whore: dressing this way is a type of armor.

I take four concrete flights up to a loft north of Chinatown on Lafayette near Cleveland Place. A letter-board at the head of the stairs lists classes and events. Fridays at four is NYPD combat Tai Chi. *Today's guest is boxer and Olympic trainer Harrison Rourke.*

Twenty-five guys sit in a semicircle listening to a diminutive Chinese man in a canvas robe and loose pants—Mr. Xinwu. The Chinaman. The room is lined with trophies and banners with Chinese lettering. To my right there are framed quotes and photographs of famous Tai Chi masters—Yang Chengfu, Zheng Maqing, Ben Lo, Wang Shujin. There is a huge parchment paper document with a line by Lao-Tsu from the "Tao Te Ching."

> *Those who master others are strong;*
> *Those who master themselves have true power.*

Right away I find Rourke, the way a magnet finds north. My throat tightens. His large back is there among all the other large backs, his cotton jacket taut across it, wrinkled at the arms same as the other wrinkled jackets; still, I would know his back anywhere.

"Body makes root in earth for *chi* power." Mr. Xinwu explains as he demonstrates drills—silk-reeling, push hands, sparing gong. "Root prevents fighter from being thrown. A blade of grass does not attack wind or hide from wind. It *yields* to wind. It has *root*. Meaning of root is same as good woman—keeps man straight in unbalanced time." Everyone laughs, then gravely he adds, "Root more lethal than gun.

"Special guest Mr. Harrison Rourke is Western boxer. Tai chi helps Mr. Rourke," he continues. "Western boxer stands too much upright, a stand-up body go down. Body hitting ground is too painful!" Everyone laughs again; Mr. Xinwu laughs too. "Number one objective for boxer—*incorporation of pain*. Boxer has to stay standing when getting hit. Tai chi teaches Mr. Rourke to *yield*—like grass in wind."

Mr. Xinwu nods to Rourke, and Rourke rises to join him. Rourke sets his feet shoulder-width apart, bending at the knees and tucking the hips. He breathes deeply, hollows his chest, and raises his back like the hood of a cobra. I try to imagine him preparing for a fight; I follow his actions as though witnessing a metamorphosis. I can almost see the leathering of the skin, the shoring up of the under-muscle, and beneath that, the organs shrinking back; the pulse stopping up, the steadiness of his body dropping to the steadiness of the floor, dropping to the steady chill of the earth. It suddenly looks as if he is holding an invisible ball.

Mr. Xinwu refers to this empty space, calling it *peng*. *Peng* is protective energy, he says, that helps ward off attacks.

When Rourke turns in profile, he sees me. He does not look, or divert his gaze, and yet, I feel his attention attach. Something shoots through me, like a charge. Physically, there is desire, and shock—it's been so long. Immediately after come things borne of the mind—the pity of wasted time, the injustice of lost access, the sick lie of myself, the way I am dressed. The idea of being alone with him is suddenly terrifying. I step back, thinking to leave, but I stumble. I step back once more and lean against the wall.

"Yield to overcome," Xinwu admonishes, his eyes flickering in my direction. "Bend to be straight. Feel for your opponent, ask what is weak, what is strong? What is solid, what is empty?"

Xinwu readies himself. Rourke also readies. They incline their heads and chests ceremoniously. "When my friend was a small boy, he was making street fights," Xinwu relates haltingly as they begin formally to spar. "When he came to me, he was big mess—very brave, very lacking skill." Rourke snaps a kick, which Xinwu blocks with incredible economy of action. "I say, 'Mr. Rourke, you think too much. Do too much. You act when you need to wait.' I say, 'You use *power*. You need to use *direction of power*.' "

They break, moving again, like sculptures painstakingly positioned and repositioned. They stop, they turn. They go lightning fast, then dead slow. It's beautiful, really—Rourke towering over his friend, and yet he is no match. Xinwu anticipates every next move almost as if he can read the objective of Rourke's muscles.

"Recently my friend returned—still very brave, now more skillful, still big mess. I say, 'Mr. Rourke, first control emotion to control body. First find *silence*.' " Mr. Xinwu moves in and finishes to the body. Rourke's body is hard, like brick; but anyway, it gives, folding in and down, going gracefully to the floor. I suppose there are tender points, like hinges. Even skyscrapers can collapse.

Rourke stands and everyone applauds. Mr. Xinwu nods, excusing him, and Rourke passes through to me.

We meet in the hall. His hands locate my waist like picking a flower at the exact right place on the stem. I snap off the floor as he lifts me. His face has changed over the past three years. There are infinitesimal lines and recesses in the muscles, like code writing only I can read.

"I thought I saw you earlier," he says. "On Prince Street. But it wasn't you." He pulls me tighter, then he lowers me, stepping back.

"When did you get in?" I ask.

"A few hours ago."

"You haven't seen Rob yet?"

"No," Rourke says. "I came here straight from the airport."

"He's meeting you later?" I want to know when they will talk, when Rob will tell him everything.

"Yeah, he'll give me a ride to my house."

Mr. Xinwu is talking about throwing an opponent's balance without causing harm, about trying to feel love for those things one hopes to protect rather than hatred for the adversary.

"How is it out west?" I ask.

He shrugs. "Not much different than here. Ever been there?"

I nod, clumsily, clumsy to admit that I've been to his particular part of the world without him, to invoke Mark even by implication. Mark and I went skiing in Aspen twice.

Rourke's eyes stir; his weight shifts. Though I say no more, I've lost him. I can read his intent before it is manifest. I am like Mr. Xinwu. A master.

Would it help Rourke to know that I looked for him everywhere— every restaurant, every bar, every street. I tried so hard to see him that sometimes I did see him, only it was not him. Didn't he just say, *I thought I saw you. It wasn't you.*

We turn awkwardly and stare into the main room, watching the cops drift into pairs. One of each set turns his back to the wall, and the other faces him. "Remember," Xinwu is saying, "confrontation is inevitable. Those who resort to violence have not mastered nonviolence. Keep control. Neutralize pushes. The only separation between you and a man in jail is control. And for police, control is a special obligation."

I try to think of something to say. I ask Rourke if this is what he taught at the prison that time.

"More or less," he replies stiffly. "More respect. Less combat."

"Do you still do it?"

"Go into prisons? Not too much. Xinwu does it regularly."

"And boxing? How does boxing fit into this?"

"This teaches control," Rourke replies. "Boxing takes control."

"As opposed to street fighting."

"With organized fights there's shared weight or class; with street fights, it's a match of intention. How much something means to you versus how much it means to your opponent. You could lose everything."

Everything, yes. A wife, a son, your life.

"Well, I'd better head back in," he says.

"I guess I—should—you know, get going too."

The staircase is tight and fireproof gray. I start down, gripping the rail. He's there, near me, leaning. Over the harp of bars we kiss.

"Goodbye," he says courteously. "It was good to see you."

I've never been the victim of his courtesy before. He hands it off like a bomb. His elbows are on the rail. He is bending and his jacket splits and I can see inside to where it is beautiful. I don't simply see that it's beautiful, I *feel* that it is beautiful. I *respond* to beauty. I can't remember the last time I responded to anything. I have so much at stake. I have only seconds. I am about to say, *Rourke*. But he speaks first.

"Tell Mark I said congratulations," Rourke says, stripping the towel from his neck, shaking it at his side, looping it back over his shoulders.

The GTO skids up as Mark and I exit the apartment building. It moves alongside us, plowing into the asphalt like a grounded meteor. My first thought is that I haven't seen the car for so long. Seeing the car is different from seeing him. It's as if there has been no car since, as if his car is the *only* car. It was the place where you kept your clothes and heard your music and ate and slept and had sex; it was a car when you needed to move. Since then there have been only vehicles. My second thought is that Rourke is angry. Rob must have told him everything on the drive down to the shore. I wonder if he saw his mother, if she'd told him of my visit.

Mark leans to the roof, and his foot slips off the curb. I'd never seen him slip before. "Harrison! What a surprise. What are you doing here?"

Rourke just says, "Get in."

"Thanks, but my car's right there." Mark points to the garage.

"Mine's right here." Rourke leans to pop the door. "Get in."

Mark bites his lip. "Let me tell the garage to repark it." He jogs across the street—not fast, not slow, but calculated, like arithmetic. It kills him to leave me at the door of Rourke's idling car, but he has to pretend at least to trust I'll be there when he returns.

Rourke's arm rests on the seat back: he stares down its length to where I stand. My body is conspicuous through my dress. A gust of wind hits my hips; I lean into it, the dress impressing deeply. With him there I feel like something soaring, something engaged in flight. I bend to pull the seat lever, knocking it forward with my knee. I climb in back and sink into the corner of the car, feeling secure. When Mark surfaces and cuts back over the street, Rourke simply observes him, his eyes like an assassin's.

Mark shuts the door. "Cirillo told me you just got in from Colorado. How is it out there?"

"It's all right," Rourke says, shoving the stick into first.

"When did you land?" Mark asks.

"This morning."

At the traffic light on the corner, Mark says, "Where to?"

Rourke turns south on Ninth Avenue. He replies, "Around."

At Old Town Bar on East Eighteenth Street, we take a table—Mark and me with our backs to the wall and Rourke facing us. It's like we're at an interview. Rourke draws his chin into his neck and drops his head to the left, and a girl appears as if in response to a silent whistle. What an obligation to be him, to possess such formidable powers of seduction, such dread competence.

"I'll take a Beck's," he says. "Bring one for her as well."

"Do you even *want* a beer?" Mark asks me, laying his elbow on the table and pointing lazily to the waitress, to me, to the waitress. "Actually, she'll have some white wine. What kinds do you have?"

"What kinds of what?" the waitress replies.

"Wine. What kinds of wine."

She furrows her brow and says, "House!"

"House," Mark repeats. "Would that be something you people express in the basement? Why don't you go check on the available vintages and come back with your findings?"

"Don't worry about it," I say to her. "Whatever you have is okay."

Rourke just sits, almost meditatively.

"Tell you what," Mark snaps. "Bring the most expensive bottle you can find. And a Stoli. Double. Rocks." As soon as she returns with the drinks, he tells her, "Gimme another Stoli."

I check his glass. It's true. It's already empty.

Mark dumps vodka after vodka down his throat, and Patty keeps my wineglass filled. Her name is Patty; I know, because Rourke asked. He turned his head insinuatingly into the tonnage of his own shoulder, just as a boa caresses its own mass and mean, and as she bent to exchange glassware, he asked, "What's your name?"

She reddened, fast and strange, like a flower infused with artificial color. Beneath her wispy black hair, she said shyly, "Patty."

I'm jealous of the way Rourke admires her, the way she is pretty and hardworking and uncompromised. I used to be that way too, uncompromised at Heartbreak and prior to that, uncompromised at the Lobster Roll, and pretty when I paid my own way and possessed firmness of will. I too used to be modest. Now I am at liberty to be immodest and indecent and indiscreet. I belong to Mark—to his circle and legion—like a cadet belongs to the military. I am a recruit, a conscript, an instrument. I cannot be hurt; I have an army. I am anonymous and inaccessible. Like most disciples, I was chosen because my need exceeds my reason. I was chosen because, unlike Rourke, I am without character.

I wonder how many glasses I've had. Eleven, I think.

Rourke says not quite. "More like three."

He hasn't been drinking at all; Mark doesn't even realize. Mark keeps ordering more rounds, and Rourke keeps exchanging full bottles of beer for new full ones. Him winking at Patty, her smiling back.

Mark jabs loosely at the air. "So. Who do you—plan to, you know."

"Spar with?" Rourke says. "Whoever's around. There's a kid from Ghana who's pretty good."

"Well, you'd better figure it out. You only have—what do you have?"

"Eight days," Rourke says.

"Eight days? And you're out drinking beers? You'd better get serious. It's been a long time for you. I hear Tommy Lydell's chomping at the bit. What happened to the old guy—the one you used to train with?"

"Jimmy Landes? He's still down in Florida."

"Better find somebody new."

Rourke shakes his head. "Nobody's like Jimmy. I'd rather go it alone."

"Well, as I like to say, everyone is replaceable."

"Not everyone," Rourke says.

Mark hangs his head and studies the tabletop as though he is taking an exam. He is exceedingly drunk. His tongue protrudes when he talks, making me think of Venus flytraps. Once Denny told me flytraps have throat hairs that are stimulated by motion, that's why they eat only living things. The movement is important because they get just about six meals per lifetime. "Can you imagine," Denny said, "wasting one of the six on a twig or a rock or something?"

"Be right back," Mark says. He stumbles to a stand and staggers into the shoulders of the crowd.

I look at Rourke exclusively. It's been a long time since I've seen him exclusively. Earlier in the day, he was in a room full of people. Men. Cops. Earlier in the day he knew nothing about Mark, about what Mark had done, about how far I'd fallen, how weak I was.

"It's strange," I say. "Do you feel strange?"

"Little bit." His words slip like pebbles across ice, shooting off and away as they are dropped. His eyes are adamantine, like black diamonds. He leans across, and the glasses make way, parting like a sea. There is a song playing.

With her killer graces and her secret places that no boy can fill.
With her soft French cream standin' in that doorway like a dream.

He presses into me, knocking forward, his hands locking down my shoulders. My arm tears a little, I make a sound—"Oh"—shooting out, and I bite down hard on my lip accidentally drawing blood. We kiss, and the red seeps in. The taste of him is sweet. He pulls back, an inch, less, the thickness of paper.

"Is that how you kiss him," he says, foully, like I am foul.

Maybe it's all the alcohol or just the flavor of blood stitched to the perfume of his saliva, but I feel something animal. I wonder what it would be to kill him. If I held a knife, would it be easy to employ? I think of the virile final feel, the passage of his influence. His throat, turning limp, hot as he collapses into me like a dying gargantuan thing, like an anvil plowing.

I have to get away, so I pull myself up and head to the bathroom. The floor heaves beneath me as I walk through a slough of saloonish greens and browns. Mark glides past me in the opposite direction, not even noticing. In the bathroom I decide to vomit. Alicia says it is easy, which it is. The liquor shoots out, *plop, plop,* and then a barrage of plops, and, okay, I feel better. I wipe icy paper towels on my face and my neck and rinse my mouth with water.

At the bar, I ask for a lemon wedge, and I stand there, leaning, eating it. Mark and Rourke are toasting; I cannot imagine to what. Living in a world with men is like being in the center of a ring with hands spinning you in a circle. It's like being spun, three-quarters one way, one-half the other, one full time back around. Wherever you land, there's another set of hands. Men like you to believe they are dangerous when typically they are not. How can they be dangerous when there are so many things they want that they won't talk about? When secretly you want a thing, you make mistakes.

I thank the bartender for the lemon.

He gives me another one and says, "Anytime, sweetheart."

I'm not a sweetheart, I've never been a sweetheart, but it's nice of him to call me one and to remind me that things don't always have to be that way. Someday maybe I will be someone's sweetheart and that someone will take me to Great Adventure on a Saturday in June and camping in Vermont and he will buy me running shoes for Christmas. I return to the table and wonder what would have to change before I could become a sweetheart. Something big would have to change, I think.

———

Rourke parks far enough away from the entrance to the building that none of the neighbors will see Mark, who is passed out in the front seat.

Rourke steps out of the car and offers me his hand, helping me out of the back. He comes around to the curb with me and he leans on the rear fender, quietly regarding the quiet street. I lean too, gripping the trunk to anchor myself. In Rourke's face there is a light. It brightens, it dims. I don't know where the light is coming from. The west, I think. I look for the river. I don't see it, though it's not far. There is hissing from the sewer beneath us; blasts of smoke skulk around our ankles.

"So," I say, "next Saturday." I try to speak without slurring; I hear myself trying.

He doesn't answer. His arms are folded against his chest. I look at his arms in wonder; I think of me inside the ring of them, of him inside me. It's been years. How many women have there been? For some reason I can't stop thinking of the volatile mechanics of his sex, of him fucking other women—though I suppose just one would be bad enough. Actually, one would be worse. One gives me an indication of how he feels about Mark.

"Well," I continue, my head swinging a bit. "Good luck."

Him not moving. "You'll be there."

"I won't be there."

"You'll be there," he repeats.

"I don't think I—" I wave one hand, ending there.

"Mark won't let you miss it. He's betting I get killed."

Carlo steps out to help the Morrisseys unload luggage and sleeping children from their car. The kids are two and four with matching bear slippers. Carlo looks over and notices me and gestures; he'll be right over.

"And if I refuse?"

"You won't. Rob needs you."

"Rob needs money. I have no money."

Rourke shrugs. "You *pull* money."

"And you?"

"Me? I pull a crowd. I fight and go home. I'm like you. I'm helping a friend. I don't care who wins."

Carlo's footsteps. Him jogging over, waving apologetically. Together he and Rourke hoist Mark from the front seat, and when they stand, Mark sags down, hanging out at the knees and in at the chest, like a scarecrow. "Got him, sir!" Carlo declares, and Rourke ducks, leaving the two to shuffle off into the overbright lobby.

I turn to Rourke, tipping in, taking hold of his shirt. The front of me on the front of him, my face by his chest. I breathe in. I study him. I feel for the remains of other women—memories of breasts, of legs, quivering throats and swollen lips, the smell of them, the taste. I should be able to find his memories, the chain that they make. But when I touch him, I find the same man I touched the first time I touched him, only now there is no openness. That's because I closed it—closed him. In feeling for others, I simply find myself.

He looks back, unflinchingly. I don't mind. I don't mind to lose a little grace when by his eyes I possess so much. "You're wrong, Harrison," I say, using his true name for the first time ever. "I *do* care who wins."

In the morning Mark rolls off the couch. Immediately he talks. Everyone says it's good to talk, but frequently those who do are no better off than those who don't.

"What the fuck was that all about?" he says, rubbing his head.

I check my watch. Rourke is awake. Thinking, not talking. By now he's at the gym; he's already been running. Eight miles, ten miles.

"What a fucking idiot," Mark says on his way into the kitchen. "Showing up like that."

Despite his hangover, he looks fine, like an antique. He has begun to gray prematurely, and the new pewter tinge suits his doggish capitalist charm. Any woman would be happy to have him. He punctures a can of tomato juice, fills a glass, and drains it. He peers at me through the framed passage over the hygienic white counter that separates the kitchen from the dining room. The counter is bare. Mark does not allow things on counters. No fruit, no papers, no vases, no dish rack. *Dish racks harbor bacteria,* he says. That's why there are no sponges, only paper towels. In public restrooms he flushes with his elbow and pulls towels from the dispenser before he washes his hands. One for turning the faucet, one for drying.

He lays the glass in the sink and wipes his mouth. "Did he *confide* in you? Did he tell you that he doesn't *care* who wins? That he's just doing Rob a *favor*?" He approaches me, coming around. "Don't be stupid. There is no fight. There's a scam, a fraud, a hustle. It's pre-arranged. Harrison's taking the fall. That's why he came last night. To prepare you. It's gonna kill him to get beaten. But Rob's in too deep with the wrong people—he has to have a guarantee. A loss is the only way he can guarantee the outcome. He asked me for the money, but I told him I can't get involved. Believe me," Mark says, "I'll do my part. I'll fill the house. But I have a reputation to uphold. I have *you* to think about. That's why, after this, that's it. We're done with this ghetto crew. We can't walk into our future dragging this shit behind us."

Mark is in front of me; we're face-to-face.

"Harrison's an animal," Mark states, "just like his murderer father. Did he tell you that his father was a murderer? Of course not. Because he's a liar. He lied to you all along." Mark reaches out quickly, but I don't blink my eyes. He slaps his hand around the back of my neck and folds me into his arms. "I feel bad for you, sweetheart, I really do. He lied about everything."

"Yes," I say. "Yes. I see that now."

46

The day of the fight he fucks me very hard, like he knows it will be the last time. "Shit," Mark says when he is done, "you are a sweet taste in the mouth."

The Cougar is double-parked outside Astor Place haircutters. I toss my bag through the open window onto the front seat. I get in and shut the door and Rob takes off.

"Nice haircut," he says. "Reminds me of the old times out in Montauk. You gotta check out this French flick, *Breathless*. Jean Seberg plays this little American girl with chopped hair and Jean-Paul Belmondo's cut really tight."

He bounces in his seat as he drives. The night is hot and Rob likes when it's hot. That's because he's a Leo, and Leos are sun kings, and Napoleon was a Leo. On Rob's chest is a new tattoo—inside the globe of a plankton-green sun, it says *Roi de Soleil*. He got it in New Orleans, at Mardi Gras. Mardi Gras tattoos bring luck. I switch on the radio.

Cisco Kid was a friend of mine. Cisco Kid was a friend of mine.

The car turns widely off Houston and onto the Bowery. Outside my window the skies are marbleized blue-black, like out of mythology. Skies like a storm is coming, only no storm is coming. Skies that make you homesick, only there is no home. When we hit Delancey Street, the prostitutes tap the hood of the car. They wave to Rob. *Hey.*

"A case of mistaken identity," Rob says to me. "I mean it, baby, I swear."

In the Cirillos' driveway, Rob's sister, Christine, says, "Everybody in the pool. That's the law." Christine works the watch counter at Bloomingdale's. If you want a watch, go to her. "I'm giving you five minutes, Evie," she warns. "A grace period. Then I'm coming to find you."

The first time I went to Rob's parents' house, I made the mistake of heading for the front door. "What are you," Rob asked, "the mailman? The last people to go in that way were relatives from Italy." *It-lee.*

The back door by the barbecue leads to the kitchen, which is full of aunts and grandmothers and elderly female neighbors. You can see the ladies through the screen, briefly making contact, like flies against a window. Arms to the elbows appear to hand off trays of peppers and sausages to fry.

Mrs. Cirillo works the grill. "In most families, Eveline," she explains as she flinches into the charcoal smog to flip a rack of ribs, "this is a man's work. But, what happens is, Dom gets to talking and everything burns."

"I'll do it, Ma." Rob grabs at the tongs. "C'mon."

"No, Robert," she says, "take care of the company."

From the upstairs bathroom window I can see the family swept up in a sort of insular and happy confusion that is enviable but that can't possibly last. Christine has everyone running in the water to make a whirlpool, while Rob's father leans wearily on the ladder, spraying non-comers randomly with the hose.

"Christine's the ambassador of the pool," Mr. Cirillo calls out. "I'm the artillery."

In the far corner of the yard, Joey hovers protectively over his wife, Anna, who sits sideways on a lounge chair feeding the baby, who's almost five now, though they still call him "the baby," and their older son, Charlie. Everybody pretends that Rob is no good and Joey is the family man, but Joey's the one they worry about. Rob's lawlessness has a complementary decency, but Joey's righteousness is forced, like he's bored of it, like any day he's gonna snap. There's another brother, in L.A., Anthony, good-looking. No one mentions Anthony; there are no pictures—except one buried deep inside Rob's wallet.

Joey removes his shirt and adjusts the band of his shorts. "C'mon, Charlie. Let's go swamp Aunt Chrissie."

Directly beneath the bathroom window is the back porch and the keg, and Rob filling pitchers. I can see the top of his head. Christine splashes at him. "Rob. Get *ova* here." Without even looking, he steps casually to the side so the water can't reach, like he knows the exact measurement from the pool to the keg.

"Forget about it," Joey taunts as he climbs the ladder behind Charlie. "He won't let Evie see him in a suit."

"Nonsense. Robert hates to get wet," Mrs. Cirillo chides. "He always has. He's like a cat."

"In my day a kid never passed up water," Mr. Cirillo says. "It's not natural."

"What do I want to get cold for?" Rob says. "It's been a long winter. I'm just starting to heat up again."

When I come back out, I join the tangle of bodies, strollers, and pocketbooks clustered around the tables in the driveway. Christine's Dominican boyfriend, Ray Peña, is passing out clear keg cups high to the brim with daiquiris decorated with umbrellas and naked ladies. Rob says the plan is to get people in the *betting mood*.

"Big bets are already down," Rob explained to me earlier on the car ride over, "but ringside is critical. You can really rake it in ringside."

Lorraine is there with a bunch of girls, cousins probably. Everyone's either a cousin or they work in the meat or the fish market. All you hear is, *eat the fish—it's fresh; eat the beef—it's fresh.* Lorraine lights a cigarette on one of those mosquito coils, and the live ash reddens her French tip manicure. I haven't seen her in a while. Her hair is straight and she's skinny. She's wearing a sleeveless white blouse and a straight black skirt.

"Lorraine looks pretty," I tell Joey.

"Yeah, well, she's on her way," Joey says. "First Chris DeMarco got her that job at the Newark DA's office as a receptionist. Next thing you know, she enrolls at Fordham Law. Now she's a paralegal. She only wears pinstripes," he adds, "even on weekends."

Rob comes over for two coladas. "Who you guys talking about? *Ironside?*"

I go to see her. I say, "Hey ya, Lorraine."

"Hey ya, Evie." She kisses me. I kiss her too.

"You look pretty," I say. "Your hair and everything."

"Thanks. I like yours too," she says, taking a look around at the back. Touching it. "Jeez, you really went ahead and chopped it off."

"Yeah, well. Summer's coming."

"I can't believe it. Summer already."

"I hear you're going to Fordham. That's great."

"Yeah." She smiles. "Upper West Side. Right by your apartment— Mark's, whatever. I saw you one time, you were on the other side of the street. With Mark's sister."

"You should have stopped me."

"I didn't want to bother you."

"It wouldn't have been a bother."

"Next time," she says, and she nods.

"Yeah," I say. "Next time."

"Mark's here?" She looks around. "I didn't see him."

"Not yet, I guess."

"He's coming here, or there?"

"Not here. I think there. Either here or there."

"Big night tonight," she says, turning to face me.

"Yeah, I guess it is."

"You ever seen him fight?"

I shake my head.

"Sit with me. Just in case." Lorraine looks down at her table. "Hey, did you ever meet any of these guys?" she asks. "This is Anne, Kathy, Allegra, Donna—Donna's my cousin. This is Evie," Lorraine tells them. "A friend of Robbie's. A friend of mine."

At seven, everybody makes their way to the street, drifting in twos and threes. Nobody gets into cars. They just get ready to get into cars, sitting on hoods, cleaning out glove compartments. Rob pops open all the doors to the Cougar and puts in an eight-track. Then he turns the volume up real loud.

> My cherie amour, lovely as a summer day.
> My cherie amour, distant as the Milky Way.

Christine and Ray Peña start dancing in the street, and everyone starts dancing, even Mr. and Mrs. Cirillo. When Christine dances, her pool-damp hair swings, and all the kids come to see. In the neighborhood, she is the one to emulate. She is defiant in her contentedness, outward about having accepted the small circumstances of a small life. As with a priest who has actually done some living, there is a dangerous intelligence to her limited aspirations that makes her behavior especially worth the watch.

Rob takes my arm and draws me close; we dance too. It's good to dance on the city streets in summer, the narrowness of the road and the expanse of the sky, the heat bleeding up through your thin shoes.

> You're the only girl my heart beats for.
> How I wish that you were mine.

Three cars slither up the street in a lights-on procession, and the dancing ends. There is a conversion back to the sweeping contagion of real time—people breaking apart, fixing clothes and hair. Rob's mother steps to the darkened rear window of the first car.

"Late as usual, Tudi. Everything's ice-cold."

Uncle Tudi creaks out to kiss her, and over her shoulder, through the inky rounds of his jumbo sunglasses, he eyes me in Rob's arms.

He says to Rob, "You ready to head out?"

Rob says, "Yeah, I'm *ready. You* ready?"

"Yeah, I'm ready. I *been* ready."

"What do you mean you've *been* ready?" Rob releases me. "We've all been waiting for *you.*"

"You wanna stand around all night and discuss technicalities?" Tudi asks.

"Shit no. Let's go."

"All right, then, let's go."

What I feel at that moment is a start, an ignition, a sense that what is happening belongs less to what has preceded it than to what is yet to unfold. Rob discharges me to Lorraine, who is somewhere behind me, calling my name. It sounds like calling a child through an open window: sweet, faraway—*Eveline.* Ray Peña's powder-blue Lincoln pulls up readily, like it's been idling nearby, and Rob and Joey get in, kind of getting vacuumed down or going fast-motion in reverse. They take off, and when they make a right at the end of the street, I see Rob's forearm hanging out the window, striking against the door frame. It has a warlike look, and in my stomach I get a sick feeling. It's not usual for him to reveal himself.

Christine, Lorraine, and I arrive at an auditorium somewhere on the Jersey shore, a decrepit building with a grand, tame face like that of a former picture palace. There are lots of people arriving. The look of them rushing to get in is anarchical—oblivious and opportunistic and everywhere at once, like rats shooting through dumpsters. We drive past twice looking for a place to park.

An empty ticket kiosk in the center of the clamshelled entrance is filled with framed memorabilia from the fifties and sixties of performers like Sammy Kaye at Point Pleasant and Fred Waring in Ocean Grove.

There is a vintage *Drink Coca-Cola* sign and a Pokerarcade mini-marquee. Christine stops to find her reflection and apply lipstick. It amazes me how like Rob she is. Her lack of shame is somehow forward-reaching and mature. While most of us linger reticently on the sill of adaptation, she is already over and on the other side, surviving just fine.

She pats my waist. "Don't look so glum, kid. It'll be over before you know it."

Through a set of double doors leading to the main arena, through the congestion of the crowd, I see the glow of the preliminary fight. This is the first thing I notice, the location of the glow, which is the location of the ring. The girls cut in through the right. I follow.

Mark is in the center of the auditorium, surrounded by people. Everyone he knows is there—Richard, his boss, and Richard's fiancée, Mia; Brett; Anselm; Miles and Paige; Jonathan and Alicia; Marguerite, his shopaholic lawyer friend; Dara; that guy Swoosey Schicks; cousins and co-workers and guys from the pit whom I've never met. I can tell they're from the pit by the pens in their pockets.

"Sorry I couldn't make it to Rob's parents' house," Mark says, pulling me from Lorraine, helping me down the aisle, giving me a kiss. "I was leading the convoy. Twelve cars!"

He passes me to Jonathan and Alicia. Alicia takes my hand, squeezing tightly. Lorraine is about ten feet behind me. She smiles before heading in another direction, as if to say, *Sorry, but what am I gonna do?* She shouldn't feel sorry. I'm used to it. Everyone does what Mark says. Everyone believes in the supremacy of money.

The first fight is almost over. To prepare myself, I think back to all the times I've seen Rourke on display—a field, a gymnasium, a theater, a classroom. I remind myself that nothing I have seen so far has been random. I've been made ready.

There is a way they tell you to draw trees. A tree should not be a blot on the landscape, stripped of obliquity. A tree should express contour, core, *crevasse*. A tree should lift off the paper. To render contour, you have to draw back and forward and down. To render core, you must envision center. Center is not the dead point between two edges, or the geographic median of some object you happen to see, but the soul of the *O*, the heart of vastness, the umbilicus, the basic order of the nature of a thing, the fixed innerness from which unfixed outerness originates. To render its scars, seek the tree's fortune. Conceive of the tree wholly. Every tree grows up and down and out with an equivalency of energy. If you look you will find a carnival of direction—perpendicularity and pendancy, lift and transverseness, convexity and indentation. A tree rises with grandeur when it meets with no obstacle; it skews sharply to prevail against adversity; it thickens incrementally, gaining girth with years; it bears down into the bed of the earth with its talons. Like a child, it bruises back in response to cruelty and obstruction. Like a saint, it drives to the light.

In every tree there is a system of softness beneath the armature, a velvet refuge, an underside, a whisper-sweet sanctuary where potential is stored. Underside, because there is truth and beauty in what is rejected by sight. Underside, because in every king there is a boy.

Antonio Vargas has gypsy skin and black hair tied back. He looks like the kind of guy who is good to kids and aging relatives and to the girls who love him. As it turned out, Tommy Lydell backed out at the last minute. When Mark got the call, he kicked the coffee table and broke it. After Mark heard Vargas's stats—twenty-two years old, one hundred ninety pounds, six-foot-one, 25–3 with 20 KO's, and a lefty—he felt good enough to kneel down and check the damage. The leg had split, so he had Manny take it to the basement.

"You want me to glue it?" Manny asked, leaning at the door with the table. It looked like he was holding a dead Labrador against his chest, legs out. "I have the clamp!"

"Throw it out," Mark said. "I'll buy a new one."

Rourke is double-jabbing, steering Vargas backward around the ring with ambling, edgy grace, his feet hardly touching the canvas. He fights easily, like it's nothing. I don't get the feeling I often get from seeing him in public, when he's there but not there, and transcendent somehow to his own performance. From the first bell, when he walked out to center, he looked at Vargas, lifted his hands, and began to fight. Vargas seemed caught by surprise, by the lack of formality. I know how he felt. I know what it is to be completely unprepared for a being so instinctive. I know what it is to face him that way, when it is just you he sees.

In the fourth round, Rourke gives Vargas a sickening combination—a right to the jaw, followed by a smooth uppercut left, also to the jaw, then a clean right to the face in the indent between nose and cheekbone, and there is shouting, in a roar, like a train popping from a tunnel. And a bell. And a retreat, to the corners. I keep my eyes on Vargas, watching in spite of the blood. His nose sheds an amber stream from one nostril. His mouth guard gets slipped out, and water goes down his face and chest from the corner man squeezing a sponge. Ice goes on the cheek, and the cut man checks the eyes. His head tilts back and people talk at him, giving coarse encouragement.

Rob appears opposite from where we stand, on Vargas's side, about ten feet from the corner, talking to Vargas's brother. I think it is the brother, by the resemblance. Rob's face floats mat level. It surprises me to see him there, though I suppose it doesn't matter where Rob stands. The men in the ring and out of it are the same: there is an equivalency between the sides. Mr. Xinwu spoke of respect between adversaries, and I honestly feel no animosity toward Vargas. What I feel primarily is curiosity. His heart, his mind. The bed he sleeps in, the layout of his kitchen, who talks to him through the bathroom door? I have the feeling people talk to him through doors, that, like me, he is never alone. No one talks to Rourke that way.

Seconds remain before the next round. Corner people pull back. Vargas is joined by his brother, who hangs down, just for a moment, one arm linked to the corner post. As the brother speaks to Antonio, both look over to Rourke, like they are viewing a horizon. Is Rourke watching; does he see them? I don't look; I can't. I haven't once looked in his corner.

"Two grand," Swoosey shouts to Mark, "for every round Harrison lasts after this one."

Mark and Swoosey shake. Not really shake so much as touch hands. "*Four* grand," Mark wagers, "that he won't last this one."

A bell rings. I don't know which—the fifth, I think. Vargas shoots over like a junkyard dog. There is a roar of approval as he crosses into Rourke's vicinity. With his right arm and his body, he keeps Rourke in a limited region as his left fist makes contact. Rourke's abdomen, Rourke's face. Vargas goes at him, again and again, five times, ten times. Rourke accepts the force of each short thrust, trembling thickly like a gong, withstanding, absorbing, not losing footing—he has *root*. I think back to Montauk, to the stoic self-sacrifice, to the almost ghastly oneness, to the minuscule and endless preparations required for such a massive exertion. It is awful to see him hit, but worse to see him step so expertly into pain.

Rourke's right eye swells and turns hard. I imagine the blood inside gathered like sheep, though blood does not come in flocks; I just picture it that way, caught inside, lost and stray. He's having trouble seeing: he has to dodge blind. On the next strike to the face, Rourke's head flies back as if he is following the trail of a jet. For a moment, his neck is exposed before the weight of his head rolls back around onto his chest, reminding me of a swan getting shot. The referee is there, giving a standing count. Everyone in the room is waiting for Rourke to fall. Maybe Mark was right, maybe the plan for Rourke is to go down. A part of me wishes it were true; yet, another part wants him to keep fighting. *Needs.*

Vargas trots triumphantly; his people call his name. *Vargas. Vargas.*

I grip the seat in front of me. My eyes begin to admit just color. The brown lines in his body, the brown lines in the ring, and in the room beyond, the brown sea of heads. If anyone is calling to Rourke he doesn't hear—I don't think he *can* hear—and yet he is still standing. Though it doesn't surprise me that he won't go down, I do wonder who it is that he is fighting.

The next moment is impacted. I have the sense of multiple end points, of time spilling over like water to define adjoining, previously hidden places. I see Rourke testing those places, preparing to test them. The stiff hull of his skin and muscles, superficially hard but on the inside open and opening further to pain, to all the pain he has not yet incorporated. It's like he is allowing himself to feel, which moves me more than his blood and blindness. I see his father missing. I see his reluctance to claim the space left empty by his father to which he felt by nature disentitled. I see the inability to protect and to be protected. I see down, all the way down, down into the mat—it's like a well—and I think how good it must feel to go back, to return to the place he was left alone, the place he was marked. I know the feeling. I often go back. To the day, the hour, the minute of losing him.

No one sees me leave. I retreat to the back of the auditorium. I look one last time as the crowd begins to roar. Rourke is coming off the ropes on the deep left. He seems to stand in glowing water. He tries to right himself. He rises then tips, and his gloved hands jerk toward his ears.

The referee holds one hand back, keeping Vargas in check. Rourke staggers forward; one step, two steps, each time getting closer to Vargas. Every eye in the house is on him. He arrives at center, finding it despite his confusion. Time seems to stop; the ring hangs from his feet. He turns at an angle to face Vargas, as if to say to some acquaintance on the street, *Oh, and by the way*—then out of nowhere, Rourke hauls his right arm back and cracks Vargas across the jaw. Vargas flies, stunned. Rourke takes the moment and moves in, starting on the body. Clear and sure. Again, again, a machine.

From where I stand, there is light, a spilling visionary light, from where it comes I don't know, possibly my imagination. The light spawns globes about the heads of the fighters like the pre-Renaissance halos of Giotto's saints, like these are men of sacrifice, like they are martyrs, though in fact there is nothing epic about them. They are common, common because we all begin with dreams but end with nothing, nothing more than what we, in our battered humility, can make of ourselves.

And voices, a hot sea, chaos rising. *Rourke, Rourke, Harri-son, Harri-son.*

RIVER

June 1984

Farewell! Thou art too dear for my possessing.

—WILLIAM SHAKESPEARE

47

The last time I saw him was on Broadway, half a block north of Houston. It was dark and cold, and Mark and I were walking downtown to an opening. It must have been my third year at NYU. In the middle of the street, a junkie was blocking traffic. There's a gas station with a car wash right there—anyway, there used to be a gas station, by now it may be gone—and the fluorescent pink light it produced made the street into a kind of theater. In the vortex of this enormous auditorium was a hunched body—Jack's.

"How disgusting," Mark yelled above the car horns.

Jack. Death-like and emaciated and stalled in a choke of municipal chaos. Mark was right, it *was* disgusting. I could almost see the venom through the sheerness of Jack's skin, like a million insects crawling.

"C'mon. Let's go." Mark tried to steer me away.

Would he come to me, would he know my voice? There was a way I used to say his name; if I used that voice, maybe he would come. If I tried to lead him from traffic, to a storefront, to a doorway, to some place of relative safety, would he let me?

But Mark didn't know Jack or anything about Jack, and it would have been bad if I'd run out onto Broadway and reached for Jack's hand, and Mark shouted not to touch the stinking filth of it. I would not want Jack to feel filthy or stinking in my eyes. If there were trouble and the police came, Jack would be taken into custody, not Mark. Never had I wished so desperately for a friend, for Rourke or Rob or Denny, for someone who trusted me. Usually you think of a friend as someone you trust. I'd never thought before of a friend as someone who trusts *you*.

Mark got me onto the curb. "You really are a sweetheart. The way you worry about people. And birds."

Jack is so small, I thought as we walked to the corner. Perhaps it wasn't fair to think that way when his version of manhood resisted dimension. Usually, you had only to look into his eyes to locate the power of him. But I had not seen his eyes; they'd been closed. Later, if there was to be a later for him, there would be shaking and profane rocking, a triangle of city streets to navigate that would seem to span miles—a stoop, a fire hydrant, the bumper of a car, and after that, a feeble search through some garbage cans, for what, not for food, he would not want food, a little left-over wine, maybe, in a precipitately trashed bottle. Later, in the ruthless and overbright morning, there would be a dilating consciousness more odious than I had ever encountered, as it labored like a half-chewed animal against the withdrawal of the pacific state he had found in his high.

Before turning west onto Houston Street, I looked back. I saw Jack bend lovingly into his addiction as debris from the street whirled like a symphony around him. The seat of his jeans was black. I wondered if he smelled like vomit. It occurred to me that I was fascinated by the look of him because the look of him was the feel of me—we were no different; we had ended up exactly the same, friendless and anonymous, ravaged on the inside. Whatever deficits had drawn us together in the beginning continued to bind us.

"These junkies are totally desensitized," Mark informed me, throwing a shearlinged arm about my waist and tugging me. "You or I would end up dead, but that guy can drink out of a puddle and be back on the street tomorrow."

It's strange sometimes, the way stories interlock, like those plastic monkeys that connect by the elbow. I never imagined that Rourke's and Jack's lives would conform again in terms of theme or episode, but they did, coupled as they were by my peripheral involvement. When you allow your story to connect with the stories of others, you are either kind or crazy. There is a fine line, I think, between compassion and madness.

It did not occur to me during the fight to think back to Jack on the street, though I might well have—the drug making Jack's skin a wall like Rourke's skin had been a wall, protecting him against being hit. Each sought to pervert a natural gift—Jack by silencing his voice, Rourke by defacing his form. Each possessed enormous confidence, yet felt himself socially lame, utterly alone. Vargas beat at Rourke from the outside to weaken the underlying flesh, just as the heroin masticated Jack's vitality, beating him on the inside with a lighter touch but greater strength. Every time Vargas made contact with Rourke, it was as if he were pounding a child's body, no matter that Rourke was strong and had made himself hard. To me his flesh was tender, because all I'd ever done was treat it tenderly.

How could a man as clear as Rourke ignore the gross arithmetic of cruelty? How could a man so physically disciplined permit the consequence of his efforts to be defiled? And Jack, raping his treasured reason, making himself stupid. But me—I loved them both, and by both I was loved. What was it that I wanted so badly I needed it twice?

Andy's Place is an all-night diner in Margate, New Jersey, two blocks south of where Rourke's fight had been. When I left the auditorium during the fight that night, I had no idea which way to go. The streets were empty and the wind had turned wild. My clothes were whipping as if I were on a speedboat. As I walked, I could hear my name, near and far, as though the sea itself were calling. *Evie! Eveline! Ev-e-line!*

I discovered the diner and slipped inside. It was surprisingly good. It had a clean foyer with a clean working pay phone, and posted on the wall by one of those toy-grabbing games was a laminated list of numbers for car service companies to Manhattan. I got through on the first try to Monroe Limo and was told by a polite dispatcher that it would be about fifteen minutes before somebody came. I figured I should wait in back in case anyone came looking for me. I informed the waitress that a car was coming, then I ordered toast. I was a waitress once too. I didn't want her thinking I had bad manners.

She had her elbow on the counter in front of the pass-through to the kitchen. She said, "White or rye?"

"Uh, rye."

"Jelly?"

"No jelly." I pointed to the bathroom. "I'll go wash up, you know, and stuff."

"G'head," she told me knowingly. "I'll knock when the cab's here."

———

Carlo wasn't on duty, Al was. Al gave me forty dollars to cover the ride up from Jersey, plus a seven-dollar tip. I'd planned to keep the driver waiting while I went up to get cash, but Al pulled out his wallet. Mark would give him an extra twenty for the courtesy, so I said fine.

I got upstairs at 2:00 A.M. I know the time because the first thing I did was pack, starting with the sterling alarm clock Dad and Marilyn had given me for Christmas. I had no idea why the clock came first—maybe because of its honest, bright numbers or the effort they'd surely put into choosing it, debating its virtues against the virtues of all other clocks. For some reason they'd settled on this particular one, and, I don't know— I just felt bad about it.

After that I packed my books, and last, all of my clothes. Luckily, Mark had just purchased a set of luggage for the trip to Italy we were supposed to take. I carried the four stuffed suitcases and a knapsack into the living room, and I arranged them in size order. Then I stacked them so they would consume the least amount of floor space. Then I stared at them, considering where to go and how to get there. No matter where I went, Mark would follow, and anyone who tried to help me would be dragged into a double mess, that being the mess of my reality, plus a whole new mess of Mark's making.

When the phone rang, it was a relief. I hadn't expected the phone. I'd expected the door—and Mark, standing there. It was Dan Lewis. "Sorry to call so late," Dan said. "Hope I didn't wake Mark." Dan attended Juilliard, which was around the corner from Mark's place, and often our paths would cross. Sometimes Mark and I went with friends to hear Dan play at the American, a dinner club in the theater district.

For a while he was quiet and I was quiet. It was 2:47; the silver clock was still in my hand. On the other side of the living room window, the wind was kicking up like crazy, like it wanted something out of me. Pieces of the street were making it up twenty-five floors. It was the same wind I'd felt outside the auditorium in Jersey, when I thought I heard my name in it.

I remember thinking, *I guess tonight is the night.* And then, *of course tonight is the night.*

"They found him in the woods. About two hours ago. At my grandfather's farm."

I'd been to the Lewis farm once during a February break when Dan's grandparents had been in Florida. There was a blizzard, and we got caught upstate near the Catskills with no food and no phone. We tried to go snowshoeing with tennis rackets. I remember Jack informing us over a candlelit dinner of canned beans and toasted marshmallows that a wood pussy is a skunk. He and Dan argued that night, as usual, about changing the name of the band.

"How about 'The Void'?" Jack had suggested.

Dan shook his head. "Sounds like emptying your bladder."

"Not 'to void,' dumb ass, '*The* void.' "

"Oh," said Dan, "as in space, as in illimitable distance."

"Exactly," Jack had said. "As in the gap between your fucking ears."

Dan cleared his throat. "You okay?"

I didn't know. I said, "Are you okay?"

"I'm okay," he said.

"How did they know, you know, where to look?"

"I guess he wasn't showing up in the place he usually stayed. One of his friends, *acquaintances,* whatever, called Manhattan information for 'Fleming' and got Elizabeth, and his family started inquiring. My grandfather had called me from Florida just the day before to say that his caretaker had reported a missing gun. He described it to me because he has lots of guns. I knew exactly which one he meant. I just said, 'Yeah, I know it. That's the gun Jack loves.' So I told Elizabeth, and the local cops started searching the property yesterday morning. They went through the night in case he was still alive. They looked for twenty-six hours. You know, there's six hundred acres there. Mr. Fleming drove up today to identify him."

I leaned over the suitcases, crushing the high part of my stomach into one of the handles. I couldn't help but think of boots through leaves. And of dogs. Most likely they'd used dogs. I thought also of the freckle in the center of his lower lip and the blue of his eyes. And the gunshot—

"How long—was he—there?"

"One cop said three or four days. But according to my father, a second guy said maybe less, that Jack was, you know, 'thin' to begin with."

"And his mom?"

"Not good. I just got off the phone with her. She decided to have a memorial service next week. On Friday evening. She's hoping we'll speak. A couple of us. You, me. Elizabeth."

An enormous gust rattled the windows. Dan heard it too, since he was only a few blocks away. "It's windy tonight," he said. "Like November. Your birthday's in November, right?"

"Yes," I said. "Funny that you would remember that."

"How can I forget the night Jack gave you that necklace in the refrigerator box? The opal."

I said, "Yeah, that's right, the opal."

"Well, take it easy, Evie. I'll probably talk to you tomorrow. Tell Mark I'm sorry to call so late."

"Don't worry about it, Dan. He's not even home."

48

Sometimes you hear someone say, *It was like seeing a ghost.* By that they mean that they have experienced a penetration of the present by an agent of the past; they have experienced a destabilization. They call the sensation "ghost" because the occasion inspires curiosity and fear and touches on the twin marvels of space and time.

"Evie?" Kate says.

Her voice comes through plainly, though I am in my mother's house in East Hampton and Kate is in France. Laurent sent her there after her graduation from McGill. She's staying with her mother's sister Yvette in Brest, a city by the sea, in Brittany. Yvette is a pharmacist; she has an *apothecary.*

"It sounds like you're in the next room," I say. Maybe "next room" is not what I mean. Maybe I mean somewhere closer. As I tell her about Jack, she is silent. I wonder, *Am I speaking too softly? Can she hear me?*

"I hear you fine," she says. For a long time there is nothing but the sound of intermittent sighs. Kate seems angry about the news, which is not what I'd expected, though it has a consoling effect on me. I feel as if I am somehow off the hook—*a* hook, *some* hook. Every time I think to fill the silence, I remember that it's Kate on the other end, so I don't have to. Besides, in my head is just random nonsense, like the time she, Mom, and Jack were trying to catch a rat, or the time Jack brought Steve Schumacher's goat over to show Kate and it ate Aunt Lowie's new walking cane, or the Valentine's Day when Jack bought us the heart-shaped pizzas.

"I don't know how this could have happened," Kate states bitterly. "It's just so absolute. It's absolute."

She obviously can't attend the funeral, but there's a place she can go in Brittany on Friday, an island called Ile d'Ouessant. "It's flat with cliffs overlooking the Atlantic, and there are massive rolling waves that smash against the rocks. It has a bird reserve and wild rabbits. I can take a ferry."

She says something else, but I miss it. The phone is heavy, so I switch hands. I have to keep switching hands. I have the idea that my wings have been broken. That's not just a figure of speech; I actually *feel* broken wings, like parts of my upper self are unpinned and hanging.

Kate falls silent, still there, on the other end, in a cottage, in France. When the phone rang it made the funny European phone sound. She seems to know about my wings, or at least guess about them because finally when she talks again she says that after arriving in Paris from Canada last month, she took a train to Brittany and on the way she stopped in Chartres to visit the cathedral. "We went there with the French Club, remember?"

I do. There are kings and queens carved into the door jambs.

"In the Royal Portal," Kate confirms, "that's right. In other doorways there are some saints and biblical figures. Remember we kept skipping all the tours and going to cafés to drink coffee and draw? You were like, 'Who wants to go all the way to France to be stuck with loud, badly dressed people from home?'

"But that day in Chartres I was afraid we would miss the tour bus and get lost in the middle of France. And you said, 'Kate, you speak the language. You can't get lost. Getting lost just means not understanding.' Do you know I always think of that?"

I suppose I'm fortunate to have someone think of me when they visit a cathedral. Mark's friend Marguerite says that shopping at Saks makes her think of her mother. *Those were our happiest times,* Marguerite says, tears in her eyes. *Just shopping, not caring.* As for me, I don't think of Chartres where Kate is concerned, but of a day in ninth grade when she was in marching band. Before her mother died, before Jack. The parade started at the East Hampton Library and ended at the Windmill on North Main Street, where there were speeches, mostly about the sacrifices of war. The kids didn't listen since it was pretty much guaranteed that they were heading into lives free of public sacrifice. They just kept poking one another, making noise, stealing hats.

Kate and I sat on the curb by the Methodist Church, and Jay Robbins joined us beneath one of the old giant elms, the three of us forming a leggy adolescent row, with them in those white polyester band pants with side stripes. He laid his trombone on the lawn, and the length of brass grazed a patch of purple tulips. The instrument was shining and gold, making a regal loop against the flowers. Jay had brown eyes and his nose was covered in a fan of freckles. When we were in fourth grade, he did one hundred fifty sit-ups for the presidential fitness test with all the boys looking on, and that same year he'd given Kate an I.D. bracelet for her birthday. She returned the gift, but she did so kindly, the two of us riding our bikes over to his house on Sherill Road after dinner one night. I waited in the driveway while they sat on the porch and talked. In the end, Jay seemed content with the fact that he'd been treated respectfully, more so than he might have been with actually going steady, and as it turned out, their friendship lasted a long time. Jay had driven Kate and Maman in to Sloan-Kettering several times, and he had taken Kate to both proms, though he had a girlfriend who lived about an hour up the island, in Mattituck.

I always think of that parade and of Jay Robbins with his trombone. Kate's natural femininity had allowed him to respond with natural masculinity, and in the end everything had been resolved. I didn't feel as scared about boys after that. But that was in the time preceding infiltration—by other girls and by ideas of propriety. Before infiltration, you could really count on girls like Kate to guide you through the labyrinth. Unfortunately, girl guides go from being trackers in the Native American sense to being hostesses in the crowded steak house sense. Who knows how it happens.

If friendship is like a cathedral, then forsaken friendship is like roofless ruins, like a formerly glorious structure. In the World War II photos my dad has of bombed cathedrals in Cologne or Dresden, they're not merely blackened ribs; they're hollowed houses of worship, still symbolic of something, just as significant as what they stood for originally—intention, faith, place. I felt connected to Kate, but also sort of out in the open.

"On Saturday we leave for Grasse. In Provence. It's where perfumes are made."

"That will be nice. You'll see lots of flowers."

It must feel good to possess a genetic immunity, to take shelter in your ethnicity, to vanish into your ancestry. Exactly as I form the thought, I set it free. I wouldn't want to live in France or anywhere else, not when the story of America is still unfolding. Not when I speak the language, when there is no getting lost, when there is still so much to understand. For me there is no security greater or better than entrepreneurial security, cowboy security, the security of infinite possibility. We say goodbye and I hang up first. I don't mean to be rude. It's just that there is nothing to keep me from putting the phone down first, nothing that makes me think—*Slow.*

49

I go first to the mimosa. It does not appear to have grown, and yet it has, which is the remarkable thing about trees. They are secretive about their growth. My mother is next, in the backyard; her face in the daylight, how I know it, the shape of her eyes and the color. She has been cleaning. In her hand is a towel and a spray bottle full of vinegar and water. She does not use chemicals anymore, she informs me, wiping her hair from her forehead with the back of her free hand. "The water table is fucked."

Tomorrow there will be a party in the yard, a birthday party for a friend from the college, Jann, who was formerly Jan when he was a she. Did I remember Jan? I must remember.

"I do remember. She wore half-glasses."

"Bifocals."

"Exactly, yes, bifocals."

My mother rubs the film from the tabletops—there are all these tables but no chairs—and she tells stories. She is not insensitive; she simply talks around my feelings for my sake. Possibly she has always talked around my feelings for my sake. It occurs to me that maybe I am difficult, that I've always been difficult, especially for her, as we are so unalike. Possibly she gave more than I knew. She trusted I would be okay, even if she could not trust herself to make me that way. *Good night, my Eveline,* she used to say. Didn't she used to say that?

I lean to give her a kiss. She kisses me back, then returns to the tables, setting down candles, the kind with plastic nets. I lift one, smelling it. It smells of citronella, of Jack.

"There's mail for you in the barn," she says. "I put it in a basket and tied it with a blue ribbon."

In the barn there are several boxes. I cannot say exactly what it is I'm searching for, but I stop at a stack of journals. Inside I find an account of my past so vivid that it's like looking at myself through special instruments for the observation of the very small or the very far. But just because there is evidence of me doesn't mean I can be found; in fact, I am irrecoverable—*we* are irrecoverable. I meant to say *we.*

It's difficult to come upon yourself at the genesis of your own path, when everything was beautiful and new. The loss of newness has less to do with gaining years than with shutting down to possibility. You start to become selective about pleasure because you no longer trust life to bestow it at random. You refuse to wait for fortune, you lose faith. You become someone who looks into another person's eyes but refuses to see the story there. As the protective net for the self tightens, the net for others widens. This is how Jack fell through.

I read somewhere that the word *nostalgia* derives from two Greek ideas—*nostos,* meaning return, and *algos,* meaning pain—together suggesting a *painful return.* And yet, though I feel pain, I can't say I long to go back. I don't miss the way I was; I don't regret what I have come to be.

What I feel has only to do with time. I am simply too late. I've learned so much, but ironically, it is impossible to revisit ignorance with knowledge. *These* keys cannot unlock *those* doors.

The bluestone at the base of the barn steps is washed in sunlight. The warmth rushes into my bare feet; it's an old warmth, a same warmth. To my right is the bed of wildflowers I planted, tangled at the base like siblings sleeping. Shooting through the thicket is a cluster of rose vervain that Marilyn and I planted one day when she and Dad visited. We stopped at Miss Amelia's Cottage in Amagansett for an antiques fair, and Marilyn bought a starter tray of the flowers and two tufted Chinese benches that I'd admired. Dad said the seats were probably made in Pittsburgh, but I imagined they had belonged to imperial Chinese children. I could see the children sitting, upright and attentive, listening to a tutor, their slippered feet dangling. When Marilyn took them to be re-covered on Grand Street, the upholsterer offered to buy them from her for fifteen hundred dollars. She refused, though they'd cost only two hundred.

My father said, "We could've bought a new car!"

"No, Anton, we'll keep them for Eveline, for when she gets her own house someday," Marilyn told him emphatically. "We never would have seen their value."

I go farther into the grass, toward the driveway, to the train tracks. There is this sensation, long lost to me, of lightness of being, of oneness with the atmosphere, of looking into sky, this very sky, with nothing before me and nothing behind. Despite the little I knew and the little I had, I recall the feeling of inalienable possession.

What I miss, what I'd possessed, may be no more than immunity. If modern life can be seen as something high-speed and pathogenic—replicating and duplicating and by necessity unoriginal—then childhood by comparison is a period of blessed insusceptibility. Maybe the loss of innocence is part of some practical operation. Maybe there are lessons in its fleeting frailty. Possibly through such sacrifice we remain captivated by joy, bound to its safekeeping when we come upon it.

Oh, the crossing bells, and the train thundering by. I hold my ground at the tracks, the meeting place of two converging lines—the vertical pole connecting heaven to earth, the gods to the dead—and the horizontal pole, the crossbar, the tracks, the line connecting start to finish, the place you imagined *from* to the place you imagined *into.*

Alone again and left to wonder, *Am I lost, or do I remain—am I perennial? Have I stopped becoming, or do I prepare?* There are pilgrims who walk and walk, through years, through nations, seeking answers to questions they don't know how to formulate.

I walk at night in East Hampton, and the world tips and turns. I stumble along, thinking dead thoughts. Skateboards and scarecrows and spitting contests, the circus star antics of boys, tipping cows and three to a bike. Soaring twilights in November, walking home late from the movie theater, kicking through fallen chestnut leaves, green with crispy borders, like melting stars or witches' shoes. The heat of the hood of a car in summer, the cupped pop of softballs. I don't know whether or not this is home, whether or not it would have me, whether or not I would be had by it. I know only that I reached a plateau on these streets, some dead end of understanding.

I call my mother from the pay phone in the alley near White's Pharmacy. A stranger answers. He sounds British, with a swarthy Manchester accent. In the background there are the sounds of a party. The one for Jann. I ask for Irene.

"'Ang on, *luv,*" he says. There is a portly plastic clunk as the receiver drops. I hear him shout to someone, "Get down, then, and give us twenty!" Then raucous laughter, then unanimous counting. "One, two, thirteen, fifteen, twenty!"

Cheers and more shouting and more counting and the party again, and when no one retrieves the phone, I hang up. The heels of my socks are damp from popped blisters, so I sit on the back step of the pharmacy, tearing away the dead skin.

By the time I return to my mother's house, everyone has gone. A note for me is on the door. *Went to the Sea Wolf. Meet us down there!*

I linger in the doorway. I don't feel like going out, but I don't feel like going to bed either. I'm not hungry; there is no television. I don't want to go into Kate's old room. I don't want to go into my old room. The whole thing feels dangerous, just being here. Going back home is like reentering a burning building. You evaluate the necessity. You map out a safe course. You decide to go sequentially and in reverse, one room at a time so you don't lose your way—it would be so easy to get lost in there. You wish you had another choice; you do not. There is something you must rescue.

As always when my mother leaves, the house is unbearably free of her presence. The living room is unusually still, as if it has been recently and rapidly evacuated. Darkness is broken by the weak mustard glint of a kerosene lamp. Glasses are half-full, pillows and sweaters lie about, the sound of Bob Dylan seeps through the cigarette smog. Three more albums are queued on the spindle; two are stacked on the turntable.

My feet stick as I walk. It must have been a good party. *Ha ha,* my father once said on a New Year's visit. *I lost a shoe there in front of the stove.*

I tour the somnolent blue living room, feeling tranquil, feeling numb, in an elegiac sort of trance. The legion of her belongings forms an evidentiary matrix. These artifacts of the heart prove presence and endurance of presence—that is to say, her own. Like a vessel in marble she channels through the objects around the house, aberrant and sheet-like, frozen-in. I recall myself as a child waiting stubbornly among these very things for something vital and real to appear or to transpire that could move me, reach me, touch me. I come upon the archaeology of my need with delicacy. One must confront one's innocence with caution when it has gotten you nowhere, when it has proven itself fallible, when no more remains, when you discover that you have outspent the purity of your heart.

It is not an easy memory—me, awaiting requital or redress, hoping for someone to take responsibility for me. Though I quickly remind myself that, as a child, I endured no more than mild disequilibrium, nothing perilous or vile, that I was loved in a sense, and cared for, and so on, and et cetera, just as instantly, I acknowledge that I am brushing off as usual the accountability of my parents, absolving them of inattentiveness because it was benign, assuming responsibility because I am capable. Capable is what they made me to be.

For the first time ever I recognize something dangerously polemical about the point of view I have long maintained. When I remind myself that professed love cannot compare to something desperate and original, which part of me is speaking? The part at peace with my own competence, or the part that detests it, the part that longs to be swept away?

Have I been in pursuit of emotional detachment because personally I prefer it, or because it is all I have ever known? How curious to have found a defining love, the tenderness for which I believe I've longed, something reciprocal that moves the spirit and bears time, and to have lost it. How resourceful of me to turn a story of achievement into a more familiar one of loss. Such loss is a form of control. Have I been working all along to secure my own failure, to collapse the machine that was made of me?

I go back around, one final time. I do not touch the things my mother has chosen to keep; they are not mine. If it is evident that I am not present here, that there is no shrine to me, I feel close to her, uniquely. It is as though I have moved from behind to make her acquaintance, growing taller every step. I feel grave with an understanding of her that is new.

I move to the picture window. I remember when nights were starlit but black. I remember the clear air and the sharp strike of footsteps and the fever of Rourke's voice. I loved him, I love him, from the very beginning I loved him. I cannot understand how it happened, how it turned to this, when the view is the same view, when the tree does not appear to have grown, when her face is the same face, when once I was a girl.

50

The clicking of the bike slows to a sharp staccato as I lean across Newtown Lane and cut toward the park. Herrick Park in East Hampton Village dangles as if by magic in the redolent air, like a tin marionette. It reminds me of the abandoned World's Fair site off the Long Island Expressway in Queens. My parents brought me to that fair in 1965. I remember running through the grass into my mother's outstretched arms. And my father, behind her, our three figures pebble-like in the wake of the colossal, skeletal globe. The *Unisphere*. Besides a brief memory of walking with them beneath a movie marquee in winter, of me with my head against my father's shoulder and the soft bounce of my mother's head moving alongside us, that is all I have of the three of us together as a family.

The bike pops onto the curb, tumbling over mounds of grass like a billiard ball. On the bench near the bike rack is an elderly black man in a baseball cap. In his mouth is an unlit cigar. I wonder what he takes when he leaves the house, probably the cigar and the hat, maybe a five-dollar bill, some matches.

By the sun, it is nine. Six hours to go until the service.

A young couple in khakis, loafers, and Lacoste shirts with upturned collars reads the papers while their two children gyrate on the rubber tire swings. I wonder if they have all they ever wished for. It must be nice to have all you ever wished for, if that's even possible. It might be that every time you get one thing that you want, another wish pops up automatically, like in that hand-stacking game. Not only do the mother and father have matching clothes and haircuts, but they share height. I don't remember women and men matching so well previously. Somehow it's a sign of the times—physical equivalency, emotional economy. It all refers to an eradication of risk. Rourke and I would not have been good at matching. That is why we failed. It's shameful to have failed where lesser people have triumphed. On my womb is a reminder of my insufficiency, an imprint, forever impressed, like a cave painting, like a running horse etched ten thousand years ago.

Sometimes Mark says, "What's wrong?"

I tell him that my uterus aches.

"Still?" he asks. "Is that possible?"

The swings are free. I take one, tucking the chains inside my elbows. My chest slumps down, my shirt bellows out, and my heels make quarter moons in the dirt. When I was little, I drew a field filled with swing sets on manila nursery paper—pairs and pairs of inverted *V*'s connected at the top by horizontal lines, very big and very small—small implying distance. I must have been four. It is strange to think about why I would have been experimenting at such an early age with perspective.

"You felt friendless," Jack once explained. "Friendless when you drew it and friendless into the future, as far into the future as your miniature mind could calculate. And it doesn't just represent a fear of future friendlessness—look at the clarity of those lines—it represents determination. *Sensational!*"

I gave the drawing to him. He and Dad framed it, then he hung it near the porthole window across from his bed so it would be the first thing he saw in the mornings. Mornings were hard for Jack. I wondered if the drawing was still there.

The slide is across from me. It swells and recedes as I swing. Slides are deceptive—all that climbing just for a shot back to no place. That was how Jack lived in the end—in a rut, working for the ride. But when you swing, there is no ground to gain, no peak, no low. You learn to linger, to be airborne; you are like a final chord suspended. If nothing comes next, nothing comes full, weighted, exquisite. I lean back, making my body straight, swinging and hanging upside down. I wish my hair could drag on the ground. Sometimes I dream it can.

A little boy chases a ball, and his father catches him, flipping him over his shoulder. The boy squeals. It has been a long time since I've heard a squeal. The old black man rolls the ball back to the child, a redhead in overalls. It is a striped beach ball so big that the boy can't see beyond it when he holds it. I know what it is to hold that ball, to crane my neck but still not perceive my steps, to feel unreliably the path before me, to read the world in terms of hot and unabashed colors, to inhale the sweet ambrosia of melting plastic.

"Goodbye, sir," I say as I collect my bike.

The man on the bench nods. "Good day, good day."

I take my leave, slowly clicking away.

Last night I dreamt of the sea. I dreamt of water all around, tossing and rocking a house, my house. It was a dream of Jack. We were in the house, and the water was high, and he sang, and the house rocked. And we rolled, gently also, like babies in a cradle. I rolled, and he rolled especially, and his singing was beautiful.

51

A girl stops at the end of the aisle. It's really hard when you're a girl to imagine yourself to be the way other girls are. They can look so soft. Not soft like how they feel when you touch them, but soft like they look when they hurt. She has burgundy hair pulled back at her shoulders and large breasts like she would be warm in winter. Her eyes are bright and small and blue, and her mascara is smeared. She wears a straight cotton skirt with multicolored stripes and a camisole beneath a fringed orange jacket that is fastened with a vintage white plastic belt. She looks like Dusty Springfield, except for the red hair and the tattoos.

"Eveline?"

"Yes," I say. "Hi."

She offers her hand. "I'm Jewel. You know my cousin. Dan."

"Oh sure. I've never met you, have I?"

She shakes her head. "I was abroad for high school, in London."

"Oh, okay."

"You used to live by the train."

"Yes, that's right, by the train."

I wonder what she's saying. She seems to be saying something. I take up my sweater from the seat alongside mine, inviting her to sit. I was saving the place for Denny, but he's late, as usual. Jewel folds into the chair as if the string that had been holding her got clipped, and she begins to cry. It's funny, I can hardly make out her sobs; they're getting mixed among the sobs of all the other people. It's one of those kinds of funerals, the communal sobbing kind, where it comes together and makes a kind of music.

Despite the sounds of grieving, the warm marine after-light of day coming through the tents in the Flemings' backyard is beautiful. I feel as though I am in a swimming pool. People have begun to creep up politely on the outer side of each aisle, brushing against the white hydrangeas, which means there are no chairs left and almost two hundred guests have come. I know the exact count of chairs because I signed for them when they arrived this morning.

"One seventy-five, right?" the driver double-checked before letting his men unload. The driver was Billy Martinson from high school, from European history class. Nico Gerardi's friend. Billy seemed happy to see me. He told me he'd dropped out of SUNY Oswego after one year, that he'd gotten out of the "party business," so to speak, and into the party *rental* business, *the delivery aspect of it*. Billy had the dubious distinction of having clocked more deliveries than any other party trucker in the Hamptons, whatever that meant. Probably just that he was a menace on the local highways.

"The secret to success," he informed me, "is the ability to be in two places at once."

"One seventy-five, that's right," Mrs. Fleming confirmed, tying her robe tighter. She kept making her robe tighter and tighter all morning, though it wasn't even slipping open.

One hundred seventy-five chairs sounded like a hell of a lot to Mr. Fleming, who appeared from the kitchen, Bloody Mary in hand, complete with celery stalk stirrer. When his wife reminded him that the service was scheduled for Friday afternoon and that colleges were out for summer, she sounded stretched and wilty, like she would not have been able to withstand an objection from him should he choose to make one. He ended up saying nothing, which had less to do with the fact that he agreed with her than that Billy and I were standing there, staring at him. As usual he seemed gigantic, though that was more in attitude than actuality. It was true that the service would most definitely be crowded, not only for the reasons Mrs. Fleming had mentioned. Though he may have had damaged relationships, Jack had had messages.

Mrs. Fleming shrugged and shook her head, quaking with her mouth agape as though she didn't know what to say, or how to speak, or what it was that anyone even wanted. She drew a strand of white hair behind her right ear and tightened her robe again, trying to collect herself. It was the nearness of her husband that had thrown her. I did not surmise this; I knew it absolutely. Just Mr. Fleming standing there, with that Bloody Mary, looking, well, looking exactly like Mark.

Billy asked, "The chairs, Mrs. Fleming? Where do you want them?"

"This way," I said, taking over, and the men followed me up the driveway around the west side of the house to the service area.

Billy examined the tautness of the tent ropes and the fixedness of stakes. "Who did these—Party Animals or Monumental Tental Rental?"

"Monumental, I think."

He shook his head. "You should have called us." He handed me a card. "Next time."

I'd arrived at the Flemings' at about nine-thirty that morning. I'd been thinking about going over all week, only I hadn't. I just kept driving by the house, making sure things appeared normal, that lights came on at night and cars moved around in the day. When my mother found out what I was doing, she got mad and told me to knock on their damn door. She told me this was no time for *bullshit city manners.*

"I don't want to impose," I said.

"Kindness is not an imposition."

"Maybe they need space."

"They don't need space," my mother said. "They need someone to answer the fucking phone."

I was pretty sure the Flemings didn't like anyone using their phone. Jack always said how his mother would bleach it every time someone touched it.

"There's no one better equipped than you to make sure the family is holding up—especially that woman—and to see to it that Jack is properly represented. You are a diplomat," she said, and liking the sound of that, she added, "A diplomat of the dead."

"Your mother's right," said Powell, who had flown home from Anchorage for the funeral. "Imagine you had died first. Jack would be sitting right there where you are, telling us what and what not to do—what music to play, what clothes to wear, what stories to tell."

My mother looked at Powell quizzically. "Do you really think he'd be sitting?" she asked. "I imagine he'd be *lying.* You know, sprawled out on the couch."

Powell nodded as he considered that. "I suppose so. Lying and crying."

"And being a tremendous pain in the ass," Mom added.

"You're right, Irene. He wouldn't be worth shit."

Though I could not exactly imagine the Flemings giving me a warm welcome, I trusted my mother's opinion. She'd been to hundreds of funerals. She was always the first to volunteer in cases of crisis. If anyone tried to discourage her from attending yet another memorial service, she'd say, "There's nothing worse than poor turnout at a funeral. I certainly hope *you're* not alone on the day you bury one of your people."

When the chairs were set—in curves rather than lines, no lines for Jack—I came in from the yard and found his mother sitting in the living room, dressed at last. She was wearing a taupe pant suit and on her lap lay a closed book, an album of some kind. Though she said nothing, there were two cups on the table and a plate of those triangular sandwiches without crusts. I figured I was supposed to join her.

She transferred the book to my lap as though passing a clipboard in a doctor's office, without fanfare or emotion. It was a photo collection of Jack's life that she had assembled from family events—weddings, graduation parties, birthdays. She intended to display it at the memorial. I didn't have to look hard or long to see that Jack was miserable in every shot, despite the fact that he had successfully bastardized all his dress-up clothes. There were Boy Scout badges Superglued onto his wide-lapeled Brooks Brothers suit and flames painted onto his one silk tie, and Wacky Pack stickers varnished onto his good shoes. I could not see the shoes in the photos, but I knew they were there. The shoes were legendary. Denny had borrowed them for the senior banquet even though they were two sizes too small, and when we'd danced, he'd moved like magic, not missing a single step.

I was overwhelmed. I hadn't seen pictures of him in so long. I wanted desperately to restore him. I couldn't understand why it was not possible to do so. Me just thinking, *his voice, his voice. His face, his eyes, his voice.* I realized that I had not neared the bottom of my pain, that my sorrow was stronger than I could ever be, coupled as it was with the sickening knowledge that I'd wasted years with Mark that could have been spent instead with Jack—helping him, if that would have been possible. I held the book close to my face, squinting.

"Is something wrong?" Jack's mother asked in her deflated sort of monotone, not looking up from the book.

"I forgot my glasses," I said, lying.

"Glasses," she said dismissively. "You're awfully young for glasses."

I stayed that way with her for the better part of an hour, going through photo by photo, squinting and sinking further into despair, because I couldn't exactly leave her alone with the wretchedness of memories on the day of the funeral. After the funeral it was going to have to be every man for himself. And, besides, Rita the housekeeper had made a fresh pot of coffee, and though I'd often walked past the Fleming couch, I'd never sat on it. It was actually quite comfortable. Mrs. Fleming didn't seem worried in the least about me holding a cup of coffee and eating sandwiches while flipping through the overstuffed album and blowing my nose, despite the very real potential for spills, which led me to wonder whether Jack had not made more of her cleanliness neurosis than she deserved. I kept looking up, half-expecting Jack to walk in, to join us. I thought it was something we could have gotten through well together—not the funeral, but coffee with his mother. I was sorry we'd never tried.

I heard myself say, "Do you mind if I open the drapes?"

She struggled with the suggestion as though having some cognitive lapse, as though a word or term I'd used were foreign to her. She moved her mouth, but nothing came out.

I stood and drew back the curtains on each window. "It's pretty today," I said. Rays of sunshine charged in at varying angles like they'd been waiting. "Isn't it pretty?" *Pretty* as a word might not have been an appropriate choice for a funeral day; however, I used it with authority. The day was mine, I'd decided, and even if it wasn't, I intended to take it. In old film noir movies, the detective takes on someone else's problem, and in the process of solving it, solves his own. He works backward through the crime while moving forward in his mind to crack his own riddle. In such narratives the crime is a metaphor, and the riddle is a metaphor, and quite possibly, beginning at the end is also a metaphor, a prescriptive for successful living. The way it goes is this—*The story starts when I enter it.*

Mrs. Fleming flinched as though stunned by the flare of oncoming headlights. Then she settled back, looking wide-eyed and stony.

"Are you okay?" I asked, not sure if she knew who I was anymore. She didn't seem flustered or disoriented; as a matter of fact, she appeared to have made her way back to safety. This was nothing new, I realized, and here lay the riddle of her chill—she was incalculably depressed. Of course Jack would have wanted to save her. Of course he would have tried. And, of course, his every effort would have been undermined. Yes, this is where he'd gotten lost. How sad. In his little-boy mind, he'd been her failure. Rourke had felt this way too, except that Jack had felt a companion disgust unknown to Rourke—Jack's father was no hero as Rourke's had been.

And the riddle of Jack was the riddle of us. Him not wanting to smother me as his father had his mother, but him not being able to stop. Him psychologically resorting to the tools and terms that had given his father power over others. Him holding me, teaching me, coming whole to my need with his need, and in the end, him leaving as he came, carrying away his pain as if in a suitcase, because I'd done nothing to relieve his burden.

"Look at this one," Mrs. Fleming said, tapping a page we'd passed at least twice before. I opened my eyes wide.

It was a picture of the two of them, Jack as a baby. In it his hair was white and hers was white. They looked lovely, mother and son, and hopeful with the new bond between them. He was no more than twenty pounds with his symphony-shell ribs poking over his diaper and his ankles like twigs. And his eyes, searing blue as though the color had been branded onto his face, as though he'd been awakened already to the nonsense of inequity.

"Never side with your husband over your children," she confided in a hiss. I turned to find her eyes. There was something eerie about the vacancy there, the hollow helplessness, the pathological refusal to invest in anything beyond the sphere of her own unhappiness. Looking at her, I felt the way others must have felt when they looked at me. She looked as if she were suffering from vertigo. "They'll tell you to do that. Never do that. Men are disposable. Children are not."

We were interrupted by a crash from the floor above. My hand jerked, and coffee spilled narrowly onto the saucer. The china shook unevenly, and I carefully lowered my cup to the table. The house had been so quiet, I'd presumed we were alone.

Mr. Fleming shouted, *"Susan! Where did you put my cuff links?"*

More unnerving than the sound he made was the fact that she had invoked him only seconds *before* the sound. She had detected him before he'd become detectable. Just as she'd been seducing me into doubting her connection to him, she demonstrated the strength of the bond.

"I didn't *put them* anywhere," she replied to the banister. "They're on your dresser."

She waited in case he was going to yell some more, then she returned to me with a joyless smile. "Jack loathed him. I loathe him too. I stayed married because I had no alternative. I had to consider *their* college, *their* future," she said. "What would I have done? Aging, with two children. Who would have hired me? Who would have loved me?" She took back the book. "At least my son had the courage to die. His father will cling to life until the bitter end. Unless I kill him first. I'd like to kill him first."

A procession of somber guests passes the row of Jack's belongings that Elizabeth and I arranged on the garden wall before the service. There's the stuffed mouse I made, the harmonica my mother had given him, his drawings, his skateboard, his surfboard, his books, his mother's photo album.

Jewel is still next to me. "Did you love him, Jewel?" I get the feeling she did.

She hunts through her tapestry purse and nods.

"From when?"

"December 1980," she whispers, withdrawing a tissue. "Dan and I ran into him at the John Lennon vigil. Jack was high. He hardly recognized us. He hadn't seen me in years, but Dan, well— We took Jack back to my parents' apartment on West End Avenue and we hid him in my room. He didn't talk for two days. The third morning he was gone. I didn't hear from him until he showed up at my apartment at Yale two months later. He was in bad shape again, so I cleaned him up and drove him back to school in Boston. That summer we got a room together in the East Village. In September, he dropped out of Berklee and came with me to New Haven."

Yale. I remember Alicia saying she thought she had seen Jack.

"For a while it was okay. We'd go to concerts and movies, and I would borrow books for him from the library. I bought him a guitar," she says. "I guess he got bored or restless, so he started to go down to the city. At first he would stay with this bass player on Fourteenth Street and Avenue A—they formed a new band—but soon he started disappearing for days at a time. His family tried an intervention, but it was excruciating for him. All of them in Elizabeth's living room on First and Seventy-seventh with a therapist and these pickled kitchen cabinets. He couldn't get over the cabinets, like why anyone would go to all that trouble.

"The family apologized; but he felt they'd just been coached to assume blame. He said they hadn't genuinely changed, they'd just replaced their own authoritarian ideas with someone else's authoritarian ideas. He said they were only motivated by AIDS and the homosexual connotations they'd have had to face if ever he'd contracted it.

"According to his family, Jack sabotaged the whole thing," Jewel says. "If only they could have seen how upset he was. He just kept saying, *They're programmed, they're programmed.* His mother especially. I think he'd been wishing she'd been shocked into feeling some effect. I didn't know what to do. I called. I wrote letters. I went to see Elizabeth."

"I'm sorry," I say.

She shrugs. "They wanted him to go to this rehab place in Minnesota, but he refused, so they cut him off. They asked us to do the same. I objected because I knew it would drive him further into the hands of the wrong people.

"Last time I saw him was Christmas, six months ago. I had a sweater for him. He didn't want the sweater; he wanted a hundred dollars. I said I couldn't do that, and I didn't have a hundred dollars. He was like, *Fine, forget it.* And that was it. A month ago, I got a call about the guitar. He'd sold it. My number in Connecticut was scratched onto the back, and the guy Jack sold it to had been arrested. The cops figured it had been stolen."

I hand her a new tissue; she's used her last. People keep coming by to kiss me and say hi, or just pat my shoulder.

"He never called you, did he?" she asks, her sad soul swimming. "No,

I don't suppose he would have." She looks to her lap. "There was a book. He carried it everywhere. When he slept, I would read it. Songs, poems, pressed flowers. Letters to you, from you. Do you know the book?"

"Yes," I say, "I do."

There is a murmur of activity in front. "I'd better get back to my family," Jewel says. "I just wanted to—to say, sorry."

"Don't be sorry to me. I betrayed him. You never betrayed him."

"No, Eveline, you didn't betray him. You treated him like he was a normal, healthy man. You didn't let it descend to pity or need. When you couldn't be honest, you walked away. He loved you all the more for it."

Father Michael McQuail of Braintree, Massachusetts, begins the eulogy by admitting that he has never met Jack, that he has come as a favor to his friend Cecilia Hanover, Jack's maternal grandmother, who is too infirm to have traveled from Boston to attend the service.

"Although I am a priest," he says, gently bending the microphone out of range, then stepping away from the podium altogether, "I have not been invited to speak in a religious capacity."

He stands before us in a sort of informal traveling priest outfit—black slacks and a short sleeved black shirt and a handsome stainless steel watch. His arms are tanned and healthy. I heard him talking earlier to Reverend Olcott about running—their *other* mutual interest. Father McQuail runs in the Boston Marathon every year.

"I understand that Jack was a plain-speaking boy, and I'm a plain-speaking man, so I won't bother to carry on about a life unnecessarily lost or precious gifts wasted. I will just say that what this individual did to himself and to his family and friends was a transgression of the worst kind. First of all, drug trafficking and drug use are illegal, and the toxic damage caused to the body and mind by substance abuse represents a desecration of the natural to a perverse degree. Secondly, suicide is a crime. On some other occasion we might have a leisurely discussion as to whether suicide constitutes an *ethical* crime or a *religious* crime, but judging by the pain I see in the faces before me, I don't think that anyone will disagree that it is a *civic* crime. His death cost all of you. You have been robbed of your ability to provide assistance, to tender compassion, to ask forgiveness."

Father McQuail speaks quickly, in a kind of nasal bark. Before one sentence is complete, the next begins its tumble from his mouth. He gives the impression of being smart and sincere and in a bit of a fervor. One thing is for certain, he has everyone's attention.

"But you know about your own pain. Let's discuss instead what is a mystery. Let's discuss feelings that are at risk of festering if left undiscussed. Let's speak of the idea to which each of you is clinging, *That those who fail were failed.* You want to know, is it outside the realm of possibility that Jack was the victim of a crime of a magnitude equal to the one he committed? Not some gross solitary act, perhaps, but fine crimes, subtle crimes, crimes of *omission.*"

A new round of crying begins. It takes minutes for the crowd to settle down. "I didn't travel seven hours to make anyone feel worse than they do already. I came because you are all assembled together just this once, and I embraced an opportunity. If anyone is too distraught to listen, you are welcome to take a walk around the block. It's a beautiful day." Father McQuail lifts the stem of a rose from the fence alongside him and inhales. He waits, but no one leaves.

"I don't have to have known Jack to know that he was difficult. Mrs. Hanover, his grandmother, whom the boy is said to have resembled, is extremely difficult. Ours is a strenuous friendship. Some might ask, *Why bother? Life is short, don't work so hard.* To me that is tantamount to saying, *Life is short, don't grow so much.* If Mrs. Hanover is acerbic, she is brilliant. If she is self-righteous, she is uncompromising. If she is stubborn, she is trustworthy—if I am made irritable by the fixedness of her opinion, I depend upon the fixedness of her ethics. If she provokes me, she expects to be provoked in kind. If she questions my meaning, it is because, indeed, my meaning needs to be questioned.

"If my relationship with her were any *less* difficult—if she did not challenge me, did not test me, if she accepted me too easily, at face value, then she would not be a friend but an acquaintance. Certainly, at this level of intensity, one cannot have many friends. This is not a bad thing. Reduced circumstances are a consequence of truthfulness.

"I don't have to have known Jack to see that he chose his friends carefully. Obviously he chose well. Surely he started out as all children do, giving what they hope to receive. An unfortunate misconception is that as we age, we need to move beyond the perfection of that childhood barter to something more abstruse. I am going to wager that Jack was terrified about making the transition into maturity that you all made with relative ease, that he claimed it was a compromise, and that he tested you—unfairly, no doubt. Some of you moved on, retreating to the safety of acquaintanceship. Terrified by your distance, your *politeness*—he removed himself in kind. He didn't need narcotics to feel alien; he felt that way already. Narcotics confirmed his feelings and numbed them."

Father McQuail paces absently in front of the Flemings. Elizabeth is shaking, trilling really, like a cold dog, and Mr. Fleming is slumped with his face in his hands. Jack's mother's head is like stone. She is a bust of herself.

"There are things that cannot be held to common external standards," Father McQuail says, "because they possess an uncommon internal nature. To be kind, to be compassionate, to be a *friend*—if, in fact, it is a friend we want to be—we must struggle to look past outward manifestations in order to see the essence of what we admire."

He rests an elbow on the lectern and looks out at us as if memorizing faces. "Being Jack's friends, you're probably resistant to simplistic analogies. However, I beg you to indulge me. If one is a gardener, one cannot treat a rose as one would any other flower. A rose wants coddling, and to be sure, few people have the patience for it—so much of the product, so much of the time, is a wall of thorns. Why does God give us the rose? To humble us, to better us, to encourage forgiveness and understanding. And for those who show forbearance, the reward is divine. Yet it occurs to me that the rose is not only the *reward*, but the *acknowledgment* of the success of our efforts—the sensitivity, the tenacity. It is the proof of the virtue of faith. *The rose singles out the tender.* God has strategically placed the pure in the midst of the perilous to separate out those who can and will strive to reach for an ideal. My suspicion is that once you have been called upon to love this way, once you have proved your capacity, you will be called upon again.

"I traveled down from Boston to let you know that your experience with Jack was not a failure; it was an *experience*. We can't rewrite Jack's life. But we can redouble our efforts the next time we meet someone like him. I ask you to be courageous of heart. I ask you to remember that if you were hurt in this instance, it was not because you deserved to get hurt, or were foolish to get hurt, it was because you *risked* getting hurt. I ask you not to forsake the willingness to risk."

Elizabeth looks ravaged. Her eyes are swollen and pink and big for their sockets, like thyroid eyes. The pace of her speech is the opposite of Father McQuail's. She speaks into the microphone as if she is sedated, though having spent the afternoon with her, I know she is not. She is simply determined to own up to her part.

She thanks Father Michael on behalf of her family, then she says, "I'm two years older than Jack, but Jack was ahead of me in everything. School, music, art, ideas, and now, suffering. He became a vegetarian when he was ten. That didn't stop the rest of us from eating meat several times a week. I remember sitting at the table, tormenting him with steak. He would stare back with a blank stare, marveling at the spectacle of me being an animal eating an animal, and sure enough, I would start to feel like an animal eating an animal. After dinner I would make myself throw up. I never touched meat again after leaving for college. I can't even stand the smell of it. I've moved from two apartments because of the odor of cooking flesh. I won't let my parents cook it when I visit, or before I visit—and for my sake, they don't," she says, "though they didn't offer Jack the same courtesy. I honestly don't know how he coped."

"At nine, he hung a sign he made from a torn sheet out of his bedroom window to protest the Vietnam War and the Kent State killings, and, at thirteen, he boycotted toothpaste containing nonessential additives. He used apples and dental floss for weeks until Dan found natural stuff at the health food store. My parents used to have him play piano like a trained pet at their cocktail parties until the time he said, 'Here's a little song I wrote just for you,' and the lyrics were the ingredients of sliced white bread played along to this really bad piano bar tune. They never asked him to play again. In high school—I don't even know why I'm telling you this—I used to hide my feminine hygiene products in a box in a dresser drawer. Once Jack walked in on me going through the box. I screamed for him to get out, but he only came farther into the room.

" 'Elizabeth,' he said, 'don't be ashamed. Please. I'm saying this because *they* never will.' " She wipes her eyes. " *'Please,'* he said to me. *'Please.'*

"Jack loved the blues from the time he was a baby, which was uncanny considering that in our house we never listened to anything but Bobby Vinton and the Carpenters. Just to show you what kind of an asshole I was, I used to tell him, *'The blues suck.'* Last night I locked myself in his room. I don't know how many of you have seen his room, but it's the coolest space. I was on his bed crying when I saw his collection of albums on the floor. For the first time I thought to look at them, *really* look at them, and I did, and I, and I—couldn't believe I, I never—there are milk crates full of—"

She bends over the lectern, supporting herself. I look away. Although she's standing before a crowd, the moment is her own. I feel Jack in the tent—the leaden livingness, the way it used to be, with a premium on honesty. It comes like a minuscule change in humidity. Her father stands to help. She waves for him to sit.

"Full of rare recordings—seventy-eights, forty-fives, in perfect condition, alphabetized, labeled, exactly the way he left them, because he *loved* them." She continues through her tears. "My first thought was to give them to Dan or Evie because I didn't deserve them. Then I realized that Jack could have sold them when he needed money. But he *refused* to do that. He preferred to shoot himself. He must have known I would receive them. He must have."

After helping Elizabeth to her chair, Dan takes her place. Minutes pass before people become quiet again. Dan waits patiently. The more patiently he waits, the more emotional everyone becomes.

"When I first found out," he states simply, "I thought, I can't say I lost anything. Whatever I lost, I gave up voluntarily, long ago. I actually felt *lucky* that I'd gotten out before getting hurt. I figured, nothing's changed. His absence is his absence, and his presence—the things we did or the music we wrote, that's still a presence, you know, meaningful and ongoing.

"But after listening to Father McQuail, I think it's safe to say I fell seriously short."

Dan tugs his shirt from his chest and adjusts his glasses. "I used to argue with Jack quite a bit. As we grew older, I stopped, because it was easier to not engage, and because I figured it's what adults are supposed to do. I mean, who wants to be interfered with?

"The bizarre thing is that the more tolerant I became of his extremism, the more extreme he became. It was like he was begging me not to be mediocre, challenging me. Instead of recognizing his tests, I ignored them. The more outrageous his behavior, the more distance I put between us. As Father said, reactions like that terrified Jack. Especially in his frame of mind, especially with the company he'd been keeping." Dan looks up at us. "I guess I could have worried less about the damage he might have caused me and more about the damage he was doing to himself.

"I've known Jack since we were two. Jack did not stumble unconsciously into adversity. Jack chose adversity because he believed himself to be a casualty of prosperity. Unfortunately, heroin use is not the kind of thing anyone can control, and loneliness, well, loneliness accrues. I asked my dad how it happened, how Jack went from using drugs sometimes to using them a lot to committing suicide. My father said it's a matter of *time in*. Like becoming a musician. Spend more *time in* than time out and you become an expert."

Dan reaches into his pocket and removes a small strip of paper, unfolding it carefully while he talks. "There's a book of his that Elizabeth gave me yesterday, *The Anatomy of Melancholy*, by Robert Burton. Here's a quote Jack had underlined. *If adversity hath killed his thousand, prosperity hath killed his ten thousand*."

Dan plays with the paper on the lectern. "Jack could scale any building. He liked to walk as the crow flies, and if a house was in his way, sometimes he would go straight over it and meet me on the other side. He might come down scraped up, but he would tell me how beautiful the stars were from the rooftop. When I heard he killed himself, the first thing I thought was how he always did like to walk as the crow flies. Next I thought, *I hope the stars look good from wherever he is*."

From the front, I can see most everyone, though it's impossible to take them all in. Mr. and Mrs. Fleming are on my left, next to Elizabeth and Dan and Smokey Cologne, who is wearing a suit that's briny green like a cartoon ocean. Smokey maintained the closest contact with Jack until the end, and there are things he has in his head that he will not share. When he arrived this afternoon, I ran down the Flemings' driveway to meet him, and he held me. I never figured we were close, but that moment helped me more than all the others. Holding him, I thought of Jack but also of Rourke and Rob, of their friendship, and I hoped in my heart that everything had been done for Jack that could have been done, but nonetheless I knew otherwise—and I started to cry.

Alongside Dr. Lewis is his wife, Micah, with Jim Peterson, from their band, and our old music teacher, Toby Parker. Dan's babysitter, Bitsy, is wearing turquoise beads the size of golf balls. Dad and Marilyn are also on the left, back by the screened porch with Denny and Jeff and Denny's mother, Elaine. Behind them, all the people standing. Mom's friends take up two and a half rows on the right—Lowie and David; her handicapped friend, Lewis; Nargis; and several people I don't recognize. Powell is there too, but separate. He's standing at the end of the aisle in case he has to catch me.

I see teachers—Mr. McGintee and Principal Laughlin and Mrs. Kennedy and tons of people from high school—Alice Lee, Min Kessler, Marty Koch. Ray Trent and Mike Reynolds are there, and so is Dave Meese, who once borrowed fifty dollars from Jack and probably still owes it to him. Rocky Santiago and his wife, Laurie, who swam with dolphins on their honeymoon, are next to LizBeth Bennett, who worked at the movie house, who is standing with Rick Ruddle, the Outward Bound counselor from Portland. I never met Rick, but I know him from hiking pictures. Funerals are bizarre—Dino, one of the brothers from the pizza place who was always antagonizing Jack, is sitting next to Jack's cousin, Monroe Fortesque. Monroe attended Phillips Academy in Andover, then Princeton. Jack called him "the Preppy Hangman." I am horrified on Jack's behalf to see Monroe there, all muggy and serious. Though Monroe is Jack's relative, he is one of those types of relatives you never imagine when you are conceiving your own funeral. If Jack had thought in advance about the Preppy Hangman being invited, he probably would have looked down the barrel of the gun and said, *Jesus, it's enough to make a guy want to think about living.*

I didn't tell Mark about the service, so he is absent. But Alicia is there, standing in back. I smile at her, then I adjust the microphone so I can be heard. I want my voice to go far.

"The Teton Mountains are in northwest Wyoming. The highest peak there is 13,766 feet. I've never been to the Tetons, but I know the average annual temperature at night and the average rainfall in May because Jack wrote it all down on the leg of my favorite jeans. Every time I washed the jeans, he would rewrite everything. I've never been to Yosemite either, but I know there are granite domes that look like hooded monks and sequoia groves that stand like clusters of elephant legs. There are boreal forests in Wrangell–Saint Elias National Park in Alaska, and carpets of wildflowers on the banks of Lake Clark in Anchorage, and petroglyphs of bighorn rams near the Arches National Park in Moab, Utah.

"Jack buried a picture of me in the ancient Blackfoot hunting grounds on the Continental Divide in West Glacier, Montana, and also a silver fork I had as a baby with my name etched on it. He said it would keep my spirit safe. He drew a map for me to find the spot, in case I'm ever out that way.

"Elvis Presley's 'One Night with You' was originally recorded in 1956 as 'One Night of Sin' by Smiley Lewis, the best rhythm and blues man New Orleans has ever seen. Jack never forgave Elvis for not giving Lewis credit. If you dared to suggest that it wasn't Elvis's fault, that in general he helped to popularize black music, Jack would say, '*Bullshit*. He should have done all the originals as B-sides.'

"Besides Dave Brubeck's 'Take Five,' *Trois Gymnopedies, Number 2* was Jack's favorite piece to play on piano. It was written by Eric Satie in 1888 as an accompaniment to athletes. Jack's favorite year in music history was 1959. In 1959, Miles Davis recorded 'Kind of Blue' with Bill Evans, and Oscar Peterson did a version of Cole Porter's 'In the Still of the Night,' which we would listen to whenever there was snow. If you happen to find a copy of that song, listen to it when there's snow and you'll know a place in Jack's head that's really nice. *Was* really nice.

"I can draw sixty-two species of wildflower from memory. Jack used to quiz me, and I would get points for speed. I've worked since I was six-teen, first in a restaurant and then in an art gallery, but the only money

I've ever felt good about earning has come from flower drawings. I've sold sixteen so far, two last week, on Tuesday. They say Tuesday is the day he died. I thought of Jack that day, how proud he would have been, how the money was like *our* money. I keep wondering if I was thinking of him at the moment he was sitting with that gun, maybe thinking of me.

"I can name every snake and every cloud. Jack's favorite cloud was cirrus because cirrus clouds are far, and he liked to look far. 'Look, Evie,' he would say, 'they're like horse's tails!' He wanted them to be my favorite too. I agreed with him as often as I could, only not in the case of clouds. I preferred stratus. Stratus are the brooding ones, low like anguish, like neglected boxcars in the rain, like crying in your favorite hiding place—like Jack.

"Turgenev wrote of nihilism in *Fathers and Sons* in 1862. Jack did not teach me that; my mother taught that to Jack, and I happened to be in the room. He was complaining about morality, how it's a hollow construct, how the only possible reform is revolutionary reform. 'Go read Turgenev,' she told him. 'Then talk to me.' And he did. Possibly she meant to show Jack that he was thinking like the great thinkers. Possibly she meant to show him that his thoughts were not necessarily original. In either case she felt it was his duty to go further. She always spoke to him very fast, like it was a race, like she had to hurry, like Jack needed to get out of his head as quickly as possible.

"I should mention how hard this is for my mother. Like the rest of us, I'm sure she wishes Jack would have called when he was in trouble. *Unlike* the rest of us, she has to live with the knowledge that she actually would have done something about it. She would have thrown herself on him, like he was on fire."

There is crying, ongoing like a faucet running. Under the tent the air is hot. I bend my knees and hold the lectern tight. "Those are the easy things. There are other things. Not so easy.

"Jack believed that society is hypocritical to place so much value on the sanctity of individual human life, while tolerating famine, war, extreme poverty, racial cleansing, environmental destruction, capital punishment, species extinction, and other crazy stuff, such as fattening calves in cages or force-feeding geese with tubes.

" 'It's so stupid,' he would say. 'Suicide is intolerable but all too frequently, genocide is not. Why the double standards?'

"It's hard to say whether Jack felt instinctively that suicide was the
best possible solution to his problems or if he became intellectually convinced of a pro-suicide position because he found the anti-suicide position to be so condescending. He hated therapy, probably because he had
been sent so much at such an early age. He rejected the theory that over-
simplified rhetoric would inspire desperate people in desperate circumstances to discover the previously elusive joy of living. 'Besides,' he would
say, 'every therapist is on the family payroll. They have the incentive to
find problems and side with their employers. We might as well ask the
housekeeper her opinion.'

"His body was his alone, he said. He said that by the time he found
himself in trouble, any feelings of entitlement others might have would
not be real reflections of real relations. They would be false or residual. 'If
love isn't getting through,' he would say, 'it's not real. If we're not sharing
it, it's not love. It's fanaticism. It's Pentecostal. *The gift of tongues.*'

"It all used to make sense. But now I see it was only Jack making
sense. Because despite his having prepared me, I'm bereaved. Despite our
separation, I've lost a piece of myself. Despite the fact that I tried to be
fair, I wonder if I behaved irresponsibly. If I can't say that my moving on
with my life was right or wrong, or him ending his despair was right or
wrong, I *can* say that today is worse than yesterday, and yesterday was
worse than the day before. When Dan called to tell me Jack was dead, I
was not surprised. Now I feel that the day should never have come, and
I'm ashamed of myself for expecting it. I feel more guilty and more betrayed as time passes. Guilty because I should have done something, and
betrayed because he promised I wouldn't feel this way.

"If I have to give up my right to sorrow in order to respect his right to
die, I'll never recover. If I absolve him of this crime, he stays an invalid,
a freak, a victim. If I don't hold him accountable, I make a choice, as if I
am godly. I'm not godly. He has to share his burden of the blame for not
finding a solution. I mean, look around. We're not talking about Jack's
one life, or *my* one life. We're talking about at least as many lives as are
here today. It's inconceivable that we *all* failed."

Powell is straight ahead, looking at me with concentration, staring evenly, attentively, as he stares perhaps at the sea.

"I wasn't sure I was going to come up here. I kept trying to think of what he would have wanted, for me to talk or for me to not talk. If you had it all figured out that Jack wanted you to do one thing, it usually turned out that he wanted the other."

People laugh, though I didn't intend to be funny.

"I thought of trying to reach him. I used to be able to reach him. I don't mean like calling up a spirit. I mean the difference between mindless thinking and *really* thinking—it's like combining everything outwardly known and everything inwardly known and letting it shuffle together like cards. And then in a way, invisible things really do begin to appear.

"Elizabeth reached him. You probably noticed the change in the air when she was up here. When she spoke, she was very brave, and all we'd forgotten of Jack became clear—*he* became clear—and we reclaimed him from his own terrible version of himself. The way he was good, the way she's always known that he loved her, the way she loved him too. The way he felt himself beyond repair but held out hope for her.

"I spent this morning with Mrs. Fleming, talking and looking at pictures, and Jack was clear then too. But his mom was also clear. I found myself wishing that I'd spoken to her sooner, that I hadn't depended upon him to arbitrate, that I'd been as willing to question his ideas of things as he'd been mine. That I'd been a better friend. His view of her was not entirely accurate or fair. Jack could be so unforgiving; above anything else, that led to his isolation. It was after sitting with his mom that I decided to speak today, not worrying what he would have wanted, just making his job of forgiving her *my* job.

"Not everyone who kills themselves lives as Jack did at the end. Many violent suicides are committed by supposedly normal citizens—parents, teachers, scholars, doctors, bankers, movie stars. Some just kill themselves over time, through more acceptable means. Pills, alcohol, smoking, reckless driving, bad diet. You have to question the discrepancy between their public accomplishments and their anti-social behavior. What face did they show, what lies did they live, what passed for love that was not love at all? You have to wonder whether an extreme need to please or to succeed is not just a convenient, socially approved way of encrypting the darker corridors. And if that false face is accepted by others, it breaks the wearer doubly: the person isn't known, and the attention they receive isn't trustworthy. The wearer of the disguise proves what they believe deeply, that people around him are just stupid.

"Jack was different: he hid nothing. He was known, and so whatever love he received was real. Everyone acts like his honesty came easily, like he had it and we didn't. But it was the product of an arduous labor. Look at the photo album on the back table. When he *was* forced to comply socially, he did so as a fully formed Jack, not as anyone who could ever be mistaken for the rest of us. His was a stylized resistance; he was an artist. And Mrs. Fleming admired Jack's will. If she made an error by concealing in the secret support of his ideals her own secret need for freedom, it was only because she'd hoped he would live more freely than she did. Today I was thinking that every challenge he made to the established order came across to her more or less like a grasp for liberty. It's obvious to me that she loved him very much, and for the same reasons we did."

I stand a little straighter. "What she didn't count on is that he would only become free if she would as well. I think he was making her a bargain. He had no intention of getting out alone."

52

The valets are dressed for the wedding in polo shirts and khaki shorts. Alicia didn't want them wearing red, white, and black, looking like waiters from a cheap restaurant, so she bought them outfits. Mark has been complaining for weeks, saying that the degree of planning that the wedding has required is obscene, though I know he actually envies Alicia and Jonathan the storm of attention.

I leave the car with the valets and cross the lawn. I make it as far as the enormous copper beech tree when I hear my name. *Eveline!* Alicia is peeking through the vertical window in the foyer. She looks perfect from far away, girl-like, like a wife in an advertisement for diamonds. As I go to her, I feel the burden of every step and inside something waning. I look at my new shoes. They seem inadequate, like they cannot possibly be counted on for support.

The house is cool, bustling but organized. Girls in satin A-line shifts with bouquets of sweet William surround Alicia, bucking coyly, like a pack of does. They are pretty in taupe and pink and with the pillbox hats Alicia made them, though it's hard to tell the difference from girl to girl. The taupe of the dresses is the same taupe Jack's mother wore to the funeral. Taupe must be *the* color. Alicia's cousin Mirelle is wearing the dress that had been made for me before I dropped out. I wave and smile, saying thank you for helping out, and how pretty she looks.

Alicia's raven hair is parted in the center, just as she likes it, flat to mid-skull, where cumbrous braids accumulate into a type of turban or hive in which six blood-red roses are enwreathed. During discussions with the florist, Mrs. Ross had suggested pink or yellow, but Alicia had refused. When my opinion was solicited, I just said that Alicia was an artist, and she knows about such things. Mrs. Ross, always an adoring mother and art enthusiast, was satisfied with that. I'm glad now about the red; Alicia looks beautiful—truly, she *is* an artist. Her neck is bound in a choker of freshwater pearls, at least ten strands thick. Her beaded gown is fitted at the bodice, becoming full at the hips. The beads catch light, making motion. With her high forehead and hollow cheeks and ravishing stillness, she looks like a black-figure silhouette in an Etruscan tomb painting.

Tears fill her eyes. "This feels bad," she says. "Unbelievably bad."

I scrape a square of glitter from her cheek. What has she been glittering? Menus maybe, or gifts for the kids. She's that way. It's unfortunate that Jack's suicide has touched her wedding, but that is life and she is part of the living. Marriage of all things has to withstand its share of troublesome associations. Anyway, there's nothing I can do. She seems to think I can do something.

"What you said yesterday at the funeral, about normal people with the need to please, people with a false face—"

I wave my hand, stopping her. I can't tell her the truth and I don't feel like lying. It would be nice to think that her super-social sensibilities will lead her to some place of relative freedom and self-empowerment, but I'm not sure they will, and besides, such sensibilities didn't exactly help her father. I reach into my pocketbook and withdraw a piece of onyx onto which I carved a flower.

"For you," I say. "For luck."

She clings to me. In her dress she feels stiff, like underneath is corrugated stuff, like a hurricane could not raise her. Maybe that's the point. In a gown the bride cannot get away. She cannot turn back. She belongs to man, to family, to community. Like a hot air balloon moored by sand and ropes. "I wish you would stay for the reception," Alicia says.

Mrs. Ross taps us apart. "That's enough, girls. Evie, dear, go sit."

Jonathan's brother, Evan, meets me at the base of the center aisle. Evan didn't want to be a groomsman. He wanted to play guitar during the service and sing "Turn, Turn, Turn," but Mr. Ross said no. He'd have enough on his mind without having to worry about a goddamned minstrel.

"Sorry about your friend," Evan murmurs as we walk, him leading me, grand and slow. In the middle of the section on the left is Rob. Next to him, Rourke. My body becomes desirous, though truly I mourn. Jack was right to call me feral. I force down the life of me, like snapping a whip at a beast. I think of Elizabeth eating meat and Jack staring. I tell myself, *Jack is staring*.

Evan delivers me to the second row, to a padded white folding chair behind Mark's grandparents, who are so small I have to lean to kiss them. As I lean, I am completely conscious of Rourke and Rob, mute and upright, eight rows behind me, observing the supple arc of my spine. The string quartet begins Mozart's "Minuet in G," and Mark and Alicia's cousin Sam and his second wife, Abby, who is seven months pregnant, join me. Abby is not in taupe, she is in teal. A teal net hangs off her teal hat. Abby and Sam own a baby furniture company on the Upper West Side. One of her gloved hands touches my arm. "We heard about your friend last night at the rehearsal dinner. Are you okay?"

"Yes," I say. "Thank you."

Sam leans over. I see the map of his goatee, the grand plan of it. "We're terribly sorry."

Mark's father made the announcement at the rehearsal dinner the night before. The dinner was at 1770 House, a historic inn and restaurant on Main Street in East Hampton, which the Ross family had taken over for the weekend.

Mr. Ross explained to family and bridal party members that a friend of mine and Alicia's had died, and that due to my particularly close relationship with the deceased, it would not be appropriate for me to participate in a wedding just one day after the funeral.

I didn't hear the announcement; I was at my mother's. But I'd come to the Ross house to finish the place cards hours before the wedding, and Mr. Ross informed me of what he'd said. By the time I arrived there, Mark had gone to play some tennis with Brett, and the bridesmaids were lined up waiting for stylists. I opened the shoe box of cards I'd finished two weeks earlier and added all the table numbers. Mr. Ross waited patiently. As soon as I wrapped up the calligraphy pens, he said, "Let's get the hell out of here."

Mrs. Ross suggested I stay. "She's had a rough week, Richard. She might like to be included in the styling session. I don't know what we could do with that hair, Eveline, but how about nails and makeup?"

"Don't be conniving, Theo. She has no intention of staying past the ceremony."

"Richard, I—"

"We've been through this a dozen times. She's leaving after the ceremony. Besides, have you seen these girls when they come out? They look like hookers."

Mr. Ross and I strolled past the fountain and the newly erected tents. I was relieved to think that the tents were not the same ones used by the Flemings. Had the events been separated by more than one day, it might have been possible. All those sedimentary tears, caught in the vinyl, dripping down and around the wedding party.

I'd given away my bridesmaid dress to Mirelle, so I had to stop by Mark's cottage to collect a spare dress and a pair of shoes for the ceremony, and when I did, Mr. Ross waited for me in the hallway. Though the cottage was in fact theirs, he and his wife had always afforded us the strictest privacy. In the three years I'd lived with Mark, they'd never stopped by without an invitation, though Alicia would walk in all the time.

My suitcases were in the center of the room. I hadn't seen them since I'd packed to leave the city after the fight. I ended up going without them when I got the news about Jack, just taping a note to the top and heading for Penn Station.

Took a train to my mother's. My friend died. Eveline.

Mark brought the luggage out with him on Thursday. He said he assumed it was for Italy. My graduation present. He'd planned for us to leave directly from East Hampton on Monday morning. A car was coming. No matter what he said, I knew he suspected otherwise.

The sight of the luggage brought back memories of the fight, of Rourke being beaten, of him beating back, of the screams of the crowd, of my run down the desolate boulevard to the Greek diner, of the cab ride home, of packing and Dan's phone call, the little silver clock and the mad wind. These elements fused in my mind so that no detail could be removed without collapsing the memory as a whole. Just as flames, smoke, and heat mean *fire,* the suitcases meant *Jack is dead.*

"You okay?" Mr. Ross called up.

I called back that I was. "Want something to drink?" I asked from the landing. "A glass of ice water?" At breakfast he'd had three coffees.

He was lighting a cigarette. "I'm fine," he said, distractedly.

I jogged down the steps, and he held the door for me. We paused by the pool, where he hooked my dress for the wedding on the crosspiece of an umbrella, then we walked in the opposite direction of caterers, florists, and landscapers.

"I hope you don't mind my having said anything at the rehearsal dinner last night," Mr. Ross said, "but Mark has had a solid week to inform people. You were up-front and timely, and your choice is honorable. Considering the quality of your friendship with our own children, Theo and I would be fools to want it any other way." He extinguished his cigarette against a fence post. "I'm not happy that Mark waited until the last minute. Not happy at all."

"He was hoping I'd change my mind."

"He wasn't *hoping* anything. He was *entrapping*. I'm not sure what Mark's up to. I hope this trip to Italy will be a good thing," he said, not sounding particularly convinced. "It should be nice for you to get away."

I didn't have the heart to tell him otherwise, so we continued to walk lingeringly, with him making inquiries into the memorial, and me describing the things I'd heard and said. I told him about sitting with Jack's mother, and he liked to hear about Father McQuail.

The BMW Mark had given me sat waiting on the front lawn, balmy and adorable, lanolin-green like chewing gum. Mr. Ross attached my dress to the hook above the rear passenger door and thoughtfully scooped up the bottom, laying it across the seat. At the driver's door he took both my shoulders and he kissed me on the forehead. I could smell the stale nicotine on his breath and I felt my heart swell. I recalled my own words from the funeral about Jack never having been forced to become something he didn't want to be. Some people live their entire lives holding true to the promises they'd made to those who depend on them.

"We're kindred spirits, you and I," Mr. Ross said. "Poets."

In the heavily contrasted light beneath the trees, it became clear to me that he was thinning. I considered attributing the change to a haircut and new eyeglasses, but I confronted the possibility that he was sick again. I hoped someone was paying attention. I couldn't bear to lose one more person. That's why it was a relief to me that Denny had settled down. One night, before Denny and Jeff made a commitment, Rob had had to get Denny out of a bad situation over on Gansevoort Street, and afterward all Rob had said was, *It's a good thing I took a gun.*

"Yes, Mr. Ross," I said. "Poets."

I twisted the side-view mirror and observed his return to the house. As he neared the porch, Alicia and her girlfriends rushed to the window like he was a celebrity and they were his fans. They knocked on the glass, calling and laughing. He waved in feigned annoyance as he mounted the steps, and when he opened the door they engulfed him. I watched Mr.

Ross rededicate himself to the monster kinetics of family life, allowing himself to love and be beloved despite the private concessions of his heart and mind.

Mark had shown up at my mother's house at seven o'clock Friday night, one hour before the rehearsal dinner to try to pressure me into attending. I'd just returned from Jack's funeral. We all had—Mom and Powell, my father and Marilyn, Lowie and David, Denny and Jeff, Dan, Troy, Smokey, and Jewel, Dr. Lewis and Micah, and several of my mother's friends. Mark came upon us in the living room, a disheveled black circle.

He had met most everyone over the years but never all at once and never with them sober and nicely dressed. Usually when Mark visited, he would get this look of unfolding shock, as though viewing a particularly revolting striptease. But that evening, like a politician suddenly recognizing the voting power of a marginal constituency, he walked in and worked the room, shaking hands, offering condolences.

"Thank you for being there for Eveline," he said as he passed from person to person. "I would have been there too, but my grandparents flew in from the coast for my sister's wedding, and I had to pick them up at JFK. Considering the tragic circumstances, I should have sent a car for them, but my grandfather's ninety, and my grandmother has Crohn's disease."

In the kitchen, Mark sat at the table, in the chair nearest the stove, the place he'd sat the night we met four years before. As it happened, I was standing where I'd stood then, against the counter in front of the sink. Like dominoes, the days fell flat; I returned to the time when I knew what I wanted but had no means of achieving it, as opposed to having the means to achieve without the knowledge of any exceptional end.

"Do we *have* to sit in here?" Mark wanted to know.

Looking in his eyes, I could see the things I'd missed when we'd first met—the undisclosed designs, the skimmingness about the mind, the restless arrogance. Before going further, I was visited by a second memory—one of Rourke—in the same room, back on that same night, and me, caught in the crucible of adolescence but braver than I'd ever been. The memory of Rourke was so positive and tactile as to clear my mind. I felt a gaping sorrow, elegant and actual. Me thinking, *Oh, what I'd lost, what I'd become.*

Sensing crisis, Mark changed directions. It was amazing, how well he knew me. "You're going to break my father's heart if you don't come to the dinner tonight. Never mind the wedding tomorrow."

I called upon the only authority I possessed—artistic instinct and imagination. I established a scene, and I entered it. The kitchen, so overrun with memories of family and friends, became something purely physical, a set or stage, something onto which Mark and I had been thrust. He took on the look of a puppet, only not innocuous, and the things of which we spoke began to sound stilted. I could interpret his script. I could see that his promise to shelter me was based upon the premise of my homelessness. I wondered what was it he wanted from me in exchange. What did I possess that he needed to take away?

My feet were bare; I set them firmly into ground, all points touching. Though it was June, the floor was cold. It was the same coldness that had always been. The coldness that belonged to my mother's house, and so to my memory and perception of it and of me. That coldness was precisely what I needed to name; it was *the paintable thing*. And in my head there was a quote my mother used to say that always made me think of facing facts. It was T. S. Eliot's, I think.

The ways deep and the weather sharp. The very dead of winter.

I walked myself through the years. I had attended college and I had a job in an art gallery. Mark and I shared an apartment on West Sixtieth Street, and there was a car for me to drive. In the bank I had eleven thousand dollars. Any time I paid for something during my time with Mark—books, food, gifts, clothes—the money reappeared in my account.

I tried to think of Saturdays, any Saturday. I had some fractional memory of him on the grenade-green leather couch in the living room, phone in one hand, channel changer in the other, pulling me down to join him. And Saturday places—restaurants, nightclubs, benefits, Nantucket, the Vineyard, Cape Cod, East Hampton. Balding men, spidery women, the superfluous sounds of sex from his friends in adjoining rooms. Mark's sex was silent. It was stealthy and habitual like some dark routine, like he was addicted to the feeling of getting his money's worth.

And me, there with him, imprisoned by the impregnability of his position, lost in a world purged of sincerity and rife with conceit. Like him and every other member of his society, I was just another creaturely thing, defined outwardly by my appearance and inwardly by the ungainliness of my aspirations, the ugliness of my compromise. I was rendered most precise not by what I possessed, in fact, but by all that I had not yet attained. In the end, I was left only with an obscene sense of having participated in one long masquerade.

Mark was reminding me of my obligations to his sister, his parents. "They *have* to supersede," he said, "any conceivable obligation you might have had to this, this—"

"Jack."

He was right. My obligations to Alicia and to Mr. and Mrs. Ross *did* supersede my obligation to Jack: they were living and he was not. They had treated me as family and I had agreed to be a member of the wedding party. However, these obligations did not supersede my obligation to myself—and this was something I needed to understand: the ongoingness and the wholeness of the self regardless of external circumstance. I tried to think about what *I* wanted. I considered the toll of my continued avoidance and denial: I'd lost everything—home and Jack and Rourke. Though I might have been passive, beneath my passivity there had been agency. My life had never been *Mark's* version versus *mine*—rather, it had been one of my creations versus another. Nothing had happened that I had not allowed to happen. I had been stronger than I'd realized. Now I felt like I needed time. The coincidence of Jack's death afforded me exactly that. Jack would not have minded. He would have insisted. Part of me wondered if he had not arranged the entire thing.

"I'm sorry, Mark. I just can't."

When Mark left, everyone in the living room took a break from telling stories about Jack to discuss Mark.

"What a straight shooter!"

"He's not so bad!"

"And I always thought he was kind of an asshole!"

Except for my mother, who hadn't spoken more than a few dozen words since my speech at the memorial. From midway up the stairs, she brought conversation to a halt when wearily she stated, "If you'll all excuse me, I'm going to bed." Then she turned and went, moving uncharacteristically slow as if there were marbles in her shoes, as if she dare not move as she usually moved, as if she feared shooting off to someplace faraway.

Jonathan and Mark appear from behind the ivied trellis. They are joined by the groomsmen who had been ushers. Mark looks like a movie star in his tuxedo. He winks. Poor Mark, with Rourke looming directly behind me. *Rourke,* I think, clinging to consciousness, trying not to drift.

I fix my dress, flattening the thin cross of ribbon that binds the bodice. I'm in gray, dove-gray, like a bound dove. He likes me in gray, though I didn't think to make him like me. I didn't intend to think of Rourke today. I don't want to live any more of my life in absentia. Such living is cruel to those who need you truly. When the service commences, I listen carefully. I never want to forget how close I've come.

Outside the tent, guests assemble loosely before forming a line to congratulate the families. Musicians disband and begin their exodus to the patio near the pool so that the ceremony tent can be reconfigured for dessert and dancing. The wedding planner and her staff appear, dressed like the parking attendants in white oxfords and khakis. They move us out with false smiles and stiff backs and stretched-out arms as if they belong to the Secret Service. Mrs. Ross asks me to escort her parents to the kitchen, where they can rest until the reception.

"Thank you, darling." Mr. Sacci's head goes in circles like it is following the trail of a tightly flying fly. He grasps for his wife's hand, and she grasps for his, both of them missing repeatedly. I take a hand of each and walk them slowly behind the altar to the kitchen, the province of tea and cookies, and Consuela.

Unlike at the funeral, there are children—wearing pluffy taffeta dresses and little-man suits, running, swinging, climbing. Jack did not know any children or anyone with children. I suppose in his circle he was the *last* child.

After the memorial service cleared out, Jack's mother had summoned me privately into the house and given me a shoe. A baby shoe. White with a soft graying lace and scuffs by the heel and toe.

"For you," she'd said breathlessly. One foot remained on the lowest rung of a stepladder, and in her hand was a half key. On the edge of the closet shelf was an opened fireproof box. "For the Blackfoot hunting grounds. If you ever make it out there. Something of Jack's to bury."

I'd turned the shoe in my hands. I'd wondered if it was a gift from Jack or from her. No matter, the message was unmistakable—in it I could see the stubborn will to walk.

"Take it," she'd insisted. "I have the other."

"Yes, Mrs. Fleming," I'd said, and we'd embraced for the last time, the shoe in my hand, and my hand resting on her shoulder. When I got to Denny's car, he and I had waved, both of us. And driving off, we'd waved once more, leaving her alone at the head of the driveway.

Rourke has already said congratulations. He is not far from the end of the receiving line. His suit is a midnight-blue with fine white stitching, cut flat to his body. Beneath is a light-blue dress shirt. Both the blue of the suit and the blue of the shirt have considerable red in them, giving him an electric appearance. He's laughing with Rob and Denny and Jeff, his head modestly lowered. The right side of his face is bruised black and inflamed. I can't make out his eye. I wish I could go to him, to them, to my friends, but I can't. There is still so much to do. Besides, I feel kind of groundless and spinning. Like Mark's grandparents, grasping blind, one hand for the other.

"Here's Evie! *Evie!*" Alicia beckons, and she pulls me to the bridal party side of the line. "Is my makeup okay?" she asks overloudly, her face hovering by mine. "Did you see his eye?" she whispers. "They say it's never going to be the same."

I kiss her, then Jonathan. The photographer demands a picture. There is an awkward pause, a flash. Alicia winks at me, then brightens professionally for the next person. I move on to congratulate the others, and finally, Mark.

"It's been a long week," he murmurs suggestively as he squeezes me, his hips pushing in, his eyes looking behind me, to see if Rourke notices. Mark says, "We're going to take a drive to get photos. Meet me over by the limos." As I walk away, he yells, "Stay out of the sun."

Rob takes my hand and leads me across the garden, turning the corner by the summer room and going in, standing where Mark can't see from his position in the receiving line. Rob raises his green aviator glasses to the peak of his head. Beneath the glasses his eyes are green as well, only softer, more receptive. He adjusts the fallen strap of my dress, and gives me a light hug.

"You smell like coconut," he says.

My chin rests on his shoulder. "My aunt gave me some lotion."

"Oh," Rob says. "Lotion. Very nice."

I push away. I'm crying, and I don't want to get his suit wet. His suit is cream-colored, a linen ecru, and his shirt is snow-white. His tie is the color of purple irises.

"You look handsome."

He reaches in his pocket for a tissue, and, taking up a tiny piece, he pats beneath my eyes. "You like the suit, huh? Lorraine picked it out. She's into fashion now, so I gave her a call. We went to Barneys over in Chelsea. You gotta see her rip through ties. It's like a special aptitude, like those autistic kids who know Mozart. We went to the Russian Tea Room after. She always wanted to go there, so I figured, *What the hell!*"

"That's great, Rob."

"She's dating some lawyer now. Short kid—five-eight. He's got a two-bedroom condo in Jersey City. I go, 'Rainy, any short guy with a two-bedroom condo is wife hunting.' And she goes, 'That's right, Rob. And any guy living with another guy and a rabid dog in a trailer with no job and a penchant for gambling *is not*. It took me ten years, but I finally figured it out.'" Rob laughs. " *'Penchant,'* she says. *'For gambling.'* "

"She loves you."

He looks over my head and sucks one cheek to his teeth. "You all right? You seem shaky. You shaky?"

"I don't know. I guess."

"Suicide," Rob says. "That's rough. But what are you gonna do? You can't change people. Look at my brother. He's dead. Practically. Soon, he'll be dead."

"Anthony?"

"That's right, Anthony, in L.A." Rob reaches for a cigarette, removes his hand, and finds a stick of gum instead. "Tony. All any of us ever heard growing up was how handsome he was. Had any girl he wanted, aged fifteen to fifty. A guy like that gets a complex, know what I'm saying, like, *Who needs a real job?* So Tony goes out West and takes an excursion through the magical world of porn. Strictly straight stuff, but still. I tried talking to him. I tried everything. But forget about it, the money was too good."

I sit on the rattan sofa. Rob adjusts his tie and sits too.

"That's the reason me and Harrison stayed in L.A. after college. My uncle was ready to go make Anthony ugly, so he couldn't shame anybody. I'm like, 'Uncle, what are you gonna do, cut his dick off?' I mean, once you start that shit, where do you stop? I asked for a chance to use a little positive persuasion. You know, spend some time, hang around, get inside, pry him loose. I offered to stay on at UCLA—at Anderson, that's the business school—my mother wanted me to get an MBA anyway, so I figured this way I'd make her happy. My father and my uncle were a little chilly on the plan. They knew I was a pushover where my brother was concerned. That's when Harrison agreed to stick around too. And then that whole Diane thing happened soon after. Even so, I got caught up. That world sucks you in. Sex and cash. Blow clouds your judgment. That's what's up with Mark, by the way. Too much coke. Those Masters of the Universe assholes keep at it all day. It gets to be like popping aspirin."

At the mention of Mark, we both shoot a glance in the direction of the bridal party. Through the screened walls of the porch, we can see that half the guests are still waiting in line. We're sitting low, so there's no way for him to spot us. Rourke is still out there, so Mark won't think to worry.

Rob turns back. "Long story short, two years later, worst morning of my life—grad school graduation and it's like, *Time is up.* My whole family's flying in and I haven't gotten through to Anthony. All that's happened is *he's* compromised *me.* Remember I told you about cheaters?

Their job is the failure of *your* character. So I'm crashed on the couch in his, whatever, *bungalow,* out of my mind high from the night before—from *an hour* before—and there are scumbags all over the place—girls, guys, guys dressed like girls, and vice versa. And I'm scanning each face. How did these fucking losers ever look okay to me?

"In my mind, deep down, I'm thinking—*praying*—that Tony's gonna walk down the stairs in some sharp suit like it's Easter in the neighborhood and I'm seven and he's seventeen, and he's gonna chase everybody out, and he's gonna say, *Let's go, kid. You got a big day ahead.* Or else my family's gonna pull up, and Joey'll be there all tight with Pop, with my mother in the backseat of the rental car at the end of the driveway, her hands folded on her pocketbook, and my old man'll go, 'Go up and get your brother, boys. Tell Anthony we're going home.'

"But nothing. *Nothing.* Nobody wakes up, nobody comes. Hours go by. By nine o'clock I'm freaking out. *I gotta go. I gotta go.* My heart is speeding like it's gonna bust, and I want to grab something, a lamp, a golf club. I'm looking to start breaking shit. Get the cops there. Cops would be better than nothing.

"Just when I think I can't take it anymore, the front door creaks open. Harrison. He doesn't set foot in the place. Too contaminated. I don't want him in there anyway. I jump up and meet him at the doorway.

" 'Let's go,' Rourke says. 'You've done what you can.'

"I snap. 'Fuck you, you fucking prick. I'm not leaving.' I go to him, 'You don't know about family because you don't have one. I'd rather be dead than leave my brother.' All of a sudden, *boom.* Harrison hauls back and knocks me down. Full force. Flat. It was like getting hit by a train.

"Then he looks down and says, 'He's not your brother. I am.' "

I think of Mrs. Rourke saying, *Do you know, I still wonder what "the wrong thing" could have been.* I wonder, was it the part about Rob taking death for granted, or the part about the brother, or the part about Rourke not having family? All, possibly all.

"Harrison pulls me up, and I'm sitting there—bleeding and crying on the front steps for—shit, it's gotta be twenty minutes. I know Anthony fucking heard me. *Everybody* heard me. All down the street people were coming out of their houses.

" 'If he doesn't come down,' I said, 'it's gonna be the last time I see him.'

" 'One time is gonna be the last time,' Harrison said. 'Let's make it today.'

"He waited until I was ready. Then he picked me up and took me over to the gym and got me iced and stitched. I couldn't even stand, I was so screwed up on blow and no sleep and adrenaline. He had the doctor over there make sure my cheekbone wasn't shattered. It was a double fracture. See?" Rob points to the left side of his face.

I've seen it before. I touch it, fingers flat, going over. "This eye is smaller, isn't it?"

"But the vision's twenty-twenty. That's all I care about. I could've had surgery, but I don't give a shit, except for the sinus problems. Besides, girls are into it. So Harrison takes me to our place in Ventura, gets me fed and cleaned up, and we make it to graduation on time. My family saw me, and they practically shit. My mother starts sobbing and Mrs. Rourke goes white, but you know what?" Rob drags his fingers across his lips, zipping. "Nobody said nothing—*Harrison was with me.*"

Rob looks at me. "Sometimes you love somebody and it's like you can't see the top of the building because you're hugging the ground floor. I know you know what I mean."

"Yeah, I know what you mean."

"That's why I give you credit for letting go of your friend—Jack."

"I'm not sure I did the right thing."

"C'mon. You were just a kid, and you let go before you had to. Most people wait for a warm bed. Not you. There was no guarantee with Harrison. In fact, odds were against it. But you treated Jack with respect, and that respect probably kept him going more than you realize. Not me. I just hung around with my brother, stealing time. Now Tony is lost. I got off easy with a busted face—my brother's got *the sickness.* Last time I talked to him, he was down to 148 pounds from 190."

"Shit. I'm sorry, Rob."

"I'm just saying, you would think for all that time in I would've gotten better results. But you gotta keep your own world pretty fucking tight if you want to control other people's outcomes. You can't start sacrificing yourself to someone else's twisted view. Like Harrison said, 'You've done what you can.' I think about that a lot. You do what you do and hope for the best. Once you hit a place of diminishing returns, you have to back off, regroup. I couldn't save my brother because he didn't want saving. Neither did Jack. Harrison saved me because I wanted it, I wanted to get the hell out. Biggest lesson of my life—there is no family other than the one you make for yourself."

"Jack used to say that."

"Well, there you go. Smart kid. But there's math involved," Rob says. "You don't just *need* friends; you've got to *be* a friend. If there's nobody to track you, to challenge you, to offer resistance, put up a fight, you become some phony fuck doing constant reinvention. Believe me, it's not easy. My brother Joey is a pain in my ass, we argue a lot, but someday it'll be worth it. When one of us needs a wall, we'll turn around and it'll be there. Other times, there's no work involved. You got an automatic fortress. Like Harrison. Like—"

"Lorraine."

"Actually, I was thinking of you."

We leave the porch and walk to where the limos and the people wait, over to where the bride and groom will pass, where the flower petals will fly. Where I thought Rourke might be, but he's not.

"I gotta tell you," Rob says, "I lost it last week when I found out you left the fight. I coulda killed my sister. I told her to keep an eye on you." He points to the top of his hand. There's a crescent burn along the length of his knuckles. "Next morning she hit me with an egg pan. *'Self-defense,'* she told my father, as if I would ever set a finger on her, that she-wolf. My mother bandaged me up and called Mark's apartment. Mark said you were *all right.* That's it. No news about a dead friend. Nothing. I grabbed the phone. 'Lemme talk to her,' I said, and he goes, *'Forget about it.'* "

"I left before Mark got home that night," I explain. "I went back early to pack my bags and leave, but then the call came about Jack. So I just walked out and left my stuff and took the first train to my mother's."

"I didn't expect you to make it through the whole fight anyway, though I didn't quite count on you leaving the premises either. I just figured you'd sit in the lobby, the car. Not vanish into the dead of night. I keep forgetting who I'm dealing with."

"Sorry."

Rob shrugs. "So you packed your bags, huh? How come Mark doesn't seem to be aware of his single status? He's telling everyone you two are jetting off to Italy on Monday."

"I haven't had the chance to talk to him. I will tonight."

Oh, *there's* Rourke. On the far side of the garden with a redhead—Diane Gelbart. Diane will be sitting at table three with her parents, which I'd hoped would be six away from table nine, where Rourke and Rob will be, but in fact the tables are back-to-back, because the caterer plotted them in loops. I saw the blueprint this morning. It looked like a drawing of intestines.

Diane's poppy-red hair moves in unison, like it's covered in plastic wrap. Her flower-print black-and-red wraparound dress reveals perfect knees. She seems to have been plucked from a photograph in a vintage issue of *Vogue*. She's like one of those giant fashion models—all clothes, all posture, huge and hard at work. She spies me from beneath the wide brim of her hat. I must be of enormous interest to her, just as she once was to me. Now I feel nothing—not exactly nothing.

I look to the street. "How is he?"

"Twenty grand richer," Rob says. "So I guess he's fine." He kicks at the grass. "I don't suppose I have to tell you it was a straight fight. Whatever Mark thought or said—"

I wave my hand, silencing him. I knew Rob would never set Rourke up for a loss. Mark only had to *think* Rob was desperate enough to do that. Mark had been suckered. Of course it had to be a legitimate purse and a legitimate gamble: Rourke works as a trainer for the Olympics. He would never damage the reputation of the organization or the guys he trains. At the Cirillos' barbecue Joey said it was gonna be the best year ever for U.S. fighters, that thanks to Rourke the team had a chance of taking twelve out of twelve golds in L.A. Rob didn't disagree. Like the numbers man he was, he just said, "More like ten out of twelve."

Mark was also wrong when he said Rourke had lied to me. Rourke never lied to me. He didn't have to. There was nothing a lie could have secured from me that the truth would not have. And as for Rourke, he wouldn't have wanted anything he needed to lie to attain. The only thing Mark got right was that Rob *did* need to control outcomes. That's why Rob relied on Mark's hatred of Rourke, Mark's ignorance of true friendship and true love, and Mark's idea of Rob as criminal and corrupt to help raise the stakes of the match. *In the end, need brings you down,* Rob had said. Mark's other mistake was in thinking Rob needed cash. Rob never needed cash. Rob would never even suggest he needed cash unless he was trying to scam somebody; it would have been too much of an implication of incompetence.

"There were, like, six hundred people there," Rob says. "Harrison still has a huge following, and Vargas is a sweetheart. Everybody loves that kid. Throw Mark and his buddies into it, and forget about it, the money was flying. It was like duck or get hit. Uncle Tudi fronted for licenses, fees, purses in escrow. The take at the door covered expenses three times over. But milking Mr. Tennis Togs was worth the whole thing. The look on his face when those numbers were read—shit. I can't believe you missed it. Vargas nearly lost his skull in the tenth." Rob enacts it minimally—hissing and closing one eye, stuttering his head back to the right.

"Harrison was down three years, so I had excellent odds. But use your brain, you know he's gonna take it—his record, his style, his character. He trains fucking Olympians. He's in the ring every day. He's got the whole martial arts thing. Add to that the incentive to burn Mark, and, well, let's just say I kept my mouth shut and made a few bucks."

"Uncle Tudi too."

"Sure. He set the odds. And a couple people I had to take care of. My old man, Ray Peña, Joey, Harrison. You."

"Me?"

"That's right, you. You know what's the matter with you? I finally figured it out. Ninety percent of the time you think smart. Numbers and letters. Regular stuff. The other ten percent, I swear, you read pictures in mist or some shit."

There is more to what he feels he owes me, more he isn't saying, such as what gave Harrison the "incentive" to burn Mark.

Vivica comes by with rose petals. Vivica is Brett's new girlfriend, the fifth since I've known him. Brett waves to Rob through the thickening crowd. He taps his watch impatiently.

Rob drags his head to one side like he's annoyed. "I got an *hour*," he calls over. "What's wrong with that kid?" he asks me under his breath. "I got a tip on a horse. He wants to rush over to OTB in Southampton to place a bet. Meanwhile, I could make it all the way into Belmont in an hour. Feel like taking a drive with us?"

"Actually, I'm leaving."

Rob furrows his brow. "Where to?"

"My mother's."

"Oh, sure, right. It's not right for you to be out," Rob says, then he laughs. "That's gotta be killing Mark, you going AWOL in front of Harrison and Diane at the family wedding. He's one sore fucking loser. You know, I had to take Uncle Tudi to his office to collect for the fight," Rob says indignantly. "Like somebody stole my lunch money. That's a seriously nice office, by the way, with the double-paned glass and those carved African heads. What do you call them?"

I shrug. "Carved African heads, I guess."

"How long has he had that space?"

"A couple weeks."

"Anyhow, I offered to clear all debts in exchange for the Porsche. He said he'd rather send it off a cliff. My uncle told him that could be arranged—*anytime*. Tudi was pissed off because he don't like Wall Street. Besides, Mark ran a check on the licenses and permits, which I figured he would. Believe me, I dotted every fucking *i*."

The bridal party is on its way. I can't see over the heads of people around us, but there's a cheer, which means they're on their way. Rob scans the approaching faces. "Damn. If you leave, who am I gonna dance with?"

"You'll find someone."

"Last time you said that, I ended up dancing with your friend Dennis all night. I got, like, three guys' phone numbers." Rob shoots a glance past me. Mark must be close. "When did you say you're gonna talk to him?"

"Tonight. Before everyone leaves."

"Why don't you come back in the morning?"

I shake my head. "It won't work. He'll come find me. He'll come to my mother's in the middle of the night when it's too late for me to object."

"I suppose I oughta be happy," Rob mutters. "But to tell you the truth, I got a sick feeling in my gut."

I feel the compression of the major vessel in my arm as Mark draws me away from Rob, neither of them acknowledging the other. Rob just crosses over to his car, which is next to Rourke's car, both of which, unlike all the other hundreds of cars going in either direction down the street, are simply parked in the neighbor's driveway. He lowers himself slowly into the Cougar and takes another look at me. I've seen this look on Rob's face before. Like he wishes he didn't have to get mixed up with dames. Like he wishes he could just go make a bet and grab a beer. I feel sorry for him. Men hold your doors and pull your chairs and carry your bags when they're too heavy, but they can't protect you from the one thing that scares them most—you and another man.

He gets into his car and starts his engine, and it's like thunder.

Alicia and Jonathan charge through a rain of petals. There is a convivial uproar. Everyone hoots and whistles and claps, except me, except Rourke. He is tall and grave across the way, with Diane at his side, his eyes momentarily on mine, and then they are gone, he is gone, with the white of the veil whooshing past, and the black of her hair, the blood of the roses, the heads going down against the storm of lights. *Whoomf.* The door. The second and third limos pull forward. These are for the bridal party. They are going to East Hampton town pond to take pictures.

"If you still insist on leaving," Mark says to me, "the limo driver will take you to your mother's house after he leaves us at the pond. I'll have someone pick you up later."

"I'll drive myself. Where's the BMW?"

"I had it parked on the far side of the house. I'd have to have twenty cars moved to get it."

"It's okay," I say. "I'll walk."

"No," he states emphatically. "I cannot have you *walk*."

"Denny will drive me."

"Must Alicia lose *all* her guests? Why not just ask my father to take you?"

The limo driver taps on the horn. Mr. and Mrs. Ross are in the front seat, watching through the windshield. Mark waves and smiles brilliantly, giving the thumbs-up sign.

"C'mon," he says. "They're waiting."

53

It's nearly dark at Georgica Beach. There is no one there but me. I walk west, my legs pressing into the sand. I climb the jetty to the end, though the rocks are slippery. At the end I stand tall and lean over, like a carved figure on the prow of a ship, like a wooden mermaid. The wind makes gains; the sea surges, pounding the shore. Rain is coming. The clouds are walking to me, approaching like armies—shields very raised.

After the wedding, the limo driver left me in front of my house. No one was home so I went to the barn. I heard the familiar shotgun snap of the door as it ripped to the side—*chuck chuck*. I thought of Jack opening the door and Rourke standing once alongside it. And of Kate coming through it, and Denny too.

The inside was saturated by twilight; the room seemed to be the recipient of an interior rain. The wood walls were bare except for old pin marks from my drawings. My mother had taken them all down to protect them. Last year, or maybe the one before, my father had made a beautiful box lined with acid-free paper, and together my parents had given me my own drawings as a gift. They wanted me to open the box, to go through my early work, but I wouldn't, not with Mark there. I just thanked them and returned the box to the barn.

The box of drawings was still on the dresser where I'd left it; I was about to open it when I saw the pile of mail. *There's mail for you in the barn,* my mother had said on the day I'd arrived, one week before. *I tied it with a blue ribbon.*

I steady myself on the wet rocks and pull the package from my sweat-shirt. The envelope is crimped and rumpled. The postmark is legible even through the clouds—New York, New York. There it is, not quite faded, not quite lost—in one corner, May 28, 1984; in the other, my address, my name, Jack's handwriting.

Eveline Aster Auerbach

This is the last object he and I will have touched, an object with in-tention and direction, with energy passing direct from him to me—life energy. The water slaps the jetty, filling in around me. The ocean. Jack drifting, Jack alone. Alone again, alone some more. Jack, out there. I can almost feel him through the mist. I hold my breath and close my eyes to break the seal. The envelope doesn't open easily. I have to tear it, and it saddens me to think how well he secured it. The contents slide into my hand—his black book. It's been so long. The cuts and the scratches, many, many more than there were four years ago. It looks *deepened.* I flip through until I find a card stuck between two pages. It was the card he'd found in his room under the carpet that time, the holiday card: *Eveline.* On the pages themselves are two blocks of writing: a letter and a song. The song is written alongside musical notations and dense, uneven bars.

Jack's handwriting is linked as if the pen never left the paper. Often we would write that way.

for the girl in despair
you must be in despair
foreigners always are and you are
a visitor to compromise, a seer, pity me i couldn't
build a life to keep you in it.
beyond experienced time
and lived time there is pure time
together we found it what we found you can find again

every man needs to be a hero, i learned by your eyes
we all want the secret of your eyes—
    your eyes say that it's better to love than be loved.
you are the supreme generous and brave like hell
for giving the only gift that matters—
the soul, they say the soul transcends this is a fact because here
in the last hours there is only you.
and so i'll be a bird to find a bird,
since a bird is what you'll be.
you'll know me, i'll be the one who says,
there was a girl, there was a life
I used to lead in the grass in the sand through the air beneath the sky
under the waves through the rain
through the wind. I'll say,
you remind me of the wind.
so until we meet again, listen for me.
I will sing to you, nightly

p.s. this is not an explanation of why im doing this since
you know that every time i cried no one came
only you made me numb, music made me numb dope made me numb
but you and music, well,
you have to practice that, play at it night and day
and dope, jesus, the shitty illiterate company you have to keep—
the one reassuring constant for me has been
the bizarre grandiosity of my despair it is
the closest thing i have to a friend. i really hate to lose it.
a few messages to the derelicts and limbless losers,
all the fakers at the funeral—
to my father—nothing, he is Satan in plaid.
to my mother—that's good just like that. To my mother—
to liz—those records are not for you they're for your kids
tell dan stop playing for the crowd he's too good for the crowd
tell smokey take it easy and pick up the box i left
    for him at duke's on 14th street.

And tell jewel, i don't know, you'll think of something good.
tell Rene thanks for going in where no one else would go—
i've done what i had to do, tried to make it right can't think of
anything else, for what it's worth i loved you i love you
don't come i don't want you here it is not good here.
this is the song, ask dan to play it for you,
it's called pretty when you wanna be
it goes, you are pretty but just be pretty when you wanna be—

I close the book. My first instinct is to run, fast and far. I make my way off the jetty, scrambling to the end, then I dive into the sand before cutting back across the beach. I go as fast as I can, making my way toward the parking lot. The wind draws down from behind to carry me along, and I feel like something light and dry and long forgotten. I push harder, using the wind to trample the spine of the earth. I want to move forward to reach prior points. I want to run back in time, to arrive at the day he died, to find the spot where his body lay. I want to lift him into my arms, clean him, dress him, fill the hole he made. I want to close his eyes. I want to mark the place he died; the leaving place. And then, running more, running again, not stopping until I collapse. Until a wall, there must be a wall. *Am I mad?* Yes, I think I must be. There is no wall in life, nothing to meet, nothing to hit, there is only running, and then more running.

I circle the block twice, checking for cars. When I'm sure it's not there, and that Rob's car is not there, I ride my bike onto the front lawn and lean it alongside the porch. I enter the main house through the porch door and go to the kitchen. The dishwasher is churning and cleaned crystal glassware is stacked on the pantry counter. The radio is playing Vivaldi's "Summer." I go to Consuela's bedroom door. She appears in a red terry cloth T-shirt and matching shorts. Behind her, a television shows a weather map of Connecticut. Hanging over the single bed like mournful eyes are two wildflower drawings I made for her.

I am breathless and my legs are wet from sitting on the jetty.

She hands me a towel. "You okay?"

"I'm okay," I say. I thank her. Then I thank her again. *For everything.* For the flowers in the cottage, the careful pressing of my laundry, the foods she knows I'll eat. "It's been hard," I conclude.

Her eyes twinkle. "Yes, *sí*. Too different." Meaning me and Mark, I know.

"I hope someday you can bring your son." When she came to work in America she left her five-year-old son in Ecuador with her husband, who died one month after she went away. "The alcohol," she confided when we first spoke of it. "When I leaving I begging him not to kill himself. *Take care of the baby,* I say. But anyway, he kill himself. That was with the drinking. Now I talk to my son on the phone but he don't know me. He calling my sister *Mommy*."

"Goodbye, Consuela. I'll miss you."

"I miss you too," she says, as though I'm already gone, which I suppose in a way I am. "You do what you do," she states, not meaning me, necessarily, but people in general.

"Yes," I agree. "You do what you do." That's the whole tragedy.

A few wedding guests are still in the dance tent, about thirty of them. Another dozen or so are around the pool. It is nearly midnight. I pass unseen. In the cottage hallway, the bulb is blown, and the doormat is kicked out. I straighten the mat, then climb into a nest of cigar smoke. The smell is of many more cigars than Mark could possibly have finished alone. I wonder who has been there. At the top of the landing I take off my sweatshirt and leave it on the landing with Jack's book. A chalk-white scuff marks the base of the built-in cherry closet where I am standing. I make a note in my mind to have it repaired—then I remember that I am leaving. The apartment door is open; in the living room area the stereo plays the Smiths' "How Soon Is Now?"

> *I am the son and the heir, of a shyness that is criminally vulgar.*
> *I am the son and heir, of nothing in particular.*

Mark is on the terrace, specter-like against the artificial radiance in his seven-hundred-dollar tux, leaning back in his chair, his legs on the wooden rail. He looks exhausted, but powerful, like a movie director surveying the glow of a just-emptied set, like he is the master of his exhaustion. His hair falls around his face; his hair is nice, straight except around the edges, where it curls now that it's long. *It's just hair,* I tell myself. His eyes, only eyes. Remarkably, I feel a failure of nerve.

Though leaving him is something I expected, it feels no less traumatic than something unexpected—the grief of losing Rourke, losing Jack, of cherished things passing—Maman, a baby. When I ask myself whether I love Mark, the answer is yes. Because we were brought together, because we stayed together, because we are, in the black regions, compatible. Ours has been a parasitic compatibility, but it has also been an enduring one, and the sense that he is mine is uncomfortably clear.

Mine, not mine. There are things we feel we must possess; we believe that they define us. And yet there are the things that chance would have us possess, and these also define us. The difference between the two is like owning the tree you have purchased for your yard versus befriending the bird who comes by chance to nest in it. I don't know which is more true, more real. I know only that the gentler acquisitions enter and honor you, simply by living freely alongside you, whereas the things taken and held by force—people, objects, ideas—stagnate, like standing water. They separate from their original purpose, lose their first nature and design. They become objects, and the holder the objectifier.

I sit alongside Mark, and together we watch the wedding's uncivilized conclusion—girls in wet dresses shivering by the side of the pool and guys in pink shirts arguing across cocktail tables. The commotion could be miles away. In the space immediately around us there is a stillness, curious and taciturn, but charged, like the dynamic silence following a bomb blast.

"They told me about a girl," Mark says, wiping his jaw with the back of his wrist. His hand is brown from sun, and the hairs are red like iodine. I know the weight of that hand, the persistence of it. "A girl." He laughs. "Some girl."

It doesn't surprise me that he goes back to the night we met. I went there too, yesterday evening, in my mother's kitchen. It's as if he is responding belatedly to my half of that conversation. He speaks with abandoned reluctance, tired of feigning ignorance to my position, bored with keeping my state of mind separate from his state of mind. From reality.

"In your cheap thrift store clothes. In that shitty little shack by the train tracks." He gazes into his drink, a full clear glass—vodka. I look for a bottle. I see broken pieces, a toppled chair. "God, you could dance." He searches my face. "I felt like I was fucking you already."

I appreciate his candor. More men should try speaking so honestly; it must be good for the soul to set the filth free. They all think such thoughts. Why not just say them?

His legs drop off the rail, slapping the deck. He leans forward onto his knees and liquor splashes on the leg of his pants. He doesn't even try to wipe it off. "I thought Harrison would try to kill me that night. When he didn't, I knew I'd won. He didn't want you seeing him for what he is. An animal. That's why I told you—*he's a liar.*"

Listening to Mark, I have the feeling I've taken part in a lockdown. This is how Jack felt his whole life. Like there was a plan for him, only he'd had no part of it. I go to the railing; Mark follows. In the tuxedo he seems smaller, shoe-black and knife-like. Like he is slicing through the haze.

" 'Bernadette,' " Mark snarls. "Do you remember?"

"On the jukebox."

"You said you would never be loved so much."

"You said you doubted it."

"Do you know why?" Mark asks.

"Because you knew how you felt about me?"

"Because I knew how *he* felt about you." Mark laughs. Not really. Not a laugh at all. "But he knew nothing about you. He thought you were independent. You're too insecure to be independent. He thought you would wait. You're too impatient to wait."

That's funny—*impatient.* I'd been waiting for years. I'd wait forever.

He catches my thinking. "You don't think you're impatient? Think again. Every time he hesitated, you penalized him. The first night we met. A year later, when he took off the second time. That's why I never wait. I make sure not to. 'Timing is everything to you,' you always tell me. No, Eveline—timing is everything to *you.* I'm just a fast learner."

I listen closely. Mark is good at talking. His reasoning is specious, but beneath the sophistry there is a plan. I can't tell—is the plan to win, or simply not to lose?

"I did my part," he says. "Affection, distraction. I led the way. You refused to follow. You stayed faithful to him in your mind. I let you have your mind. Frankly, the mind is overrated compared to the body. Unfortunately, your loyalty didn't register with him. The only place that counts to a man like that is *this*." He slaps his hand between my legs, stroking upward to my pubic bone, stopping and jamming in with his wrist. The heel of his palm hits my low belly, and his fingertips shoot up into me. Using that axis, he clamps down, pulling me closer. Mark whispers, "He'll never forgive you."

I knock the inside of his elbow to break his hold, but he returns, tighter and harder, practically sealing the gap between us.

"He knew I'd get to you. He came back to Montauk that summer because he couldn't risk leaving you to me. He hid you away. He tried to infect you. I infected you back. I gave you more than love, more than money. I reversed a history of neglect. I trained you to live on impulse. You want to drive—have a car. You want shoes—buy six pairs. You want to paint—don't work. You want food—there's more than you can eat.

"What are you going to do now? Work in a restaurant? Sell your art at yard sales? Face it. You can't go to him. He can't afford you." Mark's face closes down quick on the right in a sort of spasm. "Go anywhere you like. The world will be empty without me."

He releases me but doesn't move. It's a dare. If I run, he'll grab me; it's safer to stay. There are three or four inches between us. I can see the broken glass near our feet. I think I'd better get rid of it. I bend straight down to pick it up, my body in a line, and he lets me. First I get the circular base and use it as a canister for the rest. There are two stems among the shards. Maybe there was a toast, one of those wild party toasts. It suddenly occurs to me that Mark isn't slurring. That he's perfectly sober. He doesn't even smell like liquor. Either the drink in his hand is the first, or it's water.

He grabs a fistful of my hair and jerks me forward. I fall to my knees, swinging the hand with the broken glass just in time, keeping the palm raised. Mark holds my skull, and pulls my face into his thighs. I reach blindly to the rail, and twisting my left hand through the bars, I let go of the glass. It cracks against the brick below.

"Bleeding on the streets," he says to the top of my head. "Destitute." He spits when he talks. Specks of saliva prick the back of my neck. For a second I think it's the rain, finally arrived. "Without that abortion you would have ended up dead. Like your junkie friend."

The smell of his penis through his pants—it smells like soap or detergent. I turn my face away.

"It wasn't an—"

"Spare me the revision. If your body hadn't had the sense to dispose of the offending organism, you would've killed it anyway. You wouldn't have gone to him. And though I was happy to pay for an abortion, I never would have raised his offspring. You might have taken it to your mother, she relishes subsocial behaviors, but you'd just gotten out. You had no intention of going back. And, by the way, you could have called *anyone* from the hospital that day—Dennis, your aunt, Sara, even asshole Rob. But you were quick. You were devious. You called *me*. You knew it would crush him. You knew I would tell. And you knew how I would characterize the loss. I was impressed by the efficiency of your cruelty. I was shocked, actually, by how hard he took it." Mark bends. "He was *crying*."

He waits for a response. I say nothing. It's hard to say nothing. It takes everything. I think of Jack, his moments alone with the gun. Deliberating, agonizing. Sitting there, back against a tree, coping with a lifetime of fear and failure, waiting and waiting, for nothing and for no one. Pulling the trigger in a final concession to solitude. *Proof.*

"Didn't I tell you? He came to the apartment. To give me money. He's so *honorable.* The night of that pathetic Mexican dinner. The night I took you back to my parents' place. I told him, 'I don't need your money.' Harrison said, 'Then give it to her.' I said, 'Trust me. She's not going to need it either.' That was the first night we slept together, Eveline. You actually *rewarded* me."

I say, "You should have just left me in the hospital."

"No, no. You were too good to pass up. Besides, I liked the way you played—an eye for an eye. *Biblical.*" Mark kneels now too. He takes me down to the ground. Pulling me around, following with his chest, ready to bear down. "What did I say, earlier tonight, how long has it been— a week?"

Oh, that's the part about his not drinking. He kisses me hard, and his tongue in my throat makes me gag. If I could scream, I would scream, but a scream—

There's a noise. Something hits the cottage. The wall or the door, I don't know, a rock or a brick. Our heads look toward the rail. In my mind is a picture of us that way, Mark and me, grafted like skin from one part of a body to another. Like living onto dead. "If you're thinking it's Harrison," he says in a sort of under-growl, "you're mistaken. He left with Diane. He's probably screwing her right now."

I have very little time. I look at his eyes. They look like discs of clay, like there is no soul on the other side. I look steadily, careful not to show lenience or restraint, not to enrage him further with highness or compassion. If he is a monster, I cannot help but wonder whether it was I who helped make him one. Didn't I stay too far outside? Didn't I stay untouchable? Didn't I console him by turning slavish? Didn't I give him access to places in me that were persuadable—poverty and heartbreak—in order to stay persuaded? I answered to something preexisting in him and he in me, and so what I threaten by leaving is far deeper than the motive to hurt Rourke.

He peels back my shirt, and I wait patiently, like getting dressed in bandages after an injury. My jeans—he starts on the buttons. Though there are five, and he knows there are five, he races through to three, and starts to pull.

I say, "Mark."

He did not expect this, my speaking. He tilts his head, as if I can't be heard completely, as if he's picking up on an echo. And it's weird, but I actually hear myself that way—his way, ringing out, bouncing back. I find my voice, capturing it, steering it center.

"It's true you saved me. And it is possible I wouldn't have survived without you. You never broke a promise, and you never left my side. I know you feel like you forced me into something. Like I never loved you. But you didn't force me, and I do love you. It's true that I have nothing and nowhere to go. Don't you see? That's not why I *should* stay; that's why I *can't* stay. I never want anyone to do that to you."

He pauses. One hand, the hand supporting him, is on my arm, the other lingers on my abdomen. His eyes are ten inches from mine. I have pierced something, and yet he's been stunned, not stopped. Minutes, I have minutes.

I say, "Don't let hurting me be the measure of your manhood."

Mark looks left again, then bleakens, then collapses, rolling off the top of me. We are side by side.

"I'm so fucking tired of this place," he says. "You did that to me."

"You were born that way. You're like your father."

"Like my father." He laughs. "That's brilliant."

"The only difference between you is that he tries to destroy himself and you try to destroy everything else."

"That must be why he hates me."

"He doesn't hate you, Mark. He envies you."

For the brief remainder of our time together, we lie corpse-like beneath the gray sky above the Ross home, beneath the portion of the planet defined by them and for them. After the rain comes and goes, daylight will puncture the pallor, making way for a choir of ultramarines. In the morning comes the pacific drone of the pool filter and the premonitory stifle of the summer air and the dry creak of wicker as his mother sits to remove her shoes and lay out her robe before she swims. The mild slap of her arms hitting the water. And after, the distant tink of her spoon in a cup.

I remove the ring. I hand it to him.

"Sell it," he says, refusing to take it. "You'll need the money."

I rise in degrees. I make it as far as the balcony, where I linger and fix my clothes. The gardens have never appeared more beautiful than at this moment, the moment of my leaving. Maybe once, maybe the first time, which is incredible when you think about it, since all through the middle they've been as good as mine.

"You almost went through with it," Mark says. "Two more days and we'd be in Italy. You would have forgotten about him. You would have fallen in love with living well. You could have been set for life, Eveline. Now you're straight back to nowhere. Cirillo fucked it up. He got in over his head. I should have loaned him the money instead of letting him bring that stupid fuck back—twenty-five grand. Pennies to keep you."

"What would you have gotten?"

"Something pure," he says. Adding, "Nothing's pure."

On my way out I leave the ring on the kitchen table. There is a substantial clink. I grab my sweatshirt and Jack's book, and before hitting the stairs I hear Mark shout, "You'll be back."

The rain begins, lightly at first, like upward-floating flurries when it snows. I take my time cutting through the garden, in case Mark's watching, and when I reach the sunporch I break into a run, leaving my bike behind. It's harder to hide with a bike. At the street, I run faster. Beneath the lamplight the rain looks like jagged tinsel or chains of mercury. I tell myself to hurry. He'll think me more likely to change my mind in the rain. At the corner I turn right toward Main Beach, heading away from town, away from home. He'll go to town, to my mother's house. I'll wait under the pavilion at the beach until morning.

With the wind and the rain on my face, I don't hear the sound of tires; I only think *car* when a fortress of light encroaches on me from behind and my own shape materializes on the ground. I stop. The car stops. I start, it starts. I think to hide—a yard, a garage. I look right, for a break in the hedges. When I look back, I realize that the light is not narrow but broad. Like a blockade. The car moves up, flanking me on the left. It is white, square. Not the Porsche. The GTO.

The door opens. Rourke says, "Eveline."

Eveline—I've never heard my name spoken like that, as though there is some indivisibility between it and me. I take one instant, just one, learning the sound by heart, feeling—I don't know—just feeling.

I climb in, fall in, exhausted, shocked, but grateful to have a friend, in the night, in the cold, in the rain. A friend who is knowledgeable of my heart. It's not the first time I've received his help. Rourke was there when I broke up with Jack, only that night was dry and I was seventeen. And things were different at seventeen. I thought about what Rob said at the wedding about friendship, about needing someone to track you, challenge you. About a friend being a fortress.

He makes a series of deliberate turns until we arrive at a private road—we've been here before, the first night we were together. Soaking overgrown branches slap the windshield until we emerge on a grassy plain. Directly before us is Georgica Pond. He puts the car into park and reaches into the backseat for a towel, which he uses to dry me. The towel is stained with blood, blood from his eye, which now I can see. It is slit and stitched on top and hugely swollen, hemorrhaged and violet.

"You okay?" Rourke asks.

I shrug. "I'm okay."

He draws the towel down my arms.

I ask him how long he was waiting.

"I watched you go in."

"That was hours ago."

"About an hour and a half."

"I didn't see the car," I say.

"I wasn't in the car. I was on foot."

"By the street?"

"By the balcony. Where you were."

"Did you hear?"

Rourke looks past the steering wheel toward the pond. His profile and his jaw look like a drawing of a profile and a jaw, the lines are that hard. "I heard enough."

"He said you left with—"

"Diane? She left with her parents. He knew that." Rourke turns back to me, turning very serious. "It would have taken me seconds to scale that wall. But you did fine on your own," he says. "Better than I would have."

Better than I would have. That's what Mark had been waiting for. For Rourke to come. So he could trap him, confront him, have him arrested. I can't even think about it.

My hand reaches for his eye. He does not pull away but breathes into my touch. His normal lid drifts closed, and beneath my fingertips the distended one throbs, as if the eye below is straining to see. In his heart there is a girl; she is me. No contract keeps her; she goes with him, she goes alone, precipice to precipice, on every ledge agreeing again to leap. She is with him, she has been with him, every minute. No one can know what we know. Just us. If you listen, you can hear it. In the wide sound of the rain—*us.*

54

We go into Manhattan to an anonymous hotel. No one knows where to find us. There are no messages, no calls. One call, one call out. I knew because I woke to the sound of his voice talking on the phone, though I'd heard no ring.

I'd spoken with my mother before we arrived, saying I was safe, that I needed to figure things out, that I'd call again soon. I called for Rourke's sake more than for hers or my own; I intended to preempt Mark. I wouldn't give him the opportunity to suggest to everyone that I'd been taken against my will. He would never hurt Rourke again.

Being there with Rourke feels right; it feels like the only possible thing. It's like being in a command center in a movie, one of those steel-fortified tents where the power congregates while war is raging— strategizing, studying maps, decoding messages, drinking cognac. We have shut ourselves in to accomplish something brainy and strategic. We prepare, but for what?

We sleep in the day if we sleep at all. At night we walk through Manhattan—up Broadway or across Central Park or down Tenth Avenue into Hell's Kitchen, through scaffold castles, past lapsed construction sites where the plywood ramps rumble when you stomp them and the makeshift walls are covered with graffiti. Rourke walks and people make way. He is fierce and exact and his face is a terrifying mass of bruised flesh. If there is trouble, I don't doubt the outcome. It's like walking under an umbrella through a heavy storm. I never realized before how frequently I am concerned for my own safety, not only physical, but psychological. For three days I claim sanctuary—I can be me, think me, show me.

There is a piano bar on West Forty-fourth Street that we pass every night when we are out. Through the window it seems somber but sincere, like it was once popular but now is on its last legs. One time going by Rourke asks if I feel like going in, and I say I do. Inside the ceiling is low. His head seems to touch.

"This one is for all you Johnny Mathis fans," the piano player says, though counting everyone, we are seven. He plays "Misty."

The Ukrainian cocktail waitress leans on the far side of the grand piano; there are smudges in her reflection on the instrument. I know about the Ukraine because I asked when she brought us drinks and a small dish of salted nuts. She has a visa for school to study nursing and an aunt in Brighton Beach. Watching her across the piano, I wonder whether I will be alone like her someday, working in a bar in a foreign country, living with a distant aunt and going to school, not necessarily for my subject. I wonder whether Rourke will come for me at forty, whether at forty I will be waiting.

"If only there were a way to live in night," I say.

"There is no way," he says, watching me watch her. "I tried. After you, I tried."

He turns off the air conditioning, and the room goes hot. When he knocks the windows up and open, he leans for a moment, looking out. Past his wrists, night slips in, bringing the sounds of the city.

He moves and I memorize him. Though I know him, though I have lived with him, everything he does is new. If I am conscious of the fact that time is of the essence, that there are practical means to attend to, I can't move past the smallest moments with him. He is tranquil and orderly. When he touches things—buttons and keys and combs and me—he touches without false delicacy, as conscious of his strength as of the refinement of his object. The authenticity is somehow crucial to me, more so than talk.

One night we heard a girl crying in the hall. "Luis, Luis."

I saw his instinct fly to life. He reached automatically for his jeans and shirt. He buttoned two buttons and walked out. Through the closed door I heard him speak, just a word or two. There was the sound of sobbing and the sound of voices, mixing imperfectly down the hall, first two voices, then three.

While I waited, I decided to dress. I opened his suitcase where my clothes were kept, next to his clothes. I pulled out a pair of jeans and a T-shirt. I brushed back my hair and found some lipstick in the pocket of my jacket. I looked out over West Fifty-eighth Street, waiting with confidence that the right thing would be done for that girl, complete in the luxury of being a partner to a man like Rourke, thinking, *Why can't the world be mine—when I need no more of it than this?*

I wake to the sound of his breathing. Someone said, *Should my eyes be lost and my hearing remain, my ears could see the sound she makes.* A painter, I think. Degas, maybe, though I'm not sure. By Rourke's breath he is sad. I unbury my face from his arm and slide my chin up his chest, where I can see from my perch the distance between his eyes.

"What are you thinking?"

"If we'd had a son," he says, "would he have been gentle like you."

He sits on the edge of the bed; I curl around his back. A composite of sea-pink and frost-yellow light presses and swells past the gold drapes. The room is like a jewel box. In the light, his skin appears uncommonly fair. He looks like a white wolf or the fragile product of a hothouse, though he is neither. There is a painting, a Caravaggio, of John the Baptist. John is naked and thoughtful—boy and man, object and subject. You feel the promise of masculinity, the anticipation of action, the crisis of uncertainty. He is ready; you are waiting.

"I'm sorry," I tell him. "About everything."

He pushes into the sound of my voice as if rolling his head into a rush of wind. Reaching back with an arm, he finds my waist and pulls me closer.

"I should never have asked Mark for help in the first place," I say, and I add. "He said I did it to hurt you."

Rourke's eyes close. The bad one is healing; the blood has gone down. I touch it every day, running my fingertips across, dragging them over, bringing the nerves back to life. "I know what he said."

"Mark says I used him."

Rourke looks at me, dipping over. I don't have to wonder what it is he sees because I feel myself appear. Like a flare cutting through space, erupting into a sea of stars, I see me. He says, "Use is the thing he exchanges."

In the muscles on his chest, there are shapes. Beneath his collarbone, a whale, surfacing. By his abdomen on the left, a flattened swan. I move in, coming in around his hip bone, resting my head on his thigh. I know he feels guilty, for going against his own instinct, for thinking somehow I'd be better off with Mark. Deep down it made sense to Rourke that Mark should win. It proved his worst fears—the value of money and lies, the uselessness of strength and character.

His throat stretches to the ceiling. "I'm not sure how far back to go," he says. "How much to ask." When he speaks, his manner is steely but not disapproving. It seems we have come up against something he understands better than I, something at the hands of which he has suffered uniquely—me. "You could have been hurt Saturday." Rourke waits, but not for an answer. "Once I leave, he'll be back."

I know that. That's why we didn't stop at my mother's after meeting in the rain. Why Rourke drove straight to the city. Why we are here, unable to leave without a plan.

"Next time he comes," he says, "I don't know what I'll do."

I think of the trust Rourke has always placed in me, the constancy of it. I consider the elusiveness of happiness, and the fact that the reason I don't have it is that I have not yet earned it. Rourke is not alone in his guilt; I am also to blame. From the start I've been content to remain more conscious of his effects than his cause, which is like admiring a bridge without acknowledging the land the structure joins. He never once expected more than I could give, and yet I abused that. I gave away what he would not take.

I confront the myth of self-determination. Independence has not made me free, nor has it diminished my devotion. In spite of my liberty, I loved him—I love him. I think what it means to love. First, of course, there is the fact of you, then the sensation of loving a person, then somewhere along the way, there is the fact of the person. This last fact you cannot ignore. What you do with it—accept, adore, deny, or suppress—determines everything. There are points of intersection, these divine assignments of the heart that complete you.

"My mother lost one of us to fighting," he explains, slowly. "I can't let her lose another."

I tell him that I understand.

"I need to get back to work. I need two months to get through the Olympic Games. I have obligations. I need to know you're going to be all right until I get back."

"I can stay with Denny."

"No. Mark's too credible to the outside world. He'll get reckless and irrational. He'll blame others for whatever mess he makes."

Rourke waits a minute or two, then he draws my hands down. "You said at the funeral that you should have done something when you had the chance, that you should have held Jack accountable."

The funeral. He was there. *They* were there. Rob saying, *You seem shaky. You shaky?*

Jack's name from Rourke's lips. Him saying *"Jack"* like he knew him.

I sit up, coming next to him. "What do you think we should do?"

Rourke says, "I was thinking Spring Lake."

The phone call he made from the hotel room when we first arrived. His mother. The house, the baking, the books, the furniture, the attic. A policeman's widow. Mark wouldn't stand a chance. If she called for a restraining order against him, there would be no question. Besides, she probably has a gun in the house—no, she *definitely* does. And she knows how to use it.

"The Games end mid-August. I'll be back then. You can come visit me anytime. With Rob, without him. Whatever you want."

"Does she expect me?"

"I think she's been expecting you since you two met."

It would be nice, I think, to spend a summer there, drawing flowers in the yard, listening to her typing. "I'd like to go to your house," I say. "It's a nice house."

One thing I never thought I'd see is tears. Even the bad eye, it cries.

The sheets are soft and dry, like cooking flour when you are little and you dig in with a metal spoon. Lying there with him is like unfurling in clouds or swimming in silk or crossing from air to water. He holds me like he is unwilling ever to release me, and though his face is rough, I feel no roughness. He braces himself on one elbow, his fingers going down each rib, counting them as though I might have lost one since last he checked. His palm trails the underside of my left breast. He secures my hips; his knee slips up between my legs, bracing them apart. He looks into the gap between our bodies. I look too, at his chest tapering into the drum of his waist, at his abdomen, at the curvature of me beneath.

He breathes in. "The first time I saw you," he says, "it was like seeing a river. Something that could be touched but not held. Something there but not there. I never wanted anything so much in my life."

Before checking out, I spoke to Mark's father. My instinct was that it would be right to call, and Rourke agreed.

I reached Mr. Ross at his office. His secretary put me through directly, which broke my heart. I didn't mention Mark, I couldn't. I guess he couldn't either, because he didn't.

"And your things, Eveline?" Mr. Ross asked.

"I guess they're still at the cottage."

"What would you like me to do?" he asked.

"Maybe someone can take them to my mother's."

"I'll take them myself," he said. "I'd like to see your mother."

I thanked him. I felt Rourke's hand on my shoulder, staying, waiting.

"Am I overstepping if I ask whether you're all right?" Mr. Ross asked. "I'll keep your confidence, of course, but I do feel—well, you understand. It's as though you're—"

"I'm all right. I'm fine."

"You're with Harrison?"

"Yes, sir, I am."

"Well, then," he said, and he repeated, "Well, then." He didn't sound sad, but he didn't sound happy; he sounded like he felt what I felt, which was a little of both. "I suppose it was meant to be."

"Yes, I think so," I said, and I thanked him again, from the bottom of my heart. Those were the last words we ever spoke. Six months later he was dead.

———

The GTO is brought around to the hotel entrance, and he helps me in. The door closes and also the trunk, and those closing sounds join other closing sounds from other cars and cabs with other luggage. In the heat it all makes a thick and thumping collage.

We regard the changing landscape as we drive from Manhattan to the airport. There is that colossal cemetery in Queens with all the forgotten dead, looking like a knee-high metropolis, with its skyscraper tombstones. We pass beneath furry tails of jet exhaust, letting every other car go by. Even school buses outpace us. If he is trying to miss his plane, he won't. Not today. Today I feel a way I've never felt. In a cup on the dashboard are the pieces of beach glass we found that first day in Jersey, the day at the shore. I reach for them, pouring, palm to palm.

My mind draws pictures. The house I was born in—a brownstone, a door leading to an apartment on the left, another door, a couch behind it, the television my father watches at night, the one my mother collapses in front of, crying when the president is assassinated. The tub where I play when I bathe, twirling and sliding, up and down; and my mother—when she walks past, she sings. I remember a tune that haunts me still.

When you're lost in the rain in Juarez, and it's Eastertime too—

Mornings are cold. My clothes are warmed on the open oven door, me sitting in front, wrapped in a blanket while she moves, singing still. There is one dress of magenta velvet, a dress she made for me. It has a tiny trail of pale yellow flowers on the collar. To this day I try to paint the colors.

In another home, I am five. Five is not three. Three is when you see things and do not know enough to remember. Five is when you see and try to forget. My parents stand together, though they are no longer married, which means I am sick. A doctor is there. Another Sunday in that same room, my father returns me after a weekend spent with him, and my parents talk in the hall. And I draw and draw, my face very close to the paper, and when I erase it all, my dad comes to say goodbye, towering over me. *Not too fast, Evie, you'll tear the paper.*

And other places, other homes, all with the same reeling loneliness I felt until Rourke.

"The first time I saw *you,*" I confess, "I had a premonition. I had the feeling I'd found the thing I'd been waiting for. The next time I saw you, it was the same. And every time after it's been the same."

His hand reaches for me.

"I don't want to lose you again."

"You won't," he says. "You can't."

At the terminal, we get out. The sun beyond the concrete awning is high and the hot air is brutal, though there is wind. There is always wind at JFK, even in suffocating heat. I tie my sweater around my shoulders. I slide my sunglasses to the top of my head, and wait—for nothing. There is no more next, no more longing, no more separation of the soul. The feeling of nothing is so profound, so sure, it's a guarantee.

Rourke draws his bags from the trunk. There are two; one is a garment bag. The trunk closes, *thoom.* One of his hands holds the luggage straps, and with his free arm he reaches for me. When we hold each other I feel it everywhere, low and high. I go closer, and he comes in as well. I remember how I used to look out the window for animals in the night, for creatures keeping warm beneath leaves; I remember being relieved that they could. I hope that we are that way, he and I, that we'll be okay. I hope that love is a miracle, this love and all love and love like ours that is contingent upon nothing—and enriched wholly by concessions.

Rourke looks at me with gratitude, as if he knows what I'm thinking. *Every man wants the secret of your eyes,* Jack wrote. *It's better to love than be loved.* Rourke kisses me—once, twice, his lips to my cheek.

He hands me the keys to the car. "So you know where you're going?"

"Yeah," I say, touching the GTO—careful, like it's alive. "I know."

"August," Rourke says.

"August," I say, "yes." August. "Or sooner."

I go on my toes, and he comes down—and in the middle we meet. My lips print against his lips, soft. There it is, the stain of my devotion. And once more, then, he goes. And I follow him through the lens of the terminal glass, watching him fold in and away. How meager the bags look, how small the crowd. The bodies and faces are real, and the colors real, and the stories real, and yet, only he stands out.

Three planes mark the horizon. It's roulette to guess which is his. Planes are modern angels, silver-winged and supernatural, carrying away cargo that is precious. I don't like to think of him up there, in airborne machinery, though it is right somehow for him to vanish this way, cutting through the flat dividing lines of time, soaring West.

And him. Does he search the paling membrane of the planet from the brightness of his cabin? Does he find me—minuscule, anonymous? Does he see me the way I once was, or the way I have become? In August I will thank him—for leaving me rich, for leaving me courageous, a fighter. For leaving me with everything I have ever wanted. I am an American girl. I stand with my feet firm on the soil of a nation.

"Oh, Jack," I say out the car window, the world flying by. "Now that you're gone, I swear to be filled with twice the life."

Acknowledgments

As Eveline says, "Everywhere there are angels." And since I have received more than my fair share of divine assistance during this process, I close with expressions of gratitude to those earthbound angels who extended themselves to help me achieve my purpose.

I am thankful to Meghan-Michele German, one of the original novel's first readers, who arrived by my side in 2007 during a particularly rough moment and provided me with the encouragement and practical support I needed to give *Anthropology of an American Girl* new life. Next, I am indebted to my sister, Penelope Leigh Hope, who has read the manuscript in its various incarnations so many times that surely she knows it as well as I do myself. Penelope has given her time and attention unconditionally, and in doing so, she has helped me through more difficult moments than she will ever know.

I am fortunate to have a remarkable set of friends on whose daily support I was able to rely during the course of rewriting and editing. I am grateful to James Benard, for his early and continued faith in this project and its author; to Deborah Silva, for her loyalty; to Tucker Marder, for his steadfast friendship; to my parents, for their willingness to gamble once again on my competence; to my eldest daughter, Vee, for her uncanny ability to remain rational and advise well in the face of chaos; to my youngest children, Emmanuelle and Rainier, for their tireless cheer and inspirational artistry; and to Silas Marder, whose tender attentions on my behalf to each and all of the aforementioned gave me the safe space I needed to complete the manuscript.

My experience with Spiegel & Grau has been overwhelmingly positive. I thank everyone there for their kindness—in particular, Julie Grau, for making me feel welcome, and Hana Landes, for maintaining her serene composure while giving me very real support.

I am most obliged to my agent, Kirby Kim of William Morris Endeavor, for his level-headed enthusiasm, sound judgment, and artistic intuition. The success of this version of the novel can be attributed in large part to his conscientious willingness to read my submission cover to cover within days of receiving it.

And finally, I thank Cindy Spiegel, my editor and publisher, under whose careful guidance this book was reshaped. *Anthropology* has been as improved by her insights and influence as I have been by her friendship. I could not have done this without her.

Permissions Acknowledgments

LITERARY WORKS

Page ix   LITTLE GIDDING, T. S. Eliot, from The Four Quartets, © 1943.
Published by Harcourt, Inc., Orlando, Fla., and Faber & Faber
Ltd., London.

Page 1   From Kurt Vonnegut's Introduction to OUR TIME IS NOW, NOTES
FROM THE HIGH SCHOOL UNDERGROUND, edited by John Bir-
mingham, © 1970, Praeger (Greenwood Publishing Group),
Santa Barbara, Calif. Reprinted by permission of the author's
agent, Donald Farber.

Page 49   EVANGELINE, Henry Wadsworth Longfellow, c. 1847.

Page 135   SEDUCTION, Jean Baudrillard, © 1990 by Jean Baudrillard.
Reprinted by permission of St. Martin's Press, LLC.

Page 141   A VISIT FROM SAINT NICOLAS, Clement Clark Moore, c. 1823.

Page 164   THE POEMS OF EMILY DICKINSON, Emily Dickinson, c. 1858.
Edited by Thomas H. Johnson, (Cambridge, Mass.: The Belknap
Press of Harvard University Press), © 1951, 1955, 1979, 1983,
by the President and Fellows of Harvard College. Reprinted
by permission of the publishers and the Trustees of Amherst
College.

Page 183   SONNET 94, William Shakespeare, c. 1609.

Page 273   STRANGERS TO OURSELVES, Julia Kristeva, translated by Leon S.
Roudiez, © 1991. Reprinted by permission of Columbia University Press, N.Y.

Page 331   THE MASS ORNAMENT: WEIMAR ESSAYS, Siegfried Kracauer,
c. 1920s. From THE MASS ORNAMENT: WEIMAR ESSAYS by
Siegfried Kracauer, translated and edited by Thomas Y. Levin,

(Cambridge, Mass.: Harvard University Press), © 1995 by the President and Fellows of Harvard College. Reprinted by permission of Harvard University Press.

Page 331 THE MYTH OF SISYPHUS, Albert Camus, 1942. From THE MYTH OF SISYPHUS, by Albert Camus, translated by Justin O'Brien, © 1955, renewed 1983 by Alfred A. Knopf, a division of Random House, Inc.

Page 367 SOME MEMORIES OF DRAWINGS, Georgia O'Keeffe, edited by Doris Bry, © 1974, 1988 (Albuquerque, N.M.: University of New Mexico Press). Originally published in 1974 by Atlantis Editions, N.Y.

Page 413 THE ELEMENTS OF DRAWING, John Ruskin, 1857. Reprinted by permission of Dover Publications, Inc., Mineola, N.Y. Originally published in 1857 (London: London, Smith, Elder & Co.).

Page 497 TAO TE CHING, Lao-Tzu, c. sixth century BCE. From TAO TE CHING, A NEW ENGLISH VERSION, WITH FOREWORD AND NOTES, translation by Stephen Mitchell, © 1988. Reprinted by permission of HarperCollins Publishers, N.Y.

Page 521 SONNET 87, William Shakespeare, c. 1609.

Page 550 ANATOMY OF MELANCHOLY, Richard Burton, c. 1621. A New York Review Book, published by the New York Review of Books, 2001.

Page 563 THE JOURNEY OF THE MAGI, T. S. Eliot, 1927. Published by Harcourt, Inc., Orlando, Fla., and Faber & Faber, Ltd., London.

MUSICAL WORKS

Page 18 FOLLOW YOU, FOLLOW ME, Words and Music by Tony Banks, Phil Collins, and Mike Rutherford. Copyright © 1978 Gelring Ltd. and Hit & Run Music (Publishing), Ltd. All rights controlled and administered by EMI Blackwood Music, Inc. All rights reserved. International copyright secured. Reprinted by permission of Hal Leonard Corporation.

Page 113   CAN'T FIND MY WAY HOME, Words and Music by Steve Winwood.
            Copyright © 1970 (Renewed) F.S. Music, Ltd. (PRS), All rights
            administered by Warner-Tamerlane Publishing Corp. All rights
            reserved. Reprinted by permission of Alfred Publishing Co., Inc.

Page 133   YOU'RE ALL I'VE GOT TONIGHT, Words and Music by Ric Ocasek.
            Copyright © 1978 Lido Music, Inc. All rights reserved.
            Reprinted by permission.

Page 147   COW COW BOOGIE, Words and Music by Don Raye, Gene
            DePaul, and Benny Carter. Copyright © 1941, 1942 Universal
            Music Corp., Bee Cee Music Company and Hub Music Com-
            pany. Copyright renewed. All rights reserved. Reprinted by per-
            mission of Hal Leonard Corporation.

Page 175   HERE I AM, COME AND TAKE ME, Words and Music by Al Green
            and Mabon Hodges. Copyright © 1973 Irving Music, Inc., and
            Al Green Music. Copyright renewed. All rights controlled and
            administered by Irving Music, Inc. All rights reserved. Reprinted
            by permission of Hal Leonard Corporation.

Page 193   WHO'S GONNA BE YOUR SWEET MAN WHEN I'M GONE? Written by
            Muddy Waters. Copyright © 1972 (Renewed 2000) Watertoons
            Music (BMI). Administered by Bug Music. All rights reserved.
            Reprinted by permission of Hal Leonard Corporation.

Page 205   AIN'T WASTIN' TIME NO MORE, Words and Music by Gregg
            Allman. Copyright © 1972 by Unichappell Music Inc. and Elijah
            Blue Music. Copyright renewed. All rights for Elijah Blue Music
            administered by Bug Music. International copyright secured.
            All rights reserved. Reprinted by permission of Hal Leonard
            Corporation, and of Alfred Publishing Co., Inc.

Page 206   TURN THE PAGE, Words and Music by Bob Seger. Copyright
            © 1973 Gear Publishing Co. Copyright renewed 2001. All
            rights reserved. Used by permission. Reprinted by permission
            of Hal Leonard Corporation.

Page 215   JESUS MET THE WOMAN AT THE WELL, Adapted and Arranged by
            Peter Yarrow, Mary Travers and Milton Okun. Copyright ©
            1964 (Renewed) Pepamar Music Corp. All rights on behalf of
            Pepamar Music Corp. (ASCAP). Administered by WB Music

Corp. (ASCAP). All rights reserved. Reprinted by permission of Alfred Publishing Co., Inc.

Page 240   ROCK ON, Words and Music by David Essex. Copyright © 1973 Stage Three Music Ltd. Copyright renewed. All rights in the U.S. controlled and administered by Stage Three Music (U.S.), Inc. All rights reserved. Reprinted by permission of Hal Leonard Corporation.

Page 249   BERNADETTE, Words and Music by Brian Holland, Lamont Dozier, and Edward Holland. Copyright © 1967 (Renewed 1995) Jobete Music Co., Inc. All Rights Controlled and Administered by EMI Blackwood Music Inc. on behalf of Stone Agate Music (A Division of Jobete Music Co., Inc.). All rights reserved. Reprinted by permission of Hal Leonard Corporation.

Page 250   TELL ME SOMETHING GOOD, Words and Music by Stevie Wonder. Copyright © 1974 (Renewed 2002) Jobete Music Co., Inc., and Black Bull Music c/o EMI April Music Inc. All rights reserved. International copyright secured. Reprinted by permission of Hal Leonard Corporation.

Page 278   BENNIE AND THE JETS, Words and Music by Elton John and Bernie Taupin. Copyright © 1973 Universal/Dick James Music, Ltd. Copyright renewed. All rights in the United States and Canada controlled and administered by Universal—Songs of Polygram International, Inc. All Rights Reserved. Reprinted by permission of Hal Leonard Corporation.

Page 289   MAINSTREET, Words and Music by Bob Seger. Copyright © 1976, 1977 Gear Publishing Co. Copyright Renewed 2004. All rights reserved. Reprinted by permission of Hal Leonard Corporation.

Page 294   WHAT'S GOING ON? Words and Music by Renaldo Benson, Alfred Cleveland, and Marvin Gaye. Copyright © 1970 (Renewed 1998) Jobete Music Co., Inc., MGIII Music, NMG Music and FCG Music. All Rights Controlled and Administered by EMI April Music, Inc., on behalf of Jobete Music Co., Inc., MGIII Music, NMG Music and FCG Music and EMI Blackwood Music Inc. on behalf of Stone Agate Music (a division of Jobete Music Co., Inc.). All rights reserved. International

Copyright Secured. Reprinted by permission of Hal Leonard
Corporation.

Page 309   HEY YOU, Words and Music by Roger Waters. © 1979 Roger
Waters Overseas Ltd. All Rights for the U.S. and Canada administered by Warner-Tamerlane Publishing Corp. All rights reserved. Reprinted by permission.

Page 355   MADAMA BUTTERFLY, from the opera by Giacomo Puccini (1858–
1924). Based on the play "Madame Butterfly" by David Belasco,
story by John Luther Long.

Page 395   FIRE, Words and Music by Ralph Middlebrooks, Marshall Jones,
Leroy Bonner, Clarence Satchell, Willie Beck, James L. Williams,
and Marvin Pierce. Copyright © 1974 by Play One Music
Publishing, Rick's Music, Inc., and Segundo Suenos Music.
Copyright renewed. All rights for Play One Music Publishing
administered by Unichappell Music, Inc. All rights on behalf
of Rick's Music, Inc., administered by Rightsong Music, Inc.
All rights for Segundo Suenos Music administered by Bug
Music. International copyright secured. All rights reserved.
Reprinted by permission of Hal Leonard Corporation and of
Alfred Publishing Co., Inc.

Page 439   LET THE SUNSHINE IN, Music by Galt MacDermot. Words by
James Rado and Gerome Ragni. Copyright © 1966, 1967,
1968, 1970 (Copyrights renewed), James Rado, Gerome Ragni,
Galt MacDermot, Nat Shapiro, and EMI U Catalog, Inc. All
Rights administered by EMI U Catalog INC. (Publishing) and
Alfred Publishing Co., Inc. (Print.) All rights reserved. Reprinted
by permission of Alfred Publishing Co., Inc.

Page 464   CAN'T TAKE MY EYES OFF OF YOU, Words and Music by Bob
Crewe and Bob Gaudio. Copyright © 1967 (Renewed 1995)
EMI Longitude Music and Seasons Four Music. All rights reserved. International Copyright Secured. Reprinted by permission of Hal Leonard Corporation.

Page 470   ROMEO AND JULIET, Words and Music by Mark Knopfler. Copyright © 1980 Straitjacket Songs, Ltd. International copyright secured. All rights reserved. Reprinted by permission of Hal
Leonard Corporation.

Page 493   POINT BLANK, by Bruce Springsteen. Copyright © 1980 Bruce Springsteen (ASCAP). International copyright secured. All rights reserved. Reprinted by permission.

Page 503   SHE'S THE ONE, by Bruce Springsteen. Copyright © 1975 Bruce Springsteen, renewed 2003 Bruce Springsteen (ASCAP). International Copyright secured. All rights reserved. Reprinted by permission.

Page 508   THE CISCO KID, Words and Music by Sylvester Allen, Harold R. Brown, Morris Dickerson, Lonnie Jordan, Charles W. Miller, Lee Oskar, and Howard Scott. Copyright © 1972 Far Out Music, Inc. All Rights administered by PolyGram International Publishing, Inc. International copyright secured. All rights reserved. Reprinted by permission of Hal Leonard Corporation.

Page 511   MY CHERIE AMOUR, Words and Music by Stevie Wonder, Sylvia Moy, and Henry Cosby. Copyright © 1968 (Renewed 1996) Jobete Music Co., Inc., Black Bull Music and Sawandi Music c/o EMI April Music, Inc. and EMI Blackwood Music, Inc. All rights reserved. International copyright secured. Reprinted by permission of Hal Leonard Corporation.

Page 580   HOW SOON IS NOW? Words and Music by Johnny Marr and Steven Morrissey. Copyright © 1984 Marr Songs, Ltd. and Bona Relations Ltd. Copyright © 1984 Artemis Muziekuitgeverij B.V. and Universal Music Publishing Ltd. All Rights for Marr Songs, Ltd., in the U.S. and Canada controlled and administered by Universal-Polygram International Publishing, Inc. All rights in the U.S. and Canada for Artemis Muziekuitgeverij B.V. administered by Warner-Tamerlane Publishing Corp. All rights reserved. Reprinted by permission of Hal Leonard Corporation.

Page 595   JUST LIKE TOM THUMB'S BLUES, Words and Music by Bob Dylan. Copyright © 1965 by Warner Bros. Inc. Copyright renewed 1993 by Special Rider Music. All rights reserved. International copyright secured. Reprinted by permission.

ABOUT THE AUTHOR

HILARY THAYER HAMANN was born and raised in New York. After her parents divorced, she was shuttled between their respective homes in the Hamptons and the Bronx. She attended New York University, where she received a BFA in film and television production and dramatic writing from Tisch School of the Arts, an MA in cinema studies from the Graduate School of Arts and Science, and a certificate in anthropological filmmaking from NYU's Center for Media, Culture, and History.

Hamann edited and contributed to *Categories—On the Beauty of Physics* (2006), an interdisciplinary educational book that was included in Louisiana State University's list of top twenty-five nonfiction books written since 1950.

As the assistant to Jacques d'Amboise, founder and artistic director of the National Dance Institute, Ms. Hamann produced *We Real Cool,* a short film based on the Gwendolyn Brooks poem, directed by Academy Award–winning director Emile Ardolino. She also coordinated an international exchange with students from America and the then Soviet Union based on literature, music, and art. She has worked in New York's film, publishing, and entertainment industries, and is co-director of Films on the Haywall, a classic film series in Bridgehampton, New York.

Hamann lives in Manhattan and on Long Island.

ABOUT THE TYPE

This book was set in Garamond, a typeface originally designed by the Parisian typecutter Claude Garamond (1480–1561). This version of Garamond was modeled on a 1592 specimen sheet from the Egenolff-Berner foundry, which was produced from types assumed to have been brought to Frankfurt by the punch-cutter Jacques Sabon.

Claude Garamond's distinguished romans and italics first appeared in *Opera Ciceronis* in 1543–44. The Garamond types are clear, open, and elegant.